D0187958

The Bend in the River

A Novel by Susan Gibbs

HAWKSHADOW PUBLISHING COMPANY
MICHIGAN, U.S.A.

A Hawkshadow Publishing Company Book, Published by Hawkshadow Publishing Company, Copyright © 2001 by Susan Gibbs www.hawkshadowpublishing.com

Edited by Julie Steiff, Ph.D. Contact Mrs. Steiff through Hawkshadow Publishing at the address or e-mail below.

Cover art by Linda Lindall. Contact Ms. Lindall via e-mail at LINDAL7@prodigy.net.

Library of Congress Catalog Card Number: 2001 135410

ISBN 0–9714667–0–X

Printed in the United States of America by Cushing-Malloy, Ann Arbor, Michigan

Hawkshadow Publishing Company Edition: One
Second Printing: 2004

Dedication

To mom and dad

and

To my husband who makes my dreams come true

Acknowledgments

I particularly appreciate the skills and talents of my editor,
Julie Steiff, Ph.D.

Thanks go to my gifted cover artist, Linda Lindall, whose fine oil painting
is on the cover of this book.

Preface

A portion of this story takes place in what is now Washington State, but in the late Nineteenth Century, before Washington became a state on November 11, 1889, the territory was often called Columbia. To avoid confusion, I have called the region Washington.

I also refer to the Indian Territory in this narrative. The Indian Territory is the state now known as Oklahoma.

Susan Gibbs

Chapter One

Emma was crouched and huddled tight under a lone tree on the prairie. Her back was to the fierce west wind. Her worn shearling coat, thin calico dress, old boots and a couple of threadbare blankets were all that insulated her from the rogue October snowstorm of 1877. The air was bitter cold and the wind chafed her exposed face. The tree offered no protection against the mighty prairie blizzard.

Her eyes closed. The pain in her frozen limbs was fading, no feeling left. Three days alone on foot were now exacting the price. She felt herself sliding away from the tree trunk to lie on the hard ground dusted with fine, powdery snow. Oblivion was moments away and her mind drifted. She was sitting near the hearth in the sod house where she was born seventeen years ago. The voices of her parents swirled through her memory.

The smell of acrid smoke woke her and she opened her eyes. Her earlier surrender to the elements was quickly replaced with relief. She was in some sort of small shelter, out of the cold and warmed by a crackling fire pit surrounded by stones.

She stirred and groaned. Her throat burned from too many hours in the cold sitting under that tree, giving up, surrendering.

A man hunkered down beside her and studied her, expressionless. "How do you feel?"

The shadowy firelight gave Emma a look at the man's dress and long black hair tied with feathers. An Indian! She was suddenly, terribly afraid. He reached for a bowl of water and held it to her lips as she sipped. It did little to cool her throat and she winced as she swallowed.

"I found you yesterday. I thought you were dead from the cold." He spoke good English.

"I was trying to get to Bockmeier's," she said.

"The trading post is north. You are far south of it now. You are in the Indian Territory."

He looked puzzled and Emma knew why. The Indian camps were south

1

of her Kansas home that bordered the Indian Territory; Bockmeier's was twenty miles to the northeast of her family's homestead.

Admitting little memory of the past few days, it was obvious that she had become terribly lost. Her father, Arthur, had repeatedly warned her about crossing the border between the homestead and the Indian Territory. Only well–armed troops would dare venture where the savages lived, he had told her.

"I must've got lost. Thank you for helping me, but I have to go." She tried to rise, but every muscle in her body revolted, stiff and sore. She flopped back upon her bed of blankets. Then, the shock of her predicament slammed into her. She hoped that she could reason with this Indian. Maybe he would take pity on her and let her go. She vastly preferred to take her chances in the open and get to Bockmeier's, rather than be a prisoner of an Indian. She had grown up with stories of young girls and women being taken by Indians and forced to marry the braves and bear their children. Those were the lucky ones who were permitted to live.

"You are not well enough to go anywhere," he said.

Her heart thudded with rising panic. "Am I your prisoner?"

He looked mildly amused. "No. But it is better if you come with me. I will take you to Fort Reno. It is near our camp."

"Your camp? How far?"

"The Cheyenne Agency is three days south. That is where I live."

"No. I'll go to Bockmeier's."

"You are too far from Bockmeier's now. I passed it days ago. The weather is closing in. You do not have enough supplies to get there—and no horse."

"Why are you so far from your reservation?" she asked in her slight drawl, reaching for the bowl of water. She knew that the Cheyenne lived miles south of the border between Kansas and the Indian Territory.

Her eyes now adjusted to the darkness and she saw the man better. His face was rugged, with fine chiseled features and the characteristic high cheekbones of an Indian. His mouth was wide and thin–lipped and his nose narrow and pointed. His face was finished with a firm chin and angular jaw. His skin seemed unusually fair, but his deep set eyes startled her—a clear light blue. He wore a homespun red shirt, like those worn by whites, but with Indian–style buckskin leggings and moccasins that laced up to his thighs. In spite of the cold day, he wore no coat or cloak. Heat radiated from him; she could feel it.

He did not answer her question; instead he handed her a bowl of dried berries. She shook her head. He frowned, his gaze steady into her large, round, deep blue eyes. "You must eat."

"I can't—my throat hurts." She coughed then asked, "What is your name?"

"Shea Hawkshadow. What is yours?" he returned.

"Emma Jorden."

"Why were you out alone?"

Tears burned her eyes and her answer was a long time coming while she coughed and sipped more water to cool her throat. "My parents—they died—left me alone." Her eyes closed tight. "It was cholera, I think. After they died, I couldn't stay on the homestead alone, so I was going to Bockmeier's trading post to winter there." She wiped tears along her sleeve, in grief for her parents as well as relief for having been rescued from freezing to death. The devastating loss of her parents finally penetrated and she wept bitterly for them. It had happened only days ago, but the memory was already hazy. It had been a traumatic time for Emma, who had watched helplessly as her parents died and left her utterly alone.

His look upon her was intent. "If you were on a farm, why did you not ride a horse or mule to the trading post?"

"They ran off when I tried to saddle them. I had to walk." When she swallowed, her throat seared with pain. "Why are you so far from your reservation?" she asked again.

"I was in Colorado. I have family there among the Arapahoes. I have been traveling for days, avoiding settlers, soldiers, and Cherokee. We are on Cherokee land."

"I don't understand."

"Cheyenne are not allowed to leave the agency near Fort Reno. No Indians can leave this territory. I had to sneak away and travel at night."

"Isn't that dangerous?"

"I wanted to see my cousins," he replied with a shrug.

Without the strength to leave, Emma submitted to Shea's care for two days, uncertain what he planned to do with her. She had gone outside his *tepee*, a small conical tent, now and then, trying to get her bearings. The flat country was dusted with snow and she saw nothing familiar, not even the tree where she had huddled against the storm. She slowly realized that she had indeed headed south when she meant to go north. She had lived off the land all her life and felt ashamed for making such a simple mistake; she attributed it to grief over losing her parents.

The morning of the third day she seemed stronger so Shea took down the *tepee* and packed it on his horse. "Can you ride?" he asked.

Emma nodded and he pulled her up behind him on his tan pony. "How far are we from Fort Reno?"

"If we avoid other tribes and the weather holds, three days."

Emma reluctantly put her arms around Shea's waist as the sturdy pony trotted south. The featureless plain was devoid of people and civilization. She saw no trail and wondered how Shea knew the way. She felt utterly alone and frightened, with this blue–eyed Indian as her only hope. Uncertain what awaited her, and with no one else in the world to help her, she resolved to cooperate with him and get to the safety of the fort.

Shea did not talk much, but made sure she stayed warm during the ride. Hoping to avert any harm he might do her, she cautiously got to know him a little. His answers were distracted, as his eyes were constantly scanning the tall prairie grass and horizon for signs of other Indian tribes hostile to the Cheyenne.

When she asked him why he risked the journey to Colorado, he replied, "I wanted to see my family. They are cousins to my mother and took us in when we came south from Montana years ago. And I was bored at the agency near Reno. There is little to do there."

"Why don't you live with your cousins in Colorado?"

Shea said, "After the Custer fight, your government punished the tribes of Little Wolf and Dull Knife for being a part of the battle. We were forced to leave our home in Montana and come here. Little Wolf is a Soldier Chief and I am one of his Dog Soldiers." Emma looked mystified. "Dog Soldiers are warriors—a soldier's society. I am loyal to Little Wolf, so I followed him here."

That night, camped inside the *tepee*, she said, "Your English is good, very good. Where did you learn it?"

Shea sat down beside her and offered her several pieces of dried meat he had pulled from a pouch. "My father was white, an English trader. He was married to my mother, Little Hawkshadow."

"Was? What happened to him?"

"He left to go hunting when I was seven and he never came back. We do not know what happened to him. He taught me his tongue and the ways of the whites, but I chose to stay with the Cheyenne. I was named for him— Shea Russell. To hide our disgrace after my father left, my mother made me take her name."

His gaze unsettled her. She looked away. For a brief second, she saw the pain of the abandoned little boy in Shea's eyes, but he quickly masked it. His pain was old, but still very near the surface. Her pain was fresh and she wondered how long it would be before she felt normal, felt something other than loss and grief. She was abandoned too and sympathized with the look she had briefly seen in his eyes.

"Your mother lives at the camp near Fort Reno?" she asked.

"She died four winters ago."

"And your wife?" His lips thinned in exasperation. She realized too late that she had touched a nerve.

"I am a half–breed. Cheyenne maidens will not take me as their husband. My white blood taints the blood of my Cheyenne ancestors."

Emma simply did not understand the implications of the question and was embarrassed. It struck her how being half white carried such a stigma among the Indians. It was a corner of her attitudes that she had never troubled to examine.

"I'm sorry. I didn't mean anything by it."

Shea shrugged.

On the third day of their journey, another blizzard roared across the flat prairie. Shea's pony could not carry both of them in the deep snow, so Shea let Emma ride and led the animal through the drifts. Emma was frightened, the biting cold a bitter reminder of lingering near death under that tree mere days ago. Shea hardly seemed to notice the worsening weather, but he did remark that they had to keep moving for his supply of food, meant for one person, was very low. Emma had little food with her, except for some corn-meal, flour, lard, sugar, and coffee.

"How far from the fort do you think we are?" she asked.

"Because of the weather, two or three more days."

They slogged through the snow, the wind unstoppable as snow drifted three feet, sometimes more, in places. They could only make about ten to fifteen miles a day, instead of the usual twenty in good weather. Emma was very hungry, but said nothing to Shea. He doggedly kept on. Emma was chilled and shivering and took great pains to hide her discomfort from Shea. He had kept his word so far and had been kind to her. She would do nothing to upset him. However, her strength was failing and she fought to stay atop the pony.

The morning of the sixth day, she perked up, smelling wood smoke on the air. She scanned the horizon and soon saw wisps of smoke miles away.

"That has to be the fort!" she cried. "We made it!"

Shea had been intent on moving through the high drifts of snow. He stopped to catch his breath and squinted into the distance. "That is Little Wolf's camp, where I live."

"So how far is Reno from the camp?"

"Another few days in this weather. We have to stop to rest and get food at my camp before we go to the fort."

For hours they traveled and to Emma's frustration, the camp seemed no closer. She looked to the east where Shea had said the fort lay, but she saw nothing but flat, endless prairie. "If we head for Reno now, maybe they will give you enough supplies to get home."

"If the trails to Reno are anything like this, we will run out of food. We have to go to my camp first."

Emma became afraid. She was lucky, because Shea had been kind to her, but she was aware that she would not likely encounter a warm welcome among the Indians. She had heard about how the savages made captured whites run through a painful gauntlet, in which the captive was beaten with clubs. She tried to bargain. "I have money. Can I buy a horse and supplies from your people? Then I can head to Reno myself."

He stopped walking and faced her, exasperated. "The fort is two days away when the weather is good. You have lived on the land. Look at the sky and tell me what you see. More snow is coming, you know that. Besides, we need our horses. We do not need your money."

Emma backed down, plainly seeing that he was worn–out, just as she was. "I'm sorry. I figured the quicker I got to Reno, the better for everyone. It's the only way I know how to repay you for saving me."

He looked away. "You repaid me already. I did not have to dig a grave for you in the frozen ground."

She fell silent at his comment and concentrated on staying on the pony as the cold stiffened every joint in her body.

Near nightfall, small fires of the camp were seen in the distance, but the deep snow kept them plodding at a snail's pace. The cold made Emma feel unusually sleepy. She lolled in the saddle of blankets.

Finally, they entered the camp. Shea led the pony to a lean–to and helped Emma dismount. Her legs were numb and she immediately sank to the ground, utterly exhausted. He carried her inside a lodge and laid her on a mat of woven bulrushes covered with blankets and hides. Shapes moved around her in the dark shadows thrown around the walls by the firelight. Voices nearby spoke a language that she did not understand, but she recognized Shea's deep, gravely voice.

An old woman with a face like a dried apple came into view and hovered a moment. Her long gray braids brushed Emma's cheek.

"I'm so cold," she said between chattering teeth. She was too disoriented and weak to care if they harmed her. She just wanted to be warm again.

"Okay," the old woman said with a strange accent. Emma realized that the old woman probably did not understand English.

The old woman grabbed a blanket, smiling as she gently tucked it around Emma.

Shea knelt beside her. "This is Red Leaf Woman's lodge. She is a widow and both of her sons are dead. She and her niece, Little Fox, will care for you. The trails are blocked with snow, but the soldiers will come soon with our winter rations. Then you will go with them, eh? You will be here a few days." A blast of icy wind slipped inside the warm lodge as Shea left.

Red Leaf gave her water from a wooden bowl. "Thank you very much," Emma smiled. Her only defense was to be as polite as possible and get out of there as soon as her strength returned.

The old woman felt Emma's forehead, then brushed her knuckles lightly against her cheek. "Okay. Sleep."

Emma heard the old woman rustling around, going in and out of the lodge. Before she drifted off, Emma looked at her hands. The work gloves she had worn did little to protect her hands which were red and swollen from exposure. She clenched them into fists to restore some circulation. Finally, she burrowed in and slept.

She woke the next morning feeling better, but still stiff and a bit feverish. A young girl sat nearby weaving a basket from long, dry grasses. She smiled and put down her work, offering Emma a tin cup of hot liquid warming near the fire pit. She untangled herself from the blankets and accepted the drink, which she thought was some sort of coffee or tea. It tasted strong and bitter, probably distilled from bark, but Emma did not care. It was hot.

She nodded her thanks. "You must be Little Fox." The girl smiled and returned to her weaving.

Then, hoping to find a way out of camp, but even more urgently needing to make her toilet, Emma found her shearling coat, patted the pocket and ducked out of the lodge. She trotted on wobbly legs to a clump of bushes as far from camp as she dared. The wind had at last died down and the sun was dimmed and dull, stuck behind gray clouds. She looked back once to see that Little Fox had followed her at a distance and was joined by another girl. The girls looked to be a few years younger than Emma, maybe thirteen or fourteen, with wide, pleasant faces and dark hair in pigtails tied with leather thongs. They wore calico dresses, similar to Emma's own, but with long leggings underneath and moccasins on their feet. They wore no cloaks against the cold.

Emma quickly surveyed the landscape, noting sandy hills to the north and a rather pitiful stream to the east, trying to imprint an escape route on her memory. The ground was mostly flat, so if she made a break, it would have to be at night through the hills, she reasoned. As she hunkered down behind a screen of tall grass, she pulled a small tobacco tin, encrusted with caked dirt, from her coat pocket and assured herself that the wad of bills was still inside. She tucked the tin between her breasts for safekeeping, then headed back to the camp.

Perhaps sixty lodges occupied the shallow valley. Many were colorfully painted with stars and animals. They had a simple, regal appearance, rising tall against the snow–dusted hills. The lodges looked otherworldly in the white stillness with smoke from cooking fires curling around them. Emma felt as if she were dreaming and, for a moment, wondered if all this was a vivid dream. Maybe she was still slumped against that tree where she had nearly died in the cold. But she was here; she was quite alive—her aching muscles attested to that. But she missed her parents. She missed the sod house, shabby though it was. She missed the familiar horizon of their land and the little creek that ran through it. She missed the only world that she had ever known.

The camp was busy with activity in comparison to the quiet, isolated one–hundred and sixty–acre farm where she was born and raised. Many Cheyenne women were bent over cooking fires and children and dogs ran and played throughout the camp. Everyone was busy cooking, sewing, or weaving baskets. Several women were using fleshers and scrapers on animal hides staked to the ground. Few men were evident, out hunting, Emma supposed, and she did not see Shea's tan pony in the lean–to. People watched her curiously, but pleasantly. She was relieved that no gauntlet awaited her.

She surveyed the flat, gray sky knowing that more snow was coming even though it was only October. Panic tightened her chest. Her father had been right. He had said that winter would come early this year. She had no time to lose. Tonight she would get away and head east to the fort. Shea had said it was across the river and Emma resolved to find a shallow crossing somehow.

The two young girls followed her back inside the lodge, grinning and giggling softly. Little Fox handed Emma a bowl of dried berries and said, indicating her companion, "This is Porcupine Girl." The girl smiled shyly.

"My name is Emma," she said.

"What does your name mean?" asked Porcupine Girl in a thick accent.

Emma shrugged. "I have no idea." She jumped as Porcupine Girl reached out and tugged her long auburn hair .

"*Ema'o*," Porcupine Girl said with a smile to Little Fox.

"No. My name is Emma."

Porcupine Girl touched Emma's hair again. "*Ema'o*."

Emma was a little perturbed. She repeatedly tried to teach Porcupine Girl to say her name correctly, but she eventually gave up. The girls dissolved into giggles and whispers. Emma smiled weakly, not understanding what was so amusing. Her name was not that hard to pronounce.

Despite her raw throat, she gobbled the berries and was pleased when Little Fox gave her more. She would need to eat as much as possible to fuel her escape, now that she had her bearings. She dug around the lodge, hoping to find the bundle of food, clothing, and books that she had packed before leaving home. She found it under a pile of hides and blankets. Everything seemed to be there except the pistol she had tucked in there. It was gone.

Nevertheless, her plan to run was in place. She would sneak out of the lodge that night while Red Leaf and Little Fox slept. She would head upriver and look for a place to cross.

That night, a gusting, icy wind tugged at the lodge skins. Emma was nervous and wakeful. She heard the patter of rain on the skins stretched across the lodge poles. In the wee hours, she crept to the lodge opening and peered out. A cold blast brought an involuntary shiver. Rain had changed to heavy snow. For a moment she reconsidered, then pulled her shearling and bundle to her as quietly as she could. Just as she crawled out, a strong hand on her ankle grabbed her and she spun around. It was Red Leaf. The old woman pulled her back inside and guided her back to her bed place without a word. Emma laid down, clutching her coat and bundle, feeling guilty that she had been caught. Red Leaf sat by her throughout the night and did not sleep.

The next morning, Emma woke with a start feeling a presence near her. Shea sat cross–legged next to her. Red Leaf and Little Fox were gone.

"Red Leaf told me what you tried to do last night. Do not try to leave. The soldiers will be here soon. I told you that."

Emma sat up and crawled to the opening and looked outside. Nearly three feet of snow had fallen overnight. "I had to try."

"Why? Is this how you repay me for saving your life? Did I not take care of you—have not my people? Have we not fed and housed you?"

He was right. So far, she had been unharmed; she just did not know how long it would last. "But I don't belong here!" Emma complained.

"Neither do we!" Shea shot back, his voice low and rough. "You will wait for the soldiers!" He rose to leave.

"Where is my pistol? Did you take it?" she questioned Shea.

"Yes. I took it. You will not need it."

With her plan exposed, she had no choice but to stay. Everywhere she went, she was watched. If she strayed too far from camp, Little Fox and Porcupine Girl called her back. When the warriors started to dog her as well, she became afraid but resigned herself to settle in to wait, hoping that the soldiers would come soon. To her surprise, Red Leaf Woman and Little Fox were kind to her, seeing that she ate and teaching her to weave baskets and cook simple foods. Red Leaf also taught Emma the customs when entering a lodge: Always turn to the right when entering, and never pass between the fire pit and the owner of the lodge. And most especially, never go to the part of the lodge where the sleeping mats were. That area was considered private space for the family.

One morning, Emma was with Little Fox who was cutting cattails along the river's edge. Emma had not bathed in days and decided to brave the cold water. She kept her camisole and breeches on and bathed quickly in the freezing river. Shea had been riding out to hunt and saw her through a stand of spindly trees at the river's edge. He stopped his horse and quieted it, watching. As she emerged, her copper hair clung to her head and her thin cotton camisole stuck tight to her slim body. She looked up and saw him looking at her. She defiantly stared back at him, making no move to cover herself. He rode away.

The early storm was no freak; it snowed steadily over the next few weeks. Stuck in the camp for the winter, Emma eagerly scanned the horizon each day, watching for the soldiers with the winter rations. But each day she was disappointed. No one came to the little camp.

One afternoon Emma, Little Fox, and Porcupine Girl had returned from gathering firewood. They had walked a long way to bring back only a few armloads of branches. Little Fox and Porcupine Girl left Emma to stack the firewood outside Red Leaf's lodge. Shea walked over to Emma.

"Are you getting used to living here or do you still want to run away?" he asked with a teasing lift of his eyebrows.

"You made your point on that," she answered, contrite. She looked away from his piercing blue eyes. She now regretted being so bold that day he had seen her bathing at the river's edge. Since that day, every time Shea passed her in camp, he watched her with a look of discomforting intimacy. "But I'm getting used to how things are around here."

"Winter has not been too bad so far and you have room to roam. If you were at Fort Reno, you would be closed in by walls. I do not think you would like that," he affirmed.

"You're right, Shea. My biggest problem is with the language, though. Red Leaf is getting better at speaking English, but I can't get Porcupine Girl to say my name right."

"How does she say it?"

"*Ema'o*," Emma answered. "No matter what I do she keeps saying it wrong, then she and Little Fox start giggling."

Shea laughed. "They think it is funny that your name and our name for the color red are nearly the same."

"Emma means red?" Emma asked, puzzled.

"*Ema'o* means red in Cheyenne. The girls think it is funny that you have reddish hair and that your name is Emma."

As Shea walked away he said, "They are playing a prank. You should learn more Cheyenne so you will understand. We have a sense of humor."

Gradually, Emma became used to living with the Cheyenne, with Red Leaf and Little Fox to guide her, especially when her period started and she was hustled off to a lodge whose only purpose was to house menstruating women. Emma thought it very odd, until Red Leaf explained in her sparse English that their laws forbade men and women to be together during that time. Emma asked, why, if no men lived in their lodge? She was told that it was what they had to do in case a man ever entered the lodge. Emma spent an awkward few days there, trapped with several other women and young girls.

With little to occupy her, she started learning Cheyenne. Little Fox's English was fairly good so she was able to teach Emma many words in her language. Red Leaf understood more English than she spoke, which made conversations between them tedious and brief, but it gave Emma something to do to pass the time.

The old woman seemed affectionate and motherly toward Emma. Her behavior went against all Emma's parents had taught her about their uneasy neighborhood composed of white settlers and Indians. Emma accepted the old woman's ministrations, finally sure that no one in the camp would hurt her—as long as she conformed.

As the weeks passed she grieved for her parents, but stifled anger at being abandoned to this uncertain fate. In rare moments alone, she wept bitter tears.

One afternoon in November, the sun was bright and made sitting outside pleasant. Emma alternately stirred a pot of squirrel stew and read one of the tattered books that she had bought from Bockmeier's for ten–a–penny during the last trip there with her parents only a few weeks before. A lot of travelers dumped books by the side of the trails or gave them to Bockmeier, admitting that they were added weight as their journey west became more difficult. People stopping at the trading post had little use for them, so Bockmeier sold them cheap, especially when the shelves overflowed. Emma had largely been educated with them, purchasing as many as she could with the few cents her parents gave her.

She looked up and saw Shea approaching. She closed her book and rose to meet him.

"How are you doing?" he asked, his gaze taking her in from head to toe.

She was determined to appear fearless for as long as she was held here. But it did feel strange that she did not feel uneasy around him, even that day he watched her bathe in the river. "So you're not mad at me anymore?"

He shrugged. "You did what you thought you had to do."

"I'm sorry for trying to run off, but I was scared. I've heard stories about how whites are treated by Indians." Hoping to appease him, she added, "Those stories aren't true about your people. Everyone has been kind." The awful fate she envisioned had not materialized and she was becoming more unafraid by the day. "When will the soldiers get here?"

He frowned. "The supply wagons cannot travel in deep snow. If we get anything, it will not be until spring."

She was deflated; no help would come until then. "So your people have no food rations for the winter? What will you do?"

"We will go farther to hunt, we will eat fish from the river. If there is little food, we will eat less." He told her that promised shipments of food and tools rarely got past corrupt Indian Agents who sold them to other people before they could reach the camps.

"I have money with me. Can we buy food at the fort?"

His voice was sullen. "No amount of money will get them to sell us food. The Indian Agents make more money selling to other whites—more money than you have. The food is probably not even waiting for us at Fort Reno and will not be brought here in spring. It is how things are for us."

"What can you do?"

He rolled his eyes at her ignorance. "Nothing."

Emma was embarrassed, realizing that she indeed knew nothing of the privations the Indians endured. "I'm sorry. I didn't understand."

"Your offer to buy supplies shows you have good manners, but you cannot help us. If the rations the government sends get here, they are spoiled with bugs or mixed with sand. Most of it is impossible to eat." Shea looked her in the eye. "My people starve. The whites have killed nearly all the buffalo. Now we live on rabbits, squirrels, dogs, and skunks."

"I have some dry goods with me—flour, lard, cornmeal, sugar and some coffee," she offered. "It's not much." She felt ashamed for not offering it in all these weeks, reasoning that she would need it for herself when she finally was allowed to leave.

His look softened. "I will let you know if we need it."

After a long pause, she said, "Can't you farm this land? With the river nearby, it should be easy to get a few crops going. I can tell you how."

Shea shook his head as she spoke. "The *veho* government says we will get seed, plows, food, and medicine, but it never comes and we are never in one place long enough to grow anything. We have a home for a while, then the army comes and tells us we have to move to keep peace because more whites want our land."

She was quiet a moment before asking, "What does *veho* mean?"

"Spider. It is what we call the whites," he replied as he helped himself to a piece of squirrel meat from the pot. Emma learned another Cheyenne word.

Emma knew less than nothing about the politics concerning Indians. Although she had always lived on the border of the two lands, she had had little exposure to them; her father had seen to that. His perpetual order was that she was to remain out of sight if a wayward group of Indians left their reservations to trade with them. Emma obeyed her father, nonetheless, and she and her mother, Jane, automatically retreated to the soddy when Indians were spotted in the distance.

This day, Emma was surprised that Shea seemed to want to spend time with her. Since she had tried to escape, he had been curt, brusque, even. Today, he was unusually talkative. He told her of the bitter privations of the Cheyenne, Sioux, and other tribes of the plains and how their numbers had been decimated by war and white man's diseases. A once–strong tribe of thousands had been reduced to mere hundreds, scattered across the frontier, with two main camps of Cheyenne. This camp, the southernmost, held three separate groups headed by soldier chiefs, Little Wolf, Dull Knife, and American Horse. The larger northern agency, Red Cloud's Pine Ridge, was in northern Nebraska with the Oglala Sioux, cousins to the Cheyenne. That agency was to be moved to South Dakota in spring.

"We are trapped here. If we try to leave, the army will bring us back here—and kill some of us to make their point."

"I've lived so near all my life," Emma began. "I never knew that it was this bad for you. I guess you think I'm really stupid."

"No," he interjected. "You have little understanding of the world around you. Maybe that will change now. Your own life has been hard, right?"

"I never thought so." And she had never thought about it before, knowing little else. The only surviving child of her parent's union (three children had died in infancy before she was born), she had worked the farm and been to Bockmeier's a few times a year to sell the harvest. That was all that she knew.

As she watched him walk away, she noticed his lean, hard muscled body and the easy way he moved with strength and a lanky grace. She willed herself not to notice and returned to stirring the pot of squirrel stew.

She was now becoming aware of a larger world and a violent one, one consumed with self–interest and corruption. Her parents had tried to shelter her from it, hoping that she would eventually marry one of Bockmeier's many sons (he had eight boys), or snag a soldier from Camp Supply in the Indian Territory to the south of the homestead. At once, she understood their choice of such an out–of–the–way homestead, far from the Santa Fe Trail, but wondered what was out in the world that made them so afraid of living near a town. When she was forced to abandon her home, she had found a tin of money, rusted and coated with dirt, hidden behind a loose stone in the soddy's hearth. The tin held more than a thousand dollars and Emma wondered why her parents had not purchased better land or moved near a town.

December turned sharply colder and more snow fell, settling a fresh muffled blanket upon the camp. The stream had not frozen over and some small fish were caught, but unless large game was killed soon, already meager food reserves would run dangerously low. While Shea and the other braves hunted desperately, going farther and farther each day, Emma was grateful for Red Leaf Woman who kept her occupied. She spent the days learning Cheyenne ways and visiting with the women as they worked. Her knowledge of the language was improving. She found the soft tongue as gentle as the people. Other languages, German, Dutch, French, and others which she had heard from people at Bockmeier's, did not compare to the soft inflections of Cheyenne. Out of sheer boredom and with more than a little guilt, Emma pitched in with youthful energy, learning how to dry meat and fish and prepare dinners for Red Leaf and Little Fox. Her first attempts were inedible, but Red Leaf was patient until she got the trick of it.

Many afternoons she worked with Red Leaf Woman on her English. The two spent much time together during the short winter days. Red Leaf Woman had a unique insight into Emma in her isolation from her own people. The little round woman made her feel safe—and she clearly knew how to survive. That Emma plainly inferred, noticing there were few people anywhere near Red Leaf's age in the camp.

Another afternoon, Emma sat outside the lodge fixing a broken basket, a newfound skill, while enjoying a wild snowball fight among the children.

Even the dogs joined in, catching the balls in their mouths. Red Leaf Woman sat nearby chewing on a hide to soften it, one eye focused on avoiding the flying snow.

Shea had just returned from the hunt; Emma had seen him in the distance riding in on his pony toward the corral. A short time later, Emma grinned, seeing Shea, pelted by snowballs, making his way toward them.

"How was the hunt?" Emma asked.

"Good today," he said, holding up several rabbits. "These are for Red Leaf's lodge." Red Leaf thanked him in Cheyenne and quickly began skinning and butchering them with a knife that she kept in a sheath at her waist.

Shea looked uncomfortable. "Can I talk to you—alone?"

"Okay," Emma said, perplexed, as he led her away.

It took him some time to screw up his courage. "Can you teach me to read and write?"

Emma stared at him. "Uh, sure. But why? Your English is really good."

"Since I speak English better than anyone here, Little Wolf has told me to learn to read and write it." Something in his face foretold more.

"What has changed, Shea?"

"We are being moved to Kansas next summer. There will be a treaty, as usual. Even though the *veho* will break it, Little Wolf wants it read to him by someone he trusts."

Emma had seen Little Wolf as he walked through camp. He was an older man, lanky and with a face chiseled by a life in the open. He always nodded to her, but they had never spoken. He seemed hardly concerned that she was in his camp. Red Leaf had told her that Shea was Little Wolf's most trusted warrior.

"I'll help you, but why are you being forced to move again? Red Leaf said that your people have only been here for a couple of years."

"It is the way things are for us." He stopped and looked back at the camp. "There is one thing. You have to teach me in my lodge so no one can see."

"Why?"

"It is embarrassing for a Cheyenne man to be taught by a woman." Emma was not insulted. She was finally understanding. "It will be a surprise for the *veho*. It is a weapon they will never suspect." It was the first time that she had seen him smile.

"All right," Emma said. "When do we start?"

"Tonight," he answered. "I have to learn much before you leave in spring."
The only time that Emma could teach Shea was in the evenings when
he returned from hunting. Entering his lodge was awkward. It was on the
edge of camp with other families of Dog Soldiers; all warriors' lodges
ringed the camp as a first line of defense. She attracted much attention as
she went to Shea's lodge each night and ducked inside. The lessons went
late into the night, so Emma and Shea often ate dinner together. Red Leaf
openly disapproved of the fact that they were unchaperoned and wanted
Little Fox to accompany her. Emma stubbornly refused.

"I'm his teacher, nothing more," she defended.

Shea's progress was remarkable. He had a natural ability to recognize
words and within a month he was reading very well. Learning to write (on
paper torn from Emma's books) quickly frustrated him; however, he persisted, anxious to please her.

Little Fox had once mentioned that Shea liked coffee, so Emma gave him
her pouch of grounds one evening before their lesson began.

"It is not proper to give a Cheyenne warrior a gift."

She smiled. "I'm not Cheyenne."

He returned her smile. "No, you are not."

One night while they shared supper she was feeling restless and admit-
tedly baited him a little. "Shea? Why don't you call me by my name?"

"What do you mean?"

"You don't call me anything except for *you*."

"I never thought about it."

"I have a name. It's Emma. Why don't you call me Emma? Then I'd be
sure that you were talking to me."

The way he looked at her made her heart jump. His blue eyes ran over
her fluidly, appraisingly. When he spoke her name it came out soft, tender.
"Emma."

She blushed deeply.

Red Leaf Woman was resolute that Emma should not be alone with
Shea and went to Little Wolf to argue her case. Little Wolf, overwhelmed
by the task of relocation in summer, paid little attention, telling her that
Shea was aware of the level of conduct expected of a Dog Soldier.

In many ways, Red Leaf had become a surrogate mother to Emma and
she admonished Emma to keep her conduct above reproach when alone
with Shea.

This made Emma smile. "You worry too much, Red Leaf." For the first time in her life, Emma was pleased with herself, feeling a sense of pride. Her grief was masked by this temporary contentment and distraction. It kept her demons, which hovered just outside her consciousness, at bay.

One afternoon, Emma crouched at the river's edge, distractedly washing out some clothes. She wore a buffalo robe that Shea had given to her; she liked it despite the weight and smell because it was warm. Because she had kept careful track of the days, she realized that it was Christmas Day. Her memory drifted back to the many happy Christmases spent with her parents, but what really bothered her was that she had become absorbed in her life with the Cheyenne and was starting to forget her past. And she felt terrible guilt for not mourning for her parents better—longer. Worse yet, dates were fast becoming meaningless. Nearly three months had passed and she had become completely enveloped in life on the quiet reservation. She quickly wiped away tears when she heard a horse approaching. It was Shea, returning from the hunt, leading his pony. He had a dozen rabbits dangling from a rope over the horse's withers, the snares still around their feet.

He could see that she was upset but said nothing as he tied the pony to a sapling. He beckoned her to sit beside him on a fallen tree trunk at the river's edge.

"It's Christmas," she said.

"Ah! My father told me about it. It is part of your religion."

"I never cared much for religion. I mean, I've never been to church, but Christmas was always a special time in my home." To her surprise, Shea's arm curled around her and more surprisingly, she rested her head on his shoulder. All these months, she had been untouchable and she had longed for simple affection. His warmth and attention served as some solace, but she felt this was wrong. She was enjoying it too much.

"We should get back." She pulled away, gathering up her wet, stiff clothes over her arm, and fell in beside Shea. Both of their hands reached to untie the pony from the branch and as their hands touched, Emma felt a shock run through her body. Shea kept his hand upon hers. Across the waist–high barrier of the branch, he kissed her softly. She did not pull away. Neither of them spoke as they returned to camp.

The next night, Red Leaf accompanied Emma on her walk to Shea's lodge. She spoke in her language as they made their way through camp, but Emma did not understand a word. Red Leaf was obviously very agitated about something as she gestured to Shea's lodge, shaking Emma's arm as they walked.

Shea had not yet returned, but Red Leaf went inside his lodge and glanced around, talking to herself.

Emma followed her inside. "What is wrong?"

"You and Hawkshadow. I see you by river," she scolded.

So, Red Leaf had seen the kiss—she missed nothing. Emma had no defense and did not want to offer one. Her feelings for Shea had undergone a profound change. She had been afraid of him at first, but as they spent time together, he revealed a thoughtful intelligence that attracted her. She respected Red Leaf, but her feelings for Shea were strong.

Just then, Shea returned home. Emma remained inside while Red Leaf went outside with him. She peered out and saw him standing mute under a verbal barrage from Red Leaf Woman who shook her finger at him. Shea heard her out and mumbled something as he ducked inside the lodge, pulling the flap down behind him.

He shot an amused, sidelong glance at Emma as he knelt and pulled several pieces of dried meat from a skin pouch and placed them in wooden bowls. "She is our oldest watchdog." He handed supper to her without ceremony. The meat, buffalo or deer, Emma hoped, not dog—was dark in color. She sniffed it, then ate it anyway.

"She saw us by the river yesterday. That's why she's mad."

He looked directly at her. "I do not care, do you?"

"No, I don't," Emma admitted, but she wanted to drop the subject of their budding relationship. Thinking too much about the situation would upset the delicate emotional balance that she had been maintaining.

At length Shea spoke again. "She is angry because it is improper for you to be here alone with me."

Emma's eyes widened and she paused in mid–chew. "I don't understand. We're not doing anything wrong."

"She wants someone here while you teach me." He seemed more hungry than concerned about Red Leaf's objections as he bit into the dry, tough meat.

"Do you want that?"

"I do not want anyone here but you."

When their lesson concluded near midnight, Shea pulled her to him and they kissed and held each other for a very long time.

The next afternoon, Emma and Red Leaf Woman walked along a path cut in the deep snow to the river, carrying water skins. She knew that she was in for it just from Red Leaf's carriage. Her eyes never left Emma and she was clearly angry. The old woman knew exactly what was going on.

"What he do with you is bad. No girl be with man until wedding. Cheyenne do not do this!" Her tone was emphatic.

"We haven't done anything wrong!" Emma countered. "I'm doing what Little Wolf wanted. I teach Shea to read and write. So we kissed. So what?"

"You doing more than teaching. I know. You must stay away from Hawkshadow."

"No!" Emma cried. "We like each other. What's wrong with that?"

Red Leaf grabbed Emma by the shoulder and spun her around. "He Cheyenne, you white!"

Emma fell silent. She was caught up in her first infatuation and unwilling to see their differences. "He's so lonely and he has no wife."

Red Leaf grabbed Emma's water skins, pushed past her to the river and proceeded to fill them, slapping them on the riverbank. Emma followed.

"I want this—Shea wants this, too, I know he does."

"You both too young. He is not twenty summers old—and you too young to know better. You stop this!"

Emma took her water skin from Red Leaf. "I don't want to."

Red Leaf gripped her arm hard. "You must be sure. You will have a hard life if you stay with him."

"I can't change how I feel. We are both alone and we make each other happy."

Red Leaf's words held a stern warning. "Do not become a wife to him before you marry!"

Chapter Two

January of 1878 came and although neither Emma or Shea spoke of their relationship, it was now behind all they said and did. She looked at him differently and saw herself differently, too. Her feelings and attitudes were changing, growing, maturing; of that she was sure. Many days, she felt that she could stay in this peaceful valley with the Cheyenne forever, as long as it was with Shea. She had forgotten all about going to Fort Reno in spring.

Emma felt special and safe with Shea, and, in her heart, admitted the thrilling shock whenever he turned his blue eyes to her. She had wicked thoughts about what it would be like to be with a man.

Red Leaf had reluctantly backed off for a while, confused because Emma was not a Cheyenne and not subject to their laws. Nevertheless, the old woman watched the two intently.

Emma continued to teach Shea most nights, but when the lesson was over, they lingered together long into the night. They had not progressed past kissing and for the time being this was fine for Emma. Shea's growing affection for her supplanted her sorrow, but some of Red Leaf's words had wormed through. Emma wondered what in blazes she was doing. Was she encouraging something that could never be? What was Shea thinking of her? But she came to believe that somehow her future and his were becoming inexorably linked.

As January froze into February, Shea allowed Emma to teach him outside his lodge on warmer days, for all to see. Finally, some braves approached Little Wolf asking for Emma's tutelage, so she formed an evening class for the men for an hour each day. She found many contrary and resistant, and they had a terrible time accepting instruction from a female. She persisted, knowing that they had to use any means to get what they could from the government. Some men stayed; many left, unwilling and with little patience to learn. Emma was unable to persuade them to stay and was soon left with a half–dozen male students, mostly young men, in her humble classroom built of sticks and hides.

One morning, she was summoned to Little Wolf's lodge. He told her to soften her demeanor while teaching the men, but Emma countered, speaking in Cheyenne, "There is no time for that. I am all they have, so they will just have to get used to me." Little Wolf's eyebrows rose at her reply, but inwardly he had to agree. When she asked if she could hold classes for the women and girls, Little Wolf's response was an emphatic no. She had won a small victory with the men's classes, but she did not pursue the issue. She now knew that teaching the women and girls was impossible—for now.

"I do not like sharing you with the others. It takes you away from me and I have no one to talk with when I return home," Shea said to her one evening when she arrived late.

Emma returned his smile as he fed the fire. Over dinner of roasted rabbit, they exchanged searching glances and looks, each trying to appear not to do so. They accomplished little that night. The talk turned to the progress that she was making in her school with the men. He encouraged her to keep at it and not be intimidated.

That night, whatever the topic, the undercurrent was intimate as they talked. Both were nervous and Emma giggled, she thought, a little too much. Emma caught a look in his eyes—a look of desire—and resisted the temptations pounding within her. She allowed him to kiss her, but nothing more.

The thaw began in early March and with the ground exposed again, Emma was encouraged by Red Leaf Woman to go out with the women and girls to dig roots—anything to keep her and Shea apart. Emma had little idea of what roots she was to dig up, but she was given a root digger, a long curved stick, and spent many days with the girls. They had to travel far and Emma's success was disappointing. The girls tried to teach her how to spot the wild turnips they sought but Emma usually found little or nothing, to her continued embarrassment.

One afternoon, as Emma returned to camp with the root–digging party, they were suddenly set upon by several mounted young braves riding fast toward them. Frightened, Emma broke and ran but quickly realized that this was some sort of game when she heard the laughter and squealing of the girls. She recognized Shea on his tan pony riding with the braves. The women and girls quickly formed ranks after positioning hastily gathered rocks a few feet in front of them. Little Fox explained that only men who counted coup (hitting an enemy with a quirt or stick—a sign of bravery for a warrior) could cross the line of stones.

"What happens then?" Emma asked.

"The man can take all the roots he wants."

Emma sat down with the others and watched the men swirl around them, laughing, calling, and teasing. Several girls had already had all their roots stolen. Then, suddenly, Shea crossed the line of rocks and dismounted in front of Emma.

"I will take your roots."

"Huh?"

"Your roots. Give them to me."

"Uh, I didn't find any."

Everyone laughed. Shamefaced, Shea remounted and rode away with the other men, their mock raid ended.

The women giggled and talked as they gathered up what roots were left and resumed their walk to camp.

Porcupine Girl came beside Emma. "Hawkshadow like you." She looked wistful. "When man go to only one girl to steal her roots, he like her."

"But I had no roots."

"You will have to learn to find them, *Ema'o!*" She giggled and scampered away.

Disquieted by Porcupine Girl's statement, and guessing that probably everyone in camp knew about her and Shea, Emma battled strong feelings whenever she was near him. She was very attracted to him. And Shea made his feelings very public during the mock raid. She was at once confused and exhilarated by his attention.

A few evenings later while in Shea's lodge, she rose to leave. "Well, I think we're done. I can't teach you anything else. You've done really well, Shea. I'm proud of you. But you read as well as I do, even though I was educated by my mother. You don't need me to teach you any more."

"You are right. I do not need you to teach me reading anymore."

"Okay, well, good-night, then." She reached for her shearling, but Shea's hand on her arm stopped her.

"I still need you, Emma."

She knew what he meant and she did not pull away. He pulled her down to him and his mouth was on hers in a lingering kiss, followed by another and another. His hands moved over her body; she touched his muscular chest under his shirt. They parted from the embrace, their eyes locked. They both knew where this was headed and impulsively came together again. She felt swept away as Shea embraced her in his strong arms and unbuttoned her dress, his hands reaching in to caress her breasts. She pulled off his shirt. Soon, they were naked beneath the warm robes and blankets. Shea lay on top of her. She felt his hardness against her belly, but he made no move to do more than kiss and touch her. She felt nervous, aroused.

"Are you a virgin?" he asked, his sharp features softened in the firelight.

"Of course," she said, her whole body tight with nerves.

Trying to be gentle, he began to probe, but she recoiled several times in pain. But each time she rolled away, she pulled him back on top of her to try again. Finally, with a grunt, he was inside her and moved slowly, trying not to hurt her. She was tense and he kissed her tenderly. "Relax—relax. It will not hurt as much if you relax."

Her eyes were wide as the mystery surrounding sex unfolded. But as he moved within her, fear fell away and pain had abated somewhat. His race mattered not to her now; he was a man and she a woman and this ultimate expression of love was what she had been craving. She lay very still for a time, but soon began to move under him. A sensation of pleasure thrummed in her loins and she moaned with passion.

Soon, he began to move more urgently and straightened his arms, his chest making a sucking noise as it pulled away from her breasts. He sweated freely as his hips moved, thrusting himself deep inside her, and moments later, he grunted and flopped back on to her, panting. She did not know how to react or what to do. Correctly, she figured that he was finished, and she was sore where he had entered her. A few minutes later, he withdrew and rolled over beside her, stroking her breasts and belly.

"It hurts the first time. Next time it will be easier for you."

Emma lay enfolded in his arms, wondering at the desires awakened in her heart and body.

Reading and writing were no longer the subjects of their nights together. He became her tutor. Over the new few weeks, he made love to her again and again. It gradually became less painful and she enjoyed the sensations he had awakened in her. They lay entwined under the warm robes, mindful to be quiet and not betray the affair.

She enjoyed watching him as he took her each time and found places to touch him which gave him pleasure. He was particularly fascinated by her breasts, taking them into his mouth and tonguing her nipples until they were erect. She loved to see his nude body as he came to her each night. Some nights he finished quickly, some nights, he lingered in her, moving a little to keep himself erect. He covered her with kisses and caresses.

One night, he rolled her on top of him and her instincts took over as she moved sensuously on him and came to orgasm. She lay on him afterward, her long hair trailing across his shoulder.

"I love you, Emma," he said, kissing her deeply.

"I love you, too," she said. However, that night as she reached another orgasm, her incautious cry alerted the sharp ears of Red Leaf Woman who, unbeknownst to them, hovered nearby Shea's lodge.

No one was more surprised than Emma that she had fallen in love with a half–breed Cheyenne warrior. Just a few months ago, the thought would have been inconceivable, but here it was reality and a sweet surprise, and a welcome one. For since the day of her parents' deaths, her loneliness had increased to the point that she could hardly bear up. She was grateful to the Cheyenne for saving her life, but she had no trusted companionship except that of Shea and Red Leaf Woman. She felt that Shea understood her better than she understood herself. He knew what she needed and she accepted his passion and tenderness.

Shea had formed a strong attachment and need for Emma. On that day near the stream he had taken a chance by kissing her and she had not re-coiled in horror (something that had happened to him many times when he had tried to steal a kiss from Cheyenne maidens). Since he was a half–breed, he was considered somewhat undesirable, despite his handsome face and his status as a proven warrior of many coups. He accepted the fact that he would never marry; it was simply that Cheyenne women preferred bear-ing full–blood Cheyenne children nowadays. He had been an outcast, but that had dulled. Now, he was a young man in love.

Emma gave no thought to the fact that she might get pregnant. All she knew was that Shea loved her and that was enough.

"Who taught you?" she asked one night, enfolded in his arms.

"To make love?"

"Yes."

He smiled. "An Arapaho girl I knew in Colorado. Little Neck."

"She wasn't your cousin, was she?" Emma giggled.

"Of course not."

"Is that why you went to Colorado months ago?"

He grinned. "Partly."

"That's a long way to go to be with a woman!"

"Cheyenne maidens guard their virginity. Not some Arapaho women."

"You're glad I'm not Cheyenne?" she quipped.

"I am," he said, cradling her.

One thought struck Shea again and again as he and Emma coupled and their love for each other deepened. He wondered if she would leave him in the spring; he also worried about what they would do if she became pregnant. These thoughts weighed heavily on him and he spoke to her as she lay naked next to him under the robes.

"You need to decide which world you will live in. If you stay with me, life will not be easy. If you want to leave in spring, I will not stop you."

Emma rolled over and laid her head on his chest. "I don't want to leave you, Shea. I love you. I need you." She sat up, her full breasts brushing his chest. "Do you want me to go?"

He shook his head. "No—but you can go, if that is what you want. You might change your mind."

"I won't. I promise."

He traced the outline of her delicate face with his fingers. "Do you really love me, *nameh'o*?"

"*Nameh'o*?"

"My beloved one," he answered.

Emma smiled. "I do love you, Shea." She placed her mouth on his.

Neither Red Leaf Woman nor the majority of the Cheyenne missed the change in the relationship between Emma and Shea. They had been sleeping together for weeks, and, despite the wagging tongues of the women, Shea had not asked Emma to marry him. Even though they took pains to disguise their passion, everyone guessed their relationship had become sexual; the frank meeting of their gazes and the little smiles tossed back and forth between them were a dead giveaway. But neither of them wanted to face the next step in their relationship. Shea was Indian, Emma was white.

After grudgingly allowing the relationship to go on for a few weeks, Red Leaf Woman confronted Shea as he tended his horse in the paddock on a sunny March day.

"Hawkshadow! Send her to Fort Reno or marry her!"

Shea smiled crookedly as he watched Emma playing with the children in a patch of snow a short distance away. "She does not want to go back to the *veho*. She wants to stay with me," he answered.

"Then you have wedding before the week is out. Her child will need a name." With that, Red Leaf Woman turned on her heel and stomped back to her lodge.

Later that night under the skins, at rest after love, Shea made his decision. "Emma, will you marry me?"

She lay on her side, her slim body against his. She was momentarily startled, but considered it for a few moments. Unable to foresee the consequences, she impulsively answered. "Yes, I will!"

"Good," he said, nipping at her hair. "We will marry tomorrow."

"Tomorrow?" She sat up, surprised.

"When a Cheyenne man asks a girl to marry him, the wedding happens in a day or two. It is how we do things." Shea took one of her exposed breasts in his mouth and Emma slid beneath the skins giggling.

They were safe in their own world, inside the quiet, isolated valley. The outside world had not intruded for months and although Shea knew full well what an outsider's opinion of a mixed marriage would be, he was blinded by his beautiful Emma and felt nothing but her soft, slender body as she gave herself to him. In those moments, truly, nothing else mattered.

Shea had a difficult time convincing Little Wolf that his marriage to Emma was legitimate. The ceremony was hours away and the two men argued in Wolf's lodge.

"The *veho* soldiers will come soon. They will not understand. You put everyone in danger," Little Wolf warned.

"I can protect us."

"What about the people in this camp? Can you protect all of them from the rage of the whites when they find out? They will think she is a captive and try to take her away by force. People could die."

"But I love her. No other maidens want me. Do I have the right to take a wife and raise a family like everyone else? It is not my fault I am half white."

"A family—yes—what about that? Your children will be mostly white. Where will you live then?"

"Are you telling me I cannot live here with my wife?"

"No," Little Wolf interjected. "Only that you are trying to live in two worlds. You cannot. You must choose one or the other."

"Emma has chosen. She wants to live with us."

Eventually, Little Wolf gave his permission for Shea to marry Emma. "When the soldiers come, if she wants to go, you will let her—without a fight. She must realize the truth and make her choice. And if she stays and there is trouble, you both must go. I will not sacrifice lives over this."

Shea agreed and returned to his lodge to dress for his wedding. Since Emma owned nothing, the traditional Cheyenne wedding dowry of horses, food, and buffalo robes was overlooked. Neither of them had immediate family to provide such things. For the ceremony, Red Leaf Woman lent Emma her own wedding dress of white doeskin, elaborately beaded and butter–soft to the touch. When Emma put it on, she realized how tiny the now rotund Red Leaf had once been. Although it was a bit short on Emma's tall frame, it fit. She placed an affectionate kiss on the old woman's cheek in thanks.

Red Leaf smiled. "*Nahtona*," she said.

"What does that mean, Red Leaf?" Emma asked.

"How do you say in English? If I was your mother."

Tears filled Emma's eyes. "You mean daughter?"

"Yes. Daughter. You daughter to me."

The ceremony, conducted by the shaman Bridge, was simple and asked both Emma and Shea if they agreed to live as man and wife. Red Leaf Woman had coached her on her manner and the proper responses in Cheyenne. Minutes later, Emma Louise Jorden became Emma Hawkshadow, wife of Shea Hawkshadow, Cheyenne Dog Soldier.

After a feast of venison and roasted rabbit, accompanied by singing and dancing, the women scooped Emma up in a blanket and carried her to Shea, who waited outside his lodge.

They loved throughout the night. Shea was an intense lover and made her forget her recent trials. When he held her, he clutched her as if she would disappear if he did not hold tight. Emma reveled in the passionate feelings that he had awakened in her. Except for the times she had to retreat to the menstrual lodge, she made love with her husband almost every day.

One morning, after Shea made fast, frantic love to her, Emma lay nude under the blankets and skins and smiled, watching him dress. He returned her smile, then she saw his smile fade.

He could not bear hurting her, but Little Wolf had been right. It was time for truth between them. "The trails are clearing. The soldiers will come soon."

"I am not leaving, Shea," she said, all stubbornness, having read his expression aright. "My life is with you." She hesitated, then said, her eyes looking anywhere but at him, "I'm old enough to decide what I want, but can they take me away against my will?"

"No," he lied. He knelt, placing a kiss on her forehead. "I will never tell you to leave, Emma."

"What if the soldiers try to take me?"

"Whites have lived among us before. The soldiers would not take you against your will," he lied again, then rose and headed for the lodge opening.

"I love you," she said, emerging from the skins, walking toward him, her nude body shadowy in the firelight. Her mouth was on his and his hands moved greedily along the curves of her body. She knew that she had him; he was a willing slave to her. She felt a curious power over him and used her sensuality to keep it.

"I will return tomorrow," he said, playfully slapping her hip and brushing her breasts with his lips.

As he rode away that day, Shea felt guilty for losing his nerve. What he told her was not altogether true. The soldiers could indeed take her away if they really wanted to, regardless of the fact that they were married. He would be powerless to stop them. He sent silent thanks to the Wise One Above that she was not pregnant yet. He feared losing her for he loved her dearly and hungered for her in the night. She quenched his loneliness.

When Shea came home the next evening, he swept her up in his arms and pulled off her clothes, barely getting his own off as well, as Emma pulled him down to her. They forgot to eat supper that night.

In April, a troop from Fort Reno rode into the Cheyenne camp with several wagons loaded with much–needed supplies. The Cheyenne swarmed around the wagons, curious to see what the government had sent them— and they were surprised and grateful that they had received anything at all. Their natural politeness kept them from touching the myriad of goods until the soldiers began unloading the wagons.

Red Leaf pointed out an officer who led the troop, Major Lawrence, who, she said, had always been kind to the Cheyenne. Emma watched him. He rode tall, looking very dashing in his blue uniform. His brown hair was rather long and stuck out from underneath his hat. He also sported a couple of days' growth of beard.

He looked bewildered when he spotted Emma and instantly rode for her, saluting as he dismounted. "I'm Major Adam Lawrence. What are you doing here?"

"Hello, Major, I'm Emma Jorden," she said, mindful to use her maiden name.

Sweaty from his long ride, he took off his hat and ran a hand through his dark hair. She got a good look at him. He was well–built and handsome, with light brown eyes flecked with gold.

"What are you doing here?" he repeated, pausing to look her over carefully. He was not leering, but rather checking her outward appearance to ensure that she was uninjured. "How did you come to be here?" he said again in a brisk tone. He was used to dealing with soldiers and Indians, not young girls.

Emma informed him of the circumstances that brought her to the Cheyenne camp—her parents' demise, then the snowstorm that had interrupted her journey to Bockmeier's.

"Where is the property? We patrol as much as we can, but I can't think of where it is. I know most families living near the Kansas border of the Indian Territory."

"We lived on a homestead near a creek that fed the Cimarron."

Her beauty unsettled him; his thoughts were momentarily unfocused as she spoke. "Were there any other people—other children—with you at the homestead?"

"No. I was an only child," she answered.

She made him nervous, looking so lovely in the bright sun; when he became nervous, he tended to babble. "Oh, I see. Well, I'm real sorry about what happened. When I was sixteen, my parents died days apart from small pox. There are few doctors in these parts, really. I understand how you must have felt."

She took a deep breath knowing that she must be careful. *He is a stranger to me*, she thought. "There was nothing I could do to save them. I never felt so helpless in my life."

"Don't be so hard on yourself, miss. Cholera takes people very quickly."

"We came back from selling the fall harvest at Bockmeier's in October. That night, both my parents complained that their stomachs hurt. They went to the outhouse a lot and got weaker by the minute. By the evening of the next day, both of them had died. I can't think of anything they ate or drank that was different from what I had. Maybe they drank water at the trading post that was tainted. But I can't remember anything unusual that day."

"But why would you go back to Bockmeier's if you believed that the cholera came from there?"

She looked down at the ground. "What other choice did I have? There isn't much out here. Believe me, I had no intention of coming here. I got very lost. Shea Hawkshadow saved my life and was going to take me to your fort, but the weather closed in and I had to stay here for the winter."

When she looked up, he saw that her face had drained of color. He pitied her, aware that she had spent the entire winter with people so unfamiliar to her, hard on the heels of losing her parents.

"I was at Bockmeier's a few weeks ago. There was no mention of an illness last fall. Look, why don't we walk a little, miss? It'll take time to unload the supplies."

As the major ushered her away Shea, alerted by Red Leaf, emerged from the lodge. He came to Emma's side moments later. Major Lawrence immediately saw the protective posture in Shea's manner. Shea fell in beside her, and the hairs on the back of Adam's neck prickled with apprehension. He tried to forget the beautiful girl at his side and allowed the soldier in him to take control of his roiling emotions.

He looked to Shea in an effort to dismiss him. "With all she's been through, I'm grateful to all the Cheyenne for taking care of her." Shea nodded once but did not leave. "Well, then, it's a good thing that I came today. Miss Jorden. I'll take you to Fort Reno. I'll have one of my men help you pack."

Emma's thoughts were a jumble. "Major, I understand your concern, but I want to stay here. It's probably hard to understand but as you can see, I'm well and safe."

"What? Well, you can't!"

The thought of being taken away from Shea deeply frightened her. He was her security, her strong warrior husband—her only grounding. "The Cheyenne rescued me, cared for me. I do not want to leave."

"Shea, help persuade her to come with me. She'll be safe, I promise you," Adam said.

"What harm does it do, Adam? Why can't she stay?" Shea asked.

"Shea, you do know that your tribe is being moved to Kansas very soon."

"I will go wherever they do," Emma cut in.

"You don't understand. When the tribe moves, settlers and soldiers will see you traveling with them. People will think that you're being held against your will."

She did not want to bring trouble to the gentle Cheyenne, but her dependence on Shea was very strong. "I will disguise myself then, so no one notices me. It won't matter once the tribe is resettled," she said.

Major Lawrence tried, unsuccessfully, to rein in his growing exasperation. This girl was stubborn and immature. "Miss, there are no fences or walls around Indian lands. Word will spread that you are among them, no matter where you live. The army can't police every inch of border. It's not safe for you. If you care for the Cheyenne, you must leave."

Emma stopped walking. "I cannot. I'm sorry."

"I can take you by force if necessary, but I don't want that."

"I'm not making any trouble," her voice rose. "Why can't you leave me alone? I just want to live in peace with—" Emma bit back her words.

"With who?" Adam's eyes widened, flicking to Shea then to Emma. He hoped that he was wrong.

"I want an answer. Who keeps you here?" Adam demanded.

Emma stood mute, looking pleadingly to Shea.

"I am her husband," Shea revealed. "We married this winter."

Adam staggered back a full pace. "You're joking!"

There was a long, tense silence. Emma cursed her slip, but perhaps it was better that the truth was out. But Shea was edgy, ready for trouble. Major Lawrence gaped at them, searching for words.

Emma broke the silence. "Major, we just want to be left alone." Sensing that Adam believed she was coerced into the marriage, and with a look to Shea to stay behind, Emma led Adam away. Shea watched them, his arms folded tightly across his chest, his expression grim. "Believe me, I didn't enter into this marriage lightly, Major Lawrence. I'm not a child."

He stopped and faced her, his voice low, but tense. "You can't be more than, what, eighteen? Were you forced into this? 'Cause if you were, I can get you out of here right now. Just say yes and we're gone."

"I wasn't forced into anything. This is what I want."

"It's not that simple. There is no place you two can live in peace. People will hurt you. You both could pay with your lives." Adam took her by the arm and pulled her farther from camp. "I understand you feel obliged to repay the Cheyenne for saving you, but people will not understand why a young girl wants to live with Indians." He paused to think for a moment. "Your marriage doesn't officially exist off the reservation. You could leave with us then stay at Fort Reno. I could get you some money and you could go anywhere you want."

"I'm not leaving. And when the Cheyenne move, I'll go with them."

"You are taking a big chance, more than you realize. Look," he continued, glancing at Shea in the distance, "I don't want trouble either. You're a naïve, foolish girl and I don't say it to be mean. Regardless of the feelings that you have for Shea, this can never work." He walked off several paces, slapping his gloves in his palm, and stood in silence for a long time. The situation was too volatile at the moment with Shea and Emma's marriage so new. He did not technically have the authority to take her and decided to get advice from a superior officer. He had to acquiesce for now. "Since the weather's broken, soldiers will be here often. They will be under orders to safely convey you to Fort Reno any time you want. All right?"

Emma walked him to his horse.

"It's dangerous for you, but more so for the Cheyenne. Be prepared to live with the consequences." Adam mounted his horse and rode away to meet up with his troop. He glanced back at Emma, reminding himself of what this young girl had recently endured, but he battled to squelch his consternation.

Shea came to her and she tried to head off his anger. "I'm sorry, Shea, I know I slipped. But I thought if I talked to him alone it would help. He thought that I was forced into the marriage."

His look was troubled. "He will be back and he will ask you again."

"I won't leave you."

"Are you sure you want to stay?"

Emma placed a soft kiss on his mouth. "They will have to kill me before I let myself be taken from you. But if you say go, I will." She had him hemmed in, but there was suddenly a look in his eye that told Emma that he was thinking about something else entirely.

Shea brooded for days. He knew that Emma was young, innocent and caught up in living with a people much different than anything she had ever known. And she masked her grief in her newfound life, but Shea knew full well the hardships a young girl alone in the west would endure. He figured that his love and protection was the best security that he could offer. Deeper down, he had to confront the terrible loneliness he would suffer if she were taken away. She had become his best friend and he, her ardent lover.

In May, Shea and Emma walked along a ridge above the camp. They stopped near a grove of spindly trees and rested, watching the shadows of fast moving clouds on the valley floor below.

"Emma, we go to Kansas soon. The journey will be hard." He studied her as he spoke. "It will be hardest on you. Stay at Fort Reno until we are settled, then come later."

"No!" she cried, full of misguided boldness. "I'm not afraid. I'll go with you, no matter what." But her face fell with foreboding. "Why are you bringing this up now? Are you telling me to go?"

Shea looked at her somberly. "Not yet, but one day you may have to. I have to keep you safe, remember that. It is what husbands do."

She still had no idea what she was facing living with the Cheyenne; she was love–struck and refusing to see the realities closing in around her. Major Lawrence would come again and Shea feared that she would change her mind and leave him. Unable to let her go in his heart, he pulled her close and kissed her. Soon she lay under him and they made love under the canopy of trees. He was hopelessly addicted to her.

Chapter Three

Although he had decided not to pressure Emma for now, Major Lawrence hoped that the ill–considered marriage of Emma and Shea would run a brief course. A week after the journey to the Cheyenne camp, his patrol endeavored to find the Jorden homestead. What he found there confirmed Emma's story. Two new graves were dug into the hard prairie next to three others, which were years older.

The sod roof of the house was abloom with wildflowers from seeds borne by the relentless prairie wind. The orange and golden flowers sprouting from the roof looked strangely cheerful in this deserted place. Lumber was scarce in this part of Kansas and the outhouse and small barn were the only structures built of wood. Adam found it a depressing, lonely place. The house's sod walls were more than three–feet thick and the floor was planked with wood. The flooring did little to deter insects and mice from invading. Next to the door was a large window protected by a crude wooden shutter that had become unlatched and swung in the wind, making a muffled thump–thump–thump against the earthen wall.

The interior was dark and dank. Adam stepped over a large upended sawbuck table and chairs. The few possessions that remained in the house were strewn everywhere. The main room was fairly large with posts that held up the roof. A blackened hearth built of smooth river rocks had several stones missing. Two bedchambers flanked the main room. Each bedroom had a small glass window. The house was ransacked, but he figured that passing trailers or Indians had done it after Emma had abandoned the place. Emma was right, he thought: The Jorden homestead could not have been further from civilization. Bockmeier's trading post would have been her only refuge. After spending a half hour looking over the place, Adam and his troop returned to Fort Reno.

Revealing Emma and Shea's marriage was unnecessary for the time being, but Adam was obligated to report her presence to his commanding officer, General Considine at Fort Robinson in Nebraska. A white living among

Indians was not all that unusual; however, a beautiful young girl was another matter. If she came to her senses and agreed to come to Fort Reno, that would be the end of it. He was unwilling to put her through more turmoil in the grief of her parents' passing, but he had a duty. He would wait her out.

Considine read Adam's report without much reaction until its significance washed over him. The delicate negotiations with Little Wolf could fall apart and delay the relocation if this girl were used as a pawn by either side. He could not afford to irritate the Cheyenne. They were peaceful and more reasonable than most Plains tribes, but formidable warriors when provoked. He continued reading Adam's report.

"A personal observation, General," Adam wrote. "Emma is seventeen or eighteen, attractive, with long reddish hair. She'll stick out when they relocate. She's serious about staying, but she could not be more naive if she tried. Shea Hawkshadow found her collapsed and alone on the prairie. Hawkshadow gives no explanation for being so far from the Cheyenne reservation at that time. Miss Jorden informed me that her parents died, apparently of cholera. I have personally investigated her story and found it to be true. The Cheyenne took her in and cared for her. I suggest that we do nothing at this time, as she may change her mind or fate may intervene." Adam half–hoped that Shea would succumb to typhus, measles, or dysentery, to name just a few possibilities, and she would have no reason to stay. "Let her play out her show with the Indians; I believe that she will come to her senses and will leave them soon."

Considine filed the proper report with the new Pine Ridge Agency office in South Dakota. The report was perused by a young clerk who tossed it aside, unconcerned, and eventually filed it away.

Many weeks went by and spring warmed the prairie. Emma taught her school during the day but in the night, she was Shea's. Since Major Lawrence's visit, Shea could not bring himself to tell her to go to the fort, even though he knew that it was the only safe place for her during the relocation. She asked many questions about when and where they were going. The new reservation was hundreds of miles away and they would have to travel on foot, a journey Shea knew Emma could never make. She assured him that she could do it and outwardly appeared brave in the face of the hardship. He admired her resolve, but doubted her endurance.

Already, much strife over this newest place for an already disenfranchised people was causing dissension among the leaders of the southern Cheyenne camps. Relocation to Kansas was unacceptable. Shea and the soldier chiefs met with Little Wolf and Dull Knife, and together they hatched a daring, desperate plan to flee north, back to their lands along the Yellowstone and Missouri Rivers. The southern Cheyenne would need the support and influence of Red Cloud's Sioux, at his new Indian agency in South Dakota. After the Custer fight the Cheyenne had been forced to live in the Indian Territory, but Little Wolf was promised by the President that he and his people could return north if they did not like living in the south. Little Wolf soon advised the government that he did not care for the southern lands, but when his requests to return north were ignored, he knew the Cheyenne were in for a struggle someday. That day had come.

The break would involve every able–bodied person in camp, but Shea knew full well that Emma could never make that journey; they would be pursued by the army and likely caught and killed. He worried over her fate should the soldiers capture her. If she were installed at the fort before the break, no suspicion would fall upon her and, by some slim chance, she might return to him. But if she were captured with the fleeing Cheyenne, she would be arrested and tried or worse. He feared angry soldiers might beat and torture her, and it plagued him. He had to somehow convince her to get to the safety of Fort Reno. Part of him regretted his impulsive involvement with her. She would be better off among the whites; reservation life was bleak and difficult. Although winter had come early, hunting had been fairly good. They would not be so lucky in Kansas, which was called the 'dead country' by the Cheyenne. A small tribe had lived there some years ago and nearly all of them had become ill or starved to death. There was no game to hunt, and farming was impossible for they did not know how.

Sometimes when he held Emma in the night, he had terrible waking dreams of her sick and dying from the myriad of diseases that afflicted the Plains people, or being hunted by the soldiers. The thought of her suffering was more than he could bear. Although it went against all he felt in his heart, he would have to give her up. He brooded over the devastation and betrayal she would feel. He came to accept that these few months together would be all they would ever have.

But spring brought terrible sickness to the camp, delaying the planned escape. The Cheyenne called it the lingering sickness, but Emma recognized it as dysentery (she had contracted a case of it when she was five). Measles broke out, too, and although Emma suffered through it when she was ten, courtesy of one of Bockmeier's children, she was stunned when the Cheyenne began to die from it.

While Shea and several other braves had gone on a desperate two-week-long hunting trip, she herself fell ill with diarrhea and had lost a lot of weight. With her strength barely restored, she struggled to help in the middle of the epidemic. Emma saw to it that everyone boiled the river water before using it, for she was sure that was where the dysentery had originated. Bridge, the medicine man, backed her edict and employed her as his nurse. He brewed black sage tea to treat those with dysentery. He also had a salve for those afflicted with measles sores, but many were near death from high fevers, and several young children and old ones had already died. Emma was heartsick, confronted with the awful reality of suffering endured by these gentle people. She tended the sick as best she could.

The healthy women pitched in, including Red Leaf, who remained in good health despite her exposure to the sick. The women managed to bring in small game, but they fell ill, too, and soon, few were able to hunt. What little food remained was spoiled. Emma had to do something fast; four people had died that week and many more were perilously close. Their situation was desperate; no medicine had come with the government's shipment. While the hunting party was away, things got much worse. Two, sometimes three people a day died. Emma was depressed and her outlook pessimistic.

She was relieved when Shea's hunting party was sighted coming over the ridge. She ran through the tall grass to greet him. They hugged and kissed. The other hunters rode on ahead, their ponies laden with fresh kill. Shea dismounted and walked beside Emma, leading his pony.

"Welcome home. Are you well?"

His eyes searched her lovely face. "Tired. I missed you."

"Missed you too. How was the hunting?"

"Good. Three deer and a buffalo, but we had to go very far to get to them and go quickly before the Pawnee spotted us." He eyed her carefully. "You are pale."

"I was sick for a few days, but I'm all right now. I'm glad you're home." She did not have the heart to spoil his homecoming. She tenaciously held onto those few remaining moments of normalcy.

"Come. I'll fix you something to eat."

Her sweet welcome did not last long. As he unsaddled his pony, she saw his gaze go to the horizon. He saw the new briers and mounds at the burial grounds. "What has happened?"

She swallowed hard. "Shea, things got worse after you left. Nearly everyone is sick. Six have died this week alone." She fought tears, remembering the burial of the disease–ravaged bodies of the thin, frail children. "Arrow and his wife and two children, Flat Nose and Singing Crow, have died from measles. All the people who went to trade with that wagon train that passed a few weeks ago are sick or have died. That has to be where the measles came from."

He said nothing and walked off alone to the briers to offer prayers for the dead. She took his horse and tended it for him. He was gone a long time.

Emma's love for Shea was little protection against the diseases ravaging the camp. Although she boiled all water and cleaned everything they ate carefully, Shea quickly succumbed and fell ill with dysentery. She watched helplessly as it weakened him day by day. His cheeks hollowed and his skin sank against the bones of his body, and he was so terribly weak. She forced food down his throat and he seemed to be on the mend. In late June, he seemed stronger, but other Cheyennes still suffered.

"Shea," she said one morning. "I have to go to Fort Reno to buy food and medicine. I'll need to take someone with me to show me where it is, and we'll probably need a couple of pack horses. I will have Red Leaf look after you while I'm away."

He managed to rise up on his elbows, shaking his head feebly. "No, Emma, they will not help us. The army will do nothing."

"I'll go to Major Lawrence. He'll help."

"No, Emma. It will not work. And it is too dangerous."

"I can do it. I have my money, remember?" She produced the tobacco tin and showed him the contents. "Now it can do you some good. I was saving it for an emergency and we have one."

He sighed and spoke at length. "Okay. Take Black Deer with you. He is not sick and the soldiers know him well. But," he added, "be very careful."

Emma kissed his cheek and ran to find Black Deer.

A bewildered corporal in the guard house of Fort Reno signaled to open the gate. Emma, accompanied by the Cheyenne Black Deer, rode in, leading two pack horses. The sun glinted on her auburn tresses as it whipped in the wind. She wore a pink and blue striped dress that had belonged to her mother, and a pair of her father's large gloves covered her hands. A small bundle tied on a thong was draped across her shoulders. Activity in the yard ceased in waves as the soldiers beheld perhaps the only white woman within a hundred miles, and a strikingly beautiful one, too.

Black Deer pointed out the commander's office and they headed across the yard. Emma slid off the pony quickly, feeling very self–conscious, and headed inside alone. There she encountered another bewildered soldier, a young blond lieutenant.

She smiled prettily, showing her dimples. "I'd like to see Major Lawrence, please." The lieutenant rose and tripped over his own feet as he knocked on the door of Lawrence's office and disappeared inside.

Adam came out quickly. He seemed pleased to see her, despite the tensions of their last encounter. "Emma!" he gushed, forgetting himself at the sight of her.

"I need your help, Major Lawrence."

"Of course. Come in, please."

She removed her gloves as she stepped inside his office. He was terribly distracted by her. The color in her cheeks was high from the ride and her hair shimmered in the sunlight sliding in the room's only window.

The lieutenant resumed his seat outside and sat very still, straining to listen to the goings–on within.

Adam regained himself quickly as he closed the office door behind him. "Sorry I used your first name."

"Emma is fine," she replied, trying to act more grown–up than she was. She came straight to the point. "Nearly all the Cheyenne are sick and they have no medicine. They're very low on food, too. I've come to buy what they need. And could your surgeon show me how to dispense the medicines?"

"Buy? You have money?"

Her answer was very pointed. "I never said that I didn't have money. My mother saved it up."

He struggled to understand this girl, who at once was so naive, yet so unwavering and stubborn. "So, you could've left any time you wanted."

She ignored his comment and took the proffered chair. "I think it's dysentery and many have the measles, too. They traded with a wagon train a few weeks ago and I heard that they were carrying many sick people. I think the river water is tainted, too. I'm no expert, but you'll agree this wasn't their fault and they need proper food and medicine. So far, twenty–seven have died, mostly little children and the old ones."

"I am sorry. Are you all right?"

"I was sick for a week. I think I had food poisoning. Please help us. I have my pony, Black Deer's, and two pack horses. We'll buy as much as we can carry, as much as you can spare."

She tried to appear composed, but her stomach fluttered with nerves. She knew precisely what Major Lawrence was thinking as his eyes moved over her. Helping Shea and his people was uppermost in her mind, and she did not have the patience for his judgments today.

Adam rose and stood at the window behind his desk, then turned his attention back to her. Without taking his eyes from her, he called in the lieutenant from the anteroom. "Please escort the lady to the supply house and load a wagon with food and meat for the Cheyenne, and any other supplies that she requires." Emma heard the flat disapproval in Adam's tone, but she was getting what she needed, so she ignored it. "Have Doctor Malley see me right away. Dismissed." His tone softened some as the lieutenant closed the door. "We have guest quarters that you can use for the night, Emma. It's too late to get everything loaded today."

"Now, how much do I owe you?"

"Nothing. We'll get the supplies to them. We'll leave in the morning. I'll lead the contingent."

"Thank you. By the way, where will Black Deer sleep tonight? And will he be fed as well?"

He was not a cold man, but clearly disturbed by Emma's allegiance to the Cheyenne. She had little idea of the realities around her but for all her ignorance, she was trying to do the right thing.

"Well, he can't stay in the barracks. I'll find him a place, maybe in the stables, and I'll make sure that he has food," Adam promised awkwardly as he came around the desk. "Would you join me and my officers for dinner tonight? I'll come for you at seven?" Emma nodded and shook his sweaty hand as she departed. "Good. I'll see you tonight, then. And, Emma, you can call me Adam when we're alone if that makes you more comfortable."

Emma smiled then went outdoors with the young lieutenant in the lead. She waved to Black Deer to follow.

Adam fell heavily into his chair, rubbing his forehead. "My God," he muttered. He had a crushing headache.

All eyes turned to Emma as she walked across the yard and she felt the power of her sexuality for the first time. She inwardly enjoyed the attention, but her mission was not forgotten. She felt strong, noble, a savior.

In the supply house, a soldier was pressed into service, helping Black Deer load a wagon. Emma pitched in, but the soldier quickly grabbed the bag of flour from her arms. "Miss, this work is too hard for you."

She grinned. "I'm used to hard work." She easily lifted the fifty–pound bag and hefted it into the wagon.

A short time later, a thin, dark–haired, middle–aged man with an angular face came into the shed. The soldier stopped loading and saluted. "Miss, this is Major Malley, our fort's surgeon."

"Call me Roarke," he said to Emma. "Major Lawrence ordered me to accompany you and the troop to the camp and do what I can to help the Cheyenne. We'll leave at dawn if that's all right."

"That would be fine."

When the loading was finished, after including boxes of medicines, Roarke offered to escort Emma to the guest barracks at the far end of the yard. "Major Lawrence told me that you live with the Cheyenne."

"Since last October."

"He also told me about your parents. I am very sorry."

"I wish I could've done something more, but to this day, I just don't know what it was. It happened so fast."

"Ma'am, you can comfort yourself knowing that they didn't linger in that state for days or weeks." He shot her a sidelong glance, noting her reaction when he called her ma'am.

She looked at him with some exasperation. "Adam told you everything, I see," she said, her voice flat.

"He told me that you're married to Shea Hawkshadow."

"Yes," she breathed, bracing herself for his admonishment.

"I won't say anything unless you give me leave to do so. Adam told me because I'm a physician, in case you need medical advice. In case you found yourself, ah, in case you are—you should find yourself with child."

Emma blushed. "I'm not pregnant, doctor."

Malley could not help exhaling a long breath of relief. "Mind me asking how old you are?"

"Seventeen last August."

"You're sure that you're not pregnant?"

"I'm sure. My mother did tell me the facts about that, at least the basics. I remembered how embarrassed she was about it."

"I only worry that you won't get proper care living in that camp."

"Cheyenne women have babies all the time. They're fine, during and after."

"Yes, but Indians are made of sterner stuff that we. I can advise you how to plan your pregnancies. It's not foolproof, but—"

Emma was embarrassed that Dr. Malley would broach such a personal subject with her hard on the heels of a first meeting. She understood his concern, but was not prepared for his frankness. "Thank you, doctor. I'll let you know." She went up the steps of the guest quarters.

He smiled at this strange girl. "I'll see you at supper tonight."

She entered the building and found it clean; her belongings were already in one of the four rooms that occupied the building. She peered out the window and saw the ponies and pack horses being led to the stables by Black Deer. She looked around the sparse room, which was furnished with a bed, dresser, chair, and a washstand; these accommodations were far better than what she was used to in the humble soddy or Shea's lodge.

The two–day ride had tired her and she napped throughout the afternoon until a knock at the door woke her. "Be right there," she called, her voice thick from sleep. She quickly smoothed her dress and tied her hair back into a pony tail while Adam waited outside.

When she emerged, his eyes widened. She looked even lovelier with her hair pulled back. The subtle outline of her cheek showed. He tried to rein in his smile, but failed miserably. "Shall we?" he said, offering his arm.

"Sorry to keep you waiting. I fell asleep. And I don't have a watch." Adam smiled and they walked to the officers' private dining room at the rear of the mess hall. "Adam, it's all right if you tell the men that I'm married to Shea. Everyone will find out when we reach camp anyhow."

"Are you sure, Emma?"

She nodded.

The ten officers at a big table fell silent and rose as Emma entered the dining room on Adam's arm. He seated her to his right then took his place at the head of the table.

The table dazzled Emma's eyes, used to wooden bowls, tin plates, and crude utensils. It was set with pretty blue dishes, silver flatware, and drinking cups made of glass.

Adam was more nervous than Emma as he announced, "Gentlemen, this is Mrs. Shea Hawkshadow. She will be joining us tonight."

Everyone, except Adam and Roarke, gaped at her. All of the men there knew that Shea was a Cheyenne.

The dinner of beef steak, roasted potatoes, and beans was the finest meal that Emma had enjoyed in more than a year, and the glass of wine offered to her soothed her nerves. It was the first time that she had drank wine and she liked its sweet, light taste. But the men watched her and it made her uncomfortable. She took another glass, then another with supper. It calmed her nerves quite a lot.

Attempting to hide their shock that she was the wife of a half–breed, most officers tried to be pleasant and affable, and paid particular attention to Emma. For a while, she forgot the Cheyenne's troubles. Dessert was cake with maple syrup glaze and she was presented with a huge piece. She ate it slowly, relishing every sweet bite.

One of the men, Captain Derek, addressed her. "Ma'am, Shea Hawkshadow's a Cheyenne. I know he's a breed, but he lives with the Indians on the reservation, right?"

"Yes." She resented his use of the word 'breed' to describe Shea.

Everyone fell silent as Derek asked the question that had lurked beneath everyone's polite conversation throughout supper. "Forgive me, ma'am, I don't quite understand why you married one of them. I heard that Hawkshadow found you after your parents died. Is it because you feel that you owe something to the Cheyenne?"

Emma looked to Adam who watched her, awaiting her reply. Emma saw a little triumph in his eyes. She reached for her wine glass before relating her story to the young, plain–faced man. "The Cheyenne have taken care of me, and yes, I feel I owe them, but that's not why I stayed."

"But," Captain Derek persisted, "to marry someone of another race— I'm curious from an empirical point of view."

Emma did not understand the word but understood his meaning. She would always remember his look and tone of voice, that of open disapproval and thinly veiled intolerance.

"Well," she began, swallowing another mouthful of wine, "the fact that my husband's half Indian makes no difference to me." Several of the men muttered in low disapproving tones to one another. Emma felt attacked and was on the defensive. She wondered why Adam did not intervene, but was too upset even to look to him. "To you it might be a matter of race, but not to me."

Several forks clattered disapprovingly to the plates and Emma found it difficult to meet anyone's eyes, keeping hers on her half–eaten cake, no longer sweet and satisfying. She felt the stinging silence in the room and her voice seemed overloud. "My marriage is no one's business. We hurt no one." Suddenly, a wave of dizziness made her stomach turn and she started to perspire. She felt every eye upon her and felt the weight of their judgment. She flushed and stammered, "He's half–white, you know." The room became hot and oppressive, seeming to close in around her. She bolted out of the chair and ran outside into the cool night.

When Adam found her, she was behind the mess hall on her knees, vomiting. He put his hand on her forehead as her dinner came up.

She panted and gagged as Adam held her. "You all right?" he asked with a slight chuckle, pulling her fouled pony tail away from her face.

She shook her head and, between gags, managed, "I never had wine before. I think that it made me sick." She crouched on her hands and knees, taking gulps of air.

"I don't think that it was the wine."

"How dare that man speak to me like that! How could you just sit there and do nothing?"

"Derek was out of line and I'll speak to him about it," he apologized. But the truth was that Adam did not want to stop Derek. He was trying, in a clumsy, heavy–handed way, to teach Emma a lesson, to let her feel the sting that would dog her as long as she was married to Shea.

She heaved again, but her stomach was empty. She sat back on her heels, resting against him. Her forehead cool and sweating, she shook from the spasms of nausea. Malley had followed them outside, but Adam motioned him away.

"Everything you think about me is right. I am naive and foolish. But I'm trying to help the Cheyenne in only way I know. I didn't know what else to do or where to go. And your men must think that I'm mad. The looks on their faces—oh!" She whimpered, but did not possess the energy to do so much as weep. "I am so embarrassed!"

Adam helped Emma back to her room. She crawled across the bed and slumped, face down. Adam poured water from the pitcher on the washstand, soaked his handkerchief and applied it to her forehead.

"Do you want Dr. Malley to bring you some medicine for your stomach?" She shook her head. "I'll leave you to recover, then. My quarters are across the yard if you need anything." Emma mumbled thank you. His previous amusement had evaporated. "I'm sorry. I didn't think they'd be so rude. But I warned you that people wouldn't understand."

"What gives them the right to judge what I do? They don't understand and neither do you! And I get the distinct feeling that you're angry at me!"

Adam closed the door and sat on the room's only chair. "I am not angry. I just find myself wondering why a beautiful, intelligent young girl would sentence herself to such a hard life. I'm trying to understand. We all are."

Her eyes narrowed. "If I were ugly and stupid, no one would care? I don't consider living among them to be a sentence."

"That's not what I meant. You certainly caught me off guard that day at the camp. I do what I can to help the Cheyenne because I respect them and because of the negotiations with Little Wolf, but don't fool yourself. You are living in conditions where disease, starvation, and violence are very real."

"I love Shea," she stated. She slipped off her boots which thumped on the floor; Adam saw how old and worn they were. She lay back down, still dizzy and sweaty. She was still pretty, Adam thought with a disconcerting thump of his heart.

"Someone else could've done this errand. You didn't have to come," Adam said.

"I figured that a Cheyenne messenger wouldn't be taken seriously. Those people are in real trouble. Would you rather I let them all die?"

"Of course not."

Emma's mission of mercy fell around her in pieces and she bit back tears. "I was so worried. People were dying faster than I could get to them."

"Disease has killed more Cheyenne than bullets, do you understand that now?" he said, knowing his painful point had been made. He softened his manner. "How was Shea when you left?"

Her voice was faint. "He had dysentery, but he was getting better."

Now that he believed he had torn her down, he tried to rebuild her spirits. "You were very brave undertaking such an errand, Emma." Adam came to her and felt her forehead. "But do you think you'll be well enough to travel tomorrow?"

"I have nothing left to get sick on," she said with a crooked smile, "but I have to get back. They need me."

The few remaining healthy Cheyenne scouts spotted Emma riding with Major Lawrence and Black Deer at the head of a column of a dozen soldiers and a wagon laden with supplies. Few people greeted them as the group entered camp.

Emma looked for Shea, expecting him to meet her, but Red Leaf Woman came to her, saying that he had not been out of the lodge since she had left. The old woman looked in on him and had done what she could but Red Leaf could not hide her worry. Emma ran to her lodge, leaving Adam, Black Deer, and Dr. Malley to the unloading.

"Shea? Shea?" she whispered. "I got everything we need, and Adam brought a doctor, too." He did not stir. His face was still and the outline of his skull showed clearly against the skin. Alarmed, she put her head to his chest and heard a faint heartbeat, but his breathing was shallow and weak. "Shea!" she cried, trying to rouse him. Just then, Adam entered. "Help him!" Emma was shaking and pale as he knelt beside Shea, feeling for a pulse.

He put his canteen to Shea's dry lips and spilled water upon them. "Get Dr. Malley." She sprinted outside and returned with the doctor in seconds.

Malley opened his case and examined Shea quickly, then listened to his heart and breathing. "He's in an advanced stage of dysentery. He's very weak, he's dying." He spoke insensitively and Emma recoiled in alarm. At that moment, Shea was attacked by an uncontrolled bowel movement. A foul odor filled the lodge. "I'll clean him up. Get me more water and boil it and add several drops of this," he said handing her a bottle of iodine. He then took out a metal syringe and filled it from a small bottle of amber liquid and plunged it into Shea's arm. "Go—we're fighting time."

Adam followed a panicked Emma as she ran for the stream and filled the water skins. He took them and carried them back to the lodge for her. Soon, a pot was boiling and Adam added the iodine to the water. Using his handkerchief as a sieve he poured the water into a hollowed–out gourd to cool.

Shea's clothing had been changed and he was wrapped in clean blankets.

Doctor Malley spoke. "Mrs. Hawkshadow, you were right to demand the supplies. If his condition is any indication of the others, we have an epidemic on our hands."

Emma braced herself. "Will he live?"

This time the doctor spoke with a little more consideration of her distress. "His chances are good if he survives the next couple of days." Emma sank to her knees next to Shea. "Give him clean water as often as you can and call me if he seems—call if he gets worse. Keep him warm." Emma watched Shea's thin, frail form as his chest rose and fell with great effort. "I have other patients to see. I'll be back later."

Adam leaned over Emma. "Pray," he said as he departed.

"Don't know how," she whispered after he left.

Emma kept watch over Shea the entire night and dribbled water into his mouth as he reflexively swallowed. For many endless hours, she awaited each rise and fall of his chest and kept the fire burning to keep him warm, fighting to keep him alive.

Just after dawn, Dr. Malley and Adam returned. After a short examination, Malley pronounced, "He's better, but follow my instructions to the letter and try to get him to eat something soft. Give him gruel or whatever serves for that here."

Adam gave Emma a tight smile, then left with Malley. Weary, Emma laid next to Shea, took his hand in hers and finally slept.

The contingent stayed several days. Adam watched Emma tend Shea with great care and tenderness. He spent many hours with Shea and the two men struck a guarded friendship.

One night, Emma and Adam were on watch in the lodge while Shea slept.

"You really love him, don't you?" Adam said with resignation.

She smiled. "Yes, I do." She caught an odd look in Adam's eyes, but was too worn–out to wonder about it long.

When Adam made his farewell to Emma days later, he was sure. This farm girl raised in a sod house had inadvertently stolen his heart with her powerful combination of naiveté, courage, stubbornness, strength, and extraordinary beauty. Thing was, she did not know how lovely she was. He envied Shea Hawkshadow's luck. He tried very hard to not betray his true feelings when she hugged him in parting.

"If there is anything else you ever need, send a message to the fort. I'll see you soon."

Within two weeks, despite four more deaths from measles and two from dysentery, the Cheyenne began to recover. The hunters went out and brought in antelope and rabbits. The fresh meat, coupled with the medicine from the fort, rejuvenated them quickly. To Emma's amazement and relief, Shea quickly recovered.

In the summer of 1878, the situation for the southern Cheyenne worsened. The government of the Indian Territory and Indian Agents ordered that they relocate to Kansas, despite Little Wolf's demands to take his people back to the Yellowstone country. Little Wolf protested and stalled as long as he dared, but the fact was the government wanted the camps of the Cheyenne split north and south. Together, they were a powerful, formidable foe, especially with the large Sioux reservation nearby Red Cloud's reservation in South Dakota. The Sioux were cousins to the Cheyenne and their combined forces could not be ignored. A common belief was that distance would quell uprisings.

Little Wolf knew this and was left with no choice but to execute the planned escape from the camps and flee north in defiance of the proposed treaty and resettlement. The council decided that the Cheyenne tribes in the Indian Territory would make the break for freedom, whatever the cost.

Shea's marriage to Emma came to a crossroads. Each time he returned from council meetings, he tried hard to hide his deep sadness. He would have to leave Emma behind, for she could never make the journey. He counted on Emma's relationship with Adam to save her. He knew that the army would be in hot pursuit once they jumped the reservation. He also knew many of his people would die along the way. The south country held only sickness and famine for them, but their backs were against the wall. Shea would have to break his promise and tell Emma that it was time for her to go.

Shea had told Red Leaf Woman who wept bitter tears, but knew it was the right thing to do. She kept up appearances, but inwardly mourned the loss of her *nahtona*, her daughter.

Unsure of the actual date of his birthday, Shea had told Emma that he was born in the month the Cheyenne called 'the time when the horses get fat.' He said the whites called the month June. He believed that he was twenty–years–old. To celebrate, Emma choose a day in June and prepared Shea's favorite foods. That night they made tender love to each other. This act of devotion made Shea feel all the more guilty that he had to leave Emma behind.

Emma turned eighteen in August, cheerful and oblivious of what was to come. She did note, however, that no one spoke of the move to Kansas anymore.

Then one morning, several companies of soldiers encircled the ridge above the valley, training cannons on the camp, ensuring that the Cheyenne would not mount a rebellion before the relocation to Kansas.

"Why is the army here, Shea? What have we done?" Emma asked, watching the soldiers pitch tents and light cooking fires.

While Shea appreciated her use of the word *we*, he could tell her nothing apart from the fact that the army was taking out insurance that the Cheyenne would remain peaceful and in their camps until the move to Kansas. He went to the paddock and mounted his pony.

Shea rode out alone to meet Adam under a white flag of truce. "Why do the soldiers train guns on us?" His pony was impatient and stomping, in imitation of its rider's mood.

Adam looked very troubled. Although it was a breach of duty, he had to warn Shea somehow, not so much for his sake, but for Emma's. Shea could take care of himself. In this situation, Emma could not. He sidled his horse close to Shea's pony and spoke quickly in an undertone. "We've heard rumors that the Cheyenne plan to fight the relocation. Tomorrow, we're to collect all weapons—guns, knives, spears, bows and arrows— everything except the tools needed to prepare food. The women can keep their skinning knives, but that is all."

Little Wolf had been right after all, Shea thought. The army wanted submission, plain and simple. "You would starve us? How can we hunt without weapons?" Much more was at stake—more than a simple, albeit forced, relocation. He watched the soldier's faces nearby. They were nervous, afraid. "You would let this happen to us—to Emma?"

"I have to follow orders of the territorial authorities." Shea made a crude pumping gesture with his hand to show his irritation. "Little Wolf left us no choice. He will not negotiate. He refused the land in Kansas. We went to American Horse's camp and he refused to talk. Even Dull Knife refused when we met at his camp last month. And if Emma and you are caught up in this, there is nothing that I can do. Emma said that she'd take her chances and I guess she's going to have to prove it. I've done all I can."

"I guess we have no choice, eh?" Incensed, Shea wheeled his pony around and quickly rode off, but Adam's warning had not gone unheeded.

Under cover of night, the Cheyenne hid rifles and guns, along with the few bullets they had. Some rifles and revolvers were disassembled and put into the bundles that they planned to take with them on their flight and buried nearby. Women hid the ammunition under their clothing, hoping that it would be missed if soldiers searched them. The warriors buried their guns and bows and arrows in the ground.

When Adam and his men arrived the next morning, Little Wolf saw to it that a token amount of guns, knives, and revolvers were produced when the lodges were searched. The soldiers were smug and laughed; many weapons were broken and rusted, and little usable ammunition was found.

Shea watched Adam from a distance, noting that he did not participate in the search, a deliberate act of quiet defiance, he knew. Emma wanted to speak to him, but Shea stopped her.

"He is doing his job. Leave him alone."

Shea's guilt over leaving Emma heightened as the night of the fleeing drew near. The escape would be daring and dangerous and might not succeed. Little Wolf's camp was to meet up with Dull Knife's people at the north branch of the Canadian River many miles north of the Cheyenne camps. As for Emma, Shea reasoned, Adam would take her to the fort and at least she would be safe. He steeled himself to tear his lovely Emma from his life. He feared for her being left alone, knowing that it would wound her deeply. And he dreaded being alone again. After brooding for days, he spoke to her in their lodge a couple of nights before the outbreak.

"Emma, you have to do something and I want your promise that you will ask me no questions."

Emma slid over to sit beside him. The fire threw distorted shadows around the lodge. She grinned. "Oh, this sounds serious. What is it?"

He did not return her smile. "I want your promise."

Her smiled faded and she pulled up her knees to her chest, wrapping her arms around them. "Okay, what's this about?" she said in an offhand manner.

"Emma," he complained.

"All right, I promise. No more questions."

As he spoke, he could not look at her. "Tomorrow, you are to take a horse and ride up to the ridge and tell Major Lawrence that you want to go to Fort Reno."

Her head snapped up. "What?"

"Listen to me and do what I tell you! Do not question me!" he barked.

She shut her mouth. She had rarely seen Shea angry. It unsettled her.

"Tell him that we are not getting along—that we fight a lot—and that you want to go away from me. You are to tell him that you made a mistake marrying me." He saw a thousand questions knocking at her lips and a look of hurt and bewilderment. "Ask for—" He searched for the right word in English.

"Refuge?" she finished, deflated.

"Yes—yes, refuge. After you are at the fort, go someplace else with your money—a city or town—anywhere but here." Her face crumbled and her eyes welled with tears. "You will be in terrible danger if you stay. Adam will look after you and see that you get to safety."

"You want me to leave."

He swallowed hard. "Yes."

"Aren't you going to tell me why?"

"You promised no questions."

"You're telling me to go away and you won't tell me why. What did I do?"

"You have done nothing wrong. I cannot protect you here anymore."

"Protect me from what?"

"You must go."

"Don't you love me?"

He touched her cheek, slippery with tears. "I love you, Emma. I always will."

"What if I don't want to go?"

"Emma, you have no choice!"

She held onto a shred of hope. "You want me to wait at Fort Reno, then follow when you're resettled in Kansas. Is that why? So I won't be seen with you?"

"It is too dangerous for you to stay here." He pulled her to him. "I ask you to do this because I love you. Say you will obey me."

Her voice trembled. "If that's what you want, I will do it."

Late in the night, he reached for her. She was still awake, frightened and uncertain about why he had asked such a thing of her. He made tender love to her.

"Shea, please don't make me go," she begged.

He could not answer. He did not want her to go, but he could not let her stay.

However, the next morning, Emma made no move to pack her few possessions. When Shea asked her why, her answer angered him.

"I am not leaving."

"Yes you are. You promised me last night."

"This morning while I bathed in the river, I heard about the outbreak planned for tomorrow night." Shea's eyes slowly lifted to meet hers. He saw both love and misguided defiance in her eyes. "I've picked up enough Cheyenne to understand what's going to happen. I want to go wherever you go."

"Emma, you will never make it. I wanted to send you away to protect you. We tried to leave this place once before and failed. This time we will get away or die trying. I do not want you dead. You cannot live off the land as we do. You are not Cheyenne."

"I've lived off the land all my life! And I'm strong! I can do it, I know I can."

"No!"

"I have no life without you," she pleaded. "I will not be left behind. And if I'm left here and questioned, who knows what they'll do to make me talk? I am safer with you to watch over me."

"You do not know where we are going. What if you get lost? I have to watch over the people. I am a Dog Soldier."

"I can find my way. Just don't leave me behind!"

Shea saw the obstinate set to her jaw and he knew there was no getting around her when she got this way. He hated to admit it, but her argument made sense. Since she knew the plan, she would be interrogated and could break; after all, she was only a girl. He could not bear the thought of her suffering.

He took her into his arms. "You are brave, *nameh*'o," he said, his lips touching hers. "You will come, but you will do everything you are told. I will not let you out of this promise."

"I promise—I mean it. I will do what I'm told if it means being with you. Where are we going?"

"Home."

Chapter Four

September ninth, 1878, was the beginning of the Cheyenne Outbreak that would last more than five months and cause the Cheyenne to run fifteen–hundred miles to their homelands along the Yellowstone and Missouri rivers. Broken hearts and broken promises compelled more than two hundred eighty–four men, women, and children to run north, to run home.

Under a new moon, the flight began. Shea crept out of camp, leaving Emma to Red Leaf Woman's care, and left with the other Dog Soldiers. The warriors' job was to guard the rear until everyone who was going was away. Some of the elderly and sick had to remain, and quiet, tearful good–byes had already been made. In the sand hills, Shea found the few possessions he had buried there many nights ago. He then took up his post.

The Cheyenne sneaked away by twos and threes under the cover of night through a cleft in the valley, in a daring bypass of the soldiers' guns on the ridge, taking advantage of the new moon which gave no light. Shea and the other scouts watched for hours as all got away unobserved, with not a single shot fired from the cannons. Then came the signal that all were away and it was time to leave. As Shea was about to descend behind a hill, his glance lingered a moment on his lodge where he had savored some measure of happiness.

Shea soon found Emma with Red Leaf and Little Fox and was impressed that she moved as quickly and quietly as the rest, treading on tufts of grass to hide her footprints. Reassured, he went back to the rear guard. To keep the escape secret until dawn touched the shallow valley, the people moved along the ridge instead of heading for the open sandy hills. Soldiers rode patrol around the valley and it took great effort to avoid them. The Cheyenne's sharp ears heard them and, at a prearranged signal, the Cheyenne became still and flattened themselves against the walls of the gullies that snaked through the broken hills; even the children and babies were silent, somehow sensing the great danger. Several times, soldiers passed within mere yards with no idea that another living soul was so near. In the moonless sky, stars winked on when clouds parted and frightened many who flattened themselves on the ground, certain that the soldier's guns and cannon would begin firing. But all was silence, so they rose from the shadows and moved on. Later that night, a figure moved swiftly past Emma and Red Leaf. Emma did not know the woman's name, but she knew that she had been very pregnant; now she held her newborn close as she ran to catch up. Emma was astounded at her stamina mere minutes after giving birth. The group kept on until dawn without rest.

The next morning, it took several hours for the army to realize that the camp was deserted. Large fires had been built the night before and many still smoked, screening the camp from the watching eyes on the ridge. Adam had his suspicions, but never thought the Cheyenne would dare run with so many guns trained on them. Through his binoculars he studied the camp a long time, seeing no movement. With great caution, he led a small but well–armed troop down into the camp.

The only people found were the very old and the sick. Lodges had been abandoned and nearly every comfort left behind. Angry that they had been duped, soldiers began tearing down lodges and heaping them upon the dying fires before Adam ordered it stopped. As he searched the deserted lodges he also had a hard time burying his anger. He faulted himself for not being more suspicious of Little Wolf's acquiescence, his sudden acceptance of the relocation to Kansas, and his tolerance of the guns pointed at the camp for the past weeks. Adam had intentionally warned Shea that they were going to collect weapons and he knew the Cheyenne had produced only a token amount. But he was in command; he had to bottle up his consternation and do his duty. As he searched the lodges, his fears surfaced with the knowledge that Emma had gone with them. The desperate plan would not work. The army would catch them in a day or two, and they would be sent to Kansas. If Emma were among them, most likely she would be taken away by force and shipped east, if she were lucky. Slapping his gloves in his palm, he ordered the remaining Cheyenne taken to the nearby camp of American Horse, hoping to find a few Cheyenne still there—and possibly information about the breakout. A rider was dispatched to Fort Reno with a message to telegraph to General Considine in Nebraska, informing him of the outbreak; the return message from Fort Robinson ordered Adam to round up the renegade Cheyenne and bring them back, but avoid bloodshed at every possible cost.

Military forces at Fort Reno, Fort Robinson, Camp Supply, Fort Dodge, and all others in the area had been alerted and troops were dispatched to catch the Cheyenne. Arapaho and Cheyenne scouts hired by the army found the trail and the soldiers followed.

The fleeing Cheyenne traveled by night as much as possible, snatching sleep when they could, huddled near fires hidden behind screens of brush. As they ran through September, anxious heads turned to look back, watching for advancing soldiers, cowboys, and buffalo soldiers hired by the army. Food was short. Wild fruits, plums, chokecherries, and grapes were snatched in passing, but it was not enough; meat had to be brought in soon. Children's eyes sagged in hunger; after several days, few had the strength to cry, much less travel. Then, advance scouts reported that buffalo had been sighted not far away. Using the few mounts they had, hunters took off after them, and the people gathered together and waited for the hunters to return.

The Cheyenne's swiftest runners acted as spies to track the army's movements. These braves crept near the soldier's fires in the darkness, overhearing conversations, then silently moved off and ran back with reports. Shea was one of them and each time he left on his dangerous mission, Emma worried until she saw him emerge from the darkness to join her beside a shielded fire.

Little Wolf and Dull Knife were not surprised, but disheartened when they learned that American Horse had given a full report of how many people were now scattered through the canyons and sand hills. Little Wolf and Dull Knife knew that there was nothing they could do but elude the patrols as best they could and keep the people moving.

Emma saw little of Shea during the ensuing weeks. He was away scouting ahead or guarding the small groups who struggled to keep up. When he joined her at the fire in the wee hours, he fell asleep immediately, completely worn–out. Emma did not bother him, even though she had fallen ill several times, vomiting virtually everything she ate, despite the meager rations. She quickly grew gaunt and felt her strength waning. Shea was so exhausted and preoccupied that he hardly noticed. Red Leaf Woman put together what herbal medicines she could find and made a tincture, but it did not help much. Emma kept her promise and did not complain, caring for Shea, ensuring that he ate and got as much sleep as possible. They were together and that was all that mattered.

At Turkey Springs, Kansas, a long column of dust thrown up by an advancing troop was seen in the distance. The Cheyenne quickly gathered near a rocky outcrop as the women and warriors hurriedly dug rifle pits. The soldiers were encircled before they saw even one Cheyenne. Little Wolf wanted no attack, but warned each armed man to use bullets sparingly if they were drawn into a fight. While they held off the soldiers, mostly firing warning shots, daring warriors went for more horses, raiding settlers in the area. The women and children settled into the warriors' camp, happy to see each other, but wondering when the soldiers would return. A skirmish occurred just before dark and three soldiers were killed. Some had their horses shot out from under them. Using early morning fog as cover, soldiers advanced and retrieved their fallen comrades. The Cheyenne did not shoot at them, though they were within easy range. Afterwards, Emma, still weakened, managed to help the women strip the skin and meat from the dead horses. The meat was gamey and stringy, but welcome, nonetheless.

Little Wolf was very concerned now, because three soldiers had been killed and five Cheyenne wounded during the night, including a little girl. During the fight a six–year old orphaned girl, whose parents had been dead two years past, was missing from her group. Thankfully, the warrior Bullet Proof found her. Bridge, the medicine man, removed a bullet which had shattered her ankle, but the girl, renamed Lame One, was now crippled and had to be carried.

Still the army did not advance on the Cheyenne position.

The Cheyenne moved on again and Emma tried to keep up, but lagged behind with the old ones and the little children, too footsore and weakened to run anymore. Small groups were scattered across the countryside, coming together every few days. The weather had grown very cold and several snowstorms made the way all the more difficult and desperate. Little food and game was found and everyone was weakening fast.

Little Wolf now understood why the army, always on their heels, never launched a full attack. They were being pushed—driven—until they surrendered from hunger and exhaustion. He often passed through the little camps, saying encouraging words to keep the people strong and resolute. But he and Dull Knife argued often now, and a parting of ways was inevitable.

A huge column of soldiers and hired men were in close pursuit when the Cheyenne neared the Arkansas River in Kansas. Everyone knew that there would be fighting to avenge the deaths of the three soldiers at Turkey Creek. The warriors held them off amidst much shooting, but the cavalry tried to go behind their position, intending to surround the Indians. The Cheyenne fled into the broken hills and regrouped. Rifle pits were hurriedly dug again and the Cheyenne made another stand. There was little ammunition left. But that night, the Cheyenne were able to scatter and flee once again evading the soldiers.

Emma kept moving, running on nerves now, her strength deserting her. Through October, more skirmishes took place. Shea fought well, but he was thin and worn–out. She rarely saw him anymore. He was gone, searching for guns, horses, and meat. He and his band of warriors had some success, but it did not come without a price. Emma did not know that some settlers had been killed during these raids and the survivors exerted considerable pressure; the army's resolve to find the Cheyenne was stronger than ever.

To make things worse, a warrior, Black Beaver, had been killed while trying to buy horses from a settler with money Emma had given to him from her tin. She felt tremendous guilt and sadness. Black Beaver left behind a wife and several children.

The strain began to tear the Cheyenne apart and they often dissolved into squabbles over food, where to go, and what to do next. Little Wolf kept control somehow, with the backing of Dull Knife, but one terrible incident caused one Cheyenne to kill another. A warrior, driven to madness during the run, tried to rape his own daughter. The girl's skinning knife ended up in her father's stomach, killing him. This horrified everyone, for Cheyenne did not kill each other. This crime normally meant banishment for the killer, but since she had been defending herself, the incident was forgotten when columns of soldiers were spotted converging on the makeshift camp. It was time to run again.

The next ordeal lay in crossing the well–guarded Arkansas River. Troops were as thick as flies there. Then, cholera from tainted river water struck the Cheyenne, and many died within a day. This delayed the crossing, giving the army time to deploy patrols. One night, the Cheyenne dared to camp in the open. There was nowhere to hide for the land was flat. The army camped nearby, but did not approach. Emma could not sleep due to the strain, aware that she and the Cheyenne were watched.

The next morning, the troops advanced and the Cheyenne got away yet again. In darkness and in small groups the Cheyenne got across the river, but not before another running fight. Emma saw Shea go down, his arm grazed by a bullet, but he came up and kept firing. Hidden by the smoke from the gunfire, everyone headed for the meager safety of rifle pits. Throughout the day, guns blasted and people were wounded and killed on both sides. Many horses had been shot, brought down by the powerful guns of the buffalo soldiers hired by the army. By daybreak, the Cheyenne were far away, but fewer in number. Emma wrapped Shea's wound, but he was gone again too soon to scout ahead.

They came to the Republican River, just inside Nebraska and still managed to elude the troops. They camped in a golden valley near the river to rest. Shea's raiding party had returned with meat, coffee, and sugar. When Emma asked where these things had come from, Shea did not answer. The meat was beef and Emma ate it greedily, not realizing that settlers had died defending their meager supplies. The suffering of others was too much for her to bear; she focused on survival, nothing more.

Fall faded away and winter assaulted the land; soon the tall, golden prairie grass was flecked with snow. The nights were cold and rain mixed with snow chilled and soaked everyone to the skin. The next crossing was at Frenchman Creek in southwestern Nebraska. Emma did not know the country, but overheard that they were halfway to their destination. She held up, resolving to be strong.

At Frenchman Creek, the Cheyenne were continually harassed by soldiers, but they got across the river and continued north. Things began to fall apart and Little Wolf and Dull Knife had a parting of ways. Many of Dull Knife's people were sick and unable to keep up. Little Wolf tried to convince them to keep running, but rumors spread that Dull Knife's people wanted to return to the Indian Territory. There had been snow and blinding blizzards and many groups got lost, missed days later when the people found each other in a makeshift camp and counted how many were left.

Emma felt a sense of hope as the weary Cheyenne neared a valley in Nebraska called Lost Chokecherry, where they planned to hide and set up winter camp unless the soldiers pushed them on again. Emma battled utter exhaustion. She lagged far behind the small straggling groups. They had come twenty miles in one day, and still more miles lay before them through the snow to the valley.

Then, one afternoon, troops came pounding in from all sides and the Cheyenne scattered into the low sand hills. Emma struggled to keep up, but was too weak to run. Her stomach churned. She headed around some low hills, unmindful of where she was going and fell to her knees as her breakfast of dried berries came up.

As she lay crumpled on the ground, sweating and shaking, a voice shouted, "Don't move!"

Emma was too ill to care and rose to her knees. Four cowboys who had got around the hills dismounted, guns leveled at her. She felt so sick that she almost wished one of them would shoot her.

"What the hell?" one astonished cowboy exclaimed with a slow drawl. "It's a white girl!" The cowboys lowered their guns momentarily, uncertain what to do.

Emma heaved again. The men backed away from the stench.

Another man spoke. "I heard tell there's a white girl married to one of them savages. This must be her, Roger."

"Take her," Roger, apparently the leader, commanded. Emma was unceremoniously yanked to her feet and dragged off. She was too weak to fight or scream and did not want any Cheyenne hurt trying to rescue her. "You really live with them savages?" Emma swayed from the effects of the sickness, refusing to answer. Roger looked her up and down and said, "Cover her head. I don't want her spotted with that hair. Give me any trouble lady and I'll kill you." A smelly blanket was put around her by a young man with a placid, plain face.

"Hey, Roger," one man said, "do we get a bounty on this one or is it just for Indians?"

Roger grinned, showing stained, brown teeth. "She's quite a prize if she's that girl we heard about, Slade. We may hold out for double the bounty on this one. If the army doesn't want her, we'll keep her." Emma shivered beneath the blanket at his words. "Mount up." No one made a move to take Emma on their horse. "Somebody take her. Slade, pull her up with you."

"Geez, I hope she doesn't heave all over me," Slade whined, pulling Emma up to sit behind him. "I can't stand that smell—makes me want to puke, too!"

A look from Roger silenced his complaining.

Emma suffered holding onto Slade as they rode far around the fighting. She almost fell off the horse several times and was roughly yanked back. When the cowboys got to the army's rear line, Slade pushed her off. She sprawled in the snow and rolled over, curled up, and groaned.

An army sergeant rode up and quickly dismounted, striding to Emma's side. "What are you doing? Where did you find her?"

"I think she's that Indian's woman I heard about, Sergeant Parkman," Roger answered. "Found her heaving her guts up back of them hills."

"You were ordered not to harm prisoners. She's just a girl, for Christ's sake!"

The four cowboys were not overly concerned.

"What's the bounty on her?" Roger asked with an avaricious grin. "Say a hundred?"

"Talk to the Colonel. I'm just a sergeant." Parkman lifted Emma and deposited her in a supply wagon with a guard nearby. Emma curled up, exhausted and spent.

The wagon lurched forward and Emma was taken to Fort Robinson, in northwestern Nebraska.

After the fighting stopped near nightfall, the army retreated and the Cheyenne gathered together, again ready to run all night.

Shea found Red Leaf and Little Fox. "Where is Emma?"

Red Leaf looked worried. "She went over there a long time ago," she said, pointing to the hill where she had last seen her. "She was sick in her stomach. I could not follow because of the bullets."

Shea ran off and scrambled up the hill, but did not see her. Finally, down the other side he found horse tracks and footsteps in the snow, along with a pool of vomit. His heart sank with the realization that she had been captured. There was no blood; he was thankful for that, but it was obvious she was sick. During the fight, he had seen a group of cowboys riding to the north and he had seen one of them riding double. It struck him now that the figure had been Emma. Worried and frightened, he collapsed to his knees, choking back tears. His love was gone, taken by the army's hired men to fates that he could not foresee. He touched a thin footprint in the snow that was surely Emma's. Calls to run again were heard in the distance. With a heavy heart and little time for sorrow, Shea left with his people. The Cheyenne were on the move again. With this much snow already on the ground in Nebraska, they would encounter worse farther north.

Emma was gone and with that, Shea's hope. He feared for her at the hands of the whites.

Chapter Five

The journey to Fort Robinson was long, cold, and frightening for Emma. She was transferred to a covered wagon midway. She was still ailing and could barely keep liquids down; several times she heaved out the back of the wagon. Sergeant Parkman showed a small measure of compassion for her and peeked in the wagon during stops.

"We have no doctor with us, but there's one at Robinson. You hang on till then, all right?" As he walked away, he muttered, "I hope what she's got isn't catching."

When the gates of Fort Robinson slammed behind her days later, Emma felt swallowed up. Once inside the fort she tried to climb down from the wagon, but sank to the ground, dizzy and weak. Hands lifted her and laid her on a bed in the infirmary. Barely conscious, she remembered gagging on a bitter liquid someone had repeatedly ladled down her throat.

She awoke on a cot that was surrounded by curtains. She was still weak, but the fever had broken and with it the nausea. She called out and tried to rise. "Hello? Anyone here?"

A man with thick gray hair, about fifty years in age, parted the curtains. "You're awake. Good."

"Where am I?"

His expression was kind. "You're at the infirmary at Fort Robinson. You collapsed the minute you got here. I'm Peter Cromwell, the fort's doctor." He pulled in a chair from behind the curtain. "So, how do you feel?"

"Better. What's wrong with me?"

"A fever, probably caused by bad water, something you ate, exposure—take your pick. You'll be okay in a day or two."

"Then can I leave?"

Peter sat back, his expression suddenly guarded. "That's not going to be easy. General John Considine is headquartered here. If you're who we think you are, he won't let you leave until he has talked to you. Are you Emma Hawkshadow?"

She looked confused but she knew that she had no choices at the moment; lying could make matters worse. By now, they surely knew who she was. The rumor of a red–haired white girl living with the Cheyenne had spread very quickly. "Yes."

"Since you were involved in the outbreak, the general wants to question you as soon as possible. Look, it's a good thing that you were brought in, otherwise, you might have died out there without medical treatment. Your fever was very high."

Emma found herself inwardly agreeing, in spite of a sinking feeling of foreboding. She was in real trouble.

He smiled. "Forgive me for staring. I heard that a white woman was living with the Cheyenne, but I didn't think you were so young." He patted her hand. "Don't worry. I'll stall the general as long as I can."

"And this general wants to know where the Cheyenne are going, right?"

"He wants them rounded up as soon as possible. He doesn't want any more to die. It's winter. They'll freeze to death."

"They've held out this long."

"We can debate the hardiness of the Cheyenne later. For now, you're on fluids only—no food until I say."

As he stood, Emma asked, "Can you open the curtains? I feel like I'm in a tomb."

"Sure," he said, pushing them aside. Many men were in the large ward, and their eyes went wide at the sight of her. "In a few minutes, I'm going to have you moved to a small room next to my office. More privacy for you."

"Thank you, doctor."

He smiled. "Peter," he said, hoping to ease her into what was surely to become a very difficult time.

She wanted to trust him and she needed an ally. "Call me Emma."

Unofficially, she was a prisoner by the order of General Considine until the outbreak ended. Guards were already posted outside the infirmary, but Peter did not have the heart to tell her yet. He was a healer, not a hardened soldier.

He then signaled several corpsman who lifted her, bed and all, and deposited her in a small room as the last crate was carried out of what had been a storeroom with a small window, high in the wall. There was a small wood burner in a corner and an old table. Her bundle was dropped in the corner and the wood burner stoked and lit. The room was still very cold and the thin men's dressing gown that she wore did not warm her much. She burrowed in under the blankets.

The harsh reality of her predicament hit her. Shea was probably out of his head with worry—and she wondered what this general planned to do with her, how he would try to use her.

Just before sundown Peter returned, bringing several blankets for her bed.

"I'm worried about the Cheyenne," Emma said. "This is the coldest night in a long time."

"I'm sorry for them too, but you know it's for the best that the army brings them back. And it's best you stay here until all this is resolved. I am more concerned about you right now."

"I was keeping up, really," she said with a sad shake of her head. "I was as strong as any of them. I just didn't count on getting sick along the way."

"Is there anyone that I can contact for you? Family, friends?"

"My parents are gone—there is family in Ohio, but I don't know them. No, there's no one," she said.

He opened a bottle of laudanum that he had brought. "Here," he poured a spoonful. "Take this. It will help you sleep."

Emma tasted the bitter liquid, making a face.

Peter gave her a tight smile as she drank it down. "Don't take this wrong, but I am surprised that you were caught with Shea Hawkshadow being your husband. He's been a well-known warrior since the Custer fight. I thought that he'd watch over you."

"Shea's a Dog Soldier; his duty is to the people, not a single person, not even his wife."

"Sorry. I had to ask."

"Can I get out of bed?"

"Only to go to the privy, just out the back door. A guard is posted outside your room and will have to accompany you if you go out into the yard. General's orders."

"Who is he anyway to order me held here?"

"The ranking general of the territory. He wants to speak with you tomorrow. I'm sure that you're not looking forward to it, but I couldn't delay him any longer."

Emma's mood brightened. This gentle man seemed intent on protecting her. She did not feel defensive and was certain that he meant her no harm.

She was not so sure about General Considine. "Thank you for trying to stall him. That's a kindness I didn't expect."

She and Peter talked awhile. She told him of the circumstances that had brought her and Shea together. Peter showed much sympathy for how her life had been turned upside down.

When Emma woke early the next morning, she saw that someone had rummaged through her bundle while she slept. The dose of laudanum had made her insensible throughout the night. The tin of money was missing. She wondered whether the cowboys or Peter had taken it. She felt vulnerable.

Moments later, Peter knocked at her door and peeked in. "General Considine wants to speak to you as soon as you're dressed."

"My money is gone!"

"Sorry. Orders."

She was furious that this general had ordered her drugged, then helped himself to her money. In defiance, she dressed slowly and joined Peter outside the infirmary nearly a half hour later. Her rumpled old tan calico dress looked awful, but it was all she had; her blue one had been missing since her arrival, probably, she thought, too fouled to salvage.

As they walked to Considine's office, she watched the goings–on in the yard as men drilled, horses were herded out of the fort to what sparse pasture poked through the snow, and settlers went about their business at a small trading post. Families were at the stables, getting wagon wheels fixed and horses and oxen shod. Their children played in the yard. And the tiny trading post in the fort was busy with settlers buying up supplies for the winter. Everything looked at once normal and foreign. She had become too used to isolated prairie life and the quiet Cheyenne camp. There had rarely been this many people at Bockmeier's at one time, even in summer.

Taking deep breaths Emma steadied herself as she followed Peter into a building. Down a short hallway he stood aside, allowing her to enter a small room. An aide of the general guided Emma inside another room.

A man in a crisp blue uniform stood as she entered the office. "Mrs. Hawkshadow, I'm General John Considine. I hope that you're better?" He was tall and thickly built, with a mass of white hair. He looked formidable.

"Yes, General Considine."

In spite of his pressed uniform and authoritative mien, he looked momentarily disconcerted. "Months ago I read a report about you from Major Lawrence. You were well treated by the Cheyenne?"

"Yes."

"Good," he said. "Dismissed, doctor. Thank you."

With a glance over his shoulder, Peter closed the door and waited in the anteroom with the aide.

Considine motioned to a chair. "Please make yourself comfortable." Emma lowered herself slowly, nervous and uncertain of what to expect. He sat behind a large desk and studied her intently for a few moments. "Well, I'm glad that you're on the mend. We have little room to house a lady, but you can stay in the infirmary. However, you'll remain under guard while you're here."

Emma shifted on the hard wooden chair and dared to ask, "So, I am a prisoner?"

"In a benign sense. You're being kept here for your own safety—and your health. You will be well looked after." After absently shuffling papers on his desk, he launched into the subject of the interview. "I want to ask you some questions about the breakout. I trust that you'll cooperate to help save your Cheyenne friends. I must know where they're going."

"Your troops are on their trail, not me."

"The trail is all over the place. If we knew their destination, we could round them up and do everything to avoid more fighting, then take them to where they belong."

"General," Emma said, her voice tight with nerves, "the government didn't keep its end of the bargain. Every place they settle is worse than the last, then the government makes them move again."

"You don't know much about the politics concerning the Indians in this country. They can't live wherever they want. There isn't room for them. Hundreds of settlers are coming west each day and the railroads are reaching the northern parts of the country. The Indians have to adjust, change their ways. They can't ride the range and hunt buffalo like before. They have to learn how to farm."

"I lived on the reservation in the Indian Territory. I know that the promised seed, plows, horses, and other supplies were never sent, and what little food they got was full of sand or spoiled. Most of it is stolen by the Indian Agents who are supposed to help them! Don't tell the Cheyenne to be farmers when they don't know how and don't have the tools. Too many promises have been broken. They would rather die than return to the Indian Territory."

Considine sat back in his squeaky chair. "It's an unfortunate situation and if I could fix it, I would. If the Cheyenne jump the reservation—and somehow get to wherever they're going, which I doubt they can—other tribes will try. Hundreds, even thousands could die. We have to stop this now. We have to know their destination. Is it Red Cloud? The Sioux Agency? Spotted Tail's reservation?"

"I don't know."

"Don't play games with lives, girl," the brows lowered. The general in the man asserted himself, but his voice became deceptively conciliatory. "Tell me where they're going. No one will know what you tell me today. You have my word."

"I said that I don't know."

"You're telling me that you blindly went with them? You just went with your husband when he told you to leave with him—with no idea where you were heading?" Considine was incredulous.

"It wasn't blind obedience. I went because I trusted Shea," she snapped. "And where's my money?" Considine was openly irritated, but Emma felt that she had nothing to lose. "I demand that you return it to me and let me go!"

"You have no right to demand anything! You were damn lucky you were captured, otherwise you could've died out there."

"I would've rather died on the prairie than be imprisoned here."

"I didn't say that you're a prisoner."

"Then why is there a guard outside the infirmary day and night? Am I charged with a crime or do you treat all guests this way?"

"We're giving you a chance to get well and the guard is to protect you. Consider yourself in protective custody."

"Fine, so I'm not a prisoner," she cut in, "so I'll be on my way."

His eyes narrowed. "Not so fast. I saw the money in that tin and you can afford to go where you want, but where would you go? Would you try to find your husband?"

Irritated that he thought her so stupid, she refused to take the bait. "I don't know where they have gone since Frenchman's Creek where I was captured."

"You will stay here until the outbreak ends one way or the other, or you can tell me the destination and I'll let you go after they're rounded up. It'll be better for them and better for you if you tell me what you know. I don't want to bring charges of treason or aiding the enemy against you, but I will if you force me to. You could go to prison—and I'll make damn sure that it's east of the Mississippi. Do you understand?"

Emma remained insolent. "Why on earth would I trust you? There are women and children out there and they're just trying to go home the only way left to them. If you want to hold me, you can, but it won't do you any good."

"I can do anything I want with you!" he barked. He came around the desk and stood over her. It made her uncomfortable to have him so close. She could smell the starch on his uniform. For many moments, he visibly tried to get hold of his emotions. *Foolish girl,* he thought, *she certainly knows how to infuriate.* Trying another approach, he softened his tone. "You're young. I have a daughter about your age back east. I know you're afraid, but you have the power to save these people you care so much about. Help them by helping us. For their sake and yours, tell me."

She searched for a bargaining position—anything—but quickly realized that she had none. How many times would she have to go through this? Would Considine resort to harsher tactics to make her talk? He could make his threats reality by charging her with treason and putting her in prison. If she were imprisoned, she would lose Shea forever. With him hovering over her, she felt small and powerless. Then, she made a fateful decision.

He caught the change in her eyes. "You know. You've been around them all these months."

She stared at the scuffed wood floor, searching for what to say. "I didn't know what was going to happen until the day before. Shea wanted me to go to Fort Reno so I'd be safe," she began. "Look, no one told me where we were going, exactly. They used an Indian name for the place, but it didn't make sense to me. The word meant mother. I don't know much Cheyenne." Tears stung her eyes and she fought to quell the same panic that she felt the day her parents died; the same profound helplessness crept through her. She was beginning to understand why Shea wanted to send her away before the outbreak. He knew that she was weak. *Maintaining control with this man hovering over me is harder than running with the Cheyenne,* she thought.

Her head came up slowly and her eyes met his. A tear slid down her cheek, followed by another. She looked at him, weighing the consequences of the decision she was forced to make. She thought that it was the only way to avoid endless interrogations, imprisonment, or a firing squad. She was aware that people convicted of treason were hanged or shot. She now understood the desperation of the Cheyenne. Her survival instincts took over.

"So you don't know where these lands are?" he asked.

"Not really. I heard talk of crossing the border into Canada—or returning to somewhere along the Missouri River."

"Canada? To Sitting Bull's camp?"

"I don't know for sure. I couldn't understand everything that was said." She sniffled. "If you find them, please don't hurt anyone. They are kind people. They just want to go home."

Considine decided that the Cheyenne scouts camped outside the fort could tell him more. He saw her pale, her hands trembling in her lap. He was aware that if the scouts heard that she betrayed the Cheyenne, her life would not be worth much. Considine's experience in the West was extensive and he knew how intertwined Indian family lines were. Even though their camps were far apart, nearly everyone was related somehow. Many scouts he now employed could well be relatives of Little Wolf and Dull Knife's people.

"Okay," he said. "We'll talk again. Do some serious thinking in the meantime and try to remember details. And another thing, you had better watch your tone when addressing me. It's the least I expect from you." He called for Dr. Cromwell. "Doctor, see Mrs. Hawkshadow back to her room."

Considine's eyes held a glint of triumph as she shuffled out. Breaking this girl would not take much more effort. She would tell him exactly where the Indians were heading, but he was pressed for time to get the troops on the right trail to track and push the Cheyenne and weaken them for eventual capture. Although certain that Emma knew the route, he took a step back from the situation, realizing that the girl was young, frightened, and recovering from illness. He would give her a day or two and try again. He returned to the tedium of paperwork, but his thoughts focused on his own daughter, now sixteen. He had been unsuccessful in being authoritative with Emma, but it had always worked with his daughter. Emma was far more defiant so he designed other ways to approach her. He truly did not want to badger her with endless interrogations and threats. There had to be another way to break her—or remove her from the equation. His reports said that the Cheyenne were last seen not far from the fort, and he feared they might try to rescue her if they discovered that she was imprisoned there.

Emma walked back to her room with Peter and her guard. She rubbed her aching temples. "I've got myself in quite a place. Can't go forward, can't go back."

"It didn't go well," Peter stated.

"No, it didn't go well at all. He threatened to charge me with treason if I don't tell him where they're going. I don't want to go to jail."

"Did you tell him what he wanted to know?"

"I told him what I know, which isn't much." She took a deep breath of the frigid air.

"Did he give you your money back?" She shook her head. "Emma, patrols have found many Cheyenne who have frozen to death. Everything you can remember will prevent more from dying like that. Don't lie to Considine. He's very powerful."

"I am just what I seem—an ignorant girl raised in a soddy who married a half–breed Indian. That's all I am."

Peter sensed that Emma was much more than an 'ignorant girl raised in a soddy.' Although she may have been raised in relative isolation, she was not dumb. He noticed her sturdy common sense, weakened though it was by her youth and immaturity concerning life's realities. He wanted an end to the outbreak as much as the soldiers. He had grown weary of preparing Cheyenne bodies for burial, populating a forlorn cemetery just outside the fort. He was tired of treating soldiers for frostbite and Cheyenne–inflicted gunshot wounds.

"You have the Cheyenne's best interests at heart. I can't blame you for caring because they've suffered. But the soldiers who chase them have families, too—people who love them and want to protect their own as strongly as you want to protect the Cheyenne."

She looked at him with a peculiar expression. "What would you do in my place?"

He had no answer to that and took her back to the tiny room in the infirmary.

"Emma, I heard a little of what you and Considine said to each other. Don't behave disrespectfully toward him. He'll make an example of you, believe me. Tell him what he wants to know and end this."

She slipped onto the bed. "I told him what I knew. I'm tired and I'd like to be alone."

Peter left. A guard took up his post in a chair outside Emma's door.

Answering a knock that evening, Emma discovered a corpsman carrying a tray of food and the tobacco tin. All of her money appeared to be there. She methodically smoothed out each bill on the bed. "How am I going to get out of this?" she whispered.

The next afternoon, Peter insisted that she get fresh air and walked with her around the yard. She attracted looks of loathing and hatred from the soldiers and hired men who were resupplying at the fort while on the Cheyenne's trail. Withering looks replaced the admiring glances she had received months ago from the soldiers at Fort Reno. A paunchy corporal, dirty and unkept, shouted 'Indian's whore!' in her face as she passed.

She held her ground. "Get away from me!" she snapped.

Dr. Cromwell, a captain, ordered him to shut up. The fat corporal shuffled away, mumbling to the other men, tossing contemptuous looks over his shoulder.

"Ignore him," Peter said, taking her arm. "He's just letting off steam."

"Oh, he means it. I'm an easy target."

Running on sheer nerves, Emma tried to ignore the abuse, but felt disoriented; the noise and bustle of the fort bothered her. It was a world that she did now know. The guard constantly on her heel was a reminder that she was a prisoner, despite what Considine had said.

Considine's instincts prickled, figuring that Emma had deliberately lied to buy the Cheyenne time. Whether or not she knew the actual destination, she had certainly overhead something more. He did not completely buy the story about the Cheyenne heading for Canada; their trail so far was not toward Sitting Bull's camp across the border. His only clue was that the Cheyenne called the place 'mother.' He went to the Cheyenne scouts camped just outside the fort. Black Bird Wing was their leader, so he sat with him at his fire.

Usually reticent, Black Bird Wing opened the conversation. "You hold the wife of Hawkshadow."

Considine had been afraid of this. Black Bird Wing was not a member of Little Wolf's camp and he wondered how the scout got his information.

"So you already know. We found her a few days after the Cheyenne crossed Frenchman Creek. She was quite ill and it's lucky that she was found."

"Not good to hold wife of Dog Soldier. Her husband strong warrior—brave—and she is respected as teacher."

"Teacher?"

"She teach Little Wolf's warriors *veho* tongue and marks. You should not keep her."

"Will Hawkshadow come for her? Will there be a fight?"

"Send her to the Pine Ridge Agency and there will be no fight."

"We saved her life. She might've perished without proper food and medical treatment. She's well cared for."

"She should go now. Do not keep her here." There was a veiled threat in Wing's tone.

Considine wanted to resolve Emma's situation and set her free, but time was short and he had to find the Cheyenne, for reports said that the trail was again lost. "Why Pine Ridge? Is that where the Cheyenne are going?"

"No, but Red Cloud is cousin to the Cheyenne. He will care for her."

"I can't do that. Tell me, where in Canada did the Cheyenne live before they came south?"

The Indian's head came up slowly from his repast of dried meat. "Why you want to know?"

"We believe the renegades are heading for some old campground. Could they be going to Sitting Bull in Canada?" Black Bird Wing continued to eat without replying. The general tried to be patient while he finished. "Sitting Bull would take them in, surely."

"Do not know."

"Mrs. Hawkshadow said that the Cheyenne are going to a place they call mother. Where is it?"

The Indian's face pinched. "Mother—*nahkoa*—The Great Mother—home. It was east of the Missouri, but you *veho* made us go. It was on the Yellowstone, but we had to move again. Long ago, it was Canada, but I do not know where my people lived. It was very long ago. The earth does not wants us anymore. Wherever we go, we die."

"I don't want more bloodshed. Help me."

"I cannot. And take Emma to Pine Ridge where the Sioux will watch over her. It is too dangerous to keep her here. We know what soldiers think of a white woman who marries an Indian." Black Bird Wing dropped his last statement like an anvil then left the fire. The interview was over.

Considine left frustrated, wondering if Black Bird Wing meant that he could not or would not help him. He momentarily questioned the wisdom of keeping Emma at Fort Robinson. The opinions of his men were against her, but she had to know where the Cheyenne were going; she was all he had. It was only a matter of time, so he grimly resolved to keep up the pressure. After she broke he would send her east, away from all this trouble.

When the general disappeared into the darkness, Black Bird Wing called his men together. They huddled briefly. As dawn slid fingers of meager light across the prairie, the fort's night sentry reported that the Cheyenne scouts were gone.

Emma slept deeply that night, wearied by her situation and some lingering weakness. She woke late, finding a tray of food just inside the door on a small table. The eggs were cold, but her appetite returned and she ate everything. Even the cold coffee tasted good. So began the exile and the loneliest time of her young life.

Two days later she was again summoned to Considine's office. He questioned her for nearly two hours, but she maintained that she did not know where the Cheyenne were going and stuck to her story about Canada. For weeks he tried to wear her down, but she somehow held on and told him nothing more. He threatened, cajoled, sympathized, and pleaded—and still she held up.

Peter came to see her often and worried about the way she seemed to collapse into herself. She resisted all attempts at conversation, especially after a session with Considine. The interrogations eroded her strength and he was powerless to stop it. And whatever Emma did say, she lost either way.

Peter was summoned to meet with Considine one evening.

Considine spoke. "You can bet the Cheyenne scouts who left a few weeks ago have found Little Wolf by now," he said. "Black Bird Wing warned me to send Emma to Pine Ridge under the protection of Red Cloud. I can't do that, but Little Wolf's people may try to break her out. I've got troops scattered across half the territory and the ones left here aren't exactly the cream of the crop. If the Cheyenne come for her there will be a fight, but those are my concerns." He sat back in his chair and lit his pipe. "I'll tell you alone, Peter, this girl confounds me. She was raised in isolation on some farm, but there's a recklessness mixed with a kind of courage that I'm used to seeing only in men. It's a powerful combination and she seems to fear very little, maybe because of the way she was raised. But she has to quell her insolent nature if she's going to survive—wherever she ends up. I need your help to make her see reason."

"General," Peter said, "for all her stubbornness, she's failing. Refuses meals, hardly talks, won't leave her room unless I practically drag her outdoors. You may think that she's strong, but no one can hold up under such pressure. Your talks with her are taking a heavy toll. She would've broken by now." He paused then added, "If there is any hint that she's being mistreated, we'll all pay."

"She is not being mistreated—not by me. I have a job to do. But I've got a tiger by the tail—I can't hold her—can't let her go, either. One thing Black Bird Wing said, without really coming out and saying it, was that the Cheyenne might take any opportunity to rescue her. This orphaned girl—this wife of a renegade Cheyenne—could bring this territory to its knees."

Peter had to agree with Considine. "We can't let her go, I agree. If we deported her east of the Mississippi, she would just come back again and rejoin the Cheyenne when this is over. But for her sake, please stop the interrogations. She's falling apart and I honestly think that she doesn't know."

Considine considered Peter's entreaty. "I'll think on it. She's fearless about a lot of things but there's a way to reach her, I just have to find it."

"Sir, she's not a bad person. She was shoved into the world and has lived by her wits. She's coping the best way she knows. My only concern is for her soundness of mind and her physical health."

"I realize that, doctor. Good night."

That night when Peter came to check on Emma, he saw her pallor and the dark circles around her eyes. "Are you feeling all right?" She nodded, distracted. "You don't go out enough. And I want you to. I'll go with you if that's what you want. The fresh air and exercise will help if you feel cooped up."

"It's grown too cold," she said. "Funny, I've worked on the land all my life and in all weathers but lately I've got a chill that I can't shake. I'm not as tough as I thought I was."

"I want you to get out more. It's a request from a friend."

Emma looked away. "It won't make much of a difference. Wherever I go, I have to come back here. I've lost everything that I ever had in the last year. Forgive me if I'm not cheerful. Shea and his people are out there freezing and starving—doing what they believe to be right. I sit here in relative comfort with a warm bed and three meals a day. And I've betrayed them on top of everything."

"Wish I had an answer for you." As Peter crossed the yard to his quarters, he shivered from the searching cold and pulled his coat tightly around him. Emma was constantly on his mind. Here she was, abandoned, living in a cruel limbo between worlds, stranded between self–preservation and love. He pitied and feared for her as well. Fort Robinson was not protected by high stockade walls like other forts. Anyone could get to her—anyone. To the Indians, she was one of them; to the whites, she was an Indian's whore.

Emma sat alone in the dark that night, thinking that her life had become disturbingly complicated.

A few days later she took Peter's advice and left the small room. During a walk around the yard with her guard, Emma decided to purchase a few things for herself from the makeshift trading post. She bought two new calico dresses, a shawl, new boots, tooth powder, and other toiletries. She hoped that the new things would make her feel better. They did not.

Considine again summoned her to his office. Knowing what to expect, Emma shored herself up with what little strength remained. With her guard at her heel, she again prepared to endure yet another interrogation.

To her surprise, she and the general left his office. With the guard ordered well to the rear, out of earshot, they walked together outside the fort. Considine never once asked the Cheyenne's destination; instead he asked her questions about her childhood and her time with the Cheyenne. As she talked, she was confused because Considine seemed genuinely interested. When she concluded her story, he looked at her with compassion.

"It's hard to believe that you're only eighteen. You show remarkable maturity—in some ways. I have two sons and a daughter back east in New York. My daughter's only a little younger than you. She's a good girl, but sometimes silly and frivolous. She can be very charming when it suits her own ends. She's had a safe life. Yours has hardened you—made you grow up too fast. I don't want you to regret the decisions you've had to make, only think about what your future holds. You have strong loyalty towards the Cheyenne for all they did for you. You married a strong man who could protect you and I understand that. I think that's one reason my wife, Agnes, married me, but I've been an absent husband for nearly twenty years. My wealth is her protection because I am not physically there. I know what it's like to be alone. And I have a duty to this country and that duty extends to you as a citizen."

Emma was perplexed by the marked change in his attitude.

"I have an offer to make to you. I will send you to the care of my wife in New York City and you can live with my family. You can go to school or find work. You would have everything you need."

Emma wanted to be sure that she had heard him correctly. "You want to send me to New York to live with your family?"

"I want you to have a chance at a better life." He chose his words carefully. "Don't take this wrong but I think that you might need an out."

Emma let out a long breath. This was absolutely the last thing that she expected, but she was suspicious. "Why would you do that? I am no one to you."

"You would have a chance at a new beginning—far from all this trouble. I'm not fully convinced of your commitment—to your marriage, I mean. Maybe it was an impulsive move on your part in the midst of grief and being left alone. Honestly, I can't see anything ahead of you except more hardship if you return to the Cheyenne one day. I can't prevent you from going back, but I'm asking you to stop and think. Their life is terribly hard and will get even more difficult as the years pass." Emma opened her mouth to speak, but he continued. "I don't expect an answer right now. I want you to take time to think about it."

"I will, general," she promised. "Can I ask something of you?" He nodded. "Is there something that I can do around here? Work at the trading post, or the stables, or maybe help the cooks in the mess hall? I'm going a little crazy with nothing to do all day."

He thought it over, encouraged that she was so resilient. "I don't see any harm. But if you help in the mess hall, I don't want you out front serving food. You're a pretty thing and you would distract my soldiers far too much. I'll ask around to see if Hansson at the trading post needs help. Yes, I think that it would be a good thing for you to have something to occupy your days."

"Thank you," she said, surprised that he went for her suggestion. "And once in a while, can I go outside the fort like we're doing now? You can send as many guards with me as you want. I'm not used to living in places with a lot of people."

Considine chuckled. "Ma'am, the fort is at half strength since the out-break. But I'll see what I can do."

"Deal. I'll see what I can do about your offer."

Bewildered, she returned to her room. She thought about his offer, trying to imagine what life would be like in a big city and what it would be like living with another family. It was at once tempting and daunting. What would Shea think of her? What would she think of herself for abandoning the marriage? Shea's heart would be broken again. And if she did go, what would she do if living in New York did not work out? She would only be alone again, aban-doned, again.

Considine did not press her, but had Peter make arrangements for her to work in the cook's shack to help prepare meals. Emma pitched in and duty there made the days pass more quickly. The cooks and servers were nice to her and taught her to prepare several dishes for the men. When the patrols were out and less help was needed in the mess, she helped out in the stables. Her guards were often absent since she was surrounded by other soldiers. A few men made their opinion of her very clear still, but she refused to dwell on it. Work alleviated her depression and guilt. Considine's offer was on her mind; days passed and she had not given him an answer. Yes, she loved Shea, but the chance at a comfortable life and an education beguiled her nonetheless.

November ended with freezing blizzards and below–zero temperatures. The sky was flat, gray, and sunless. Emma was eager to go for a ride out of the fort, but the general would not allow it, citing the weather.

When the weather warmed a week later, she was allowed to ride out-side the environs of the fort. With two guards at her back and Peter beside her, she rode for nearly two hours until the soldiers herded her back. The freedom was intoxicating and she longed for more.

Peter came to see her one evening and they talked about Considine's offer. "Have you made up your mind yet?"

"I don't want to lose Shea, the one person I know loves me. But this is really tempting. I always wanted to go to a real school—college, too."

"You have to make up your mind soon. Considine's getting transferred any day."

"He is? Where?"

"To Red Cloud's new Agency in South Dakota to oversee negotiations with the northern Cheyenne. You'll have to decide real soon."

She sucked in a shuddering breath. "Everything has fallen apart and there is nothing I can do. If I go east, I lose everything and have to start over again. If I stay here, I have to find Shea somehow after all this is over and rebuild a marriage. He may not even want me back after so long."

"Emma, Considine's trying to help you, don't you see? He likes you despite how the two of you started out. He's not as bad as you think."

"That's why I've had such trouble making up my mind. I thought that he hated me. He caught me completely off guard with his offer, which I know is generous and very risky for him. I'm no more than a stranger to him." She thought a moment. "He has a daughter near my age—maybe he feels guilty about hardly ever seeing her. Maybe he gets rid of his guilt by helping me."

"Is that so bad? You would have a good life in New York. What's in your way, then?"

She turned her deep blue eyes to him. "Love, Peter. My love for Shea is in the way."

During another long ride around the fort, Emma's thoughts focused on the Cheyenne. She hoped that they were nearing home—*nahkoa*. They had been running for three months. She also reconsidered the general's offer but fate intervened and her priorities and perceptions shifted once again.

Early the next day, a soldier spurred hard for Fort Robinson. Once inside the gate he barely waited for his mount to stop and vaulted from the saddle. He took the six steps up to Considine's office in two leaps.

He was quite winded. "I need to see the General immediately!" he said to the aide.

Considine heard the commotion and came out of his office. "Report, lieutenant."

In spite of the bitter cold, beads of sweat showed on the lieutenant's forehead. He gulped and swallowed, trying to wet his dry throat. He remembered himself and saluted. "General, we tried to send a wire, but the lines are down. Sir, we got them, well, some of them. Dull Knife and about seventy Cheyenne surrendered near Chadron Creek. They're about ten miles away, but the going is slow. A lot are half–starved and barefoot. They'll be here tomorrow or the day after, best I can tell."

"Surrendered or were captured?" Considine asked, mindful of the political mileage that he could get from this.

"Surrendered, sir. They've agreed to go back south if we keep them for the winter and feed them."

The soldiers at the fort prepared for their unexpected guests. Emma heard the unusual activity near the storehouse while working in the mess and pulling on her shearling, ventured outdoors. Soldiers loaded wagons with food and took them to a large shed at the far end of the camp, near an unused barracks. Catching snatches of talk in the yard, Emma overhead that Cheyenne were on their way to the fort, surrendered, the men were saying. Her heart thudded in her chest. She wondered if Shea would be with them. She hovered on the sidelines listening, but inwardly shuddering. That morning, she had decided to accept Considine's offer.

Searching cold drove her back to the mess hall, but she worked near a window, watching the preparations for the Cheyenne. If indeed Shea were among them, would Considine let them be together? Emma had to wait and wonder.

Two days later, more than seventy ragged Cheyenne shuffled into Fort Robinson. Emma intended to meet them but when she tried to get near, several soldiers crowded in around her, ushering her back to the mess hall. Craning her neck, she saw Dull Knife immediately; he was very tall, well over six feet. She looked for Shea, but virtually everyone was wrapped against the cold and she could see only a few faces. The Cheyenne were taken to the old barracks.

For days, Emma sent requests to Considine, asking to see the Cheyenne. Each request was denied. Peter had been tending them each day, so Emma had no news—no idea if Shea were there. She felt cheated and angry with Considine who, a few days ago, had acted like her friend—acted like he cared.

She went outdoors for long periods in defiance of the cold, trying to get a glimpse of the Cheyenne in the distance, but she could only venture so far before a guard blocked her progress. She tried to pick out Red Leaf Woman's rotund figure, but could not. She hoped that someone would recognize her and raise a hand; then if Shea were there he would know that she was all right. But her heart sank each day, realizing that if Shea were among them, maybe he did not want to see her. Maybe he was angry at the weakness that had caused her to get caught by the buffalo soldiers. Maybe he had guessed at her collusion with the soldiers, her role in sending them toward Canada. Insecurity wormed through her.

She needed to talk to Peter, but for days on end he was with the Cheyenne and returned to his quarters very late each night, long after she was asleep.

Willing herself to rise in the wee hours one morning, Emma intercepted Peter in the infirmary. Still in her dressing gown, she cornered him as he took supplies from a storeroom.

"Peter! Considine won't let me near the Cheyenne."

"Orders, Emma," he interrupted. "He doesn't want you with them just yet."

"Why?"

"Don't know. It's for your safety."

"Is Shea here?"

Peter looked around, assuring himself that no one was nearby. "Well, I don't know what he looks like, but I asked around. Word is that Shea stayed with Little Wolf. That group is still on the run."

She breathed a sigh of relief. "That means maybe he's still alive."

"No way to know. Dull Knife's people parted company with Little Wolf's group weeks ago."

"Can you convince Considine to let me see the Cheyenne? He'll listen to you."

"No, Emma. He's leaving next week and doesn't have time. I have a lot of work to do—so many Cheyenne are sick and malnourished. I just don't have time to plead your case."

Emma walked away, dejected and hurt. She still did not understand the massive responsibility thrust upon the fort and was mostly concerned for herself.

A few days before leaving Fort Robinson, Considine came to see her. After apologizing for denying her requests to see the Cheyenne, citing the responsibilities now upon his soldiers, he said, with a tinge of resignation, "Since I've had no reply to my offer, I'm guessing that your answer is no."

"I'm sorry, general. I almost said yes, but when I saw Dull Knife's people arrive it made things clear. I want to be with my husband when this is all over."

"I hope that you don't regret it. Colonel Wessels takes over this fort soon and he has been briefed on your situation. He has instructions to hold you unharmed until the breakout is over. When it ends, you are free to leave."

Emma allowed herself a smile. "Thank you, general. That's a relief." Although she had no idea how long the outbreak would last, it was a ray of hope. She clung to it.

Chapter Six

Colonel Wessels, called 'the Little Dutchman' by the soldiers, was a small man in a meticulously pressed uniform. Days after his installation as commander, Emma noticed a change in how the Cheyenne were treated. Considine had allowed the Cheyenne relatively free roam provided they stayed near the barracks, and they had been well treated, but Wessels, harsh and inexperienced with Indians, quickly changed everything.

The warrior Bull Hump escaped the barracks one night, so Wessels punished the Cheyenne by denying them free roam and then, angered by protests, denied them food and water as well. They were locked in the small barracks and deprived of the barest essentials of life, as well as the dignity of privacy. Emma watched helplessly from a distance. She asked to see Wessels repeatedly. Her requests were not denied, they were ignored.

Then, for some inexplicable reason, Wessels granted Emma permission to ride outside the fort with a couple of guards. What Emma did not know was that Considine kept tabs on her through Wessels and it was his order. Wessels believed it would silence her so that she would stop sending requests to see the Cheyenne. He was already tired of her despite the fact that they had never met.

It was a cold day; the wind had ceased for a change and Emma was grateful to get out of the fort. But this day she was accompanied by her least favorite guard, Corporal Seymour Fulton, the man who had shouted 'Indian's whore' at her weeks ago, along with a young corporal with light brown hair named Michael Doyle. By his surly attitude Fulton made it clear that he resented her and this particular duty. Emma ignored him and struck up a conversation with Doyle as they rode a half mile from the fort. She needed this rare bit of freedom and Doyle seemed to be an amiable young man.

Just after they stopped to eat a quick lunch Emma needed to relieve herself and headed for the only available cover, a small wood nearby.

As she returned through the woods, a dark stain on the snow caught her eye. She knelt down and, with a start, saw fresh blood. Seeing no animal tracks around it, she quickly became alert. Then she saw boot prints in the snow and an indentation where something—someone—had been dragged off. She called out for Doyle, but there was no answer. Then she huddled down and kept still, straining to see through the trees. Someone was crashing through the trees behind her. She turned just as Fulton backhanded her and wrestled her to the ground. He tore away her coat and her dress. She struggled and got away, screaming as she ran. He caught her by the hair and tossed her to the snow–packed ground.

"Bitch!" he snarled.

She bunched and rolled, trying to gain her feet and run, but she slipped on the snow. His kick caught her in the stomach and she sprawled, her wind gone. He punched her in the face, but she fought him off and rolled away. He tackled her and held her down, pulling up her dress. She felt his hands clawing at her leggings, then his finger roughly shoved inside her. She regained breath and screamed again, but his big dirty hand quickly covered her nose and mouth.

"No one can hear you, bitch. You're nothing but an Indian's whore so you should enjoy this," he sneered as he unbuttoned his pants.

She fought, kicking and trying to bite his hand, but he hardly noticed her efforts. His foul breath reeked and she fought to breathe under his big hand. The scene swam before her as she felt her legs forced apart and felt him roughly enter her. The pain was unendurable. His weight held her down. With all her strength, she fought, her screams muffled by his hand, desperately trying to breathe, but she was weakening from lack of air and pain. He quickly finished with a grunt.

"That's a good girl," he said, "and there's no one you can tell about it!"

She saw a knife glint above her in the weak winter light, then sank into oblivion.

That afternoon, Peter came to the infirmary with news for Emma that Shea had been spotted during a skirmish with troops. The news would bolster her spirits, but there was no answer to his knock on her door. "Emma? You in there?" He waited for some stirring within, but there was none. He asked a passing corpsman, "You seen Emma?"

"She went out to ride. Not back yet, I guess."

"Who went out with her today?"

"Ah, Doyle and Fulton, I think," the corpsman told him.

"You seen them around?"

"No, Doc. Haven't seen either of them."

A chill ran through Peter. He remembered that day Fulton had hurled his insult at Emma and with all three of them absent for too long, he became very concerned. He quickly grabbed his medical bag, went to the stables, saddled his horse and rode out of the fort. Low, wind–driven clouds promised more snow very soon so he rode fast. Quelling rising panic, he searched nearly an hour. Then he saw movement near the wood south of the fort and spurred his horse. Two horses from the fort's stable were tied to a tree. He dismounted, calling out and following the tracks through the woods.

A trail of blood led first to Doyle, who had his scalp opened by a blow to the head. He was mere feet away from where Emma lay; it appeared that he had tried to crawl to her. Fulton was nowhere to be found.

Peter fell to his knees beside her. "Emma? Can you hear me?" Emma's long hair stuck to her neck, stiff with frozen, crusted blood. He felt her face—it was cold and still and her chest was blood–soaked. "Oh Christ!" With little hope he felt for a pulse and felt a faint thump. He rummaged in his medical case for bandages and carefully pulled away her shearling and tore the bodice of her dress at the shoulder where the knife had gone into her chest. He quickly bandaged the wound. "Hang on, Emma."

He then went to Doyle who had woke, moaning and disoriented. He used smelling salts to bring the young man around, then bandaged his head, which sported a three–inch gash.

"C'mon corporal. Get up. Help me with the girl. She's hurt bad."

Doyle used every bit of willpower to stand and stagger over to Emma. "I saw what he did—Fulton. Beat the daylights out of her, then he—raped her."

"We've got to get her back to the fort. Help me!"

Doyle almost dropped Emma several times as they carried her out of the woods and got her on Peter's mount. He was weak and barely able to keep his seat as they rode, so Peter took the reins and pulled the young soldier's horse behind his, along with Emma's horse.

Peter rode as fast as possible, cradling Emma, trying to keep her warm. The sentries saw Peter waving frantically and shouted an alert to all within the fort. Many hands reached for Emma as she was carried inside the infirmary. The moment he got inside the gate, Doyle passed out and slid off his horse.

Several patients and soldiers watched from the doorway of Emma's room, staring and quiet, seeing the blood; Emma was barely recognizable, her face bruised and swollen.

Peter spoke to the corpsmen who pushed through the crowd. "You—stay and help me with her—and you, get me blankets, lots of them, bandages, alcohol and my suture tray. And you—see to Doyle and clean out the cut on his head. Somebody get Colonel Wessels. Everyone else, get the hell out!" Everyone reluctantly shuffled away. A corpsman closed the door and helped Peter cut away what was left of Emma's ripped clothes. Peter removed his hastily applied bandages and examined her chest wound. It was not deep, thanks to her shearling, but her breathing was thin and labored and she was icy cold. His practiced eye ran over her. The torn clothing—the bruises on her thighs and abdomen. "Son–of–a–bitch Fulton!" he muttered.

The corpsman looked sickened, stammering, "Did he—has she been—"

"Yes," Peter hissed. "Not a pretty sight, is it?"

Wessels rushed into Emma's room moments later.

Peter spoke, "Corporal Fulton did this to her. You've got to get a patrol out to look for him! His tracks will be fresh!"

"What happened?"

"She's been raped and stabbed!" Peter said with impatience. "Doyle's got a gash on his head, courtesy of Fulton." He regained some composure with a deep breath. "Around four, she hadn't come back so I left the fort and found her and Doyle in the scrub woods south of here. Fulton and his horse were nowhere to be found."

Wessels only nodded.

Peter felt both guilty and angry. Guilty because he could not be with Emma much since the Cheyenne had arrived, preoccupied with their care. He had shut her out a few days ago when she had asked him to intervene with Wessels. He was under orders, yet he had hurt her by his inattention. And news of her injuries or death would bring the wrath of the Cheyenne down upon them. His anger at Fulton was dark and seething. He hoped to watch the man hang for what he had done.

He examined the black bruises on her face. "She's half frozen and I think the knife nicked her lung. She's not breathing right." Peter looked up at Wessels. His presence was useless, standing there gaping at Emma's nude body. "Colonel, would you wait outside, please?" Wessels gladly retreated to his office.

A corpsman returned with the needed supplies and he and Peter cleaned Emma's knife wound and stitched it up. Her lung injury was small and would have to heal on its own; stitches would never hold. Her chest was tightly wrapped in layers of bandages. Then Peter looked at the red and black bruises on her thighs and large bruises on her stomach, arms, and throat. With a terrible sinking in his heart, he examined her thoroughly. She had been brutally raped. She was left nude under the blankets. "We have to warm her up slowly. Get more kindling for the wood burner," Peter said.

"Uh, shouldn't I get her a dressing gown, sir?" the corpsman asked.

"No. The skin is very fragile after exposure. Clothes can cut it apart. Go get the wood. Anyone who wants information about her is to ask me or Wessels only. That's an order."

Wessels reappeared at the infirmary just before dark, finding Peter in the ward stitching up Doyle's scalp.

"Doyle, tell the colonel what you told me."

The young man's face was slack and his eyes wide and unblinking with disgust at what he had witnessed. "We were heading back, but Emma said she had to go—so she went in the woods. I was tightening my horse's cinch when Fulton hits me on the head with his rifle butt. I ran off into the woods and blacked out. Screaming woke me up. I crawled towards the sound, then I saw what he was doing to her." He struggled to keep from crying. "He stabbed her when he was done and rode off. I tried to get to her."

"We know you did, Doyle," Peter said as he wrapped Doyle's forehead with a fresh bandage.

Wessels looked disturbed and ushered Peter to Emma's room. She remained unconscious. Peter dismissed the corpsman sitting with her, then spoke. "We have our witness and I'm certain after examining her."

"You're absolutely sure?"

His answer was impatient. "I'm sure that he beat and raped her!" The outline of Fulton's knuckles clearly showed on her cheek.

Wessels shook his head. "Will she live?" He was troubled, mainly because Considine insisted on regular reports on her. Wessels had only been in command of Fort Robinson for a short time and this had happened on top of his troubles with the Cheyenne. Considine would certainly hold him accountable for the attack upon Emma.

"Don't know yet. Being out in the cold slowed the bleeding. But exposure to the cold may take her just the same."

"I'll have a troop look for Fulton tomorrow but with the weather getting worse, I don't expect to find him."

"You mean a troop wasn't sent out this afternoon?" Peter's look of incredulity showed his frustration at Wessels' inaction.

"I don't have time to chase down one man. What he did was terrible, but I have the Cheyenne to worry about." The colonel's face was stone. "I can't keep a lid on this for long. The Cheyenne will riot if they find out what happened. I'll post more guards around her," he said, as if this would avert any more trouble, but too dull to realize that it was too late. "I need my soldiers here in case we have an uprising." He said that he would send out a half–dozen men to search for Fulton the next morning.

Peter was heartsick as he held vigil at Emma's side all night. She had her faults but she had never hurt anyone. He resolved to use all his skills to keep her alive. He would eventually get her out of this place—somehow, using every connection he had .

Hours later in his office, Wessels was writing and rewriting a wire to send to Considine. He chose his words carefully, unwilling to rile the general and for himself, not appear incompetent.

He handed the wire to the young corporal who operated the telegraph. It read: E injured by Fulton(stop)expect full recovery(stop)Fulton deserted(stop). Wessels then sent messages to the other forts in the area with a description of Fulton. He braced himself for an immediate response from Considine. No reply came.

In the tiny room of the infirmary Emma lay still and cool as death, her chest barely rising with each shallow breath. Peter never left her side.

The next morning as the troop departed a winter blow began, obliterating any tracks left by Fulton. The troop returned the next evening without Fulton; worsening weather prevented further effort.

From the barracks windows, the Cheyenne had seen Emma brought in and asked the guards about her. Wessels had ordered the guards to say that she had been hurt in a fall from her horse. The Cheyenne did not believe it and were left to speculate about what had actually happened to her.

Another day passed and Emma remained unconscious. She was very pale and her skin still hard and cool. Her bed was moved nearer the small wood stove in her room. Her eyes fluttered open from time to time, but there was no consciousness there. Peter dribbled water down her throat. She swallowed, but did not stir.

Late that night, Peter dozed, his head lolling on his chest, then jerked awake hearing Emma moan. He spoke to her, trying to coax her awake. "Emma? Wake up, c'mon, try. It's Peter. You're safe." Her swollen eyelids fluttered and she cried out, remembering. "Shh, Emma. You're all right." Her hand went to her chest, touching the tight bandages. "You're going to make it, don't worry."

"Fulton!" she gasped.

"Calm down. He's gone—deserted."

Tears slid across her cheeks and he wiped them away. "He forced me," she said though her bruised mouth. Her chest buzzed as she spoke.

"I know, Emma. Now don't try to talk."

She gasped for breath. "I saw the knife and knew I was dead. Then I saw him, plain, just as I see you now. Standing in front of me—he said come home."

"Fulton said what?"

"No—Shea."

"Emma, you're not making sense. Quiet now."

"Shea was there. He knows," she whimpered. Both eyes were swollen and half–closed and her chin and cheeks swollen with purple and black bruises. After a dose of laudanum, she drifted off, mumbling.

Emma woke with a cry late into the third night. Her eyes bulged with pain and fear. Peter calmed her best he could.

"Stay still now." She fought to remain conscious and told Peter, in painful gasps for breath, what had happened. She was particularly concerned for Doyle, who she believed was dead, but Peter assured her that he was all right and had tried to save her.

"The knife hit your lung, so quiet, okay?"

She watched him with eyes that looked much different. Deep pain and desolation were etched there. Her once gentle, innocent blue eyes had, in a few moments of terror, changed—hardened. The naive orphaned girl had been replaced by a young woman who had experienced terror, brutality, and rape.

"You lost a lot of blood, Emma, so you're going to be weak for a while. Nod or shake your head. Any pain when you breathe?"

"I feel like I can't catch my breath. And where are my clothes?"

"Don't talk. Here's paper and a pencil—and a bell to ring to call for help, but I'll be close by," he said, putting these items on a table next to her bed.

"You were near frozen when you were brought in, so we had to cut off your clothes. Your skin's warmed up so let's get a gown on you now." With great care, he helped her into a clean gown and laid her back down. "Any pain?" he asked, gently probing her abdomen. "Anything?" She shook her head slowly. "Any numbness or tingling in your arms or legs?" She shook her head no. "Any other places where it hurts?" My back, she indicated. "I'll put some compresses on you," he said, watching her face dissolve into tears. "It's not your fault what happened. I don't want to sound cold, but try not to cry. You lung needs time to heal." He gently dabbed her tears away. "Can you manage some soup?"

He helped Emma to eat a little broth, relieving the corpsman of the duty, then applied warm compresses to her back.

"What day is this?" she asked.

"It's Tuesday. You've been out nearly three days."

Another wave of humiliation and fear moved through her as the attack replayed in her mind. Panic spread through her and she could hardly catch her breath. Burrowing beneath the covers, she whispered, "I wish Shea were here. I need him. I saw him."

"So you said the other day, but you were a little rattled when you woke. Quiet now."

"I did see him. He was right in front of me. He told me to come home."

"Emma, it was a dream."

She took a painful breath. "No it wasn't. He was there. He was."

"If you say so, Emma."

"Any word on Little Wolf's people?"

"I heard a report that your husband and a troop leader exchanged words a few days back. Your husband's still alive."

"Yes, I know."

She woke the next morning alone, but the muffled voices of the guards outside her room soon caused her to doze. However the pain would not allow her to sleep very long. She rang the bell for a corpsman and got a dose of laudanum.

Later, Emma's door opened and Wessels entered with Peter. Emma was half-awake, feeling very groggy from the laudanum.

"I'm encouraged you're better," Wessels began. "Is there anything I can do for you, anything you need?" She shook her head. "Well," his discomfort was evident, "let me or Doc Cromwell know if you do. There are guards all around you. Doyle backs up your account of what happened. Did you say or do anything to Fulton that might've angered him?"

She was suddenly agitated, the drug making his statement more acute. "I did nothing to bring this on!"

"Okay, all right," he said defensively.

"It wasn't my fault," she strained for breath. "He made his feelings about me quite clear weeks ago. I couldn't fight him off."

Wessels spoke. "We haven't found Fulton yet, but I've sent word to other forts in the area. He can't get far in this weather."

"He'll come back and finish me, I know it!" she gasped.

"No one will get to you," Peter said, "not if I can help it."

She was drained. Her eyes slammed shut into a dreamless sleep.

Peter and Wessels spoke in the hallway. "I didn't know that she objected to Fulton as her guard. Why wasn't I informed about this?"

Peter told him of the day Fulton called her an Indian's whore, but pointed out that the army's best men were in pursuit of the Cheyenne. "The commander that was here before Considine was going to force Fulton out of the service, but he was transferred before he could do anything. Fulton's a problem both you and Considine inherited. He'd always been a discipline problem and he made his opinion about Emma clear from the start. I didn't know that Fulton was assigned to her the other day until it was too late."

"Considine will have my head for this."

Witnessing Wessels' harsh treatment of the Cheyenne, Peter found it difficult to feel sorry for him. Wessels had his own agenda and did not care about Emma or Dull Knife's people. It was up to him to do something. Peter went to the telegraph room and sent a message to General Considine.

That night, Wessels paced off his small office, searching for a way to salvage the situation. He had just been assigned to this weary little post, but with the coming resettlement of Dull Knife's people and the many requests that he had had from them about Emma's health, he knew he had to make himself look competent and, to his dismay, compassionate toward Emma. He dearly wanted a transfer back east. If he handled the situations with the Cheyenne and Emma ably, his chances were good for reassignment. He composed another wire to Considine telling him that Emma was on the mend, but that was all he felt obliged to do.

Chapter Seven

Another blizzard hammered the frontier, slowing the Cheyenne pursuit considerably; still, they evaded capture. The pace the Cheyenne sustained was brutal and fatal. Soldiers found bodies scattered throughout the countryside, but Little Wolf's main group still eluded them.

Due to the bitter cold and still stiff and sore, Emma spent a lot of time alone in her room. Peter let the men know that she liked to read and many books were immediately loaned to her. She was very relieved when her period started a week later; that animal, Fulton, did not get her pregnant. Peter was vastly relieved as well. He now made more of an effort to keep her informed about the pursuit of the Cheyenne and also reported that there was no news about Fulton. Emma darkly hoped that he had frozen to death on the prairie and the wolves had devoured his corpse.

Doyle had visited Emma several times, but was often tongue–tied and uncomfortable. He was thoroughly disgusted at what Fulton had done to her. Emma understood his discomfort and endeavored to put him at ease, assuring him that she was all right. Doyle soon returned to light duty in the mess hall. Discovering her favorite foods, he personally made Emma's meals for her. She was touched by his compassion.

Although the army hired buffalo soldiers, cowboys, and Indian scouts, all had limited success tracking the Cheyenne and frustration grew as the search entered a fourth month. Continued failure could spill over into a full–scale war when the Cheyenne were eventually found. Emma could not believe that they had held out so long and at last admitted to herself that she never would have survived. Shea had been right and she cursed herself for not listening to him. If she had, she would be safe at Fort Reno under Adam's care, not in this bleak fort surrounded by strangers, watching for signs of life in the dark, cold barracks where Dull Knife's people suffered.

Doyle told her that some Indian scouts employed by the army had deserted the ranks, torn between duty and the increasingly desperate plight of their people. When the army spotted a camp in the distance, they figured they had the Cheyenne surrounded, but in the night, all would sneak away, leaving frustrated troops standing guard over a deserted camp the next morning. The astounding stamina of these desperate, starving people was more than a match for the army and their mounts and proved an embarrassment to the government.

Emma's despair deepened. Her parents had been dead over a year now and she cried bitter tears of loss. She worried over Shea who was starving and freezing on the prairie, hunted day and night. Each day she hoped that he had the strength to keep eluding the patrols. Her thoughts became fixed on Shea and the Cheyenne, imagining their terrible ordeals and ignoring her own.

She struggled to rise each day. A palpable wretchedness settled over her as the heavy snow blanketed the prairie. She could not breathe deeply and sometimes felt that she was slowly smothering; this made her frantic, causing her chest to constrict, making breathing all the more painful. And it was not only her injuries that stoked her depression. She believed that she would never be released from this strange imprisonment. In her brief exposure to what she termed the 'other world,' trusting a person's word had proven not worth the bother.

Emma's feelings of helplessness lingered as the winter days passed slowly. Though her body healed, her mind did not follow and she feared the advent of madness. Since Fulton's attack torturous dreams invaded her sleep, unnerving the guards outside her room when she woke screaming many nights. Peter took to sleeping on a cot in his office, ready with laudanum to sedate her on particularly bad nights.

Surrounded by guards, Peter moved Emma to a small guest cabin, hoping that it would help her to have privacy and quiet. Wessels allowed it because he was ordered by Considine to release her in spring. Her two guards were posted in a small vestibule.

Many newspaper reporters were in the region covering the outbreak. Wessels wanted anything that she said about her stay at the fort to be as positive as possible. He was glad to soon be rid of her.

Although no one spoke of her ordeal openly, everyone knew now, even the Cheyenne. Wessels, furious, was unsuccessful in trying to discover who had talked. Many soldiers who had once condemned Emma as a traitor rallied to her now. The sight of her injuries and bruises was unsettling and, when coupled with her screams in the night, gave everyone pause. The majority of soldiers were polite and kept a respectful distance and many sympathized with her loneliness and seemingly unsolvable dilemma.

Emma isolated herself in the aftermath of the attack. She had many hours alone in the small cabin and many fears preyed upon her. Ill–equipped to handle the terror of what had happened to her, she buried her emotions. They struggled within but the wall she had built around them held. Her appetite lagged and she often refused the meals that Doyle personally delivered. She grew thin and pale. Chances were better than good that her husband would die—and if he did survive, she convinced herself, Shea would think her damaged and never take her back. She was most afraid of being alone in the world again.

After Peter removed the bandages that had kept her left arm immobilized for weeks while her chest healed, Emma began spending time in the warm stables tending the horses. The rhythmic strokes of brushing their coats freed her mind and strengthened her unused muscles. The animals accepted her care, wanting nothing in return. Her ever–present guards did not mind because the stables were warm; it was easy duty.

One afternoon, Wessels found her there. "Emma," he said, "I see you're feeling better. I have a fine stable here, don't I?" He never missed an opportunity to let her know that he was in charge and resented her presence in his fort.

"I find that animals are easier to deal with than people."

"I've been asked to give you an update on the Cheyenne at the request of General Considine," he said with a distinct note of resentment. He disliked being Considine's errand boy. Emma wondered why Considine still took the time to care. Maybe she had been wrong about him.

"Your husband's alive. During a skirmish a few days ago, a Major Lawrence spotted Shea and called to him to arrange a meeting with Little Wolf, but the Cheyenne held off his contingent for hours then escaped."

Emma perked up. "Major Adam Lawrence?"

"I think so. You know him?"

"He was stationed at Fort Reno near the reservation where I lived. I know him, yes."

Wessels looked uncomfortable. He was weighted by his decisions to subdue the Cheyenne who remained in the freezing barracks with no food or water. Now, realizing that Emma also knew Adam Lawrence, Considine's newly appointed aide–de–camp, he felt powerless to exert control over her.

The girl seemed oblivious that she had important friends, but he wondered if she was only being cagey and would use the influence when needed.

"All right, then. Let's hope that he can make progress with Little Wolf's people when they are found," Wessels said as he turned to leave.

This was the first time that she had ever spoken with him alone and took advantage of it. She emboldened herself and asked, "When are you going to help the Cheyenne in the barracks? I don't understand why you're punishing all of them for the actions of one."

"I'm not their enemy, ma'am. Just doing my job. We gave them shelter and food, but they broke their word to me by helping Bull Hump escape."

"There are women and children in there! How can you starve them and let them freeze?" She dared to speak freely and did not care what he did to her; she thoroughly disliked him and felt that she had nothing left to lose. In fact, she was no longer afraid of pain or death—Fulton's attack had left its indelible mark. Dull Knife's people suffered mere yards away because of this ignorant man.

"I was left with no choice when their demands became too much. They wanted free roam, but Bull Hump's escape ended that. Since he got away, others would've tried, so I had to lock them up."

"You mean the Cheyenne asking for humane treatment is a demand?"

"You had better be concerned with yourself instead of them. I've done you more favors than you realize!"

"Nothing you've said or done convinces me that you care about anyone but yourself and your little war of wills with Dull Knife!" Emma declared.

Her comment penetrated. Wessels was ensnared by his decision to keep control of the Cheyenne. If he relented now, he would look weak. Emma returned to brushing the large bay.

"I am doing what is right for everyone." He swallowed and continued with the message Considine had ordered him to relay to her. He fought to soften his tone. "You will be released from custody soon so I hope that you speak well of your care here. And remember what Corporal Fulton did to you was of his own volition. The army had nothing to do with it and condemns his actions."

"Whatever do you mean? I've been kept here against my will for months! And what I say about my imprisonment is my business."

"You've been housed, fed, and we've saved your life twice now. If you were still with Little Wolf's tribe, you would never have survived."

She could not bear to look at him and continued brushing the horse. "I wouldn't have needed saving a second time if I hadn't been held prisoner. At least with the Cheyenne I would never have been beaten, raped, and nearly murdered! I may have died out on the prairie, but at least it would've been for a reason. Really, colonel, you're crazy if you think that I ever wanted to be here. I was kidnapped by hired men and forced to stay here."

He was not very good with people, but he needed her to keep her mouth shut about the rape and the treatment of Dull Knife's people when she was eventually freed. He was ambitious, but somewhat dim. "I am offering you a chance to start your life over. I will give you a sum of money, then a troop, handpicked by me, will escort you to the nearest train station. I strongly advise you to go east of the Mississippi, in fact, I'm ordering you to leave the territory when you're released."

"Oh, please, colonel! This is just another cover up—let me go, but make sure that I'm surrounded by troops until I'm put on a train east. The farther east I go, the less people care about what happens out here! The army is not off the hook, believe me!" Emma saw room to bargain. "I'll take you up on your offer. I want a horse, a pack mule with supplies for three months, and a good map. And you can keep your army escort. I'll take my chances alone and find the Cheyenne myself."

"They'll be sent back south where they belong when they are found—and they will be, I assure you."

"If you feed Dull Knife's people and give them food, water, firewood, and the necessities of life, I will speak well of my time here. If not—"

"I will not be blackmailed!" he growled.

"How do you justify your treatment of Dull Knife's people? And what do you call what you've offered me? You want to buy me off with a few dollars! Forget it! When I leave this place, I'll tell everyone who will listen what happened here—to me and the Cheyenne."

"I will not allow you to leave this fort unguarded. The general's orders are very explicit," he hissed, supremely annoyed with Emma's obstinacy.

"You should be more afraid of the Cheyenne! As for me, I've had my fill of this place and of the guards who dog me every minute!"

Her remarks and spiteful anger rattled him. He did not deal well with displays of emotion. And things had become very quiet lately in the Cheyenne barracks and he was worried. "You don't understand all that has transpired with Dull Knife."

"You're a coward for not dealing fairly with the Cheyenne," she spat. "I am shocked how little you know about them. You should take the train east. You don't have what it takes to live out here!"

Taking a long moment, Wessels tried to diffuse his anger. "It has been difficult because you have endured much during your stay. My offer is meant to give you a new start, a respectable life."

"I've always been respectable, colonel," she snapped. Her patience with this awful man was gone.

Wessels was not a hard man, only foolish and inexperienced. He could not, would not, argue that her treatment at the army's hands had been just or compassionate.

She looked him straight in the eye. "Give the Cheyennes food and firewood—and give me what I want—and I'll speak well of my time here. That's my offer," she asserted.

Wessels had no choice but to relent. He sent her counteroffer to Considine who strongly advised against her foolish plan to travel alone. He ordered Wessels to get her to change her mind, but he was terribly unsuccessful. She was unyielding, feeling a small measure of power for a change. Wessels, at least, did provide some meager rations for the Cheyenne, but it was too little, too late.

Bitter cold weather slammed the fort again. Emma rarely left the cabin in December other than to spend a few quiet hours in the stables or the mess hall kitchen. When she did venture outdoors, her eyes always found the Cheyenne's barracks in the distance. No smoke came from the chimneys. They were freezing and starving and she wondered why Wessels could not admit his mistake. Had her threats to expose their inhumane treatment toughened Wessels' stance? She had believed that strong–arming Wessels would help the Cheyenne. All she had endured thus far was nothing in comparison to the suffering of Dull Knife's people. She tried to hold onto some shred of hope that Wessels would do something, but apart from finally giving them a little food and some firewood, he did nothing else.

Christmas came and went virtually unnoticed by Emma for the second year in a row. She did not leave the cabin that day despite coaxing by Peter who gave her a gift of a pair of warm gloves purchased from the trading post. She ate Christmas supper alone while Peter was obliged to attend Wessels' Christmas party in the officers' dining room. However, she hardly missed the festivities as she was preoccupied with the Cheyenne and their misery and frustrated that she could do nothing but watch the dark barracks for moving shadows as the only signs of life inside. She felt responsible for their continued mistreatment—Wessels was punishing them for her hostility toward him. He wanted submission from her. She vowed not to give in. But a part of her wondered if her stubbornness had made the Cheyenne situation worse. Uncertainty turned to despondency.

Days later, Peter had forgotten a bottle of laudanum in Emma's cabin. Although she still needed it sometimes because her nightmares persisted, she had refused a dose that evening. But later, in her brittle mental condition, she picked up the amber bottle, turning it over and over in her hands. She toyed with the idea of drinking it all down. Her hopelessness would end. She would not have to ponder her fate or that of the Cheyenne. The memory of losing her parents would evaporate. The relentless horror of the rape would disappear. And her quandary as to whether Shea would take her back would no longer exist. She opened the bottle and brought it to her lips several times, but lacked the courage and slammed it down, ashamed of her weakness in looking for an easy way out. Attempts to resist depression failed for it had outgrown her powers to oppose it . The only thought keeping her from killing herself was that maybe, just maybe, she could reunite with Shea—if he survived the run and this brutal winter—and if he could accept the fact that she had been brutalized. She would beg him to take her back if she had to.

'I can't give you the will to live,' a little voice in her head began to repeat, *'but you had better pull yourself together.'* She held on, needing to come out of this dark place and see Shea again. Being with him would make everything right. Her love for him was stronger than she had ever realized. It kept her alive.

She had never coped with her feelings of grief, loss, and anger, so successfully had she secreted them inside her heart. When times got rough she had the arrogance to congratulate herself for her strength and resolve to survive. But now she was stuck somewhere between madness and hope and holding onto Shea's precious memory as a lifeline. He was the only person on this earth, she believed, who loved her.

Events played ceaselessly in her thoughts, both joys and sorrows carrying the same sting, that winter of 1879. Her life had changed abruptly in 1877 when her parents had died and she had lived day–to–day staying occupied to block out her grief and pain. It was not working. Her mind was a train wreck, a hopeless jumble, and she was ill–equipped to deal with it.

A recurring dream tortured her. Ghostly apparitions of her parents would appear, wailing and calling out for her. Terrified, she would run away, stumbling through a dark, thick wood. Thorns and nettles shredded her clothes and punctured her exposed skin as she fled. Panic drove her towards something unseen but she knew if she reached it that she would be safe. Moans, carried on a howling wind, followed her regardless how far or how fast she ran. The tangled path through the woods ended at the steep bank of a fast–moving river, then the sky went black and a fierce wind blew so hard that it pushed her into the river and carried her along, her body crushed against boulders poking up from the rapids. Her screams went unheard. There was no one to hear. She would wake abruptly, believing that she felt the pain of being crushed against the rocks, a shriek of terror caught in her throat.

She remembered Considine's comment that her marriage to Shea had been an impulse to avoid making decisions about her future. Life with the little Cheyenne tribe had seemed to be the best choice since she had been orphaned, but she was now paying the price for denial and rash decisions. She had been swept unwillingly along by events and now paralyzing fear about her future overrode every thought, every moment. A way out seemed an impossibility.

Matters for Dull Knife's people worsened. The barracks were freezing and little food and wood were provided. She had heard that the Indians pulled up the floorboards and burned them in an attempt to keep warm. Food was so scarce that some Cheyenne reportedly ate their own clothing.

They became so wretched that they broke out the night of January ninth, 1879 and desperately scattered through the hills behind the fort.

That night, Emma woke to shouts and gunfire. Wearing only boots, a dressing gown, and an army–issue coat given to her by Peter, she ran out into the yard. She ran off fast with her startled guards in her wake. She saw Cheyenne jumping from the barracks windows. Flashes of gunfire lit the freezing night, illuminating shadows running for the hills. Many Cheyenne were shot before they got very far; men, women, and children were cut down indiscriminately. Emma ran in front of the firing line, causing the soldiers to check their aim at the fleeing Cheyenne.

"Stop! Stop!" she cried over the crackling din. "Somebody stop this!" Several soldiers quickly dragged her off and hustled her back to her cabin. Her guards would not let her out despite her angry protests. The cabin's only window faced the low north wall, so she could not see what was happening. She only heard the boom of gunfire that went on for a seeming eternity. She wept for the Cheyenne and paced off the tiny cabin. She did not sleep.

At dawn she opened up her door. "The colonel says that you're to stay inside," one guard said.

"What happened? Please!"

The appeal in her eyes affected the young soldier. The other guard was asleep in his chair so he leaned down close to her and whispered. "Dull Knife's people broke out last night. A bunch were captured and brought back, but some were hurt—some killed."

"How many died?"

"About thirty, I think. All we had to do was keep them fed and housed until spring, then take them back south. The colonel had other ideas. He shouldn't have starved them." The young man looked very troubled and quickly drew back as their voices roused his companion from sleep.

"What a waste," Emma said and closed the door.

She was kept inside the next day and only let out for a few minutes to get meals. She saw soldiers manning stretchers and wagon loads of Cheyenne, living and dead, were brought into the fort. Even from a distance she could smell blood and death fouling the cold air.

Wessels then left the fort with many men to pursue those who had escaped. He was especially keen to capture Dull Knife, who had not been among the dead or wounded. It truly never occurred to him that he was the cause of it all. He would always maintain that the Cheyenne brought on their own destruction.

Emma felt a small measure of revenge when she heard that Wessels' had been grazed in the head by a bullet while pursuing Dull Knife's people; unfortunately, he did not die from the wound. She wondered whose bullet it was—Cheyenne or army.

After Wessels was gone she pleaded with Peter to help tend the wounded Cheyenne. He was in desperate need and allowed her to help.

Wounded and dying Cheyenne were laid close together in the barracks and a tent nearby housed the dead. Blood was everywhere, making the barracks floor slick and sticky. She walked between the rows, horrified and deeply affected by their suffering. Her guards followed without arms for a change, carrying water, bandages, and medicines. Peter worked as fast as he could, completely overwhelmed and was thankful for the extra pair of hands. Swallowing her gorge, Emma learned nursing quickly, learning what to do from the corpsmen.

Day and night she worked at Peter's side with little rest. Many Cheyenne hands touched her in thanks, but some no longer possessed the strength. Many children were wounded; two of them died in her arms. She gulped back her tears and continued to help the living.

The magnitude of the Indians' plight was now finally real to her. The Cheyenne and other tribes would be annihilated before long. The government did not care, despite the promises, meetings, occasional supplies, and the meaningless treaties. The settlers and disaffected men who came west did not care. The other tribes could not care about one another anymore; their plates were too full of dispossession, sorrow, disease, starvation, and death.

Eventually she and Peter went to the tent where the dead awaited burial. Frigid temperatures provided a gruesome kind of cold storage. Emma looked at the faces, trying to put names to them, but she did not know many of Dull Knife's people. Her footsteps halted when she recognized a pair of beaded moccasins poking out from under a blanket. She fell to her knees with a cry and pulled off the blanket. It was Porcupine Girl, shot through the heart. Her calico dress was saturated with black blood. Emma was nearly hysterical as Peter pulled her away. He did not allow her to enter the tent again.

Burial details performed their grisly task for days while Emma continued to help the wounded. The grim work did not sicken her anymore. By helping them she felt truly useful and needed despite the appalling circumstances.

Each night she returned to the tiny cabin and fell onto the bed, often too exhausted to remove her bloodstained clothing. Each morning at dawn she bathed, dressed, and returned to Peter's side to work without complaint. Tears for the dead and the suffering no longer did anyone any good.

Peter was moved by her energy and determination. He resolved to use his influence, albeit meager, to get her away from Fort Robinson when the first blade of new prairie grass poked through the snow. So, taking advantage of the colonel's absence, Peter sent a telegraph to General Considine pleading for Emma's immediate release. Considine's tersely worded reply was to wait until spring. Peter did not risk Considine's displeasure again. He had sent a telegraph to Considine weeks ago regarding Emma and had never received a reply. But now he had a response and he did not like the fact that his concerns about Emma were again dismissed.

Peter needed help and admired Emma's dedication in helping the Cheyenne, but she became careworn, running on raw nerves. He ordered her to rest for a few days. She refused and kept to her strict routine. It was her last defense and only form of absolution. Peter eventually gave up, knowing her stubbornness and resolve were all that she had left.

Wessels was still away on his march to find Dull Knife. His harsh treatment of the Indians had been publicized and he was disgraced; his next assignment would make duty at Fort Robinson seem carefree. Dull Knife would be his redemption, he had believed, but Wessels returned without his trophy. Afterwards, the remaining Cheyenne at the fort were treated somewhat better. Adequate food and firewood were provided and although they could now leave the barracks, they were always surrounded by soldiers. The ragged, ravaged Cheyenne stoically waited to return to the south in the spring.

In March, a telegraph message from General Considine arrived for Emma. It ordered her freedom in April when the trails were dry. She was to be given a hundred dollars, a horse, a pack mule, and all the supplies she required. An escort would arrive to take her wherever she desired. She told Peter that the army could forget the escort and although relieved that her incarceration was nearly over, she felt guilty about leaving the wounded Cheyenne behind.

"I want to get out of here, but the thought of leaving these people is more than I can stand."

"You've done all you can, Emma. These people will remember what you did here," Peter assured her.

"What if things get worse for them? The army is expert at burying scandal, you and I know that firsthand. I'll tell people what happened here." She fell silent. The frozen corpse of Porcupine Girl haunted her so. She shook off a darkening mood.

One afternoon in late March, Peter ran into the stables where Emma was feeding the horses.

"Emma! There you are! Little Wolf's band has been found and Shea's all right. They made it to the Pine Ridge Agency in South Dakota. They have been granted asylum with the northern Cheyenne in Montana at Fort Keogh. They're being taken to a new reservation in the area. It's finally over!" Peter said.

Emma smiled and slumped against the stable wall. Her beloved Shea was safe. Peter said that the troops at the Sioux camps were very surprised when Little Wolf's Cheyenne showed up among Red Cloud's people. They slipped in one by one before anyone knew what had happened. The soldiers, who had been encamped at Pine Ridge since the outbreak, were surprised, expecting the Cheyenne to run for Canada.

Her imminent reunion with Shea was now a reality, but she was troubled. Would he take her back? And what had happened to Shea during all these months? Would they both have changed too much?

"I thought that the army was shipping them all back south, like with Dull Knife's people," she said.

"That's not going to happen with Little Wolf. He's a shrewd character and has convinced the Northern Cheyenne chiefs and the neighboring Sioux leaders to intervene. The government, probably to avoid embarrassment for never catching them, agreed. The Cheyenne will have their own reservation near the Tongue River in Montana."

"I'm glad," she said. "Now I can leave this awful place—no offense. But I will miss you."

Peter smiled at her with affection tinged with sadness. "I'll miss you, too."

Chapter Eight

Emma kept to her routine despite her coming freedom, but worried over the fates of Red Leaf Woman and Little Fox. There was no way to know if they had survived. When and if she saw Little Fox again, she would have to give her the devastating news that her friend, Porcupine Girl, was dead. Bad weather delayed the arrival of the escort sent by General Considine; Wessels would not release her until the escort arrived. But she was suddenly in no hurry to go. She would refuse to travel with the escort, however the prospect of traveling alone to Montana was daunting.

Wessels tried to appear as her benefactor to impress Considine, who was escorting Little Wolf's band to the new reservation. He allowed Emma to leave the environs of the fort again four deep in guards, with the stipulation that she remain in sight of the sentries as well. She walked along the nearby stream, enjoying the crisp April morning while her guards skipped stones on the water. Patches of snow still dotted the land, but the trails were clearing. Tantalizing thoughts of freedom were tempered by guilt at leaving Dull Knife's people behind—but the possibility of seeing Shea again occupied her thoughts.

She turned, seeing movement on the horizon. Her guards were suddenly alert, watching a rider coming from the west. A big man riding a gelding soon pulled up and dismounted. The guards quickly closed in around her.

He smiled under his shaggy, untrimmed beard and walked over to Emma. "You must be Emma Hawkshadow. Pleased to meet you. I'm Max Cody."

She took his proffered hand, but was clearly taken aback and suspicious. "How do you know me?"

"I've had a hand in making you a little famous. I'm a reporter with the Omaha Sentinel here in Nebraska."

"But how could you possibly know about me?"

He grinned, showing remarkably good teeth. "We have mutual friends."

"Omaha Sentinel—a newspaper?" she asked.

"Yes, ma'am. You look well, if I may say so. The description I had of you does not do you justice. You're far more pretty." He came as close as the guards permitted, but he did not seem deterred by them. He spoke in a low voice, almost conspiratorially. "I'm your escort. Considine sent me. I'm to take you wherever you want. Do you plan to return to your husband?"

Her guards looked at one another, uncertain if they should permit the two to speak. Not wanting to choose either way, the soldiers simply escorted the pair back to the fort. Cody strategically placed his big horse between themselves and the guards, effectively muffling their voices as they talked.

"You're my escort?" She was confused. "I thought that the general was sending soldiers."

"Nope. Just me." His look was alert, but kindly. "I have a message for you," he said, slipping a letter into her hand, "from a friend."

The guards craned their necks, trying to glimpse what he had given to her. She opened the letter.

"Dear Emma, Shea and the Cheyenne are safe here at Fort Keogh in Montana. In a few weeks, the tribe will be moved to their new reservation on the Tongue River, southwest of the fort. I told Shea that I would help you to get here, but I cannot get away. General Considine has sent Max Cody to you. Max has promised to see you safely to the reservation. I trust him and you can, too. He knows the way. Cody has another message from General Considine for the commander at Fort Robinson. Please come north as soon as you can. Affectionately, Adam."

Emma stared at Max. "How do I know this is genuine? How do I know you're who you say you are?"

"Shea said to call you *ema'o*. Then Adam said that you would remember what happened behind the mess hall at Fort Reno last year. I'll admit, I'm curious about that one myself," he chuckled.

Emma smiled. *Ema'o* was the private joke between Little Fox and Porcupine Girl and she vividly remembered heaving her guts up after drinking too much wine at Fort Reno. "It was my own bad judgment at Fort Reno. Nothing sordid," she grinned.

She believed that Cody was genuine, but he did not look like a reporter—more like a mountain man, she thought. He was very tall and broad, not fat, but husky. He wore fringed buckskin and high laced boots that went up to his knees. His light brown hair was long and streaked with gray. As he walked, the ground literally thrummed beneath his feet. His face was sharp and angular and his beard hid a wide–lipped mouth that was permanently curled into a sort of smirk.

"You spoke with Shea—so he's all right?"

"Yes, ma'am. He's a little worse for wear, but very excited to see you again—so are Major Lawrence and General Considine."

"Mr. Cody, how do you know the major and the general?"

"Call me Max," he smiled. "A good reporter doesn't reveal his sources."

"Please. I don't have the patience for games."

He grinned, ignoring her terse remark. "You have more friends than you know and they have kept tabs on you. I spent the last four months trailing various troops chasing the Cheyenne. Tell me, did you get to know the young corporal who operates the telegraph here?" She shook her head. "Ben Lawrence?"

Emma stopped walking. "Lawrence?"

"Ben has a brother."

Emma walked ahead a few paces. "Adam? Adam's brother is stationed here? I never knew that."

Cody came close to her, keeping his voice low. "I trailed Major Lawrence's troop for weeks and got the whole story about you and your husband. As for Considine, I've known him for years, back to when he was a major. He heard what happened to you from Ben. Ben had been sending secret messages about you to Adam, but he got caught by Considine when he was headquartered here. The general was angry and forbade any more messages. However, when he got transferred, he saw the value in having a spy here to report on Dull Knife's Cheyenne, Wessels—and you. Considine had little faith in Wessels' ability. We all know how that turned out," he said, referring to the massacre of Dull Knife's Cheyenne. "Minutes after you were brought in after you were attacked by that soldier, Ben got word to both his brother and Considine."

She turned away, embarrassed and ashamed. "You know what happened to me? They know, too?"

"I was stopping at Fort Laramie in Wyoming on my way to Omaha when I got a request from Considine—to do a favor, really, to come to get you right away. Unfortunately, the weather prevented me from getting here sooner."

"Did you write about the attack in your newspaper?"

He looked at her earnestly. "Ma'am, I would never have publicized the details of your ordeal. I don't deal in that kind of reporting."

"What did you write about it, then? she asked, perturbed.

"No details, just that a soldier had attacked you. That's all," he said.

Cody's words gave Emma considerable pause. "Forgive me. I don't trust many people." She walked on and said, "But it's good to know that someone was watching over me. I won't tell anyone about Ben. He took a big risk and I don't want him in any trouble over me."

"I assure you that I am your ally. My sympathies lie with the Indians—all of them. What the government tried to do to the Cheyenne was wrong. I've written a few articles hoping to drum up support for them. They worked, to a degree, I think." They walked on a few paces. "So, when do you want to leave?"

"Hold on a minute," she said, feeling pressured. "I don't know you and even though I believe Adam's letter is genuine, you're still a stranger to me."

"You'll have to trust me." Max said no more as they entered the fort.

Her desire to get away from the fort was stronger than her apprehension of Cody. "All right. We'll go as soon as possible. And I'd like to see those articles you wrote about me," she said over her shoulder as she headed to her room.

Cody then went to Wessels' office.

Knowing that he could not refuse the famous reporter of the Omaha Sentinel shelter, despite his supreme irritation, Wessels allowed Cody to stay in the troop barracks. Cody was sure to hear of Emma's ordeals, so he planned to put a gag order on everyone at the fort. However, he was further irritated that Cody already knew everything about Emma. Wessels and Cody had a pitched exchange as Wessels tried to find out who in his ranks had been leaking information. All too used to this type of behavior, Cody remained mute on that point. Cody handed him Considine's orders concerning Emma. Wessels dearly wished that the troublesome girl would get out of his fort as quickly as possible—and take Cody with her.

Max Cody was a shrewd reporter, a legend in the West, tough and fearless and a great friend to the Indians. But Peter did not like Emma being around him. She might talk too much and give rise to a sensational 'Max Cody' story. Peter burst into Wessels' office that day to complain. Wessels had already lost the battle with Cody and was in no mood to discuss it further.

"Cody has to see that she's getting the best care, otherwise he'll write a damaging article about us. Cody and Little Wolf go way back to the Rosebud

Massacre. The Cheyenne trust him. Let's concentrate on getting them both on the trail, understood?"

Considine's letter had the desired affect on Wessels. The colonel quickly arranged everything and gave Emma a horse, a pack mule, supplies, and a hundred dollars. Wessels wanted her gone as quickly as possible.

Cody admired Emma's skill as she expertly loaded the pack mule the morning of their departure. "The journey is long. I hope you can ride."

"I can stay in the saddle as long as you can," she said with a confident smile.

Later, as she returned to make sure that she had gotten everything out of the cabin, she tried to quell her fear of traveling alone with a stranger. Adam trusted Cody and Shea wanted her back, so she had to risk it. She resolved to appear unafraid and be very careful. Her next stop was to find Peter, but suddenly, he was there beside her and gave her an affectionate hug.

"Be happy, Emma. Safe journey."

"I owe you so much, Peter. I will never forget your kindness." She pressed her lips to his cheek. He blushed, then handed her a package wrapped in brown paper. In it was a warm woolen coat, shirts, socks, and trousers.

"These aren't exactly things for a lady, but I hear it gets real cold in Montana. You can wear the pants under your dress. They'll keep you warm." Then, he handed her his dog–eared copy of Dickens' *Great Expectations*, his favorite book. "Take this and remember me."

Tears welled in her eyes. After another fond embrace for Peter, she left the little cabin, mounted the study mare, and waved farewell.

As she and Cody left Fort Robinson, she saw a young man leaning against a railing. Although she had seen him frequently around the fort, she wondered how she could've missed the resemblance to his brother. As she passed, she placed her hand over her heart and mouthed 'thank you.' Ben Lawrence tipped his hat and smiled. Ben returned to the telegraph room and sent a message to his brother that Emma was on her way.

There was no need for Emma to worry about traveling with Cody. He was interesting and entertained her for hours as they rode north. He had crisscrossed the continent many times, seen many things and told many stories, some of them actually true. Max confessed that his father had been an abusive man, prone to drinking, so at fifteen he had run away from his home in St. Louis and headed west, driving mule trains and taking part in other less savory occupations that he declined to detail. His first taste of reporting had come when he had witnessed the Rosebud Massacre of the Cheyenne and Sioux in Montana while working as a scout for the army. His luck at being in the right place at the right time had attracted the attention of the editor of the Omaha Sentinel who had seen Max's story in another paper. Max had been hired to work for the Sentinel, though no one there had met him for the first year of his tenure. Max telegraphed his stories to the paper and disliked being ordered to report in once a year at the home office. He loved the frontier and shared Emma's dislike of crowded, noisy places.

Emma proved to be an interesting companion as well. During their weeks together, she told him of her life and her recent trials.

(Her tale would later become a series of articles penned by Cody that made her famous for a short time. The saga of the Hawkshadows would make Cody famous and very rich on the lecture circuit in the east.)

Emma and Max had several hundred miles of wild, open country to cover. April was rainy and chilling and Emma caught a slight cold. Despite her protests, they lost two days of travel in Wyoming because Cody insisted that she rest until her fever broke.

In May, while crossing a river swollen by flood, Emma would have been swept away if it had not been for Cody's grip on her reins when her mare put a foot wrong. Another night, a bear moved through their camp looking for food and knocked over her tent while she was inside sleeping. Roused from sleep by Emma's screams, Cody quickly shot the animal. Emma came to rely on his guardianship and finely honed instincts. She learned much about survival from this man and came to have great respect for him.

Months later, the pair came upon a huge army encampment in Montana. Emma could see just the tops of lodges in a valley beyond. The smell of cooking fires drifted on the wind, taking her back to a brief, peaceful time at the Indian Territory's reservation. Max told her that in addition to Little Wolf's people, some northern Cheyenne and Sioux had left the Pine Ridge Reservation, anxious to be near their ancestral lands.

Emma and Max pitched their tents near the army's encampment. She was astounded at the number of troops and Indians roaming about freely and without conflict.

For the moment it seemed that the Indians had the upper hand as a result of the Cheyenne breakout. With the opening of the West and more railroad routes, more and more people poured into the area and the military was not so free to do as it pleased anymore. Too many eyes watched, too many ears heard, too many photographers and reporters followed the tragic stories of the Plains tribes. The Cheyenne and Sioux had power and used it. She had overheard comments from several soldiers in camp about how stubborn the Indians had become.

Although Emma was free to roam as she pleased, she kept close to camp and to Max. A Major Grendall approached her the afternoon she arrived, informing her that the men had been ordered to keep a distance from her, but he wanted to know if he could oblige her by assigning guards for her safety. She declined his offer, deciding to rely on Max.

"Well that's your decision, ma'am. I'll inform General Considine that you're here, if you have no objections."

"No objections, major. Thank you."

"My tent is just across the way," he pointed, "so come to me if you need anything, all right?"

She felt sure that most every soldier in camp knew of and about her. For the most part, they were respectful, courteous, and kept a distance from her (by Considine's express order).

Out in the open and with fresh air to breathe and prairie to wander, Emma enjoyed a lifting of her spirits. She was almost free. The one thing that she had not done was to attempt to find Shea. Rising trepidation stopped her dead. Max, clearly sensing her conflict, left her to sort it out.

Max got word to Adam that he and Emma had arrived safely. With the afternoon and evening free before resuming talks in the morning, Adam rode through the army camp looking for Emma.

She was easy to spot among all the blue uniforms. She walked alone atop a rise nearby. The late day sun spotlighted her, shimmering on her auburn hair. After tying up his horse he sprinted up the hill.

Hearing someone fast approaching, she wheeled around, startled, thinking that it might be Shea. When she saw it was Adam, she smiled and hugged him.

"So, how was the trip?"

"Fine. Cody was a perfect gentleman and saved my hide a few times. It feels so good to be outdoors again. Never could get used to walls."

"How are you feeling?" He was just as embarrassed to ask as she was to reply.

She shrugged, knowing what he really meant. "All healed up."

"Good, that's good." Adam squinted into the late day sun. "Nice country, you think?" he asked as they started walking downhill.

"It's beautiful. Reminds me of Kansas with all this prairie, it's more rocky, though. But I do love the prairies. I've never seen the mountains before. I know the range is huge and the peaks high, but from here, they just look like a jagged gray line."

He smiled. "I crossed them when I was just a corporal. They are much more than a gray line on the horizon, I assure you."

"I know what your brother risked for me. Max told me about his secret messages to you. He never spoke to me—not once. After I knew what he'd done for me, I tried to see him but he always seemed to slip away."

"That's his way. He's a bit of a solitary."

"I'll write to him to thank him for all he did."   She and Adam walked together through the tall grass. "Wessels wanted me gone more than anything. You would've enjoyed how fast he put everything together for us," she chuckled. "He practically shoved us out the gates of Fort Robinson!"

"You haven't found Shea yet," he stated. He had seen Shea that morning and knew he did not know that she had arrived.

"I'm waiting for the right time to let him know I'm here."

"He'll hear about you—you stick out around here. Why don't you find him? I'll go with you, if you want."

"I want to give this another day or two."

"I thought this was what you wanted."

"I don't want to bother him. He's probably busy with the negotiations and resettlement."

He wondered why she was stalling. "What's wrong, Emma?"

"I—I just don't know if he'll want me back. We've been apart nearly seven months. After he hears what Fulton did to me—he might think that it was my fault."

"How can you think that? Emma, he attacked you and tried to kill you. What he did—pardon me for being blunt—had nothing to do with sex. It was an attack upon you. It was not your fault."

"We'll see if Shea feels the same way."   She quickly changed the subject. "You heard what happened at Fort Robinson in January?" He nodded. "Oh, Adam, it was horrible. They shot at everyone—even women and children. Thirty people dead, for nothing!"

"I know, Emma, but some survived and some got away. You'll have to console yourself with that. Word got around here about what you did for Dull Knife's people. You're a heroine to the Cheyenne."

"Some heroine!" she scoffed. "I am more of a coward than you know." She fell silent for a moment, her mouth working, trying to say it right. "You've been with him—has Shea found someone else?"

"No, he hasn't. I know that for a fact." In an effort to lift her spirits, he said, "Look, put all that away and have dinner with me and Max in the mess tent tonight. I think you need a good meal and pleasant company. Six? And no wine for you!"

She smiled at his admonition, seeing something different in his eyes, something that she could not read, but his easy manner kindled joy at seeing his familiar face. He helped her feel lucid again and now she wondered why she had always felt so uncomfortable around him in the past. Maybe it was because he could read her all too well. When he spoke to her, he always held her eyes. She felt that he could read her thoughts.

Adam went to his tent at the far side of the encampment. He was at once sensitive to how much she had endured—and joyful that she had survived.

As Emma waited for six o'clock to arrive she resolved, whatever the outcome, to find Shea. After her repeated declarations that she would rejoin him, she did not want to look like a fool.

She donned a green and blue dress that she had bought at Fort Robinson. It was wrinkled from being packed away, but it was the best one she had.

Adam came and escorted her to the mess tent for supper. Max was already there with a tray heaped with the free food. He signaled to them that he had saved a bench for them at one of the tables. Adam waved back as they got in the food line. Wearing the green and blue dress, the wrinkles overlooked, and with her hair combed and loose, Emma turned the head of every soldier in the tent.

"You look nice, Emma, thank you," Adam whispered, close to her ear. "I haven't seen a pretty girl in months. Come to think of it, that girl was you." They smiled at one another and moved through the line. Adam kept very close to her, almost brushing her with his body, but he just stayed out of reach, just as he had when they had walked together the day they first met. His proximity did not make her feel uncomfortable.

The hot, steaming food reawakened her appetite and she took a big helping of chicken and greens. Adam had a huge steak and potatoes. The mess tent was crowded, noisy, and hazy from the cooking fires and tobacco smoke. Emma's eyes blurred and teared, but she could see well enough to devour her meal.

As soldiers cleared out of the mess tent, others moved to vacant seats, moving closer to stare at the auburn–haired beauty. Emma was uncomfortable with the attention and intentionally kept her eyes on Adam and Max.

"Is all this too much for you?" Adam asked.

She shook her head with a tight smile.

Adam watched her intently. "I heard from Ben that you tried to stop the soldiers from shooting Dull Knife's people. That was a brave thing to do."

"I remember when you told me that I didn't know what I was doing by living with the Cheyenne. January ninth, I saw exactly what you meant. I've never witnessed anything so horrible—so desperate."

"You did everything you could," Cody said.

"Why can't they come here? There's plenty of room for Dull Knife's people."

"They wanted to return south," Adam said. "It's a sad fact of life for them, but never get used to it. The minute you accept it, you lose your soul. And then you'll lose your resolve to help them someday when you can." Adam absently returned to his meal. Much of her ignorance and naiveté were still intact, he noticed, but their simplicity struck him on another level for the first time. He was beginning to understand the reasoning behind her observations and opinions. But there was a new hardness to her tone since he had seen her last year.

She pushed her mood aside. "I'm glad to be here, don't get me wrong. And, Max, thank you for getting me here safely."

"Most welcome, madam. You were a very charming companion. It was an enlightening trip. You outmaneuvered them all, clever lady."

Emma smiled at Cody and Adam caught something suspicious in their exchange. His eyebrows arched. "How so?"

"What?" she asked, all innocence.

"Outmaneuvered who?" Then suddenly, he understood. "It was you."

Her blue eyes were cool. "What are you talking about?" Emma smiled and took a bite of the roasted chicken.

Adam lowered his voice to a hiss. "You knew where the Cheyenne were going all along, didn't you? You were the one who convinced Considine to divert troops to Canada!"

Emma studied him. "Adam, do you really think that I'd ever betray my husband? It was just a ruse to get some of the troops off the Cheyenne's trail. So a few troops were inconvenienced."

Max laughed and left the table to get a second helping of food.

Adam was not amused and leaned in, malevolent. "You played a very misguided and reckless game with soldiers' lives."

"I wasn't left with a choice. I had to do something to get Considine off my back. Shea is all I have in the world. Do you really think I'd risk losing him?"

"You're a hell of an actress, Emma." Adam wanted to hurt her for her daring scheme. "What if he doesn't take you back?"

"I'll worry about that when and if I have to. I can be alone, you know. I've had a lot of practice lately."

Adam could not rein in his anger. She was more hardened than he had supposed but he did not expect such calculated deceit. She really irritated him. "You do foolish things, Emma and I know other things about you that Max Cody could write about! Then you wouldn't be so smug!"

"I don't know what you mean."

"I found the soddy last year. I know what happened there."

Emma was thunderstruck. "I told you—"

"You didn't tell me everything, did you?"

Emma got up to go, but Adam yanked her back to the bench. "Why didn't you tell me the truth? We could've done something. I falsified my report to Considine to protect you."

"I told you the truth! You weren't there! You don't know everything!" She wrestled from his grip and ran out of the mess tent.

He followed her into the cool night. "Emma! Come back!"

"Get away from me!" she shouted.

With a full tray of food in his hand, Max Cody returned to the table and found that his companions had gone. He saw Emma and Adam arguing in the distance, but decided to keep out of it. Instead, he joined a group of soldiers to regale them with tales of his exploits. His ego needed a little stroking.

Adam chased her down, grabbed her and spun her around. "Why did you lie?"

"I didn't lie to you!" she cried. "My parents died! I had to bury them and abandon the only home I ever had! What do you want from me?"

"The truth!"

Emma pulled away and ran to her tent. He found her there, curled on her bedroll.

"Go away, Adam," she muttered.

He took a few moments to calm himself. "I shouldn't have brought it up, but sometimes you make me so angry. I'm angry at you for diverting the troops, that's all. I went too far. I'm sorry."

She sat up; a look of unmistakable worry etched her brow. "I don't know what you think you saw at the soddy, but I never lied to you. Maybe something happened after I left—maybe that's what you saw. But I don't want to know either way. I can't handle it. Why don't you just drop it?"

He looked ashamed. "I apologize. Good-night, Emma." Adam withdrew, closing the tent flap. He walked back to his tent, replaying his visit to the soddy, second–guessing what he had seen that day. In hindsight, he felt guilty for confronting Emma with what he believed to be the truth. He had pulled this acute torment out of the hat to get back at her for diverting the troops, but as he laid in his dark tent, he was filled with self–reproach. He would find her tomorrow and ask her to forgive him.

The next morning he knocked on her tent pole. "Emma?"

Max poked his head out of his tent which was next pitched to hers. "She left at first light. Headed off for the reservation."

Adam's disappointment was very evident. "Alone?"

"Yup," Max answered. "Say, what were you two arguing about last night? That girl cried herself to sleep."

"I said something very stupid, Max. Very stupid."

Max sat on the ground, lacing up his boots. "She did what she had to do, you know, about misleading the troops. She's awful young to handle all that's happened to her."

Emma's abrupt departure stung Adam. He regretted what he had done last night. He had secretly nursed the hope that Shea would reject her after their long separation. Then, while consoling her, he could be honest about his feelings. They were stronger than ever and he had a hard time disguising them. Picking a fight with a girl was a sure way of showing affection, he cursed himself—if you were eight years old.

Emma rode through the large reservation, attracting much attention from the Sioux and Cheyenne. She did not recognize anyone and called upon her meager Cheyenne to ask where Little Wolf's camp was. It was north, she was told, so she rode on for nearly an hour until she saw the lodges.

The camp of the newly arrived southern Cheyenne was off by itself in a wide valley cleft with broken hills and gullies. She sadly counted only twelve lodges—there had been sixty in the Indian Territory. As she approached, people recognized her and came running, shouting *maiyun*—a word that she did not understand. A crowd gathered around her as she dismounted. Even some of the warriors came forward to greet her.

Red Leaf Woman broke through the crowd and hugged her in her strong arms. "*Nahtona* has returned! My heart is glad! We will have a feast!" Red Leaf Woman's formidable grip curled around her hand and she kissed it, overjoyed at seeing her adopted daughter again.

Emma hugged the old woman tight, tears of relief coursing down her cheeks. "Red Leaf, I knew you'd make it. Tell me, is Little Fox here? Is she all right?" Red Leaf said yes. In spite of what she had to tell the girl, Emma was relieved that Little Fox was alive. It would have been too much if both had died during the outbreak.

Suddenly, the crowd silenced and parted. Shea stood there, his eyes locked with hers.

Emma took a few steps toward him; she could not read his face. "Hello, Shea," she said, trying not to smile too much. All the things that she had planned to say to him instantly deserted her. They stood in silence but that same pull existed between them. Both were thinner and worn, and to Emma's shock, Shea had aged considerably. Strands of gray stood out in his black hair and he had deep lines etched on his magnificent face. But his brilliant blue eyes had not changed; they caressed her, drinking her in. They faced each other separated by several feet of highly charged air. There was so much to say, so much to reconcile, so much to confess, so much to forgive.

He rushed forward and grabbed her up in his arms. She felt his tears on her neck. "You are back—*nameh'o*!" He held her and she relaxed in his embrace, sagging with relief.

Shea's lodge was larger and finer than the one they had shared in the Indian Territory. Emma felt a bit of possessiveness from him as she entered the dwelling and surveyed her new home, but then she was in his arms.

"When you are ready." Emma knew immediately what he meant and hung her head in shame. He lifted her face to his and repeated. "When you are ready." His lips touched hers tenderly in assurance.

"You know—everything?" He nodded. She held him tight, feeling his muscled frame, realizing how much she missed him—his touch—his scent. "I'm all right. And at this moment, I want you more than ever."

He settled with her on a pile of robes and slid off his clothes, then undressed her. When he saw the scar on her chest, he touched it. "This was the price you had to pay for choosing to love me."

She touched his angular cheek, roughened by exposure to the elements. "I'd go through it all over again just to relive the way I felt when I saw you today. Does it matter to you—what that man did to me?"

Shea tried to speak but lost his voice and swallowed several times as he looked upon her. He sadly realized that his memory of her exquisite face had faded. He thought that he would never see her again and had been riddled with guilt over what had happened to her. But his heart gladdened at the mere sight of her. She gave him strength, but he did not know how little she had to spare.

"It does not matter." He kissed her passionately and touched her soft skin. When he entered her, he watched her in case the memory of the rape surfaced. It did not. She pulled him deep inside her and wrapped her legs around his hips.

Later, they lay together after making love throughout the day. She told him about her time at Fort Robinson. "Living in that place was like being dead. Once, I wanted to end my life because I thought I'd never leave that place. You were so far away, suffering, and I could not help you. I had no one. I never felt so alone in all my life."

Shea leaned in and kissed her tenderly. He pulled her to him, caressing her body and soothing her. "I love you and I am happy you returned to me. You have great courage."

A flood of memories coursed through her: the first tug of affection, the first kiss along the river, the first time he made love to her.

To her surprise, he spoke in a manner unlike that of the man she had known. "I am sorry, Emma. I should have forced you to go with Adam before the breakout. You would have been safer. Leaving you behind at Frenchman Creek was the hardest thing I have ever had to do. Forgive me."

She swallowed hard at this stunning confession. He was not one to admit that he was wrong. "There's nothing to forgive, Shea. You are a Dog Soldier. I understood that from the beginning." The memory of the day she was captured was still etched in her mind; she had never faulted him for not being at her side every moment. His duty to his people was always understood.

His mouth was on hers in a needful kiss. "You are the only love I will ever have. I am sorry for all that happened to you." Emma laid her head against her husband's warm chest. "You were strong enough to survive. Now it is time to heal," he said.

She twitched a little, remembering the strange waking dream that she had had of Shea standing before her after Fulton stabbed her that horrible day. It was truly a vision, she now believed. And she was right to return to him.

Later, she asked, "What does *maiyun* mean, Shea? People called me that when I rode in this morning."

He smiled crookedly. "It means spirit, mysterious one." She looked at him questioningly. "After you were captured, the women and children keened for you. Their songs sent magic so you would be safe. To them, you became a spirit. I was out of my head—sad and crazy all the time. I had dreams of you—that you were in terrible danger and I could do nothing to help."

Maybe they did send magic. Despite everything, she had survived. She shook off a shiver. "I just lived through it. That's all I could do."

Later, he dressed and crawled to the lodge opening and looked at the setting sun. "I have to go. There is a parley about the reservation borders and Little Wolf wants me there."

"It's all right. I'll be fine."

"I will see Adam and ask him and Cody to the feast tomorrow."

"Sure," she answered.

He smiled at her. "You are thin. But Red Leaf Woman will take care of that. Go find her."

She unpacked her few possessions after he left. She felt so strange yet many things were familiar to her. She forgot herself and almost touched Shea's warrior shield, bow, and quiver of arrows hanging on the wall, but remembered that women could never handle men's weapons—it diluted the blessings put upon them by the shaman. The smell of the lodge was sweet and earthy, reawakening her love for him, reminding her of the reasons that she wanted to return. More trials were likely but they would now face them together. He gave her the one thing she craved most: love.

Later that evening, Emma found Red Leaf's lodge. The old woman quickly placed a plate of dried buffalo meat and berries in her lap.

Emma ate in silence for a few minutes as Red Leaf Woman watched her, her wrinkled face glowing with joy. Emma soon opened up and told Red Leaf and Little Fox all that had happened at Fort Robinson. The old woman wept as Emma spoke.

Red Leaf said, "You brave, like warrior. You not give your life to soldier when he tried to take it. You have strong magic. You are legend now."

Emma rested her head on the old woman's shoulder. "I don't want to be a legend, Red Leaf. I just want peace."

Before leaving Red Leaf's lodge, Emma got up the courage to give Little Fox the news about Porcupine Girl's death. "It was quick. She did not linger."

Little Fox looked very sad but did not cry. "I dreamed of her in the south. My dream told me she lived."

"Little Fox, I am so sorry." There was nothing more to say. The girl was all too used to losing friends to disease and bullets.

Adam and Max arrived for the feast the next evening. After he greeted his hosts, Max settled in easily, being much acquainted with the Cheyenne.

Then Adam approached Emma and Shea. Shea thanked him for his part in bringing Emma back to him and offered him a place of honor around a large outdoor fire pit. Emma seemed glad to see him; her behavior showed that she was no longer angry. She apologized for leaving him without saying good–bye. He did not mention their argument of the other night. Later, Emma joined in the dancing as night fell and the firelight flickered across the bodies as they stepped and twirled. She seemed to blend in so easily, Adam noticed.

"How's Emma doing?" he asked Shea.

"She feels safe with me. I am grateful to you and Cody for bringing her here, Adam. You are a great friend to Emma and the Cheyenne—and to me," he said.

"You're very lucky, my friend. She's a remarkable woman."

Shea shot a glance at Adam. "I know if I need to get her to safety, you will be there for her. My chances of living a long life are not good, I know that. If something happens to me, care for her." Adam blushed deeply, the heat of the fire making it worse. "I heard you are trying to get the liaison post at Fort Keogh. I hope you get it so you will be close."

Adam became alarmed at Shea's words. "Why are you talking like this? There's peace—stable peace. Emma's back with you. Enjoy this time.

Granted, I don't know what the country is like here, but you should have a good life."

Shea watched Emma dance, but the look in his eye went far beyond her. "After we came here, I went on a vision quest. I went into the hills for four days and nights. I did not eat and slept little. The visions were not good. Something bad is going to happen." Adam knew better than to discount dreams had during a sacred vision quest. "Little Wolf told me that the settlers near the reservation do not want us living here and have a militia. Things are not as peaceful as they seem. Little Wolf fears problems with this militia; they fear us, but we have given them no reason for fighting. All we want is to live here in peace with our families."

Adam considered the implications and Shea's warning. "If I get the post at Keogh, I swear I'll do all I can to avert trouble with the militia."

"I know you will. Thank you." Shea rose and pulled Emma out of the circle of dancers, leading her to his side, and the three of them shared in the feast. The dour predictions were forgotten and they spent a pleasant evening, laughing and talking, ignoring the uncertain future hovering somewhere out beyond the firelight.

Emma found General Considine several days later and spent nearly an hour with him, thanking him for all the kindness he had shown to her. He was glad to see a new maturity in her, but barely able to disguise his anger over Wessels' indifferent treatment of her, especially after the Fulton incident. He promised to check on her for as long as he was in the area. Fort Keogh would be his headquarters for now and Emma felt more secure knowing that she was worth his notice.

Several weeks later the negotiations concluded. The new Cheyenne reservation was established and the borders set.

Considine's squad was heading for Fort Keogh and as his aide, Adam had to leave as well. Adam came to see Emma and Shea the night before his departure, accepting an offer to dine with them. Emma simply glowed. It was obvious that she was happy to be back among those she considered her family. Using a gift of beef sent by Adam, she prepared a hearty stew. They dined in contentment and intimate friendship.

When it came time for Adam to leave, Emma hugged him, placing a kiss on his cheek. "I don't know how to repay you for all you've done." She handed him a letter. "This is so your brother knows how grateful I am to him. Would you post it for me?" He nodded. "I'm sure that you'll get the appointment at Fort Keogh, so I'll count on seeing you soon." Adam's unmistakable look of love diverted Emma for a moment as he gazed upon her face. She backed away and she and Shea watched Adam ride away into the cool night until they could see him no more.

That night, they lay wrapped in each other. Shea's finger traced the long scar on her chest. "My love, my Emma. I am so sorry." He cradled her and she drifted, dozing.

"Sometimes I think I love you too much," she whispered after he was asleep. When she closed her eyes, all she felt was his body next to hers and his heartbeat as it moved again within her breast.

Chapter Nine

The following months were full and content for Emma. As she and Shea rekindled their marriage, they could not keep their hands off each other. When he lay with her, he was mindful and gentle. She basked in his passion for her and, many nights, lay awake watching him sleep, sometimes feeling this was a dream and that she would wake up in the tiny room at Fort Robinson, alone and bereft. His love was reassuring and a confirmation of her struggles to survive.

Summer was cool upon this northern land and they spent many days riding in the hills of the vast reservation, so much larger and more beautiful than the one in the Indian Territory. Shea was obsessed with her and exorcised his guilt, trying to make up for their long separation by giving pleasure to her body, which she granted frequently and willingly.

They soon became the butt of jokes with their newlywed manner and the obvious fact that Emma was not yet pregnant. Each month, Emma joined the other women in the menstrual lodge, and, since her comprehension of the Cheyenne language was improving, caught pieces of conversations, speculating about her and Shea. Word was going around that she was barren. She tried to ignore the idle talk, happy to be reunited with Shea, but Shea had also heard the jokes and they bothered him, too. He talked to Emma about it often. However, these 'talks' started turning into arguments, leaving both Emma and Shea with bruised feelings.

One discussion escalated into a full–blown shouting match when Shea offhandedly mentioned that he was allowed, under Cheyenne tradition, to take a maiden as 'second wife' to bear him a child. Children aside, the thought of him making love to another woman shook her foundation of love and trust in him. Many people heard their raised voices and later, Emma's sobs. Wagging tongues and gossip bothered them both. Emma desperately wanted a child and thought that it was true—that she was barren. Would he really take another wife and push her aside? She felt hurt, angry, and betrayed. After all she had endured to return to him, the stinging pain went deep. After another heated argument on a night in July, she stormed out of the lodge.

Shea found her brooding at the river's edge. "Emma, do not be mad. I said I would not do it. Now come home."

"I will not be replaced! Don't play games with me. I'm not up to it," she sobbed.

"Stop worrying about it. I do not want to fight over this anymore."

"If Fulton injured me so that I can't have children, how would I know? Dr. Cromwell said that he didn't see any damage but he said there is still no way to know for sure. Damn it! I won't share you with another woman! I'll leave, I swear it!" Eyes full of pain turned on him. "I will not have you sleep with another woman just so you can satisfy your vanity by fathering a child! Did you ever stop to think that the problem lies with you?"

He took a deep breath, trying very hard to quell his anger. He reminded himself that she was still very shaky emotionally. "Emma, I promise that I will not do it."

She looked at him through red–rimmed eyes. "When I got involved with you at the camp in the Indian Territory, Red Leaf told me that Cheyenne men and women don't sleep together before the wedding. As you pointed out back then, I'm not Cheyenne. Making love together before we married didn't seem to matter. Now you're telling me that you can take another wife if I don't get pregnant fast enough for you?"

"Emma, you do not understand. I do not care if we have children. Even though I thought about it, I would never take another woman. If we do not have children, it does not matter." He tentatively put a hand on her shoulder. She did not pull away, but he felt the tension in her body. "Maybe all the jokes have bothered us more that we want to admit, eh?" He kissed her forehead.

She burrowed in next to him that night, her feelings of insecurity welling up with fresh torment. This was absolutely the last thing she needed. Resentment continually welled up in her and she fought it back time and time again.

He spoke to her in the dark. "Emma, you have never spoken of what that man did to you. If you talked about it, it might help me to understand how you feel."

She remained silent on that horror. Speaking of it would only bring back the pain and humiliation.

A few days later, Max Cody and a man named Miles Kenworth came onto the reservation. Emma welcomed Cody and invited him and Kenworth to lunch.

"As promised, Emma, here are the articles I wrote about you both," Max said, handing her a pile of newspaper articles. "I wrote a few more articles about you and Shea—nothing more about the Fulton incident, of course, but all you two have gone through. You made me famous, Emma. Papers as far away as Chicago and Boston picked up the stories. I'm leaving soon for Omaha so I wanted you to have them."

Shea took part of the pile from Emma's hands and to Kenworth's astonishment, began to read.

Kenworth's mouth dropped open. "You can read?"

Shea shot him a look under lowered brows. "Of course. Emma taught me." There was a note of triumph in his tone. Their recent clashes were forgotten when Emma smiled at him.

In the late afternoon, Kenworth found Shea in the paddock. He seemed nervous, squirrely.

"Mr. Hawkshadow, I've got a business proposition for you. Since you and your lovely wife are so famous, there might be a way to make a profit off this—for you and your people and, I admit, for me as well. What I propose is that my company conduct tours of the reservation with you and your wife as the main attraction. A white girl living with Indians can't miss! We'd both make a healthy profit and I'm sure that you could use the money."

Shea scowled at him.

Emma and Max had been strolling and turned when they heard Shea yelling at Kenworth, who took off running in fear, jumped on his horse and galloped off the reservation.

Max chucked and told Emma of Kenworth's notion. "I warned him not to do it. He works for a circus back east. He doesn't understand how things are out here; he's a rich pampered kid from Rhode Island and in love with myths of the wild west."

Emma laughed and the incident was forgotten until later, when she considered that she and Shea had become curiosities. It bothered her that people wanted to get a look at them, like young plants under a bell jar.

Max delayed his trip to Omaha at Shea's invitation to remain with the tribe a while longer. Cody stayed in the lodge of Sun at Midnight, Shea's cousin.

Assured that Shea would not invoke his right to take another wife, the marriage entered a comfortable time and Emma started her school again, teaching small groups of Cheyenne and Sioux children. She was glad to have something to do while waiting for Shea to return from hunting each evening. When he did, she tied down the flap of the lodge and they were alone, nude beneath the skins and blankets. She needed his arms around her and he needed her softness against him. He could not imagine life without her.

In late July, a small contingent of soldiers arrived and delivered a message to Shea. Adam had won the post at Fort Keogh and would visit as soon as he could. The soldiers barely contained their surprise as Shea read the message instead of Emma.

As he lay with her that night, it was Shea's turn to feel insecure. He asked, "Emma, do you have feelings for Adam?"

"Adam's our friend, Shea. I could never feel about him the way I feel about you—never. You are my husband and I love only you. Put your mind at rest, my love," she said as she teasingly traced the outline of her breasts with her fingertips. Adam was forgotten as Shea rolled her on her back and soon after slipped inside her. She moaned with pleasure.

When Adam arrived a month later, he was very excited and hopeful about his new position. "This is a good posting," he said as he dined with them one evening. "I'm still on Considine's staff, but I'm the liaison between the Cheyenne, the Sioux, and the military, as well as the settlers in the area. I'm going to do what's necessary to keep peace."

Shea looked to Emma, who busied herself over her meal. She did not meet Adam's eyes and a sting of jealously pricked at him despite Emma's words to the contrary. He now understood why Emma had become so angry when he had brought up the sore issue of taking a second wife. "Will you and your soldiers be camped on the reservation?"

"No, but we'll be stationed in small posts around the borders. That militia you mentioned months ago—you were right, unfortunately. It's formed up just north of here in Peabody. We're keeping an eye on them. But I have to warn you. The militia leader, Paul Tyler, has made public statements condemning your marriage to Emma. He's been preaching it goes against God's law for an Indian to marry a white. He thinks that Emma has been tortured or brainwashed and that's why she stays. So far, he's only words, but we're watching him just the same—you never know with these bible–thumpers. I think he's just spouting off and he wouldn't dare come on the reservation."

Something in Adam's tone made Shea think otherwise. This man could indeed be a threat to the hard–won peace. "What if Tyler and his men come onto the reservation? What will the army do? Our guns have been taken away and we cannot defend ourselves."

"If he comes, we'll arrest him and all who ride with him."

"But how much damage will he do before you get him?" Emma cut in. "It would take the army hours to get here if something happened."

Adam dismissed her concerns. "I doubt that his men would be able to slip through the mounted patrols. Tyler doesn't have the guts to do anything so daring. He just talks a good game. We can handle it. But if anything's brewing, you'll know immediately." Adam desperately wanted to change the subject. The militia was on the brink of something and he did not want the Cheyenne involved. Tyler's Militia, as it was known, was his problem and he was charged with keeping them off the reservation. He had tried to plant a spy in the group but the plan was exposed and his man was sent back, beaten and bloodied. "So, how have things been around here?"

"Best we are going to get," was Shea's reply. "It has been peaceful enough, but it has only been a few months and we still have our scouts posted all around the camps. The hunting is better than in the south. There are still buffalo and antelope here and we have made many good kills."

Adam smiled at them both and finally, Emma met his eyes with a searching look that Shea did not miss. Had she lied to him about her feelings for Adam? His regret grew over their recent arguments about children. He resented Adam's ease with Emma. There was no dismissing the new level of intimacy between them.

"Adam," Emma said, "did you know that Cody wrote some articles about us?"

Adam's expression was guarded. "I read them. The series he wrote about you and Shea is the most popular thing to come along in years. Curiosity seekers are sure to come onto the reservation to get a glimpse of you. We might have some minor trouble, so tell your scouts to keep a sharp eye, Shea."

"Oh, I can't imagine that happening, Adam," Emma interjected. "Max's articles about us can't be that big a deal and interest in us will eventually die down. Shea chased off a man from a circus a few weeks ago who wanted to put us on display. It was pretty funny. Besides, no one is allowed on the reservation and with the troops and Cheyenne scouts posted, nothing will happen. And if they trespass, the government will do something about it, right?"

"Off the record," he spoke more to Shea now, "the government doesn't care and people will find a way if they want something bad enough, so prepare yourselves for some of the inquisitive getting on the reservation. Curiosity–seekers are one thing, but the militia is something else. I'm not trying to frighten you, but be ready to get word to me if anything happens."

Shea considered Adam's words. Max's articles, originally written to help the Cheyenne, could backfire at a time when they were settled and their numbers were increasing. Emma was sometimes frustratingly ignorant of such things and it bothered Shea. The Indians would not tolerate a military presence on the reservation. The tract of land granted to them was vast and its protection always the subject of tribal council meetings.

Adam thought a moment about his own words. "Shea, can you arrange for me to meet with the council? They should know about the militia and the potential for tourists and we should work together to plan for dealing with any trespassers."

Before nightfall as Adam prepared to leave, he slipped a hand gun with a large, short barrel into Shea's hand.

"It's a flare gun," he explained as Shea examined it. "Just put this cartridge in the barrel, point it high above your head and pull the trigger. It shoots a flare that can be seen for miles, even from the outposts. If something happens, use it and here," he said as he handed him a half–dozen more cartridges. "It's just a precaution, Shea, and I'm violating the treaty just by giving this to you. Keep it hidden."

Adam's warnings about Paul Tyler were not lost on Shea. Now a member of Little Wolf's inner circle, Shea, with Adam's help, warned the council of possible tourists and Tyler's civilian militia. Little Wolf respected Adam, and took the warnings seriously, posting more scouts around the camps. Max was also at the council meeting and admitted concern because these problems were a consequence of his articles. Max asked if he could remain. The council granted his request. The Cheyenne would use him, if needed.

As feared, the fragile peace began to crumble. Settlers were coming west in droves, assisted by a new railway that extended well beyond the reservation, heading for the northern reaches of the west coast. Both the army and the Cheyenne had their hands full fending off curiosity seekers desiring a peek at the white girl who lived with Indians.

In August, three braves were killed when a group of settlers unwittingly wandered onto the reservation and attacked a hunting party. Their deaths outraged Little Wolf, who sent for Adam, who sent an appeal to the territorial governor, asking for more troops to protect the borders; the appeal was ignored. The tribal council met nearly every day as plans were hatched and honed to keep people away.

"We have to do it ourselves. There are not enough troops to help us and the *veho* government will do nothing," Little Wolf told the council.

Things got worse a week later. Tyler's men made a dangerous, deadly serious move. A group of twenty men stole onto the reservation and attacked a small camp of Sioux and Cheyenne at the northern edge of the reservation, slaughtering everyone, including women and children. More than fifty were killed. The Sioux and Cheyenne were outraged, insisting that Paul Tyler be brought to them for justice. The territorial government refused to get involved, claiming that it was a matter for the Bureau of Indian Affairs in Washington, D.C., and Adam, his hands tied by red tape, spent many hours with the council trying to find another solution, vowing that the military would take care of Tyler when they caught him. Things were getting so bad that Adam considered putting a bullet in Tyler's head himself but that would make him no better than Tyler. He chose to work within the system and came away disappointed again and again. Tensions ran high and Shea was dragged into arguments with his own people, for many blamed his white wife for drawing Tyler's attention in the first place. Shea stood firm and refused to send her away, but Emma worried when she saw him return from meeting after meeting defeated, angry, and torn.

Emma summoned her courage and spoke with him one such night. "My presence has caused a lot of trouble, Shea. This time, I'll leave if that's what it takes to end this."

"You are not the cause of this, but it is easier for Tyler and others to blame you for their actions. The *veho* government has made sure we are powerless. We do not have enough weapons to avenge the massacre." Shea's irritation was evident; his efforts to resolve the situation failed. He raged for days so Emma kept a distance and kept silent, except to assure Shea that she would leave if that was what he wished. Her love for him had matured and she would give him up if it kept him and his people out of harm's way. Trouble was that it would take more than leaving Shea to fix problems that had existed for hundreds of years; still, it was all she could offer.

Unexpectedly, weeks later in September, word was sent to the Cheyenne council that Paul Tyler would meet with them to discuss restitution for the massacre. In actuality, he was forced by Considine, who had authority over the powerful military forces at Fort Keogh. Considine met personally with Tyler, vowing to put him behind bars if he did not appease the Cheyenne and Sioux.

Under a white flag of truce, Adam's troop escorted Tyler and two of his self–appointed 'captains' onto the reservation to a large tent erected for the parley. The Indians were wary and the few guns they possessed were secretly assembled and loaded by the women, then hidden in the lodges. Shea told Emma to stay out of sight during the conference, an order she willingly obeyed.

A cloud of dust announced the contingent's arrival and Shea, Little Wolf, and the rest of the council grimly watched them approach. Before ducking inside the lodge, Emma spotted Shea talking with Adam and Considine. They stood close together and Shea's impatient gestures showed the frustration and apprehension that everyone felt. She had to admit that she felt safer with Adam and Considine's troops nearby.

After introductions, General Considine opened the meeting by reading the terms of the treaty aloud and explaining how it bound both Indians and whites and separated the lands each occupied. Tyler listened, his manner ostensibly regretful and acquiescent, explaining the massacre was touched off by a misunderstanding and that he wanted to put things aright. But Shea watched him closely, seeing another Tyler—a man who could barely contain his seething hatred when he looked at him. While he sat in the council circle, Tyler's body was contorted and tense.

Considine was speaking. "The lands granted to the Cheyenne must be respected by all who live near the reservation. It is the law. We have had no incidents of the Cheyenne or Sioux leading war parties across the border. The territory demands the militia make restitution to the Cheyenne and Sioux for the deaths of over fifty of their people. If you do not comply, you risk arrest and trial."

Tyler jumped to his feet, his tone shrill and overloud with defiance. "What do you expect me to do? I am a poor farmer and so are the men who ride with me. We are trying to protect our families from the savages! You do not understand how we feel, general! How can we raise a Christian family, living near a people that allows the races to intermarry!" Tyler dramatically pointed at Shea. "What do I tell my children when a child of mixed blood is born? It is unnatural and an abomination!"

Shea was ripe with anger and hatred for this smug little man. He sprang upon Tyler, knife drawn, but several soldiers quickly closed in around him and pulled him away before he could strike. Adam jumped to his feet and made a point of standing with Shea who panted with fury and shook off the hands that held him.

"This man is a savage and his wife a harlot who prefers living in sin instead of with her own people!" Tyler then fell silent and confounded everyone by calmly glancing at his pocket watch.

Adam's skin prickled and his hand moved furtively, unsnapping his holster. Shea did not miss Adam's gesture and their eyes discreetly met. The meeting quickly dissolved into chaos and Shea and the other tribal council members stormed out of the tent.

"You and your whore will pay!" Tyler shouted after Shea. Shea spun around and ran at Tyler but was dragged off again. "I start my mission with you, Hawkshadow!"

Adam looked to Considine who spoke with fury. "Put this man in chains, captain. He's under arrest."

Tyler smirked and folded his arms defiantly across his chest. "It doesn't matter what you do to me."

Just then, a distant thunder rumbled and the ground beneath Emma's feet thrummed. Disobeying Shea's order, she went outside and saw a large group of men spurring their horses hard from the northwest, throwing up a huge cloud of dust.

At the parley tent, men ran for their arms and horses. Taking advantage of the confusion, Tyler and his men melted into the crowd. Adam tried to grab Tyler, but was knocked aside as soldiers pushed past him to mount their horses to meet the attacking militia. The watch! Adam thought bitterly. His ambush was well–timed! Adam strained to see Shea and the Cheyenne leaders as they ran toward the camp. He and Considine ran for their horses.

Emma saw the riders coming. The fighting would converge in the center of camp at any moment. She ran through the camp gathering together women, children, and the old ones and headed for a gully a distance away from the lodges. Troops clashed with the militia with a terrifying noise and quickly had the advantage of training and firepower. Cries and shouts could be heard all around her as she scooped up two young children and got them to the meager safety of the ditch. She was astonished at the relative calm among them; they seemed too used to this and panic was not evident. She sprinted back to camp and saw Red Leaf Woman trying to make her way to the ditch. Emma ran fast for her, but another woman came to Red Leaf's side and shouted that she would take her, so she continued back to get the stragglers. Red Leaf looked at her sorrowfully as she ran past.

As Emma got nearer camp, she saw Shea running hard just ahead of the soldiers. He was trying, she knew, to get to the lodge where his rifle was hidden. She helped round up the remaining Cheyenne and hurried them away, and turned to see Shea being pursued by a man on a large brown horse. She ran back, trying to wave and warn him over the noise and smoke. The air was thick with bullets as they whizzed past her and thudded into the ground, throwing up dirt and rocks, obscuring her vision.

Terrified and powerless to help him she turned and ran for the ditch, but tripped over an exposed root and fell hard to the ground. She scrambled up, then a rough hand grabbed her by the hair. She screamed. A man, who was not a soldier, curled his fist around her long hair, pulled her with him and turned his horse east, dragging her away from the battle. She stumbled and fought, trying to loosen his grip and keep away from the horse's crushing hooves. Shea saw her and screamed her name, but she did not hear. She was taken to a narrow cleft just out of sight of the camp and thrown to the ground. She scrambled up quickly, but the man barred her way with the horse's body. She tried to dodge him and run away, but he leveled a revolver at her head and she froze, her heart pounding.

"Guess I won the reward for catching you, you little whore. I should just shoot you now, but I want the twenty bucks. Mr. Tyler has a special reunion planned for you and your pagan husband." He grinned horribly, showing what few blackened teeth remained in his mouth. "But if you try and run, I will shoot you," he growled.

She slowly backed off, fearing for herself and for Shea, but her wondering did not last long.

Moments later, three more men rode into the cleft, led by the man on the large brown horse who was dragging Shea by a rope cinched round his chest. He was gashed, bloody, and covered with dirt. He rolled and twisted to a stop then lay still. Emma made a move toward him, but the click of a revolver stopped her dead. Her kidnapper dismounted and leered.

"You're pretty feisty! Maybe a white man is just what you need to turn you around. You'll forget all about this Injun after a few minutes with me!"

Her heart thudded as he approached, rubbing his crotch. The horror of being raped again gripped her and she screamed, twisting away from his rough, dirty hands.

The man on the large brown horse cut between them. He was thin with a hawkish face and thick, short dark hair. "Enough, Louis! That is not our purpose today." He pushed the ugly, paunchy man aside with his well–trained horse and dismounted.

Another man got off his horse and roughly pulled Shea to his feet. Emma saw Shea swaying, barely able to stand. "Shea!" she sobbed. A vicious slap was delivered by the man who had kept Louis back. She staggered but remained on her feet.

"You will not speak another word to your husband," the dark man said, with terrifying composure. "I am Paul Tyler, leader of the militia." His voice then assumed a menacing, hysterical pitch. "You are both sentenced to death for effrontery and fornication in the eyes of God! You are a harlot and your husband a savage and you dare to mix the races!" He came close to her and spoke with frightening nonchalance. "I have to do this, you see. What you've done can never be forgiven. You can never have a place among decent people. I'm really doing you a favor."

A chill rattled through her entire body.

Tyler nodded to a man still mounted who produced two ropes and threw them over the limb of a dying tree that grew between the rocks in the cleft. Twin nooses dangled at the ends.

Emma looked to Shea, who briefly met her eyes, but Tyler punched her hard in the face and she fell to her knees with a whimper. Shea made a move towards her, but was backhanded by Louis. He twisted and fell, sprawling in the dust. Both Emma and Shea were pulled to standing and their hands were bound behind them. The ropes were cinched around their necks. Emma stiffened and prepared to die.

"Your executions will serve as a warning to others who dare to mix the races!" Tyler said with chilling triumph.

Louis chuckled. "Your plan worked perfectly. Catching them was easy. The parley was a great excuse. Yep, too easy."

Shea swallowed hard. The meeting with Tyler had been a ruse. He felt ashamed for trusting and dread for Emma, who was about to die beside him.

At a nod from Tyler, the rider holding Shea's rope looped it around his saddle horn and spurred his horse.

Emma shrieked in horror as Shea was hanged, kicking and gasping. Then something burned her cheek and she recoiled as a loud crack sounded a split–second later. The man with Shea's rope somersaulted off his rearing horse and the rope around the saddle horn uncoiled. Shea hung suspended a moment, then fell to the ground in a heap. Emma struggled to free her hands and twist out of the noose.

Tyler whipped around and saw Adam kneeling in the brush, taking aim again. Tyler turned back and fired his revolver at Emma. The bullet lifted her clear off the ground, shattering her left shoulder. She landed in the dirt flat on her back, her hands mashed beneath her.

Adam's next shot hit Tyler in the head and he dropped where he stood. The two remaining men mounted, spurring hard for Adam, who held his ground and took careful aim, ignoring the return fire. He fired twice expertly, killing them both. Adam mounted his horse and galloped for the cleft, pulling his mare to a hard stop.

Shea lay in the dirt, semiconscious, fighting for breath and spitting up blood. His right shoulder and leg were twisted at grotesque angles. Adam moved him carefully. The rope around his neck was so tight that Adam had to cut it away with his knife.

"Lie still, my friend. I'll get help." He cut Shea's bonds and scrambled over to Emma, who lay still, her face, hair, shoulders, and chest covered in blood. For a horrifying moment he thought that she was dead, but she took a breath and groaned. Cradling her to his chest, he moved her with care, severing her bonds and sliding off the noose around her neck. Holding her with one arm, he pulled off his jacket and shirt then checked her wound. It appeared that the bullet had passed straight through her shoulder.

As he tied his shirt around the wound, she spoke in a shaking whisper. "Shea . . ."

Adam laid her gently down. "He's alive. Lie still. I'm going for help. Those men are dead. They can't hurt you anymore." Adam allowed himself tears as he pulled his bedroll and blanket from his horse and covered Emma and Shea. Shirtless, he put on his jacket and quickly rode away to signal for a wagon. His coat was soaked; the sweet smell of Emma's blood made his stomach roll.

The battle still raged, but had moved away from camp; the army had the militia on the run. Adam found a soldier and ordered a wagon brought to the cleft immediately.

When the battle began, Adam had seen Tyler as he ran down Shea and dragged him to the narrow draw. He had also seen Emma taken, but was too far away to help. Desperately, he raced through a hail of bullets, one passing clear through his coat unnoticed, and spurred his horse hard to get to them. Needing a hidden approach, he had to stop a distance away. When he saw the ropes produced, he dismounted, fighting to remain calm and steady, aiming his rifle. The next shots he made would be the most important of his life. He held his breath as he leveled his sights at the executioner hanging Shea. Emma was perilously close to the shot and he prayed that he would not shoot her by mistake. The hot wind Emma felt moments before Shea's hangman died was Adam's bullet, which had passed so close, it had burned her cheek.

The soldiers repelled the ambush with the help of the Cheyenne warriors who were able to arm themselves. Twenty militia lay dead or wounded, wasted sacrifices to their cause, outclassed by the soldiers and the Cheyenne. But two soldiers were killed and three Cheyenne wounded, and Tyler and his lynch mob lay dead near the cleft. The twenty–five remaining militia retreated and scattered when they realized they were outnumbered and outgunned, but their only mission was to provide a diversion to give Tyler time to hang Emma and Shea Hawkshadow. The army pursued the militiamen, and they scattered into the hills and off the reservation.

The small camp was destroyed. Most lodges had been trampled and many had burned. Emma and Shea's was knocked down as well; it was lucky that no fire burned in their lodge that day. Adam ordered his men to erect it before Emma and Shea were taken there. The Cheyenne women and children soon emerged from the ditch and amid wails and cries and returned to the camp to tend the wounded and rebuild their lives yet again.

Moments later, Adam returned to the cleft. Emma stirred. "Lie, still, Emma," he said.

"Is Shea alive?"

"He's hurt bad," he said, hating having to prepare her for his possible death, which could come in moments.

Emma eyes were wide with terror. "Where's Tyler?"

"He's dead and so are the other three. Now lay back. Help's on the way." Mercifully, she passed out.

The wagon seem to take forever to come. Two soldiers put Emma and Shea on stretchers and lifted them into the wagon while Adam hovered. He vehemently refused the soldier's attempt to load Tyler and the hangman into another wagon. "Let the wolves have them," he snapped. The men obeyed, fearful of Adam's wrath.

Considine rode up next to Adam as he rode beside the wagon. "Tyler?" he asked, looking around.

"Dead," Adam replied, "back there in the cleft with another man and two others over there." He gestured carelessly to where the bodies lay in the dirt. He took a shuddering breath and spoke, not taking his eyes off the unconscious couple. "Tyler tried to hang them both and shot Emma before I got him. He hanged Shea. I don't know if he'll make it."

Considine wiped dirt and sweat from his forehead with a handkerchief, shaking his head, appalled. "Hell of a day," he said, "and we're responsible. We should've seen this coming." Adam inwardly agreed, but was preoccupied with Emma and Shea's suffering.

Many Sioux from the nearby camps came to help the Cheyenne in the hours following the raid. With an eerie quiet, they rebuilt the lodges and helped tend the wounded.

Emma woke at twilight, pain pounding her shoulder. She turned her head painfully and saw Shea nearby lying on his back, wheezing and sputtering, fighting for air. She tried to rise but was too weak. Adam was asleep slumped against Shea's backrest, shirtless beneath his blood–stained jacket. His ruined shirt lay crumpled near him, stained and crusted with blood—her blood, she rightly guessed.

Just then, Dr. Malley, who had befriended Emma back in the Indian Territory, ducked into the lodge. Adam woke immediately, in spite of his own exhaustion.

Malley knelt between Emma and Shea and spoke in a quiet voice to her. "Mrs. Hawkshadow, glad you're awake."

"Dr. Malley? From Fort Reno . . ."

"Kind of you to remember. I'm General Considine's personal physician now. I'll be with the both of you as long as I'm needed." He quickly checked under the bandages around her shoulder and ladled a dose of laudanum down her throat. "Shea's right shoulder and leg were dislocated and I set them both back into the sockets. His throat's bad, though. I'm doing all I can." Emma feared the worst. "Have hope. I still have to stitch you up but had to wait till the bleeding slowed. Give me a few minutes to check over your husband."

"Did Shea break his neck?"

Malley looked to Adam hoping for a hint of what to say, but Adam was too weary and dispirited and looked away.

"His neck's not broken, but his injuries are severe. Every minute he lives and breathes, there's hope."

Emma lay back and tried to rest, but her only thought was horrifying fear that Shea would die and she would be alone again. Coherent thought slipped away with the drug; she felt outside herself and her pain. Her eyes fixed upon the small opening in the top of the lodge as the smoke from the fire drifted away. For a moment she envisioned drifting with it, escaping this day's horrors. She wanted to float away on the wind without care or thought, but pain abruptly grounded her. She craned her neck and watched Dr. Malley work on Shea. He carefully applied salve to the rope burns around his neck, then listened to his heart through a stethoscope. She fought revulsion as the memory of his hanging replayed again and again in her mind. He cannot die, she thought, not now—not after I've come back to him—not after all we've endured. The scene swam before her as the laudanum took effect, but she fought to stay awake watching Dr. Malley.

"Emma, I'm going to get cleaned up," Adam said in a soft voice. "I'll be back in a little while, okay?"

When he finished tending Shea, Dr. Malley went outside and washed his hands with alcohol. The smell of it made Emma's stomach lurch. He returned minutes later with a young red–haired corpsman.

"Okay, we're going to stitch you up now. The corpsmen here is going to roll you over on your side. Let him do it. Don't try to move yourself." The corpsman came forward at Malley's nod.

Adam then returned, still damp from a hurried dip in the river. He helped the corpsman roll Emma gently on her right side and cradled her neck with his warm hand, which calmed her a little. Malley worked quickly, dabbing the wound with a smelly liquid that burned terribly. Emma sucked in her breath and tried not to cry out, but she yelped anyway.

"The bullet passed clean through and your collarbone's broken. I'm going to have to set it." As Malley spoke, he snapped the bone back into place. Emma nearly passed out from the deep, sharp pain. "Here we go. Sorry, but this is going to hurt. Do you want more laudanum?" She shook her head.

Malley washed crusted blood from her chest, neck, and arm. Adam looked down at her with deep sorrow. His thumb caressed her cheek.

The laudanum did not dull her pain, but the drug caused her not to care. She felt unfocused and as if she were floating. "What's the matter, Adam? You look white as a ghost. *Maiyun*."

He shook his head, not understanding her comment, and slipped his hand in hers as the doctor began to stitch.

She held his hand so tightly that it went numb, but he did not pull away. Tears wet her cheeks, but she did not cry out again, a feat that moved Adam and amazed Malley, who had been a Union doctor during the Civil War. Mercifully, she fell asleep immediately after Malley applied bandages and put her arm in a sling. With Adam on guard throughout the night, she slept.

Shea was semiconscious throughout the night and his breathing rasping and labored. He sounded as if he were constantly choking, so Adam kept close by, wiping away the blood and spittle. He spoke to his friend, assuring him that he would live and that Emma was going to be all right as well. He did not know if Shea heard him, but it made him feel better. He felt so very alone in the quiet lodge in the quiet camp stilled by tragedy.

Considine came to the lodge late that night. He was very discouraged. Although he barely knew Shea, he harbored great affection for Emma. "They never deserved this—no one does."

Adam was grim, his voice a graveled hiss. "Tyler calls the Indians savages, but he was far more brutal than any Indian I've ever known. There was no reason to do this! I'm glad I killed that animal." His eyes were wide with fatigue and regret. "I couldn't get to them fast enough. I saw them taken and couldn't get to them! When I saw what Tyler intended to do, I thought of all these two have suffered and I wanted to stop it if it meant my own life. I failed." He was dejected, riddled with guilt.

"You saved them both, Adam," Considine said, fully aware of his friendship with Shea and his feelings for Emma, which were transparent to him when Adam spoke of or looked upon her. "You did your best and that's all anyone can expect. Stay here as long as it takes to get them on the mend."

Emma woke early the following morning, finding herself flanked by Adam curled beside her, softly snoring, and Shea on the other side. She managed to sit up and shift to Shea's side. His eyelids fluttered, but he was in a deep sleep. Despite a rasp that came with every breath, he was alive, to her relief.

Her movements woke Adam. "Emma—Emma—lie back down. You'll tear the stitches. He's holding on." She kept her eyes on Shea as he gently guided her back down onto the blankets and covered her. "I've been up with him all night and he seems better—honest," he said, trying to add a note of hope to his voice.

"I don't remember much after I saw Shea pulled up and saw him hanging there."

"Shh," he soothed. "He's strong. Trust in that." He found her hand and held it, his fingers feeling the delicate bones beneath her skin. "I followed you both to the draw. I shot the man who hanged Shea, and, I can see, I narrowly missed you," he said, touching her cheek lightly. She looked at him in amazement, understanding how close she had come. "Sorry I wasn't faster." Emma squeezed his hand and tried to smile. "I got the others with Tyler. In all, twenty of the militia were killed or wounded, and two soldiers were killed—good men, too. Three Cheyenne are wounded and one is dead, but she wasn't shot." His voice trailed off. Fatigue had made him careless. He did not want to tell the sad news just yet, but now there was no avoiding what she had to hear.

She had seen that same look on his face last night. "She?" Adam could not look at her. "Tell me!" she cried.

"Red Leaf Woman. Her heart. She died in the ditch during the battle. There was nothing anyone could do. I am sorry, Emma. I know what she was to you."

Tears of shock and grief slid down Emma's cheeks. "No! No!" The loss shook her deeply. He felt pity for her as she dealt with yet another blow. After a long silence, she gathered herself and lay sniffling. "Has she been buried yet?"

"It's today."

"I'm going."

"No, you can't. If you tear the stitches, you'll start bleeding. You could get an infection that could kill you."

"I'm going," she insisted.

Arguing with her was useless. She had a right to say good–bye to the old woman who had guided her through the new life she had chosen; she had to bury a parent again.

Adam asked Little Fox, who was too upset to attend her aunt's funeral, to watch over Shea while he supported Emma as she walked slowly behind the brier to the burial grounds. The old woman's body was covered in wildflowers and laid to rest under stones.

Despite terrible weakness from her injuries and the tumultuous emotions surging through her, Emma was the last mourner to leave the grave site. Many thoughts went through Emma's mind that afternoon—thoughts of rage and enmity for what had been done—a desire for revenge mixed with anguish at Red Leaf Woman's passing and bitterness at the senselessness of it all. Nothing had been accomplished yesterday, she thought resentfully. Too many had died and although the Cheyenne had survived another day, others like Tyler would come again. Next time, the Cheyenne might not be so lucky as to escape with their lives, such as they were. The militia might have suffered a blow, but they could return.

She thought of the cold night that she had buried her parents, feeling the same desolation. It was a minute–to–minute struggle to keep from screaming, for if she did, she was afraid that she would never stop. Although Tyler was dead, his point had been painfully made. Adam finally guided her away from the grave, but on the way back to the lodge, her strength failed and he carried her home.

Sweet, gentle Little Fox had prepared supper for Emma upon her return. As she watched her, she envisioned Porcupine Girl at her side. And as she ate a little, her eyes filled with tears remembering the frozen body of Porcupine Girl in the dead tent, as she called it. Little Fox had taken her best friend's death very hard and now she had to cope with Red Leaf's death. Little Fox left to go to the burial grounds to offer her prayers for her aunt.

Emma tried, unsuccessfully, to dredge up hope in all of these events, but another horrible day overwhelmed her and she fell into an exhausted sleep soon after Little Fox departed. While she slept, Malley checked on them, encouraged that Emma's shoulder showed no sign of infection and surprised that Shea seemed stronger.

"It's still touch and go," he whispered to Adam. "He still could take a turn, so watch him. Try to get a little water in his mouth if you can to wet it, but don't force it. If he chokes, he could die."

"What should I be watching for?"

"If he stops breathing," Malley replied.

Emma had awakened when Malley had entered the lodge, but did not stir as she listened. Inside, she was breaking. She succumbed to the pain in her shoulder, which again pulled her into a dreamless doze. Adam spent a sleepless night watching over his friend and the young woman who had a distinct place in his heart.

The next morning, Shea awoke writhing in pain. Adam came to his side as he struggled to speak, gasping for air, his eyes bulging in panic.

Adam held him down and spoke to calm him. "Keep still and don't try to talk, Shea. Your neck and throat are in bad shape." With surprising strength, Shea gripped Adam's arm and he read his face aright. "She's right here next to you. Tyler shot her in the shoulder and her collarbone's broken, but she's okay. She's asleep." Shea tried to turn his head to see Emma, but could not. "Keep still, Shea," Adam repeated, trying to control him. Shea's strength was formidable, despite his injuries. "Lay quiet and I'll tell you everything." It took Shea a while to calm down, then Adam told him the events of the past two days. When he told him of Red Leaf Woman's death, Shea gestured toward Emma. Adam understood. "She somehow found the strength to go to the burial yesterday. She's taking it pretty hard, but you'll need her strength to see you through this. I won't lie to you. You've got a long way to go."

When Dr. Malley arrived that afternoon, he was relieved that Shea was coherent and alert. Malley cared about these two people and was heartened that Considine allowed him to remain as long as needed. This gesture by Considine was intended to aid their recovery, but he also knew that Max Cody was in camp during the ambush. The wily reporter might not keep silent this time. This story was too big and there were too many witnesses to keep it hushed up. Emma and Max were friends, so he wanted publicly to show that the military had done everything possible to repel the ambush and help the Cheyenne.

Max had indeed witnessed everything and had even fought the militia. He had a heartrending article to wire to his paper in Omaha, despite some interference from Considine who wanted to co–write the story. In the end, Cody wrote the story his way.

Two weeks after the ambush, Malley and Adam reluctantly departed. Both men had done all they could. Emma saw them off and with her good arm, hugged them both, bestowing a kiss on the cheek for each. Malley blushed at this attention from the pretty, brave girl that he had met at Fort Reno. He promised to return soon and went to his horse.

Emma spoke to Adam. "I'm sorry Shea couldn't come to see you off. He's still so weak."

Adam's finger traced the bullet burn on her cheek. "Take care of each other. Send word if you need anything." He was transfixed for a moment as their eyes met. "I want you to be happy. You are very important to me."

She smiled, returning his affection. "And you are to us," she said. "Tell me, did Tyler have family?"

"A wife and two sons."

"I'm sorry for them," she said. "It's unfair what he put them through, whether or not they agreed with his mission."

"His boys were young, both under ten. I heard that his wife has already left Montana. She went back east to family." He pulled her to him, hugging her gently, then he stepped away, mounted his horse and rode off. "I'll see you soon," he called, waving.

Due to his injuries, Shea slept apart from Emma and she felt lost and isolated again, just as she had at Fort Robinson. It was hard with Adam away, especially since she was left with Shea's care. Little Fox helped out when she could, but she had to maintain Red Leaf's lodge alone. She was to be married, but her intended, one of Sun at Midnight's sons, Carries Fire, had been wounded in the ambush. Little Fox spent a lot of time tending him.

Shea could not move without considerable pain and his voice was silenced. This strong, seemingly invincible warrior had, in a few weeks, been reduced to a thin, frail man who kept to his bed day and night. He was too weak to do more than swallow liquids and sleep. In her loneliness, Emma's thoughts turned to Red Leaf Woman. She missed her so. Red Leaf had kept her focused and many times the old woman's strength had shored up her own. Her common sense had always made Emma feel secure during her adjustment to life with the Cheyenne.

The only person who really helped Emma was Max. He came to the lodge daily and did what he could for them and he became a cherished companion for her in her loneliness and despair. However, he was compelled to leave a month later.

"I'm being sent to Texas. The Comanche are causing trouble down there and I have to cover it. I'll keep in touch with Major Lawrence in case there is anything I can do. I'll be back. I promise."

She watched him ride away feeling stranded.

In the weeks following the ambush, Shea's afflictions became much more than physical. His temperament, once gentle and meditative, changed drastically. Although he could not speak, his rage was clearly directed at

Emma. Still coping with her own injuries, she was unprepared to deal with the change in him. Violent bursts of anger were hurled at her and she was confused and too drained to fight back—and fight back at what? It was hard to fight back against a look or a gesture. He could not walk steadily and his breathing was still labored from his swollen throat. But he had become mean, often cruel. He submitted to her ministrations when she tended his wounds, but slapped her hand away when she tried to help him walk or sit. He had become distant, showing no affection, sympathy, or acknowledgment for her care of him.

Emma felt some relief when he was at last able to leave the lodge on his own, lurching through camp. The look on his face was malevolent and cold to everyone, but especially to her. The cuts and gashes all over his body troubled him, but he shut away the pain, trying to do for himself, sometimes failing and angrily refusing her assistance, shoving her away. Emma gave him a wide berth as she watched him struggle to lift or carry with his one good arm. He became winded easily and had not the ability to ride his pony to join in the hunt. Weakness clearly frustrated him and she was the suffering recipient of his annoyance. The qualities of tenacity and stubbornness that she had first found so attractive in him soon soured in her heart.

When he wanted to communicate with her, he wrote terse notes on paper torn from the leaves of her books, usually informing her of some task that she had forgotten to do, unmindful that her shoulder still pained her and she still had a month to go in the sling. At day's end, she was tired and sore too, but he took no notice of her struggles. It was becoming hard for her to recall what he used to be like and she tried to remember the loving, gentle, tender, intelligent man who had been a strong, noble warrior—a man that she wanted in her bed. Now, love in this home was lacking and it hurt. Emma retreated inside herself and kept her distance, hoping that the man she loved would soon return.

In early November Dr. Malley arrived with a troop, bringing medicine, food, and gifts sent by Considine for the Cheyenne. To Emma's disappointment, Adam did not accompany them. She had come to depend heavily on Adam. He was a great listener and always seemed to know what to say to her. But she was so troubled over Shea's condition that she emboldened herself to speak with Malley.

After Shea stoically submitted to Malley's examination, he limped out of the lodge. Emma was alone with the doctor.

"Will his voice come back, Dr. Malley?"

"I don't know ma'am. Has he tried to speak yet?"

"No," she said. "He hasn't."

"How are you feeling?"

"I'm all right. The shoulder's still sore. How much longer in the sling?"

"Probably two more weeks. Don't put any strain on it for another month after that, though." He was packing up his kit, ready to leave.

"Please. Wait. I need your help—advice, I mean," she began, finding it hard to open up. After a long pause, she decided to plunge in. "Shea's changed. He's so angry at me all the time. I don't know what do to."

Malley sat down next to her. "What's been happening?"

She confided in him, speaking of Shea's frequent outbursts of anger, all directed at her. "He's become so cruel—mad at everything—mad at me. So unlike him," she said. "I'm afraid to do anything because nothing pleases him."

"People dealing with such ordeals sometimes are not themselves for a while." He was trying to give her the standard clinical answer, but he could plainly see that she was deeply troubled. He schooled himself to listen to what she really meant.

"I know that," she said with worry, "but I think he blames me for what happened."

"You had nothing to do with the ambush. You were a victim too that day."

"Seems like there is always something bad happening to us. I'm tired of it. Oh, I wish we could go away from all of this to someplace where no one could find us. Someplace where no one wants to kill us. Then he might snap out of it."

Malley watched her sorrowfully. He wanted to say something to console her, but he had little experience with counseling. "I wish I had a solution for you, ma'am. Only you can decide what to do. Sometimes, there's nowhere to run and you have to fight—if the fight's worth it, I mean."

Hours after Malley left, she thought about his words. Was the fight worth it? What would she gain—and more importantly, what could she stand to lose? She felt terribly fragile, but bit back tears and resolved to keep trying.

Days later as they finished supper, Shea became angry with Emma— again. He made a slashing move to his throat, his new sign that she was talking too much. The silence of the lodge bothered her, so she combated it with nervous chatter, unaware that it annoyed him until he hurled a tin plate across the lodge, barely missing her injured shoulder. He had not hit her with his fist, she thought bitterly, he did not yet possess the strength. And what would she do if he did?

This most recent outburst unnerved her and she became truly afraid of him. She kept making excuses for his behavior and tried to be sensitive to his suffering, but her patience was wearing thin and she felt as if she were trapped with a wild animal. He might be hurting, but he had the strength to vent his anger upon her, she noticed bitterly. Since that terrifying day in the cleft, he had expressed only resentment and hostility toward her. As the weeks wore on and his stamina increased, his foul temper grew. He was out of sorts no matter what she said or did. Another night, he seemed more reasonable and she tried to express some affection by kissing his cheek, but he spurned her, gripping her arm so tightly that his hand left a bruise. All other expressions of affection, both spoken and displayed, met the same stony, sometimes threatening indifference. She was thankful that she was not pregnant, for her only respite was when she retreated to the menstrual lodge each month. Shea was left to struggle on his own those days and she did not feel guilty for that.

Without Red Leaf, she had no one to confide in, no one to lean on and felt utterly isolated. She faithfully, wordlessly, tended Shea's wounds, applying salve to his neck, which was still swollen and purple, and compresses to his shoulder and hip, which pained him. She made sure that he took his medicine, but his expression was cold and distant when he looked at her now. She felt more like a slave than a wife and found many excuses to leave the oppressive atmosphere of the lodge.

Many nights she lay awake and battled a growing desire to leave him. She felt guilty and now wondered if she had made the wrong decision to return. If not for Adam, they would be dead. And she came to blame herself for inciting Tyler's wrath. If she had stayed away, this would never have happened. And Red Leaf would still be alive. The memory of the battle continually unnerved her and the thought of Red Leaf dying in the ditch haunted her. Emma grieved for her. She had not been with her. She had not been able to say good–bye.

Shea's hostility, coupled with the realization that people wanted her dead, shook Emma deeply. Unfamiliar noises brought fears of another attack amidst the open spaces of the earth and the sky that she once cherished. Shea's belligerence drove her outdoors, but even in the busy camp, she felt exposed—a victim in waiting—and she had to face these fears alone. She wondered how the Cheyenne had survived living this way. And she had nightmares about Shea's hanging. In the dreams, she sat in the dust looking up at his lifeless body hanging from the tree. When she woke, she sometimes wished that he had died that day so that she would be free from this little hell that had become her life. Shea had his own inner demons to battle and publicly she showed devotion and did what he would allow her to do, but privately, her efforts were trivialized and unappreciated. Locked into a one–way battle for her marriage, she was frustrated and very worried.

Eventually, to escape the mounting tension between them, she had secretly begun studying with Shea's cousin, Sun at Midnight, out of sight of the camp, learning to use the bow and arrow. She felt a curious revenge when she hit the targets; Sun at Midnight was impressed with her skill. Although her range was one hundred yards, half the distance of an expert archer, it was impressive. Out of the sling, her sore shoulder hindered her at first, but she kept practicing, strengthening it.

Max Cody returned in late November; even heavy snows could not deter this man. He was invited to hospitality in Sun at Midnight's lodge, but hard upon arrival, heard of the troubles between Emma and Shea—it was gossiped about all over camp. Max spent a lot of time with her, determined to bolster her mood, and brought her his next series of articles about them.

"Max, please—I'm begging you—don't publicize what's become of us since the ambush. Our failing marriage wouldn't make a very good story for your readers."

He touched her hand with affection. "I promised you once that I'd never write about such things. I meant it."

Max encouraged her to keep practicing the bow, praising her natural affinity for the weapon and once joking that she should imagine Shea was her target. She returned his wry smile and her next shot hit the target dead center. Emma practiced with the bow daily. Cheyenne women were good hunters and some regularly went with hunting parties. Emma was determined to be the first white woman to go with the hunters, for she fully intended to go the next time game was sighted. Shea would be furious, but she did not much care what he thought any longer. She had resolved to leave Shea when winter ended and get as far from him as her money would take her.

Emma soon moved from wooden targets to squirrels and rabbits, giving away the kill to other families so that Shea would not discover what she was doing. The people, out of respect, kept their silence. It was a disgrace for a man to treat his wife badly and the tribe censured Shea, but he was unable to pull himself out of his downward spiral of anger and self–pity.

In sympathy, Sun at Midnight presented Emma with a sturdy mare, whom she named Butternut. She was responsive, swift, and easy to control. Shea wondered why Sun at Midnight had given it to Emma, but was too preoccupied with his own struggles to wonder about it long.

One night in December, she awoke to find Shea pulling at her blankets. His eyes had a strange, glazed look that frightened her. His hand moved up her thigh, pulling up her nightgown. "Stop it," she said as she pushed him away. "Leave me alone."

He kept caressing her then fastened his mouth on hers. He held her down under him and quickly made love to her. She heard his rasping breath quicken as he moved on top of her. When he finished, he pulled one of her blankets off, rolled over and fell asleep immediately. Emma straightened her clothes, curled deep into the blankets and did not sleep the entire night.

The next morning, she rose and began preparing breakfast. Shea was stirring. Emma thought that he had tried, in a clumsy way, to make up with her last night. She tried to lighten her tone.

"I hope you were warm enough last night. You fell asleep so fast afterward." Shea's eyes met hers wonderingly and he shrugged his good shoulder as if to say 'What?' Emma did not understand his reaction.

Shea looked exasperated, ripped a piece of paper from a book and scribbled. "What do you mean?"

"After we made love, Shea."

He looked confounded and scribbled again. "I did not lie with you last night."

Her breath caught in her throat. "Yes, you did." He shook his head. "Shea, I'm not crazy."

He took up the pencil again and wrote. "I do not remember."

Her heart sank. Was it possible that Shea had brain damage from the hanging? Perhaps that was what was truly wrong with him. Malley had not warned her about this! "It's okay. Maybe you thought it was a dream. People sleepwalk. Maybe that's sort of what happened."

Shea's face closed over, unreadable. Emma continued making breakfast, trying to push this newest worry from her mind.

Indeed, Shea did not remember and it deeply troubled him. He left and went to the sweat lodge, a skin–covered hut where the men gathered for steam baths. He began going there often, hoping that the vapors would heal his throat and ease the pain in his limbs. Emma was glad to be rid of him. With him out of the lodge, she had the privacy to weep unseen.

Winter only fueled Emma's desolation, especially after Max left for an assignment in Canada. Shea was still his sullen self and she held onto hope that spring would revitalize him and bring him back. Maybe he was not brain damaged—just unable to cope. If she saw him at least trying, she would stay; otherwise, she had her escape plan ready, and this time, it would succeed, unlike her abortive attempt when she had first come to the camp in the Indian Territory.

Continuing to appease the Cheyenne after the raid, Considine saw to it that several wagon loads of dry goods, meats, and medicines were regularly delivered to the camp. Although the people were grateful they knew that the supplies were only a gesture and would soon come no more. However, the Cheyenne thirsted for revenge against the militia and already had defenses in place. More scouts and many signal fires were placed around the ridge in case another attack came.

Little Wolf met with Considine in January, fearful of more trouble come spring. He was assured that the militia had disbanded and the army and Cheyenne scouts had the borders well patrolled. Some members of the militia had been captured and were in jail awaiting trial, Considine told him, but some had escaped justice, and their whereabouts were unknown. He did his best to assure Little Wolf that most of the militia had left the territory, and without a leader, the militia would not reform in the same numbers. Little Wolf did not believe him.

Emma was relieved when Adam arrived in March with a large contingent of soldiers for a parley with the Cheyenne and Sioux leaders. He found Emma and Shea just after his arrival and she invited him to supper. He noticed the change in Shea immediately. Emma looked pallid and worn–out as she put together a modest meal. She did not sit near Shea as was her habit. Supper was quiet, strained.

Unable to get her alone to talk, Adam was very concerned when he rode away to the encampment that the army had pitched nearby for the parley.

The urgency of bringing about peace between the Cheyenne and the white settlers was driven home the next afternoon. General Considine and Adam were there in the parley tent, along with many other officers, trying to figure out how to alleviate the fears of the Cheyenne and Sioux.

Everyone hushed to silence as Shea and Emma entered the big meeting lodge. Although women were forbidden in the tribal council circle, space was made for Emma as Shea's interpreter. Shea handed her a piece of paper. He had spent the previous night writing it and would not show it to her until that moment. He could not speak and had lost much weight on a diet of liquids, but his eyes were fierce.

Considine looked momentarily startled when he realized that Shea Hawkshadow could read and write as Emma took the page from his hand. In the light of day, only Adam noticed the new creases in her face and the dark circles under her eyes. What he had witnessed the night before was not simple fatigue. Dr. Malley, respecting Emma's privacy, had never told Adam of her troubles.

Everyone fell silent as Emma stood and began to read in a voice thick with emotion. Adam did not mistake it for conviction for the words she read.

"Shea Hawkshadow, Dog Soldier, has this to say to the leaders assembled here: The Cheyenne people are grateful to the army for their help in repelling the militia illegally on our land. We are sorry for the deaths of the soldiers, but our women and children live in fear on the land the Great Father in Washington said is ours. Your government ordered us to throw down our guns and arrows and we are not allowed to defend ourselves like men. We demand the government give us arms to protect our lands. We demand they give us guns and bullets. We want the storehouses of food and medicine promised by the treaty we signed. We have only received a token amount of these things. And they were given to appease us. If you do not allow us to live the way we know, we will soon die off."

Emma looked up. Adam was staring at her. His expression of admiration mingled with sympathy was not lost on her. Adam knew her too well and she could not hide from his scrutiny. She colored and turned her attention back to the rumpled page.

"We are glad Tyler is dead and his militia scattered, but we fear more raids. We have a treaty telling us we will be safe in our lodges, but we are not. My dear wife," Emma stopped and read ahead. Her eyes flicked to Shea who nodded for her to continue. Standing before the tribal leaders and high–ranking army officers, she had to continue. "My dear wife has suffered at the hands of the whites. It is men like Tyler who will come again and again to harm us, regardless of who we marry, regardless of where we live. We are human beings with families and all we want is peace on our own lands. The Cheyenne and Sioux have given much. Land—lives—and more land. It is time for the government to give what has been promised."

Adam looked across to Shea and found him staring back with eyes fresh with obstinacy, replacing reason. Despite Shea's silence, Adam could see the warrior within, speaking through white words and his white wife.

Emma was visibly uncomfortable; Adam could see her close over.

"These are the things we want. What will the army do? That's all," she concluded, resuming her place next to Shea. She looked at him. He could not remain much longer; he sat slumped and pale. She was trying very hard to dig down and find the strength to care about him. His head turned as far as it could and she could see the hard look on his face, awaiting an answer to his speech by proxy. He made no acknowledgment of her effort this day and it rankled her.

Considine took time to reply. "Shea, I'm encouraged to see that you are stronger and since I am acquainted with your wife, I'm thankful she survived the attack upon her. The government regrets the terrible injuries the Cheyenne suffered and you are right. You have, by treaty, the right to live on your land in peace. I will do all in my power to assure it. I will take your requests to the Bureau of Indian Affairs and insist that they are honored."

Then Little Wolf spoke, followed by the other soldier chiefs. All of them knew full well that the requests would never be granted, but looked for a way to get just one seriously considered. Emma kept her place near Shea as talk swirled around them. Her eyes kept returning to Adam who watched her steadily, distracted from the talks. She knew that he saw through her. Shea held up well and spoke through her using paper and pencil, but he looked exhausted.

Finally, a break was called at noon. As Shea rose, Emma put out her hand to help him up, but he refused with a shove that nearly toppled her. He shot a resentful look at her and stood without assistance. She slowly followed in his wake, head down, blushing crimson as he walked unsteadily back to the lodge. Their troubles had been no secret in the weeks following the ambush but now they had been made very public indeed.

Adam quickly came to her. His eyes bespoke far more than his words as he watched Shea go. "He seems, uh, in a bad mood. Maybe because of the meeting."

She spoke in a terse voice. "Don't make excuses for him. You can see how he's changed."

He remained close to her to keep his comments from being overheard. "I saw how he treated you just now, Emma. I don't like it. What's going on?" She shrugged her good shoulder. They walked a short distance and, trying to brighten her mood, he said, "You look much better, but I think you'll have that burn from the bullet on your pretty face for a while. I am really sorry." He smiled good–naturedly. She smiled back but kept an eye on Shea as he stumbled home. Adam placed his hand lightly on her arm. "It looks to me like Shea wants to be alone. How about lunch with me?"

Relieved, Emma put her arm through Adam's as he took her to his tent. For a while she set aside her troubles and shared his lunch.

"So, how's your shoulder?" he said, trying to keep the talk normal until she was ready to open up. He knew that she would, eventually.

"It's fine, just a little sore."

They talked of trivial things for a while, then Adam saw an opening and pressed her. He could not stand to see her in such obvious pain. "Emma, talk to me. Something's wrong. I can see it plain."

She measured him with her gaze, sure that he would never betray her. "I can't reach Shea. He's slipping away from me. I can't do anything right for him. He can't speak, but we manage to have the most bizarre arguments! There's a look he gives me sometimes. He's in terrible pain and I'm trying to be understanding and care for him, but some days—" She finally spoke the words that Adam had waited so long to hear. "I've made a mistake, Adam. I should never have come back to him. Look at what's happened. It was my presence here that caused this."

"Is that what you think?"

"Shea blames me, yes. And I think he's right."

"Hold on a minute! Tyler would've found any excuse to do what he did. He was a sick man." Adam squelched his anger at Shea for causing Emma to feel this way and chose his words carefully. "Leave him, Emma. You've done all you can and put up with more than anyone should." Words he had wanted to say for so long tumbled from his mouth. "Leave today— now. Just get on my horse and I'll get you out of here. I can hide you and protect you at Fort Keogh. I'll leave the army. I'll go anywhere you want. You'll have time to get well—someplace safe—away from all this." His steady gaze fixed on her, giving Emma's heart a serious turn. "Emma, I love you. You might feel the same about me someday and I'm a patient man. I'd make a good husband, I promise you." His expression held a disquieting look of love and affection that penetrated her more deeply than she wanted to admit.

"No offense, but no more 'protection' at forts, okay? Got a bad history at those places." Her effort at covering her conflict with a bad joke fell flat. Adam did not return her affected smile. A battle began in her heart. "Oh, Adam, I can't leave him. It's more complicated than you know."

There existed an undeniable bond between them. He let her talk out her fear and frustration. But his feelings for her overshadowed everything else. "You don't have to live this way." He lifted her chin with his hand, his dark eyes looking deeply into hers. "Emma, I'm in love with you and whatever you choose, I'll abide by your decisions. You have to be absolutely sure that you're doing what's best for you and for Shea. I saw how he treated you. Has he hit you, Emma?"

"No punches yet, exactly," she answered sarcastically.

"What hold does he have over you? Make me understand why you're putting up with this!"

"He doesn't have a hold on me. I think I'm pregnant, Adam."

"Oh, no," he breathed. "How dare he treat you like this when you're carrying his child!"

"He doesn't know. I'm only a few months along, I think."

"Then he doesn't have to know. Emma, come with me now. We'll be together. I'll raise the child as if it were my own. Shea doesn't deserve to know!"

Emma saw the love in his steady brown eyes and heard the anxiety in his voice. He was trying to save her again.

"I can't explain in words. My instincts tell me to stay because maybe he'll snap out of it. I'll tell him about the child when he's better. Maybe the news will change how he feels about me."

"Good God, Emma, how much longer until you've had enough? Until he beats you? Until he beats the child?"

"He's in terrible pain. He can't ride or hunt. He can't speak. Oh, don't you see? I finally understood today when he pushed me away in front of everyone. He's been humiliated and he's frightened, but he's too proud to admit it. I know he's taking it out on me, but I have to give him a chance. Weakness is the worst thing for a warrior. He's afraid that he won't ever be the same." She checked a tear sliding down her face.

"Emma, I can't bear to think what your life will be if he stays like this."

"The child coming must be a sign that I should stay. After all, Shea took me back. He didn't have to."

"Does anyone else know that you're pregnant?"

"Some of the women have guessed, but they're not saying anything. I think they feel sorry for us. I don't know what to do. Don't tell Shea, please," she pleaded.

He held her face and wiped away her tears with his thumbs. "What would your life have been like if I had found you on the prairie that day instead of Shea?" He kissed her.

She drew back, but her eyes betrayed genuine feelings for him. Adam's heart thudded in his chest, hoping that she might feel the same. She slid away, feeling his love coming in waves that threatened to sweep her away. How easily she could forget Shea as she looked into Adam's warm brown eyes! His words reverberated in her head, despite efforts to shut out the sad truth. She was frightened of her future with Shea and for an impetuous instant, considered leaving with Adam. She needed peace and she would never have it if things did not improve between her and Shea. But the child changed everything. She had to give the marriage another chance, but too many questions plagued her. Would Shea change when he was told about the pregnancy or would she have to endure his foul temper for the rest of her life? And what about the child? Could she let it be raised by parents who despised one another? It was all too much to bear. She locked her emotions away, a neat little trick that was becoming a habit.

She looked outside the tent, seeing the men returning to the meeting lodge. "Looks like it's time you get back and I better check on Shea."

He rose and stood very near her. "I'll take you from this place the minute you say the word. Whether or not you choose to be with me won't matter. I want this pain to end for you."

"Thank you, Adam. You're a good man and I know what you've offered me today."

151

He felt powerless to save her. "Emma, what can I do?"

"Be my friend."

"I will always be that."

She tried to lighten his mood and deflect her own struggle after his profession of love. "There must be many other women more worthy of your attentions. Adam, you should find someone who is less of a mess." She smiled at him with genuine affection.

"Unthinkable. No woman I'll ever know could match you." He took her hand and kissed it with tenderness.

She smiled. "Be with us for supper? Maybe Shea's humor and mine will improve with you around."

She left then, sure that he could see the emotions battling in her gaze. The half mile walk back to camp gave her time to think—and regret.

Shea did not return for the afternoon session of the council meeting. Silent and angry as usual, he met her outside their lodge. He slapped a piece of paper in her hand which read: "Adam is not your husband. Do not do that again." He angrily threw aside the flap and went into the lodge.

Emma followed, bracing herself for yet another battle with Shea. Surely he could not have seen Adam's stolen kiss. It was the same old fight, only with a new adversary—jealousy.

"I had lunch with Adam! So what!" Shea dismissed her with a gesture. "Shea! Look at me!" He kept his back to her, displaying his annoyance, his arms crossed upon his chest. "You didn't want me anywhere near you! You made that clear enough! Adam was only being kind. He knows that something's wrong between us. Everybody saw what you did today!" She took no pains to hide her fury. "I can't take this anymore!" She moved around to face him, her eyes narrowed and irate. She was no longer afraid of him. "You used me today! I wanted to gag reading what you wrote about me. Those words were hollow—meaningless! Now, you've resorted to spying on me and assuming things that you know nothing about! Don't you realize we owe that man our lives? How dare you be jealous!" For a change, she tossed things around the lodge in frustration—bowls, cups, blankets, and clothes. "I'm trying real hard to love you and hold this marriage together, but I can't do it alone. You won't accept the slightest help from me."

Her words met stony silence, but his anger weakened him and she exploited it. The wild river that she feared from her recurring dream carried her along and she willingly crashed upon the rocks this time. Anger freed her. She had nothing left to lose.

He bent down and rummaged, tearing a page from one of her books. He rose and took a pencil and wrote, poking holes in the paper, then snapped it out to her. It read: "Everyone saw you go into his tent instead of coming with me. You are an unfaithful wife."

She fumed, crumpled the note and deliberately tossed it in the fire. "How dare you! Unfaithful? What do you think we were doing in his tent, huh? Making love? You fool! We had lunch and talked—about you. I told him what a son–of–a–bitch you've become!" He glared at her. "All you've done is push me away, except for one night when you made love to me, but you claim you can't remember that! I thought we'd be okay after that, but you went back to your horrid self! I thought that lack of air did something to your brain when you were hanged, so I've tried to give you time to get well. But I was wrong. You're fine—you're strong! I've tried everything to reach you and you don't care, you make that plain. I've put up with your rotten temper far too long! I was hurt, too, and I needed you to at least understand. I never asked anything of you! All I do is give you your medicine, cook your meals, and stay out of your way! What kind of life is that? If you want this marriage to end, so be it!" She stood her ground as he whipped around came threateningly close. She stared him down with stoic resolution.

Backing away, he tore another page and wrote something. He held it out to her, his expression working into something trying to resemble capitulation. She did not reach for it right away. He waved the paper. She snatched it from his hand. It said: "Do not leave me. I blame myself because I could not protect you. I am sorry." She could not look at him as tears of frustration coursed down her cheeks.

"All right," she said through clenched teeth. His feeble apology did not mean that they had resolved anything. There was much more to this; she had a long way to go before she could trust his word.

Adam came that evening for supper but felt uncomfortable, immediately sensing the strain between them. Although Emma had told Shea that she would stay, she was still battling the pain in her heart. That was much tougher to overcome than her physical woes. Shea appeared acquiescent and subdued. He had weathered her formidable temper. It was the first time that she had fought back at him.

Emma made every effort to be affable and pleasant in deference to Adam as she set dinner before them, meat for herself and Adam and a thin gruel for Shea. Adam saw Shea try to catch her eye several times, but she deliberately took no notice. It was also obvious to Adam that Shea did not know of the pregnancy. He wondered why she had not told him; he selfishly hoped that she had not because she was waiting for the parley to end before she left with him. It would make sense. She could slip away more easily when the troop moved out and it would be hours before she would be missed. He pushed these thoughts away and covered his tension, talking about what happened at the parley that afternoon. Shea could only nod and felt shut out as Emma and Adam talked to each other over dinner.

Later on when Shea left the lodge to relieve himself, Adam looked to Emma. "You can cut the tension in here with a knife."

"Just another argument. Shea saw us together today and he got really jealous. But I don't care what he thinks anymore."

"Emma, if my being here is causing problems for you—"

"It's not you. He needs to realize what a great friend you are to us both. He's wrapped up in self–pity and hate. You're just witnessing a normal day. It isn't pretty, is it?"

"Do you want to leave with me?" he asked again, knowing that it was his last chance.

"No, I'm sorry, Adam. I agreed to try again. If I wasn't pregnant, I'd probably go, believe me, but something keeps telling me to stay. My hope isn't completely gone."

He heard her sarcastic undertone. "Don't take this wrong, but I think he sees you as a possession."

"Maybe he does, but with the child coming, maybe he'll see me as something more."

"But you haven't told him about the baby yet."

She shook her head. "I just can't yet, but I can't hide it much longer."

Later, Shea walked Adam to his horse. Although it pained him, Adam opened the subject. "Shea, Emma's been through a lot and needs you to help her. You have your own struggles, that's obvious. She's tough, but she has her limits, just like anyone else. She just needs to know that you love her." Shea stopped, throwing an impatient look at Adam. "It's no secret—your problems." Shea made a cutting gesture to his throat and started to turn away. "Shea, everyone saw how you treated her today. She was so embarrassed. I felt sorry for her so I invited her to lunch with me. In my opinion, she's held up well these past months, but I don't think that you realize what a remarkable woman she is. You should at least try to give back a little of what she's given you. She put her life on the line to protect you and the Cheyenne during the outbreak. Did you know that she's the one responsible for diverting some of the troops to Canada? She risked prison or a firing squad for you. Help her. Help her now or you'll lose her."

Shea stood with his arms folded, his face slack with shock.

Emboldened by the fact that Emma had not said that she did not love him, Adam persisted. "If she's going to live this way, I will give her a way out. I'll take care of her if you cannot. I am her friend and yours, too, but think about her. You'll miss her when she's gone, my friend."

Shea's jealously was stronger than his common sense. Adam could entice Emma to leave him and the thought panicked him. He realized that he had punished her for an event neither of them could've anticipated or controlled. Maybe it was the simple fact that Adam could take her, so he wanted to keep her with him. Guilt over his treatment of her assailed him, but his anger at his own weakness died very slowly. His feelings of inadequacy had been vented on Emma, the woman he promised to love, the woman he longed for during their separation, the woman who had returned to him after her own terrible ordeals. Emma was collecting far too many scars of the flesh and of the soul.

When Shea returned home that night, he made an effort to show kindness to Emma as she straightened up the lodge. He pulled her to him and hugged her. Emma could not feel the old attraction, but she reasoned that it was a start. Their troubles were temporarily closed in silence between them. That night, she clutched the page with Shea's plea in her hand as she slept, hoping she had made the right decision. She would remain—for now.

She did not regret her hour with Adam, for he treated her like a lady and was pleasant company. And she still felt the touch of his lips on her mouth. His offer was tucked away in her heart and she felt better knowing that she could be saved, should the marriage end. After all, her child would need a father. She searched her own feelings, finding, in her current state, that she could love him. He would never hurt her like Shea had.

When Adam left two days later, she quelled panic. He would be far away if she needed him. She saw one last plea in his eyes, but she had to look away. Though her heart was overloaded with loss and regret, she chose to stay with Shea. She grew up in the winter of 1880.

Chapter Ten

As Shea tackled his own demons, he remained incapable of dealing with Emma, despite his promises to shore up their marriage. Although he had convinced her to stay, he did not know how to heal the breach that remained between them. His physical stamina was returning, but his voice had not. And he was still too debilitated to ride with the hunters, his leg and hip still too sore to mount his pony. He was unable to tell Emma how helpless he felt. Emma was so strong, he believed that she would never understand.

He stayed in the lodge most days, brooding and feeding the fire. As he watched Emma work, making meals and overseeing his care, he felt impotent, feeble. She tried her best to be kind and patient, but he had worn her down. He could not see a way out without sacrificing his stubborn pride.

In the following weeks, arguments between them continued. Emma wryly noted that he would soon run out of pages torn from her books, then the fighting would have to stop. To escape she left the lodge for long periods, leaving him to deal with his dark moods alone. After her chores were finished, she practiced the bow with Sun at Midnight and Max, who had thankfully returned in April. Max commented that her skills with the bow were much improved. He also remarked that she had gained weight and that her face had a roundness to it. He guessed that she was pregnant, but she begged him not to tell anyone, especially Shea. Max was her confidant, someone from her world she could talk to.

And her pregnancy had progressed. Her stomach pouched a little and had grown hard. Shea had not slept with her since that night in December, nor had he noticed she had not retreated to the menstrual lodge for months. Her full dresses hid her belly, but not for much longer. She agonized over how to tell him—and when.

Very early one morning in April, word went through the camp that buffalo had been sighted. Emma heard the call and quickly, quietly dressed in the pants and shirt that Peter had given to her when she left Fort Robinson. No dress would do today. The pants just fit around her swelling belly and the work shirt fit loosely and was worn untucked. She pulled on her boots and her coat. When she stepped over Shea, he woke and grabbed her ankle.

"I'm going with the hunters. Breakfast is in the pot." He held her leg tight and shook his head emphatically. "Let go!" she snapped.

Perplexed, he let go and she ducked outside.

Confused looks were exchanged among the assembled hunters when Emma rode up on Butternut minutes later. Sun at Midnight handed her a quiver of arrows and one of his best bows. She slung them both across her back. Max was there on his big gelding, grinning at her, ready to join in the hunt. The women began singing a high–pitched tremolo sound. The cry was meant to encourage and cheer the hunters as they rode off to the hunt. The hunters rode north and the women prepared to follow to butcher the kill, readying pack horses and travois to haul the expected meat and hides.

Emma felt exhilarated when they came upon the great beasts grazing in a shallow defile about three miles from camp. She had seen small herds of buffalo in Kansas, but since her family did not need them for food, her father would warn them off with a blast or two from a shotgun and they would scatter. He considered them a nuisance since they trampled or ate their crops.

Sun at Midnight explained the strategy of the hunt as they dismounted. She was to stay at the rear and up on the ridge while the experienced hunt-ers drove the beasts into a dry wash beneath them on the valley floor, trap-ping them. The hunters moved along the ridge, quick and quiet. Then the shooting began. The beasts milled around several minutes, confused and unaware of what was happening.

But the buffalo were not easy to kill. Emma was midway up the ridge, stationed behind a boulder, flanked by Sun at Midnight and Max Cody, watching where the shots were aimed. She had never killed anything this large and doubted her skill.

"I've shot rabbits and squirrels up close—buffalo are big, but they're far away," she remarked.

Max encouraged her. "Just aim for the heart like you practiced with the targets. You can do this."

"You have an awful lot of faith in me!" she chuckled.

As the buffalo were killed, they did not scatter. In the distance, she saw that a small daring band of mounted hunters had formed up in front of the herd. The old bull who determined the herd's direction had been felled first, effectively confusing the rest. Arrows whistled, slicing the air. Many buffalo fell from a single arrow to the heart. Emma shot a few arrows, missing her target of a young bull. Determined not to embarrass Sun at Midnight after his weeks of training, she took her time and aimed, missing again. On her sixth try, her arrow struck the bull in the hindquarters and it fell on its side with a loud snort in a cloud of dust, but rose back to its feet quickly. With another arrow ready, she held her breath and aimed for the heart. She let the arrow go and the bull fell on its side, struggled a moment then lay still. Sun at Midnight and Max grinned. She returned the smiles, proud of herself.

When the hunters decided that there was enough meat, the remaining buffalo were herded off. The women arrived soon after, taking care of the slaughter and loading the meat and hides onto pack horses and travois. Even dogs were outfitted with small travois fitted to their backs. Only blood and entrails were left on the ground. Buzzards circled high on the thermals, waiting for the Cheyenne to depart so they could begin their grisly feast.

Emma was given the tail of the buffalo she had killed, a coveted prize. She proudly rode into camp at twilight with the hunting party. Shea came out of the lodge and watched her ride past. His expression was sullen.

Sun at Midnight jumped down from his pony and told Shea how Emma had killed her first buffalo with only two arrows—quite a feat for a beginner. He said that he was proud to be the one who taught her to use the bow. Ordinarily, this was something to celebrate, but Shea looked past his cousin, shot Emma a withering look and stomped away.

Emma dismounted and saw to Butternut, then went to find Shea. He was walking far from camp when she spotted him and ran to catch up. Her back was aching from hours in the saddle. "Shea! Shea! Please—stop! Damn it, Shea! Stop!"

He was stubborn and kept moving until his legs went rubbery and weak and he could not catch his breath.

She came up beside him at last, breathing hard. "I should've told you, but you're not interested in anything I do or say anymore." His face was stone, but she read his thoughts. "I'm not trying to show you up. You can't hunt until you're stronger. Have I made you feel less than a man since you were hurt? Huh? I'm trying to take some of the pressure off you—I am trying to help. You'll be well someday and back on the hunt." He turned his back to her. "Answer me! Have I made you feel less of a man?" After a long moment, he shook his head no. "Then, why do you treat me like I'm so unimportant? Can you do something other than be mad at me all the time? Try being nice to me for a change and see what happens. It will be something new you can try!" He refused to look at her. "Well maybe I should take Adam up on his offer!" The words tumbled from her mouth, unleashing all the anguish that she had buried. "He wanted to take me away from all this!" She flung her arms around, indicating the camp, this life—him. "And let me tell you, I thought about it!"

For many moments they stood apart in silence. Fatigue dragged at her voice as she came around to face him.

"I didn't mean that how it came out. Shea, if I had any feelings for Adam, I would've never come back to you. I wanted to rebuild our lives because I thought we were worth it. But I'm not sure of anything anymore. I do love you and we need each other if we're going to get through this. If you don't want to bother, fine!" She waited for a response, got none, and watched his face expectantly. "What is it I've done?" she shouted, then her breath caught in her throat. "You blame me for everything, right?"

His accusative look made Emma step away from him. After a moment, he nodded.

The silent indictment sank in. When she finally spoke, she fought to keep her shattered emotions under control. "So we come to it at last. I was right all these months. Why didn't you just come out and tell me, so I could leave you for a good reason?" Emma felt something break inside, shards of glass cutting from within. She backed away from him. "I—I should—I understand—all right then." She turned from him and walked away.

Shea watched her go. The damage he had done was irreparable. He regretted it now, but it was too late to stop the new torment that he had inflicted upon her. He wanted to hurt someone—she just happened to be in the line of fire—again.

When he returned home, Emma was gone. Her few possessions were missing and when he checked the corral, her horse was not there. Panic gripped him. She had come through on her threat to leave him. He mounted his pony and rode out of camp. Every eye in camp watched him go. He had not ridden since the ambush and was in terrible pain, but he dug deep for the strength. He picked up her trail at last. She was heading northeast, he knew, to Adam and Fort Keogh. Despite lingering feelings of anger, he could not bear the thought of Adam consoling her and taking her away from him.

He kept on her trail as night overtook the sky. She had gotten far ahead of him and was pushing her already exhausted mare hard. He kicked his pony to a fast trot. Many emotions moved through him—first regret, then gut–twisting guilt for hurting her so needlessly. He really could not blame her for being angry. The ambush confirmed one thing: He could not protect her from people like Tyler and it was destroying him and his love for her. She would always be an outsider among the Cheyenne, but his possessiveness was so strong that it had begun to coil and contort into something bordering on a sickness of mind. He would never forget the look of betrayal on her face this day. He thought about all she had been through in the past year and believed that she was over it. He had depended on her strength to somehow pull him through his anguish. He now realized she had no strength left.

The last bit of light faded from the sky. He finally spotted her heading up the ridge that marked the border of the reservation. He spurred his pony and caught up with her.

When she heard his approach, she tried to urge Butternut on, but the mare was beyond tired and stumbled. Resigned to one last showdown, she pulled up the horse, dismounted, and waited for him.

He found her sitting atop a promontory on a large boulder with her back to the huge valley below. The deepening blue sky framed her and a shaft of light lit her auburn hair, making it look like fine, shimmering silk.

Although she was expecting him, she jumped when he came into view, so quiet had been his approach. She would not meet his eyes. He cautiously came nearer, hunkered down, and nervously plucked at some tall grass sticking out of patchy snow that remained.

"Sorry, Emma," he croaked, his voice thin and strained. It felt as if his throat were tearing to shreds with each syllable. The pain made his head swim.

She turned toward him, at the first words that he had uttered in months. Her face was pale in the dying light and her eyes were swollen and red. He was shocked at the change in her features. She was closed, lost, hard. He came closer. "Emma? It is not safe out here." His throat burned horribly, but he continued to try to talk after several attempts to swallow.

Her voice showed how overburdened and tired she was. "You don't want me. You blame me for everything."

"No!" His voice choked off and he ate a handful of snow to wet his dry, sore throat. "I did not mean it."

She made no move. "Cheer up. I'm giving you what you want. I am leaving you. Why would you want to live with someone that you despise?"

His voice failed him for several moments. He knelt before her and shook his head, his eyes pleading with her. He held her wrists in his hands, tugging gently. He flicked his head to indicate that they had to go.

"No. You're right. I'm responsible for the deaths of all those people the day of the ambush. I'm responsible for you getting hanged. I'm responsible for Red Leaf's death, too. Adam was right. I should've never come back."

He pulled her to her feet. His voice was strained beyond his capacity for pain. "Do not hate you. Do not go! I love you! It was me. I understand now." His voice was in shreds. He pulled her to him and kissed her, holding her close. She did not resist, nor did she welcome it. Her lips did not soften against his like they once had. He felt how cold she was and tried to share his warmth in the embrace, but she pulled away.

"Your voice is back. I'm glad for that, at least," she said, "but we can't go back to the way things were. I won't do it. We have to stop looking for blame and get on with this marriage, otherwise, there's no reason for me to stay." She sighed and rubbed her eyes, sore from tears. "After all I went through at Fort Robinson—all I endured to keep your secrets! And you have the nerve to blame me for the act of a crazy man!"

He remained mute under her anger. Her losses and pain were fully exposed, combined with the lingering terror of Tyler's ambush. She could endure no more. Seeing her so lost and hurt finally got through; he realized his depth of love for her.

"What are we going to do?" She took a deep breath. "And what are we going to do about our child? Will it have parents who hate each other?" He gripped her arms. "Yes, Shea, I'm pregnant. You've been too preoccupied with self–pity to notice. It's due in August or September. You're going to be a father. What do you think about that?" It was not the way she envisioned telling him about the child but she was beyond caring.

Shea looked startled, then his face closed with a frown that had really begun to vex her. The shock of her leaving him with his child growing within her showed how desperate she had become—how far he had pushed her.

"Why did you not tell me?" he managed.

"You've been rotten to live with lately."

He shook his head, his features slack with regret.

"I'm afraid of you," Emma confessed.

He studied her a long time, his hand gripping hers tight. "A child." His voice was only a whisper. He put his arms around her and she slumped against his chest. She had no fight left. "Come," he said. "We will start over, *nameh'o*." He called her his beloved one. With surprising tenderness, he kissed her.

Emma went home to try again.

She made her pregnancy public the next day and Shea redoubled his efforts to heal his mind and body, especially after Little Wolf sought him out, admonishing him to pay proper respect to his wife, who aside from being a teacher, was now honored as a hunter.

"She is to be respected, most of all by her husband. When the child comes, do you want it to have a bitter man as a father?"

"I have changed," Shea promised.

"Your voice has returned. Use it to patch up your differences with your wife," Little Wolf advised.

April at last warmed the air and the last of the snow melted in this high country. The warmer days agreed with Shea and he worked hard to heal the breach with Emma. He would do whatever was necessary to have her love him as she did before.

He was stronger now, riding farther each day and joining in the hunt when he could. He had managed to eat solid foods and Emma made sure the meat was well stewed so he could chew and swallow. He was gaining weight and although his clothes flapped around his thin frame, he stood straighter and looked upon his wife with renewed affection and respect. The people in camp exerted steady pressure on Shea to fix the problems between them.

At the spring feast Shea recited his coup, as the other warriors did, according to tradition. He then praised Emma for her skill in the hunt and his joy for their long–awaited child. As Shea spoke, he could not take his eyes from Emma. Even she had to admire the change in his manner and his re-commitment to the marriage. To him, she was indeed extraordinary, not only in her simple beauty, but also in her courage. He reproached himself for not seeing it all this time and vowed to treasure her as long as he lived and be a devoted father to his child.

That night, and for the first time since December, he made love to Emma. Her longing for him was again as powerful as it had been in the beginning, a memory she cherished and had conjured more than once to get through the last few months.

Shea's spirit was revived and he now rode with the hunters all day without tiring. He could not lift the larger prey, so the other braves helped. Acknowledgment of his wife's hunting prowess and his survival at the hands of Tyler's men elevated him to the status reserved for soldier chiefs and wise ones. He accepted the help and always gave a portion of his kills to those who assisted him and to families in need. At last, he learned that pride was not arrogance.

Adam arrived with a supply train in late April. The problems between Emma and Shea seemed to be working themselves out. It pained him to see her happy in this existence but he had to admit that they were good together. But he still ached to take her away. When Shea announced that he was to be a father, Adam did a good job of acting surprised and said he was happy that Shea's voice had returned. Emma's breath caught in her throat when she noticed the searching look Adam gave her whenever Shea looked away.

Shea had a council meeting and entrusted Emma to Adam's care for the afternoon. It was risky, but he felt secure that he had Emma's heart and she would not run away with Adam. He had to allow both of them to resolve the undeniable feelings that existed between them.

"How are you feeling?" Adam asked as they strolled around the camp.

"I'm fine. Shea's happy about the baby."

"Are you happy, Emma?" he asked.

"My life is going to change forever when the baby comes. I have to focus on that. Things with Shea are moving along, but we have a long way to go."

"So you won't be taking me up on my offer."

"I was tempted." She smiled at him. "Yours was the finest offer from the finest man I've ever known." Adam was deflated, but managed to smile at the compliment. "Shea's getting better and we're getting closer, I think. He's trying. I'm trying."

They had walked far from camp to a stand of white birches. Adam stopped and faced her.

"Can you tell me you truly love him after all he put you through?" He touched the brown shadowy scar inflicted by his bullet which still showed on her soft cheek. His arm slipped around her waist and he bestowed a tender, lingering kiss. He nuzzled her neck and she felt a thrill shoot through her, but she pulled away.

"Adam—no," she said, breathless. "We can't. I can't do this."

"I'm sorry—sorry." He straightened. "That was out of line. Just lost my head for a minute."

"Adam," she began.

"I understand. I won't ask you anymore." He fumbled to remove a scrap of paper from his pocket. "Emma, there's a purpose to my coming today. Next week, I'm being transferred to Washington D.C., to the Bureau of Indian Affairs." Emma's eyes welled up. This was good–bye. "If there's ever a time you need anything—anything," he emphasized, "write me at this address." She clutched the paper. "Considine recommended me for the post and I can't refuse. It's something I've always wanted. I can make a difference there, I know I can." He fell silent seeing the tears in her eyes. He drew her to him and embraced her.

She stepped back from him, her eyes betraying her feelings for him. "You have no idea how much I'll miss you, Adam."

His eyes drank in her lovely face. "You'll never look at me like that again, will you?" he said.

He cherished every moment he spent with her that day, storing it away in his heart. Despite her decision to remain with Shea, he read her emotions on her face. When she was around him she softened, her colour was high, and she smiled easily. He would conjure these memories often in the future.

Shea took Adam's leaving with a mixture of sadness and respect for his friend. Adam's ideals were too lofty, but Shea knew that he had to try. But he was relieved that Adam would not be around to entice Emma to leave him. He was still jealous, but he would miss Adam nonetheless. He had been a good friend and had saved his life and Emma's.

When he and Shea exchanged farewells that day, Shea spoke. "Good–bye, Adam. I owe you the lives of my wife and child, and my own. I will never forget all you have done."

They shook hands, then Adam mounted his horse. Emma came beside Shea. "Take care of her. You're very lucky, my friend." Adam rode away, looking back once, savoring a last look at his friend and the extraordinary young woman standing beside him.

Shea kept to himself for several days and Emma did not intrude. Shea knew that he would never see Adam again.

In her heart, Emma took Adam's leaving very hard and she endeavored not to show it to Shea. She relished his kiss and his tenderness that day in the stand of birches. With only Shea in her life, the loss of her parents, Red Leaf Woman, and now, Adam, weighed on her, but she was determined to rebuild her life and deliver a healthy child.

There was no further trouble on the reservation as spring made the prairie blossom with acres of wildflowers. Emma and Shea had peace between them at last and his stamina increased. He made love to her often, but mindful of the baby, his former energies were suppressed.

"How long can we keep doing this?" he asked one night.

Emma shrugged. "For as long as we can," she smiled, radiant.

He pulled her nude body to his and made love to her.

Afterwards, he said, "Emma, I am not sure we should stay here and raise the child. I have seen too many children maimed, starved, and killed. I grieved for every one of them, but they were never my children. I cannot condemn our child to life on the reservation."

Emma looked at him in disbelief. "What are you saying?"

"We should leave as soon as we can. We should go west or north to Canada. We have to find a place where we can live away from everyone, someplace where we can raise the child in peace. He will be mostly of white blood and he should live in the white world."

Emma was stunned. Shea would leave his people—his life—behind for the love of an unborn child. But the thought of a long, perilous journey alarmed her. "Shea, are you sure—absolutely sure?"

He kissed her. "This child will be more than I ever could be. I must give him every chance. Are you strong enough for the journey?"

"If you want this, Shea, I will go without complaint," she assured him, a tear tracing her cheek.

Shea held Emma and his unborn child close. The most important event of his life drove this fateful decision. He must risk taking his wife and unborn child into the wilderness to an unknown place, an unknown future. He must leave his tribe forever to give his child a chance. He had to redeem himself in his wife's eyes after a very sorrowful and turbulent year. The need was strong for him to return Emma to the white world in some fashion. Life with the Cheyenne would only become more difficult for her and the child. He could not bear the thought of her hating him if she stayed on the reservation for the rest of her life. Fate had drawn them together and pulled them apart.

The pieces must be put aright in her world, not his. He now understood why his father had left so long ago.

Early May was the time for their leaving. The lower trails were at last cleared of snow, but some were still treacherous and muddy. The weather had turned rainy as spring struggled in this cool country.

Emma feared for the child should she meet with illness or accident along the way but she steeled her nerves against such thoughts. Shea was demonstrating his abiding love for her and the child and the consequence was that he had to leave his people forever. In moments alone, she wept when she thought about what they were facing. Nevertheless, preparations were made. Their only plan was to head northwest.

To disguise himself on the journey, Shea would wear the men's clothing that Peter had given to Emma at Fort Robinson. He stuffed his hair up into a hat, effectively transforming himself into a white settler. Emma was unprepared for this demonstration of devotion to her and the child. He also said that he would use his given name of Shea Russell, fearing that their real surname would alert people who may have read Cody's articles. Emma agreed and they rehearsed a concocted story should anyone ask about their hometown, destination, and such. They were taking no chances.

A few days before they were to leave, Emma and Little Fox rode out to a trading post near Fort Keogh. With money from her tin, Emma purchased a tent, two used riding saddles and had both of their horses shod. If Emma and Shea intended to be settlers, they could not use the Cheyenne saddles and blankets on their horses. She had also purchased clothing for Shea, dry goods, and other supplies for the journey.

Shea had been retraining his horse because it was 'Indian broke,' meaning that Indian ponies accepted riders from the right side. Horses trained by whites received riders from the left side. This was another detail that he would not leave to chance. Any white would question his method of mounting his horse from the right. Shea's pony snorted and protested the unfamiliar handling but soon became used to it.

Good-byes were made and there was wailing among the women and children, contrasted with a profound silence among the men. Little Wolf came as they were about to leave early in the morning and bade them a safe journey. Shea and Little Wolf faced each other for the last time. Little Wolf at length nodded, acknowledging that he understood Shea's reasons for leaving. He regretted losing a good hunter and proven warrior. Little

Fox gave Emma a bundle of baby clothes that she had fashioned out of her own clothing and soft buckskin. Emma wept and hugged her, her memory drifting back to the day that she met her and Porcupine Girl. As Emma and Shea rode away, they knew that they would never see the Cheyenne again.

Emma and Shea had never discussed where they planned to settle, but he assured her that they would know the place. Trusting Shea's instincts, she allowed fate and his innate sense of direction to determine the outcome of a very perilous journey.

When they had lost sight of the camp, Emma asked, "Shea, you've never said, I mean, since you're going to pass for white, are you going to live as one wherever we end up?"

He gave considerable thought to the question. "If it is safer for our child that people think I am white, then I will live as one. I have denied that part of my blood all my life, but I want our child to know his ancestors and the proud family he comes from. But if I can live as a Cheyenne, I will."

The journey began easily enough and the weather held fair, but the nights were very cold. Shea often woke during the night to make sure that Emma was warm and comfortable and so far, she felt fine. Her back ached from riding all day, but as promised she did not complain. She worried over her condition, but looked forward to a new place where they could begin again. Granted, she did not know if they would settle in Canada or somewhere in Idaho, Washington or Oregon, but a part of her was excited and hopeful to find the peace that she craved lay somewhere west of the high mountains they must somehow cross.

The small tent that Emma had bought provided good shelter. Game was plentiful on the eastern slope of the Rockies and Emma and Shea picked early berries, drying them to eat later. As they surveyed the gray wall of the Rockies that stretched from horizon to horizon, they headed for a pass that Shea knew.

At night, Shea would lie next to Emma for hours, feeling the baby's movements, utterly fascinated. She was nearing her sixth month and Shea still wanted her, but he did not penetrate too far. Despite the risks of their journey, Emma was curiously happy.

Along the way, they met many others heading west and were persuaded to join a small wagon train after camping with them for a few days. Emma was glad to be off the horse to rest and the women made a terrific fuss over her. To them, she was Mrs. Shea Russell from Ohio and she and her husband were heading to family in Oregon.

Shea kept to himself, keeping his hat on to disguise his long hair, which he refused to cut, but earned the respect of the men for he felled large antelope and deer with expert aim. More than once, his Indians skills were unwittingly praised. He could spot water from a great distance and had an uncanny sense of direction. He could read the weather, particularly one afternoon when he persuaded the wagon master to take shelter in a draw when the sky turned yellow–gray and threatening. It was worth the detour. A violent thunderstorm marched across the prairie and several tornadoes were spotted in the distance.

Since Shea's injuries of the previous summer had kept him indoors, his tan had faded some and it would be hard to spot him as an Indian. His blue eyes, wool britches, homespun shirt, suspenders, and hat, which was discreetly tied around his chin all the time, hid his true identity. But the boots he had bought with Emma's money at an outpost pained him. Each night when he came inside the tent, he could not pull them off fast enough. He also kept a bandanna tied around his neck to hide the scars from the hanging and since most men wore them, no one questioned it.

Emma enjoyed the weeks with the people of the wagon train and Shea knew that he had made the right choice, especially when he saw her chatting with the other women. She blossomed around her own people, bravely stepping back into her world.

They stayed with the wagon train for the perilous trip over the mountain passes, slick with mud, making the toughest part of the journey much easier. Emma refused to ride in the wagons, despite admonishments from the other women. She preferred to ride beside Shea. They were together and they were happier than in many months. Butternut proved a dependable and sure–footed animal and her courage grew from the animal's solid ride. After the trip over the pass, the train was heading south to California. Emma was sad to see them leave. As parting gifts, some women had given her clothing for herself, Shea, and the baby, along with food, which she gratefully accepted.

Alone now, Emma and Shea turned northwest. The lush Cascade range beckoned in the distance. June brought fair weather, marred by brief but heavy downpours. In the valleys below, meadows were greening and wildflowers sprang up everywhere, sweetening the air. Sometimes at night, the rain turned to snow in the high country, but did not settle. As they ascended the range, Emma was awed by the thick woods blanketing the foothills. Alder, spruce, and aspen grew wild among evergreens that grew to dizzying heights. It looked impenetrable, a wall of green. Emma felt safe with the lush green all around her, like a blanket on a cold night.

She had made no mention of whether they should stop, but they must for the baby was due soon. She wanted to be settled someplace as soon as possible, for her back had become a misery to her. However, she kept her promise and did not complain, deferring to Shea's judgment. They pressed on. They soon descended into a wide valley that stretched before them as far as they could see. They kept to the heights above, its slopes thick with pine and silvery blue spruce. Evidence of habitation was seen in the denuded slopes here and there from logging operations, but they had met no one and seen no towns. Traveling was slow, for the hills were rocky. They had to lead their horses over the rougher going.

Fortunately, for her strength was deserting her, they came upon a small cabin. It was situated high above the valley floor and surrounded on three sides by thick stands of Douglas fir. Shea hid Emma in the trees with the horses and cautiously approached the cabin. After a few minutes looking inside and out, he satisfied himself that the cabin was deserted. Needing rest, Emma was grateful when Shea told her they would stay for a few days. Besides, heavy rains had soaked them for days and Shea had developed a deep, rasping cough that worried her.

The little cabin was well built of huge logs with an overhang across the front to provide shade from the sun, for the dwelling faced full south. It was surprisingly clean and well kept. There was a large fireplace built of stone, two sleeping chambers, and a spacious main room in the center. The cabin had real glass windows, too, something Emma now considered a luxury after living in windowless lodges. There was a dry sink and stove along one wall of the center room. She was also pleased to find a well–stocked cupboard containing pots, pans, and tableware. A table with four chairs and a rocker near the fireplace completed the room. Judging from the tools that hung on the walls, this was someone's hunting cabin. A lean–to out the back was just large enough to shelter the horses and an outhouse was tucked under a huge fir tree. There was also a well with sweet water.

They settled into the cabin and Emma slept in a bed for the first time since Fort Robinson.

Mere days after their arrival, Shea collapsed with a high fever. His cough was coarse and dry. Emma insisted that he take to bed, which he did, after stubbornly arguing that he was fine. Although she was nearing her eighth month and very tired, she managed to look after him. Shea battled fever for several days. Taking the revolver with her, she explored the area and found a shallow stream just down the hill in front of the cabin. At least she could put fresh fish on the table. She fashioned a crude fishing pole out of a stick and a length of rope and used a hairpin for a hook.

Shea's fever finally broke, but his cough lingered. He did not rebound very quickly. Emma never voiced her fears that his injuries from last year were responsible. She spent much time with him reading aloud the few books she had with her (that did not have pages ripped out), although Shea seemed to enjoy her company more than the stories.

For two weeks he rarely left the cabin and stayed in bed for most meals. His cough lost that dry rasp and soon he seemed stronger, able to chop wood and tend the mule and horses. However, when his chores were finished, he often returned to bed. They lived on the foodstuffs they brought with them, along with fish caught from the stream and small game that Emma got with the bow. Shea was now thankful that Emma had learned to use it. Gunshots would only alert anyone in the area to their presence. He did not have the strength or enough ammunition to fight back if there were trouble. The woods were thick with deer and wild fowl, but Shea's stamina in the chase was not what it used to be. It rained a lot, but it was a clean soaking rain and never lasted very long. After it stopped, Emma came into the habit of stepping outdoors to drink in the sweet earthy scents. It was a peaceful place and she liked to listen to the rain drip through the huge trees for hours afterwards. The big firs created a sort of sheltering wall around the little cabin and made Emma feel safe, sheltered, and curiously at ease. This lovely meadow was a temporary home; either they would push on to find a better place, or they would be discovered and have to go. She hoped they would remain undiscovered at least until the birth of the baby.

As Emma carried water from the well one hot morning in July, she saw a lone rider on a narrow twisting trail in the valley below. As fast as her bulk allowed, she retreated to the cabin to alert Shea. His rifle was loaded and in his hand in moments. He watched to see if the rider approached. He did.

The stranger was very tall and broad–chested, with clean–shaven, rugged features and a mass of wavy brown hair worn long. He rode very straight on his large roan mare. His tan shirt was fringed buckskin and he wore high boots and brown trousers. He pulled up the mare a short distance away and called. "Hello! In the cabin!"

Shea hurriedly stuffed his hair up inside his hat and grabbed his rifle. He went to the door and peered out.

The stranger's eyes rested on him for a moment. He raised a hand. "I mean you no harm, sir. I saw the chimney smoke from my logging camp. This is my hunting cabin."

Emma stood behind Shea and peeked out. After placing the loaded rifle just inside the doorway Shea stepped out a pace. "We did not know. We are sorry. We will go."

"No. There's no harm done. I don't . . ." He stopped talking as the heavily pregnant Emma come into view. He stared at her with a peculiar expression. "No need to leave. I don't use this place much anymore. My logging business keeps me in town, besides," he said in deference to her, "I wouldn't throw a pregnant woman out into the wilderness." He smiled cordially and dismounted. He left his horse to graze and came nearer, relaxed and unafraid. "Jason Beck," he said, extending his hand to Shea.

Shea took it, his eyes sharp. Jason's eyebrows lifted while he waited for a response in kind. "Shea Russell. This is my wife, Emma." She stepped forward and accepted Mr. Beck's respectful bow as he shook her hand. "We stopped to rest for her," he said, his eyes never leaving Jason.

"Understandable. Your first?" Jason asked.

Emma nodded with a careful glance to Shea. They appeared both very wary and nervous and this was not lost on Jason.

"I live down there, around the bend in the river," he said, turning and pointing in the distance. "Easthope. It's about four miles north along the river of the same name."

Emma craned her neck to see where Jason had pointed, but Shea's eyes remained fastened on him.

"I haven't used this cabin for a couple of years. I didn't mean to frighten you, ma'am. You and your husband are welcome to stay as long as you like."

Emma's hands went protectively to her swollen belly, but she emboldened herself and asked, "There's a town nearby?" She saw Shea stiffen. He wanted to live away from any towns or settlements and it was obvious that he was uncomfortable with one so near. However, they needed supplies even if they moved on after the birth. She hoped that there was a doctor or midwife in town to help her when the time came. After all the time it took her to get pregnant and the luck of their journey west, she would not risk losing the child now.

"Oh, it's maybe an hour or so. Just take the trail down the hill and hold north along the river road. It's a good road, too. Can't miss it. But stay off the logging roads. There are a lot of them crisscrossing the hills. You can't miss them, either—they're lined with logs. They're dangerous, whatever the season."

Shea looked at Jason assessingly, his face pinched as his mind worked over what to do. To her surprise, he motioned to the cabin. "We are having breakfast. Join us."

Puzzled, Emma led the way. Jason ducked in, following Shea.

Shea needed to know more about this man, although his friendly, open manner had caught him off guard. He was unused to being treated as an equal by whites, despite his disguise.

Jason noticed that Shea kept his hat on inside the house, a strange habit, he thought.

Emma set tin plates on the table and finished making breakfast while Jason and Shea made small talk. Exhibiting an easy manner, Jason seemed friendly and pleasant, but Shea remained on alert.

"How long have you been here, Mr. Russell?"

"A couple of weeks. Emma needed to rest and I was ill from all the rain. We have traveled a long way."

"Yeah, it does rain a lot here. Where are you from?"

"Ohio," Emma cut in as she placed Cheyenne–style bread and hot wheat cereal before them. With a start, her eyes fell upon the bread for it was not baked in a loaf, but wrapped around a stick and baked over an open fire. She prayed that Jason would find nothing unusual in it. He apparently did not. He picked up a piece with a nod of thanks and began to eat.

"I've never been to Ohio, but I hear it's nice. So what brings you way out here to Washington?"

Emma looked to Shea to help on this one. Firstly, they had not realized they were in Washington, they had guessed Oregon. Secondly, saying that they came to see family could get complicated; they were running out of continent.

Shea covered the time needed to fabricate his reply by taking several bites of bread. Jason busied himself with his breakfast as well. Emma and

Shea exchanged a cautious look. Again surprising her, he covered very well.

"We had crop failure on our farm. We sold out and came west, looking for a new place." His explanation sounded too rehearsed and Emma feared that Jason would become suspicious, but he listened with a small smile playing about his lips and a moment later, Emma knew why.

"You don't look like a farmer," he said with a grin as Shea's head snapped up at the comment.

"I have been ill. I told you that." Shea's reply was curt, but for some reason, Jason let it go.

"I've lived here all of my life. My parents came from Minnesota in the late forties. I've traveled around some, to Oregon, California, even Canada. But I like it here best. I can help you find work in town if you want. There isn't much farmland this high up, but maybe I can find someone who can help you out."

Shea's reaction of feigning gratitude would have been almost funny if it were not for the trouble they could have. Jason was treating Shea as white and it unsettled him, but he quickly regained his composure. "We do not know if we will stay. We might go on to Canada."

"Well, I hope you stay. Easthope's a nice town and a good place to raise a child." He twisted around in the chair. "Mrs. Russell, there's a doctor in town if you need to see him. Stuart Barlow." Emma acknowledged this, saying thank you, but committed to nothing.

Jason talked about his logging business for a while and at length pulled out his pocket watch, announcing that he had better head home. He rose and again shook Shea's hand and bowed to Emma. "Fine breakfast, ma'am. Thank you both very much." He walked outside as Emma and Shea exchanged several meaningful looks, each trying to wordlessly communicate with the other.

Jason found his horse nearby, a well–trained animal, Shea admired. "Stay as long as you want," he said, mounting the big mare. "There are a few bears up here and the occasional mountain lion, but we've never had an attack. There are a few wolves in the area, too. Give them a wide berth. Bury your garbage and keep a sharp eye and you should be all right." He looked to Emma. "Dr. Barlow is in the three–storey red brick building attached to the hospital in town if you need him. I know him well, so I could convince him to come here, to save you the trip."

"We will remember that, Mr. Beck," Shea answered.

"Call me Jason. I'm in the area a few days a week, so I'll look in on you again." Emma nodded, bewildered by this big, amiable man. He took up the reins to depart, but hesitated with a smile that Emma caught earlier. "I tell you, I never expected Shea and Emma Hawkshadow would end up living in my hunting cabin." They exchanged shocked looks, but Jason spoke quickly. "Please don't be frightened. I'll tell no one that you're here. Easthope is a small town and the people, you'll find, very tolerant. I'm pleased to have met you both." He kicked his horse and trotted away down the grassy slope in front of the cabin and disappeared below the hill with a wave.

In front of the cabin Emma sat upon a fallen tree trunk that served as a bench under a fir tree contorted by the winds. "My God!" she exclaimed. "He knows who we are!" Shea stood like stone watching where Jason had gone. "How?"

He shot a keen look at her. "Max Cody."

"I hadn't realized those stories made the papers way out here. I thought that Cody worked with papers back east."

Shea stood, arms folded, his expression wary. No longer was it just himself and Emma. With an infant coming any day, they could not disappear in the night. Jason had guessed who they were right away. Jason had even offered him work knowing that he was a Cheyenne. This mystified Shea and he did not know if he should fear or trust him. He had been set up before.

"What should we do, Shea?" Emma asked, her eyes appealing to him. "He could tell others, despite what he said. Should we go?" Jason seemed nice and helpful, true, but Emma knew full well that people often appeared one way and acted another. She could not think what to do, depending on Shea to make the decision. She hoped that her instincts about Jason were right and he would tell no one, but what would they do if other people rode by? She felt anxious for the unborn child, fearing that something terrible might happen. "Do you think Jason meant it—about letting us stay here a while?"

"Probably. But if he found us, others will, too." He sat beside her, his mind working. "I do not think he means us any harm. I am not sure I trust him after only one visit. I am not used to trusting whites. We will have to be careful."

Emma tried to lighten his mood. "You trust me," she said smiling and slipping her arm around him. "He seems nice enough. And besides, you still need rest and the baby's due soon. This may be a good place to stay until then. And if Jason's right, maybe you can drop your disguise, you think?"

"Okay, we will stay as long as there is no trouble. I have the rifle in case and I want you to keep the revolver with you." He left the sentence unfinished.

As they sat in the sun, Shea placed his hand on her stomach. "He is active today."

"She," Emma playfully corrected.

Shea smiled in spite of his growing worry, but in his mind, he played out scenarios if he had to defend them.

They sat in the sun on that hot July day, contemplating the decision to remain and the unexpected, affable Jason Beck.

Chapter Eleven

Jason returned to the cabin a week later pulling a pack horse laden with dry goods, clothing, meat, fresh milk, butter, and eggs. As he rode closer, he watched Shea with an almost comical expression. Shea had not worn his hat that day. Jason took in his long thick hair, worn in braids, Cheyenne–style, but did not comment as he dismounted near the cabin.

Shea tried to turn down Jason's generous cargo out of pride, but gave in when he saw how happy Emma was as she surveyed the packages, her face flushed with delight. Inside the cabin she unwrapped a package of baby clothes, admiring them.

With an embarrassed blush, Jason said, "These were mine when I was young. They're a little old–fashioned, but I thought they might fit the baby." Another bundle held women's and men's clothing, old, but made of very good fabric. "These belonged to my mother and father. They're both gone now, so someone might as well have the use of them. You might be able to use the material."

"This is very generous of you, Mr. Beck. Some of the shirts will fit Shea, as soon as he gains back some weight! He's so thin!" she joked.

Jason had also brought fresh beefsteaks, a delicacy to Emma, and he accepted her invitation to remain for supper.

Emma was glad for the material, for she had no maternity clothes and no dresses left that fit. Her meager sewing skills would be put to the test. Her breasts had swelled along with her belly in the final months and she had to wear most of her dresses partially unbuttoned, which embarrassed her, and with about five weeks left, she knew that she would grow much larger.

Jason and Shea talked at the table as Emma waddled around the cabin preparing perhaps the finest supper that they had eaten in years. The smell of the streaks frying made Emma think of the sod house and of how much her life had changed in so short a time. She carried her parents' grand-child—a child they would never know. She held back tears at the thought and returned to cooking supper.

Cornbread and potatoes baked upon the hearth alongside a pot of coffee. Shea glanced at the pot again and again. He loved coffee.

"How did you know that we were still here?" Shea asked, still guarded around Jason.

"I can see the chimney smoke from logging Camp Three. I figured that you'd at least stay until the child was born, so I took a chance and brought you a few things you might need after your long journey." His manner and words were simple and without pretense.

"Have you told anyone that we are here?"

"Not a soul. I'll tell no one unless you say it's okay."

Emma's head turned slightly, for on some level she did not yet understand, her instincts about Jason were correct.

"The entire town read Cody's articles about you, me included. It was the topic of conversation for weeks." Shea flinched, obviously disliking the fact that he and Emma were unwilling celebrities. "If you need supplies, I don't see any reason why you can't come to town. We have a lot of Indians around here. There's a small reservation of Yakima nearby. Many work for me at my logging camps. Things are different in Easthope. Winters are harsh and the summers are short. If we don't help one another, we don't survive up here. The nearest town is Millersburg, fifteen miles away. Millersburg has a train depot, so that's how we get goods shipped up here. If you decide to come to town, just let me know and I'll take you," Jason offered.

Shea knew that Emma should see the doctor before the birth, but he was afraid of what might happen should their appearance in town cause a problem.

Jason sat back as Emma poured coffee for them all and took her seat at the table.

"It has been a long time since I have had real coffee. I wish that I could pay you," Shea said, dropping a hint to Emma that she should offer him some money from her tin. He had told her long ago that he felt no right to it. It belonged to her.

Emma picked up the hint. "Mr. Beck, we have some money put by. Please, we must pay you for the things you brought us and for staying here."

Jason shook his head, liking her soft drawl. "Everything I brought is meant as a gift. And paying rent isn't necessary, either."

Emma smiled and Shea was letting down his guard.

Dinner was quiet while the steaks were devoured, along with the cornbread and baked potatoes. It was not an awkward silence. A bond was developing between them, Emma could feel it.

Jason smiled and leaned back in his chair. "Another fine meal, Mrs. Hawkshadow."

Emma jumped a little, for few had ever addressed her as such. She had become used to answering to Mrs. Russell.

"I hope I didn't alarm you last week, but your names are well known. I knew who you were right off. And, Shea, your accent gave you away some."

Shea looked at Jason, trying to reconcile this man, the only non–judgmental white man that he had known besides Adam. He smiled, understanding Jason's comment about his accent which he had endeavored to cover.

"Well, I'd better head home. Thank you again for a fine meal. Is there anything I can bring you next time?"

"No, Mr. Beck, thank you all the same. You've already done so much," Emma said.

"Please call me Jason." His green eyes sparkled as he smiled at her.

"Emma," she allowed.

Jason came again later that week, again bringing dry goods and other small comforts, blankets, lamp oil, and many tools, which he said he no longer needed. Shea accepted them with gratitude, especially the nearly new ax, which replaced his worn hatchet. Wanting to try it out, he left, taking the rifle with him, leaving Emma and Jason alone. As usual, she asked him to stay and eat, an invitation he accepted and a courtesy Emma was glad to extend.

She poured coffee for them. "Jason, you said that you own the lumber business in town?"

"Yes. I inherited it from my father. My brother Karl is a silent partner. He lives in Tacoma, so we don't see each other much." He then asked, "Does Shea need a job? I'd be happy to set him up."

"No, Jason, thanks. I don't know how long we'll be staying after the baby comes."

Jason let the subject drop, so began telling her about the business, but it sounded almost like a confession. Beck Lumber sustained the town exclusively. Virtually everyone he met on the street worked for him or in some business related to or dependent upon his own. He felt pressured to behave like a figurehead, which distanced him from the townsfolk. What went unspoken was his ease around Emma and Shea; with them he could let down his guard. They wanted nothing from him but acceptance and the things that he did for them were appreciated.

"Tell me, does anyone else know that we're up here? I mean, have you heard any talk in town?" Emma said, breaking eggs in a frypan.

"I haven't told anyone. Why? Has someone come here?"

She was mindful not to offend. "No. But it worries Shea. He doesn't trust many people, especially whites, with the exception of you and me and a friend he had who was in the army. He keeps that rifle loaded and near him all the time and I always carry the revolver."

"Well, I suppose that some people have been wondering where I've been going off to, but I'll keep it a secret for as long as I can. Few people ever come up this way and that's why I chose this spot to build this hunting cabin."

"Jason, since you won't take money, is there anything we can do to repay you? I could do mending or laundry, ironing." She trailed off, realizing that he had never revealed anything personal. "I'd like to do something, but if your wife objects, then—"

He replied, "There is no need to repay me." Emma smiled at him in thanks. "If I hear of anything brewing in town, I'll be up here to warn you, but I doubt anything will happen. This isn't that kind of place, my father saw to that, but that's another very long story."

Emma pursued her earlier comment. "Are you married, Jason?"

He grinned, suddenly nervous and shy, a boyish blush colouring his cheeks. "No."

"How come?" she asked with a grin.

His blush deepened and he seemed to find the table top very interesting. "I just never found the right woman. Of course, all the old biddies in town seem to have an endless supply of daughters, sisters, and nieces to introduce me to, but honestly, so many of them are looking for nothing more than to marry well. I'm considered a catch," he said with a nervous chuckle. "I'm twenty–six, unmarried, and make a good living; that's very attractive to a young girl wanting a husband. Some people figure I'm holding out or that there's something wrong with me." He spoke simply and without guile, but he was very self–conscious, shifting in his seat.

"You seem perfectly normal and nice to me," she giggled. "Don't let them push you into something that you're not ready for. If it's meant to be, you'll know. I grew up in a sod house in Kansas with very few prospects as far as education and marriage. I imagined my life turning out very differently. And look at me now."

They exchanged smiles as she served him scrambled eggs. She accepted his assistance as she settled her bulk into a chair. Emma had kept a discreet distance from Jason and was happy to find a gentle, thoughtful man who stubbornly refused to settle. She liked that about him.

"I've spent my life working in my father's business and when he died a few years back the business was left to me, lock, stock, and lumber. My mother passed on a year later. All I've done since is run the mill and the logging camps, so there has been little time for anything else."

"Do you live in town or in these beautiful hills?"

"In town. I built my own house next to my mother's."

"Why don't you live there? Or was it sold after your parents passed away?"

"No. Closed up the place after my mother died. Too many memories there." He seemed to want to drop the subject.

"I'm sorry," she said. She wanted to know what bothered him about his mother and the house but did not want to pry. Jason would tell her if he wanted her to know. "I was barely seventeen when my parents died. I know what it's like to be alone. Is there any other family besides your brother?"

"No. Just Karl. He's married with four kids already and he's not thirty yet."

"So the children will take over the business someday?"

"My nieces and nephews would have to hire a manager. I doubt any of them would recognize a peavey or know what a quartersaw is. They're city kids."

"Well, I wouldn't know the difference either, but I can use a plow and a butter churn and can slaughter livestock!" She laughed and rose, intending to refill their cups, but Jason's hand on her arm reseated her. She smiled as he poured more coffee for them and resumed his seat. Although Shea was himself again, he had not babied her during the pregnancy. Cheyenne women somehow kept up with their work even when pregnant and worked until their first labor pain, had the baby, then returned to their tasks hardly missing a beat. In a flash of memory, she remembered the young Cheyenne woman who had given birth the night of the outbreak and ran to catch up mere minutes later. No one else thought it unusual. Emma had received the same treatment from Shea and although it did not bother her, a little break from her chores was welcome.

Jason fiddled with his eggs and asked, "How did you meet up with Max Cody?"

She looked away and took breath to speak but hesitated, remembering her interment at Fort Robinson.

He had intruded on private and painful matters and regretted the question, but Emma answered.

"I met Max at Fort Robinson in Nebraska. He'd been sent by our friend in the army, Adam Lawrence, to take me to the Montana reservation to rejoin Shea. During our journey north, I told him all about my life, such as it was. The following autumn, he returned to the reservation and showed us the articles, but I never thought that they'd been printed this far west." Emma felt that she could trust this man with anything.

"Did you know that Cody wrote more articles late last year? He wrote about what that madman tried to do to you and Shea."

"We saw Max this spring and he gave us the clippings. After the ambush, he had a lot to write about."

Jason saw her visibly sadden and wished that he had not pried.

Just then Shea came back, his arms loaded with wood and hefting the ax, nodding his appreciation to Jason. He came to the table while Emma poured him a cup of coffee and served him the rest of the eggs.

During the afternoon, Shea told Jason their reasons for leaving the reservation.

"My child will be part of the white world," Shea said. "We left the reservation to find a place to live in peace. Cody's articles helped us for a while, but after the ambush, everything was clear. Such people might come back again and I could not let my people suffer because of us. We could not remain any longer."

Jason easily accepted the fact that Shea was literate. "I understand. I try to help the Indians in the area. I hate how they're forced to live on the scrap of land granted to them by the government. Their poverty is terrible. The children suffer most. I'm a member of the town assembly so I do all I can, even though my suggestions are sometimes unpopular. If I can't get the townsfolk to help them, I do what I can on my own. It's the least I can do for them."

Shea was impressed with Jason's efforts, hoping that it was not just talk.

Jason spoke to Emma. "The articles said that you were injured while at Fort Robinson."

Emma looked uncomfortable and looked to Shea, whose expression became closed, guarded. Cody had never publicized the rape, but he had mentioned her rough treatment at the hands of a soldier.

"I lived through it."

"I didn't mean to be nosy. I'm awful sorry."

"You're not prying. It was just a dark time—stuck in that place and being apart from Shea. You've been a friend and you deserve to know why we shy away from people and want to live apart."

Shea reentered the conversation. "The day of the ambush in Montana forced me to see the truth in a lot of things. If it had not been for our friend Adam, Emma and I would be dead. Adam sent Tyler to his God with a hole in his head." He paused for breath. Since the hanging, he often became winded when he talked. "I was not myself afterwards but Emma stayed with me and endured my foul temper." He looked into her eyes with a profound look of love and gratitude, moving her. Emma never loved him more than at this moment. The flare of animosity that had sometimes remained between them was finally extinguished that day.

"It's a hard thing to leave your home," Jason said, "but I understand why you want to live away from other people. I can't say that I blame you."

Emma smiled at him and rose to clear away lunch. Automatically, Jason rose to help her, and a second later, a puzzled Shea did as well.

After lunch, Jason produced cigars and Shea showed particular delight in a good smoke. Emma worried about the affect on his throat but seeing his obvious pleasure, kept silent.

Jason departed at dusk and ducked out the cabin door. "I'm sorry if I've caused unpleasant memories for you. My questions were too personal. Chalk it up to my excitement at meeting you two in person."

Emma said, "Other people have been through much worse. We owe you much for allowing us to live in this beautiful meadow."

"It's nice to have a reason to come up here again. I didn't realize how much I missed the quiet up here. I'm glad you like it here as much as I do."

"We do," Shea said, shaking Jason's hand.

Jason mounted his horse. "Shea, you might receive a visit from the Yakima Indians. Their reservation is just south of here and I'm sure they know that you're here. They're peaceful, so don't be afraid if they come."

"We do not want trouble, Jason," Shea said.

"You won't have any," Jason assured him. "I'll see you soon."

As the day cooled and the sun dipped behind the trees, Shea was fatigued and Emma insisted that he rest.

Emma and Shea came to like Jason and looked for him to return, which he did every few days.

Emma's worry over the baby increased as she grew larger and her stomach dropped, a sign, she knew, that the birth was very near. The only way to calm her fears was to see the doctor, but she first had to broach the subject with Shea. Her maternal instincts were powerful and the baby's health uppermost in her thoughts.

"Shea, I should go see that doctor Jason mentioned. I'd feel better if I knew that everything was all right. I know the birth is close. Will you promise to think about it?"

He sat brooding over breakfast. He saw the worry in her eyes and he worried too. He did not commit to anything, but the matter was decided for him later that morning.

Jason arrived bringing fresh milk and eggs. It was a pleasant afternoon, so the two men sat outside on the fallen log outside the cabin while Emma was indoors putting away the food.

"Jason, Emma needs the doctor," Shea began.

Jason's head jerked up. "Is something wrong?"

"She is nervous," he said, unable to voice his own fears. "We do not want to take any chances. We have waited a long time for this."

"We can go now. On the way down we'll pass Camp Three and I'll get a wagon for her. Or if you want, I can have Dr. Barlow up here by nightfall."

Emma overheard them as she came outside. "No, there's no need to bring him all the way up here, Jason. I feel okay, I'd just feel better if I saw a doctor. Could we go today, Shea?"

"Maybe just you and Jason should go."

"No!" she exclaimed. "I want you to be there. Please."

Shea frowned, but grudgingly agreed to come.

Shea prepared to go to town by putting on trousers and a shirt and tucking his long hair up inside a hat. Jason was now accustomed to seeing him bare–chested, wearing only leggings and moccasins with his hair in braids. He hid a smile under his hand when he saw Shea emerge from the cabin. Shea looked visibly uncomfortable in the clothing, and with the heavy boots on his feet, he walked awkwardly. Before they left, Emma produced a bandanna. Shea tied it around his neck to cover the scars from the hanging. Jason's smile faded as Shea completed the disguise.

Emma donned a heavy cotton shawl, knowing that the trip back would be late. The night air was often chilly, but the shawl also covered the back of her dress, left partially unbuttoned due to her bulk. Across her shoulder she carried the buckskin pouch, strung on rawhide, that contained the tin with the money. If their initial visit to town went well, she hoped they might purchase a few supplies. It took both men to get her atop Butternut and she had to assure them she was fine a half–dozen times before they stopped fussing over her.

Shea spoke to Jason out of Emma's hearing. "I left my rifle behind. I do not want to go to town carrying a gun, but I think we are making a mistake. Maybe you could take her."

"I know these people and I don't think they'll be anything more than curious. Besides, you look like a perfect, meek, white settler in those clothes." He laughed aloud and so did Shea.

On the way down the trail, Jason told them the history of the town. Easthope was nestled in the lower valley along a wide sparkling mountain stream. The town's name, Easthope, was his mother Evangeline's maiden name. An isolated logging town in the high mountains of the central Cascade Mountains, it was a new settlement, founded in 1846 by Jason's father, Quincy. He had seen the beauty of the lush mountains, yes, but also the potential for logging and with the stream running through the valley, his entrepreneurial spirit awakened. The river, a clean, clear run off from the high country, was perfect for floating logs to barges, for it joined the great Columbia River many miles away.

In the beginning the town was far from railroad lines, so Quincy built roads that radiated out from the town to link up with established routes, most of them cut by settlers who came through many years before. There was no stopping Quincy Beck when he was determined to do something. Business boomed when the rail lines reached Tacoma.

The town was spread along the bottom of a long, wide, meandering valley, its slopes carpeted thick with Douglas pine, oak, aspen, cedar, and redwood. Hacking the town out of the untouched wilderness was a formidable task, but with the help of his two young sons, Jason and Karl, both born in the 50's, and even his young wife, Evangeline, a town was born.

An intelligent and opportunistic man, Quincy used the labor of the local Yakima Indians who lived on small reservations in the area. Due to the isolation of the town, the Indians made a fair wage and were fairly treated by Quincy Beck. As an incentive, Quincy guaranteed each worker a house built, within certain specifications, after completing five consecutive years of work in the town's sawmill or logging camps. He was motivated by the plight of the native peoples, crammed onto small patches of land almost devoid of game, but he also wanted to guarantee that his workforce would not desert him. They were far from civilization and he needed dependable workers. Labor for each house was shared by all workers, which built an interdependency ensuring that those workers would remain and repay the favor. It worked for the most part; there was a time of peaceful coexistence between the Indians and the few whites in Easthope.

In the 1860's settlers, many lost in the mountains, came upon the small town. Some moved on but some remained, creating a variety of businesses that supported the town. A general store was first, financed and built by Quincy, for an Irish couple and their twelve children. Soon a blacksmith, Elmer Brody and his family, set up shop. Farming was difficult in the hilly terrain, but a few families had been moderately successful. They supplied the town with apples, corn, wheat, and livestock. A veterinarian then settled in Easthope, happy with his monopoly for animal care.

In 1870 Quincy chartered a bank, but did not run it, enticing a young and ambitious, albeit naïve, Jewish man named David Ginsberg, from Massachusetts who passed through town, intending only to winter over. Quincy realized his knack with numbers and persuaded him to remain. A young Presbyterian minister, Frank McCormick from Ohio, passed through town as well and was persuaded to remain after Evangeline entreated Quincy to build a church and meeting hall, financed, of course, by Beck Lumber.

Other businesses followed as more people found Easthope. The town was thriving in its isolation but Quincy had not been able to find a suitable teacher for the children, so he built a large schoolhouse and hired a photographer from Tacoma. He sent the photograph and a letter to colleges in the east, extolling the virtues of his quiet town that was so desperately in need of a teacher. To his astonishment, a young woman riding alone on an exhausted horse arrived one summer afternoon, announcing that she was

Prudence Styler of Danbury, Connecticut, coming to claim the job. She had joined up with a wagon train and trekked across the continent on her sturdy horse. A woman traveling alone was something rarely done even during the mass westward migration of the time. She took great care presenting her diploma, somehow preserved on her long ride across the continent. Impressed with her spunk in undertaking such a journey, Quincy hired her on the spot. She was charmed by the simplicity of the log schoolhouse and set to organizing classes. Jason and Karl were under her tutelage and Jason admitted a boyish crush on her from the start, which kept him motivated and adept at his studies. She was called Miss Prudence and she remained so for many years, despite the best efforts of the loggers who courted her. When Prudence married, it was to the young Jewish man who ran the bank.

Evangeline Beck became the grand lady of Easthope. Always quiet, reserved, dignified, and religious, she became a nurse to the sick and benefactress to those in need. She never tossed her considerable wealth around and chose instead to reinvest it in local businesses and the people with the courage to live in the town. She and the preacher were great friends as well and organized many social events for the town. Despite the fact that few loggers ascribed to any religion, Evangeline, with a light hand, drew many to the church with the soaring ceiling and new organ shipped all the way from Pennsylvania. Jason said that he remembered finding his mother sitting in the church alone on many occasions, basking in the sun streaming through the colored glass windows.

But a very real danger of living in Easthope, Jason warned, were the avalanches that had twice destroyed large parts of the town in just one winter. Small slides still occurred throughout the winter, especially along the steep eastern slopes. Quincy learned where most of the dangerous zones were and forbade building along the avalanche routes. Avalanche bells were installed all over the valley and dogs were trained and kept near the camps to help find victims buried alive under the snow.

Another danger came from white settlers passing through Easthope. Fights occurred, caused by those who took offense at seeing Indians working next to whites at the mill and logging camps. There was a time of considerable trouble between the white and Indian workers at the camps and mills, and fights were frequent in the early 60's. Quincy did what he could to keep the peace and defended the Indians, risking his own life numerous times. He never hired a constable, preferring to mediate these matters himself. This was his town and no one was going to spoil it. With the help of the loggers, troublemakers were run out of town. In the aftermath, Quincy redoubled his efforts to reward his workers and the town as a whole.

Soon, Beck Lumber became a large company, challenging the large mills just north of the border in Canada. Other mills were often bypassed in favor of Beck Lumber. Quincy even initiated a sort of profit–sharing with his workers, white and Indian alike. Fighting soon ceased. It was hard to argue with success.

The main street was just that. All businesses fronted it, with homes radiating out from the road. Mindful of the prevailing winds, Quincy's sawmill was at the far end of town, with three millhouses and several warehouses built along the river, so that barges could be loaded with logs and floated downriver to the Columbia. The lumber was then sold to brokers in Tacoma and Spokane.

In the 1860's smaller towns sprang up nearby, the first being Millersburg in 1862, founded by a big German doctor named Deiter Miller. Jealous of Beck's monopoly on the logging, he set up his clinic in Millersburg, intending to be the area's only physician and surgeon and hoping that people would move to Millersburg, rather than make the fifteen–mile journey from Easthope for medical treatment. However, Easthope lost few families to Millersburg.

Despite jealousy, relations between Deiter and Quincy became more amiable and the two men partnered to build hospitals in both towns along with a good road through the forest to link the towns. Everyone went to Dr. Miller, even the Indians; this unsettled Deiter, until he realized that they had money with which to pay, so he forgot his misgivings.

Millersburg was more refined than Easthope, with better access to the main roads, which allowed more specialized goods to be brought up. Still, Quincy knew that he must partner with the businesses in Millersburg and soon convinced store owners to open shops in Easthope as well. Both towns flourished.

By the time Karl and Jason were old enough and strong enough to work, Quincy set them to task, first in the logging camps, then at the sawmill, before they learned the less exciting financial and management end of the business. His sons would inherit the company and he insisted that they learn from the bottom up to gain full understanding of what the business entailed and what workers endured. He would not let his precious town go to lazy, rich sons who had no idea of the pressures workers faced.

In 1867, Doctor Stuart Barlow, with his wife and seven children, settled in Easthope at Quincy's urging and outright bribery. Dr. Barlow's services were needed in the small town and Quincy showed off the new Easthope Hospital. Dr. Barlow accepted Quincy's promise to build a house large enough for his family as a downpayment for his services. Deiter was glad for the help by then since his practice was too large for one doctor straddling two towns, and since he was not getting any younger. Due to the many accidents that befell workers in such a dangerous business as logging, having a doctor in town was indispensable. There were always some half–dozen woodsmen and mill workers in the hospital, with logging–related injuries. Catastrophic injuries, such as amputations and crushed limbs were becoming less frequent, but in the early years, Dr. Barlow had his hands full. He started a safety council that implemented better working conditions, but despite their efforts, horrible accidents and swift death still befell several men each year.

As Karl and Jason were set to work in the logging camps Quincy noted Karl's disinterest, but kept up the pressure. If Karl did not take to logging, at least he would have a work ethic for another profession. Karl preferred college when the time came, so Quincy sent him to a university in San Francisco. But Jason, the younger, took to the hard work with a sort of benevolent conqueror's zeal. Jason was physically larger than Karl, and grew broad and muscular. He blended in with the other workers, white and Indian alike.

Jason never acted like the owner's son and never suggested that his tenure on the steep slopes was temporary. He learned fast and suffered some injuries, reveling in what he perceived as a great adventure. To the present day, he appeared at the logging camps unannounced, pitching in where needed.

One day when Jason was eighteen, a sluice that sent logs down to the river broke apart. Huge logs rolled down the slope and Jason, as well as many others, was in their path. He pushed everyone to safety and paid for it by colliding with a log that rendered him unconscious for two days. He soon returned, ax in hand, ready to begin again. He loved his work in the cool, beautiful mountains. He convinced his father to begin replanting efforts on denuded slopes, astutely arguing that the land must keep producing to keep the business running. Little could deter Jason and in that way he was like his father.

Karl remained in San Francisco after college, working odd jobs, while Jason remained in Easthope. Jason worked every day on the slopes, despite his father's decree that the eighteen–year–old would now learn the sawmilling and business end of the lumber trade. It was hard for Jason to leave the cool, shady hills and the camaraderie of the men, but he reluctantly moved to the mill, where most of the white men worked.

But when he became bored with the tedium of the books, he could be seen at the camps, chopping and sawing, delighting in the sweat and his sore muscles at day's end. One day at the sawmill, a new worker who did not know who Jason was picked a fight with him in the yard during a lunch break, trying to establish dominance over the youngster. Jason took the man easily as Quincy watched. When the man discovered who Jason was, he intended to quit; when Jason heard this he caught up with him that evening in the shack that the man and his family occupied. He convinced him to stay, saying that he would rather have a man who could work and play hard, rather than one who slunk away at the first hint of trouble. The man became foreman of the mill years later.

Karl had later moved to Tacoma and set himself up in the insurance business, a budding industry in the northwest. He married and as of 1880 had four children.

Jason's mother worried over her remaining son who seemed consumed with work. He expressed only cursory interest in the young girls in town and courted no one girl in particular. She applied subtle pressure, but Jason did not cave. Acutely aware that he was wealthy, he did not want a wife who wanted to marry his money. His few dalliances proved him right about this fact time and again, making him reclusive. He built a wall around himself to insulate his tender heart. He would find the right girl in time, he was certain of that.

In 1877, his father died. A year later, his mother, succumbed to a heart attack. Jason was alone, and although he was very wealthy, it did not make him happy. Single women redoubled their efforts to engage him, but to no avail.

Jason kept to a strict routine: Up at four a.m. to oversee the day's work at the three logging camps, then open the mill at eight. He would closet himself in his office, preoccupied with the books and orders, and was the last to leave at four in the afternoon to return home to a solitary dinner in his big log house.

Once a year, Jason sponsored a lumberjacking exhibition, an event which entertained the townspeople. Tables laden with food and drink were set up along the river and a brass band, imported from Tacoma, entertained. Sometimes, a small traveling circus would come to town as well. The logging competition was grueling yet exciting and although he was the sponsor, Jason sometimes participated and was terribly humble when he won an event. With his strong upper body strength, he consistently won the ax throwing and pole climbing contests.

Like his father and mother, Jason was the town's benefactor and always carried the burden of owning the sustaining business of the town. Without logging, Easthope was nothing. If he did not keep the business running at a profit, he would lose his quiet home near the river and the hard–working people who allowed him to have it. When Jason found himself envying his brother's comfortable life in the city, he would ride alone up to the ridge above town, drinking in the sweet scent of evergreen and lush beauty of the woods to reassure himself that he had made the right decision to remain.

After his mother's death, Jason built his own imposing log cabin next to his large, echoing childhood home. He could not cope in the house of his dear mother for all the memories that it held. He closed his mother's house, leaving all the furniture in place. It was a sad shrine. Jason went to the old house once a month alone—to clean it. He did not have the heart to rent or sell it, and was waiting for a reason to reopen it; he just did not have one yet.

Now, the town was settled and tensions between white and Indian had turned to cautious acceptance. When the workday was over, the Yakima retreated to their reservation some miles away. Despite the best efforts of Quincy and later Jason, Indians were still not welcome in the town's establishments, especially the new hotel and restaurant, the ice cream parlor, and the general store. The stores would only wait on Indians if they came by the back door. Jason brooded over their treatment as second–class citizens. He knew that it was their labor that built the town. It rankled him that they were not allowed to live in town or enjoy its advantages. His treatment of the Indians had always been respectful and kind, and in secret he helped families in need, just as his mother had. Dr. Barlow was also enlisted by Jason to treat the sick at the reservation.

When Jason went hunting he always shared his kills with the tribe. His example was dismissed by many townsfolk, but the gossip did not dim his commitment. To the Indians he was respected as the man who tried to help them improve their impoverished lives.

Jason was well–liked among the work crews. He sometimes joined the men at the Pry Bar Saloon for drinks after the workday ended. The barkeep was glad to have Jason in his establishment. Jason's presence discouraged flare–ups between workers that could disintegrate into fistfights that had destroyed the saloon more than once.

On rare occasions, Jason accepted dinner invitations from neighbors, most of them having one or more daughters to display, but he always showed polite, noncommittal interest. He hated the reason that he was invited, but loneliness drove him to attend these occasions. Jason attended all of the dances held in the church hall and although he danced with the eligible girls and they swooned over him, he treated all the young women with polite detachment. There was no chink in his armor until the day he met Emma Hawkshadow.

Shea walked his pony and led Emma's mare as they descended the track toward the road. Soon they heard, then saw, one of the logging camps, Camp Three, Jason called it, the highest and steepest. The smell of freshly cut wood and sweet pine hung heavy in the air.

As a caution, Emma and Shea rode ahead under the cover of the trees while Jason got a wagon at the camp and met them up the trail. Emma was deposited in the wagon and her horse and Shea's were tied to the rear. Jason rode his mare while Shea drove the wagon. Shea needed something to do while he battled waves of nervousness as they headed for town.

The outskirts of town had many modest well–kept homes framed by thick stands of evergreens covering gentle slopes. The Easthope River ran beside the town, wide and indigo blue.

They turned onto Main Street. At the far end was Jason's sawmill, marked by a beige veil of sawdust hovering in the air. Jason explained that sluices carried the logs down the mountain to the booming grounds on the river.

"Booming grounds?" Emma asked.

"The logs make a booming sound when they hit the water," Jason said.

Just then, a heavy, thundering splash was heard that reverberated through town. "You'll get used to it. I don't even notice it anymore," Jason grinned. "The sawmill was built next to a natural current in the river where the logs can be corralled before being fed into the saws. Some logs are hauled out to dry before sawing and some are loaded on barges heading down to the Columbia River. From there, the wood goes to the brokers in Spokane and Tacoma. But lately, some lumber has been shipped north to Canada. Other mills in this region can't beat my prices."

Their progress through town was slowed by a man driving a water wagon. It held barrels of water in the back. Spigots on the barrels sprayed water on the road to keep the dirt and sawdust down. The sweet, earthy tang of freshly sawn wood pervaded every corner of the town.

Emma occupied herself cataloging storefronts along Main Street. There was a bank, a general store with a post office inside, a hotel, a saloon, men's and ladies' clothing stores, and a livery stable at the end of the street near the lumber mill. A large white church with a tall spire was in the center of town, flanked by a shady park and a cemetery. Next came a barber shop, a shoemaker, the schoolhouse, a butcher shop, and a small library. The fire-house was next to the newspaper building that had a telegraph office inside, the sign outside read. She pictured a line of people waiting outside its door, waiting for Max Cody's next installment of their story. But all in all it seemed to have a wealth of businesses and shops that she hoped to explore.

Jason pointed out his childhood home that was built on a rise with a view of the river. It was the most beautiful house in town, a soaring Victorian, painted deep red with white fretwork, with a large wraparound porch and twin balconies on the second storey.

Several people paused and watched them pass by but Emma did not feel the disapproval she had become accustomed to, perhaps, she reasoned, due to Shea's disguise.

Shea kept his gaze on the people, bravely meeting every eye. Emma saw his hands whiten with strain on the reins. He did not look Indian in his white clothing and his hair stuffed up in the hat, but he was naturally wary and watchful.

Jason pointed out the doctor's office, which was connected to the hospital by a covered walkway. The doctor's office and the hospital were the only brick buildings in town. Outside the doctor's office hung a sign that read 'Dr. Stuart Barlow—Physician.' They pulled up and Shea and Jason helped Emma climb down from the wagon. As Jason showed them inside, several women walking with their young children stopped to inspect the newcomers.

Thankfully, the waiting room was empty. Jason knocked on the inner office door and a short, stocky, graying man opened it a moment later.

"Jason!" he said, shaking his hand. "Good to see you. Don't tell me you're ailing? You're never sick."

"I'm fine, Stuart. I have some new friends that need your help if you have a few minutes."

Dr. Barlow had been aware of Emma and Shea as he emerged from his office, but he had not looked them over too closely until now. "Dr. Stuart Barlow," he said, extending his hand to Shea and with a nod to Emma. "Ma'am."

Summoning his courage, Shea said, "This is my wife, Emma," pausing for a split second, "Hawkshadow. I am Shea." Emma's eyes widened at Shea dropping the pretense of the name Shea Russell. "She's—"

"About eight months along?" Dr. Barlow said as he ran his practiced eye over her. "Come in, Mrs. Hawkshadow, come in," he said as he guided her through the doorway. "Wait here," he said to Shea. "This won't take long." With that, he closed the door.

Shea took a step back and landed in a chair near a window. He saw several people outside, forming little groups, talking and pointing to the doctor's office and Jason's wagon. Jason smiled and Shea returned a crooked grin.

"Well that is one person down, how many more to go?"

Jason chuckled. "About two hundred forty." After a short silence, Jason said, "So you've decided to use your real name?"

"If you figured it out, others will. I would rather explain the truth than live a lie," he replied.

Half an hour later, Emma emerged with Dr. Barlow. "Everything's fine," she said, beaming. "How much do we owe you, doctor?"

Stuart Barlow had the course of a half hour to think about where he had heard the name Hawkshadow before and as he got a long look at Shea, he put it together. He seemed to jump a little as he answered. "Ah—ah—a dollar is sufficient, ma'am. Thank you." Emma pulled a bill from the tin in her buckskin purse. His eyes returned to Shea who now came beside Emma. "Hawkshadow," he said, tapping his fingers on his chin. "Hawkshadow. From the stories in the paper?"

Shea nodded but his look was proud and fierce, ready for the fear and rejection he expected. Suddenly, Barlow grabbed Shea's hand and shook it. Shea met the man's eyes, leaning back, puzzled.

"This is indeed a great pleasure, sir—ma'am. I read the series about you. This is indeed an honor, Chief Hawkshadow!"

Emma giggled and Jason's grin widened.

"I was never a chief," Shea replied, fighting a smile that threatened his guarded expression. "Nice to meet you," he said, unfamiliar with such words.

"Your wife and child are just fine. She should deliver in early or mid-August. Are you staying in town or just passing through?"

Jason broke in. "They're staying at my hunting cabin, Stuart."

"Oh. That's far from town. Are you sure you won't consider staying in town until the birth? It's a long ride up the mountain. I'm not saying that you'll have any problems, but you never know. Maybe stay at the hotel so I'll be nearby when the time comes."

Emma looked to Shea, then they both looked to Jason. "No, thank you," Shea said, his voice even. "We like the cabin for now."

Dr. Barlow did not push, seeing that Shea was ill at ease. In his excitement at meeting them, he had forgotten that Indians were not welcome at Murdock's Hotel and Restaurant.

"Of course. But, Mrs. Hawkshadow, if you have any bleeding or unusual pain, get here with all speed. Ride in a wagon. No lifting, no running, no climbing, understood? And get lots of rest."

"You can have my wagon as long as you need it," Jason offered.

"Thank you, Jason," Shea said as Jason opened the door on the bright July day.

Dr. Barlow walked them out. "The less jostling around, the better off you'll be. If I'm not here or at the hospital, I live in the blue house down the street," he pointed. "It was indeed a pleasure meeting you. Good day."

A small crowd was still clumped together across the street, trying to appear nonchalant, yet get a glimpse of the newcomers. Emma felt shabby and self–conscious, unable to meet their eyes, but Shea met every one. Some looked away, some did not, but he could see that they were merely curious for they believed what they saw: A young white couple, travelers passing through town to see the doctor.

"How about a tour of the mill, eh?" Jason said as he offered Emma his arm, and a moment later, Shea took her other arm.

She walked between the two men, glancing up now and then. She gripped Shea's arm tight for support and felt very out of place. She had never been in a regular town before. She felt fat and dirty in her old worn dress and the cotton shawl.

Small knots of people casually followed the trio. They crossed the street and went to the mill at the edge of town. Shea knew that Emma was tired, so Jason found her a shady bench outside his office while he showed Shea around the mill, going so far as to offer him a job, once they were alone. Shea respectfully declined.

About twenty townsfolk stood across the street, watching Emma. She felt very exposed, now eager to leave and return to the quiet cabin up on the mountain, but her eyes involuntarily flicked to the people again and again. The women wore fine new dresses with matching hats. Many carried parasols, and Emma saw that many women had their hair stylishly pinned up or curled. Their clothing was far from elegant, but smart and practical. Emma felt coarse, common, and embarrassed—in between worlds.

After a time, a young woman broke from the crowd and walked straight toward her. Without preamble, she seated herself next to Emma. She was broad, but not heavy, pretty, brown–eyed, and round–faced with the high colour of her Irish heritage in her clear skin. Her curly brown hair stuck out from underneath the blue bonnet that matched her dress.

"Hello, I'm Rachel Barlow," she said, offering her gloved hand.

Extending her own hesitantly, she said, "I'm Emma. Emma Hawkshadow." She prepared for the usual reaction and was wholly unprepared for the one that she got.

"I knew it! I was right!" she exclaimed, her gloved hands muffling a clap. "I had a feeling when I saw you two ride in. Is that Shea Hawkshadow, the Cheyenne Chief?" she said, pointing to Shea across the yard.

Shea was keeping an eye on her and had turned his attention from Jason. She saw him take a few steps toward her. Jason turned as well, putting a hand on Shea's arm. Jason said something to Shea, but he kept an alert eye on Emma.

She shifted on the hard bench for her back hurt. She repeated Shea's answer to Dr. Barlow a few minutes ago. "Shea's not a chief, but yes, he's my husband."

"I read the stories about you and your Indian husband."

"He's half Indian," Emma felt she had to say.

Rachel seemed not to have heard and spoke very melodramatically as her hand flew to her chest. "Such heartbreak and tragedy! I felt so terrible reading about what you went through! Persecuted for loving each other! I always wished that Max Cody finished the story, but since you're here now, you can tell me everything!" Emma was completely astonished by this aggressive young woman. "You're staying in town, aren't you? Oh, wait, I know! You're the ones staying in Jason's hunting cabin, right?"

"Um, yes, just until the baby comes."

"Jason's a good man. Very kind. I see that you're pretty pregnant there," she said with a slight chuckle, freely touching Emma's belly. "When are you due?"

"Soon," she answered. She was in the same position as Shea weeks ago when he first met Jason and had to decide whether to trust a veritable stranger. This woman was bold, open, and ebullient. "I just saw a Dr. Barlow—"

"He's my father–in–law. Oh, I hope you'll be staying a while. I want to know everything about you. At first we all thought Cody made you two up, but I can see that you're real. You've led a very interesting life for one so young! I'm twenty–four," she volunteered. "And you?"

"Twenty in August."

She switched subjects very quickly, now back to the baby. "You must be excited. Is this your first?" Emma nodded. "I have two. One is six months, that's Helen. She's got curly brown hair like me. The other is Martin, he's four. He's dark haired like my husband, Caleb. Don't you fret about the birth. I'll tell you everything to expect. It's not as hard as you think. It's hot out here. How about coming with me for a cool drink?" She stood, smiling. "Shall we?"

With Rachel's assistance, Emma rose. Beads of sweat dotted her forehead. Town was much warmer than the cabin in the cool hills. "Well, okay. I—I have to tell Shea. Be right back." She waddled across the yard, fighting the urge to look back at Rachel. As she told Shea where she was going, he looked over her shoulder, scrutinizing the woman in the blue dress.

Jason smiled and waved to Rachel. "That's Dr. Barlow's daughter–in–law. There's no harm, Shea."

"Enjoy yourself," Shea said with a conflicted tinge to his voice. "We will find you later."

Emma realized in those few moments with Rachel how lonely she had been for female company and impulsively kissed Shea's cheek in thanks.

Shea watched Emma walk away with a slight waddle, then reluctantly turned his attention back to the tour of the lumber mill.

Rachel took Emma's arm as she escorted her up the street, chattering, relaxed, and affable. Emma tried to concentrate, but this reception was so unexpected. The little crowd that had kept them under surveillance gradually dispersed. Rachel and Emma made their way along the wooden walkways to a little restaurant inside Murdock's, the town's only hotel.

More curious stares greeted Emma as she and Rachel entered the establishment. Rachel took a table in a quiet corner. Emma took the seat facing the wall. Unable to cope with the attention that she attracted from the patrons, she presented her back to them instead. She smoothed her windblown hair as Rachel seated herself.

"You have the most beautiful hair," she remarked, removing her gloves. "It's a lovely color and so long." Emma knew that Rachel was doing her best to put her at ease. A waiter brought menus. "Two lemonades?" She looked to Emma who gave her a tight, nervous smile. "Unless you're hungry. You are eating for two."

"No, lemonade is fine." The waiter took his time writing down the simple order on his pad, his glance returning to Emma. She was hungry, but her stomach fluttered with nerves and she was afraid that she would keep nothing down.

"Mine's so wild. Curls all over the place. I can't seem to control it."

"What? Oh yes. You're lucky. My hair is so straight." Emma said, straining to keep her mind on the shifting topics.

"Maybe, but it's so thick. I'll trade you any time!" Rachel laughed.

The waiter brought the drinks moments later. Emma drank the sweet tart lemonade. It tasted so good, she smiled in spite of her nervousness.

"So, how long have you and your husband been at Jason's cabin?"

Emma looked worried. "Does the whole town know we're up there?"

"We've all seen the chimney smoke. He gets occasional squatters there, trappers and lost travelers, but Jason doesn't mind. He's been heading up there more than usual, from what his men say. He went loaded with supplies, but he didn't have his guns with him for hunting. We figured somebody was up there, but Jason's such a private person that no one had the gumption to ask about it, not even me! When he took out armloads of clothing from his mother's house, he had us all going!" she said with a snicker.

"Yes, he told us that his mother passed away not long ago."

"She was a very kind woman and Jason's a lot like her, but more private. He keeps to himself."

"He's been very kind to us. Jason is one of the few whites that my husband trusts." She regretted her slip of the tongue thinking that she had offended Rachel.

"Well, if all I read about you two is accurate, I can see why he doesn't trust us whites."

Emma finished her lemonade and Rachel signaled the waiter for another. As it was placed before her, Emma grimaced and leaned back in her chair.

"Are you all right?" Rachel asked, rising from her seat.

"The baby liked the lemonade. He just gave me a good kick to say thanks."

Rachel resumed her seat. "So, do you want a boy or a girl?"

Emma thought for a moment. Shea's hopes were pinned on a son, but she answered, "Just a child that's healthy and can grow up in safety. Whether it is a boy or girl, its life won't be easy because of being part Cheyenne. I've watched Shea struggle with it. It's not easy to live in two worlds. If you deny all that makes you what you are, it can make you crazy." Emma was revealing too much to this stranger, but she was struck by the normal–ness of the conversation. It seemed at once foreign yet familiar. As they talked, she kept her sentences short and clipped, a habit picked up among the Cheyenne. She tried to relax, sipping her second lemonade and reaching back to a time when she knew a little of the art of conversation.

"What did Stuart have to say? Is everything all right with the baby?" Rachel asked, genuinely concerned.

"Dr. Barlow? He said I'm fine," Emma replied.

"We're lucky to have him here. After my mother–in–law died a few years ago, we thought he'd go back east to Massachusetts. But he stayed, I think, because all his children live here or in Oregon. My husband, Caleb, is the youngest. He's got two brothers and two sisters in Portland, Oregon, but a sister and brother still live here. George is a shoemaker and his sister Ruth works at the millinery."

"Dr. Barlow was very nice, but he seemed concerned that we're living up on the mountain so far from town."

"Oh, I know! You could stay with us until the baby comes," she said, Emma thought too loudly. Several heads turned in their direction. "I have plenty of room. My house is huge—six bedrooms! It belonged to Stuart and his wife. They raised all seven children there. When I married Caleb, the house was a wedding present. Stuart's wife, Millie, passed on three years ago, so he's much better off in a smaller place. My parents moved to Spokane just after we married. My father's a carpenter. He helped build some of the houses here, but he was lured away to Spokane by the offer of a partnership in a construction firm. My younger brother, Stan, was only twelve when my parents moved, but he visits me once in a while. He's now a partner in my father's business. But I stayed here. I've always liked it here in Easthope."

"It's a nice town," Emma agreed, bowled over by Rachel's outpouring of her family history. She had to struggle to keep up with Rachel's quick mind and the shifting subjects. "Big families. It must be nice, even though you're far apart. You're lucky."

Rachel took a sip of her lemonade. "I do want to help you. Our home is open, if you want. Oh, say that you'll think about it. It would be wise for you to stay nearby."

"Thank you, Rachel, but we like the cabin. It's our home—for now."

"My house is so big, we'd hardly see each other. You'd have privacy."

"I appreciate the offer, but I think it's best we keep a distance. We're not used to being around a lot of people. Shea isn't used to being in a place like this and neither am I." She again thought that she offended Rachel.

She did not seem to notice Emma's slight about civilization. "The offer's always open." Rachel prattled on, talking about pregnancy and the changes it imposed on a woman's life and body—a subject hardly spoken of in private, much less in public. She spoke of how to get through the labor and what Emma should expect. It was the first time that Emma had heard anyone be so open and honest about such an event. Emma found her amusing and fearless.

Rachel spoke about her own experience with childbirth and its aftermath. "I gained so much weight with my Martin, I didn't think that I would ever lose it, but you're so slim you won't have a problem."

Emma did not feel slim, but smiled, appreciating the compliment. But she felt dizzy, struggling to keep up with Rachel's chatter.

A short while later, Rachel spotted Shea and Jason on the walkway in front of Murdock's. Emma pulled a bill from her buckskin bag and held it out to Rachel.

"Oh—please allow me," she said, gently pushing Emma's hand away. She paid the waiter and came around the table to assist her. "I enjoyed this.

I hope you and your husband come to town again soon—or maybe I could come up and visit you, if that would be all right."

Emma heard herself saying that she would like that very much. Rachel took her arm once again and led her out into the warm day.

Shea moved to Emma's side, asking after her.

She grinned. "I feel wonderful."

Rachel greeted Jason with a sly pirate's smile. "Now I know your secret, Jason. We've all been wondering who's been up at the cabin."

"So now that you know, you'll tell everyone?" Jason asked, fully aware that Rachel was not going to keep this tantalizing morsel to herself.

"No," she said. "The secret is safe with me at least for a while, but I can't guarantee that Stuart won't tell."

"Well," Jason said, leaning down close to Rachel's ear, "try to keep it to yourself for now. They need some peace and quiet."

Emma introduced Rachel to Shea. "This is Rachel Barlow. Rachel, this is my husband, Shea Hawkshadow."

Rachel shook his hand. "It's a pleasure to meet you, sir." Her smile broadened as she took him in close up. "You have the most incredible blue eyes—so unusual for an Indian." She tried to cover her embarrassment for her last remark. "Would you like to step inside for a cool drink?"

Emma's smile faded. Shea shook his head and frowned. "Indians are not welcome in such places." Jason and Rachel looked uncomfortable, knowing that Shea was right. "Come, Emma, we have to get supplies now." His hand tightened around her arm and he pulled her forward a few steps.

Rachel was still blushing with embarrassment. "I'd better get home. Martin's at the Neilsens' and my sitter's probably wondering where I went. Helen will be up from her nap by now." She found Emma's hand, squeezing it fondly. "I'll visit soon, I promise." Emma smiled after her newfound friend as Rachel trotted down the street.

Jason drove Emma and Shea to the general store a short distance up the street. "Looks like you've found a friend," he said. "But be a little careful, Emma. Rachel is better than a newspaper when it comes to spreading news."

Emma smiled, her face bright. "She seems nice."

Jason grinned, seeing how fast Rachel moved in, trying to put Emma at ease. To Rachel, Jason knew, Emma and Shea were celebrities—and she would be the first to befriend them, then brag about it to anyone who would listen.

They entered Carruthers general store where Emma and Shea purchased dry goods, molasses, beans, potatoes, eggs, and a lot of coffee. Emma shopped with Jason's help since he knew where everything was in the store. Shea had never been in a store before and occupied himself looking at the myriad of goods on the shelves. Even Emma was astounded, only knowing shabby, out–of–the–way trading posts. Emma indulged herself a little and bought a journal and new shoes. At last she could get rid of the worn–out boots that she had bought at Fort Robinson.

As Shea and Jason loaded everything into the wagon, Emma waited on the walkway while Jason's horses were unhitched and replaced with Butternut and Shea's pony. Unused to the heavy, restricting harness, both animals snorted and stomped in protest. With a farewell to Jason, Shea helped Emma aboard, hopped up and snapped the reins, departing for home.

The following week at the cabin, Emma moved the rocker outdoors and wrote in her brand–new journal—an extravagance, she knew, but it freed something in her. She wrote for hours until her hand cramped.

Their reception in town had been cool, but that, she reasoned, was because they were newcomers. Rachel's reception was the bright spot and Emma found that she liked her. Shea worked nearby splitting wood, shirtless and clad in leggings and moccasins as usual. She drank in the peaceful summer's day as if it were honey. She was content and although their trip to town had been brief, both of them laughed that night when they revealed their level of tension during the visit. She knew that word of them would spread and the next trip might not be so pleasant. If she had learned anything over the past few years, it was to be cautious.

Shea was disconcerted that he would have to keep his hair in a hat and wear white man's clothes since people had seen him in such dress, but at the cabin, he dressed in his Indian clothing and let his long hair hang loose. Emma knew of the pride he took in his appearance as a Cheyenne and hoped that someday, he could dress as he wished in town. "We will go back to town soon," he promised, knowing what it meant to her.

That same afternoon, Emma heard a wagon approaching. Coming up over the hill Rachel appeared in a large wagon, driving identical dappled grays, strong and magnificent. She waved as Emma went to greet her.

"Hello!" she called. "I brought a few things for you. I hope you don't mind." As Rachel alighted from the wagon, Shea assisted her, imitating what he had seen Jason do for Emma.

Rachel took in his appearance. As he was shirtless, she could see the scars from the hanging around his neck, but she did not miss his lean hard–muscled body as her own slid against him as he helped her down. He helped carry the packages that she had brought into the cabin.

Smiling, Emma led Rachel inside and Shea remained outdoors chopping wood. As she opened the bundles, tears filled Emma's eyes.

"There are baby clothes, diapers, blankets, and some of my maternity dresses. I hope they fit. You're taller than me." Emma wiped her tears on her sleeve. "Oh, please, take them. I don't need them right now and I'd rather someone use them. Some things are hardly worn at all." Rachel pulled out a few garments, running a careful eye over them just to be sure.

"Thank you, Rachel. I don't know what to say. Between you and Jason, we've received so much." Her voice choked with emotion.

Rachel hugged her. "I wanted to help without seeming like I'm giving it as charity. I think we're going to become good friends and that's what friends do for each other."

Emma smiled and composed herself. "I get so emotional over everything lately, it seems."

"That's normal. I cried and raged for months when I was pregnant with both of mine. I don't know how Caleb withstood it all. I was a monster sometimes!" she laughed.

They spent the afternoon oh–ing and ah–ing over the tiny baby clothes, which were of fine quality, and, as Rachel promised, nearly new.

"They grow so fast, few things get worn out, which is good for when the next one comes along."

"It took me a long time to become pregnant. This might be our only child," Emma sobbed then quickly checked her emotions. "Oh! I'm being silly!"

Rachel put her arm around Emma's shoulder. "Don't dwell on that. But it's all worth it, no matter how many you have. C'mon, let's try on the dresses. It will cheer you up."

The maternity dresses were short on Emma, Rachel commented, but they fit everywhere else. Rachel saw the scars on Emma's chest beneath her camisole as she undressed in the bedroom. Her gaze fell on them, with a look of sad fascination that Emma did not miss. She decided to keep on one dress, a lovely double pink calico with a lace collar and deep ruffled hem. It felt so good to be out of her tight, worn–out clothes. She was grateful, for if she and Shea went to town again, she would not be self–conscious in her shabby old dresses.

Later, Emma prepared tea and cornbread biscuits and she and Rachel sat and sipped and talked at the table.

Later, Rachel produced a brush from her handbag and stood behind Emma brushing her hair. "Next time I come, I'll bring my scissors and trim your hair—you know, even it out. It's so thick and soft."

Emma's thoughts drifted as the rhythmic strokes of the brush relaxed her.

Rachel commented, "You're used to it, Emma, but to see a man like Shea, dressed in his Indian clothing—it's, so . . ." she trailed off, searching for the right word, "so exotic to someone like me. Sometimes I go for a ride past the logging camps just to get a glimpse of the men with their shirts off!" she said with a husky chuckle.

Emma was surprised at Rachel's unrestrained candor, but she did not feel jealous hearing her husband being spoken of in such a manner. Rachel said it playfully, so she did not mind.

Rachel became serious for a moment. She stopped brushing and rested her hands on Emma's shoulders. "Those scars on Shea's neck—they're from the hanging, right?"

Emma nodded and rubbed her face, for she knew well the questions that were to come.

Instead, Rachel surprised her again. "That must've been terrible for you, watching your husband hanged right before your eyes. And you would've been next if it hadn't been for that soldier who saved you."

Emma reached back and squeezed Rachel's hand. For the first time since Adam, someone else expressed understanding for all she had endured that terrible day.

"I couldn't wait for Cody's articles in the paper each day. Sometimes, a bunch of us would line up in front of the newspaper office to be sure to get a copy. I tried to imagine you as Cody described you and when I saw you both come into town last week, I knew it had to be you. Your hair gave you away." She resumed brushing Emma's hair. "Do you mind me talking about Cody's stories?"

"No. It's just—it was a bad time." Rachel closed her mouth on all the questions knocking at her lips and listened as Emma's quiet voice filled the room. "I thought that we would be safer at the Montana reservation, but we weren't. After the ambush, we were both in bad shape. Shea couldn't talk for months, so we communicated with pencil and paper. Even so, we had many arguments—it was more than I could take."

"Sometimes people say and do cruel things when they're in pain."

"I know. I almost left him because of it."

"I felt the same way with Caleb once." Emma's comment about pencil and paper had been lost on Rachel until now. "Wait. Shea can read and write?" She looked genuinely shocked.

"I taught many of the Cheyenne to read and write. Shea was the first. We were good company for each other at the time. Shea's father left when he was very young and his mother had died long before I came to the camp. We were both very lonely. An old woman, Red Leaf, had become like a mother to me and when she found out that Shea and I were in love, she warned me about the troubles that we would face. She was right about that, but I was too infatuated with Shea to understand what she meant."

Rachel's eyes sparkled with excitement. "Did you and him—*you know*—before you were married?"

Emma nodded, a small smile playing about her lips. "The Cheyenne have very strict rules about that sort of thing among themselves, but they didn't quite know what to do about me. They had bigger problems than an orphaned white girl."

Rachel bit her lip. "So you did it? Before the wedding?"

Emma smiled at the memories. "I never saw anything wrong with it. It seemed natural. But we married in March of '78 and that made Red Leaf happy." Emma saddened, remembering her. "She died the day we were attacked by the militia. I miss her."

Rachel stopped brushing Emma's hair. She put the brush back into her satchel and sat down next to Emma at the table. "What sort of things go through your mind—on a day like that, I mean that day? I've never been in real danger, you know, life or death. What's it like?"

Emma rose from the table and went to the window. "Survival—that's all you can think about until you realize that you're not going to make it. Then you resign yourself and you get real calm and many things become clear. It's not that you give up, really. It's amazing how fast you can prepare yourself to die. I believed that I was living the last moments of my life. I felt cheated that I'd die so young. I was only eighteen but if I were to die, at least it was beside my husband. Everything that day had the quality of a dream, not a nightmare. I was no longer afraid. I heard shots and shouting. I remember screaming, then in an instant I was on the ground. I heard Shea somewhere near me—he was choking. Then I heard a horse and rider and I thought it was more militiamen coming to finish us off. But it was Adam and I knew that we'd be safe—if we lived. When I saw the look on Adam's face, I thought that my arm had been shot off. I couldn't feel it."

She came back to the table and poured more tea for Rachel. "I was so naïve, so foolish. I didn't understand Shea's feelings—how powerless he felt that day—and afterwards. I was helpful, kind, patient, and as loving as I could be, but it wasn't enough. Shea hated me for a while. When I discovered that I was pregnant, I couldn't take any more of his foul temper, so I left him—but he followed me and convinced me to try again. It was one of the hardest decisions that I ever had to make." Heeding Jason's warning that Rachel was 'better than a newspaper' in spreading news, Emma kept her plan to go to Adam to herself. She patted her stomach. "This little person growing inside of me brought us back together. But I think—no," she turned to Rachel, "I know that I made the right decision."

Rachel watched her intently. "Where did you get that other scar on your chest?" Emma's eyes filled with tears. Rachel immediately backed off. "I'm sorry. I'm too nosy. It's a flaw in my character—can't help it sometimes."

"It's all right, Rachel. It's just another pathetic story about how trouble seems to follow me wherever I go. I hope that things will be different if we decide to stay here."

"I know what it's like—marital troubles, I mean. Caleb and me had some problems just after Martin was born. He'd been with another woman who lives in Millersburg—Elsa Swenson—spinster. Nothing but a whore, pardon my speech. She makes a career out of preying upon weak men and my Caleb was weak back then. He tried to become a lawyer, but failed the exam several times. He didn't want to work at the mill or the logging camps and it bothered him to borrow money from his father. I was pregnant and not all that nice, because I felt sick the whole time. We didn't, *you know,* and Elsa moved in like a crow picking at an animal's carcass. Caleb began going to Millersburg more and more, supposedly looking for work and it made me suspicious. A few weeks after Martin was born, I left him with my mother-in-law and followed Caleb. I caught him in bed with Elsa."

"I worried about the same thing when Shea and I were separated during the outbreak. I thought that he had found someone else," Emma said.

Emma watched Rachel pick at the wooden tabletop with her fingernails, pulling up tiny splinters. It was plain to Emma that Rachel had unresolved anger over her husband's affair.

"So, we have even more in common," Rachel said.

"But you came back together and had Helen?" she said, trying to ease the pain etched in Rachel's face.

"She brought us back together, much as your child has. I think our marriage is stronger now, I can't explain why. Maybe he wanted to see what he was missing and realized that it wasn't much!" She smiled wryly, taking a sip of tea. "But soon after, he got a job at the bank and he's vice–president now. Who would have thought that he had a head for figures?" She shook off her mood. "So how are you feeling?"

Emma's brow creased. "I didn't tell Shea, but the baby's not moving as much as before. I'm worried."

"It means the time's close. I think the baby stores up energy before the birth." Rachel continued with questions, but Emma had become fatigued and longed for a nap. Rachel was relentless. "I just can't picture you running around the countryside after the Cheyenne jumped the reservation. It must've been so bleak, so terrible to have no home."

Emma looked at her assessingly, pausing before she spoke. "Imagine the entire town of Easthope leaving in the night without a sound from babies, children, animals—everyone just gone." She sighed. "But I wasn't Cheyenne. Shea knew full well that I couldn't make the run and he wanted to send me away. When I knew what they were facing I refused to leave him. Along the way I was captured and taken to Fort Robinson. I was really sick so in a way, it was a good thing that I was captured, but," she paused as that terrible time worked through her mind again, "I was forced to stay at the fort for months. I ran out of hope."

Remembering what she had read in Cody's articles about Emma's time at Fort Robinson, Rachel asked, "What happened when that soldier at the fort attacked you?"

She shook her head and could not, would not give details. "It was just a dark time for me."

Rachel persisted. "Emma, tell me. I swear I'll tell no one."

Emma looked at her a long time, trying to decide if she could trust her. No, not yet—not with what Fulton did to her. Her answer was strained with weariness. "I would rather not go into it, okay?"

Shea returned some time later, carrying a bucket of water and an armful of wood. He was cordial to Rachel, but very circumspect of her. Emma announced Rachel's generosity as Shea noticed the new dress and the piles of clothing scattered around the room. He mumbled a thank you to Rachel, grabbed up a crude fishing pole and headed to the stream to catch fish for dinner.

Rachel ended her visit, seeing that Emma was very tired. Emma watched her depart with a small longing to live in town.

That night in bed, Shea lay next to Emma. Although she was too far along to make love, they lay nude touching and stroking each other in the warm room, lit by a single lamp. He laid his head on her stomach. "That woman gave you so much for you and the baby. I wish I could do that."

She tugged at his long hair. "Hey, don't feel that way. She was being kind. I like her. She has a good heart. But I'll return everything if you want."

"No. That is not what I meant. As your husband, I should give you those things."

She shifted and lay on her side facing him. "My love, you've given me this child. It is the greatest gift you could ever give me. We're together again and safe and that's all I need." He kissed her holding her close. "The money I have is for both of us to use, I don't care what you say to the contrary. I would've bought those things for the baby but Rachel and Jason beat me to it. You saved my life the day you found me. I lived through Fort Robinson because of you. You gave me my life back—gave me a purpose. No material things can replace that. I have no regrets."

Chapter Twelve

The first week of August, Emma was pleasantly surprised one afternoon when Jason arrived. As usual, he stayed for supper.

She moved slowly as she cooked, refusing any assistance. She felt enormous, but had spent many hours in bed lately, so moving around felt good. She wore the pink calico maternity dress of Rachel's and felt pretty in it, despite her size.

As she stood at the cupboard slicing bread she cried out, "Oh!" Both Shea and Jason jumped up, knocking over their chairs. "The baby—my water broke!" With a grunt, she doubled over as a labor pain jolted her. Shea held her up as her legs crumpled beneath her. "I have to change. I'll ruin Rachel's dress," she said breathless.

Shea laughed with nerves and helped her into the bedroom. He pulled the room's curtain and helped Emma into a bed gown. He paused a moment and brushed her hair from her face and kissed her. "I guess this is it, Emma. I love you."

He left the room and spoke to Jason. "What should we do?" He looked helpless and a little afraid. "Cheyenne women do not need help with their babies."

Jason felt unnerved as well. "We need a clean knife to cut the cord. That's all I know. She has to do the rest." His statements came out more as questions and Shea lifted his hands in uncertainty. "I better get to town and fetch Dr. Barlow."

"Yes," Shea said with a quick glance around the cabin. "I will get a knife and put it in the fire." A pain hit Emma and she yelped and breathed herself through it as Rachel had told her. Shea ran to the bedroom and stood in the doorway.

"Shea, we'll need water boiled and cooled to wash the baby—and a clean knife to cut the cord—and blankets—and don't get the navel wet when you bathe him." She yelped again.

Shea froze. "Cheyenne women have their babies alone."

"I am not Cheyenne!" she declared, then another pain hit her. Shea dropped on his knees next to the bed and held her hand, for he knew little else to do. Emma panted with effort and beads of sweat showed on her face. The pain abated for the moment. He tried to reassure her, patting her hand. "Shea, it'll be all right. Women have babies every day."

"Not my wife. We have waited a long time." He was trying to sound brave and confident.

Jason peeked in the bedroom. "I'm going to get Barlow. You hang on, okay Emma?" She turned her head, panting, trying to smile.

Hours went by as Shea sat with her, doing what he could as the pains came and went, wiping perspiration off her face and sponging her off to keep her cool. Jason had been gone over three hours and Shea's ears were sharp for any sound outside. Just after dark he heard a rider. It was Jason.

"Stuart's miles away delivering another baby," he said, out of breath from his frantic ride. In the dark, he had somehow managed to cut a half hour off the ride to town and back. "I left word with Rachel and put a note on Stuart's office door to come. We'll have to manage till then. Rachel wanted to come, but it's too dark and she doesn't know the trail well enough. She'll be here at first light, she told me to tell you that, Emma."

Jason set himself in charge of boiling water and soon every pot was full, cooling on every available surface. He grabbed the knife from the coals and placed it on a towel and brought it to Shea. Both men stood at the foot of the bed, waiting, watching her. Emma grinned, watching them watching her.

In the wee hours, Jason sat near the fire still surrounded with the bowls and pans of cooling water. Emma's contractions continued and Shea sat behind her, helping her push. She had her knees up and was sweating and yelping from the contractions. Shea fanned her with a bunch of pages torn from her journal. Soon, the contractions came closer together and he called for Jason. He wiped her face as she leaned back, panting. She was tiring and he was very worried. Jason came in.

A strong contraction hit and she screamed. "It's coming, I can feel it! Shea, it's coming!"

"Jason, quick—get behind her and hold her!"

Jason took Shea's place and Shea went to the foot of the bed, pulling the blankets back over Emma's knees. Her hands found Jason's and she gripped them with amazing strength.

"I can see it!" Shea exclaimed.

She yelped with pain and sat up, pushing, her face red and contorted. She fell back against Jason, then lurched forward again. "Oh! Oh!" she screamed. "It burns!"

Her gown had fallen off at the shoulder and Jason saw the scars on her back, shoulder and chest. For a moment he was transfixed.

"I see the head!" Shea's voice was tense and overloud.

"I have to push!" Emma gasped. Jason got behind her and held her. She screamed as the final push came, digging her nails into his palms. The baby slid out and began to cry immediately. Emma flopped back against Jason, exhausted. He worked one hand free and wiped her face with the edge of the blanket.

It took a few moments for Shea to wipe off the baby and cut the umbilical cord, then he lifted the child and placed it in her mother's arms.

"We have a daughter," he said, a look of pure wonder on his face.

Her face assumed a look of exquisite euphoria as she looked upon her baby girl. She's perfect, Emma thought. The child's eyelids fluttered and her tongue worked in her tiny mouth. A shock of black hair covered her head. Emma kissed her cheek as tears of happiness flowed down her face.

"Oh! You're so beautiful!" she cooed.

Quiet minutes passed as Shea and Emma greeted their daughter. The baby cried softly.

"What are you going to name her?" Jason asked.

"Katherine Shea Hawkshadow," Shea answered.

"Katherine was my mother's middle name. Oh! Take her," Emma said, as the contractions started to expel the placenta. Shea took Katherine a moment and placed his first kiss on the cheek of his long–awaited child, then handed her to Jason, who held her awkwardly at first, then began talking gibberish to her, fiddling with her little pink hands.

As dawn brightened the cabin, Shea gave Katherine her first bath while Emma dozed. Shea was fascinated. She was chubby and had the required ten fingers and toes. It was hard to tell who she resembled because her face was red and pinched, but she had fine black hair, just like his. Jason stood behind him, watching the infant, captivated.

Shea wrapped the baby and placed her next to Emma who awoke. He fought tears. "She could not look any different, could she?" he said, holding his daughter's small hand in his large rough one.

"Jason, thank you," Shea and Emma echoed as Jason peeked in.

"She's beautiful. But it's time I head home," he said, not wishing to intrude on the new family.

"Oh, no, Jason, stay. It's the wee hours and you must be exhausted. Stay and sleep. You'll fall off your horse if you try to ride," Emma begged.

Jason did not argue and headed for the small bedroom. He was snoring in minutes.

Shea took one of the many pans of water that Jason had boiled hours before and washed Emma, then helped her change into a clean gown. After changing the bedding he sat with Emma, gazing upon the little girl who would become so important to them. Emma soon slept and Shea took his daughter and sat by the fire and held her for hours, unwilling to sleep. He marveled at the miracle he had witnessed and thanked Wise One Above for giving Emma the strength. Seeing the perfect little person asleep in his arms made his heart swell with adoration and pride.

In the early morning, Shea heard a wagon coming. Rachel and Dr. Barlow rushed in moments later. Shea held Katherine as he greeted Rachel and Stuart. Rachel cooed over her while Stuart went in to examine Emma.

Rachel heard snoring in the other bedroom. "Jason?"

"He was up all night with us."

She studied the look on Shea's face. "They steal your heart right away, don't they? How did Emma do?"

"She did just fine." His voice choked off with the emotions he found swelling within his heart. "Remarkable."

Rachel voiced her approval of the child's name. "She looks like a Kate."

Soon, Dr. Barlow entered the room. "She's okay. I want her in bed for a week—no less—and if she tires, make sure that she lays down. And no relations for six weeks, all right? Now, let me take a look at your little one."

After Stuart's exam, Rachel carried Katherine in to Emma.

"Isn't she beautiful?" Emma said, drained, but glowing.

"Nice work, Emma. She's gorgeous. How do you feel?"

"Good—I feel good—sore though! Why didn't you tell me about that part?" She giggled.

Rachel shrugged. "That's a part I prefer to forget."

"Shea's in love with her more than me—different than me."

Rachel smiled. "I saw the way he looks at her, Emma, and he's in love, that's a fact."

While Shea struggled to make breakfast for them all, Jason woke and he gratefully accepted his help with the cooking. Later, Jason looked in on Emma.

"Jason! Come in, please." He came in and kneeled by the bed, his hand going immediately to Katherine's. "Thank you."

Jason's eyes met Emma's for a long moment, then he turned his attention to Katherine, lightly tickling her chubby cheeks. "Any time," he said smiling at the baby.

When Rachel returned home that afternoon, she kissed and hugged her children, feeling a newfound appreciation for the miracle they were.

When Jason returned home, he felt lost in the big log house, wandering from room to room, not tired as he should have been, but spoiling for something to do other than the ledgers. He had realized something last night and both cherished and feared it. His relationship with Emma these past weeks culminated as he held her in his arms as she gave birth. Her stamina affected him and when he saw the terrible mottle of flesh upon her shoulder and chest, his heart broke. He marveled at her strength and her beauty. In that moment, he realized he loved her.

In the weeks after the birth, Emma's strength quickly returned. She was joyful and content with her new role as a mother. She sat in the sun nursing Katherine and realized with a start that her twentieth birthday had passed on August twenty-seventh without notice.

Shea wanted her, but the six weeks were not up yet, so they found other ways to amuse themselves in the bedroom. Rachel came often and Emma enjoyed her company and advice. Many days, Rachel stayed late and Shea fell into the habit of guiding her down the steep trail to the river road if it was near dark. Emma was glad that Shea had come to like Rachel, for he had been so circumspect of her in the beginning.

"Shea, I'm glad that you and Rachel are getting along. I thought that she was too overbearing for you."

"She is your friend and I will treat her with respect, but sometimes she says things that she should not."

"She embarrasses you sometimes?"

Shea nodded. "Yes, that is it."

"She means no harm. Just sometimes she says everything that's in her head."

Shea smiled and kissed her. "I am glad you do not act like that. I love you, Emma, I always will," he said.

Emma and Shea's sex life revived after the six weeks were up and he made frantic, passionate love to her. "I have missed you, so . . . missed you," he said nuzzling her.

Emma said, "Maybe this is the place we've been looking for."

He kissed her throat tenderly and said, "We will stay as long as you want."

"I love it here. I have everything I need now."

With Jason's escort as insulation, Emma, Shea, and Katherine came to town in October. People gathered around as they walked through town, stopping to admire the baby. For the moment at least, their plans to push on were forgotten. Their sorrowful lives had struck a cord and the townspeople were proud to have them as residents and frontier celebrities.

In a turn of sentiment peculiar to isolated areas in the west, Emma and Shea gained acceptance in the town of Easthope, first as curiosities, later as legitimate members of the community. Doubtless the Cody articles were the catalyst, but Emma and Shea earned a measure of respect from the people in the small mountain town.

They always stopped in to visit Rachel and had come to know her husband Caleb as well. He was a tall man, but slightly built and very thin, looking rather frail with a haggard expression. He looked the perfect banker. At first he was wary of Shea. Having an Indian in the house at first unsettled him. Shea knew this and always made excuses and departed, saying that he had business elsewhere. It bothered Emma, even though she tried to hide it by backing up Shea's excuses to depart, but eventually, Caleb relaxed and Shea came farther than just inside the front door to drop off or pick up Emma and Katherine.

After negotiating with a stubborn Jason, Emma and Shea purchased the cabin and the surrounding acres for a ridiculously small price and made their home in the hills of Easthope.

Fall was fast approaching and the days grew shorter. Leaves turned to deep golds and russets. This was Emma's favorite time of year. Rachel still came often and Shea always escorted her down the hill in the evenings, a perfect gentleman, Emma thought.

Not long before snow locked them in until spring, Rachel arrived at the cabin one morning. She managed a tight smile when Emma greeted her, then found out why later on as they sipped coffee near the hearth. It was Emma's turn to prod until Rachel said what was on her mind.

"Emma, I'm pregnant."

She hugged her. "That's wonderful! Katherine will have a playmate her age! When's it due?"

"June, I expect."

"How did Caleb take the news?"

"He's happy. We wanted another child, but I didn't think that it would be so soon. Helen's only ten months and having two little ones in diapers is going to be hard, but I suppose other women have gotten through it, right?"

Emma smiled, longing for a brother or sister for Kate. She then packed up Rachel's maternity dresses and promised to return the baby clothes that Katherine would soon outgrow.

As usual, Shea led Rachel's team down the steep hill at twilight. When he returned he said, "It is getting very cold. Snow is coming, so we might not see your friend for a while."

In March, Emma strolled outdoors holding Katherine, bundled against the cold. Snow had been heavy, but Emma was getting a little cabin fever, so she took a walk and stood overlooking the valley. Evergreen branches were laden with snow and the river cut a blue streak between the snowbound hills in the valley far below. Muffled sounds from the logging camp were heard in the winter quiet.

Shea sat on the fallen log in front of the cabin fixing some worn bridles. Suddenly, he stood and whipped around. Before him stood several Indians. He moved cautiously with one eye on Emma and Katherine. One of the men approached from the tree line.

"Chief Lame White Deer. I am Yakima," he said. He was very tall with broad shoulders, deep set eyes, long gray-streaked hair, and chiseled features. He approached confidently but solemnly.

"Shea Hawkshadow of the Cheyenne."

Lame White Deer pointed to Shea's neck and he understood. He unbuttoned his coat and pulled his shirt collar down, displaying the scars from the hanging around his throat.

Lame White Deer said, "No trouble."

Emma heard the voices and turned, clutching Katherine close to her when she saw the Indians standing at the tree line. She stood stock–still, her heartbeat quickening in alarm.

"What do you want with us?" Shea's keen instincts were primed. He was within arm's reach of his rifle, a fact not lost on Lame White Deer.

"Are you man or spirit?" he asked.

Shea was perplexed by the question. "I am a man. I live in peace with my wife and child."

Emma began to make her way toward the safety of the cabin. Her movements caught Shea's eye and he motioned for her to stay put.

"Cheyenne call your wife *maiyun*. She spirit?"

"She is to my people," Shea replied, now understanding why the Yakima had come.

Lame White Deer motioned to another Yakima brave who came forward and handed him a large bundle wrapped in buckskin and a wooden carrier for the baby. "Gifts for the *maiyun* and her child." He held the two items out at arm's length and Shea accepted them with a solemn nod. Without another word, Lame White Deer and the others melted back into the woods.

Emma came to Shea's side moments later. "What was that all about? Who are they?"

"Yakima," he answered. "Chief Lame White Deer with gifts for the baby."

"Do you know them?"

"No, but they know us. They have been keeping an eye on us from a distance. They believe that you are a spirit and so is Katherine. The gifts show their respect for you and Katherine." He smiled with a hint of wonder. "He called you *maiyun*. Looks like the story Red Leaf Woman and the children made up about you made it all the way here. We will have no trouble from them."

"How can you be sure? Should we tell Jason about this? Maybe he can head off any trouble."

Shea shook his head. "Yakima would not lie about their purpose, especially when bringing gifts to honor the local spirits—you and Kate. They are a little afraid of us and that is how I want it to stay."

Indoors, they unwrapped the bundle. It contained handmade rattles and animal shaped toys carved from soft pine. There were also tiny buckskin dresses for Katherine. Shea examined the back cradle, pronouncing it very handsome and well made.

"Do you think they'll come again?"

"They will keep watching us from a distance to see if you or Kate perform any tricks of a *maiyun*, but they will not harm you."

"You're so sure?" Emma felt uneasy.

Shea shrugged it off and did not seemed concerned.

Winter ended reluctantly in the high country, but a dry April allowed Emma, Shea, and Katherine to travel down to Easthope once again.

Rachel was huge, nearing her seventh month. She said that she felt fine, but Emma could not help notice a look she caught in her eye sometimes. When she asked what was wrong, Rachel always dismissed her concerns.

"I can't help it. I always feel strange when I'm pregnant. This is my third child, but I can't shake the feeling that something will go wrong."

Emma promised to help when the time came. In mid–June, Emma took Katherine and stayed at Rachel's awaiting the birth. Shea remained at the cabin and came to town now and then, but he never stayed long at the Barlows, excusing himself and spending a lot of time with Jason or with Harris Brody, the son of the town's blacksmith and wheelwright, who had taken over the business for his aging father.

Stuart and Emma were beside Rachel when the final contractions came and Emma was first to hold Rachel's newborn son, Randall Stephen Barlow. He had Caleb's dark hair and slim build. Rachel held her newborn son and wept.

"He's a little early," Stuart said to Rachel, "but he looks fine, just fine."

Caleb was pleased with another son. Later, Shea came and took a long look at the boy. Emma knew that Shea was slightly disappointed that their first child was a girl, but they were actively trying to have another, despite their history. She remained a week until Rachel was up and around again. Caleb's sister Ruth then stayed with Rachel.

The next five years were peaceful and rich for the little Hawkshadow family. The town had formed a sort of protective shell around them, with Rachel and Jason their staunchest allies. They came to town most every week except in winter, and had made a few friends. Each April, they always made the trip down the mountain to celebrate Jason's birthday on April 28.

Emma was especially keen to be with Jason for his birthday since he had no family in town.

Shea accepted the peaceful existence set before him in Easthope and doted upon his daughter.

Jason's business grew and for many months he seldom had time to visit. But Jason still held the annual logging exhibition in the summer and the Hawkshadows never missed it. Shea tried his hand at the various wood cutting contests, but his wind did not support such exertion. Still, he proved a winner two years running with logrolling, in which competitors stand on floating logs and roll them with their feet. He was agile with remarkable balance.

Just after Kate's fifth birthday, a photographer passing through town begged to take Shea's portrait after discovering who he was. Some townspeople had assumed bragging rights that the Hawkshadows were residents of Easthope. At Emma's urging, Shea reluctantly agreed and the young man found his way up to the cabin on a rented mount, loaded down with his camera, tripod, and plates. He took several photographs of the three of them standing together outside the cabin, then asked Shea to don his native clothing, which, to Emma's surprise, he did. Many photos were taken of him, some close–ups of his magnificent face and others showing details of his dress, bow, arrows, and shield. Months later, Jason delivered a package from the photographer. It held a dozen of the photos, free of charge. Kate treasured them and kept them beneath her bed in a cigar box that Jason had given her.

Years before, Emma had persuaded Jason to allow her to invest in his mill and logging business and the dividends were enough to support them as the years passed. They were able to afford two proper pull horses for the wagon, relieving Butternut and Shea's pony of the chore. Besides, Emma's horse and Shea's pony were growing old and were left to graze in a small paddock that Jason helped Shea to build.

Emma often wondered where Adam was now and often wrote him at the Bureau of Indian Affairs in Washington, D.C., but she never received replies. Either he was no longer there or did not want to answer, she thought.

Emma fought off bouts of depression, in particular that her parents would never have the pleasure of knowing Kate. Even though she had everything she could want, having no family to share Kate with was often difficult. Her lingering sadness was fought off with her habit of locking up her emotions and proceeding with her day–to–day life.

Her friendship with Rachel deepened as well and Helen and Randall were Kate's favorite playmates. When in town, Emma and Kate spent their time with the Barlows. Emma and Rachel visited and watched the children play. Shea, uncomfortable around what he called 'women's talk,' always went off to see Jason or Harris Brody.

Kate had grown into a female version of her father, whom she openly worshipped. Shea spent every spare minute with her, teaching her Indian ways and the ways of the land and its animals. Her resemblance to him was remarkable, with the same thick black hair, narrow face and high cheekbones. Her eyes were shaped in half-moons like Shea's, but were the deep blue of Emma's. Kate had inherited Shea's stubbornness as well, for she would not come when Emma called her. This made Emma frequently impatient. She could not tear Kate and Shea away from each other, but she loved to watch them as they played, fished, and wrestled. Shea and Kate even built a small fort just inside the tree line where the two of them spent hours together, continually improving and expanding the structure. Shea's face brightened with joy, absorbed in his child. He was happy for the first time in his life.

Despite diligent efforts, Emma had not become pregnant again and they had given up, but when they took to bed after Kate was tucked in, their passion for each other burned as brightly as ever as their bodies entwined, then later parted, sweating and sated. Emma's figure was still slim but had lost that girlish straightness; her hips and breasts had rounded and become more womanly. Shea found her more desirable than ever. Another child mattered less and less as the years passed and Shea and Emma spoiled their vivacious child.

Chapter Thirteen

In the spring of 1887, Shea suddenly became ill. He had a deep, persistent cough and weakened very quickly doing daily chores. Although he had no symptoms of fever, aches, or pain, he became easily winded with any exertion. He looked healthy, but Emma worried about him and convinced him to see Stuart.

Emma had stayed alone in the tiny waiting room, leaving Kate at Rachel's that morning. Jason poked his head in several times during the morning, but each time she had no news for him.

In the early afternoon, Stuart emerged from his office. "Come in, Emma." He looked weary, but his tone was brisk and clinical.

Shea sat in a chair before Stuart's desk, impassive and staring. Emma sat in the other chair.

"I'm afraid that the news isn't good," Stuart began. Emma's chest felt tight and she held her breath. "Shea has tumors in his throat caused by the hanging, I believe. I can't tell if they're malignant until I get in there and see what we're dealing with, but this is serious enough to operate, tomorrow if you agree, Shea. I want you to go to the hospital today to prepare."

"Shea?" Emma paled and fought back tears. "What do you want to do, Shea?"

His eyes met hers, eyes filled with dread. He cleared his throat, fighting another coughing spasm. "Whatever Stuart wants to do is fine." He drew a quick breath and coughed.

He had surgery the next morning, on Saturday.

Rachel found a sitter for Kate and her own children and stayed with Emma in the waiting room at the hospital. Stuart called in Allison Carruthers, who, in addition to running the general store with her husband Gale, also had been a surgical nurse during the Civil War when she and her husband had lived in Maryland.

Before the operation, Stuart allowed Emma and Shea a few moments alone.

"I love you so much. We'll get through this somehow. After all we've been through, nothing can take you from me." She kissed his lips and backed out of the room. He smiled at her, but he was scared. She was frightened, too; she could do nothing to help him.

Her stomach rolled with waves of apprehension during the endless hours of waiting. Rachel prodded her to eat something, offering to get her a meal from Murdock's, but Emma refused. As soon as he could get away from the mill, Jason came to sit with them. He was quiet and brooding.

Just before five o'clock in the evening, Stuart came and asked to speak with Emma in a small office. His face was unreadable.

"He's sleeping off the ether. He came through fine." He stood next to a desk, motioning Emma to a chair. Her face was hopeful, searching. "I removed the tumors that I could, but Emma, some of them appear malignant. I can't remove them without damaging his esophagus. We bought him some time, but the cancer will continue to spread." He sat on the edge of the desk. "He has six months, maybe, I can't be sure." Her face crumbled and her mouth quivered as tears fell unchecked, wetting her face and trickling down her neck. "I'm sorry, Emma, real sorry. Towards the end, I'll make sure he's in no pain." Stuart's own sadness was evident. He had great respect for and a long friendship with Shea.

"Does he know?"

"No. He'll wake soon. You should be there when I tell him."

"Can I see him now?" she asked. Her own throat felt constricted in response to the tragic news. She wiped her tears away and fought to compose herself as Stuart took her to Shea's room. His neck was heavily bandaged. She pulled a chair next to the bed and kissed his cheek.

When Shea awoke, Emma leaned close and touched his face with tenderness. Shea read her face even before Stuart gave him the grim news. He could not speak, but accepted it with characteristic stoicism. But in his heart, he was devastated. Most of all, he regretted that he would not see Kate grow up. Stuart quietly closed the door after him, leaving them alone.

Emma's face was ashen and her eyes were red–rimmed and puffed. She trembled in spite of all the control that she could summon. "Maybe there are doctors in the east who have more experience with this. Maybe we can borrow money from Jason for the trip. I love Stuart like a father, but maybe he doesn't know everything," she said through tears.

Shea shook his head and she read his answer in his eyes. He knew no other doctor would help an Indian, no matter how far they traveled, no matter how much money they had to spend.

Taking a pad of paper from his bedside table, he wrote, "It is all right, Emma. I am not afraid."

She touched her lips to his. "I am."

Rachel gripped Jason's arm when Stuart came to the waiting room and told them the sad news. They sat together in shocked silence.

When Emma emerged an hour later, Rachel rushed to her. "Oh, Emma! We'll do all we can to help, of course. Whatever you need."

Jason stepped forward, his eyes brimming with tears. Emma stepped into his embrace, his strong chest and warmth a much–needed comfort. He tried to speak several times, but his voice kept choking off.

Emma read the question on his face. "He doesn't seem afraid." She stepped away and landed in a chair, breaking into sobs. "I don't know how I'm going to tell Kate! She worships him!" She was shaking and breathing too fast. Jason caught her as she sagged. He held her as Rachel ran to find Stuart.

"I'm all right, Rachel. Don't bother Stuart. Just give me a minute." She took several deep breaths to steady herself. "I have to go to tell Kate."

"No, Emma, wait," Jason pleaded. "You're in no shape right now. I'll talk to her for you."

"No, Jason. I have to do this myself." With Jason and Rachel flanking her, she held herself together during the walk to Rachel's house. The cool evening air revived her a little, but it was the longest walk of her life. She dreaded what she had to tell her six–year–old daughter. The town swam before her tear–filled eyes, its colors mixing and smearing. She had made a promise to herself when Kate was born that she would always be truthful with her, but she had not bargained on telling her little girl that her father was dying. Jason had an arm around Emma and his grip felt sure and solid. Rachel exchanged sorrowful looks with Jason as they walked, wiping her own tears away.

Kate had been sitting on Rachel's porch and she ran to her mother's waiting arms. Rachel cleared Caleb and the children out of the house and along with Jason, waited on the front porch while Emma and Kate went inside. Emma came out much later, holding the weeping child, her shoulders soaked by her daughter's tears.

"Stay here, please, Emma, to be nearby for Shea," Rachel said.

Emma looked to the street. She had intended to stay at Murdock's hotel, but decided to remain with Rachel. Jason and Rachel's boys were leading the horses and wagon back to Rachel's stable. Later, Caleb brought in Emma and Kate's clothing, packed in burlap bags. Emma nodded thanks to Caleb and cradled and rocked Kate on the porch swing. Kate cried herself to sleep and Emma carried her inside and deposited her in a spare bedroom that Rachel had already set up for them.

That night in bed, Caleb held Rachel. "It's not fair. Those two have been to hell and back. What will Emma do without Shea? And poor Kate. To lose her father. I don't know what I would do if I lost you, Rachel." For the first time in many weeks, Caleb and Rachel made love. Shea's illness had given both of them a new appreciation of how fast everything could change.

Over the next several days, Emma slept with Kate to reassure her that she was not alone and to assure herself of the same.

Emma spent a week with Shea at the hospital, feeding him, helping him change clothes, and seeing that he slept as much as possible. Kate begged to see her father, but Stuart would not allow it, nor did Shea want her to see him yet. Stuart's incision had effectively cut Shea's throat from ear to ear. Emma had a very difficult time explaining this to the child. Depriving Kate of her father for even a day wounded Emma deeply.

The Barlow family made them welcome and made sure that Emma and Kate ate, sometimes having to force the issue, especially with Emma.

"Emma, you need your strength," Rachel prodded.

But with every bite Emma took, she knew that this simple act could no longer be enjoyed by Shea. Stuart had warned her that his diet would now be almost entirely liquids. Her memory drifted back to his injuries after the hanging. He had lived through that horrible ordeal, despite the fact that their marriage had splintered. But even then she had a shred of hope. This time there was none—nothing to steady her. When alone she broke down in sobs, sometimes to the point of nearly fainting. And perhaps in sympathy for Shea, she found it hard to catch her breath. Sleeping was fitful and brief, which only fueled her dread. She grew thin, failing in unison with Shea. Rachel and Caleb appealed to her to talk to them, Stuart—anyone. Rachel watched Emma crumble as she tried to cope alone.

Emma was punishing herself. She still held onto the belief that her presence at the Montana reservation had sparked the ambush. She was blaming herself for Shea's cancer and there was little Rachel or Jason could do to change her mind.

Jason went to the cabin each day, keeping up with the chores and feeding and exercising Shea's pony and Butternut. He even brought down clean clothing for them and some of Kate's toys and books.

Stuart wanted Shea to stay in the hospital until the end, but he would not hear of it.

After a week in the hospital, he wrote, "I want to die on my own land, in my own house. I want to go home."

Emma, Shea, and Kate were shepherded up to the cabin by Rachel, Caleb, and Stuart in their wagon. Jason rode beside them on his mount. Shea was carried inside on a stretcher and lifted onto the bed.

Jason paused a moment at Shea's bedside while Emma and Kate bade good–bye to the Barlows.

Shea motioned for a pencil and paper and wrote. "After I am gone, take care of them for me."

"Of course I will."

The next note read, "I know you love Emma. She will come around if you give her time. She will have a good life with you."

Jason did not dispute the truth of Shea's words. Such pretense was unnecessary between them. He took his friend's hand firmly in his.

Jason, Rachel, and Stuart came often to help and Emma did appreciate their presence, but alone at night, she fought to hold together. She masked her troubled soul, tending Shea with tenderness and cheerfulness, but inside, she was broken, panicked about what she would do in the aftermath. The fact that she would soon be a widow shadowed her constantly. With weakening self-control, she tried to push away the shadows.

Unable to speak for weeks, Shea communicated via pencil and paper, holding long conversations with Emma. Shea's eyes fell upon her beautiful face in the dim lamp light and his heart swelled with love. Kate tried to amuse him by telling him made–up stories. He cherished every moment with her and his beloved Emma. But he felt a creeping dread, sometimes impossible to keep at bay, that soon he would never see Emma's delicate features again, that he would never again hold his daughter's chubby, soft hand. Tears were not part of a warrior's life, but in moments alone, he wept.

In June, he left the bed and soon tried his voice. It was weak, a shadow of what it had been. He had to strain for every word, but Emma was encouraged and heartened by his stamina. He tried to resume his usual chores, but he could do little heavy work. Emma took to chopping wood and Kate carried heavy loads, despite her youth. As Shea watched them toil, he became withdrawn, spending many hours at the stream fishing, coming to terms with his imminent death. But Emma was not coping. She watched him through eyes rimmed red from frequent crying spells that sprang upon her. He tried to comfort her and although he did not have the strength to make love to her, he held her tight in the night.

Emma tried to rally by holding a party for Kate's seventh birthday in August. The Barlow children came up and Shea seemed to be his old self, enjoying the afternoon. But the thought that Shea was witnessing his child's birthday for the last time devastated him—and Emma.

Jason came often and Shea visibly brightened when he arrived. He helped chop wood and tend the animals and even cooked supper sometimes, for Emma lacked the energy many days.

One such afternoon Jason and Shea sat at the edge of the stream, their fishing poles in the water.

Shea's voice was frail. "Jason, after I am gone, I do not want Emma and Kate living up here alone. She says that she wants to stay up here, but she cannot. It is too dangerous and too far from town."

Jason knew what Shea was asking and tried to put his mind at ease. "I've been thinking about that, too. I wanted to offer my mother's house to them, if that's all right with you. I would be next door to watch over them. They would want for nothing."

Shea was relieved. "Thank you. That would be good. Very generous, Jason." His voice faded and he cleared his throat several times. "You have kept the house shut up all these years, but I do not know where else they can go. Emma needs to be someplace where she feels safe and Kate should be near her friends."

"I've had that house shut up for too long. I would be honored to do this for you."

"I will tell Emma tonight."

Jason looked at Shea thoughtfully. "Shea, are you afraid?"

Shea's eyes seemed to spark a little and he smiled crookedly. "I would be lying if I said no, but I always knew that I would not live long."

"What do you mean?"

"All my life I have had dreams about dying. I would die bravely in battle, defending my people or I would give my life to save another. I always knew that my death would serve a purpose."

"Purpose?"

"Most everything bad that has happened to Emma is because of me. She has been through a lot and it is time Wise One Above takes me from her so that she can have peace. She will not be alone. She will have you to care for her. I know how you feel about her, I think I knew the day you first came here. She will always have you to look after her and Kate. I can die easier knowing that."

Jason looked at once sad and embarrassed. "So it shows, eh?" He sat back against a rock and breathed out a long breath. "Shea, I never had designs on your wife."

"You are a man of honor and you have been a true friend to us. I see how you watch Emma. She is not even aware of it, but I see. You love her."

"But, Shea—"

"I am not angry or jealous. The funny thing is that I thought I would be, but I am not. Somehow you are the right man for her." He smiled. "Years ago, I almost lost her to Adam Lawrence. She would have left with him if she had not been pregnant with Kate. I was so jealous and afraid to lose her."

"Emma loves you. I can't take your place in her heart. And Kate—I could never be what you are to her."

"You will be. But give Emma time." He landed a fish, pulled out the hook, and put it in the creel. "Emma is very tough, but she lives her life in each moment. Her past and her future do not exist. You will be her future, but you have to know her past to understand her. You need to know everything." The two men talked a long time.

Later, Shea was very tired and Jason helped him to standing, then the two of them walked back towards the cabin. Jason looked troubled after hearing the details of Emma's past. "I had no idea that she's been through so much. Cody's articles left out a lot. I'll help her, I promise."

"Jason, when I die I want to be buried underground. Emma may want to bury me in the Cheyenne way, under rocks, but I cannot stand the thought of an animal digging it up. I do not want them to see such a thing. Will you do this for me?" he rasped.

Jason could only nod, fighting tears.

That night, Shea told Emma that he wanted her to move to town after his death.

"This is our home. I want to stay here."

His voice was thin and strained. "It is already settled. You cannot live here alone and you know it."

"But, Shea, I can't leave you."

"It is not my choice, but I have to leave you. I go with you wherever you live. My body remains, but that is not me. I am in you and Kate. Do this for me. I have to make sure that you and Kate are safe and cared for."

Rachel came up often to bolster Emma, trying to get her mind off her growing despair. She brought Helen and Randall as playmates for Kate on weekends and in this way they all held vigil around Shea. Rachel often broke down when Emma did, the two women crying on one another's shoulders.

Emma saw the pain etched in Jason's eyes as he watched his friend deteriorate and weaken as the cancer spread. Shea's condition held until mid–October when he took to bed, his strength failing.

Each night when Emma tucked Kate into bed, the child came into the habit of asking, "Will Daddy be here in the morning?" Biting back tears, Emma always replied that he would.

Emma watched her once–strong husband grow thin and frail as the cancer chipped away at his body and at her soul. He was entirely on liquids now and had lost a lot of weight. Jason came to stay, knowing that the end was near. He had constructed a bed for himself, which was wedged in the main room against the wall near the door. Emma lived and slept in the rocker at Shea's bedside, refusing the same bed, unable to cope with the fact that he would soon not be there.

One night very near the end, Emma and Shea were alone in the bedroom.

"I have to tell you something," he said in a strained whisper. "This will not be easy for you to hear." She sat forward, his hand in hers, straining to hear him. "After Kate was born, Rachel and I—Rachel and I were together. I did not mean for it to happen. She is your friend and you should not blame her. I was weak and a fool."

Tears of shock slid down her cheeks and her hand fell away from his.

"It did not last long. I do not know what was wrong with me. I loved you then and I love you now." He lay quiet a long time, a single tear sliding down his cheek. "I did not feel like a man then. I could not give you the things you needed." Emma became very still as they sat together in silence. Shea watched her face for some reaction. "I am sorry, Emma."

She soon stood, smoothing her dress and wiping away her tears. "It's time for your laudanum. You need to sleep." She smiled and went to a small table and measured out the medicine, taking great care as she gave it to him.

His hand gripped hers. "I love you, Emma. I always have." His voice was nearly gone. "Forgive me."

"I love you, too, and I think I understand. Rest now. I'll be right here in the morning."

Jason was reading to Kate by the fire when Emma entered the main room later that night. Jason saw something in her face that alarmed him. "Emma? What's wrong? Is it Shea?"

"He's sleeping."

They stayed up late, talking about many trivial things after Kate was in bed. Emma was distressed and Jason sensed that it was something other than Shea's illness.

"You look all twisted up," he said. "Do you want to talk about it?"

"No—no offense. It's something between me and Shea. It's all right though," she said mostly to herself. "It's all right."

Emma woke early and tended to Shea as if nothing had happened the night before. She sat with him a long time, reading to him. Jason and Kate played and sledded outside.

Days later, Shea's voice failed him. He was weak, but communicated using pencil and paper. Soon even that became too difficult. He was failing very fast and Emma's dread grew, but she held it in check—she had to. She had Kate to consider.

Emma joined Jason outdoors one afternoon as Shea slept. "He's very weak," she said. Jason put an arm around her shoulder. He felt solid, strong, warm. For a few brief minutes, they watched Kate make another snowman; she had made a dozen already. Emma looked up and saw Jason's eyes well with tears.

"I'm really going to miss him, Emma."

She lacked the strength to console him, but wished that she could take his pain away somehow. If it was anything close to what she was feeling, Jason was in bad shape as well. And Kate coped by staying occupied, alternately playing by herself and entertaining her father, building strength in herself as her father slipped away from her.

"I have to get back to him," Emma said at length.

Late that afternoon, Stuart and Rachel came up on Stuart's sledge. Emma steeled herself as they pulled up. She had been so numb since Shea's confession that she had no idea how she would react around Rachel. She had bigger things to worry about and somehow the affair did not matter so much in the face of what was to come.

Rachel reacted when she saw her face. "How's he doing, Emma?" she said, bracing herself for the worst.

"It'll be any time now, I think. He's so weak."

Everyone went inside out of the cold. Stuart examined Shea and emerged from the bedroom, shaking his head in sadness and speaking in a hushed voice. "I gave him some stronger medicine that will make him comfortable." He put a hand on Emma's shoulder. "You should be with him."

She and Kate went into the bedroom and Kate took her place on Emma's lap in the rocker. Shea dozed fitfully that afternoon and Emma remained by his side, refusing the dinner that Rachel prepared.

The November skies darkened fast and Stuart regretted that he and Rachel had to go to beat the dark home. "I would stay if I could, Emma, but I've done all I can."

"Stuart, I thank you. You've allowed him to go with dignity."

Rachel came to her. "We'll come tomorrow, I promise." Emma nodded and accepted Rachel's affectionate hug.

After they left, Jason came in with a chair to sit with Emma and Kate at Shea's bedside. Kate soon fell asleep in Emma's lap. This night, she did not ask if her father would be there in the morning. Emma held her tight.

On the night of November 12, Shea woke, his eyes clear with a hint of the old intensity that Emma knew so well. He fought the final battle, summoning his remaining strength. Kate woke as Emma handed her to Jason. Emma sat with Shea on the bed, cradling him in her arms.

"I love you, Shea, and I forgive you, *nameh'o*," were her last words to him.

He closed his eyes and died minutes later in Emma's arms.

Jason wept as he watched his friend take his last breath then slump. He had fulfilled his promise to Shea. He was there at the end and his job now was to bury his friend and care for Emma and Kate, according to Shea's wishes.

Emma sat with Shea in her arms, holding him tight. She had not the strength to cry, but felt a profound emptiness invade her heart as his life slipped away. She looked at Shea's magnificent face, peaceful and free of pain; she could not help but feel some level of relief for him. He was free.

Soon, she gently laid him down. She softly called to Kate and the child ran to her mother's arms. She rocked her precious girl as Kate cried herself asleep.

Jason's voice was barely audible. "Emma, why don't you put Kate in bed. I'll take care of Shea." She rose and carried Kate to her room. Jason pulled the curtain behind her, then washed Shea's body and covered it.

Emma waited in the main room, leaning against the mantel, her face pallid in the dim light from the fire in the hearth. Jason went to her and held her as tears finally flowed and she sobbed on his broad shoulder. He cried, too, gripping her so very tight. Neither of them slept that sad night.

Early the next morning, Rachel, Caleb, and Stuart arrived. Rachel knew that Shea was gone. A peculiar quiet pervaded the air. Emma sat on the log outside the cabin, barely visible in fog hovering just above the snow, her arms wrapped around Kate, rocking her. As they drew nearer, they saw Jason digging a grave a short way up a small rise east of the cabin.

Stumbling through the deep snow, Rachel fell to her knees before Emma. "When?" she asked out of breath, tears stinging her eyes.

"Last night." Emma hugged Kate tight.

"I'm so sorry," she said, not knowing what else to say.

Emma looked at her, unable, hindered by grief and fatigue, to condemn her for the affair with Shea. She saw true friendship and love in Rachel's face as she knelt before her in the snow. "He was in no pain at the end. He woke for a moment, then just fell asleep, it seemed. He's at peace now."

Caleb and Stuart came to her, offering their condolences.

"I wish I could've done more, Emma," Stuart said. Emma took his hand, the look on her face telling him that she knew he had done all that he could.

Caleb was overcome and shook his head with sadness. Caleb had acquired an unusual respect for Shea and his death hit him hard. "I'm real sorry, Emma. I'll miss him. We'll go help Jason," he said.

The fog burned away as the sun rose high. Its light shone upon the glittering snow. Stuart, Caleb, and Jason went into the cabin with a stretcher from the sledge. Shea's body was put on it and the three men carried him to the grave. Emma, Kate, and Rachel followed. Shea was clad in his old leggings, soft buckskin shirt and moccasins. His bow, some of his arrows and his shield were carefully arranged at his side. At the graveside, his body was covered and lowered into the ground. Emma wept and Kate clung to her, wailing.

Emma felt faint and drained, too overcome to speak at the graveside. Her memory drifted to the day Shea kissed her for the first time, the moment she knew she loved him, their reunion after the outbreak and their joy at Kate's birth. She would not trade a moment, except for this one. She reached down and petted Kate's hair. The child's arms remained locked around her mother's waist.

Stuart said a few words of comfort and Caleb recited a prayer. Then Jason stepped to the head of the grave and spoke, his voice thick with emotion.

"Today I bury the finest friend I've ever had, Shea Hawkshadow of the Cheyenne." He sniffled and cleared his throat several times before he could continue. "We became as close as brothers. He trusted me, something I know he didn't do easily. He was a man of great strength and dignity—a survivor." He looked to Emma and Kate. "He loved you both so dearly. He told me often, but I never got tired of seeing the look on his face when he spoke of you. You were his life. I grieve with you because I've lost my best friend. Shea has many people who will always remember him." Jason could not continue and stepped back, allowing everyone to say their own silent prayers.

Rachel tried to lead Emma away as Jason, Stuart, and Caleb filled in the grave, but she refused. No flowers grew in winter, so Emma and Kate knelt together, placing boughs of evergreen upon the mound. Hand in hand, Emma and Kate shuffled back to the cabin through the deep snow. As they did, a fine, glittering snow began to fall, its particles lit by the sun, diamonds falling from the sky. Emma felt them melt on her face, mingling with her warm tears. Kate held out her hand, catching the sparkling bits in her palm, sure that her father's spirit sent them as a gift. She raised her face to the sky, smiling for a moment.

Jason and Stuart put together a meal while Rachel and Caleb worked in the sickroom, changing the linens and airing out the room, making it fit for Emma. Kate curled on Emma's lap in the rocker gazing into the fire, silent.

The flow of tears had stopped for now, replaced by numbing grief. Jason offered Emma coffee and Kate some hot cider, but both refused, shaking their heads in unison. Later, they did sit at the table. Kate stayed glued to her mother's lap and ate some, but Emma only picked, her appetite lost. To combat the stillness, Jason and the others talked among themselves, trying to keep Emma company on this, the saddest day of her life.

Near nightfall, Rachel, Caleb, and Stuart departed, but Jason remained. Before Stuart left, he gave Emma laudanum to help her sleep. She gripped the bottle. With an inward shudder, she watched them disappear into the darkness down the hill. She hated it when people left. She always felt cut adrift.

After putting an exhausted Kate to bed, Emma came to sit with Jason before the fire and cried. Jason kneeled before her and held her. The sweet smell of earth from the grave was still on him.

"Get some rest now," he urged. "Rachel and Caleb cleaned the room for you."

"I can't go in there just yet." She spent the night sleepless in the rocker by the fire.

Jason rested on the bed against the wall, but he was wakeful, watching over Emma who did not leave the rocker all night except to check on Kate and feed the fire.

The next morning dawned bright, mocking Emma's profound sorrow. Kate slept and although it was approaching noon, Emma left her alone. Jason came in after a very quick dip in the stream. His hair was frozen into spikes.

Emma managed a small smile at his appearance. "I should try to reach Adam. He needs to know what's happened. Maybe he'll answer my letters now." Her face was set and still. "Jason, I don't know what I would've done without you. But you should go home and rest. You look exhausted. We'll be okay."

Jason could not bring himself to say that she looked worse. Yellow circles of fatigue showed beneath her eyes.

Jason understood her need for solitude but would not leave her alone. He broached the subject carefully. "Emma, please come to town as soon as you're able. I'm staying with you until you do, all right? Caleb has been overseeing a crew from the mill working on my mother's house. It's ready for you and Kate. Just let me know when it's time."

"I know that I should come down. Kate should go to school in town, too. We'll come down soon, I just can't say when right now."

Kate rose soon after, her eyes red and puffed from crying. "I want my Daddy back," she said through sobs. "I want Daddy . . ." Emma swept her up in her arms, soothing the child and stroking her long black hair.

Twilight fell upon the cabin and on the woman inside. That night, while Jason was in a deep sleep, Emma donned her coat and left the cabin, walking through freshly fallen snow to Shea's grave. Light faded from a purple and orange sky.

"What am I to do now, Shea? I'm afraid, so afraid." She remained at Shea's grave a very long time, her sobs muffled by the snow that began to fall again. She felt as if the flow of tears would never stop.

Later, she summoned her courage and returned to the cabin. She pulled off her coat and went into the bedroom that she had shared with her beloved Shea. Jason woke for a moment and saw her go in, but he said nothing.

Rachel and Caleb had erased all traces of a sickroom. Clean blankets and fresh quilts covered the bed. Emma curled onto the bed, still dressed, too consumed with worry to cry any longer. She was twenty–seven and alone with a young child. Only a small cabin and a few acres marked what she owned in the world. When she moved to town she would have to find work. She had lived off the land all of her life and had no idea what work she could do to support herself and Kate. Sure, the dividends from Jason's mill were generous, a little too generous, she knew, for she always suspected that he put in a little extra toward her monthly payment.

Emma and Shea had talked about selling the cabin back to Jason and had intended to move down the mountain, but now his grave lay yards from the door in the only place that they had ever had a measure of happiness and peace. Many worries kept her awake. She put out her arm behind her, an old habit of reaching for Shea, before she checked herself. It grieved her that he would never be there again. A turbulent chapter of her life had closed, along with her heart. She lay awake for a third night.

Unbeknownst to her, Rachel knew of Emma's desire to mourn in private and discouraged visitors to the cabin in the days following news of Shea's death. Rachel obligingly published Shea's obituary in the town paper. It was the first time that a death notice for an Indian had ever been printed in the Easthope Post. She even paid for a wire to Max Cody at the Omaha Sentinel and another to Adam at the Bureau of Indian Affairs in Washington, D.C., hoping that it would somehow reach him and Emma would have another friend to mourn with her.

Caleb continued to oversee preparations at Beck House in Jason's absence, returning home each night exhausted from double–duty at the house and his job at the bank, but he never complained.

Rumor spread that Emma and Kate would be moving to town. Friends awaited their arrival daily, watching the trail above town for Jason's sledge. The merely curious residents anticipated the reopening of the grand old Beck House, as it was known, for it was obvious that Jason intended for them to live there. The Hawkshadows had made an indelible mark upon the towns-folk, and many intended to offer Emma work. Her grace and strength were touching, along with Shea's unaffected dignity and devotion to his wife and daughter. He had ceased to be the renegade Cheyenne and had become, at least to some, a friend, a neighbor.

Chapter Fourteen

In the days following Shea's death, Rachel's house had become a storehouse of gifts; food, toys, money, and household goods donated by the townspeople were ready to greet Emma and Kate when they came down off the mountain.

A week after Shea's passing, Jason again broached the subject of Emma and Kate moving to town. "Emma, we need to go. Winter's closing in fast up here. You'll start to feel better with a change of scenery. I know this is hard for you, but we have to go."

She sighed and tried to deflect Jason's reasoning. "Jason, you've been up here for weeks and I'm sure that your business has suffered. I can't hold you here any longer. I promise to come down soon. It's just that I can't deal with it right now."

He spoke honestly, but mindful of her apprehension. "Emma, it has to be now. In town we can all watch over you. You and Kate can't be up here alone. What if the weather gets worse and you get snowed in?"

"My husband died!" She drew away and looked out the window toward Shea's grave. "The man I loved is here. Our lives are here. Jason, you shouldn't worry. The Yakima watch over us. I've seen them around and I've seen their tracks in the snow."

"Emma, they do it out of respect for you, Kate, and Shea, but you have to think of Kate now—and yourself."

"I know," she said as a sob escaped. "But I'd be leaving Shea behind—leaving all the memories."

He hugged her. "I felt the same way when my mother passed away. With my brother in Tacoma, I was so alone. I closed up that house because I couldn't stand the memories. I know what it's like. Please. I'm begging you. Come with me."

Grief made her unable to make a decision. "I know you're right, but I can't take any more charity from you—living in your mother's house and everything."

"I promised Shea that I would watch over you both. It's time to leave."

She met his soft green eyes and, at length, relented. "Okay. You're right. That's one thing I can't argue about you. You're always right."

He sighed, relieved. "I'm not always right, Emma. This is what's best for you and I realize that you aren't thinking straight right now. I'm only here to help. Come, there's a lot to pack up. If we get moving now, we can be in town before nightfall."

She turned to him. "Jason, I'm so grateful to you."

"I would do anything for you, Emma."

"Jason, what will people think of me living in such a grand house?"

"I don't believe that I care."

The contents of three lives were loaded into Jason's sledge and they climbed in. They took one last look at the cabin and at the grave just before descending the hill. Emma felt strange and empty, uncertain of the new life facing her. She felt that she betrayed Shea by leaving, but was forced to admit that it was safer to live in town, and it was his wish. She recalled little of the trip down the mountain, preoccupied with fear of what lay ahead with life in town. Kate sat close to her, wrapped in a blanket. The child was quiet, subdued, also uncertain of what her life would be like without her precious father.

The crews at Beck House had departed mere hours before Emma and Kate arrived late that afternoon. Emma at last understood Jason's need to bring her and Kate down off the mountain. It seemed that half the towns-people had heard them coming. Dozens of people followed the sledge, then saw to the unloading of their belongings and carrying them into the house. Rachel, Caleb, and the children came laden with all the gifts that they had been storing. As Emma watched the armloads of generosity from these kind people, she blessed them, but cursed the soul of Paul Tyler and his lynch mob who had taken her husband away from her at the age of thirty.

Few people, other than the town gossips, evinced disapproval of Emma living in Beck House. She was bolstered by Jason's kindness and did not have the energy to care what people thought about her, but she could not shake a feeling of hopelessness. The death of someone she loved had again forced her to leave behind her home.

Evangeline Beck's home was indeed splendid, the grandest house that Emma had ever seen or imagined. Although she had been past it dozens of times, Jason had allowed no one inside for years. It stood next to his own log home on the adjoining lot, three storeys of understated Victorian design on a rise overlooking the river. The facade was stained deep burgundy, with off–white fancy trim around the porch, balconies, and windows. Dormer windows looked down from the third storey. In spring, a perennial garden would line the path to the half–dozen steps leading to the porch, which was painted off-white to match the trim. The covered porch was huge. It was at least fifty–feet long and fifteen feet wide; it spanned the first floor and wrapped around to the back of the house. Two smaller balconies were at the second storey, balancing the massive porch below. Tall, straight lodge–pole pines dwarfed the house, looking fragile as if the snow–laden branches might snap at any moment.

Inside, Emma was further impressed, not only by the sterling condition of the rooms, but by the comfortable elegance of the old furnishings, well made and done in golds and muted reds. She smiled for the first time in weeks, watching Jason as he went around the house lighting the lamps in anticipation of the grand tour. He seemed very proud of his boyhood home, anxious to show it off. Kate kept her hand in Emma's as they passed from room to room as if they were in a museum, touching nothing, humbled by the grandeur. Each room had thick rugs on the floor, as well as beautifully carved clocks that hung on the walls. The ticking of the clocks echoed throughout the house.

Two parlors occupied the front of the home; one was very formal and a casual keeping room was next to the kitchen. The huge kitchen had an indoor water pump, a luxury to Emma, and a water heating tank hooked up to the wood–burning stove. A large washroom adjoined the kitchen. Adjacent to the kitchen, down a short hall was a bathroom with a sink, and the newest indoor luxury—a commode.

Jason blushed. "It works well, no odors, but there's another out the back in a shed in case this one stops working if the pipes freeze."

Kate pulled the chain on the toilet, finding the flushing action particularly fascinating. "This is where we . . ." Emma nodded, smiling and blushing a little herself. "No more outhouses!" Kate giggled.

Jason grinned. "There is another bath upstairs with a tub and shower. You have all the modern conveniences. Maybe Easthope will have gas light soon. There's a pipeline being built in Spokane that might come up here someday."

A huge dining room with large windows and an ornate fireplace spanned nearly the width of the rear of the house. A larder, which joined the kitchen and dining room by a narrow hallway, was tucked behind pine paneling with a secret door that Jason pointed out, demonstrating the spring mechanism that opened it.

"I hid here as a kid, but my mother always knew where to find me. I could always be found where there was food!" Kate noted this hiding place for anticipated games of hide–and–seek.

On the second floor was a huge bedroom suite, complete with built–in closets and a separate dressing room. Large bay windows with upholstered window seats in blue fringed damask fabric overlooked the front and back yards. French doors next to the windows allowed access to balconies, one facing the front and one overlooking the back yard of the house. The bed was huge and dressed in coverlets of pale blue and off–white. The ornately carved headboard of the bed was taller than Emma. A vanity and mirror with a blue tufted chair occupied a corner and across the room was a huge dresser with a dozen drawers. The carpets on the floor muffled their footsteps as they walked back out into the hallway.

"And this," Jason said, opening a door midway between the main suite and two other bedrooms, "is the other bathroom. I have to get the boiler working, though. It hasn't been used in years and it needs some work. For now when you need a bath, you can get hot water from the heater next to the stove and bathe in the washroom. In the meantime I'll have the pipes checked so the water pressure is high enough to bring the hot water up here."

The third floor held three more bedrooms, generously sized with dormer windows, light and sunny from the southeastern exposure.

While descending from the third floor, Emma asked, "Jason, which room was yours?"

His eyes flickered with a mischievous twinkle as he opened a door farthest from the large suite. It was old, but the brown, burgundy, and tan wallpaper had held up remarkably well. An armoire and tall chest of drawers occupied one wall, with an upholstered chair, a bed, and a nightstand on the other. Emma smiled when she saw the bed.

"Yes, I outgrew it by twelve. My father had to lengthen it for me," he said, pointing out the eighteen–inch long boards that extended the bed frame. Kate went to the French doors that opened out to a balcony that overlooked the front yard. Emma called her back inside as she and Jason headed for the stairs.

Jason smiled while he showed Emma and Kate the grounds, especially the huge, hilly back yard. "My mother had a lot of parties here. Once, she had two hundred people here for a barbecue on a September night after the logging contest. It was quite a party—one of the best nights I can ever remember."

"But the logging competition is held in summer, right?" Emma asked.

"Usually," Jason replied, "but that year it rained for weeks and the contest had to be postponed."

He then led them through the snow across the vast yard. "There's a carriage house and stables for six horses and a wagon. And there's a spring house over there. Behind that is a windmill–powered well that pumps the water into the house. A tool shed's back here, too. I hope you don't mind if I borrow things from it now and then."

Emma smiled. "Of course I would never mind that, Jason. It's your property after all."

He shook his head. "This is your home now."

Emma became quiet. Kate wandered off, looking for ways to cut through the fenced yards to get to the Barlows' place on the next street and two houses down. Emma called Kate inside as she and Jason went inside through the back door that opened into the kitchen.

"So, what do you think of the place?" Jason asked.

"I think it's grand—beautiful. You grew up in a palace. I've never seen a place like this before," she said, touching the blue curtains that covered the window in the back door.

"It may look grand, but we were a normal family with problems like everyone else." A shadow crossed his features as he spoke. Emma caught it, but did not pry.

"I can't afford this, Jason."

"You can afford it."

"I couldn't afford the coal to heat the place. It's more of a museum, pardon me for saying. I'm used to much simpler living."

"I'm offering it to you for the bargain price of two dollars a month. I'll take it out of the dividends from the mill. How's that?"

Emma tried to imagine living in such comfort. She felt embarrassed. "Jason, this is too much. I can't accept this."

He looked around, ignoring her refusal. "This is a great house and someone should be living here. I want it to be you." In a tender show of affection,

Jason took both of her hands in his, feeling their softness. "You are so dear to me and if I can give you a safe, comfortable home I'll count my life as worth something. I give this house and everything in it to you. Shea asked me to look after you and this is the best way I know how."

Emma was touched and tears filled her eyes. Jason's strong, warm hands still held hers. She looked into his eyes. "Under such circumstances, I can't, Jason, not this time. It's the most generous offer that you've ever made and you must know how grateful we are to you for everything you've done over the years, but it's impossible. What will people think? They'll know that I can't afford a place like this."

Jason's face fell. Emma saw his reaction and made a counter–offer. "What if we stay the winter, then look for something smaller in spring—something that's in my budget?"

Jason's hands tightened around hers. "Why deplete your money when you don't have to?"

"You don't understand what I meant. I feel embarrassed living in such a grand house. People are kind in this town, but I know some people will gossip and spread rumors. They'll think that you're keeping me."

"I told you before that I don't care what they think! Why do you think I came to the cabin so often? I could be myself around you. I'm so tired of people tiptoeing around me because I'm their boss. No one ever tells me what they really think because I own so much of the town and the mill that gives them their jobs. You and Shea were always honest with me. Everything I ever did, everything I ever brought, was out of friendship. And if the old biddies in town want to wag their tongues, fine with me! The people who know you will stand by you. Forget everyone else."

"Momma, I like it here. Can we stay?" Kate asked as she came in from the back yard.

The stalemate continued as they went to the front parlor, but Jason won out. He did not accept victory smugly or exultantly; he just smiled when Emma acquiesced after a pitched exchange. But she insisted that a lease be drawn up for the rent so that she would not feel like she was taking advantage.

Jason impulsively hugged her when she accepted his offer. He withdrew, embarrassed. "Uh, sorry."

Emma chuckled. "Oh, Jason, don't be silly. But if you were any happier, you might've crushed me!"

The matter was settled at last. Emma and Kate Hawkshadow became permanent residents of Easthope.

Rachel stopped by with Caleb just before dark. Rachel tentatively peeked in the door. "Why, this place is grand, indeed, Emma!" she said with an affected English accent. "You'll need two maids to keep it for you!"

Emma smiled as she stood aside to let them in. "I can't afford to hire myself, Rachel. Maybe I can hire your kids to work for me. They'll work cheap, right?"

"Sorry, Em. I've got them enslaved for the next ten years! My, this place is something!"

"You've never been inside before?" Emma was genuinely surprised.

"All the years that Jason and his family lived here, we were only here once, but it was packed with people and we didn't get a chance to look around. When his mother died years ago, I remember him saying that he hoped to have a reason to open this place again. Looks like he's found his reason."

"We argued over rent for a while, but he won."

Rachel gushed. "Oh, Emma, we can see each other whenever we want to! Just cut through Jason's yard to mine. There's a gate between the two fences."

"I know. Kate's already discovered the shortcut."

Kate jumped into her mother's arms and hugged her neck. "Which room is mine?"

"Any one you want, except for the big one, that's mine, sweetie."

Kate wriggled down and ran up the stairs, examining each room before choosing Jason's former bedroom.

Ever practical, Caleb offered to chop wood for her. "Oh, Caleb, thank you, but I can do it."

"Nonsense," he said. "You need rest and quiet. I have two strong sons who will help you with anything you need done. No arguments now."

The ensuing weeks cheered Emma as word spread that the 'Widow Hawkshadow,' as she was now known, and her daughter were installed in Beck House. They had many visitors jostling with Jason's crews who still had work to finish in the house. Freezing temperatures had frozen the plumbing so there was a lot banging on pipes and heavy footfalls of the men echoing through the house while Emma tried to entertain waves of visitors paying sympathy calls.

The third floor was unused so Emma kept it closed up, but first she nailed all the windows shut on that floor, fearful of a break–in, even at that lofty height. With a pang, she remembered how secure her warrior husband had always made her feel. Now she could not help feeling exposed in the large rooms of the house and she often found it difficult to sleep. The big old house creaked and groaned and she could not shut out the noises. And she could not shut out her grief.

But she loved the huge kitchen and spent much time there with Rachel. She never broached Shea's confession about the affair with Rachel and resolved never to mention it. Emma masked her pain and turned her thoughts to what kind of work she could do to make money. She tried her hand at baking and found that she was pretty good at it. Every time that Rachel visited she left with a basket of cookies, cakes, and pies. Emma toyed with the idea of starting a bakery business, but doubted that her pastries were good enough, or that she had enough money to make the investment. Asking Jason for funds was out of the question. She had taken too much from him already.

Kate virtually lived at the Barlows and it was difficult at first for Emma to let her go, but Rachel calmed her fears. "It's good for her to have other children around. It keeps her mind off things."

Emma began to hate the fact that Rachel was right.

Jason visited often and enjoyed the fine dinners and treats that Emma prepared. He joked that she would make him fat, but he kept coming by. She did feel a little more secure with him just next door and they spent many late evenings together, but still, Emma could only sleep when she was exhausted.

But as Jason watched her one Saturday afternoon, he noticed fatigue dragging her movements.

"Emma, you didn't sleep again last night, did you?" he asked, concerned. "I'll watch over Kate. Take some of Stuart's medicine and sleep."

"I'm just getting used to a new place, that's all. It will pass when I feel more at home here."

Jason knew that was only an excuse and rummaged through a cupboard for the laudanum, untouched since Shea's death. He broke the wax seal.

"Here." He poured a spoonful. "Take this and go upstairs." She shook her head. "You need to rest." He set the spoon on the table, but spilled its contents for all his care. He took her gently by the shoulders. "After you've slept, you'll feel better. I know what I'm talking about." He refilled the spoon and held it to her lips. She obediently swallowed the medicine. "Don't worry about Kate. I'll take care of her." She went upstairs without further word.

Jason peeked in her room an hour later. She had changed into a bed gown and was sprawled across the large bed in a deep sleep. She slept throughout the afternoon and evening.

Noises roused Emma the next morning and she found Jason in the kitchen preparing a breakfast of eggs, bacon, biscuits, and tea. He ceremoniously pulled out a chair for her as she came into the kitchen.

"You look much better. Breakfast's ready. Kate?"

The child shuffled in and slipped into a seat at the table.

"You stayed all night? Why didn't you wake me? What will people think?"

He grinned, relieved that her wry sense of humor was returning. "You know my opinion on that, Emma. Now have a seat and eat something."

"Oh Jason, I couldn't eat a thing."

"Let me show off a little, okay? Sit and eat," he said. She took a sip of hot tea and in a few minutes her appetite returned. She ate everything that he placed before her. Jason sat opposite her at the table, smiling.

She returned his smile. "You were right. I do feel better. I didn't know you could cook."

"Been cooking for myself a long time and I'm pretty good at it, I think."

"It's good, Jason," Kate said through a mouthful of crisp bacon.

Jason skipped church services that morning. Kate was restless, so the three of them ventured outside and played in the yard. A snowball fight ensued, caking them with snow. Jason heard Emma laugh for the first time in months. It gave him hope that she would be all right and come out of the cruel limbo that she had been in during Shea's illness. The Barlow children arrived after services so Emma and Jason retreated to the safety of the porch to escape the flying snow.

"Jason, I'd like to borrow your sledge some morning and go up to the cabin," Emma said as the children chose up sides for another snowball fight. "The weather's held so I think the trail will be in good shape."

"You mean go up alone?"

"I just need to visit Shea, that's all. It's hard to explain. I can get there myself. I don't want to inconvenience you."

He understood her need, but he could not allow her to go alone. "You don't inconvenience me at all. I can drive you both up today." Her head turned, ready to protest, but he continued. "You're not going alone." Emma did not argue. He knew the trails so well and she had to admit that she felt safer with him.

As the three of them came up the hill to the cabin, Jason pulled up the horses as they beheld more than a hundred Yakima beside Shea's grave. Emma smiled, not surprised. She recognized Lame White Deer, Eagle Claw, Far Walker, and several others that she had come to know over the years. She put her hand on Jason's sleeve as he moved to investigate. "They mean no harm. They've come to pay their respects."

Kate watched intently as a low chant began, a haunting song of mourning. When the chant ended, they departed. Lame White Deer brought up the rear and nodded to Emma.

"They consider us strong magic, you know," Emma told Jason as he helped her down from the sledge. "They know about Shea surviving the hanging and they also know that the Cheyenne called me the spirit, *maiyun*."

Emma walked through deep snow to Shea's grave. Kate expressed no interest in going with her for the moment, so Jason engaged her by building a snowman.

Emma spoke to the snow–covered mound. "When will I stop missing you, Shea? I can turn and see you coming up the hill with fish from the stream for dinner. I can still feel you here. I don't know what to do without you."

Kate came beside her a while later. "I miss Daddy."

"I know, darling. So do I. If you want to talk to him a while, I'll leave you alone." The child nodded and Emma went to Jason, but before they departed, he went to the grave alone and had his own private moment at Shea's grave.

On Christmas Day, and for the first time in their lives, Emma and Kate went to services at the town's only church, Easthope Presbyterian. Unsure of themselves, Emma and Kate watched Jason for cues during worship. It seemed foreign to Emma, who had read the Bible a lot during long winter nights in the soddy when she had exhausted her supply of penny books bought from Bockmeier's. Emma liked the warm church with its stained–glass windows spilling colors across the congregation, but was at somewhat of a loss to understand the sermonizing, which she knew many people felt was so important. To her, it seemed like common sense to treat your neighbor with kindness and live a life of pride in hard work and charity. Why did people need a reminder so often, she wondered. She felt somewhat out of place there, but knew it was something that people in town did every Sunday, so she joined in.

The Reverend James Thomas seemed nice enough. He was young and this was his first parish, so he wanted to acquit himself well. His sermon was peppered with a little fire and brimstone, but his message seemed to center on what he termed the virtues of a Christian life: faith, hope, love, and charity. Kate liked the singing and joined in when she got the hang of the tune.

Later, Emma and Kate spent Christmas morning by themselves. Emma had turned down invitations from Rachel and Jason, but she promised that she and Kate would join Jason at the Barlows' house for Christmas dinner.

In the formal parlor of Beck House, a small sapling evergreen was decorated with dried berry and paper garlands. Kate had fashioned a star from tin foil saved from candy bars that she had received from Jason, who made sure to bring her such treats often. Emma had fashioned a rag doll for Kate from scraps of fabric in the style of the Cheyenne, a skill that she had learned from Red Leaf Woman. As her hands worked, she sent up a silent prayer to the old woman, wherever her formidable spirit now existed, asking her to watch over Shea. Kate's gift to her mother was a picture she drew of herself and her mother and father, standing outside the cabin, with big smiles drawn on their faces. Emma's breath caught in her throat, seeing that Kate had also drawn Shea's grave in the background.

"I don't want to forget him, Momma. Daddy had a nice smile." Emma hugged Kate tight.

Jason joined the festivities at the Barlows' Christmas afternoon, bringing armloads of generous gifts for all. To Kate he gave dolls and candy, to Emma, a brooch of amethyst surrounded by silver filigree work. Emma had little money, so she filled a large basket with fresh cakes, pies, pastries, and cookies for the Barlows. Rachel gave Kate and Emma warm flannel bed gowns.

Emma gave Jason one of Shea's arrows. He was touched and honored by such a gift. He held the arrow reverently in his large rough hands.

"I saved this for you. I knew that you would want it."

"This is the finest gift I've ever received, Emma. Thank you," he said, deeply moved.

Jason had sent a freshly killed turkey to Rachel's that morning and they feasted on roasted turkey late into the night. Aside from Stuart, Caleb's brother and sister were also there with their spouses and children, making a total of twenty people in the house. Emma felt isolated among the crowd, often retreating to a corner to watch the family's interaction. Everyone seemed to get along; the children played and tussled; the adults moved easily among one another, talking and laughing. Emma observed how they seemed so natural and at ease with one another. She felt like an outsider, but was curious as she watched. Kate blended in with the children, something that Emma was grateful for. Jason caught her eye now and then, smiling at her.

Later, Emma retreated to the kitchen intending to help clean up, but she really needed a moment alone, finding herself a little envious of the closeness of the big family—it was something that she would never enjoy. She turned as Jason entered with an armload of dishes from the dining room. He set them on the counter and came to her, placing a soft kiss on her cheek.

"Merry Christmas, Emma."

"Merry Christmas, Jason." Their eyes locked for a brief but eloquent moment, then Emma moved away and started cleaning up the kitchen.

Jason walked Emma and Kate home that night. She stood on the back porch, watching Jason disappear into his house and felt very alone and lost. She barely suppressed an urge to call to him and make him stay just a little longer. He was just next door and she told herself to stop being so foolish. But she had come to depend on his quiet good company. He came daily before the mill opened and did all heavy work around the place. He chopped wood, stoked the boiler, tended the horses, and fixed anything that needed repair. She could not be selfish and tie him to her, but part of her crumpled every time he left.

That night, she wrote a letter to Adam addressed to the Department of the Interior, Bureau of Indian Affairs in Washington. Even though her previous letters received no reply, she prayed that this one, with the news of Shea's death, would find him. Jason took the letter with him the next morning and posted it for her.

Despite frequent outings with the Barlow children, Kate was lost without her father. Emma strained for ways to amuse her, but Kate had an extraordinarily close relationship with Shea. Emma learned to read Kate's mood, knowing the bad days when the child's thoughts were preoccupied with her father. *She's only seven—she didn't deserve this,* Emma thought bitterly. Emma tried every diversion that she knew of and encouraged Kate to talk about her father in hopes that Kate would start to heal.

Jason noticed the change in the child and bought Kate a big sled to amuse her. The two of them had hours of fun sledding down the hills together. Jason also bought ice skates for Emma and Kate. A pond near town always froze over in winter and ice skating was a favorite pastime of the townsfolk. Despite Jason and Kate's outright begging on these outings, Emma was only a spectator. She punished herself for Shea's death and increasingly kept a distance from those most able to console her.

Kate now regarded Jason as a very large playmate and, on at least one level, a substitute for her father's attention. One afternoon, Emma grinned when she saw him playing dolls with Kate in the parlor. Despite her depression, her appreciation for him grew each day. He brought not only material things they needed but more importantly, he was salve for their souls.

Assured that she was ready so soon after her father's death, Emma put Kate in second grade midway through January of 1888. Kate's first day of school was eventful indeed.

She remained brave until her feet touched the steps of the schoolhouse. Then, she ran back to her mother's arms, pleading. "I don't want to go in there, Momma. Please don't make me go. Keep teaching me at home like before."

After much patient prodding and reassurance from Emma, Kate stomped up the stairs and joined her class. Despite a tussle in the school yard during a recess with a boy who baited her for being part Indian, Kate's first day ended and her routine of attending school began.

When Emma asked Kate how she felt when the boy made remarks about her Indian blood, her reply surprised her.

"Hart Engles is a stupid boy. He doesn't know anything about Indians or their ways. Daddy told me that I would meet people who were afraid of what they don't understand. I made sure that Hart understands now."

But winter became an empty time for Emma, left alone during the day. The winter beauty she had once loved depressed her and she kept indoors except for chores that forced her outside. The nights were long and lonely without Shea. To sleep, she had become so dependent on laudanum that she had asked for another bottle. Stuart was a bit reluctant to give it to her, but Emma assured him that it was only to help her sleep. Stuart did not know that she was also buying laudanum from Carruthers general store. She had bottles of the drug hidden throughout the house. Lethargic from the effects of the drug, she found it harder and harder to rise each day. Her body and mind felt heavy, listless.

Kate kept to herself as well, rarely leaving the house when she returned from school, despite a steady stream of children asking her out to play. The days were very cold, so Emma reasoned that was why Kate stayed home.

Emma had little energy to cook, clean, or spend time with the child. She depended on Jason's visits to interrupt her desolation and restore her for a few hours. Soon, Kate seemed to rebound and started to go outside to play, now eager to go, unable to cope with her mother's obvious sorrow and inattention. Each night, Emma took a drink of laudanum so that she could sleep through the night.

Rachel came often and for those few hours each week, Emma put up a good front, convincing Rachel that she was doing better. But by February, deep despair, unlike anything that Emma had ever experienced, overwhelmed her. She was unable to give voice to her feelings and buried them in a numbing emotional void.

At Jason's insistence, Emma and Kate joined him for rides in the sledge through the back country while he showed them the spectacular sights of the Cascade range. He sensed that Emma was barely holding together and wanted to divert her and help her open up to him, Rachel, Stuart, someone. Kate thrived on the trips, plaguing Jason with questions while Emma was polite, forcing small talk, understanding Jason's intent, but unable to enjoy herself. She was so alone inside, the depths of her loneliness seemed fathomless and preoccupied her more each day. Sometimes, Jason stayed very late into the night; Emma found any excuse to keep him nearby. She worried about Kate. She should've worried more about herself.

Chapter Fifteen

Despite the best efforts of Jason and the Barlows, Emma was sliding out of reach. Her addiction to the laudanum grew and the excuses she made to Stuart were growing thin. Stuart worried over her, but reasoned that she was still grief–stricken. He would keep a close eye on her until spring, then wean her off the drug. The narcotic muddled her thinking and sapped her energy, dragging her down as she struggled to rise each day and keep to a routine. Few things gave her joy anymore. Only Kate and Jason had the power to snap her out of it for short periods. Emma was foundering, both unable and unwilling to do anything about it.

Rachel felt powerless and spoke of Emma's deterioration to Stuart many times. Stuart visited Emma often hoping that she would break out of it, but he had to admit that something had to be done. He then refused to let Emma have any more laudanum. She became incensed one day when he wanted to search the house and remove the drug. Emma ordered him out of the house. She did not want him to find the hidden bottles of laudanum that she had bought from Carruthers' store.

The cage that Emma had constructed around her emotions during the past years was rapidly falling to pieces. The laudanum numbed her and, she thought, gave her time to heal. It did the opposite and made matters worse. Her decline had already begun and was impossible to halt until she wanted it to stop.

Dazed by the drug, she could not remember how to do simple tasks. She put things away in the wrong rooms, once finding the iron in the vanity in her bedroom. She got lost in the big house and panicked when she could not get her bearings. Dark thoughts dogged her of Shea's slow death, her own trials at Fort Robinson and most acutely, watching her parents die so long ago. It was like a spring thaw that brings huge chunks of ice downriver to dam up the course. Emma could not break through her addiction without help.

Torturous images ran through her mind, some hauntingly real, some induced by the drug's cunning effects. She had to visibly shake them off.

These waking visions were fast becoming out of her control and too real. Her periods had stopped and she knew, of course, that she was not pregnant. She was worried over her health, but did not dare tell Stuart after being so rude to him.

Rachel tried to talk with her but met with stony refusal, buttressed by claims that she was fine and just adjusting to life in town. Emma did not know how to ask for help. There was much more to her problems than grief and she was at last starting to realize that; she just lacked the strength to face the issues.

Kate still had crying jags over her father but held up remarkably well for a seven–year–old. Emma could see how lonely she was and did what she could, though she lacked the imagination that Shea had to amuse and create play for the child. Kate did not know what to do with herself and sometimes spent hours alone in her room. When she played outside, she never ventured far from the door.

Jason invited Emma and Kate to supper at his house one night in February in an attempt to bolster Emma's spirits. "I owe you dozens of suppers already," he had said.

It took all of Emma's energy to dress and ready Kate that evening, but she managed to get them there on time, at six o'clock.

Jason grinned as he opened the door, happy for the company. Emma had been in the house many times, but only for short periods and had never appreciated how big the log house was. Jason had a wood–burning heater in his large, comfortable keeping room. A kitchen occupied the rear of the house. There were three bedrooms upstairs, each with a large fireplace built of smooth river rocks. The home's furnishings were large, sized for him, but deep and soft. The house was like Jason—open, warm, and strong.

Jason proved again that he was a good cook, serving beef steaks with roasted potatoes and canned beans that he had borrowed from Rachel. He also served wine, which relaxed both Emma and Jason. Kate gobbled up her supper, then was excused to explore the house on her own.

Kate peered in the dining room later. "Is that your bed upstairs?" Jason nodded. "Boy, that's the biggest bed I've ever seen!" she said. "I could roll over three times and still not touch the other side!" Soon, Kate was lulled to sleep on the keeping room sofa after the big meal and the cozy warmth of the house.

Over coffee, Emma said, "Jason, thanks for letting us stay in your mother's house." She stirred sugar into her coffee. "But I'm still concerned about what people think of you. They know I can't afford that place."

He spoke with honesty and sincerity. "Shea wanted you and Kate to live near people. Easthope is your home now. Living here is the best thing for both of you. I would've brought you here even if Shea hadn't asked me to." She nodded and let the subject rest at last, but she noticed Jason watching her. "Kate seems to be doing better. She told me that she likes school after all. How are you doing?"

"All right. I'm wandering through new territory. I never expected to be a widow so young. And I worry about the effect on Kate. She keeps up a brave front, but I know how much she misses Shea. Your visits do a lot for her. Thank you."

"And you? You keep up a brave front, but you seem all shut up, just like my mother's house used to be. How about a party? Would that cheer you up? Maybe a trip to Seattle with Kate?"

His kind words and soft eyes had breached the wall holding off her emotions. She buried her face in her hands. "Oh, God, I miss Shea! I didn't think it would hurt this much!"

He reached over and put his arm around her and pulled her to him. "It's all right, Emma. You have a lot of people to help you through this. Give yourself time, all right?" He cupped her face in his hands. "You can talk to me any time about anything. Shea wouldn't want you to mourn him forever, but don't be ashamed about how long it takes or asking for help."

She sniffled. "I can't see anything ahead of us. I have to make a living for us somehow. I can break sod, that's about all. I'm scared," she confessed.

"Shh," he soothed her. "I will help you."

The next morning, Emma woke to noises in her yard and saw Jason there splitting wood before sunup. She went downstairs to the kitchen window and watched him work as he stacked the wood on the back porch. She stood within reach of the door, but she backed away, not wanting to be seen. She watched a long time, amazed that he did not seem to tire. Telling herself to stop hiding behind the curtain in the door, she stepped outside, inviting him in for breakfast. He accepted with a grin.

As they ate, he mentioned, "Em, I have to go to Spokane for a couple weeks. I've got to leave today. I've put off the trip as long as I could. I've got some new contracts there and a lot of people to see. I should be back by the end of the month. But I'll ask Caleb and Rachel to look in on you. Caleb will make sure the wood is cut and that the boiler is running properly."

Her chest tightened with apprehension even though she knew that she was not alone in town. "I can take care of myself, so don't trouble Rachel and Caleb. Have a safe trip. I'll miss you," she said.

"See you in about two weeks," he said. "You're sure there's nothing I can do before I go?"

She smiled. "Is there anything I can do for you?"

He returned her smile. "Just be here when I come home."

Emma barely held herself together until Jason's return. Seeing him come down Main Street on his big mare a day earlier than expected filled her with relief. He came to see her immediately, but Emma could see that he was exhausted and begged him to go home to sleep.

That night, Emma, dressed for bed, sat reading in the parlor after she put Kate to bed. She jumped, hearing footsteps crunching on the snow outside. She quickly went to the front window and peeked out between the curtains. A large figure was coming towards the house. He went up the stairs and onto the porch. A heavy hand knocked on the door.

"Help me!" a male voice pleaded. "I'm lost. I'm freezing! For the love of God, please let me in!"

"There's a church down the road. You should go there," Emma said, her voice quavering.

The man began to force the locked door. Emma jumped a full yard back in one leap. Her heart was in her throat. "I have a gun!" she yelled, as she grabbed the shotgun that Jason had left her in a compartment under the staircase. She rummaged in a nearby chest, frantically looking for the shells. As she was about to give up, her trembling hand fell upon the box. She shoved two shells into the breech.

Kate had been awakened by the voices and had crept down the stairs.

"Kate! Go back to your room!" Emma ordered.

"Momma? There's some man outside."

"Go—now!"

Kate stood frozen with fear on the stairs.

The man pushed the door with his body again.

"Go away! Stay out!" she shouted.

The door gave way, swinging in swirling snow.

"Don't you remember me, Emma?" Seymour Fulton slammed the door behind him.

Emma recoiled and before she could raise the heavy gun to fire, he rushed her, sending it spinning from her hand and clattering to the floor. Kate screamed, ran down the stairs and bolted away.

Emma struggled and screamed as Fulton tackled her to the floor. The old terror sprang upon her again and she fought with every bit of strength she possessed. She was determined not to endure another rape, knowing full well that he would succeed in killing her this time.

"I work for your new man, that Beck fella. Been waiting for my chance. But I couldn't get near you until that filthy Indian you married died. Took him long enough!"

She spat in his face and he slapped her.

"Settle down, bitch. We're not going to do anything we haven't done before." He tore her gown, grabbed her breast and bit it hard. Emma screamed. "Shut up!" he yelled. With one hand, he pinned her arms above her head and pulled his pants down with his other hand. His full weight on her pushed the air from her lungs. Emma could not make a sound. He punched her hard in the jaw, knocking her nearly senseless. She kept struggling, trying to bite him and kick him. "Later, I'll make the acquaintance of your daughter!"

Emma regained her wind and screeched, "No!" Her screams were quickly muffled by his hand. She twisted and fought to no avail. He was too strong. She wondered where Kate had gone—and prayed that she had run for help.

His sneering mouth, full of dirty teeth, stank. She dug her nails into his hand, but he did not flinch. "I like a woman who fights back! Did the Indians teach you that?" He leaned down and put his foul mouth on hers. She bit his lip and he recoiled, wiping the blood across his cheek. He snarled and slapped her.

Suddenly, Emma felt something in her hand. Kate jumped back as Emma took the knife that she had dropped there. With all of her strength, she twisted one of her hands from his grip and stabbed him in the stomach. Blood poured from his wound, soaking her. He rolled off her and crawled towards the door with a look of astonishment. Emma bunched and rolled to get away from him and watched him creep across the floor, leaving a trail of sticky blood.

"You bitch!" he sputtered, trying to pull out the knife as his guts spilled onto the floor.

Jason burst in the front door, his shotgun in his hands.

Fulton pulled himself to standing at the staircase railing. "You weren't due back until tomorrow!" he gasped in surprise.

Jason herded Fulton towards the door, the gun pointed at his chest. "Frank Reid! What in the hell are you doing?"

Emma stumbled to Jason's side. Her shotgun was in her hands. She fired both barrels. Fulton staggered out through the open door and was dead before he landed in the snow at the bottom of the steps. Emma sank to her knees, trembling, the smoking shotgun lying across her lap.

Jason froze in shock. "Why did you do that, Emma? I had him."

Emma did not answer him. Kate came in from the kitchen and ran to her. Emma pulled her close. "Are you all right, Kate?"

"Yes, Momma," she answered, her voice tremulous with fright. She saw the blood soaking Emma's night gown. "Momma! You're bleeding!"

"It's his blood. It's all right now."

Kate pulled her mother's torn gown over her chest, her small hand shaking. They huddled together in the doorway as the freezing night hurried all the heat out of the house. Fulton's body lay in the snow, his blood soaking it black. Jason went outside and made sure that Fulton was dead, then came back. He fell to his knees and put his arms around Emma and Kate. Kate pulled away and went to the sofa, grabbing a throw and putting it around her mother's shoulders.

A shadow fell across Fulton's body. The town's new constable, Roy Nesbitt, stood there, revolver drawn, then he bounded up the steps. "Are you all right, ma'am?" he asked, out of breath and seeing the blood and Emma's torn clothing. "What happened?" he asked, kneeling beside her and looking to Jason.

"One of my men attacked her. I heard screaming and came running. I shot him." Emma looked to Jason in surprise. "It was Frank Reid. He works at Camp Two. I don't know why he would attack Emma."

"No," Emma said. "He's not Frank Reid. He's Fulton. Seymour Fulton."

Jason's head snapped around. "What?"

Emma looked towards the door. Townspeople, startled from sleep by the screams and gunfire, were filling her front yard. "He was at Fort Robinson when I was. I'll tell you about it later."

Jason's face fell. "Oh my God. Shea told me what he did to you."

"He did?"

"This man's been working for me since November. Oh, Emma, I had no idea."

Emma tried to soothe Jason's shock and guilt. "There is no way that you could've known."

"Let's discuss that later," Nesbitt interjected. "She needs medical help." Jason and Roy helped Emma to a sofa. Kate curled in tight next to her, breathing hard, still frightened.

"You know that man?" Kate asked.

"A long time ago," Emma answered.

"What did he do to you, Momma?"

"He tried to kill me when I was kept at that fort in Nebraska." Kate's arms went around her mother's neck and she kissed her bruised cheek. Emma returned the kiss and gazed at her precious girl. Then, she turned to Nesbitt. "Is he dead?" Emma asked.

"Yes, ma'am," Nesbitt answered.

"Good."

Several people rushed into the house, but Nesbitt ordered them out. They left too slowly, so Jason crossed the room and herded everyone out and shut the door.

Outside, Stuart pushed through the crowd. He rushed into the house, medical bag in hand. In his haste, he slipped and fell in the blood on the floor of the foyer. Jason helped him to standing.

"I heard the commotion and the shotgun fire. What happened?" Stuart asked, breathless from his fall.

"We'll tell you what happened while you work on Emma," Jason said, leading Stuart to the sofa.

Stuart checked Emma over and made up compresses for her bruising, then did what he could to stem bleeding from her nose, mouth, and a cut on her cheek. She would be all right physically, but he saw the terror in her eyes and was bothered by a hardness to her voice as she recounted this night's shocking event to Nesbitt.

Over the next quarter hour, she explained what had happened that night, as well as her violent history with Fulton. She was careful not to give details of the rape in front of Kate. As she spoke, Jason's mind flashed to the night that he had held her as she gave birth to Kate, remembering the two scars on her chest when her gown fell away from her shoulder. He knew that one scar was from Tyler's bullet. This night, he learned the history of the other. Jason paled, feeling guilty for ever hiring Seymour Fulton.

"This wasn't a chance break–in. He wanted to finish what he started years ago. When he heard that I was here, I guess he bided his time, waiting for Jason to leave, only he didn't know that Jason came back a day early."

Roy was amazed at Emma's composure. She had just been attacked, then a man had been killed on her doorstep. She did not seem to care, other than to be assured that Fulton was dead. His instincts prickled, but he had to proceed carefully with his investigation. Emma Hawkshadow was newly widowed and the favorite of the powerful Jason Beck.

Just then, Rachel and Caleb rushed in and Emma went to meet them in the foyer. Rachel wore only a nightgown, robe, and heavy boots that belonged to Caleb. "Emma!" she cried, hugging her and seeing the cuts and bruises on her face. "We heard screams and shots! What happened?" she gasped, seeing the blood all over Emma. "Dear God, are you all right?"

"We're all right." As Emma looked out the door, she saw half the town still standing around Fulton's body.

"Who is that man?"

"It's a long story, Rachel. I'm not up to telling it again just now." Emma closed the door and shuffled back to the sofa. She sat down and cradled Kate.

"I'll take care of these," Caleb said. He picked up both shotguns and took them to the washroom just off the kitchen. He returned and sat with Rachel on the parlor's other sofa.

Emma returned her attention to Roy. "Is there anything else you need right now? I have to calm down my daughter and I have to change out of this nightgown."

"We'll talk tomorrow. Do you want to stay at the Barlow's house for the night?"

"Oh, please, Emma," Rachel begged.

"No," Emma said with a determined shake of her head.

"Then I'll stay here with you," Jason offered.

"No one's going to make me afraid to stay in my home."

Jason looked grim and she saw a flash of temper in his green eyes. "Don't argue with me, Emma."

"I'd like to get a written statement from you both as soon as you're able," Nesbitt said to Jason and Emma.

"Tomorrow, all right?" Jason asked.

Roy stood. "Okay. I'll get the body out of here as soon as I can."

"That would be good, Roy. Thank you." Jason dismissed him with that.

Roy left, bewildered and unsure how to proceed. This was the first murder that he had dealt with and the first ever in Easthope. He was the town's constable, but his power went only as far as Jason allowed. Overlooking a brawl at the Pry Bar Saloon and an occasional knifing between loggers was one thing. Overlooking murder was quite another, despite the circumstances.

Nesbitt ran over the details of what he had seen that night. Mere seconds had passed between the screams that had brought him running and the blast of the shotgun. Then Jason had appeared outside for a moment, then had run back into the house. The gun had not been in his hands. Running up the steps, Roy had seen Emma huddled on the floor inside the house, a gun across her lap, yet Jason had confessed to the shooting. Her face had been badly beaten and it was obvious that Fulton had attacked her, but he could not reconcile what he had seen. Had Jason just handed her the gun when he went outside to look at the body? Why would he do that when he went out to make sure that Fulton was dead? Roy knew that he had to tread very carefully.

With Rachel and Kate's help upstairs, Emma changed into a clean gown. Kate saw the bruise on Emma's breast left by Fulton's teeth. "Momma! Look what he did to you!"

Emma's look at her daughter was peculiar. "He did far worse to me the last time. I'll be okay."

"What did he do to you last time?" Kate asked, upset that she didn't get a straight answer before.

"You're too young, my love. Maybe when you're older," Emma said softly. Kate looked sullen and felt left out, not understanding that she was indeed too young to hear of such horrors. "Anyway, it doesn't matter anymore. It's over."

"Stay with us tonight," Rachel pleaded.

Emma was resolute, taking Kate's hand and heading down the stairs. "No, thank you. That man is dead and that's the end of it. I'm not afraid."

Emma felt safer knowing Jason was there that night, sleeping on a sofa. She dozed in the wee hours of the morning, the events of the previous night replaying over and over in her mind.

Jason woke up early and fixed the broken lock on the front door. Rachel later arrived with her three children who were admonished to stay in the kitchen and keep quiet. Rachel set to scrubbing the blood–stained floor in the foyer. The stain did not come out. The floor would have to be sanded and refinished, she told Jason as she placed a rug over the stain. She then prepared breakfast and carried a tray up to Emma's room.

Emma was awake, sitting at the window seat overlooking the front yard, staring at the blood–stained snow and the impression left by Fulton's body. She turned when Rachel entered.

"Brought up your breakfast," Rachel said, placing the tray beside her.

"Thanks."

"Should I bring up a tray for Kate?"

Emma turned and looked at the child who was in a deep sleep in her bed. "Later. Let her sleep."

Rachel's hand touched Emma's. "How are you doing?"

She spoke in a low voice so as not to rouse Kate. "Years ago, you asked me where I got the other scar on my chest. I'll tell you how I got it."

Rachel's face was tear–stained as Emma recounted her rape and near murder at Fulton's hands. Later, as Rachel descended the stairs with the breakfast tray, she passed Jason.

"Be real quiet. Kate's in her bedroom and she's still sleeping." Rachel's pallor was not unnoticed by Jason.

"You all right?" he asked.

Rachel nodded and continued down the stairs.

Kate woke as Jason's heavy footfalls woke her. She mumbled good morning and shuffled off into the bathroom.

Jason sat beside Emma, who was still at the window seat. "I don't want you in any trouble over this, Jason. I'll go to Nesbitt today and tell him what really happened."

"No," Jason countered. "I shot Fulton, not you."

"But Jason, you could end up in jail—despite what he did to me. I won't let you take the blame."

"And what would happen to Kate if you, by some freak chance, go to jail? Nothing's going to happen to me or to you, I can promise you that."

"Jason, I shot him in cold blood. I was so afraid, but I had to finish it. And I think Roy Nesbitt knows that I'm the one who did it."

"I said not to worry. I'll take care of Roy." Jason then spoke of his guilt over inadvertently hiring Fulton.

"You could not have known who he really was. I never saw him in town. He must've kept to the logging shacks up on the mountain. This is all a terrible coincidence, that's all."

Jason saw forgiveness in her eyes, but he harbored awful guilt in his heart for unwittingly putting Emma and Kate in great danger. It would take years for him to learn to live with it.

Later, Kate reentered the room and curled on her mother's lap. "Kate, are you okay?" Jason asked.

The girl spoke with directness that reminded him of Shea. "He was a bad man and deserved what he got." Jason's eyes widened. She looked wise beyond her seven years. "Momma didn't do anything bad to him, but he did something bad to her."

"You saved our lives last night by giving me the knife. You were so brave," Emma said. "Now I need to ask you a question. Did you see who shot him?"

"No, Momma. After I gave you the knife I ran to the back door to get Jason. I heard the gun go off when I was in the kitchen."

Emma's face was filled with relief. Kate did not know the truth. "My brave Cheyenne girl." Emma kissed Kate's forehead and hugged her.

After Rachel was sure that Emma was looked after by Jason, she returned home. She was very concerned for Emma, especially at the change in her demeanor. A new hardness was there, a peculiar detachment. While the fact remained that she did not provoke the attack, Emma seemed unemotional, except for showing deep satisfaction that Fulton had at last paid for what he had done to her so many years ago. She had not seen Emma cry and thought that she was holding back, or more frighteningly, did not care overmuch. Rachel tried to make excuses for her behavior, figuring that Emma was being strong for Kate, but she could not quite bring herself to believe that was all there was to the situation.

Jason remained throughout the day and later prepared lunch. Emma sat at the table, picking at her food, distracted. While they cleaned up, Jason was bothered by the haunting expression pervading Emma's features. "You all right, really?"

"Yes," she sighed, putting away dishes in a cupboard. "I'll be fine. Sorry to ruin your homecoming."

"This is my fault."

"Jason, please stop," she snapped, then regained herself with a deep breath. "You can't spend every waking moment worrying about us. The chances against this man finding me again were astronomical." Fulton's brutality flooded her thoughts and she fought back the horror again. Jason hugged her. His warmth calmed her and she felt bad for being abrupt with him.

"I don't want to leave you alone, Em."

Emma smiled a little. "The danger is over and we're all right. Don't worry."

"But I do. I always will."

She wished to be left alone. "You need to rest and Kate and I need to be alone. No offense."

"None taken, Em." He looked around the house, noting which windows needed locks on them, vowing to return the next day to fix them. Leaving was hard for him. He looked back at the house several times during his short walk across the yard.

Just after Jason left, Emma left Kate to play in her room, then went to her bedroom and took a dose of laudanum. She did not bother to use a spoon to measure how much she took this time, but drank it straight from the bottle.

Roy Nesbitt came to Jason's office the next afternoon to get his statement concerning Fulton's attack on Emma. "I heard Emma's screams and came running, along with half the town," he was saying.

"You have sharp ears, Roy."

"Well, as I ran toward the house, I saw Fulton standing in the doorway. The next thing I knew, he jumped about a foot off the ground from a shotgun blast and rolled down the steps. Then you ran outside and looked him over, then ran back in. I saw Mrs. Hawkshadow sitting on the floor with the gun across her lap. When I came in, another shotgun was near the stairs. Which gun was yours?" Jason said nothing. Roy chided himself for not sniffing the barrels of the guns to determine which one had been fired. "The only weapon Fulton had was a knife and it was still strapped in its sheath under his coat. He broke in and he attacked the lady, but Jason—"

"What are you implying, Roy? Fulton's weapons were his fists. He didn't need a knife to threaten Emma."

"She shot him, Jason. I could smell the gun smoke on her."

"No. She stabbed him with a knife that Kate gave her. I shot him." Jason sat back in his chair. For the first time in his life he used his power as the town's owner, its employer. There would be no Easthope if it were not for the lumber business. He had always sworn never to exert such pressure, but he was protecting Emma and young Kate. His choice was clear and he would harbor no guilt for what he was about to do.

"Roy, Emma was fighting for her life. She was raped and nearly murdered by this man once before. If that's not reason enough for killing that animal, I don't know what is." He leveled his steady gaze at him. "It doesn't matter who shot him. There's nothing to be gained by further investigation without putting her and the child through more grief."

"I'm doing the job you hired me for, Jason. Charges won't be filed, but I just want the truth."

"Roy—let this go. They've been through enough."

The constable looked dejected and stood. "I understand. I'll resign."

Jason sat up, startled. "I don't want you to resign. You've done an excellent job of keeping the peace around here. This is the only time I'll ever ask this of you—just this one time. Let it go."

Jason Beck's subtle, steady pressure had the desired affect. Nesbitt was compelled to close the case on Seymour Fulton. The body was not allowed in the consecrated graveyard next to the church and was buried in the woods far from town. The grave marker had no name, just the date of death. This was Jason's doing. He did not want Emma seeing Seymour Fulton's name or knowing where his body lay—ever.

Two windows of Jason's first floor faced Emma's house. He pulled up a chair near the one which afforded the best view and slept there night after night so he could watch over Emma and Kate.

Fulton's attack unnerved Emma and she found it difficult to go outdoors, feeling exposed and weak, dreading people's reaction to her bruised and cut up face. She did what few errands she needed to do late in the day, just before the shops closed, to avoid as many people as possible. Some towns-folk exhibited kindness, but some looked away, unsure of what to say to her.

Emma kept Kate close by when she came home from school, watching her from a window when she played outdoors. When she ventured too far, Emma always called her back. The child seemed to be dealing with the attack much better than Emma and she envied her. Emma knew how close to death she had come once again. Fear and uncertainty spiked now and then, followed by full–blown panic attacks that started to tear her down.

The laudanum did not help keep the demons at bay when Emma slept, which was not often or for long. Disturbing dreams plagued her sleep and she often woke with a start, feeling a presence in the room. Jason's intentions in offering his mother's house were out of friendship, but she now feared living in the big, creaking house. Despite being in town with neighbors on all sides, being without Shea, her protector, frightened her. She could not voice her fears to anyone—she tried not show weakness. *I was the wife of a warrior and I should be braver than this*, she told herself. With supreme effort, she held her emotions in check and tried to convince everyone that she had put the harrowing Fulton incident behind her.

That spring, the darkness seemed to lift. She left the laudanum alone for the first time in weeks and the warm spring renewed her spirits. She felt ready to face the world again.

The summer of 1888 was healing for Emma and Kate. Emma seemed to be coming out of her depression and she did not request any more laudanum from Stuart; he did not know that she had one last bottle stashed away. Even though she had resolved to stop taking it, she could not bring herself to throw it away. Although the stupor caused by her heavy use of laudanum took weeks to dissipate, she at last felt clearer than she had in months.

Jason talked her out of looking for another housing arrangement and she and Kate were now permanently installed in Beck House. Emma felt a part of the community for once and pushed aside Fulton's return and the paralyzing fear that accompanied the aftermath. Everyone knew of her struggles in the months following Shea's death, but the Widow Hawkshadow and her charming daughter could do no wrong. The townsfolk embraced them and applauded their bravery that terrifying night.

Summer was a whirlwind of picnics, parties, and the thrilling annual logging exhibition. At the contests, prizes were awarded to all comers, whether or not they won an event. The evening ended with fireworks shipped in for the occasion from San Francisco. The crowd was awed by the sparkling beauty in the sky, a fitting climax to a wonderful day. Emma watched the show, remembering the plaques and ribbons that Shea had won in the logrolling competitions. The memories made her feel very lucky and proud to have enjoyed those times with Shea.

It was also an end to a dark time in both Jason and Emma's lives. Emma and Jason were inseparable and the way Kate held onto Jason's hand in town, a newcomer would've assumed that they were a family. But respecting Emma's year of mourning, Jason kept a discreet emotional distance and paid no unseemly attention to her other than to act as her escort. He had coped with his guilt about Fulton and come out of it stronger and much wiser when it came to hiring workers. His instincts were sharpened by his unfortunate mistake.

To Emma, Kate's welfare was uppermost. Grateful to Jason, but still preoccupied with mourning, she had not guessed his true feelings. As a consequence of the night of Fulton's attack, Kate remained close to home and had become an obedient, helpful child. She feared leaving her mother alone for long, believing that someone might hurt her.

Jason's attentions to Kate were affectionate without being patronizing or courting favor. He let the girl come to him and her favorite perch many evenings after supper was on Jason's lap while Emma read aloud.

Jason's attentions to the pretty young widow set tongues wagging, particularly that of Fiona McBride, queen of the town's gossip circle. Every Tuesday afternoon, a half dozen women met at her house for tea and a sewing circle. The favorite topic of late was how Jason Beck was 'keeping' the Widow Hawkshadow.

"He'll wait until a year after the death, then he'll move in. You know what I mean," Fiona said to the ladies. "Taking advantage of a widow's grief—and did you see how he garnered the favors of the girl at the logging exhibition last month? I thought I knew Jason Beck."

Martha Hamlin disagreed. "Jason's known the Hawkshadows for years. I don't think he's doing anything wrong. He likes Emma, everyone knows that. And that house of his mother's had been empty for ages and it was only right that he offer it to them. Besides, I hear that she's paying some token amount for rent. She doesn't have much money."

"Don't be naive, Martha. Jason sees that she wants for nothing. It's obvious what's going on. He lives right next door. He could slip in and out of there without anyone seeing. He's angling around to marry her and may already be helping himself, if you know what I mean."

"I like Mrs. Hawkshadow and I don't care what you think, Fiona," Martha replied, defending Emma, whom she hardly knew. "Maybe they have romantic feelings for one another, but Jason would never do anything improper. There are plenty of unattached women in this town and if he were a cad, he would have done something by now." After a moment's thought she added, "We should invite Emma to tea sometime. She'd feel more welcome among us. And, you, Fiona, would get to know her a little better."

"Excellent idea," Fiona said with a satisfied grin. "More tea ladies?"

A week later, Emma accepted an invitation to Fiona's sewing circle. She knew many of the women, but disliked the gossip that peppered the conversations. She declined later invitations and besides, she did not want to advertise her limited sewing skills. However, she and Martha Hamlin struck up an acquaintance. Martha's husband Tom was the foreman of the three logging camps and worked long hours leaving her alone, for their children were grown and had moved to Seattle.

In September, while Emma was at the general store, Gale Carruthers came around the counter and handed her a letter. Emma had never received mail and for a moment thought that it was a letter from Adam, but the return address was from Philadelphia, Pennsylvania. She went outside and sat on the bench in front of the store to open it. A piece of paper fluttered to her lap. It was a bank draft for $5,000. She read the signature at the end of the letter, then trotted home, pale with shock. Alone in the kitchen, she read it.

The letter was from Shea's father, Shea Russell.

Emma and Kate borrowed Jason's dray one fall afternoon to visit Shea's grave. Although Jason wanted to accompany them, Emma's desire to be alone with Kate won out. He reluctantly let them go but kept one eye on their progress up the mountain trail from his office window.

At the cabin, Emma's thoughts became lost in the life that she had led there and she felt some comfort as she sat in the sun. Kate sat near Shea's grave. She talked to her father, telling him all that she had done in the past weeks. Emma indulged her and let her talk for as long as she wished. When they departed, Kate kissed the mound and told her father that she loved him.

This ritual was what they both needed. Unused to living in town, Emma was sometimes bothered by its noise and crowds. The quiet open spaces of the mountain property did more to rejuvenate her than sewing circles or parties. With little to occupy her days, besides preparing meals, cleaning the house, and waiting for Kate to return from school, she needed this quiet time, this quiet place. Kate liked visiting her old haunts, the trees she liked to climb, the stream, and the fort that she and her father had built together.

Emma's panic attacks waned and she almost felt normal again, but something dark threatened to drag her down; she fought it every waking moment and even battled it in her dreams. Still, she managed to leave the laudanum alone.

November 12, 1888 came and with it the first anniversary of Shea's death. Emma awoke in tears, burrowing herself deep under the blankets.

A while later, Kate tiptoed into her room and curled up next to Emma. "Do I have to go to school today?" she asked.

"No. I thought that we might spend the day together. Maybe there is something special we can do."

"Are we going to visit Daddy today?"

"If you want."

"Can Jason come?" Kate asked.

"He's at work, Kate. Besides, I think just you and me should go today," Emma answered.

Later that morning, she and Kate went to Jason's barn and borrowed his sledge. She harnessed the horses and drove up the mountain with Kate.

Emma was confounded as she came up the hill to the cabin and she and Kate got down off the sled. Many sledges were pulled in under the trees. Waiting beside the grave were Jason, Rachel and Caleb with their children, and many townspeople. As Emma walked nearer with Kate in hand, she saw a canvas cover upon the grave. For an irrational moment, she thought that his grave might have been disturbed, but as she drew closer she realized that was not the case.

She came beside Jason, her face questioning until he pulled off the canvas. A crypt had been placed over the grave accompanied by a headstone:

Shea Russell Hawkshadow
Cheyenne Tribe
Born, June, 1857 – Died, November 12, 1887
Warrior, Husband, Father, and Friend
Rest in Peace

A tingling spread through Emma. For a moment she felt light, almost weightless. Kate's hand in hers seemed to fade away for a moment as she approached and knelt, touching the headstone, her fingers resting on the word *husband* carved in granite. Kate kneeled beside her.

Jason leaned down and spoke close to her ear. "We had spies placed around town because we took a chance that you would come up today. These people started coming up when you were hitching up the horses in my stable. The townsfolk wanted to do something to remember Shea. We took up a collection and had this made for him. We hope you think it's fitting."

Through a haze of tears, she rose and hugged him. Her voice was no more than a whisper. "Shea, wherever he is, thinks it's fitting indeed and so do I. Thank you." Overwhelmed, she looked around the ring of people, remembering every face. Kate pulled out a small bunch of dried flowers from her coat pocket and placed them on the grave.

Emma felt Shea's presence in the quiet meadow patched with snow. She spoke to Shea in the privacy of her thoughts. *The people of East-hope are taking good care of us. Rest in peace, my love.* Something in her let go of some of the guilt over his death. Shea's precious memory had a lasting monument. He would not be forgotten.

Kate seemed to make her own peace, too, that day in her eighth year. She understood what she had witnessed that morning. She remained beside her mother as Emma made a point of speaking to everyone, shaking hands and offering thanks for this touching gesture.

Emma at last addressed the crowd. "We're so grateful. Your acceptance of us since we came here has moved us time and time again. I don't know what more I can do except be a good neighbor and repay you all when you are in need. Katherine and I thank you all from the bottom of our hearts." The people soon returned to their sledges. Emma found Jason through the crowd. "You made this possible. I thank you, my dear friend."

He smiled down at her, his soft green eyes caressing her face. She smiled, feeling shy when he looked at her. There was something penetrating in his look these days. Emma felt self–conscious.

"Em, we did something else. A sign will be put up after the spring thaw. The trail below the cabin to Main Street has been named Hawkshadow Road."

Her eyes glistened. "Oh, my. I like that."

Emma and Kate spent Christmas with the Barlows and Jason was invited as always. Emma gave Jason a string tie with a pendant of a bear carved in ivory. She had bought it from a Yakima woman who reminded her of Red

Leaf. The old woman peddled her intricate carvings to people getting off the stage in front of Murdock's Hotel.

Jason's large fingers touched the fine carving and he smiled at her with open tenderness. To Emma, he gave a lovely watch on a silver chain. Rachel winked at her when she opened it for she had helped Jason pick it out at a jewelry shop in Millersburg. Jason was delighted when he saw Emma's smile. She had never had a watch before.

"I have no excuses for being late, do I?" she giggled. "Jason, it's lovely. Thank you."

Winter soon passed over into spring which came early for a change with warm days and cool evening breezes.

The following April Jason came to Emma's for dinner one night and was very honored when Kate asked if he would tuck her into bed. Emma smiled and busied herself clearing the table while Jason read Kate a bedtime story upstairs. When he returned, she had set two glasses and a bottle of wine on a table near the fireplace. This had become their habit of late.

"She's asleep," he announced as Emma offered him his usual chair near the fire. "Dinner was superb, as always."

She poured him a generous glass of the local vintage. "Oh, I forgot, I have cake. I'll be right back."

She stepped into the kitchen with Jason at her heel. As she set out plates and sliced the cake he stood very close, watching over her shoulder. "It's coming, it's coming," she teased. Then Jason put his arm around her waist and she turned within the circle of his arm. "Jason—what?"

His mouth was on hers and she fell against him in the kiss.

His voice was soft and passionate. "I'm in love with you, Emma. I have been for a very long time. You see, all these months, I couldn't tell you, the time just wasn't right. I thought we might try, but we've been friends for so long that I'm not sure if you feel the same way about me." He exhaled as if a great weight had lifted.

There was a long silence as she chose her words. This big, handsome man could easily sweep her away and she resisted, but was not sure why.

"Oh, Jason. I never dared to think that you felt that way about me. It's a welcome surprise, believe me." She was quiet again, but her look was far off. "I've tried so hard to close the chapter on Shea, but I have Kate to consider. She adores you and so do I. You have a special bond with her. You spend time with her and I'm always so grateful for all you do for us."

He wanted to help her, heal her, love her. But would she be able to give up Shea's memory, still so clear, so near to her heart?

"Do you feel the same about me?"

She looked at him with a mixture of relief tinged with confusion. "I'm not sure how I feel."

Jason smiled tight with resignation. "Okay, I understand. I'm sorry I mentioned it."

"Jason, please." She took a deep breath. "I'm not saying that I don't have feelings for you. Just give me a little time. I'm just no good to anyone else right now because I'm concentrating so hard on Kate. I'm flattered, Jason, really. To be chosen by you is an honor."

Emboldened that she might feel the same someday, he decided not to back off. He kept her close in his arms.

"Em, I was wondering if—well, you know the spring dance is next month at the church hall. You've never been to it." He sucked in a deep breath to summon his courage. "Would you go with me?"

She slipped from his arms, blushing crimson. "Oh Jason, thank you—I couldn't."

His courage remained. "Why?"

Emma's mouth worked, trying to form an excuse. "I—I can't leave Kate alone," was all she could come up with.

"We'll find a sitter." Emma's hands gripped the edge of the soapstone sink. He took a step closer to her. "You've locked yourself up in this house for months. It's time you got out and did something fun. Come with me."

"There's a reason I've avoided the spring dance every year. I've never been to a dance before. I can't dance," she said hoping to sidestep the invitation.

He came a step nearer. She could smell the warm sweet scent of freshly cut wood on him from his day at the mill. It ran a thrill through her and she jumped a little in response to her awakening feelings.

"Emma, nothing would give me more pleasure than to escort you. Whether or not you want to dance is of no concern to me. I just want to be with you." Another step closer. He put a hand to her cheek and lifted her lips to his and kissed her again. "I meant everything that I said. I love you and I want to be with you."

She slid away from him, but he moved with her, keeping his body close. He kissed her again. His warm lips spread a tingling to every part of her body. She slumped against him as her hands loosened their hold on the counter and gripped his shoulders. Then she pulled away from him.

"I can't—Jason, I—I . . ." She realized that she was out of excuses.

"Why not? I'm telling you that I love you. I'll give you all the time you want, but be honest with me. You've been alone far too long and so have I. Will you give us a chance?" She looked at him, unblinking. "Will you?"

"I'm afraid of losing your friendship, Jason," she said at last. "Love changes things."

"I'll always be your friend, no matter what." He looked into her dark blue eyes searching for the affection he craved. "I'm asking if you could love me someday. I've never said these words to any woman before. I love you, Emma Hawkshadow."

The wall of grief that had kept her feelings dammed up began to break and she could no longer deny her love for him. Yes, she said to herself, I love him, but she lacked the courage to say it, fearful of the fate that all men important in her life had endured. She had lost them all.

"I have feelings for you too, Jason," she managed, her throat feeling tight and dry, "and I'd love to go to the dance with you."

Jason held her body against his, kissing her again.

He had freed something in her as his kisses swept her to a place of peace for her injured soul, a secure place filled with longing. There came a point in their newfound passion when Emma could've easily succumbed to him, but they both broke the embrace. Jason's face was flushed and he looked at her with eyes dilated with desire. She felt warm, light, and although her heart was racing, she felt calm, so at ease with him. Her courtship and marriage to Shea had been quick and their times too often stormy. Her body craved the release of intimacy, but she knew what trouble it could bring. Love did change things and her friendship with Jason was so very precious to her.

After wine and cake, Jason kissed her good-night. As he took his coat from the peg rack near the back door, he said, "It's on May eighteenth at six o'clock. I'll come for you at five–thirty?"

She smiled as she closed the door, lingering a moment to bask in the tender, sweet excitement that he had released in her. It was like being freed from a dark, cold pit, much like the way she had felt when she was released from Fort Robinson. There were definite possibilities, she thought to herself.

That night in bed she entertained daring fantasies, imagining making love with Jason. She had only been with Shea and wondered, a little wickedly, what another man would be like. When she imagined Jason with her, the bad memory of the rape melted away. Jason would be gentle with her should they ever . . . but she felt a pang of guilt, feeling that she was being somehow unfaithful to Shea. And how would Kate react if Jason started courting her? But her body ached for those intimate feelings. She soon drifted away to sleep thinking of Jason as a lover and a most cherished friend.

The only person Emma told about Jason's declaration, was, of course, Rachel. Rachel was overjoyed, but promised to keep it a secret.

"Don't let the past get in the way of you two finding happiness," she said. "He's the best man I know and he's loved you all along."

"Really?"

"Emma, maybe you didn't notice, but I did from the start."

Emma sighed. "He's sometimes too good. I wonder if he has some darker side that I've never seen. And I wonder about the affect on Kate. I mean, is she ready for this? She likes Jason, but maybe it's too soon."

"It's been well over a year since Shea died. Kate adores Jason—and so do you. As for a dark side to Jason, he's just what he seems. He's kind, generous, and will always love and protect you and Kate."

"Believe me, Rachel, I know what kind of man he is." The night of Fulton's break in and how Jason saved her life sprang to mind. He had been unwavering in his treatment of her. It mystified her that Roy Nesbitt had never come to get her statement about the attack. Jason had taken charge and fixed things somehow, but he had never told her what he had done. "I have feelings for him, but they're not clear. I rushed into one marriage. I don't want to rush into another."

"What's the rush?" Rachel echoed. "Jason's a very patient man and he'll wait until you're ready and he'll wait for Kate to accept him, if that's your worry. Just give him a reason to hope, that's all he's looking for."

"I've never had this happen before."

"What?"

"Being courted. I don't want to get it wrong."

Rachel smiled. "Follow your heart—okay?" She saw Emma's worried look. "C'mon, out with it, Emma. What else?"

"Jason asked me to the spring dance."

Rachel rubbed her hands together with delight. "Oh, I can't wait to watch the two of you together!"

"What do you mean? We're always together."

"Oh, Emma, when he's with you on the street or here in your house, he always keeps his feelings for you in check, but now he can be open about how he feels about you. It's so right, you know?" Rachel smiled that sly pirate's smile that she did so well. "He's a very desirable man."

Emma's brow wrinkled at her comment and she wished that Rachel would not refer to the men in her life in such an intimate, provocative manner. She remembered Rachel's comment about Shea being exotic years ago and pushed away a mental picture of the two of them coupling during their brief affair.

She fought to return her thoughts to her situation with Jason. In the light of day, her head was ruling her heart. Their brief encounter last night now gave her pause. She didn't want to make any mistakes. "I told him that I'd go, but maybe I've made a mistake. Maybe it's too soon."

"Ah! Maybe, maybe, maybe! Give up, Emma. Jason's been in love with you for years! You need to get out and do something before you grow as old and dusty as this house."

"Hey, I keep a clean house! It's not that dusty!" Emma joked, hoping to deflect the speech she knew was coming from Rachel. And Rachel ignored the comment, just as Emma feared.

"It's just a dance. And be careful, you might have a good time. I'll watch Kate if you want," she said, guessing her next objection. "You and Jason are perfect together. Everyone but you seems to know how much he loves you. I see the way he looks at you when you're not looking. I hear how he talks about you when you're not around. Besides, what's behind all those dinners that he has here? I'm glad that he did something about it. And isn't it time for both of you?"

"A part of me always knew, but I don't want to mess this up. He's too important to me."

"Do you feel the same?"

"I'm not sure yet. I told him that I still had some reservations because of Kate."

"Emma, Shea's gone but you have to do what's best for you and Kate. Jason would make a fine father and a great husband. You would want for nothing. It's time. If Shea could tell you so, I know he would."

"Oh, don't do that, Rachel, that's unfair."

"You've mourned for Shea and you'll always miss him, but your life didn't end."

"But others did. The men in my life have a terrible habit of being tempo-rary. My father—Adam—Shea. If anything happened to Jason, I don't know what I'd do."

"Emma, everything's a risk, but that's life. You've faced far worse than a man expressing his love for you."

Emma remembered another declaration from Adam long ago and the guilt that she felt when she refused him. "When Jason kissed me, I wanted him. I could hardly stand it."

"So why didn't you?"

Emma scoffed. "Don't be crude, Rachel."

"It's a beautiful thing when a man and a woman are in love. I know you. I can tell that you love him deep down. If you two are careful, no one will know! It will be like, well, getting a free sample of your cakes!"

"You're just trying to shock me, aren't you?"

"Is it working?" Rachel taunted.

Emma wished that she had not brought up the subject. Again, a picture of Rachel and Shea making love flashed through her mind. "Let's drop this, okay? I need a little time to figure this out."

Rachel said, "Okay, but give him a chance."

"That's what he said."

"Well, he's right. He's in love with you and he's handsome, rich, and the kindest man that I know. What more could you want? Besides, you get red as a beet when you talk about him."

"I think I love him, but it's so different from what I felt for Shea." Emma sat opposite Rachel with her head in her hands. So many fears now rose up in her mind that she had difficulty sorting them out.

Rachel's jovial mood disappeared and she thought that she heard a soft sob. She put out her hand and ruffled Emma's hair. "Hey, I'm sorry. Me and my big mouth. But what are you so afraid of?"

"Oh, Rachel, there's so much more to this. You just don't see. I know that people in town have treated us well, especially in their treatment of Shea, but they saw him as a curiosity more than anything. I'm not the type of woman who marries the richest man in town, not by a long shot."

"What on earth are you talking about?"

Emma raised her head and Rachel saw tears in her eyes. "I was wife to an Indian. People tried to kill us because of it—Fulton came back all these years later to kill me because of it. People see me as being tainted—low—

too low to marry someone like Jason. No one speaks of it, but I've felt it. As long as I'm the 'Widow Hawkshadow,' I'm safe and everyone's all right with us living here. Jason's reputation could be ruined."

Rachel came to sit beside her and tugged Emma's head to her shoulder. "It matters how you feel about each other, not what the townsfolk think. Here is a chance for you and Kate. If you don't take it, you'll regret it for the rest of your life. Don't bury yourself here because of what a few gossips might say. And don't worry about Jason's reputation. He owns the whole damn town. No one would dare say a word against him." She comforted her, producing a handkerchief to wipe Emma's damp cheeks. "Jason has never courted a girl. He would never have told you how he felt unless he was sure. What have you got to lose?"

A week before the dance, Emma appeared at Rachel's door with Kate in hand. As Kate scampered inside she said, "I have nothing to wear next week and I can't dance." Rachel grinned and yanked her inside.

"I'll get my apron off then we're going shopping," she announced. "I'm sure that Ruth, Caleb's sister who works at the dress shop, can find something stunning for you to wear."

After trying on ten ensembles at the millinery, Emma settled on a deep green dress with a lace collar. The deep emerald polished cotton set off her long auburn hair. "Should I put my hair up?" she asked.

Rachel expertly gathered up Emma's hair, grabbing a silver comb off the counter to secure it. "How's that?"

She turned to the full–length mirror. "Oh Rachel, I look so grown up," she chuckled. The outline of her angular cheek showed with the hair away from her face.

"Well, you are grown up, Emma," Rachel said. "You're not seventeen anymore. You look lovely."

Emma smiled at herself, for once seeing herself as a woman, not as an ignorant girl raised in a soddy. "Rachel, thanks for kicking me in the rump about Jason. You were right."

Rachel grinned. "You're welcome. Now for the dancing. Change out of this and let's get to my house. We've got work to do."

Jason stopped by Emma's one afternoon after work, catching Rachel giving Emma a dancing lesson in the parlor. He watched from a window on the porch as the two women giggled like girls and Rachel complained about Emma's big feet as they clomped around the parlor. Smiling, he retreated home, waiting until Rachel went home to supper, then he came in by the back door for dinner as usual. Emma was flushed and her hair was disheveled. To Jason, she had never looked lovelier. When he departed that night, he held her in an embrace. She cuddled against him as they lingered over good–night kisses.

Chapter Sixteen

Saturday the eighteenth arrived. Emma spent most of the day roaming around the house, her stomach fluttering with nerves. She doubted that she would get through the night without making a fool of herself. The spring dance was an annual event and in all the years she had lived in Easthope, she had avoided it like the plague.

As she dressed and put her hair up with many hairpins, Kate sat on Emma's bed, teasing her to behave and not to stay out too late. Then she grabbed her overnight bag and bolted out of the room when Helen knocked at the back door.

"Don't do anything I wouldn't do!" Kate shouted as she pounded down the stairs.

"Where have you heard such talk, young lady?" she called down after her, but Kate was already out the door, anticipating spending the night at the Barlows'.

Ready a half hour early, Emma sat straight backed on the parlor sofa, out of view of the front porch as twilight spread deep pinks and lavenders in the sky. She fiddled with the beaded drawstring bag that Rachel lent to her, trying to calm her nerves.

Jason arrived at five–thirty with a bouquet of flowers for her. He noticed her hands trembling as she placed the flowers into a vase in the kitchen.

"We don't have to go if you don't want to. We can do something else, a walk maybe, or a ride in my carriage."

She took a deep breath. "I want to go—really. It's my first dance and I'm a little nervous. I spent a week taking dancing lessons with Rachel. If I back out, she'll kill me!" Jason smiled then helped her with her shawl. She touched her lips to his. He smiled down at her, his eyes soft and warm.

They strolled down the street to the church hall, along with many other couples. Jason felt proud that many men and women admired the beauty in the green dress on his arm.

As they entered the hall all eyes turned to them, including Rachel and Caleb, who had left Martin to mind the children so that they could go to the dance for a while. Rachel beamed at Emma from across the room.

The band was playing. It was a simple ensemble of a fiddle, a banjo, a snare drum, and a concertina. Couples were already dancing, filling the large room.

"You are the most beautiful woman here," Jason whispered, his breath warm against Emma's cheek.

That night was one of Emma's finest. She had dreamed of such an occasion since childhood, accepting the fact that it would never happen as long as she was trapped in the isolation of the soddy. But fate had intervened many times over and here she was, dancing with the kindest, most handsome man in town. Although she danced awkwardly at first, Jason's warm hands and strong lead helped her to relax.

"Look at me," he whispered to her. "Keep focused on me and follow along."

He was a smooth, sure dancer and held her close every chance he got, especially during the slow waltzes. At times, the music faded away and both of them felt like they were the only people in the room; their gazes seldom left each other as they whirled.

Rachel and Caleb did not stay long but Rachel moved through the crowd, heading off single men wanting a dance with the beautiful young widow in the emerald dress. There was little need for her efforts. Emma and Jason's attraction for each other was obvious; no one dared to cut in on them.

The sewing circle women were huddled in a corner, their talk centered on Emma and Jason.

"Well, it's time the Widow Hawkshadow got on with her life. I knew all along that Jason Beck was the one for her," Fiona McBride said.

"That's not the tune you were singing a few months ago, Fiona! You practically branded Emma a gold–digger," Martha Hamlin retorted.

"You're right about that, Martha," Allison Carruthers agreed, "Don't they look perfect together."

Fiona feigned a wounded look and returned to her silent appraisal of Emma and Jason's dancing.

During the band's first break and eager for fresh air, Jason and Emma strolled into the cool night. Once they were around the corner, out of sight in the shadow of the church, he pulled her close and kissed her.

"I'm so glad you came with me tonight. I'm repeating myself, but you look so lovely." They strolled, talking and holding hands, and rejoined the dance much, much later.

The dance ended at midnight. Emma and Jason strolled along, bringing up the rear of the crowd as clumps of people melted away in the dark toward their homes. At her front door, Emma invited him in for a cup of coffee.

"No thank you. I should be going. You must be tired," Jason said.

"I'm not, honestly. I had a wonderful time."

He said good-night and trotted home.

Emma went inside and lit a lamp in the kitchen. She slipped off her shoes and was about to put on a pot of tea when she heard a soft knock at the back door. She peered out between the curtains and saw Jason. As she opened the door, he rushed in and took her in his arms, his lips caressing her face and neck.

"I didn't want anyone to see me come in. Oh Emma." His hands swept along the curves of her body. She tangled her hands in his long hair and her lips returned his impassioned kisses. She pulled away, blew out the lamp, took his hand and led him upstairs to her bedroom. He followed her very willingly.

She lit one lamp, keeping the flame low as Jason removed his jacket, tie, and shirt. She came to him. He fumbled with all the pins until her hair fell in an auburn wave around her face.

"Jason, I love you," she murmured. She stroked and kissed his broad chest as he groaned, enraptured.

He unbuttoned her dress and it fell to the floor in a heap, along with the rest of her clothes. His hands were all caresses on her soft, fair skin. The rest of his clothes soon fell beside the green dress. He held her nude body against his and she felt his massive hardness against her belly. He lifted her onto the bed and lay next to her, touching her and fondling her breasts. She touched him intimately, feeling his erection. He shuddered and rolled on top of her. His back arched as he penetrated deep. He thrust and circled his hips, exciting her to orgasm, and as she pulsated deep inside, he became still, enjoying the sensation of her pleasure. He leaned down and kissed her, his tongue firm in her mouth, then his hips began urgently driving against her, plunging him deeper and deeper as he came. He lay on top of her panting, still erect in her and moving a little, causing her to come again. Her lips found his and she drank in his feverish, urgent kiss.

She thought his energies were spent as he cradled her and dozed, but soon, he rolled her on her stomach and was inside her from behind as she lay prone before him. She felt his sweat trickle down her back as he moved within her and she came to another shuddering orgasm. He loved her until daybreak.

Just before dawn he dressed, but was reluctant to leave her. She dressed in a light cotton gown and walked him to the back door. As they kissed, he could not resist her, and, lifting her onto the kitchen table, he pulled up her nightgown and took her once again. As the first light of day searched out the darkness, they parted. He dressed, kissed her and returned home, jumping the fence rather than bothering with the gate. He turned and grinned before disappearing into his house.

The only neighbor who was awake to see Jason's departure was Rachel at her kitchen window. She was glad that she had risen early that morning. "About time," she grinned.

Those summer days were glorious for Emma and Jason as they explored the depth of their passion and love for each other. Emma let her guard down, basking in this newfound passion. She managed to push away the dread that had dogged her for so long. Kate was in school until June and they took full advantage of the privacy. Jason came into the habit of stopping at Emma's for his lunch hour, but he rarely ate lunch. As their passion burned, lunch time became an hour of frantic lovemaking. Many people noticed that despite frequent lunches at Emma's, Jason Beck seemed to be losing weight.

Young Kate sensed something in the air right away and began her own campaign to make sure that Jason would be her 'new daddy.'

Emma blushed one evening during dinner when Kate said, "You know, if I could pick a new daddy, I'd pick Jason, Momma. He's nice. Is he a good kisser?" Emma was so absorbed in thoughts of him that she did not chide Kate for the remark.

Spring rainfall was heavy and Emma had to keep indoors for days on end. To break her boredom while Kate was in school, she baked, perfecting her specialties. An idea had congealed and she wanted to ask Jason's advice about opening a bakery.

In addition to joining her for 'lunch,' Jason still came most evenings for the standing invitation to dine with Emma and Kate. He always made a point of helping to clear the table and clean up, something that Emma was still unused to. He always brought wine for them to enjoy after dinner. After Kate was in bed, they would linger over a glass or two by the fire in the front parlor, just to talk, without the sweaty passions that bound them at other times. It was a much needed respite, as their affair had become quite intense.

Emma and Jason had to quell their passions for the summer with Kate at home all day. Jason still came daily at noon to Emma's and ate lunch for a change. However, a few passionate afternoons were stolen when they drove up into the hills and spread blankets upon the long grass and they made love. She craved his touch. She quenched his longing.

Emma was cheered by his company, whether it was in or out of bed, and a quiet ease developed between them. Kate enjoyed his company and often perched beside him on the sofa after dinner while her mother and Jason exchanged accounts of their day. Emma was mindful of Kate's feelings and had not told her of their changing relationship, but the girl was smart and had not missed the looks they exchanged.

One such night, Emma mentioned to Jason that she was thinking of testing out her baked goods at the general store before opening a store outright. "It would give me an idea of what people like, if they like it at all. And I wouldn't have to make a huge investment."

"I've sampled what you've made and I think everything's delicious." His eyes sparkled. She knew what he really meant.

"I'll talk to Gale Carruthers tomorrow."

Although Gale was reluctant, Emma offered the first batch of cakes and cookies on approval. "If they don't sell out in three days, we'll forget it. Deal?"

Her baked goods did not sell out in three days; they sold out in one, and customers clamored for more. In a few days, Emma had a thriving business in a corner of the general store. As word spread, she was commissioned to make wedding cakes and pastries for parties. She was earning good money and grateful for something to occupy herself between Jason's lunch–hour visits and preparing dinner.

Sometimes Emma fell behind in her baking and joked that Jason's attentions were ruining her business, but when he took her in his arms and touched his lips to hers, her cottage business was forgotten. Jason could not get enough of her and Emma was insatiable, but to Emma's growing dismay, Jason made no proposal of marriage.

Emma pushed those nagging thoughts from her mind and threw her energies into planning Kate's ninth birthday party in August. Kate was popular at school and more than fifty children filled the house for the celebration. Emma grinned as she watched Kate act more grown–up than she was while she went through the rituals of games, presents, and cake. She was reserved and polite and she took special care to keep her new dress clean when the games began in the back yard. As the children departed late in the afternoon, Kate escorted them to the door and shook everyone's hands.

Rachel came up behind Emma. "Is Kate nine or nineteen?" she laughed.

"Sometimes I believe that she's older than me, I swear it!" Emma joked.

"How are things with you and Jason?" she asked.

"Fine."

Rachel was about to start digging for more detail on Emma and Jason's relationship when a crash was heard in the parlor. Someone had upended a tray of glasses, so Emma set about cleaning it up.

But shrewd Rachel knew what was going on during the 'lunch hour' between Emma and Jason. She visited one afternoon in September, careful to arrive after Jason's one o'clock departure. Emma was flushed when she answered the door.

"You two are like clockwork!" Rachel chuckled as she stepped in.

"Huh?"

"You don't fool me, Emma. I know what's going on around here during lunch hour. Now, tell me everything!"

Emma blushed and walked back to the kitchen. She fiddled with several platters of cookies and pies, stacking them in a large basket for the trip to Carruthers' store. "I don't know what you're talking about, Rachel. You have a dirty mind sometimes."

"Oh yeah? I can see from your face and your disheveled appearance that I'm right." She looked at her hungrily. "C'mon, you can tell me. Look, I'm your best friend. I swear I'll tell no one."

Emma turned away, her hands working in her apron. "We're getting along."

"I want more!" Rachel complained, with a mock pout.

"Rachel, it's personal."

"Well, that's what I want to hear!"

She stared at Rachel. She was very reluctant to tell Rachel anything, feeling very pressured by her. "All right. We're not having lunch—well sometimes we do."

"How many times have you two had lunch—or have you lost count?" Rachel grinned. "Tell me something! Things are cool between me and Caleb right now. I have to live through you. I know it started after the dance."

"Are you spying on me?" Emma said with shock and embarrassment.

"No, Emma. I saw Jason leave the next morning, that's all. It wasn't hard to figure out. I think it's wonderful!"

"Please don't tell anyone. We've already gone too far too fast and I have to pull up and slow this down."

"Don't slow down. Things are just beginning for you two. Leave all those sad times behind and enjoy this. When's the wedding?"

"He hasn't brought it up. I'm getting worried." She sat down at the table. "I know he loves me, but marriage hasn't been mentioned once. I've known him for years. He wouldn't use me, would he?"

"Absolutely not. Jason's not the type but you know he's never had a steady girl. Maybe he's got cold feet. He'd be taking on fatherhood and the memory of Shea. That might be hard for him. Give him time and enjoy yourself, but don't get pregnant, okay?"

"That's one thing that I'm grateful for. It took a long time for me to get pregnant with Kate."

"But what if it was Shea? I mean, what if your difficulty getting pregnant was his fault? What would you do if Jason got you pregnant?"

The thought struck her full force. Maybe it had been Shea. Then, Emma thought of Shea and Rachel's affair years ago; she was now grateful that Shea could not get anyone pregnant easily. A nagging thought began to bother her but she pushed it aside.

But getting pregnant out of wedlock in a town that had done so much for her, Shea, and Kate would disgrace her forever. She would lose Jason, of that she was certain, even though he would be half responsible. After all, Jason's business sustained the town and he was its most prominent member. She was the widow of a half-breed Cheyenne.

Emma covered her fears and said, "I don't sense that he's afraid of marriage. He's a very strong man. He faces everything else head on."

"This is new territory for him. Be patient. I'm sure that he's just waiting for the right moment. He wouldn't have poured his heart out to you if he didn't mean it." She paused, smiling, her look far away for a fleeting moment. "You know, Caleb asked me to marry him just after the first time we did it."

"And you acted so shocked when I told you that Shea and I had done it before we got married! Why, you little hypocrite!" Emma cracked.

Rachel giggled. "We just couldn't wait and I discovered that Caleb is quite vulnerable afterwards. He'll say yes to anything!"

Another vision streaked across Emma's mind of Shea and Rachel lying together. It was becoming too hard to continually forgive Rachel, and anger at her inappropriate comments began to fester in Emma's soul. She was sleepless that night as these thoughts gnawed at her.

When Jason arrived the following day at noon, Emma pulled away from his embrace. "Jason, I want to talk to you. We have to talk about—well, where this is going."

"I love you, Emma. I thought you knew that."

"I do. I love you, but how much longer are we going to sneak around? I suspect that everyone in town knows what we're doing in here during your lunch hour. It's embarrassing to know people are thinking of us like that."

"I thought you didn't care what people thought of you."

She cut across his words. "I do care. These people have been very kind. I owe them to act a certain way. I admit my half of guilt in this." Jason's look stopped her. "What is it?"

He touched her cheek. "Emma, I love you more than anything—anyone. I didn't want to pressure you into something that you were not ready for. I don't feel what we're doing is wrong. I want you to be sure that you want to be with me. You go to Shea's grave often, and there's nothing wrong with that," he added quickly. "I decided long ago that I would propose marriage once in my life to the woman I loved. And that woman is you, Emma. There's no one else for me. And Kate is like a daughter to me already."

"Shea's death knocked me over good. I had a very hard time letting go, but I did it with your help. But maybe you're right. I guess I need time to think."

Jason left after bestowing a soft kiss. Out of respect for her, he did not return for lunch or dinner, or, for that matter, for the rest of the week.

That Sunday after church, Emma and Kate went up to Shea's grave and spent the afternoon wandering the meadows. Kate shored up her fort with found sticks and branches while Emma sat nearby at the creek. Being there always brought back a flood of memories for Emma. But this day as she sat in the sunshine and lost herself in the sound of the bubbling creek, Shea's favorite place, the grief over his death was fading. She no longer felt that dreadful shock of pain when she thought of him. The day was soft and gentle with a light breeze, barely enough to ruffle her hair.

"I have to let you go, Shea," she said in a whisper to herself. "I loved you and you will always be a part of me and you'll always be Kate's father, but I have to get on with my life. I need to feel loved again. I need Jason and so does Kate." She closed her eyes as the wind sprang up; she felt its touch on her cheek, like a caress. She believed that she had felt Shea's spirit move through her, and she was not afraid as a mysterious whirlwind enveloped her. She opened her eyes after several moments, feeling at peace for the first time in over two years. Then, movement off to her left caught her eye. Lame White Deer was watching and raised a hand to her. She smiled and waved after him as he turned and disappeared into the tree line.

Later, Lame White Deer told his people of the strange wind that had enveloped the *maiyun* up on the mountain that afternoon.

That evening, Emma sent Kate to Jason's to ask him to supper. He came a half hour later. He looked like he had not slept well in days, his eyes slack with fatigue.

"Welcome, Jason. How have you been?" Emma said. Kate giggled as Emma stood on tiptoe and kissed his cheek as he entered by the back door.

"Fine, fine. How are you?"

"Fine—no—I feel great. Hungry? We're having chicken and dumplings. It's Kate's favorite."

He helped set out the plates and flatware on the dining room table then sat in his usual seat at Emma's right.

If it were not for the ebullient Kate talking about her classmates at school, Jason and Emma would not have exchanged more than ten words during dinner. Both of them were tense, struggling with what to say to each other.

Jason was indeed hungry and had three helpings of the chicken. "That was delicious," he said as he wiped his mouth with a napkin. "Thank you, Emma."

"Jason, will you help me with my arithmetic?" Kate pleaded.

He looked to Emma for consent. "I'll clean up. Go ahead." As she bustled between the kitchen and dining room, she half–listened to the two of them talking over Kate's math problems.

Soon, it was time for Kate to be in bed. Emma saw Kate to her room then returned downstairs.

Jason was in the kitchen. He had his coat in his hands. "I should be going, Emma. Thank you for dinner."

"Jason, please stay," Emma said. "I need to talk with you.".

She led him to the formal parlor where they sat apart from each other on the sofa. A fire burned in the hearth to ward off the night's chill.

"This afternoon, I went to the cabin with Kate." She stopped talking when she noticed the downcast expression on Jason's face that he no longer tried to hide.

"I know. I saw you driving up the mountain road again today."

"You think that we go there too often, don't you?"

"It's not my business, Emma," he replied, dejected. "You don't have to explain why you go up there. If it's for Kate's sake I more than understand, but if it's because you're having trouble letting go of Shea, that's something else. I can't share you in that way and be a substitute for Shea's love. Understand that Shea was my closest friend and I honor his memory, but he's gone and we both have to get on with our lives."

She was suddenly fearful that he was withdrawing his affections from her and she was shaken to her core. Her inability to let go of Shea's memory was indeed driving him away. "But that's what I want to talk about, Jason. Please hear me out."

"All right," he agreed, guarded and sullen.

"We spent the afternoon at the cabin, as we always do, but today was different. I thought of Shea and all we had gone through together. I remembered our pain and our joys, and gave thanks for Kate. He found me that day years ago, alone and near death on the prairie and saved my life, cared for me. No one was more surprised than me when I realized that I loved him. We had hard times, but things smoothed out when we came to Easthope. A large part of our happiness here was because of you. Your friendship to me, but especially to Shea, was so important. You'll never quite know how much it meant to him. You were responsible for our acceptance in this town and you were there to help Kate and I when Shea got sick. I needed someone and you were there." She paused for breath and for courage. "And now, I find myself in love with you. It's a different love than the kind I had for Shea and that's why I've had such a hard time sorting it out. I was so young when I married Shea. I made a lot of mistakes. I rushed into the marriage to hide my pain after my parents died. But what I feel for you is—different—deeper. I do love you, Jason, if you still want me."

His morose expression suddenly lifted. "Of course I still want you, Emma. Shea knew how I felt about you from the start and it didn't bother him. He asked me to care for you after he died and I tried, but I failed. You were almost killed by Fulton—again. I've felt so guilty over that. I want to make those dark times go away for you, but I don't know how."

She reached out and touched his cheek. "None of that matters, do you hear me? I don't blame you for anything." She searched his face. "Oh, Jason, I love you and I don't want us to be apart anymore. This past week has been hell. I can see it's been hard on you, too." She slid across the sofa and burrowed into his shoulder; his arm closed around her.

Jason stared into the fire for a long time, then sat up straight and took her hands in his. "Emma, I've been in love with you since we met. I never believed I would have the privilege and the honor of your hand. Will you marry me?"

Truly, Emma had not expected this. Her slender hands tightened around Jason's and tears filled her eyes. "I want nothing more than to be your wife, Jason. I will marry you."

From his pocket, he produced a gold ring with a single garnet that was encircled by seed pearls. Taking her left hand, he placed the ring on her third finger. He kissed her. "I've been carrying this around for weeks," he said with a smile filled with relief. "It belonged to my mother. Please accept it and know that I love you and always will." Jason took her into a tender embrace. Emma slumped against him with joy—and relief.

Jason made sure to arrive at Emma's the following morning just before Kate left for school. Together, they told Kate that they were to be married.

Kate nearly broke Jason's neck with her hugs. "When? When? Sooner the better, that's what Rachel says!"

Emma smiled indulgently. "It will be soon, but we haven't set a date yet. Now run along to school."

"Can I tell anybody?"

"You can tell anyone and everyone," Jason said as Kate pounded out the door calling the news to Helen and Randall who waited on the walkway out in front of the house. The children trotted off around the corner.

Emma and Jason stepped out onto the porch, hand in hand, drinking in the cool morning air.

Minutes later, Rachel came running with hugs for them both. "Kate told me the news! It's about time! Have you set a date?"

"We'll decide on a date soon," Emma promised.

That evening, the soon–to–be family sat in Emma's parlor after sup-per. Jason sat on the sofa with Kate next to him. She bombarded him with questions. "Where will we live now? When's the wedding? Can I be in it? Will I have a brother or a sister soon? If I get a brother or sister, do I have to share my room?"

Jason smiled and patiently answered each question, savoring every moment. Emma, relaxed and content, sat in a wing–backed chair bent over some needlework that she was trying to learn.

"Well, Kate, we were thinking about next June or July. What do you think?" Emma asked.

"Why wait so long?"

"We need time to plan the wedding. We want it to be nice and we'd like to have it outdoors, since the whole town will be invited."

"But Daddy told me that you got married to him the day after he asked you."

Emma smiled. "Well, that's how the Cheyenne do it. We're going to do it a little differently."

Kate sighed melodramatically. "I wish the wedding was tomorrow, then Jason could stay with us all the time."

Chapter Seventeen

Jason and Emma planned their wedding for next June seventh, a week after Kate's school year ended.

Just after the logging exhibition that year, Jason had to head to Tacoma. He was very concerned about leaving Emma alone, worried about her ordeal of last winter. Rachel urged Emma and Kate to stay in her home, but Emma refused. Jason did not push the point and had to satisfy himself that Rachel was only a few houses away. He also asked Roy Nesbitt to keep an eye on Emma and Kate, just in case.

But when he returned, Emma seemed distracted and listless. She slowly moved around the kitchen making coffee the morning after his return.

"I had to go to Tacoma," he said. "And I hated leaving you alone again. I thought you would be okay with Rachel nearby. But something's wrong, I can see it in your face. What is it, Em?"

"Just tired."

He pulled out a chair at the table for her and took the kettle from her hand. "Then sit down. If you need help around here, I can hire someone. This is a big house."

"That's not it—it's not that kind of tired," she snapped. She felt irritable and bristled with anger, but anger at what, she had no clue. She just felt aggravated, crabby.

"Did something happen while I was gone?" he asked, trying to keep his tone calming, fearing that indeed something had happened.

Emma stepped back and sat in the proffered chair, her head in her hands. "No—nothing happened! I can't put words to how I'm feeling. Maybe we're moving too fast."

"I understand."

"You don't understand." She looked up at him. "It's not you, honest. I don't want you to take this the wrong way. But—see—I felt like I faded away the day Shea died."

"You have me, Rachel, and Caleb to help you through it."

"Rachel—right," Emma muttered.

Jason was very worried. "Did you and Rachel have a fight?"

During a long silence, Emma made a decision and tried to open up, as much as she was able. She had kept so many serious issues bottled up for so long, she feared that she would be a nervous wreck if her deep-rooted problems escaped her carefully built prison. "There are things bothering me. And I'm not even sure if they matter, but sometimes I think I'm going crazy."

"You can tell me anything, Emma. And I'm sure of one thing—you're not crazy," he soothed.

"There is one thing I am sure of." She drew breath several times until she was able to say it aloud. "Rachel and Shea had an affair after Katherine was born. Shea told me just before he died. I can't seem to get it off my mind. I've tried to forget it but it won't go away. Some friend, eh?" Jason was not shocked, a reaction that she had fully expected.

"Your last words to Shea were that you forgave him. Now I understand why you said it."

"I forgave Shea, but I'm having trouble forgiving Rachel."

After a long silence, he said, "So you know. And you're okay about Randall, too? You have more strength than I would in the same situation." Her jaw dropped. He slumped, realizing that she did not know all. "Oh, Emma, I thought he told you everything."

She blinked in shock. "Guess he didn't. What about Randall?"

"I thought you knew. Oh, Emma, I'm sorry."

"Are you telling me that Randall is Shea's son?"

He looked stricken, knowing how deeply he had hurt her. "From what Shea told me, the chances of Randall being his were good."

Her face drained of color. "You knew all this time? Why didn't you tell me?"

He struggled to find his voice. "I couldn't stand to hurt you. Just after Kate was born, I was coming back from Camp Three. I was riding along the trail below the cabin to the main road because the deer trail I normally used was flooded. I saw them together, but they didn't see me." He rose and went to the window over the sink, looking out so she would not see the pain on his face. "Next time I was alone with Shea, I told him what I saw. I was mad at him for being so foolish. He regretted the whole thing. He was having a hard time back then. He couldn't give you the life you wanted and all the things you should've had. He was always afraid that you would leave him. He talked about his army friend, Adam, and how you almost ran off with him. Anyway, he didn't tell me about Randall until years later. He and Rachel were never sure." He swallowed hard and turned back to her.

She felt numb. "Now I understand why Rachel wasn't happy about being pregnant. I thought it was because Helen and Randall would be so close in age. What a fool I was!" As she put together the pieces, the deep pain of the discovery struck her full force; the repercussions were enormous. She doubted that she had the strength to recover from this staggering blow.

Jason's own guilt was sharp. He swallowed tears. First he had hired Fulton who had tried to kill her, now this. He searched for anything to say. "Randall's like Caleb, you know, tall, slim with the dark hair."

"I'm glad Randall's coloring was so convenient!" Tears of humiliation pooled in her eyes.

"This is my fault," he mumbled, busying himself by putting the coffee kettle on the stove.

"I don't hold you responsible. You were caught between both of us."

"Em, Rachel's marriage was in trouble long before you and Shea ever came to Easthope. Rachel wanted to hurt Caleb like he had hurt her when he had that affair with Elsa Swenson. She made her discovery about Elsa very public and humiliated Caleb to get back at him, but it wasn't enough. That woman can sure carry a grudge." He looked to her. "What are you going to do?"

"What can I do?"

"Will you tell Rachel that you know?"

She looked distracted. "Huh? I have to think about that. Not much I can do about it now, is there? It's already done."

"Emma, what can I do to make this up to you?"

"Nothing, I'm afraid. I need to be alone for a few days. Do you mind?"

"No, no. I'll go, then." He walked to the back door and searched for something to say to comfort her. All he could say was, "I'm sorry."

"It's all right, Jason. I'll see you soon." When she knew that Jason was out of earshot, she crumpled to the floor and sobbed.

For several days, Emma kept to herself. Jason saw her out in her yard hanging laundry and waved, but respecting her desire to be alone, he did not approach. Emma went about town with Kate in tow as usual, doing errands, but she felt ridiculous and insignificant. Her husband and her best friend had betrayed her. She thought that she could forgive the affair, but the added shock of Randall's possible parentage rocked her already shaky foundation. It was another loss, another burden, and emotionally she was shattered. She was distracted and irritable. Kate noticed the change in her mother's behavior, but being a child, there was little she could do. She was obedient and sensitive to whatever her mother was going through.

Rachel still visited Emma often, but did not notice the change in her demeanor right away. But Emma's torment grew to the point that she could hardly stand to be with Rachel.

One afternoon many days after the discovery, Rachel came over to Emma's and sat at the kitchen table while Emma pulled freshly-baked bread from her oven. Emma was distracted and quiet.

"Emma, are you feeling all right?

"I'm fine."

"Everything okay between you and Jason?"

"Sure, Rachel. Everything's fine."

"You look a little pale. Are you getting enough rest?"

"I'm fine," she repeated.

"Emma, I'm just concerned."

She slid another tray of bread in the oven and slammed the heavy iron door. "Will you just leave me alone?"

"Emma!"

"Tell you what," she snarled, yanking out the chair from under Rachel, "why don't you go home to your family and quit worrying about the widow down the street! I'm sick of everybody asking me if I'm all right! I'm fine! And when you get home, send my daughter back. She's my child, not yours!"

"Emma, calm down. What did I do?"

"You've done quite enough! I have been tolerant, I've let things go, but I can't do it anymore! There are some things I can't abide—like liars!" She faced Rachel. "I know."

Rachel was mystified. "Know what?"

Emma shot an accusatory look at Rachel. "About you and Shea and I know about Randall, too. How could you do such a thing? Now get out of my house!"

Rachel staggered. "Oh my God! Emma, it's not what you think. Please let's talk about this!"

"No! Leave my house now!"

Rachel burst into tears and fled the house. She sent Kate home as ordered and did not see Emma or Kate for days. She wanted to explain, but she did not dare approach Emma now.

In her anger at Rachel, Emma did not want to involve Kate so after a week, she relented and allowed her to spend time with the Barlow children. She never intended to punish Kate, but she felt a pang every time Helen and Randall were in her house. She avoided them as best she could without seeming rude. The boy was an unwitting reminder of the betrayal. The scene she conjured of Shea and Rachel making love played in her mind again and again. This scar was not upon her flesh; it was on her soul.

Rachel had told Jason that she and Emma had had a bitter fight. Since he had guessed why, he began visiting Emma again. He was responsible for her desolation and he would do anything to console her.

Kate often spent the night at the Barlows which Emma allowed, but she and Rachel had still not spoken since that day in the kitchen. At night, alone, Emma felt exposed in the big house. She could not sleep for very long and roamed the house at night, checking and rechecking all doors and the window locks that Jason had installed. Every noise made her jump. Her fears grew so irrational that a horse's whinny caused her to run to the window to see what was the matter. She was not comfortable with being alone and wished that Jason could hold her in the night and push the demons away, for she lacked the courage to face them. In desperation, she uncorked a bottle of laudanum and began taking it several times a day to numb herself.

In bed, in a haze before the laudanum pulled her into sleep, her turbulent life replayed in her mind. She was powerless to stop the memories. The oppressing emotions weighed her down and broke her.

On nights when Kate stayed overnight at the Barlows, Jason tried to initiate love–making, but Emma refused him. It bothered him but he had to give her time to sort things out. He hoped that soon she would open up and rid herself of the conflicting emotions that beset her. But as the days passed, he sadly realized that he could not reach that part of her. She had become defensive, quarrelsome, and sarcastic. He endured the brunt of her grief and anger without complaint, believing that his love would help her recover. He remembered the day that she had confided in him years ago, telling him of Shea's treatment of her after he was hanged. The roles had reversed. He understood Emma's desperation during that time, and understood that Shea's wrath had come from a profound feeling of helplessness.

Unfortunately, business called him away again. After his return from a week–long trip to Tacoma in October, he was unprepared for the change in her. She was in the kitchen pulling fresh biscuits from the oven when he knocked and entered by the back door.

"Welcome back. Just made some fresh coffee," she said, trying very hard to smile and be pleasant. "How was your trip?" She poured him a cup of coffee as he sat down at the table. "Did you see your brother while you were in Tacoma?"

"Uh, no," Jason replied, suddenly uncomfortable. "Didn't have time."

"Why not?"

"I wanted to get back. How are you?"

"Fine. Just been busy with the baking. Gale Carruthers wants more all the time and I can't keep up. Maybe I should open a bakery, then I could hire help."

Jason did not take the bait to change the subject. She seemed small, slumped—and moved like an old woman. "I'm worried about you, Emma. You're so unhappy. What can I do?"

She leaned against the soapstone sink watching him, expressionless. At length, she took breath to speak. "I can't dodge you, can I, Jason?"

"I hope you don't feel that you have to."

Her reply frightened him because it was so affecting. "Things are happening—in my head—my mind. I'm having bad dreams and some of them are still with me when I'm awake." She turned away and upended a tray of biscuits into a market basket. "Maybe it's because I miss you when you go on a trip. I just have to get used to it. It's not your fault, Jason. I just have to get a grip on things."

"I postponed the trip as long as I could. But if you're having problems sleeping, why haven't you seen Stuart? He'll help you."

"Stuart can't help with this. I'm sorry that I said anything. I don't want to worry you."

"What I said about Randall caused you pain and I'm more sorry than I can say. I wish that day never happened."

"There are a lot of days I wish had never happened," she said with a far–off look, then her manner abruptly changed. She seemed too calm. This really frightened him. "In a way, I'd rather know the truth, but I won't lie to you that I'm past the shock. It just takes me time to get over things, that's all."

"This is a big problem, Emma. You were betrayed by two people you loved. That's not easy to get over—or forgive."

"What would you know about it? This has never happened to you! Don't sit there and tell me how I should feel!" She caught herself and apologized. "I'm sorry, Jason."

She could not mask the awful pain that her best friend had seduced Shea. For so long, she worked very hard to appear that she did not know about the affair and kept the friendship going despite the anger chipping away at her resolve. After venting her anger on Rachel that day, she had felt more guilt than anger, but there was nothing she could do about it. One of the 'animals' had escaped from her cage. She could not take back her words to Rachel and she could not heal herself by burying her pain this time. *I lived through worse—I survived—I can live through this, too,* she told herself. But she was afraid of what living with it was doing to her.

She spoke after a long silence. "I'm sure how you feel about me—"

"But you're angry with me, I know."

She shook her head. "Not really—no. I don't want to hurt you, Jason. I love you, I do. But another piece of me was torn off when I learned the truth about Shea and Rachel. My life has been coming at me so fast, I can't keep up anymore. You've been my only grounding besides Kate. But something's unresolved about—about a lot of things, I guess."

"Talk to me, Emma. I won't be hurt by anything you say or feel. If we work together, it will be easier for you."

She smiled at him. "Jason, don't take any of this to heart. Know that I love you so much that it scares me a little."

He saw her knuckles whiten as her hands clenched the countertop.

"I should have never returned to Shea when he ended up in Montana. My presence there brought about his death. If it hadn't been for that goddamned Tyler and his lynch mob, Shea would be alive!" She turned away from him. "Sometimes I get so mad that I don't know what to do with myself. And Kate—she's so fragile sometimes. I can't replace her father and I'm angry—so helpless to fix things for her. Tyler got his way in the end by taking Shea from us." Her shrill laugh made the hairs on the back of Jason's neck stand up. "When Shea confessed the affair, I couldn't bring myself to condemn him. I forgave him, but I waited so long to tell him. He held on for weeks, waiting for me to say those words. I made him suffer for no reason." When she turned to face him, she held out her hands. "I was so selfish and

I was hurt so deeply. I kept tending him and gave no thought to his feelings, to what he needed. I thought that I forgave Rachel by not mentioning the affair, but you know how that ended up. Every time I look in a mirror I see the toll of my life on my face and my body. I'm covered in scars, inside and out." Then her voice faded to a whisper. "But, there are no guarantees. You never know what's going to happen next, do you? I keep losing everyone important to me. If I lost Kate or you—"

"Emma, you're a good mother. Nothing's going to happen to Kate. As for me, I've never had a sick day in my life, except for getting in the way of a log rolling downhill once. Knocked me out for days." He chuckled, but she did not join in.

She had lost her way after Shea's death and the discovery about Randall's possible parentage had shaken her trust in the people she loved. It was not the most horrible thing in the world that could happen to her, but it was the last thing that she could endure. Emma's disorientation and grief were profound and she would take a long time to come out of it.

Jason wanted to assure her that she would be all right. She had cleaved to Shea's strength all these years and now that security was gone. He had hoped that he could fill the void and it struck him hard that he could not. He could not give her his strength and it frustrated him.

She went to the stove, wiping away tears. "Do you want more coffee, Jason?"

"Emma, sit down and talk to me. Let's get all this out in the open and deal with it."

She sat at the table opposite him, pouring them both coffee. "Okay, here's what I want, Jason. I want to marry you. I want Kate to grow up and be happy. I want to patch things up with Rachel, but that's a ways off. I want to be free of these awful feelings, these awful thoughts."

"What awful thoughts?" he asked, pale with worry.

She sipped her coffee. "Just memories—dark memories. I have to let them go, I know that, but it's not easy. They've been my dark little friends all these years."

"Talk to me," he urged.

Jason gave her leave to talk about anything, holding her hand, holding her when tears flowed, and reassuring her all that he could. They talked for hours, but he knew that she was still skirting the real issues, holding back.

But the relief Emma needed so desperately did not materialize. Jason's shoulder was always there, along with his tenderness and understanding. She expected time would heal everything, just as the scars on her body had needed time to mend. But this disease of the soul needed attention other than time. Once again she had to fight to regain her balance.

She struggled to keep up with her baking business, but it was losing its charm. Jason's visits and outings momentarily diverted her, but the torturous dreams and creeping despair overtook her until she was convinced that she was crazy. She let her business slide and kept to her bed for days on end. Jason was very upset because his visits and their long talks did not possess the restorative powers he had hoped for.

Emma's dreams had taken on the terrors that had plagued her. Horrifying nightmares ripped through her, replaying and intermingling her parent's deaths, being stabbed by Fulton, Shea's body hanging and twisting, and Tyler's revolver leveled at her. Emma awoke sometimes with a shriek, scaring Kate who heard her cries echoing down the hallway.

Jason came often to see her and did what he could to get her to talk, but Emma started to keep him at a distance emotionally and physically. He begged her to see Stuart but she refused, claiming that she would snap out of her doldrums soon.

Worn out by continuous lies to Caleb about the reason for her and Emma's falling out, Rachel continued to mourn the shattered friendship. She had no one to confide in, no one to trust but Jason. On a snowy morning in October, she knocked at Jason's office door at the mill and poked her head inside.

"Jason, I have to talk to you."

Rachel had never come to his office before and he knew why she had come. She was subdued, not at all like herself.

He rose from his chair and indicated for her to sit in the seat near his desk. "Sure, come in. Sit down."

She stalled, looking around the office with feigned interest, then said, "I didn't know who else to go to. I need your help, Jason. Emma and I had a terrible argument." Jason's guilt about his role in the whole thing pricked him as Rachel continued. "It was a terrible scene."

He spared her the pain of admission. "She knows about your affair with Shea—and about Randall."

She recoiled, thunderstruck. "You know that was what the fight was about?"

"I saw you two together years ago below the trail. Years later, Shea told me that Randall might be his son." He fiddled with ledger books on his desk. "Rachel, this is all my fault. I'm the one who let it slip. Shea told Emma about the affair just before he died. Emma told me about it and like a fool, I just assumed that she knew about Randall. I thought she was handling it very well, considering. I'm scared for her and I will do all I can to put it right."

Rachel wept. "I wondered how she knew. Oh, Jason, we never wanted to hurt her. We didn't love each other, believe me. I used Shea and I was willing to pay the price; I paid for it by living a lie. But Emma shouldn't have to pay for our mistake. Shea loved her. Caleb and I were having such troubles before and after I discovered his affair. I wanted to get back at him. When I realized that I was pregnant, maybe by Shea, I was so confused. I practically raped Caleb to cover myself." Rachel felt an odd lightening of her guilt knowing that someone else knew her shameful secret. She knew that Jason's sense of honor could be counted on to help her. "I need Emma to know the affair wasn't Shea's fault and how sorry I am. She's my best friend."

"I made a wreck of things. Maybe I should've come to you right away, but I didn't know how Emma was going to deal with it. Unfortunately, she's not coping with it very well."

"Please help me, Jason," Rachel pleaded. "Please do what you can."

After he came home from the mill that afternoon, Jason was changing his clothes. He planned to head over to Emma's for dinner.

Just as he was about to leave, Kate pounded on his back door shouting. "Jason! Jason! Come quick!" He bounded down the stairs and flung open the door. "Momma's sick! She won't wake up!"

Jason's heart was in his throat as he ran next door into Emma's house. Kate followed. In a few leaps, he was upstairs and at Emma's bedside.

Emma lay sprawled across the big bed, pale and perspiring. Her breathing was shallow and labored. Jason picked up a brown bottle of laudanum that was on the night table. It was empty.

"Fetch Doc Barlow, quick!" Jason ordered.

Kate ran down the stairs and outside as fast as she could.

He felt Emma's forehead. It was very hot. "Emma? Emma? What have you done?" She did not stir. He rushed down the hallway to the bathroom and grabbed a handful of towels. He threw them into the sink, turned on the cold water then wrung them out. He returned to her beside and placed the cool towels on her forehead. "Em, can you hear me? Talk to me."

Her eyes fluttered open, but they were unfocused and hazy. In a whisper, she said, "Take care of Kate for me."

"Why did you do this?" Jason's voice rose in panic. "How much did you take?"

She looked at him with sad, solemn eyes. "Promise me that you'll care for her. Be her guardian. Please, Jason. In my dresser there's money. It's yours. Take it for Kate."

"How much was in the bottle, Emma?" he persisted.

"I love you," she whispered. "Just let me go."

"You have to tell me—how much did you take?"

The drug pulled her into delirium and her words slurred. "I was a lousy daughter. I was a lousy wife. Why else would Shea want to be with Rachel? And I'm a lousy mother, too. I can't reach her—Kate's better off with you."

Just then, Stuart arrived with Kate at his heel. Kate stopped at the bedroom doorway, unwilling to come any further.

Jason's voice had risen to a shout, born of pure fear. "Emma, how much did you take? Answer me!"

She blinked away tears. "Jason, raise Kate for me."

Kate backed out of the room and sat on the steps.

"No! You're not leaving me and you're not leaving Kate, either!" Jason yelled.

With surprising strength, Stuart yanked Jason away. "What the hell are you doing?"

Jason was scared, unmindful that Kate was nearby. "She drank laudanum. I can't find out how much she took. She wants to die!"

Stuart began examining Emma. He listened to her heart through his stethoscope. "What brought this on?"

"She's been troubled. I thought that I could help her through it."

"How long has she been like this?"

"Weeks—several weeks," Jason answered. "I didn't know she was this bad."

"Why the hell didn't you tell me?" he scolded. "We've got to get her to the hospital now. Jason, help me get her to my carriage out front."

Jason bundled Emma in bed blankets and carried her down the stairs to Stuart's carriage. Kate grabbed her coat then followed them outside. She hopped up into the carriage and sat next to Stuart in the front seat. Emma slumped against Jason in the back seat, mumbling in a drugged delirium.

As Stuart flicked the reins, Kate turned around in the seat.

Jason's voice choked with emotion as he spoke to Kate. "She just took too much medicine. It was a good thing that you came to get me."

"But why did she need medicine? She didn't seem to be sick."

Jason had no answer for her.

Stuart said, "Don't worry, Kate. We're going to take good care of her."

"Am I going to get sick, too?"

Jason looked at Kate. "What she's got isn't catching."

"Will Momma come home tonight?"

"You can stay at Rachel's until your mother comes home, okay?" Jason said.

"Can I stay with you, Jason?"

"I'm gone all day. Rachel's at home to care for you." Jason did not mean to be short with her, but he was terrified that Emma would die in his arms. He could feel her going limp.

Kate fell silent and turned away.

Many people on the street watched Stuart's quick progress down Main Street in his buggy. Stuart pulled up to the hospital and Emma was lifted out and carried into the hospital by Jason. Rumors spread quickly.

Emma was placed in a room on the first floor. Two nurses disappeared inside the room with Stuart. Jason and Kate waited, sitting on the cold, hard wood floor, unwilling to go far. Kate would not leave her post near the door.

Jason did not know what to say to the child. His thoughts were focused on why Emma had committed such a desperate act.

They heard Stuart's voice and the clinking of metal instruments, then a nurse came out carrying blankets and Emma's nightgown, soaked in vomit. Kate's eyes were wide, but she was silent. The smell of the vomit made Jason's stomach roll. More nurses and orderlies went in and out of the room. It was an hour before Stuart emerged. He looked shaken.

"Can I see Momma?" Kate asked, popping up from the floor.

"Not right now. She's asleep." Kate's face fell and a look from Jason caused Stuart to acquiesce. "Okay, but just for a few minutes and be very quiet."

Kate went in and tiptoed to Emma's bedside. She was in an exhausted sleep, curled up tight. The child tucked the covers around her mother. A nurse was in the room, filling a syringe. When she plunged it into Emma's arm, Emma did not move. Kate flinched instead, as if the pain had been her own.

Stuart and Jason spoke in hushed voices in the hall. "It's going to be close the next few hours. Some came up, so that's good. It'll take days to get the laudanum out of her system, though. She's in bad shape. Take Kate to Rachel's then come back here. We have a lot to talk about."

Jason mumbled that Emma and Rachel recently had an argument.

"I heard that days ago. I don't buy that excuse." He looked at Jason assessingly. "You're a terrible liar. There is more to all this."

Jason rubbed his face. He felt drained. "It's everything that's happened to her. Her life hasn't been easy and I think the fight with Rachel was the pebble that caused a landslide. She's been shaky for weeks and I wanted her to see you, but she refused. Is she going to make it?"

"We'll do all we can. Withdrawal from laudanum is very difficult. I will be sure that someone watches over her for the next few days."

Jason joined Kate in Emma's room. He observed the look in the girl's eyes. It was a gaze that was withdrawn and defensive. It was the way that she looked near the end of Shea's life. Back then and despite her youth, she had distanced herself emotionally as she watched her father fail. Kate could lose her mother, he thought sadly. Of course, he would care for her, but he knew that he could not keep her because he was not married. He feared what might happen to her if she were sent to an orphanage. He resolved to ask Rachel and Caleb to adopt her if the unthinkable happened. He would use all his money, all his influence to make it happen.

Jason left with Kate in hand and borrowed Stuart's carriage. While Kate packed a bag in her room at home, he cut through the yards to Rachel's. He told Rachel and Caleb what had happened.

Rachel and Caleb stood in the doorway, shocked at the news. "Of course. Kate can stay as long as needed," Caleb said.

"How's Kate taking it?" Rachel asked.

"She's scared, but thank God she knew to get help."

Rachel and Caleb readied an extra bed and put it in Helen's room. As they worked, Rachel started crying and Caleb hugged her.

"Maybe it was accidental. Laudanum's tricky stuff. Let's concentrate on Kate now. Stuart and Jason will take care of Emma."

As Jason drove Kate around the corner to the Barlows, she asked, "Is Momma going to have an operation like Daddy?"

"No, Kate."

"Daddy's operation was what made him die."

"Is that what you think? No, the operation gave him more time, Kate. Your mother will be fine in a few days and she'll be back home."

Kate was withdrawn when they reached Rachel's. Jason helped Kate unpack then returned to the hospital. He fought claustrophobia as he walked down the narrow hallways. The low ceilings were depressing and the place smelled musty.

He entered Emma's room. Stuart was stationed at her bedside in a chair. He was alternately watching Emma and reading a book on mental illness.

"How's she doing?" Jason asked, keeping his voice low.

"So far, so good. She didn't take a lethal dose, but it was close. It's my fault for giving it to her after Shea's death. I was careless. I'm guessing that she stashed away a bottle of it. I just didn't know."

"Can I stay with her tonight?"

Stuart stood and rubbed his sore back. "No argument there. I'm going home to grab supper. When I get back, I want to know everything that's been going on. Call a nurse if she gets sick again or wakes up."

On his way home, Stuart went to Carruthers general store. He strode in and went behind the counter. Allison and Gale greeted him, but were puzzled by Stuart's look of grim determination. Stuart found the brown bottles of laudanum on a shelf. He scooped every bottle into his medical bag.

"I cannot allow you to sell this poison anymore. If anyone wants painkillers, tell them to come to me." He dropped a twenty dollar bill on the counter and walked out.

"What was that all about?" Allison asked Gale.

While Stuart was gone, Jason read the book on mental problems. He did not get far. The detached, clinical descriptions of mental disorders and treatments only further depressed him. He sat there, wondering what it was that had pushed Emma over the edge—and how he had missed it.

Later, a nurse stayed with Emma while Jason went to Stuart's office.

Jason told Stuart about Emma's deepening depression, discreetly leaving out her discovery about Randall. "I was wrong," he confessed. "I couldn't help with Emma's problems. I should have come to you."

"Emma hasn't been too happy with me lately. I refused to give her more laudanum, so she tossed me out of the house a few months back. I should've searched the house when she wasn't home to find the bottle she apparently hid away."

"There are a lot of things we both should've done," Jason agreed.

"Well, now we have to get her well. It's going to be a long road back for her. It won't be easy."

That night, Jason was again at Emma's side, putting a cool towel on her forehead. She moaned and rolled on her back, her long auburn hair spread across the pillow. She forced open her eyes and looked around at the sparse room; it had been stripped of all sharp objects and unnecessary furniture.

"Jason! Where am I?" Her speech was still slurred.

His smile quivered as he stroked her hand. "You're in the hospital. Do you remember coming here?"

Her look said that she did not. "Where's Kate?"

Jason hesitated before answering. "At the Barlows'."

Emma's brow knit for a few moments. "Oh," she said. "Is she okay?"

"You scared her, Em. Good Christ, why did you do this?"

She rolled on her side away from him. "I don't want to talk about it."

He touched her shoulder. "Why won't you tell me?"

"I don't want to talk about it!" she hissed.

Jason spent the night dozing in the hard chair, waking with a start every time she moved or moaned. It was a very long night.

Stuart returned the next morning. He woke Jason, who was slumped in the chair. "How did she sleep?"

"She was restless. I wouldn't call it sleeping." He stood and stretched. "I have to open the mill. I'll be back later."

"We have nurses who will keep an eye on her. You don't have to do it."

"Emma has lost so many people in her life. I will not desert her now. I have to do everything I can to help her."

Stuart went into the hallway and waved to a nurse who came into Emma's room moments later. Stuart spoke to her. "Wake her up and take her to the washroom. Get her bathed and in a clean gown. See that she eats breakfast, too."

"Yes, Dr. Barlow," the young woman answered.

As Stuart walked him out of Emma's room, Jason asked, "Can I bring Kate in to see her?"

"It's too soon."

"Stuart, Emma's all she's got. Please."

"All right, but keep it brief—and supervised."

Before he left the hospital, Jason arranged to pay Emma's bill at the reception desk.

"That's a very kind gesture," Stuart said. "I had intended on paying it."

"I'll spend every cent I have to help her."

Jason went home, washed up, opened the mill, and left the business in the hands of his foreman. He came to Rachel's later in the morning.

Rachel glanced back to assure herself that Kate remained in the kitchen where she was kneading bread. She kept her voice low. "I told Kate that she could stay home from school for a few days. Jason, rumors are all over town about Emma. People are saying that she overdosed on laudanum. It's just a matter of time until Kate hears it."

"Great! That's all the kid needs. Look, I'm taking Kate to the hospital to see Emma. Stuart said that it's all right."

Kate and Jason drove up Main in his carriage a while later. Many people watched them as they passed. The truth was out—Jason could see the pity in their faces.

Jason ushered Kate into her mother's room. Emma was sitting up, but her eyes were closed. She was pale with beads of sweat shining on her face. Jason watched her whole body tremble and her skin looked waxy. Her long hair was damp from her bath and she had changed into a clean bed gown. His footsteps roused her. Jason smiled at Emma as he led Kate into the room. He left the room and waited in the hallway.

Emma's face brightened at the sight of Kate and she held out her arms for her. Kate sat upon the bed, wrapped in Emma's embrace. Tears fell unchecked as Emma realized all that she would've lost if she had succeeded in the suicide. When she was at last able to speak, she said, "Are you okay at the Barlows'?" Kate nodded. "I made a mistake with my medicine. I'm so sorry if I scared you."

"It's okay Momma. When can you come home?"

Emma's breath caught in her throat and she found it difficult to answer. "I—I don't know. The medicine made me pretty sick."

"By Sunday?" Kate asked. "I wanted to go up and visit Daddy."

Panic welled up. Emma's mind was mired in guilt for what she had put her daughter through yesterday and for all the days leading up to this desperate act. At length, she answered, "If I'm not home by then, maybe Jason or Rachel and Caleb can take you."

"No. I want to go with you, like always. Get better and come home, Momma."

"I will. I promise."

Jason came in to collect Kate later. She left reluctantly after bestowing a kiss on Emma's cheek. Emma managed a smile, but there were tears in her eyes. Jason gave Emma a reassuring nod. He returned to the hospital after seeing Kate back to the Barlows'.

After roaming around the hospital, Jason found Stuart in his office. He told him that the truth about Emma's condition had leaked out.

Stuart sighed. "I already know. I heard three different versions just this morning. I've spoken to the staff, but it's too late. We'll worry about damage control later. So, how did Emma's visit with Kate go?"

"All right, I think. It's so hard to read either of them."

Later, Jason sat with Emma as she picked at her lunch. Her hands shook. "Stop looking at me like that."

"Like what?" Jason asked, surprised at her hostile tone.

"I'm not crazy!"

"Yesterday was quite a shock. I need a little time to sort it all out and so do you. Please," he said, his voice controlled and non–accusatory, "tell me why."

"It just seemed like a good idea yesterday." She was sarcastic.

He lowered his voice and leaned in close. "Emma, I've got all the time in the world to listen. I want to help."

She overturned the tray of food and shot out of bed. "Help? I've never asked for help from anyone—ever! What possible good would it do? I can't change anything that's happened. I thought I could live with it all, but I can't do it anymore!" She leaned down close to him and gripped his hands tight. He fought not to flinch as her nails bit in and he felt her draw blood. Her eyes narrowed. "You think you can help erase everything that I've gone through? From the day my parents died, my life has spun out of control—and I deserved every bad thing that ever happened to me!"

"I can't make it all magically disappear, but I'm here to help you to learn to live with it."

She spun away from him and paced around the room. "That's the point. I don't want to live with it anymore. Don't you get it? Everyone around me pays the price for my selfishness—for my cowardice—I never do! Well, it's time for me to pay up!"

Jason rose and moved near her. "I want to help you get well. Look, if you don't want to talk to me, maybe you could talk to Stuart."

"None of you know me! You don't know what kind of person I really am. Quite frankly, I don't know if I want to tell anyone the truth. If I did, I doubt you'd see me as the same person. You wouldn't want me in the end."

Jason was fearful of her mood, which was growing more despondent by the moment. "Knew what?"

She watched him cannily. "I've only told you what I wanted you to know. The world would be a better place without the likes of me."

"You want to leave Kate an orphan—like you were?"

Emma turned to him. "I bring misery upon everyone I've ever loved!" Her face was damp with tears.

"C'mon, Emma. Bad things have happened to you, but you didn't cause them."

She lifted an eyebrow. "You want to bet? Let's tally the people that are dead because of my selfishness. Let's see, first my parents, Red Leaf, Shea— even Fulton and Tyler. The only one who really pegged me was Adam. He escaped to Washington so that he wouldn't be next. He doesn't answer my letters because he knows me all too well."

"You're not responsible—" he began.

"I had to have my way, no matter what. I couldn't help my parents. Then I came back to Shea after the outbreak and forced him to take me back. People died because of my presence at the reservation. Leave me alone. I don't need your pity!"

"Emma, I don't pity you!" He tried to hug her, but she shoved him away, her fist connecting with his chin. Stunned, he staggered back. She lunged at him, but he grabbed her around her waist. Her strength was formidable. He held her tight, ignoring the kicks and punches she delivered.

"Let go of me!"

"I won't let you beat me up," he hollered. "Now settle down!"

"You're hurting me! Help me somebody!"

Her strength held and Jason almost lost his grip as she twisted and kicked. He lifted her clear off the ground and dropped her in bed and pinned her.

"Emma, stop it!" he shouted in her face.

Two orderlies ran into the room and pulled Jason off her. Emma made a break for the door, but ran smack into Stuart, knocking him hard against the jamb. He quickly grabbed her. "Get her back to the bed! Get straps—now!"

She was hustled back to bed by the strong orderlies. Stuart and Jason held her down as she screamed and struggled in their grasp. The orderlies ran out and quickly returned with heavy leather straps and after a prolonged struggle she was tied down to the bed.

"What the hell did you say to her?" Stuart growled.

Unable to cope with the creature in the bed, Jason ran out. Her screams echoed through the hallways and Jason thought that his head would split from the sound. Winded and sweating, he ran outside, slipping on the new snow and falling to his knees, dizzy and sick. He wiped his face with handfuls of snow, trying to recover from what he had done. He had pushed too hard. He had not expected such violence from her, nor was he prepared for her strength. He sat back on his heels, breathing in the frigid air, trying to stop trembling. Several passersby stopped and stared. He soon rose, brushed the snow from his trousers, then resolutely returned inside the hospital.

The door to Emma's room was blocked by two large orderlies who denied him entrance. Jason stubbornly remained and paced back and forth in the hallway. Nurses went in and out of Emma's room. He could hear her ranting, demanding, then begging to be let loose of the straps.

A while later, Stuart came out of Emma's room. He was understandably fatigued and irritable. He spotted Jason pacing down the hall and strode up to him. "What did you say to set her off like that?"

"We were talking. She started saying that she didn't deserve to be helped. Then all of a sudden, she hit me. She scratched me up, too," he said, showing Stuart the gouges left by her nails. "I had to subdue her."

Stuart's anger died quickly. "Violence is a symptom of withdrawal from the laudanum. She's not ready to go home. No, not by a long shot. I don't want you with her right now. She has to settle down on her own. I can't give her any sedatives because of the laudanum still in her bloodstream."

Jason let out a long breath. "Shea warned me that this might happen."

"What?" "

"Come to my house tonight. I'll tell you what I know."

"It'll be quite late," Stuart warned.

"It can't wait. I'll be up. Come by when you can."

When Jason returned home, he allowed himself tears, tears of guilt and frustration. He had broken through his shyness by admitting his love for Emma and felt secure in that love—until today.

He went to the Barlows' late that afternoon. Rachel saw that he had been crying and told the children to go outside to play. Martin, Helen, and Randall bounded out the door. Kate shuffled past, bringing up the rear. As she closed the door behind her, Rachel caught the look of betrayal Kate shot at Jason. Word of the scene at the hospital had already reached her somehow, Rachel told him.

"What really happened with Emma?"

Jason dropped down on the stair steps, his formidable strength failing him. He did not speak for a long time, running his fingers through his long hair, his nerves raw. "She attacked me. It was all I could do to hold her off."

Rachel leaned down and got a better look at his hands and bruised face. "Did she do all that?" She was aghast.

"I pushed her when I shouldn't have. She's sane enough to be afraid—no—she's terrified. She's lost inside herself and instead of coping with it, there's just anger there—at anything, anyone. But a part of her is fighting back—it's just the angry part. I just don't understand why she tried to kill herself."

"She's told us about her life. We've even witnessed some of it, but she never talks about how these things made her feel—how they affected her. She reports her life like she's telling a story about someone else."

"That's how she protects herself, Rachel."

"Kate thinks we're keeping Emma in the hospital against her will. She heard that she's been strapped down."

"Well, that much is true."

Rachel tried to reassure him. "If she gets rest and quiet, someone can reason with her and get to the bottom of this."

"She's not crazy. It's just that too much has piled up on her all these years. She has spent a lot of energy denying it by burying it all inside her."

"It's hard to watch someone you love suffer so."

He colored. "She hates me."

"Jason, don't take anything she says right now to heart, okay? You know she loves you." Rachel mustered a smile, trying to lift his mood. "Hey, come in the kitchen and we'll talk and have something to eat. I'll put a cool cloth on those bruises and dress the cuts on your hands."

"No, thanks, Rachel. I need to be alone for a while." He was obviously distraught. "But I'm not giving up on her. I've got to go back to take her some of her things. Maybe she will have calmed down by then."

"I'll take care of her things. I'll come by and get the house key from you then I'll pack up what she needs and take it over."

"Thanks. Here," he said. "I carry a spare key." He stepped out onto the porch, longing to retreat home. He watched the children playing in the snow. Kate stood apart from them, then her resentful gaze turned upon Jason. "What about Kate? What's going to happen to her if Emma doesn't recover?" he asked Rachel.

"If she's committed, she'll lose Kate and she won't be able to live with that. If she thinks that everything's lost, she'll succeed next time. I know how determined she can be. More than anything, her determination put her in this situation. She can't reason everything away and bury her feelings any longer. Please Jason," she pleaded, "see that Stuart takes away anything that she could hurt herself with."

"He already has. Her room is stripped bare. Look, I'm going to go home and sleep for a while. This has been a rotten day." As he descended the steps, he approached Kate who stood defiantly with arms crossed, so like her father, he thought. He kept his distance as he spoke. "Kate, your mother's going to be at the hospital a while longer. She needs rest."

"You hurt my Momma. I heard what you did! I hate you!" she shouted and ran away in tears.

Stuart saw Rachel at the front desk of the hospital, took the bundle of Emma's things and handed it to a nurse. Emma's brush and comb were removed, as well as the laces on her shoes and undergarments. A hand mirror was taken, too, and each garment inspected for loose trims; all buttons were unceremoniously ripped off. Even Emma's tin of tooth powder was inspected. And the books that Rachel had included were fanned, checking for a stray hairpin.

"We don't want any accidents," Stuart said as the illegal items were handed back to Rachel.

Once home, Jason felt lost and very guilty. His well–meaning but heavy–handed approach had wounded Emma further. Now, he had a taste of Emma's own desolation. Her cruel words of that day invaded his soul. Seeing how she had changed in so short a time perplexed him. If he could trade places with her, he would, but she had to face her pain alone; he was powerless to take it from her. He relived the horror of seeing the empty bottle of laudanum on her nightstand, nursing unfathomable guilt for forcing her to take it after Shea died. He convinced himself that he had helped fuel her addiction to the drug.

When he changed his clothes he saw a half–dozen bruises on his arms, legs, and chest, inflicted by her fists and kicks. Intending to nap, he slept through the night, utterly spent. Stuart came to his door near midnight, but the house was dark and there was no answer to his knock.

Stuart spent the wee hours of the morning reading his few books on mental illness, but he was a surgeon. Find the bad tissue and cut it away, that's what he was good at. He read and reread until his eyes were dry and sore.

Jason arrived at Stuart's office in the morning. "Sorry I missed you last night. I was pretty tired."

"No matter," Stuart said. "Let's talk now."

"Can I see Emma?"

"No, sorry. She's no better than she was yesterday. I know that she's lashing out because you're closest to her, but it just shows me that she's not ready to see you."

"I have to see her."

Stuart wanted to say no, then acquiesced. Jason had to face reality and understand that Emma needed help, despite how much he loved her. Emma and Jason had a special trust, although it had been damaged the day before. Jason wanted to protect her, but he had to see how sick she really was. "All right, but just for a few minutes." Stuart clapped him on the shoulder and they walked over to the hospital.

As they came down the hallway toward Emma's room, Jason said, "Shouldn't someone be at the door? What if she tries to leave?"

"There's no need," Stuart said as he opened the door.

Emma lay, still strapped to the bed. Her hair was messed and tangled from struggling in the bonds. Her eyes flicked open. She struggled against the straps. "Let me out of these! They hurt!"

"You kept her in these overnight?" Jason was utterly shocked.

"We had to. She raged all night."

Without a word of consent from Stuart, Jason began to undo the straps.

"Don't, Jason!" Stuart ordered, signaling an orderly into the room.

"Get out!" Jason glowered. "Out! I can handle her!"

Stuart was angry and the orderly froze in the doorway, uncertain whom to obey. His father worked as a sawyer for Beck Lumber.

"I want you out of here, Jason!"

The two men stood toe to toe. "I know what I'm doing, Stuart," he growled. "Leave me with her. If she's going to vent her rage, she can take it out on me."

"That isn't going to help her!"

"Get out and let me try to get through to her. I know her better than anyone. Trust me," he said, fighting to sound rational.

Stuart had never seen Jason so determined—or threatening. He backed out but remained to listen at the closed door.

Jason freed Emma from the straps and she bolted out of the bed. He caught her when she lunged for him and held her tight against him. She struggled, but her energies were quickly spent. She sobbed and buried her head in his shoulder. Her head came up and her eyes seemed to clear for a few moments. Tears slid down her cheek.

"What's happening to me? I can't think straight."

"It's the drug, Emma. Look at me. Focus on me. Remember when we went to the dance last year and you were so nervous? I told you to look only at me—and you did. You trusted me that night. Trust me now."

She broke away and backed herself into a corner. "That was just a stupid dance!" Her expression suddenly changed. She smiled, but her eyes were calculating. "Can you get Stuart to stop strapping me down? If you could do that—"

He knew that she was trying to manipulate him. "If you promise not to bolt again. I want your solemn promise."

"Sure, I promise," she said too quickly. "Jason, I feel like I'm back at Fort Robinson. I'm watched every minute! There's a courtyard out back of the hospital with tables and chairs. Can we go out there? Please? I promise not to run."

"It's too cold, Emma. It's been snowing for days."

She looked out the window as if for the first time. She seemed startled by the thick blanket of snow. "What month is this?" she asked, genuinely confused.

"October," Jason answered.

"October?" she mumbled. "It's October?"

Jason was shocked that she had completely lost track of time. He began to understand what the drug had done to her mind. She was adrift and helpless. "Please promise me that you will work with Stuart. Will you?"

"I can't stand being locked up in here," Emma whimpered.

Jason sat in the chair next to her bed. He saw her muscles tighten and did not miss her glance at the unprotected door, but she did not bolt again. He spoke in a whisper. She strained to listen.

"Emma, I don't want you kept here, but I can see that we have no choice."

"What choice do I have?" she shot back, her voice harsh, sarcastic. "I'm kept strapped down like an animal! And it's your fault! You and your big mouth!"

Jason continued, ignoring her words, which was not easy, for he was hurt by them. "Kate's fine, but she misses you. She needs you. I'm so sorry I caused this. I agree. I should've kept my mouth shut about Randall. The sooner you get well, the sooner you can be with Kate again—and the sooner you can begin hating me in earnest."

The mention of Kate brought a sudden stillness to her heart. She fought to concentrate.

"No one, least of all me, wants this for you. You're frightened and you need help. I don't want to lose you and Kate, but if that's the price I have to pay for seeing you well, I will pay it." He paused and sat back, composing himself. He began to battle his own little demons and could only imagine the huge ones that Emma had kept at bay for so long. "And if you don't want me to come see you, I won't." He waited for her to speak, but she said nothing. "Well, that's all I have to say."

He replaced the chair against the wall and headed for the door. As he opened it, Emma pleaded. "Don't leave me."

He came to her, took her in his arms and stroked her hair. For a few moments, he thought he saw the Emma that he knew. He kissed her.

"I want to get well, I really do," she began, "but you see, it's not just about the affair between Rachel and Shea. That's what set me off, but it's not the reason."

"I'll listen, Emma. Just talk. That's all you have to do."

They talked of many things over the next two hours. She was starting to open up and Jason was encouraged. He hoped that his presence would reassure her and let her know that she was safe, no matter what she revealed.

When his time for leaving came, Emma said, "Tell Kate I love her more than anything and I'll work hard to get better. Tell her not to forget me."

"How could she forget you? You're an extraordinary woman, Emma, and you will get through this." He kissed her deeply.

Later, Jason met with Stuart in his office at the mill. They talked for two hours more. When the conversation was over, Stuart looked uneasy.

"Helping her is going to be harder than I thought," Stuart said. "I don't know too much about mental breakdowns. Her problems go very deep."

"We have to try, Stuart," Jason stated. "We owe her that. I will do anything you ask."

That evening, Jason had to deliver Emma's message to Kate through Rachel. Kate had placed all blame for her mother's collapse squarely upon him after hearing the rumors circulating around town. The truth was tangled with outlandish rumors. Kate didn't know what to believe. Even Rachel's attempts to tell her the truth made little difference.

The next day while on his way to see Emma, Stuart saw Jason on the street. Stuart spoke first. "Emma seems calmer. You did all right yesterday." This was high praise from Stuart, who was having trouble keeping a professional distance from Emma. He was not all that sure of what he was doing, but he was encouraged that he could use Jason to reach Emma.

Stuart told Jason a lot of people had been asking after Emma. The whole town knew about the scene at the hospital, and her outburst had been exaggerated and embellished. "Wait until I find who's spreading the lies about her. I'll fire them so fast, they won't know what hit them. If anyone asks you what's wrong with Emma, say it's exhaustion. Let's hope that replaces the rumors flying around. I don't want her branded as crazy. And spend time with Kate when you can."

"Stuart," Jason said, "I'm the last person that Kate wants to see. She thinks I'm responsible for putting her mother away."

"Give her time—give them both time, okay? But I want your word you'll be patient with Emma. This situation will take a bit of finessing, if you know what I mean," he said, referring to the conversation they'd had the night before.

"Then we agree," Jason said.

During the ensuing days, Emma still struggled to control angry outbursts that threatened to overwhelm her. Jason visited every day and weathered her fits, sarcasm, and tantrums. But when he returned home, he often skipped supper and went upstairs to bed. Being with her thoroughly exhausted him.

On the sixth day, Emma's demeanor had undergone a profound and startling change. She sat by the window in her room, dressed in a fresh bed gown. Her waist length hair hung loose and shimmering. She had even straightened up her room and the bed was made, nice and neat.

Jason stifled an eerie feeling as he entered, despite the order of the room and her outward appearance. "Hi, Em. How are you doing?"

She put on an affected smile as she turned to him. "Much better. Over the worst of it. I hope to go home in a few days. I don't want Kate to be stuck at Rachel's any longer than necessary. I wish that Stuart would let her come in to see me again."

"Did Stuart say that you can leave?"

"Oh, you know he's a worrier. He wants me to stay, but I'm feeling better. What I did was selfish and wrong. The quicker I get home to Kate, the better off we'll both be. I've owned up to what I did. That's it."

Emma was putting on the most convincing act that she could muster, covering everything—again—burying her pain and troubles under a facade of order mixed with complete denial. Jason knew that she was determined to win her life back, but there was no way she would go home any time soon.

For days she kept up the pretense, agreeing with Stuart's analysis of her problems, cooperating with the staff, and no longer trying to bolt for the door. But she was no closer to the real causes of her collapse.

No homecoming came over the next week. Exhaustion caught up with Emma. She slept sometimes fourteen hours a day and had to be awakened to eat her meals. Only Jason had the power to coax her to stay alert and focused on their conversations. But his uneasiness heightened as she seemed to slip away, unable to keep her train of thought. She rambled when she spoke and often forgot her point. And she did admit that she felt betrayed and hurt by Shea and Rachel's affair, and rightly so, Jason agreed. She spoke of her troubles, but seemed to get nowhere near resolution. But he knew that some plan to deal with her reticence needed to be devised, like figuring the angle for the fall of a tree—one way was disaster, the other, safety. Some days, he felt like he was being sucked in to the shadowy, wretched darkness where she concealed her depression. He had a fair measure of torture, dwelling on his own remorse in revealing the whole truth of the illicit affair.

To alleviate the constant strain and pressure of dealing with Emma, Jason began regularly coming up to the logging camps in the afternoons. With fanatical energy, he climbed tall pines with the strong and quick stepping high-climbers, men who worked high in the trees, their task to top off the tallest trees before they could be felled. Back on the ground, he chopped wood and hauled logs right alongside the loggers. He worked until dark, worked until his muscles revolted with the strain and his weary mind briefly cleared of his preoccupation with Emma's condition. When he was done with the back-breaking work, he was too drained and weary to think about anything or anyone.

Despite Stuart's effort to put around the story of simple exhaustion, people knew the truth about Emma. Many attributed her illness to grief over Shea, followed by the brutal attack of Seymour Fulton. Those who had read the Max Cody articles years before hailed her determination to survive at all, and it never occurred to them that her current suffering was a direct result of the numerous tragedies that she had endured. Most people believed that collapses were caused by a single, devastating event. If they had to choose which devastating event in Emma's life had caused her 'collapse,' they would be hard put to choose just one.

Emma languished in the hospital. No date for leaving had yet been discussed.

Chapter Eighteen

The territory of Washington was to become a state on November 11, 1889. Jason struggled to put on a celebration for the town. Main Street was festooned with red, white, and blue bunting and banners declaring statehood were draped across storefronts. That night, fireworks sparkled in the clear winter sky while a brass band played patriotic songs. However, Jason was too preoccupied with Emma's illness to enjoy the festivities.

Days later, Jason was invited to dinner at the Barlows'. Jason had little appetite, aware he had been summoned for a reason that he would not ultimately like; Stuart had come as well. After the meal, the children had been excused and were playing in the parlor. Rachel closed the door of the dining room to give them privacy. Jason's instincts prickled.

Stuart then brought up Emma's situation, a subject carefully avoided during supper with the children in the room. The word 'situation,' Jason thought, had a long–term sound to it. Stuart had something in mind, something that Jason was sure to oppose.

"She's talking more about her troubles, which is encouraging," Stuart said, "but she's not coping with other, long–standing problems and with losing Shea. Jason, your efforts are helping, but not fast enough." Stuart met Jason's skeptical gaze. "Like you said, Jason, there was a pebble that caused a landslide. Physically, she's better. Emotionally, she's not. But if she doesn't improve soon, we'll need to take further steps."

"Further steps?" Rachel broke in.

Jason knew what he meant. "An asylum, you mean! Out of the question!"

"The hospital in Millersburg is better equipped to handle these cases. It's a last resort, Jason, so settle down. I don't want her committed—none of us do. She was coping with a dying husband for months. That's hard on anyone, whether or not the death was expected. She's had a lot of hard times in her life. She's fragile despite attempts to convince us otherwise."

Jason had never considered her fragile until this moment. For weeks now, he had counted on her inner strength to pull her through this, just as it always had. All the terrors she had endured in the past eleven years were now exacting their toll. His love for her did not figure in the equation and it hurt. She had not opened up enough to confide in him—trust him. "I will not let you lock her up." His tone held an open threat.

Rachel tried to diffuse Jason's growing anger over Stuart's suggestion and took his side. "I don't want her sent away. It'll do more harm."

"I understand you both, I do. However, I'm going to give her a few more weeks to improve, then I'll see about getting her into Millersburg Sanitarium," Stuart said.

Jason was shaken and angry. "You can't be serious, Stuart! She needs a little more time, that's all. I see her every day. I know I'll get through. Don't do this to her."

"Jason, I applaud your intentions. But you're an amateur in these matters, as am I. She needs professional help. She's stuck someplace and we're having no success helping her and wearing ourselves out in the process. There are qualified doctors at Millersburg Sanitarium and I would see her twice a week. It won't be as bad as you think."

"If she had to go, how long would she have to be there?" Rachel asked, hoping that it would be very brief. Her mother had told her about a cousin she had never met that had been institutionalized. The horrifying stories of the asylum flooded her mind: Unsafe, unsanitary, brutal—with rats and vermin pervading these prisons for the insane. Despite the falling out with Emma, she would do what she could to prevent committal. She had resolved never to admit Randall's possible parentage to Caleb because it would destroy her family. She hoped that it would not destroy Emma in the process.

"Hard to say, but she'll be safe there, that I can guarantee. It's not set up like an asylum, it's a hospital for people with mental problems. She'll be supervised—"

"You can't guarantee anything, Stuart," Rachel broke in. "I've heard what those places are like. We won't be able to watch over her if she's far away."

"Then I'll care for her," Jason interrupted.

"You can't do that, Jason. She's a woman. You can't do everything for her," Rachel began.

"Then I'll hire someone to help me until she's well. She's not insane."

All of them spoke at once, piling remarks and opinions upon one another until Caleb rapped the table for silence. "Jason, Emma's not insane. I agree with you. She's suffering from a deep depression brought on by grief and too many shocks and losses. We can't cure her no matter how much we want to. Let someone who is not so close to it all try to solve this."

Stuart nodded in agreement. "One more thing. Kate is a problem if Emma is committed. She'll become a ward of the state and could be sent away. I don't want that, so I've already got that new lawyer in town, Donald Sternin, looking for next of kin. We're trying to find Emma's father's family, just in case. If Kate has to be sent away, even for a while, the law says that she has to be with family."

Kate crept away from the door. She ran upstairs and cried herself to sleep.

Days later, Stuart entered Emma's room and pulled up a chair. She had been dozing, but stirred and propped herself up with the pillow. "I want to go home! I can't stand it here anymore," she complained.

"I'm sorry. It's up to you, not me."

Her voice rose. "Why am I being forced to stay here? And by the way, that medicine you give me is making me sick!"

"It's to help get the laudanum out of your bloodstream, but I'll prescribe something milder, all right?"

Her eyes welled with tears of fright. "How do I get through to you? Do you want me to admit that I made a mistake? Okay, I did and I regret it. Was I crazy at the time? Maybe! I fell apart, but I'm better—I understand why I did it and I promise never to do anything like that again. I want to go home. I want to see my daughter. It's been over a month since I've seen her. What about the effect on her?" She looked worn–out, but a fire was in her eyes that had long been absent. "I'll do anything to get out of here."

"Well, you've made a start. You're at least willing to bargain. Shows shrewd thinking."

"Tell me what to do, Stuart," she pleaded.

"You may believe you feel good now, but I'm looking out for your welfare as well as Kate's. Everyone understands your grief about Shea. But after observing you over the past few weeks and despite your efforts to convince me otherwise, this has gone far beyond your ability to cope alone."

"I don't know what you want from me, Stuart. I'll admit I was addicted to laudanum. It was a stupid thing to do. By the way, how many addicts have you treated?"

"Just you." He betrayed a little smile.

"Oh, great! You're new at this, too?" She chuckled, then fell silent for a moment. "Tell me about Kate. How's she holding up?"

"She's doing all right. But I'll tell you plain, I won't allow her to be with a parent who isn't well. I wouldn't be doing my job as a physician and as your friend. You haven't convinced me that you're ready to cope yet."

"I can cope. I know it. Besides, I don't want Kate at Rachel's. She belongs with me."

"Emma, Rachel's doing you a great favor. I know that the two of you had some sort of falling out, but you've got to put that behind you and concentrate on getting better. Kate is comfortable and well cared for. That should be your only concern."

"What Kate is going through makes me feel so guilty—so selfish. Can she come to see me? Please?"

"Soon. But you have to earn it by cooperating with me. That will prove to me that you're serious about getting better. You can't take on all the blame for things that have happened to you. You held up well, but this is bigger than you can handle without help. You're a strong woman and you have endured hardships that few people could understand. We have to break down the problems into manageable pieces and deal with them."

"I've spent the last decade dealing with loss. I'm an expert at it."

"But you've become an expert at burying your pain and battling through another day. The people who care for you can't stand by and watch you struggle. I've been concerned about you since Shea's passing. You weren't the same after that."

"Why didn't you talk to me about this before?"

"Would you have listened?" She gave no answer. "Maybe now you're ready. You've got a lot of people on your side."

She knew that he was right. But memories and fears rushed through her so quickly that she could not control the rush of emotion continually welling up in her. The cage housing her pain had disintegrated and she was left with scattered emotions.

"Stuart," she said at length, "I had to stand by and watch my husband die a slow, painful death. And his daughter had to watch it too." Her voice wavered. "I'm allowed to feel bad about it all, aren't I?"

"There's nothing wrong with those feelings. Your difficulties didn't happen overnight and won't be solved overnight. It's enough to make anyone cave in, and I truly believe what you're experiencing is temporary."

She looked worried and changed the subject. "Stuart, how am I going to pay for all of this? I can't afford to be here for so long."

"Don't worry about it. It's been taken care of."

"Jason?" she assumed.

Stuart's nod told her that she was correct.

Rachel intervened in Kate's continuing bitterness toward Jason. She had put up with enough of Kate's rude comments about him. She took Kate aside one evening and spoke to her with great patience.

"We've talked about this, but I need to be sure that you understand what's going on with your mother. You miss her very much and I wish that I could bring her back to you, but she's not well enough yet. I know what people in town are saying, but your mother really needed to go to the hospital. You blame Jason for taking her there, but try and forgive a little. He would never hurt you or your mother—ever. Hasn't he always been a good friend to you?" Kate nodded. "Jason feels very bad that you are angry with him, and he deserves another chance, don't you think? Next time you see him, promise me that you'll try to forgive him. If you have any questions about the state of your mother's health, come to me or Caleb, or even Jason, all right? You can depend on us to tell you the truth."

Kate looked relieved. "Should I tell Jason that I'm sorry?"

"That would be a good start. Jason is very lonely right now without you or your mom."

"Can I think about it?" she asked.

"Sure."

Kate did not think about the matter for long. Jason arrived the following evening to pick up Emma's laundry from Rachel. As Rachel handed him a bundle of clean clothing, Kate peered inside the washroom.

"I'm sorry I yelled at you, Jason," Kate said in a subdued voice. "Rachel told me that I shouldn't be mad at you anymore. But I missed my Mom, so I got mad at you instead. I'm sorry."

He knelt down and held out his arms. Kate ran to him. He hugged her. "I'm sorry, too! I'm going to see your mother. Do you have anything that you want me to tell her or anything that you want to send with me?"

"Can I come with you?"

"When Stuart says it's okay, I'll let you know."

She looked at the floor. "Tell Mommy I want her to come home. I don't want her sent away to Millersburg. I don't want to go away either.

Rachel's hand flew to her mouth and Jason was stunned, realizing that Kate had overheard the conversation in the dining room days ago.

Jason felt terrible guilt that the child had been coping with this fear on her own. He looked to Rachel, then to Kate. "Believe me, Kate" he said, "I promise you that you will never be sent away. Your mother will never be sent away, either."

"Is she crazy, like people say?"

"No! You know how strong she is, don't you? Sometimes people who are that strong need a rest sometimes. Your mother will come back to you, I promise. I see her every day. She's getting better. Maybe you can come see her soon. I'll work on Stuart," he said with a sly wink. Like Emma, Kate needed a dose of hope. He would get Kate in to see her mother—even if he had to sneak her in.

Stuart now allowed Jason to bring in Emma's needlework to the hospital. Jason voiced concern about Emma having a needle in her possession, but Stuart assured him that Emma was closely watched.

"I'm convinced that she won't hurt herself again, Jason. Having some familiar things around will be good for her. Trust me."

True to his word, Jason came to be with Emma sometimes twice a day. In anticipation of his visits, she willed herself to keep track of the days. With a shock, she realized that the second anniversary of Shea's death had passed. She had not noticed. It rattled her that time had become blurred and unimportant. Still, something within her began to fight back. It was a shaky start, but she had recovered some of her resolve. Kate's welfare occupied her thoughts, and the guilt of leaving her alone was the catalyst to move through this dark time.

Jason had the most profound effect on Emma and she had showed enough progress to be allowed into the day room on occasion. The room was pleasant with many windows, if one ignored the orderlies strategically positioned around the room. However it was a cheerful enough place and she enjoyed the time out of her austere, depressing room.

One such afternoon Jason found her there reading near a sunny window. When he sat beside her, she reached for his hand.

"Jason, I'm sorry about that day when I hit you. I was out of my head because I was so afraid. I didn't mean to hurt you. Please forgive me. I'm so glad that you didn't give up on me."

He held her close and kissed her. "All was forgiven long ago, Em."

"I hope I didn't do any permanent damage."

Jason blushed. "I always thought that I had an iron jaw, but I didn't know you were so strong!"

"Just a simple farm girl," she quipped.

He grinned. "I have a surprise for you."

Kate appeared from around the corner and ran to her mother. Emma caught her up in her arms. Tears of joy slipped down her cheeks. They spent the afternoon together, laughing and talking. Kate said that she expected her mother to be home for Christmas and had already laid out her plans for the celebrations. Emma tried to give the child hope that she would do everything she could to be home by the holidays. Kate brought in the drawing that she had given her last Christmas, the one of herself, Emma, and Shea outside the cabin. Emma's eyes welled up when she saw it. Jason hung it up over Emma's bed with wood putty. Nails were forbidden in her room.

That evening, Stuart stopped at Jason's house. Jason poured two apple brandies for them as they sat in the large, comfortable keeping room.

"So how do you think Emma's doing?" Stuart asked.

Jason took his time before answering. "Letting Kate in to see her mother did a lot of good. Neither of them seem so sad or angry anymore."

"Good. I agree. It's time, Jason," Stuart said ominously, "if you think you're ready."

He thought for a moment. "I have to think it over."

Jason spent restless days and nights, locking himself up in his house except to go to work. He did not come to the Barlows' to see Kate as was his habit, nor did he go to the hospital to see Emma.

Two days later, he appeared at Stuart's door early in the day. "Let's go."

Emma was happy to see Jason when he came in her room. He asked after her.

"I feel good. But I missed you. Been busy at the mill?" She searched his face for a clue why he had not been to see her in days.

Jason's eyes avoided her scrutiny. "Yes, the mill's been busy. There's a lot of inventory to ship out. The early snow means that a cold winter is coming. The river could freeze over."

Emma accepted his excuse. "How's Kate?" she asked, hungry for news of her daughter.

"She wants you to come home. So do I." He paused, raising his eyes to her, trying to phrase his next statement as carefully as he could. "That's the thing, see. Stuart knows you're close, but if you don't open up and get to the bottom of your—problems—he said that you might be here longer than he planned, and maybe you would be sent to another hospital."

She quelled rising panic. "I don't know what he wants to hear. He tells me I have to face up to things. What should I tell him?"

"Only you know."

"I can't stand it here much longer. I'm lonely and I miss Kate so much. She needs me. I feel better, I really do. I just want to go home. I'll be better when I get home."

Jason took a deep breath and a perilous chance. He saw the opening and plunged in. "Let's talk about something else—maybe about your home in Kansas. I've always been curious about your life back then. You've never talked about it."

She was suddenly defensive. "Why are you bringing that up?"

"Just curious. Maybe it will do you good to talk about something else. Get your mind off things." He pulled up a chair near the bed and sat down. "So tell me, what was your life like when you lived in Kansas?"

"It was all right. It was hard, lonely, boring sometimes." She looked confused and resisted giving details. "We worked hard every day. Living like that was all I knew. But I liked reading the ten–a–penny books I bought at Bockmeier's trading post. Sometimes I would play with the Indian children when they came with their families to trade with us." She looked at him. "Why do you care about this? I mean, what's the point?"

"It was your home most of your life. I just want to know what it was like. I'm tired of picking apart why you're here and why you did what you did in October. I just thought that you would enjoy reminiscing."

Stuart came into the room, bringing in a chair with him. "Good morning, Emma. How are you doing today?"

Emma saw an expectant look in Stuart's eyes that bothered her. She suddenly felt cornered and got out of bed, pacing around the room. Jason kept prodding her to talk about her life in the little soddy.

"Why are you two ganging up on me?" she cried.

"We're not, Emma. Jason and I were talking the other day and thought this might be good for you."

"I don't understand why this is so important."

"It's not." Jason rose and crossed the room. He reached out and touched her cheek. "Just talk to us."

She stepped away, her eyes flicking from Jason to Stuart. "Okay, if it isn't important, I'll tell you. It's a pretty dull story. Try to stay awake." She began to speak.

She told them that her parents, Jane and Arthur Jorden, were from Point Pleasant, Ohio. Their wedding journey and plans to homestead in Oregon were halted in Kansas by her mother's first pregnancy. They bought the Kansas land cheap as it bordered the Indian Territory, and they eked out a living. Emma said that she was the only surviving child of her parents. Three children, Aaron, Grace, and Elizabeth, died in infancy before she came along. Alongside her parents, she worked hard each day, the monotony broken by occasional visits to Bockmeier's trading post to sell their harvest. She talked about the Indians who left a nearby reservation to trade with them and how much she liked playing with the Indian children, although she was never allowed anywhere near the Indian men.

"To you, it was a little life, but it was all I knew. We survived storms, tornadoes, the grasshopper plague in '74 that wiped out our wheat crop—and worst of all—isolation. Then everything changed when my parents died. I was forced into another world—a world much bigger and more frightening than anything I knew existed, except in storybooks." She faced them both. "Not much to dissect, is there?"

After a long silence, Jason said, "Tell me about the day your parents died."

She tensed. "You know how my parents died. Why do I have to go in to it again? It doesn't have anything to do with what's wrong with me now."

Stuart spoke. "Their passing changed your life. You said so on many occasions."

"Changed it for the worse," she returned.

"Maybe, but you survived all the same," Stuart added.

"Survived," she muttered. "That's what you call it, eh?"

"Just indulge me," Stuart said.

She turned away from them. "My parents died and I ended up at Shea's reservation. I still don't understand why I have to go into this." Emma did not seem distressed; she just did not see the sense in it.

Jason's posture straightened as it hit him. She did not talk about her parents' deaths because of one fact: She did not remember. He exchanged an enlightened look with Stuart. It was time. "Emma, we know the truth about your parents."

She whipped around. "What?"

"Adam told Shea. Shea told me."

"Told you what?"

"What really happened to your parents. Adam found the homestead just after he met you. He put it together. Look, I don't know the details. No one knows the whole truth but you," Jason said.

Her breath caught in her throat and she moved to the window. Her entire body trembled. She looked out the window, yet her eyes took in nothing. Her hands were white, gripping the window sill. She lost her balance, staggering for a moment before regaining herself. "The truth," she whispered, as a flicker of memory began to coalesce.

This was the opening that Jason had waited for and now he was unsure how to proceed—how hard to push. Stuart's nod signaled him to press. "It wasn't your fault."

"Why do you want me to relive it? It was horrible!" Emma's breath came in shallow puffs and she felt lightheaded. Memories rushed through her mind in a blur and she fought to make sense of them.

Jason came behind her. "Don't be afraid."

She shied away from him. "Don't put me through this!"

"Adam and Shea never condemned you for what happened at the sod house. Why would we?"

"Tell us what you remember," Stuart said.

Emma turned around and slumped against Jason, sobbing. He soothed her, stroking her hair. Soon, she steadied herself with several deep breaths.

"Emma, you have to find your own strength. I wish I could give it to you, but I can't. But I do know you can get through this," Jason encouraged.

She stepped away from Jason's embrace. "I'm not sure how to do this." Her next request was the hardest thing that she ever had to ask of anyone. "Will you help me?"

"Count on it," Stuart assured her.

At length she spoke in a voice so quiet that both men had to strain to hear her. "They didn't burn the soddy."

"Who?" Stuart asked.

"They didn't burn out the soddy because it would've alerted any troops in the area."

"Emma, who was at the soddy?" Stuart said again.

"Pawnee," she explained. "My parents didn't die of cholera. They were murdered by Pawnee." She let out a long breath tinged with a small measure of relief. "The day before it happened, we had been to Bockmeier's to sell the fall harvest. At the post, my father heard that the Pawnee were raiding settlers. The next morning we came home. My father gave pistols to me and my mother, just in case the Pawnee showed up. I didn't think anything more about it. We'd had warnings before and nothing ever happened. The Pawnee traded with us sometimes, even though my father had to give more than he got, but that's how they were. The Cheyenne were much nicer—always kind and grateful."

Jason remained near her, leaning against the wall. "What happened when the Pawnee came?"

Her face flushed with the effort of recounting long–buried memories. "My father told me to water the horses at the stream, so I did. Later, I heard riders coming fast and saw about a dozen Pawnee heading for the house. I hid behind a bush near the riverbank." Her face was pinched. "My mother was the first to die. Then my father came running from the wheat field and was cut down by arrows before he could fire a shot."

"What did you do, Emma?" Stuart asked.

Her short laugh made the hairs on Stuart's head prickle. "I did what any good coward would do. I slunk down along the riverbank and found a hole in the bank at the bend of the river. Then I covered myself with rotting leaves, branches, and mud. Even when a warrior rode along the riverbank to steal our horses, he didn't find me. I hid there for hours. It was near dark when I dared to move."

Jason spoke. "What could you have done against a dozen warriors?"

"I had a pistol in my pocket. I should've done something besides sniveling under that rotting mess! Yards away, my parents were dying and I did absolutely nothing!"

"Emma, you were only a girl," Stuart interjected.

"I should've shot as many Pawnee as I could, before they killed me! My parents worked so hard on that scrap of land. They sacrificed three children to it." She paced around the room, fighting to calm herself. "Later, when I got to the soddy, everything was so quiet. There was an absence of—presence—around the place. It was like the lives of my parents had a sound—their heartbeats, their breath, their feet on the soil. There was nothing anymore. Things from the house were scattered all over the ground. I found my father first. He had so many arrows sticking out of him—there was so much blood. His shirt was soaked with it. I screamed, I think. I don't exactly remember. Then I crawled to my mother. She lay next to her little kitchen garden." She wiped away the tears streaming down her face. "Did I tell you I looked a lot like my mother?"

"No, you've never mentioned it," Jason answered, for she seemed to be waiting for a response.

"Well I did. I was taller than her, though, and she had darker hair, but we looked a lot alike in the face." Emma took a shuddering breath. "She had no face. It was gone. One bullet was all it took."

Hearing the details of Emma's terror moved Stuart and Jason. They exchanged mutual looks of commiseration—and shock.

"Their bodies were all swelled up. The skin was stretched so tight, I thought that they were going to explode all over me. I had to bury them as soon as I could. I couldn't leave them there for the wolves. It was getting dark and starting to snow. I went to the barn and found an old broken shovel the Pawnee had left behind. The ground was so hard, I couldn't make the grave very deep." She turned away, unable to meet their eyes. "When I dragged my father to the grave, he let out a breath of air. I was so scared, I hit him with the shovel! He was still alive!" She sank to the floor sobbing. Jason moved quickly to catch her.

Stuart spoke compassionately, mindful of what grief and terror had caused her to do. "Emma, that happens to people that have recently passed away. Air gets trapped in the lungs. The air just came out when you moved him, that was all."

"I hit my dead father with a shovel! What kind of person does that? Wasn't it horrible enough that he was brutally murdered?" She turned to face him. "I panicked!" Emma visibly battled to continue. Confessing her horrors of so long ago was fast exhausting her. "I buried them in that lonely place and knew that I had to leave my home. I had no claim to the land, since women can't own property, and I couldn't stay even if I could. The Pawnee could come back and realize that they missed someone if they saw the grave. I decided to go to Bockmeier's. It was a twenty–mile walk and I knew I could do it in a day or two if the weather held.

"That night, I slept without a fire in the house. It was so cold. I didn't sleep much. There were a few threadbare blankets left behind along with furniture too heavy for the Pawnee to carry off. I used the furniture to block the door. When it was light, I wiped off the mud and dirt that was caked on me from hiding along the river. Then I salvaged what food I could, even scraping coffee and corn meal off the floor. As I was about to leave, I remembered I once saw my mother hide something behind a rock in the hearth. I never thought much about it. I looked there and found a tobacco tin there that was filled with money. At least I could pay my way at the trading post. I packed what I could carry and got out of there. I walked and walked for days. I don't remember much until I woke up in Shea's lodge." She resumed pacing around the room. "I made up the story about the cholera. I came to believe that's what happened. I shut it all out. I didn't think that anyone would ever understand why I did nothing to help them. It wasn't until Shea died that little pieces of what really happened to my parents started to come back to me. It's been eating away at me ever since." She sighed and admitted, "That's why I took the laudanum. It was a very feeble attempt to make the memories go away for good."

"You didn't intend for them to die that day, Emma," Stuart pointed out.

Her expression changed. Her tone was caustic. "You're so sure? It got me away from that sod house, away from that dead–end life. I wonder if I was hoping, in the back of my mind, that their deaths would free me. I knew there was little ahead of me if I stayed with them, but I didn't have the courage to tell my parents that I wanted to leave. I did not want to end up a farmer's wife like my mother. I would read the books I bought from Bockmeier's and learn about other possibilities—other lives that I could lead. Chances at another kind of existence were so tempting. My life changed that day and I blamed the Pawnee, but I was to blame too."

"How would you have changed what happened, if you could?" Stuart asked.

She crossed her arms upon her chest, trying to stop trembling. "That's what I don't know. It's haunted me all these years." She shut her eyes. "I let my parents die. I had the pistol in my pocket. I should've used it on myself for being such a coward that day."

Jason was alarmed. "You don't mean that! Look at all you've accomplished—all you've survived since then. If anything, what happened to you made you strong, Em. If the Pawnee had found you, they would've killed you—or worse—taken you as a slave. You did what you had to do."

"I should've gotten to my parents when I heard the Pawnee ride off. Maybe I could've saved my father at least, but I was too scared to move."

"No one can condemn you for what you did," Stuart said.

For the first time in weeks, Stuart's words were getting through to Emma. She realized that Stuart and Jason really understood her. It helped her begin to let go of the self–pity and anger that she had nursed for so long.

"When I awoke in Shea's lodge, I had no idea how I got there. Believe me, when he asked what had happened, I couldn't remember everything. I knew that my parents were dead, but the details were fuzzy, like a dream that fades when you wake up. I tried to remember, but couldn't, so I heard myself saying that they died of cholera. I hardly mourned them because I buried the terror of that day. I even convinced myself that they had died of cholera. It was much easier than admitting the truth to anyone, especially to myself. My parents were good people and loving parents. I loved them. They worked hard and sacrificed a lot.

"The day after Shea was buried, I went to the grave alone after dark. You were sleeping, Jason, and didn't hear me leave. All the horror of what happened to my parents flooded back. When I realized what I had done, I sat there crying for such a long time. I felt like such a failure. It's been a minute–to–minute battle to keep myself going ever since. If I didn't have Kate, I think I would've done myself in long ago." Bravely, she looked Stuart in the eye. "When I tried to kill myself, I wasn't serious, whether you believe me or not. Something inside of me broke. I needed help. And it wasn't the first time that I tried to do myself in."

Jason was shocked and looked to Stuart, who was not. Stuart remained focused and calm. "When?" Stuart asked.

"It was just after my parents died, when I left the soddy. After Shea found me, I told him that I was heading for Bockmeier's trading post and just got lost. It wasn't true. I intentionally went south, into the Indian Territory, knowing that few people lived near the border. I kept walking into the wilderness, hoping that I'd die along the way. I had to pay for not defending my parents. I remember that my father predicted an early winter weeks before he died. The weather was so cold. I saw it as a sign. I saw that tree where Shea found me. I just sat down and gave up. Freezing to death is easier than you think. You just sort of slip away. Your mind keeps going, but your body fades away. After a while, there was no pain in my body or mind. My thoughts were going off in different directions. I saw crazy things: Buildings, people, animals, even boats floating on the prairie grass. I remembered moments from my childhood—playing with the Bockmeier children and the Cheyenne children, too. Then, I felt someone pick me up. I thought that I was dead and that's how dying felt, like I was light, floating, free of my body. Then, everything went black." She turned and saw Jason's face, set and grim. "Shea not only saved my life, he saved my sanity, that is, until he died. All that pain I had buried resurfaced when I lost him."

Jason's voice was subdued. "You could've trusted me with this. You know I love you."

"And I've depended on that more than you know," she said. "Years ago, Adam told me that he had found our homestead. He knew what had happened there and tried to make me face it, but I truly didn't remember. I've held back because I thought you would think me mad to have kept such terrible secrets buried for so long. Normal people don't do such things."

Stuart spoke. "Emma, you're not mad. This outgrew you, that's all. We understand." He watched her, seeing her eyes soften a little.

"You know what terrified me the most the day my parents died?" she volunteered. "How they looked when they were dead. All bloated—and there were strange bruises all over their bodies. My father was a handsome man with dark hair and eyes. He had the longest, thickest eyelashes. Even when he was mad, his eyes always gave him away. He could never stay angry very long. He was so still, lying there in the tall grass. I would never look upon his eyes again." Her breath started coming in gasps and she went pale. "And seeing my mother like that, without a face!"

She fell to the floor and wretched, gagging up her breakfast. Stuart called for an orderly while Jason held her in his arms. She sobbed uncontrollably. Jason lifted her onto the bed and held her close while the orderly mopped up the mess on the floor.

"Aren't you going to give her something, Stuart?" Jason pleaded.

"No more drugs. Let her cry it out."

It was an agonizing half hour for them all. Emma gulped for breath and her eyes burned and swelled from tears. She clung to Jason, her entire body racked with sobs. Guilt and self–reproach would not disappear with a crying jag, but she had at last spoken her horror aloud and no one condemned her. She also prepared to sacrifice her love for Jason, should he have a change in his affection for her. It was certain, she reasoned, after discovering how weak she was. *He won't be able to depend on me*, she thought. Her tears soon subsided, leaving her exhausted. Stuart gave her some water, then Jason pulled blankets over her and let her sleep.

"Leave her be," Stuart said, guiding Jason out into the hallway and closing the door. "She'll sleep for hours. This was very hard on her—on all of us. Go home."

On his walk home that day, Jason did not notice the gusting wind and swirling snowstorm that was quickly blanketing the town. His thoughts were occupied by Emma's confessions. She was seventeen when it happened, he thought. She was hardly mature enough to deal with such a tragedy. She felt weak and guilty for what she had done and it would take time to build her up. He went home for a while, then spoiling for something to do, he went to the mill for the remainder of the day. He kept to himself, which was common, but many workers noticed that he was very distracted, going from one thing to the next. But that night for the first time in weeks, he slept soundly. He knew the enemy and was ready to fight alongside his beloved Emma.

The next morning, Jason was again at the hospital. Stuart had just finished examining Emma just after breakfast. She smiled when Jason came in; the mere sight of him gave her strength.

He leaned down and kissed her. "How did you sleep?"

"Dreamlessly," she answered. "No nightmares for a change."

"Me too," he said.

"Well, Emma," Stuart began. "You told me that you've been doing a lot of thinking. Are you up to talking some more?"

She nodded and reached for Jason's hand, pulling him down next to her on the bed. "I understand some things better, I think. I woke up in the wee hours this morning and realized something. I don't know if it's important, though."

"Everything's important," Stuart coached.

"The thing is that I can't condemn what the Pawnee did. When I lived with the Cheyenne and realized how they were forced to live, I understood why the Pawnee raided us. They were starving. We had food, our own land, and livestock. To them, we were rich with our crops, cows, horses, and chickens. It's a wonder that we weren't attacked sooner."

"You had no choice that day, either. You were outnumbered and could've done little to save your parents. Do you understand that now?" Stuart said.

"Yes, Stuart. Ignoring the shocks I've had has been one of my greatest flaws. But I have to admit in a pinch, self–imposed amnesia kept me going."

Her throat was dry and she sipped water from a cup from her nightstand. "There's something else you both need to know. A few months after Shea died, I got a letter. Inside the envelope was a letter and a bank draft for five thousand dollars. I didn't tell anyone about it."

"That sure is a lot of money. Who sent it?" Stuart asked.

"Shea's father, Shea Russell." Both men looked at each other, astonished. "It was a shock for me, too. I read the letter over and over. It was incredible and so sad. Max Cody was lecturing at a museum in Philadelphia. Shea's father went to hear him. He was stunned when Cody spoke of Shea Hawk-shadow. After the lecture, he cornered Cody and discovered that Shea was his son, even though Shea's mother changed his last name. With Max's help, he tried to find Shea—more than six years he searched. The only word he got of Shea was when Rachel sent Cody a wire with Shea's obituary. Cody sent it to Shea's father."

Jason saddened. "At least he was trying to do the right thing. It's a shame that Shea never knew."

"I wrote back thanking him for the money, which was intended for Kate's education. That's what I was trying to tell you that day I took the laudanum, Jason. The cash was hidden in my dresser. If I had died, it would've given Kate a chance for a better life than mine."

She slipped her arms around Jason's neck and hugged him. Stuart saw that he was crying. Jason had his own battles, he saw. Being rich and powerful was no guarantee of an easy life, or happiness. Stuart left them alone for a little while, busying himself by taking Emma's breakfast tray back to the kitchen. When he returned, Emma was talking.

"Jason, you were right when you said that I've survived far worse, but coming out the other side of this isn't easy." She looked to Stuart. "The thing is, it's a good thing that you locked me up. In a very dark, weak corner of my mind, I thought if I were dead, that would fix all the problems. But I know now that I have to live with my choices and face my responsibilities. I haven't lived a normal life, but how could I have been ready for all that happened? It was all so fast and too often, violent. Many people that I loved died awful deaths. Adam was right years ago when he told me that I was a naive fool. He was trying to make me see the realities around me, but I wouldn't listen. I was too young, too stubborn, too stupid. The scars I have were inflicted by ignorant men. They tried to kill me, but they couldn't. I held on and outlived them." She looked to Stuart. "I haven't been a good patient, have I? Stuart, I know you're trying to help me. It seems that since my parents' murder, my life has been out of my control. Things happened so fast and I lost so much along the way. There was little time to sort it out before the next thing came at me. I don't know how else to put it. Thank you for all you've done—for all that both of you are doing."

Stuart and Jason talked with her a long time. Emma poured out all her fears, putting a voice to her insecurities and fear of abandonment.

"Being alone is the one thing I fear most," she confessed. "I can survive physical pain, but the pain of being abandoned is terrifying to me. And I nearly orphaned my daughter because of my weakness. It will take a long time for me to reconcile that—to earn Kate's trust again."

"She loves you, Emma. She'll understand," Jason soothed.

Stuart later excused himself to see to other patients, but he was reeling from what he had learned about Emma over the past two days.

Emma and Jason were left alone for many hours. It was supper time when Stuart looked in on them again. Emma and Jason cuddled together on her bed. She half laid against him, smiling and relaxed. Stuart observed how she shored herself up, drawing on Jason's unwavering strength, just as she had done with Shea. And she needed it until she could stand on her own again. He was heartened seeing how their hands remained interlocked and the ease they had with each other. She was learning to let go of the long–buried guilt and rage at herself. She was learning to trust. Stuart allowed himself hope as he went to the kitchen to order up two meals for them.

As Jason left that night, Emma saw him to her door and pulled him into an embrace. "I feel set free, no pun intended. I feel better." She bestowed a light kiss on his mouth. "Give Kate my love." She held his eyes and said, "Jason, I know that you think I'm weak for trying to kill myself."

He was somber and leaned against the door. "Of course not, Emma. I know what it's like, the desperation and guilt, I mean."

Emma saw that Jason had something on his mind. "Tell me," she urged. Jason resisted, but Emma encouraged him to talk. "You've spent weeks listening to me. Whatever it is, you can tell me. Please."

At length, Jason spoke. "My mother was wealthy most of her adult life, but she had a hard time when she was young. Her parents died a month apart during a flu epidemic in Minnesota. Her family was split apart. Her three older brothers were taken in by cousins in Wisconsin to work their farms, but since she was a girl, she wasn't wanted. Eventually, she was taken in by an aunt who lived nearby, but those years were very hard on my mother. She was beaten and abused by her aunt and uncle.

"At fifteen, she ran away and lived with a friend. While living there she tried to find her brothers, but she never could. When she was seventeen, she met my father. They married, left Minnesota, and came west. My father was a smart man, but he was rough with her. He was rough with me and Karl, too. When I was about eight, I saw him beat her up one night. I watched it all from the top of the stairs in the house where you now live. My father built this town and he was a good businessman, but he wasn't much of a husband and not much of a father. He had to control everything—everyone. At work, he did it with money. At home, he did it with harsh words, his fist, or his razor strap."

Emma pulled him back into the room and closed the door. "Oh, Jason. I never knew. Why was he like that? Was he beaten when he was young?"

"I wish I knew. He never talked about it. From that I assumed that things were not good in his family." He shook off the memories. "It's in the past. And I don't want to burden you. You're just starting to recover."

"I want to hear it all, Jason. Maybe I can help you for a change."

Jason walked over to the window. He realized why Emma liked it there. The view of the forest clinging to the mountainside was breathtaking in the snow and a waterfall was just visible in the distance. It was a moment before he continued.

"He stopped hitting my mother eventually, but he was still cruel. He said such unkind things to her. He liked to put her to shame if she didn't do something to his satisfaction. If his shirt wasn't pressed perfectly or he didn't like what she prepared for dinner, he became savage and evil. He would say that she wasn't pretty, that she was lazy—things like that—just to hurt her. She was a beautiful, intelligent woman, but he wore her down. I pitied her. I know now that my father was insecure. I tried to stay out of his way, but I did mischievous things as all kids do. I got a terrible beating from him when I was caught stealing apples from the general store. If I came home dirty from playing along the river, I'd get beaten. Karl and I lived in fear. Nothing was good enough for my father. He thought that he could beat us into his idea of perfection. Instead, he drove us all away.

"I don't know why the marriage broke down in the first place. My mother had said, years later, that the marriage began very strong and that there was a lot of love between the two of them. Maybe the pressures of building the business and the town got to my father. I don't know. Then Karl started to join in when my father would start in on my mother. The two of them were like wolves and ganged up on her. I wanted to defend her, but I was still just a kid. But it paid off for me to work in the logging camps. By the time I was fourteen I had grown bigger than them both.

"One day, my father and brother were at my mother again while she was in the kitchen cooking dinner. My father was shouting at her that he didn't want duck for dinner, he wanted venison. Dinner was coming out of the oven and it was just too late. Of course, my father hadn't told her what he wanted for dinner before he left for work. He set her up like always. Karl started in on her, too. I couldn't stand it any longer. I told them to back off. My father pushed me and we got into a fight. My brother jumped on me too and we fought—the three of us. My mother was crying and shouting, trying to break us up, then my father shoved her against the wall. I flew into a rage. By the time it was all over, the kitchen was a wreck and my brother and father were slumped in the corner, no fight left in them.

"From then on, they knew that I would defend her. Karl avoided me all he could afterwards. That's why he went to a college far away, that's why we're not close. And I was glad to see him go. I wished that my father had gone with him.

"I hated the fact that anyone could infuriate me like that. I have never been a violent person. My father gained a little respect for me, but he kept trying to find a weakness in me, something he could exploit. With Karl gone, he taught me the business, but he treated me like an employee, not his son. When we had disagreements about anything, he threatened to find someone else to leave the business to. One day he said it once too often. I told him I would expose his despicable treatment of my mother if he did. That got his attention. It was a powerful position for me to be in. If I inherited the business and my mother outlived my father, I could make a good life for her.

"One afternoon when I was eighteen, I came home from work and saw my mother sitting in the parlor by herself. She hadn't heard me come in by the back door, I guess. I watched her from the parlor door. The night before, my parents had had another fight. My father didn't hit her, but his words had cut her to ribbons. She looked so sad just sitting there. Then, I saw that she had a knife. Before I could do anything, she put it to her throat. At that second, a floorboard creaked under me and she hid the knife up her sleeve. I didn't want her to know what I'd seen, but I loved her, so I sat with her and we talked for a long time. She confided in me. Her marriage had no love left and Karl despised her, too. It was tearing her apart to lead two lives—the town founder's rich, benevolent wife and an abused woman at home. At home she tried to stay out of my father's way, but when she left the house, it was like she was someone else. She smiled at folks, checked in on the sick, and gave people gifts and money. She even helped settlers passing through town, seeing that they had adequate supplies, medical treatment, money, and fresh horses, whatever they needed. Instead of being beaten down, she showed kindness and tolerance."

He laughed with grim amusement. "Of course, this got to my father, but how could he admit to his treatment of her? He built this town and lured many people to stay and build his fortune. If the truth got out, those same people would've deserted him. He knew it and I knew it. And it was a good thing that my father was a rotten bookkeeper and left that to Allison Carruthers. Allison had guessed that something was terribly wrong between my parents, so she doctored the books to protect my mother. My father never knew how much money my mother gave away. He had a lot of money to spend as he liked and that was all he cared about. Even when he hurt her, my mother preserved her dignity. But that day in the parlor, I saw a side of her that terrified me. If she left the marriage, she would have nothing; my father always reminded her that he would keep every cent. How she got through each day is still a mystery to me."

"Oh, Jason, I had no idea. I've been too busy feeling sorry for myself with not a thought for anyone else. I didn't know. I'm so sorry."

"I did all I could to help her. My father's treatment of her got a little better in their later years, I think because he was just getting old. But he never showed her the respect that she deserved. She was a great lady, despite her private hell."

He sat beside her on the bed. "You remind me of her in some ways. You put on a brave face and get through the day, but inside, you've got all this turmoil going on. You've got to put it in a place where it can't hurt you anymore. My mother had only me to confide in. You're lucky. You have many people who want to help you."

He held back tears. "When my father died, it was like my mother was freed from prison. With Karl away in Tacoma, we both looked forward to some peace, but she died just short of a year later. Her heart just gave out and I found her dead in the kitchen one morning. I thought that she had been cheated because she barely got a year of peace. But because I kept to myself, I couldn't bring myself to talk to anyone. I had the business to run. I hid out in the mill office. It was the hardest time of my life. I do know what you're going through."

"How did your brother react to all this? Did he ever come around and realize that he had been so cruel to your mother?"

"No. My father would travel to Tacoma to see Karl and his family, but my mother was never welcomed. She knew where my father was going and it broke her heart. She still loved Karl and respected his wishes, no matter how hard it was for her.

"I realized how callous my brother had become when he didn't come for either funeral. I was alone and I had such a huge responsibility in taking over the business. I shut up the house after my mother died and lived in a tent while my house was being built. The memories of everything that she endured in that house almost destroyed me. It took every bit of strength I had to open up the house for you after Shea died. Then I started to realize, as you have, that the problems were in me. I carried them with me. You're not alone like I was, Emma."

Emma's eyes filled with tears. This was the first time that Jason had ever opened up about his earlier life. Like her, he had kept things buried, but somehow he dealt with them better than she. She wished for his strength. "Now I know why you never visit Karl when you go to Tacoma—why you never speak of him."

"I don't like rehashing things. What is in the past is past."

"There is nothing wrong with leaving the past behind, but once in a while, the past demands your attention, no matter what you do. Maybe I wouldn't be here if I had dealt with the guilt that I felt when my parents were killed. I can tell that you still care about your brother. There may come a time when you two can reconcile. You shouldn't miss the chance if it comes. It's a chance that I will never have."

Later, Stuart came in and spoke with Emma. "Well?"

She took a long time to reply, choosing her words. "I feel good. It's like a weight is off my chest and I can breathe at last. I've always been afraid because of the choices I made—and even more so of the ones I didn't make. I used to feel so alone, like I was helpless and thrown this way and that by whoever wanted to do me harm. There I was, time and time again, always wanting to escape and control my own life. I tried to shut away all those feelings, but they broke out, just like the Cheyenne did in the outbreak back in '78. Now I understand how they felt. When it came to my own desperation, I was too weak to do anything about it. I did feel responsible for Shea's death. If I had stayed away, he would be living with his own people with another family. He wouldn't be buried up on the mountain."

"You had happy years with Shea. I saw how great you two were together. Emma, all couples have hard times and secrets, too. But if you had stayed away from Shea, you wouldn't have Kate, now, would you? And tell me, can you imagine a day without her?" Her smile and her look to Jason answered his question. "That's as it should be. Forgive yourself and stop blaming yourself for things that you had no control over."

"Stuart, teach me to live with these things. They still crowd me. Please tell me what to do now. I've got a bad habit of pretending that nothing bothers me."

"I'll help you, don't worry." He rose to leave. "You haven't asked if I'm going to release you."

She looked at him. "I trust your judgment. I've taken my first step out of here. You're my doctor and my friend and I will do as you say."

Chapter Nineteen

During the next few weeks, Emma regained her balance with Stuart and Jason's help. She had committed the ultimate act of selfishness all those years ago by saving herself, but she did not perceive it as a failure or fatal character flaw any longer. The realization was cleansing, healing. Guilt and grief ebbed and she was able to deal with her feelings in ways that did not debilitate her. She bolstered herself by reflecting that after her dismal failure to protect her parents, she never allowed herself to be a victim again. It was admitting defeat that gave her strength, learning without numbing self–reproach, and admitting that she was flawed, just like everyone else. And she asked for help and got it. By facing down her darkest emotions, she allowed them to subside, their negative energies dissipating.

Stuart asked Rachel, Caleb, and Jason to his home one night in early December. "I've decided to release Emma Saturday morning." He chose his words. "Rachel, since you and Emma had a fight months ago, she may not be ready to deal with you, so don't push. Let her make the move if it's going to happen, all right?"

"Agreed. But where will she go, Stuart?" Rachel asked. "Do you think that she should be in her house alone with Kate?"

"It's her home and that's where she wants to be. I offered my house to give her time to readjust, but she turned me down. She won't hurt herself again. We all have to make an effort to be around her, but don't get too close. She doesn't want pity. Give her time to get back on track." This advice was directed mostly at Rachel.

Emma was released the following Saturday as planned. Stuart came to her room. Her stomach fluttered as she gathered her things and followed him outside into the sunny December morning. She stood a moment on the threshold, drinking in the cool air scented with pine. She hugged Stuart and kissed his cheek. "Thank you," she whispered in her ear.

On the street, Jason waited alone near his covered carriage. She went to him and he took her in his arms. "Ready to go home?" he asked, smiling.

"You bet." She looked up at him. "Thank you, Jason." She kissed him tenderly. Without a backward glance at the imposing brick facade of the hospital, Emma stepped up into the carriage.

The streets were snow packed, so Jason drove slowly down Main. Fresh snow began falling in beautiful, fat flakes that instantly coated everything, giving the town a dreamy aspect. Many heads turned as they passed, and Emma was sure that rumors would be circulating by noontime. But that was forgotten when the carriage stopped at the doorstep of the Barlows'. Emma willed herself to look around for Rachel, but did not see her or Caleb, for that matter. The children heard the carriage arrive and came out onto the porch. Martin had been charged with the task of minding Helen, Randall, and Kate and looked somewhat the worse for wear.

Without a thought for the ankle–deep snow, Emma stepped off the carriage and ran to her daughter. Kate stood a moment on the porch, her eyes locked with her mother's. Then she came running and Emma caught her up in her arms.

"Oh my darling!" she gushed, kissing her cheeks. "You look so pretty!" she said, admiring the blue velvet dress that Kate had borrowed from Helen. They embraced and kissed one another as the snow coated their clothes and hair. Kate's face twitched and fell into a frown as she buried her head in her mother's shoulder, crying with sheer relief. Emma had never felt so rich or grateful in her life—she was sure that her daughter loved her. Her peace of mind was restored as the child clung to her and she carried her into the warm house.

Rachel and Caleb had been at Emma's house all morning, restocking the larder with items that Jason had purchased. They had just returned by the back door, since it was faster to cut through the back yards to get from house to house. Rachel's and Emma's eyes met briefly as Emma carried Kate down the hallway to the parlor.

Emma cradled Kate on her lap near the fireplace, wiping away her tears. Jason closed the parlor doors to allow Emma and Kate privacy. He herded the Barlow children back into the house then back to the kitchen.

"Oh, Katherine. I'm home for good, don't you worry. I'm sorry for all that I put you through." She rocked her girl until her tears subsided.

"Are you okay now Momma?" Kate sniffled.

"Yes, and seeing you makes everything perfect. I'll never leave you again, I promise."

"What was wrong with you?"

She took a deep breath. "I was sad after your daddy died and I blamed myself, which was the wrong thing to do. He meant everything to me just as you do and I missed him more than I realized. I have been through a lot of bad things in my life, long before you were even born, and those bad things made me sick. I had to go to the hospital to learn to deal with them. And knowing that you were here waiting for me helped more than anything. Thank you for not being mad."

"But I was mad at you. I was really mad, but Rachel told me that you would come home soon, and I shouldn't be mad because you were sick."

She cupped her child's lovely face in her hands and looked deep into her blue eyes. "I love you, Katherine. Thank you for believing in me," she said, bestowing a kiss.

"I love you, Mommy."

"I'll do better, you'll see."

"When can we go back home?"

"As soon as you're packed."

Later, Emma waited in the foyer with Jason as the children pounded upstairs to help Kate pack.

Rachel passed by the open kitchen door and stood stock–still. Already, she was breaking her promise to Stuart to keep a distance. To her surprise, Emma came to her and looked around the room to satisfy herself that they were alone.

"Where's Caleb?" Emma asked.

Rachel distractedly pointed to the yard. "He's chopping wood."

"Rachel, it's taken me a long time to understand. I hope that we can be friends again—that we can talk this out soon."

Rachel fiddled with her apron and spoke in a hush. "You have every reason to hate me. I won't blame you if you never speak to me again."

Emma sighed. "I don't hate you. I'm grateful to you and Caleb for caring for Kate all these months. Thank you."

Rachel held back tears. "Emma, can we be friends again someday?"

"I hope so. There are things in myself that I need to find again. Please be patient."

Rachel nodded and went back to her work in the kitchen.

On the way home in Jason's carriage, Kate asked, "Momma, can we go see Daddy? I miss him."

"Sure, darling." Emma quelled a bit of panic tightening her chest, but she had to focus on Kate's needs, not her own. Jason gave her a searching look, silently asking if she needed his intervention. She read him and shook her head slightly. "Of course, it depends on the weather and if the trail up the mountain is safe."

Emma was surprised and heartened when she arrived home. Jason had made sure that the boiler had been lit and a blaze burned in every fireplace. When she saw all the food in the pantry, she felt a little upset about accepting charity, but she had promised Stuart to accept all the help that came her way. Jason mentioned that Rachel and Caleb had restocked the larder and cleaned the house.

"That was very generous of them. Thank you for letting me know," Emma replied.

Help came in the form of Allison Carruthers, the wife of the owner of the general store and the nurse who had assisted with Shea's throat surgery. Emma knew Allison only from quick conversations at the store. She had come to Jason upon hearing that Emma was coming home, volunteering to help with the cooking, cleaning, and laundry until Emma was stronger. Emma was at once a little embarrassed and very grateful, doubting that she had the strength to jump back into her routine so quickly.

Jason and Allison worked around the house the entire day, putting things in order and leaving Emma and Kate by themselves.

That evening after Allison left and Kate was asleep, Jason walked Emma upstairs and made a show of tucking her in bed. He kissed her. "Get better. With what I have planned for our wedding night, you'll need your strength, so rest up." She giggled and slid beneath the blankets. To Jason's ears and to his heart, it was a sweet, much missed sound. "I'll see you tomorrow."

She studied him. "What if I had died, Jason?" There was still an undeniable streak of melancholy in her, and she regretted asking the moment the words left her lips.

The lack of pretense in his look at her said what was truly in his heart. "I would've died a lonely man. I will never love anyone the way I love you."

As Emma drifted in and out of sleep that night, Rachel's kindness to her and Kate kept rising to the surface. She had to heal the breach between them. She regretted her angry outburst of a few months ago. *I should've let it go,* she thought. *What good did my telling her that I knew about the affair do, except hurt us both?*

Jason's exhaustion caught up with him that night when he returned home. He slept soundly for twenty–four hours, his formidable store of strength gone. Emma knew how fatigued he was and did not cross the yard to disturb him. She and Kate spent a quiet Sunday together, playing games and baking, leaving the kitchen a sticky mess. Neither of them cared. They were together again. It was all that mattered.

When Stuart arrived the next day to check on Emma, he was disconcerted. She seemed to be backsliding. She paced around the parlor and seemed frazzled. He thought that he had sent her home too soon.

"Coming home was draining for me. And I have had trouble sleeping," she confided.

"I'm glad that you're being honest with me. Let's give your readjustment a few more days. If you're not feeling better soon, you will tell me, agreed?"

"Stuart, I will not hide from you any longer. I promise you that," she said. "But if I'm still having trouble adjusting to being home, will you put me back in the hospital?"

"No. I think it's important for you to be home with Kate. You and I can handle anything that comes up without hospitalization. But you have to continue to be honest with me."

Days later, Stuart checked in on Emma. She seemed much stronger. She assured Stuart that she was sleeping better and glad to be home again.

Stuart was encouraged and dared to probe into another area, hoping that Emma was strong enough to face it. He had witnessed the distance between Emma and Rachel, and had at last guessed what had torn them apart. He confided that he suspected that Shea might have been Randall's father.

Emma recoiled, shocked. "How did you find out?"

"I'm a doctor and a father. Caleb told me about the troubles he and Rachel were having back then. And there were other things that Rachel said and did while Shea was sick—she was grieving as if she were losing her husband, too. I finally put it all together when I overheard you and Jason talking one day at the hospital. I confess that I was standing outside your door when you and he were discussing it."

Emma looked away. "So you know about the affair?"

"Caleb knew that she was seeing someone else, but he never thought it was Shea. And he's never to know that Randall might not be his."

She looked relieved. "Oh, I agree. Why destroy us all?"

"You have to deal with this and I don't want it to stall your recovery. There is nothing anyone can do about it."

"I'm starting to understand it all, Stuart. Rachel never meant to hurt anyone. She was in pain because her marriage was falling apart. Shea didn't love her. It was a physical release for him, nothing more."

"This is a critical time for you. It's up to you if you want to face these problems with Rachel."

Emma slumped on the sofa and regarded him, conscious of Stuart's attitude toward her question. "Does it bother you that your grandson might be part Cheyenne?"

"He's my grandson and I don't care what his bloodlines are. Too many people have been hurt by this as it is, and I want your solemn promise that you will tell no one—ever."

Emma took a long, penitent pause before answering. "Of course I won't. Randall's just a child. Why hurt him? But every time I see him, I think I see Shea—and I'm astounded that no one else does. Maybe it's because I knew Shea so well, but maybe I didn't know him after all." She clamped her mouth shut, resisting the urge to babble.

"Concentrate on getting your strength back," he said, switching to his crisp, professional tone. He opened his bag and examined her, listening to her heartbeat and looking her over. "You look too thin. I want you to gain some weight."

"With Allison doing all the housework, I don't work up much of an appetite. But I'm sure that I'll gain some back because all I do is sit around the house like an old dog," she quipped.

"Did you sleep through last night?"

"Not all the way through," she said, knowing that she dare not lie to him after all he had done to save her. "I will soon, though—and without drugs. I won't be asking for any."

He had learned to read her moods very well. "Believe me, Emma, you won't be getting any. I cleared out Carruthers' stock of laudanum. It's no longer sold in this town or in Millersburg."

She later volunteered that the troubles with Rachel were still eating at her. "I want to get it off my mind, but it just keeps coming back at me."

"Emma, these things happen. It's how we deal with tragedies, large and small, that defines our character. Shea loved you, but he made a mistake. Have you ever been tempted in that way?"

"Never," she answered, then suddenly remembered that day in Adam's tent and later in the stand of white birches when she had let him kiss her, touch her. And the time she thought about running away with him while pregnant with Kate. "Well once, but I never acted on it."

"You can understand Shea a little better, then?"

When she rose from the sofa, she got dizzy and collapsed to the floor before Stuart could catch her. "I guess I got up too fast."

He took her up to her bedroom. "Stop pushing yourself, Emma. I'll have Allison bring your meals up to you. Stay in bed the rest of the day and tomorrow, too."

"No, I'm all right," Emma assured him.

"Emma—do as I say," Stuart ordered. He went downstairs and found Allison in the washroom where she was ironing clothes.

Emma was very frustrated that her strength did not return quickly. As her recovery progressed, Jason spent time with her when he could. He had to put in many late nights at the mill to catch up on the work that he had allowed to slide over the past months.

A rare bit of warm weather in December melted most of the snow in town and the weather turned unusually balmy and sunny. Over Allison's objections, Emma insisted on sitting on the porch, basking in the sun on those comfortable afternoons. Allison took meticulous care of her, seeing that she ate well and rested—a lot. Emma accepted the older woman's ministrations and found a friend in her. Kate had returned to her routine of school and play and did not ask to go up the mountain again, sensing that her mother was not yet ready.

Allison stayed for two weeks, at last satisfied that Emma could manage light work. "I don't want you tiring yourself out. You have a lot of busy days ahead with the holidays coming, so if you get tired, call on me."

She hugged her. "Allison, thank you and thank Gale for letting you come."

"He had no say in it. I do as I please!" She smiled as she trotted down the front steps waving good–bye.

Jason came each day and chopped wood, cleaned the house, and cooked dinner on many occasions. His presence did much to reassure Emma that he loved her. She missed him when he left each evening, waving from the gate that connected their yards.

Chapter Twenty

Emma and Kate began to mend their fragile relationship. Emma started to feel revived and clear for the first time in many years and, in her newfound contentment, overindulged her child. She was acutely aware that Kate had suffered too and did all she could to reassure the child. Kate rebounded and although she had the freedom to roam and play, she kept close to home.

With Christmas coming, Emma felt pressure to make the usual preparations. She steadied herself and helped Kate decorate the house and planned her baking for the holidays, attempting to make everything appear normal.

Against his better judgment, Jason took Emma and Kate up the mountain just before Christmas. The trail was very slick, so he had to drive the team with great care and concentration. He worried about Emma. He felt that it was too soon for her to return, but Emma insisted because she did not want to disappoint Kate. The child needed to get her own feelings sorted out in her own time, her own way.

Jason was more concerned about Emma. "Okay, I'll take you," he had said, not disguising his misgivings. "But if I think you can't handle it, I'm bringing you straight down."

The cold air and open spaces refreshed Emma and although the day was cold and deep snow fell in this high country, she felt renewed, stronger, and safer with Jason at her side. When she came to Shea's grave, she realized that her guilt had diminished. Kate came up beside her and slipped her mittened hand in hers.

"Does Daddy watch over us?"

"I believe he does. I know you miss him, but I want you to always be proud that he was your father. He was a very special man and he loved you more than anything."

"I know he loved me," she confided. "So if he's watching me, maybe he doesn't miss me so much, right?"

"Yes, my little love."

Later, Emma poked around the cabin with Jason.

"My gosh," she said with a wry smile. "I didn't remember it being this small. I'm spoiled, living in the wide–open spaces of your mother's house. You were right to get us out of here, but you know my memory of those days is fuzzy. I wasn't in the best shape when Shea was sick."

Jason held onto memories of good times and friendship in this place. "Look, while we're up here, why don't I load up the rest of your things? We packed you up so fast, there might be things that we left behind."

"Yes, I think some books are still here and a few of Katherine's old toys," she agreed.

As Jason drove down the icy trail, Emma said, "Stuart said not to worry about anything for now, but I have to find a way to support us." Jason opened his mouth to speak, but she cut in. "The dividends you pay me from the mill are more than adequate, don't get me wrong, but I need something to do while Kate is in school. I want to start up my baking business again. Maybe I could rent a building someday and open up a bakery."

"I think I have an answer to that," Jason said. Kate crawled up from the rear of the sledge to cuddle between them under the blanket spread across their knees. "It's been vacant for years, but I have a building next to the general store. Why don't you open your bakery there? You're a hell of a baker." Emma smiled at the compliment. "I think it would be successful. Besides, Gale always complained that your goods took up too much space in his store, no matter how fast they sold out."

"I'm still thinking about it, Jason. As for the building, I will pay you a fair rent on the place if I do this."

He opened his mouth to protest, but decided to let her keep her pride. "Just say the word and we can argue over rent again." He grinned, slowing the horses where the trail was steep and sticky with mud and snow.

She glanced over at him, cherishing this remarkable man who had done so much for her and her family. On this December afternoon, she allowed herself to enjoy his handsome face and his easy, warm manner. She wondered at her luck, having such a man to love. She hugged Kate close to her and nuzzled her soft black hair.

Aware that her collapse and confinement in the hospital were common knowledge, Emma was very reluctant to go out in public.

After much coaxing Jason convinced her to go out. "I'll be with you the whole time."

"I don't have much else to buy for Christmas," she said, mining for excuses. "I decided on your gift months ago. That just leaves Stuart and Kate. And I can do that shopping later, when I'm stronger."

"Christmas is less than a week away. You can do this," he urged.

Stifling a tightness in her chest she did agree to go, but only if he stayed at her side.

Those people who knew Emma were sympathetic and kind as Jason escorted her down Main Street the next day. Passersby stopped, offering assistance, if she should find herself in need, they said. She accepted their wishes for her continued health with dignity and although it fatigued her, she held up well with Jason's presence and strong arm around her for support.

At the general store, Gale Carruthers, at Allison's insistence, refused her money and included a generous bag full of peppermint candies for Kate. At the millinery, she found several dresses for herself and Kate. She smiled at Jason's evident discomfort as he waited among corsets and ladies' undergarments on display. The owner, Caleb's sister Ruth, charged her half price on everything.

Ruth leaned over the counter and spoke close to Emma. "I hope you'll be better soon," she said. Emma looked away, blushing crimson. "Don't be ashamed. Everyone has problems. Fight back with everything you've got." Emma's eyes welled with tears as Ruth squeezed her hand.

"Thank you," Emma whispered.

Stuart later spotted Emma with Jason on the street. He hugged her with affection. "You look wonderful, Emma," he said with a wink to Jason. "People might think that you're married already. You stick so close to one another." Emma looked to Jason. His easy smile and adoring look upon her made her forget her troubles. He was good medicine for her, she believed, much better than laudanum.

Jason offered her dinner at Murdock's restaurant. She accepted, grateful for the private room that he procured, tucked away in the back, with heavy red curtains that could be drawn, allowing privacy. It was normally reserved for newlyweds or young lovers.

Emma slumped a little as the waiter drew the curtain after taking their order and pouring wine. "You were right. Everyone's been so kind today. It feels like I'm dreaming." Her eyes glistened. "I guess that people liked us more than I thought. I always had the feeling that we were only curiosities here, more than residents. You were right from the very beginning, Jason. Easthope is different. It somehow thrives in isolation."

"I'm glad that you and Shea decided to stay," he said. "After Kate was born, I half expected you all to be gone every time I came up to the cabin."

After a few minutes of small talk and several sips of wine, Emma said what had been on her mind for many days. "Don't be alarmed at this—it's just an idea that I've been playing with. I was thinking that Kate and I might spend a few weekends up at the cabin during the spring. It'll give us time to break away, you know, put things to rest." Jason was shocked at her idea but covered it by pouring more wine. Emma missed his look of apprehension. "I'm hungry. What's keeping that waiter?"

Jason brooded on Emma's desire to return to the cabin, knowing the isolation was the worst thing for her now. Easthope may thrive in its isolation, but Emma did not.

But he was gratified that her appetite had returned. She enjoyed a dinner of grilled salmon with potatoes and greens. He ordered another bottle of wine as they relaxed over dessert, spending two peaceful, intimate hours together. He blocked out her wish to return to the cabin. He could not deal with it at the moment and did not want to spoil this private time. He had missed her company so much over the last few months, and he knew she was still fragile, so he gave her room to talk about anything she wanted.

In the comfortable silences, Emma's thoughts drifted back to the night that she had first tasted wine and later ended up on her knees vomiting while Adam held her. She remembered how angry he had been with her that day when she had insisted on the food and medicine for the Cheyenne, but she also remembered how his anger had died that night as he chuckled while she purged. The memory brought none of the old embarrassment she had harbored. That night, the meal, the wine, and Jason's good company made her feel warm, content, and very lucky. She then wondered if her letters about Shea had ever reached Adam.

Just after dark, Jason drove her over to Rachel's to pick up Kate. He saw them home. "I have to go to the lumberyard and close up, but I'll be back to say good-night," he said as he walked her to the door and kissed her.

Once home, Kate was bustled off to bed. The child smiled as Emma turned down the lamp and closed the door part way. "Good–night, my little love," she whispered with particular affection.

Emma never minded if Jason let himself in the house. He had returned while she had been upstairs, built up the fire in the parlor, and sat down to wait for her.

She joined him on the sofa and took his hand. "Thank you, not only for today, but for all you've done. I always seem to be thanking you and taking from you."

He lifted her long, thin hand to his lips, bestowing a tender kiss. "You can consider me your truest friend," he said. "I will always see to it that you will have everything you want and need for the rest of your life. I love you."

The next morning, Emma went to the little post office inside Carruthers' store, but there was no mail for her. She left disappointed that she had received no word from Adam and wrote him again that night, hoping that this letter would reach him. She also wrote one to Shea's father, informing him that her recent illness was the reason she had not written for so long.

One evening a few days later, Emma mustered her nerve and invited the Barlows for dinner. Rachel was agitated and changed her dress four times before an impatient Caleb dragged her out of the house.

"Rachel, she's trying to make up with you. Stop fussing over what you're wearing. This is what you wanted, isn't it?"

"Yes, but just let me be nervous, all right?" Caleb shrugged as he handed her up into their carriage.

Rachel was still a bundle of nerves as she stepped into Emma's house. The children disappeared upstairs to play and Jason and Caleb retreated to the back porch for a cigar, leaving the two women alone in the kitchen.

Emma made the first move and hugged Rachel. "Let's go on and let what's happened stay in the past. Neither of us can change it. I've missed you."

Rachel hugged her tight. "Oh, Emma, I'm sorry that I hurt you. It was never intentional. Forgive me."

"I do."

Rachel was uncharacteristically quiet as tears dripped down her cheeks. Emma watched her, knowing that her instincts had been correct. It was time to forgive. They went into the parlor and Emma closed the doors.

Rachel spoke at length. "You knew, yet you stayed friends with me. Will you let me tell you how it all happened?" Emma nodded, hoping that she was strong enough to bear up. "I never wanted to hurt you and Shea didn't want to hurt you either. He told me that time and time again. It started just after Kate was born. Neither of us saw it coming. He guided my team down to the lower trail one evening and we started talking. I'm the one who took advantage of him. Don't blame him. It was me—all me. He was so handsome and exotic."

Emma cringed at her use of the word. She wished never to hear the word 'exotic' ever again.

"Before we knew it, we did it in the back of the wagon. But believe me, Emma, it wasn't love. Back then, Caleb and I were having troubles after his affair. I wasn't trying to take your husband away from you. He loved you. But being together just became routine. Every time he took me down to the lower trail, we would—" Emma waved her hand, hoping that Rachel would get the hint to avoid the details. Rachel's voice dropped. "I discovered that I was pregnant weeks later. I didn't know what to do. If you found out, you would hate me and Shea as well. I told Shea about the pregnancy and we were never together after that. He felt guilty, he really did. And poor Caleb. To cover myself, I practically raped him that night. He was mad at me over some argument, but I had no choice. I was a harlot, no better than Elsa Swenson. I was getting back at Caleb for his affair, I know that. But I don't know who Randall's father is. If Caleb has any doubt, he'll leave me."

"He won't find out, Rachel. This will stay between you and me, all right?"

"You're so calm, Emma. Tell me what you're thinking."

"It's done. There's nothing that I can do about it now."

The animosity between them died away, like smoke dissipating on the wind. Both women yearned to reform the friendship.

While the children played upstairs, Emma brought wine and cake into the parlor. She slid off her shoes and propped up her feet on a hassock. That comfort was a small renewal in itself and the wine relaxed her, too. A wicked thought crossed her mind. She should've drank wine instead of laudanum. It tasted better and had a similar effect.

Rachel broke the silence. "Jason mentioned that you want to spend time up at the cabin, but I hope you'll reconsider. It's so good to have you nearby—and safer, too."

Emma willed good memories of the years at the cabin; the only intrusion in her reverie was imagining Rachel and Shea together, but she had trouble conjuring it now. It was, as she kept telling herself, in the past. She at last understood Shea's feelings of inadequacy at the time, also accepting that he was not the kind of man who spoke of his inner feelings. But she was secure

Shea had been hers since the day they had met. She remembered their love–making with a sweet lingering tenderness that she could always treasure. In his brief bout of insecurity he may have given his body to Rachel, but she had always had his heart.

"I'll think we'll spend a weekend or two up there during the spring, but that's all. I couldn't bear to sell the cabin or the land. It's part of us and Shea's there."

"I hope that you don't go for long. And don't do it until you're strong enough, Emma."

"Well, I haven't made up my mind yet. I have to talk to Kate and see how she feels about it." She sighed. "Anyway, past that, I need to have some-thing to do when Kate is at school. I'm bored silly around this house every day. I'm thinking about expanding my baking business and renting a building from Jason. I've lived off the land all my life and there isn't much call for a woman good with a bow and arrow in these parts." Both women laughed. "I'd like to teach, but Easthope already has Prudence Ginsberg. I've offered myself as a substitute teacher should she need me, but that would be now and then." Emma's memory was drawn back to the days when she taught the Cheyenne to read and write. It was a gratifying time in her life. "But I have to find a way to make more money. Living in town costs more than I realized."

Rachel helped herself to a slice of Emma's spice cake on a nearby table. "I'm going to go ahead and spoil my dinner. You should sell this, Emma. It's delicious," she said through a mouthful of cake.

"Do you think that people would still buy baked goods from me after what I did? People are probably calling me The Madwoman of Easthope, or some-thing like that. They might think I'm dangerous."

"You're dangerous to our waistlines!" Rachel quipped. "But what do you have to worry about? When you marry Jason, you'll be a very wealthy woman."

"I'm worried. He said he still wanted me, but we haven't discussed the wedding plans since I got out of the hospital. He's been very polite and attentive, but I can't shake the feeling that he's doing the honorable thing. Maybe he feels like he can't back out. I should give him an out."

"Don't do it," Rachel warned. "You have to understand that he's been through it, right along with you. He came by after he took you to the hospital. He had been crying. He felt so guilty for what he and Stuart had to do to you.

And he had a lot of guilt for slipping about the other thing," she said, referring to the discovery about Randall. "Jason would never, never hurt you. You don't seem to realize it, but you're quite a catch, even Shea had said so." Rachel's voice faltered. "I'm sorry. I should not have said that."

"It's okay, Rachel. Don't live the rest of your life watching everything you say around me. It's all right to talk about him. It may seem strange to you, but I don't mind it so much. You saw a part of him I never did and in a way, I'm envious of that. He always tried to be strong around me, or maybe I made him think he had to be. He never quite opened up to me until he was dying."

Emma leaned across the sofa and hugged Rachel. "Once you get used to it, the hospital's not so bad. It's sort of peaceful—away from all the daily worries."

"I just might check in there someday. I could use a few weeks away from the kids!" Rachel laughed.

Chapter Twenty–One

Emma's illness was fading from her day–to–day concerns. However, it took her days to get up the nerve to ask Jason about the wedding. He looked relieved when she mentioned it; he said that he didn't want to put any pressure on her so soon, but they began planning for the ceremony and the dinner to follow. This gave Emma purpose, something tangible to hold onto.

Christmas dinner was at Beck House with Jason and the Barlows. Before Emma served the main course, Jason spoke to everyone at the table. Even the children stilled to listen.

"Em, seeing the courage you showed in putting your life back together made me think that I should do the same. I've been grieving over the hard life that my mother endured with my father." Everyone looked surprised but Emma because he had never spoken of it to anyone but her. "The strength you showed as you faced your problems gave me the resolve to face mine. You give me courage, dear lady." He raised his glass to her and his gaze rarely left her for the rest of the evening.

Later, Rachel cornered Jason in the kitchen. "I had no idea your mother and father didn't get along. All of you did a good job of covering it up."

Jason was not ready to confide the whole story to Rachel, but said, "My father was a hard man and few people know what my mother went through. I got scared for Emma when I saw her slipping away. It was too much like my mother—one face in public, another in private."

"I think that Emma is going to be all right Jason. She has you to love her," Rachel said.

Wedding plans went ahead. With Kate back in school after the holidays, Jason renewed his 'lunch hour' visits with Emma. Their bodies entwined as one. Emma had never felt more loved or secure since those early days making love with Shea in the privacy of their lodge in the Indian Territory.

In April, Emma left Kate with Caleb while she and Rachel went to Seattle to buy her trousseau. They spent the week at a very posh hotel, courtesy of

Jason, awaiting the alterations to the wedding gown. Jason had fresh roses delivered to Emma each day; each bunch had a loving note tucked inside.

Emma's dress was beige satin overlaid in Brussels lace, with leg–of–mutton sleeves buttoned with pearls. The train was short, for she was practical, knowing that the wedding would be outdoors. The headpiece was of lace and pearls with a short veil that fell to her waist. The shoes were soft beige calfskin that buttoned high on the ankle.

Rachel wanted her to get the matching parasol. "The wedding will be outdoors and the bride should not be sunburned," she said.

"Jason is going to be billed for the dress as it is," Emma said. "I shouldn't get carried away spending his money."

"He wants you to have the prettiest dress that you can find. Get the parasol. It won't put him in the poor house, you know," Rachel said

Emma shone when she put on the full ensemble the day it was delivered to the hotel. "Rachel, should I wear this? This is my second wedding. I heard that it's not proper to wear a wedding gown the second time around."

"Nonsense," she said, fluffing the veil and skirt for full effect. "You look stunning. Besides, this is Jason's only wedding and you should look the part of the blushing bride."

The day of their return, Jason and Kate met Emma and Rachel at the stage in front of Murdock's. For the first time Jason kissed Emma in public, blushing as he did so.

"Hello, my love. Thank you for the roses and your romantic notes. I missed you," she whispered. She leaned down and hugged Kate. "How was your week at the Barlows'?"

"It was all right. When can I see your dress, Momma?" she asked, full of impatience.

"As soon as we get home," she promised. Emma waved good-bye to Rachel.

Jason took the arm of his two favorite females, leading them to the new carriage he had bought while Emma and Rachel were away. He loaded up the many boxes and drove them home, glad to have Emma back.

Spring moved across the small mountain town and by late April, rains melted the snow. Jason was troubled as the melt had raised the level of the river. There was some flooding, but no homes were damaged. But it made hard work for the mill crews, trying to corral the logs in the overflowing pond next to the mill.

Still, the earth was rebounding from a long winter freeze. Carpets of wildflowers coated the meadows and the trees gained strength in the long sunny days, spreading deep green shadows over the land. At his expense, Jason had the main roads through town paved with brick and cobblestone. Easthope was noisier from street traffic, but there was much less dirt and sawdust floating through the town.

Accompanied by Jason, Emma and Kate were up at the cabin one bright Sunday afternoon.

"Jason," Emma said, taking in the emerald meadow. "I talked it over with Kate and we decided to spend some time up here. It's always so lovely here with the flowers and the warm days and cool nights. I think that I can cope up here for a weekend now and then."

"But I thought that you decided to wait until after the wedding, so I can be here with you."

"I need to be here once in a while, I guess, to work out the feelings I still have. But I feel good. I know I can do it."

"Okay. You do what you think is best," he said with reluctance, "but I'll be up here every day to check on you both."

"I may have trouble keeping Kate up here for long. She spends so much time at the Barlows', they may have to adopt her. A few days up here now and then will be good for her."

Jason made it plain that he did not want her to go, but Emma's stubborn streak caused him to relent.

However, the matter of weekend visits to the cabin was decided for Emma two weeks later. During a violent thunderstorm, lightning apparently hit the cabin, burning it to the ground. The next morning, a trickle of smoke could be seen from town. The townsfolk were afraid of a wild fire. But Emma knew the location of the cabin so well and her heart sank. She knew that the cabin was gone long before Jason took her and Kate up the trail the next morning. As she picked through the blackened ruins, her reaction was not what he expected.

"Maybe I should start going to church more often. I think God is telling me to stay put in town, eh?"

"Looks like it," he answered, then sneezed.

"Are you feeling all right, Jason?" Emma asked.

"Just a little cold." He sneezed again. "Good thing we got all of your things out last year. I would feel terrible if you lost anything precious to you."

"I have everything precious." She smiled and took his hand. "I have Kate and you."

Jason grinned with relief, for he himself had burned down the cabin the night of the storm. He knew of Emma's desire to return there and feared losing her to illness once again. He knew that he was being selfish, but he loved her and needed her close by.

The day before, the opportunity had presented itself. The storm rumbled all afternoon and broke just after dark. Jason slipped out of his house and rode as fast as he dared to the cabin. The storm brought howling winds and horizontal rain, making the trail slippery and treacherous. Jason could only see a few feet ahead as he urged on his skittish horse. Twice, large tree branches blew down across his path, making the horse shy and rear up. At last he reached the cabin. As lightning flashed overhead, he lit a torch and tossed it onto the roof. He watched the cabin burn, hoping that it would not ignite the surrounding trees. Despite the soaking rain, the wind fanned the flames, burning the cabin to the grassy earth. He had found a way to keep Emma near him and as he rode away from the cabin he had built so long ago, he harbored no regret. He arrived home, soaked to the skin, and came in through the front door so Emma would not by chance see him. He nursed a head cold as a consequence. And Emma always believed that providence had taken her cabin in the storm.

Although the cabin was gone, they still visited Shea's grave often, for Emma was resolved to give Kate all the time she needed to mourn her father. They had always been isolated living in the cabin, but Emma did not want Kate to feel isolated in town. Kate's first home had been the cabin and Emma would give her all the time she needed to grow away.

The days leading up to the June seventh wedding were bliss for Emma and Jason. The townspeople anticipated the lavish wedding of the Widow Hawkshadow and Jason Beck, one of the richest men in Washington state.

They decided to live in Beck House after the wedding. Jason was glad to be returning to a familiar place, and, after much soul-searching, was able to make peace with his unhappy memories. The fact that both his parents had died there, after years of turmoil in that place, had spooked him for years, but Emma and Kate's presence in the house brightened every corner and pushed away the old ghosts. He was glad to leave his large, echoing house as well and sold it to his superintendent at Camp Three, Kent Barry and his family.

Jason took Emma's advice to initiate a truce between himself and his brother. He wrote a long letter to Karl asking if they could put the past behind them, and inviting him to the wedding. To his surprise, Karl wired back that he and his family would come.

A wedding lunch was planned and flowers were ordered from Millersburg. Emma employed a local seamstress to create a pale blue floor–length dress for Kate, who would act as flower girl, a role that the child took very seriously. She practiced around the house, perfecting her part by scattering wood chips in lieu of flower petals along the hallways. Emma was at first perturbed, constantly sweeping the floors, but indulged her child.

On a warm Sunday afternoon, Jason lounged with Emma on her back porch. He had just returned from services and looked handsome in his suit and the carved ivory string tie that Emma had given him for Christmas one year. They were discussing how to set up both of their backyards for the outdoor wedding ceremony and the dinner to follow.

"I think the ceremony should be at the far end of the yard under the trees, where there is more shade. The caterers can leave space in between the rows of tables for me to walk down the aisle," Emma said.

"Fine," Jason said. "So in my yard we'll have the ovens and stoves. And the beer kegs and smoking tables should be in my yard, too, all right?"

"Okay with me. I just hope the majority of the guests are upwind of all that smoke!" she joked. "The gift tables can be set up at this end of the yard. That way, we have a large area for dancing. What do you think?"

He nodded his approval. "Now to the most important thing. What about the honeymoon, Em?"

"Oh!" she exclaimed. "I never had a honeymoon. It completely slipped my mind. I wouldn't know where to begin, do you?"

"You got me."

A sly smile lit her face. "Surprise me."

June seventh was two weeks away. Emma's pulse quickened when she realized that her new life was going to become a reality. Kate was excited, trying on her pretty blue dress and her new leather shoes dyed to match. She sashayed around the house, twirling round and round. Emma had to make her take it off lest she ruin it.

"I can't wait, Momma. I'm getting a new daddy." She then became thoughtful and watched her mother for a reaction as she asked, "If Daddy's watching from heaven, do you think he minds you marrying Jason?"

She hugged her. "Your father would've wanted this. Jason was his best friend. He knew that Jason would always care about us."

Two days before the wedding, Jason's brother Karl and his wife Glenda arrived with their four rambunctious children. Emma watched them arrive from her parlor window, but did not come out to meet them. She had promised Jason that she would meet them later on in the day. She saw much tentativeness between the brothers as they shook hands. Karl resembled Jason with the same color hair, but that was where the resemblance ended. Karl slicked back his hair and was built much lighter and lankier than Jason. He wore a very nice suit and hat. Glenda was a small woman with dark hair held in a tight bun. Emma could not see her face well, but she looked somewhat peaked, in her opinion.

Karl and Glenda's children, two boys and two girls, ranged in age from seventeen to eleven. They were all dark-haired like their diminutive mother. Without a word of introduction or permission, they bounded down off the rented carriage and immediately pounded up the stairs into Jason's house. Emma was very surprised when Glenda began unloading the carriage after meeting Jason. To Emma's way of thinking, the children should have helped with the luggage. When Jason saw what Glenda was doing, he immediately shooed her away and pressed Karl to help him.

The brothers' reunion was awkward at first. There was leftover tension from their turbulent childhood, in particular, the day that Jason beat the tar out of Karl and his father for shoving his mother.

Leaving Glenda and the children to settle in, Jason took Karl up the mountain to tour the logging camps. Once alone, and with many memories and conflicting emotions, Karl began to talk. He confessed to Jason that he had moved to Tacoma after college to escape the tensions in the family. Then he spoke of his fear of their father.

"I was afraid to stand up to father. When he beat us, he was out of control."

Jason remembered the beatings. His father's razor strap had left many welt marks on Jason and Karl. The beatings, even for small infractions, were always severe.

Karl continued. "I'm ashamed to say it. To save myself, I joined in with father against mother. I thought that would keep him from beating me, and it did in the end. I'll never know how you got through those beatings, especially the time he threw you down the stairs when you were thirteen. You got back up and faced him down. I acted like a monster. I've had to deal with a lot of guilt all these years, believe me. Every time I wanted to write to you and explain, I chickened out. I realized, too late, the cruelty mother had endured and that I caused some of it. I was terrified of father. Your example in the kitchen that day taught me a lesson, but it took me a very long time to really understand it. I ran from all of you. But you were stronger than me. You had the courage to stay."

"Sounds like you're becoming the brother I always wanted." Jason baited him a little, which was not in his nature, but he harbored some lingering resentment toward Karl. He stepped back from the old anger. "I'm glad to know that you didn't hate Mom. She loved you."

"I know that now. But I think about how cruel I was to her. I did not even allow her to see her own grandchildren." His voice choked with emotion. "I realized that I had become like father. Opportunistic, cruel. That's hard to live with. I hope that you can forgive me someday."

"We're brothers," Jason said with a broad smile. "And I'm glad that you came. Wait until you meet Emma."

Karl gave Jason a sidelong glance. "Emma—yes. Glenda told me that she had read some newspaper articles years ago about her and her Indian husband. We were both real surprised—no, I'll be honest with you for a change—shocked—that you got involved with a woman who lived with Indians. Don't get me wrong, I mean, I don't know the lady."

His words perturbed Jason. He knew what Karl meant—that Emma was wild, loose, and dirty from her association with Shea and the Cheyenne. Karl would never know all that she suffered to just have a little love in her life. Unwilling to halt the healing that had begun between himself and his only known relative, Jason squelched his anger.

"Then you know the hardships that Emma endured. But there are many other things she experienced that were never in the papers. Emma is the strongest, smartest, most loving woman I've ever known—and a stunning beauty. You weren't fortunate like I was to see her and Shea together. They loved each other with such intensity. And their daughter, Katherine, is remarkable. She's a lot like Shea—wise beyond her years, intelligent, and stubborn—in the best way." Their eyes met. "Karl, I love Emma. I cannot imagine my life without her. The good people of this town accepted her, Shea, and Katherine. If you do one thing while you're here, give her a chance."

Karl looked embarrassed. "I didn't mean it that way. I always thought that you would end up marrying one of the town girls."

Jason allowed himself a smile. "They never interested me. I always knew that I'd find someone and was content to wait. When I first met Emma and Shea, Emma was pregnant with Katherine. She accepted my friendship right off. Shea took some time, but he became the truest friend I ever had. The first time that I saw Emma, I was infatuated with her. After Shea died, it took me more than eighteen months to get up the courage to propose to her. We were such good friends by then; I didn't know if she would have me. What she's experienced outstrips anything I've learned by living in a small town like Easthope. By nineteen, she was already years older than me. You'll like her, I know you will."

Jason and Karl talked for many hours that day as they drove through the hills. They sometimes rehashed the past, but managed to talk things out, adult to adult. Both of them were older and wiser. Seeing the logging camps and how Jason had grown the business over the years, Karl was impressed with his younger brother.

That evening, Jason held a barbecue in his back yard. Emma liked Karl and Glenda very much and although she felt that they overindulged their boisterous children, she was glad to at last meet someone from Jason's family. He had always seemed so lonely in Easthope. She resolved that he would never be lonely again.

The day before the wedding, Karl, Glenda, and their children took a carriage ride through the hills. Kate was at the Barlows', Jason was at the mill, and Emma was home. She stood in her bedroom, admiring her wedding gown hanging on the door, touching it and hoping that it would not look too big on her, for she had lost a lot of weight from pre–wedding nerves. Smiling and humming to herself, she replaced the paper covering and carried it into the adjoining dressing room.

Answering a knock at the back door a short while later, she opened it to Jason.

"Are we alone?" he said as he rushed in, sweeping her up in his arms. He kicked the door shut with his foot. She grinned, flicking her head toward the stairs. He carried her upstairs and made love to her all afternoon. He was gentle, tender, and passionate.

Soon, he heard the carriage carrying Karl's family crunching along the gravel path to the stables. Jason quickly dressed and splashed water on his face at the washstand. He came back to her and kissed her as she lay nude in bed. "Oh, I hate to leave you looking so delicious lying there. But I'll see you tomorrow. Noon, right?"

"One o'clock!" she smiled.

Chapter Twenty–Two

Emma rose early on Saturday, June seventh. She went to the window that overlooked her back yard and opened it, relishing a warm, gusty breeze that fluttered through the lace curtains. She imagined the two–hundred guests that would soon fill her yard to celebrate her marriage to Jason. If the day looked like rain the fallback venue for the wedding was to be the church hall, but she was glad to see the deep blue sky studded with high clouds.

Kate was up early too, after battling with Emma the night before because she had been too excited to sleep. She shuffled into Emma's room rubbing her eyes with a chubby fist.

"Momma, are you scared about today?" she asked.

"Just a little nervous. Are you scared?"

"No," she lied. "I thought you were."

Emma said, "You'll do just fine, honey. Just do as you practiced and don't worry about it. I want you to have fun today."

"I don't remember—who married you and Daddy?"

"The Cheyenne medicine man, Bridge."

"What did you wear that day?" Kate asked, touching Emma's gown hanging on the dressing room door.

Emma's memory went back to that wonderful morning that Red Leaf Woman lent her the old white deerskin wedding dress. She could still conjure its scent, its incredible softness against her skin, and how she felt when she was led to Shea to be married to him. She bit back tears for a moment at the memory. She sat upon the window seat and described the deerskin dress to Kate and explained how the ceremonies were different but in the end meant the same thing. Kate sat beside Emma and laid her head on her mother's shoulder. They enjoyed a quiet moment together.

Emma thought about what the day would bring. Her life was about to change for the better and she had left her shadows in the past. She thought of Jason. Although her love for him was just as deep as it had been for Shea, it was different. She was not as dependent or subservient as she had been with Shea. She was a full–grown woman now and although she owned little, Jason encouraged her to keep the baking business after the wedding; but she would never have to worry about money again. Jason was very wealthy, but she had never once seen him lord it over anyone; in fact the reverse had occurred. In truth, she avoided any discussion of money; she had no idea how much he had. All Jason ever wanted was to be treated like everyone else and he fought his autocratic image in his own quiet way. But in bed with Emma, this gentle man was passionate, commanding, and hopelessly addicted to her. A small smile played about her lips as she thought of his brief, passionate visit the day before.

Rachel burst in later, her job today to dress the bride and see to all the final details of the ceremony. She was dressed in a crisp cotton dress of yellow and blue stripes, with white crocheted cuffs and collar. She looked like the sun and the sky, bright and warm.

Emma and Rachel laughed as Emma struggled into the corset. "My gosh, this corset is so tight." Emma had rarely worn one and shifted uncomfortably, trying to fit her breasts into it. Kate giggled from her perch on the window seat.

"Let's make room for food, all right?" Rachel teased as she tugged at the corset, loosening it.

"Ah, that's better." Emma rolled her eyes. "I can breathe now."

When Emma donned her wedding gown, Rachel's eyes welled up. "I'll never make it through the ceremony without making a fool of myself. You look breathtaking. Look at yourself," she said, turning Emma toward the full–length mirror.

Emma had to admit that she looked lovely, dreamlike, she mused. The corset nipped her slim waistline and made the gown fit much better. She needed help buttoning the twenty pearl buttons adorning the sleeves, so Rachel took one arm and Kate took the other.

Rachel pinned up Emma's hair into a chignon. "I wish you only happiness." The two women smiled at each other in the mirror. Such a bond had existed between them both from the start that Emma felt that Rachel was her sister. Rachel felt the same and although she harbored guilt over her brief affair with Shea, she was sure that Emma had forgiven her.

"Kate, go wash up and comb your hair. Rachel will be in soon to help you dress."

Kate hit the floor running. "Finally!"

It was eleven o'clock when the various elements of the wedding started coming together in the yards. Rachel was busy with Kate, so Emma cherished the time alone. A wooden arch covered with white roses was first to go up as Emma sat in her gown on the window seat, watching from behind the veil of the lace curtains that puffed with the breeze. Tables were set up along with chairs borrowed from the church hall. A wide aisle was left down the middle of the tables, just as Emma specified. Torches were set up, ringing the yards to provide light throughout the evening. The caterer arrived to set up his ovens and stoves; the bustling and shouting made Emma want to go out and general the situation, but she resisted the urge and stayed put.

She calmed down when she saw Jason, strikingly handsome in his new dark blue suit and tie, come out of his house next door. Caleb, his best man, came out with him and followed Jason across the yard. Emma saw Jason's business side for the first time and was impressed; in mere minutes, everything was coordinated. He was commanding yet understanding of everyone's needs. Cooks began filling the ovens with dozens of chickens; trays and plates were stacked nearby, ready to serve the meals. The tables were topped with crisp blue cloths and vases of flowers. The band arrived and began to tune their instruments, and the photographer arrived and set up his tripod and stacks of photographic plates.

In the middle of this glorious chaos, Emma, still hidden behind the lace, saw Jason gaze up at her window and smile. She wanted to pull aside the curtain and wave, but it would be bad luck and unseemly. She returned his smile even though he could not see her.

The Reverend Thomas then arrived and he and Jason became engaged in a serious conversation about the ceremony as Jason and he walked around Emma's yard.

Kate banged into the room in her blue floor–length dress and landed on the window seat beside Emma. She pulled back the curtains and looked into the yard. "There's Jason. Hi Jason!" she called. Jason's head came up and he smiled and waved. He could see Emma, barely visible behind the lace, and winked for her benefit. Kate wanted to go out onto the balcony, but Emma wanted her to remain indoors until the ceremony. Kate was jumpy. "How much longer, Momma?"

"I'm not sure. My watch is on the bureau."

Kate skipped over to the dresser. "It's twelve–thirty already! A half–hour left!"

Emma quelled a thrill of nervousness. She went to Kate's room to find Rachel putting the finishing touches on her hair. "It's twelve–thirty. It's almost time."

"Oh!" Rachel exclaimed. "I better get Caleb and the boys working as ushers! The guests will be here any minute. I'll send Stuart up as soon as he arrives. And I'll bring up the flowers as soon as I can corner the florist." She trotted down the stairs as fast as her stiff crinoline allowed.

"How many people are coming today?" Kate asked.

"Just about the entire town, sweetie. That's about two hundred or more. I invited the Yakimas, but I don't know if they'll come."

"Why?"

She tried to explain it in terms that Kate would understand. "I think they're bashful about being around other people. It's not that they aren't happy for us, but some people will be uncomfortable if they come."

"That's stupid, Momma."

"I know, dear."

"I wish that I was born sooner. Then I would know what it's like to live with Indians before the whites came," Kate said. "It must've been very exciting!"

Emma smiled at her girl and did not tell her the truth of how hard a life it was. She wanted her daughter to keep her innocence a while longer. Life held enough trials as it was.

Back in Emma's bedroom with Kate beside her on the window seat, they watched the guests arriving. In a break with tradition, there was no 'bride's' or 'groom's' side of the aisle. Emma and Jason felt that such a distinction would be difficult to make as their lives were so intertwined with the people in the town. Kate watched, naming those she knew and commenting on how handsome Randall Barlow looked in his suit as he performed the role of junior usher for the young girls. Emma pulled her daughter onto her lap.

"No! Rachel said not to sit on your lap because I'll wrinkle your dress."

"I don't care. Sit with me." She wrapped her arms around Kate.

Stuart arrived at twelve forty–five, dapper in his brown pinstripe suit and flushed with pride, for he was to give the bride away. He kissed Emma's cheek as he beheld her in her wedding gown. "You're a vision." His compliment was sincere. "You're one extraordinary woman, Emma and I'm proud that you chose me to walk you down the aisle." She hugged him and a tear spilled down her cheek. "Ah, now, don't waste your tears on an old man."

"You've been a father to me. You've saved my life. I love you and thank you for all you have done for us." The face of her father moved through her memory. She thought how proud he would be this day. Even her mother would approve, she knew. She became distracted for a moment, thinking of their graves out on the prairie. If they had lived, her life would have turned out so much differently. She resolved to someday return to the little soddy and if new owners had not obliterated the graveyard, she would create a proper resting place for her lost family. Now she would have the means to do it. All that had happened brought her to this time, this place and to her wonderful Jason. *Too bad I'm not religious*, Emma thought. *I would like to thank God, but I haven't been a member of the club.* Guts, determination, and self–preservation had seen her through. That was a kind of religion, she mused. Maybe her beliefs were not conventional, but neither was she.

As Emma, Kate, and Stuart descended the stairs and went out the front door, Rachel ran up on the porch, winded and excited.

"It's time! Everyone's seated. Kate, here's your basket and your flowers, Emma. Best of luck!" Rachel ran back down the stairs and around to the back yard to signal Reverend Thomas that the bride was ready.

After peering round back, Stuart motioned Emma and Kate forward. The sun was high and warm upon Emma's face. She paused a moment, looking west of town to where her home had once been high up on the mountain. In the privacy of her thoughts, she spoke to Shea: *I am happy. Watch over us, my dear Shea.*

At Stuart's signal, the band began to play. As Emma came around the house she beheld the crowd which rose at the sight of her.

Stuart patted her hand. "This is it," he said, beaming.

With a quick glance around, Emma saw all the people and was heartened at the turnout, but worried that there would not be enough food. But she pushed the thought aside and concentrated on her walk down the aisle. After Rachel started down the aisle, Emma nudged Kate and sent her to the cherished task of scattering the flower petals, a job that she performed with grace and poise.

Emma looked for Jason at the other end of the aisle. The crowd obscured him but she knew that he was there, waiting for her.

The crowd seemed to melt away and even though she heard the oohs and ahhs as she passed by, her focus was on Jason as he stepped to the center of the aisle and beheld his radiant bride. His collar–length wavy hair shone in the bright day. He looked awed as she drew near, then they came together at last. His arm slid around hers as if it had always been there, and in a way it always had.

Reverend Thomas began the ceremony and his words faded away as Emma and Jason gazed at each other. The reverend made the most of his large audience and the fact that he was officiating at the wedding of one of the wealthiest men in Washington. Then suddenly, the vows were upon them.

Jason's voice was soft as he replied, "I do."

When Emma's turn came moments later, her eyes held his as she spoke the words, "I do."

Jason placed a gold filigree ring, shaped to fit around her garnet engagement ring, on her finger. She slipped a gold band on his finger. His warm hand held hers as the service concluded.

"You may kiss the bride," Reverend Thomas said.

The kiss lingered longer than propriety allowed and the guests smiled and chuckled as Emma and Jason remained locked in an embrace.

"Ladies and gentlemen, I present to you Mr. and Mrs. Jason Beck," Reverend Thomas said in closing.

Then, Jason took Emma's and Kate's hands in his. The new family walked up the aisle to lively applause.

Emma and Jason were mobbed as people congratulated them and an impromptu receiving line formed. Jason kept a tight grip on her in the crowd, his strength reassuring as people swirled around them.

Shortly, the crowd broke up and lines formed at the punch table, the sweet table, and several tables set up especially for the children with favorite foods and games to amuse them. This was Kate's contribution to the wedding. From her vantage point next to Emma, she could see the other children swarming around the tables. She ran off to join in, or rather, not miss out on anything.

It took a while for Rachel and Caleb to reach them through the crowd. Caleb pumped Jason's hand, repeating congratulations, over and over.

Rachel's hug took Emma's breath away. "I know now why you didn't want a train! It would've been filthy by now!" she exclaimed. "I'm so happy for you both!"

The men quickly found the beer kegs and smoking tables in Jason's yard. Later, the ovens in Jason's yard opened and the smell of roasted chicken filled the air.

Then, Jason looked around and pulled Emma away to the front of the house. He carried her up the steps and over the threshold and deposited her in the front parlor. He wrapped his arms around her. "I wanted a minute for just you and me." His kiss was tender and lingering. "Today is the happiest day of my life. I will be a good husband to you and a good father to Kate. I promise to love you always and care for you and Kate." She fell into him in a long embrace as they both savored the moments alone. "We better get back to our guests, Mrs. Beck."

She smiled, extending her hand. He took it.

As they rounded the side of the house, Emma spotted Lame White Deer and several other Yakimas standing nearby on the street. Lame White Deer came to her. "I am happy for you this day. Live long together."

"Thank you. Will you all please stay and have something to eat?"

He shook his head, glancing to the crowd in her yard. "Thank you, Mrs. Beck, but we must go." With that, he nodded and walked away with the others.

As she watched them depart, her gaze went up the mountain.

"Are you thinking about Shea?" Jason asked.

"Would you be upset if I said yes?"

"Of course not. I kind of feel like he's here with us."

She kissed him. "I love you, Jason."

Scattered applause greeted the newlyweds as they reentered the yard and greeted more guests. Hundreds of faces passed before Emma in a blur. She felt surreal, floating.

As they worked their way to their table, Emma was astounded at the number of presents heaped on the gift tables. The caterer was setting up another table to handle the overflow.

The wedding feast was the subject of admiration for years. Fresh fruit compotes and cold leek soup preceded roasted chicken with potatoes and free–flowing wine, champagne, brandy, beer, and punch.

The day was a dizzying whirl for Emma, who was transcending her past and stepping into her future in mere moments. Jason stayed at her side throughout the afternoon. Later, after desserts of assorted ices and cakes, she and Jason danced their first dance as man and wife. Both of them thought back to the dance at the church hall—and what had transpired afterward. Jason held her close during the waltz. She relaxed against him, moving with him with ease and lightness of step.

Emma and Jason made sure to visit each table, thanking every guest. In the evening, Jason joined the men in his yard. They drank apple brandy and beer, made many toasts, and smoked many cigars.

Rachel found Emma off alone, watching the children playing kick ball at the far end of the huge back yard. "You all right?" she asked.

Emma wore a small smile. "This has been an incredible day. Thank you for all you did."

"Anything for you, Emma. Say, has Jason told you where you're going for the honeymoon?"

"Not yet. It's a surprise. And I've used all my persuasive powers to wheedle it out of him, but nothing worked."

"Why are you over here by yourself?"

"I'm just enjoying watching the kids play. I've never really taken the time to step back and watch how Kate is with other people. She wants to control things. I can't say that I blame her after the life she's led so far."

"She's just fine, Emma. Look at her." Kate was now organizing a rather intricate game of catch, explaining how it would work and how to win. "She's a leader. Her future will be interesting."

"I'm just thankful that she's come through the last few years so well. She's so strong, so much like Shea."

Rachel touched Emma's shoulder. "You were so lucky to have Shea in your life."

Emma sighed. "Shea gave me much more than I ever gave him. It wasn't easy for him to leave his people and all he knew. He put me into this world so I would never be alone."

Rachel wiped away a tear. "He truly loved you, you know."

"I know," Emma said, giving her an affectionate hug. "If I had one wish today, I would want my parents here to see all this. They would've been so proud of me."

"I'm sure they were proud of you," Rachel assured her. "Look, don't dwell on things. Go find that handsome husband of yours and enjoy yourself."

Emma shook off her mood and went to find Jason. When she passed through the crowd, Jason's eyes found her as she came toward him. His look of love pushed away all other thoughts except him.

It was a starlit night with a soft, warm breeze. Around ten, Kate changed into her play clothes and with her overnight satchel in hand, worked her way over to Emma and Jason.

Emma hugged her tight, kissing her. "Good night, my Kate. You were perfect today. I love you so very much. We'll see you tomorrow. Be good at Rachel's tonight."

"Good–night, Jason," Kate hesitated. "Uh, what should I call you now?"

Emma had never thought about this. From her early childhood, Emma and Shea had allowed Kate to call Jason by his first name. Emma looked to Jason and shrugged.

He grinned. "Jason will do just fine." He knew full well of Kate's continuing attachment to her father and did not want to intrude upon his memory by being called daddy. He kissed her cheek in farewell. Kate soon found Helen and the two of them ran off to find Rachel and Caleb.

The revelers stayed as long as the beer and wine flowed. The last of them departed near midnight. Breaking with tradition again, Emma and Jason stayed until the very end of the celebration.

Late that evening, Emma paused on the back porch as the tables, chairs, and ovens were dismantled and carted off. Jason swayed a little beside her, a bit drunk.

"Thank you for marrying me," she whispered. He smiled and slipped his arm around her as she lay her head on his broad shoulder. "Maybe we should open the gifts now."

"Tomorrow," Jason said, tugging her indoors.

Their love–making that night had a new freedom as they coupled as husband and wife. Jason was creative and energetic as he loved her again and again. She clung to him, delighting in his passion and in her own. They dozed through the wee hours as they lay entwined, sated, and tranquil. In the early morning, Emma rose and while showering, turned to find Jason in the tub with her. He took her again to her slippery delight.

Kate returned from the Barlows mere moments after Emma and Jason had dressed. After a quick kiss, they came downstairs.

"Sleepy heads!" Kate commented. "It's almost lunch time!"

That afternoon, Karl's family departed. Jason hugged his brother in parting. Karl looked surprised at Jason's gesture, but hugged his brother back. "I'll write, Jason, I promise." He looked to Jason and Emma. "Best of luck to both of you. Hope to see you again."

The next day, Jason began moving his belongings into the house. Many of his workers helped, curious to get inside Beck House, as it was still called. The reality of the place somewhat wiped out the myth, but they were impressed nonetheless. Emma had to let Jason confront his own demons as his possessions again became part of the spacious house.

The following day, they were to depart for the honeymoon. Where they were going was still a secret, and Emma could barely contain her excitement. She kept asking what clothing to bring, trying to get a clue to their destination, but with a sly grin, Jason told her to bring a little of everything. But more than anything, she looked forward to being alone with Jason for the next month. Rachel came to collect Kate and bade them good–bye.

On the way to the Millersburg train depot, the stage had to pass by the hospital where Emma's darkest hours had been spent while she fought to rebuild her life. She had come to avoid going near that part of town whenever possible. Today, she leaned out the window of the carriage, waiting for any lingering demons to resurface. Few did.

"It doesn't look as I remembered. It seemed much bigger and darker before," she commented.

As they boarded the train in Millersburg the next day, Jason revealed that their destination was San Francisco. Emma had never been to a big city before and hugged him, delighted.

The next month was a whirlwind in the great city. The hotel room that Jason reserved was opulent and very spacious. Each meal was at a fine restaurant and Emma thought that she would burst from all the rich food. They toured the city, marveling at its sheer size and grandeur. The parks were picturesque and they spent many hours strolling arm in arm, exploring all sorts of shops and museums.

Emma had never seen an ocean, so Jason hired a private coach to take them for a tour of the coast. She loved the sweet salt air. They convinced the reluctant driver to go down to the beach and Emma pulled off her shoes and stockings and waded in the water with Jason. Like a young girl, she laughed and kicked up the spray, her hair trailing behind her. By the time the day was over, Emma had collected a pile of shells and driftwood from the beach.

In the night in their private suite, they slept little in the bloom of marriage and desire. Each time Jason loved her, she felt whole, complete. He was an inexhaustible lover and she drowned in his passion.

Making sure not to neglect Kate, they sent her postcards and gifts while they were away. They purchased still more gifts for her and for the Barlows, to be delivered upon their return.

One afternoon they toured more shops and were awed at the myriad of goods there. San Francisco was the West's gateway to the Orient and there were such wonderful things to be had. At one shop window, Emma spied a china vanity set which held several bottles and boxes on a matching tray. The set was hand–painted with delicate pink and yellow roses.

"Oh, that's nice. Do you think Kate would like it?"

"She'd love it," Jason agreed. "Buy it."

Emma looked closer at the set though the window, then recoiled when she saw the price tag. "Jason, this is fifty dollars! That's ridiculous. We can't afford it."

"Sure we can, Em. Get it."

"No, it's too much. This trip is costing you enough as it is."

"It's not a problem, Emma."

She continued to protest so Jason took her hand and they walked away a few steps. "Emma, we have plenty of money. You can buy a thousand of them and it wouldn't make a dent."

"Huh?"

He spoke without affectation or pretense. "Emma, with the business doing so well and other investments back east, there is over four million dollars, last time I checked. We can afford anything we want."

Emma staggered back and didn't speak for several moments. "Did I hear you right? You have millions?"

"We," he corrected. "And it's yours to use as you see fit."

The shock reverberated through her entire body. "I thought that you had a few thousand. That's a lot of money to someone like me."

He laughed. "It's true—you can check."

"Jason, I don't want your money. I didn't marry you for that."

He pulled her close to his body and kissed her. "I know why you married me!"

She blushed crimson. "We're in public!" she teased.

It took several minutes to get over the shock but Jason convinced her that the vanity set would make a great gift for Kate, especially since the store owner offered to put Katherine's name on each piece in gold paint. Emma joked that she thought she would faint, spending what was to her a year's money on something so frivolous.

In the hotel one evening, Emma dressed in a new lace and satin gown and set next to Jason on a sofa. She admired the gift for Kate. "You were right in making me get this, Jason, but it may take time for me to get over the price tag! But I'm a little worried. How am I going to manage the finances? My mother tried everything, but I was never good at mathematics."

"Em, I have accountants to take care of that for me. One is here in San Francisco, one's in New York, and Allison Carruthers' daughter Juliet takes care of my books at the mill. I have stashes of cash hidden around and there's plenty in the bank in Easthope. My father may have had his faults, but he told me long ago not to put all my money in banks or investments. In fact, you've been sleeping on a small fortune and didn't even know it."

"You mean the mattress at home? It's stuffed with money?"

Jason nodded, laughing.

Too soon, the month was up and they boarded the stage for the railway station. "I loved it here, but I miss Easthope. The city is wonderful but all the hustle and noise gets to me. I used to think Easthope was too noisy. I was sure wrong about that. I can't wait to get home," Emma said.

"I know what you mean. I want to smell freshly cut wood again. I miss it," Jason agreed. "After we get home, I would like to treat Rachel and Caleb to a trip like this. They're always there to care for Kate. After we're settled, we can take their children into our home and let them get away alone."

She was glad that Jason said 'our home.' She realized that he had conquered his anxiety about moving back into the house. "That's a terrific idea, but they won't let us pay. I know Rachel and Caleb. They're very proud."

"Leave that to me," Jason assured her.

Kate ran to her mother's arms when she saw Emma and Jason step off the stage in front of Murdock's. "Momma! What did you bring me?"

Rachel laughed. "You spoiled her even though you weren't here. We got all the postcards and gifts you sent—and by express, too. I'm impressed!" She embraced Emma then handed her a large package. "Glad you're home. Your wedding pictures just arrived so I picked them up for you."

"I can't wait to see them. Thank you, Rachel. How was Kate?"

"Wonderful as usual. She, Helen, and Randall spent every minute together. They spent a day at the pond outside of town and came home filthy. I couldn't get the mud stains out of her pinafore."

"No matter. Thank you for taking her in. Oh, this is for you and the family. A small token of appreciation for caring for Kate," Emma said, handing Rachel a large box.

"Oh you didn't have to bring back a gift! We were happy to help." Rachel sat down on the bench outside Murdock's and opened the box. Inside was a silver coffee service and matching tray. She called Caleb over to her, showing him the gleaming silver pieces, each engraved with a stylish *B* for Barlow. She hugged Jason and Emma. "It's the most beautiful thing I've ever seen! Thank you, but you shouldn't have! But I'm glad you did!" Rachel let Caleb return to loading Jason's wagon with the trunks and ushered Emma aside. "Now tell me all about your honeymoon—well, what you can tell me in public. I'll wait until we're alone for the steamy details!" she said close to Emma's ear.

Emma had to suppress a momentary chill, trying to remind herself that Rachel was just the sort of person who made audacious comments. "It was a lovely city. The weather was perfect and we had a wonderful time. We even saw the Pacific ocean and roamed the beach for hours," she answered. Emma had learned her lesson regarding Rachel. She would never tell Rachel the depth and passion of her love for Jason. That was private and would remain so.

That evening, Kate tore into her many gifts, admiring the fine clothes Emma had brought, along with dolls, toys, books, hair combs, perfume, jewelry, and a kaleidoscope. She especially loved the china vanity set with her name painted in gold. The set contained an atomizer, so she filled it with perfume and proceeded to squirt them until Jason and Emma smelled like lavender bushes. Emma tensed as Kate handled the set a little carelessly, but Kate would treasure this gift most of all and would keep it for the rest of her life.

True to his word, Jason persuaded Rachel and Caleb to take a long vacation together the following spring. They chose San Francisco as well, and Jason made sure that they had the best of everything.

But having the three Barlow children around the house quickly got on Emma's nerves. Used to a single child in the house, she found that the demands of three more whittled through her composure. Helen and Randall argued and bickered and Emma felt that she spent her entire day breaking up their fights. Martin brooded and disappeared with his friends for hours, leaving Emma fretting about where he was and what he was doing. Kate seemed to enjoy having the company at first, but Emma noticed that she soon went off by herself for a walk outdoors, or disappeared with a book.

"Momma, when I stay at the Barlow's, I always behave and never fight with anyone. I help clean up and cook meals, too. I'm not tugging on Rachel's sleeve every minute."

Emma grinned. "I'm proud of you, Kate. I'll never have to worry about you. Just understand that all families have a certain way of living. You'll have to make a lot of decisions when you have a family of your own."

"Well, I won't let my kids bicker and fight all the day long!"

Kate had grown into a beauty and, at age fifteen, was the subject of much speculation as to whom she would marry. She was ravishing with long, thick glossy black hair, deep blue eyes and a small lithe figure. Boys were already buzzing around her and she enjoyed the attention.

Emma, who well knew the dangers of marrying young, discouraged potential suitors, but knew that she could not stem the tide forever. She and Jason encouraged her to attend college in order to give her what Emma had never had—choices—and time to grow up and develop her talents and interests.

"You can go to any college you want, even to one in the east. With the new century upon us soon, it's more important than ever that a girl get a good education. The world is changing fast and you have to be prepared for it. Education is the way you can hold your own," Emma told her again and again. Jason encouraged her, too, but secretly hoped that she would make a good match in an eastern college. He saw great potential in the girl, but still harbored certain beliefs about the course a woman's life should take, despite Emma's advice to the contrary.

Each time Jason escorted Emma or Kate in town, he smiled with pride. For the first time in his life he was happy and settled—and it showed.

With her newfound wealth Emma dressed well, employing a woman new to town who was an accomplished seamstress. Choosing patterns from the Harper's Bazaar catalog, Emma and Kate wore fine clothes, some trimmed with imported laces and fur. With her lean figure and height, Emma wore her ensembles with elegance and grace and she soon became the envy of many. She enjoyed her newfound wealth and preferred to order materials through the local millinery. Although the prices were higher sometimes, she wanted to allow local shopkeepers a fair profit. She owed much to the people of Easthope. She never forgot that.

She also kept her baking business, which had grown so big that she was considering hiring help and wanted to open the shop that Jason had offered to her years ago. However, he argued that it was too small so he had a new structure custom–built to her specifications.

Now a legitimate businesswoman, Emma hired a half dozen people to assist her as business increased. She hired a female manager, Juliet Carruthers Allard, the married daughter of Allison and Gale Carruthers. Jason was perturbed that she lured away his bookkeeper, but soon found a replacement. Some doubted Emma's business acumen for hiring a female manager for the busy bakery, but Juliet proved her worth. She always gave Emma credit for her faith in her and respected her for giving her a chance in a man's domain.

"People say that I have no experience in management, but I've spent my entire life doing the accounts for my father's store and Jason's mill. When my parents go back east to visit relatives for months, who do they think runs the store? How can anyone say I have no experience?" Juliet often said.

Jason's logging business grew larger during those years with contracts for Spokane, Seattle, and Vancouver. He was even making inroads into Canada, and the mill and logging camps on the mountain worked all year–round now.

On many Sundays, the Becks rode up to the clearing up on the mountain. Emma and Kate still preferred regular visits to Shea's grave and Jason came to look forward to them too. He enjoyed rediscovering the hills and meadows of his younger days. He found himself taking on Kate's habit of sitting at Shea's grave and recounting the stories of his days. Time after time, he thanked Shea for trusting him with the care of Emma and Kate.

Chapter Twenty–Three

It was a cold day in January, 1896. Emma rode up to Camp Three, laden with cornbread muffins, cakes, and cookies for the work crew, a weekly routine that she had established years ago. A rising wind and the low, gray scudding clouds extinguished the sunlight, but she enjoyed the brisk pace set by her new sorrel mare, Ruby, for old Butternut had died of a twisted intestine the previous fall. Shea's pony died soon after, from loneliness, Emma believed.

On the logging trail, she met her neighbor Kent Barry and logger Leo Esterling riding down from camp.

"Hello, Mrs. Beck," Kent called. "The crews were dismissed for the rest of the day. The weather's turning bad. There are strong winds coming down off the peaks, so we're in for a storm."

She turned her horse around to head back, then asked, "Where's Jason?"

"He was up at the cook's cabin when we left. Should be along any time."

"Thanks. I'll ride back with him then."

"Be careful on the trail, ma'am, the wind's kicking up," Leo cautioned.

"Oh, take these to your families," she said, handing them the bundles of baked delights. "No sense in them going to waste."

"Thanks, Mrs. Beck," Leo and Kent echoed as they parted.

Emma turned Ruby back up the trail. Another fifty yards along the logging road, she heard rumbling. Then Leo and Kent quickly rode up behind her. Kent grabbed her horse's reins.

"What's that noise?" She caught the startled look that Leo and Kent exchanged. "Thunder?"

"Avalanche," Kent said with an ominous tone.

"Jason!" Emma cried, pulling the reins from Kent's grip and spurring her horse.

"Mrs. Beck, no!" Kent shouted after her. "Stop!" Emma ignored him and rode up the trail. "Hell! Leo, ring the avalanche bell and get help up here. I'll go after her!"

Leo quickly rode his horse downhill to sound the bells installed along the length of the ridge. The sound meant one thing to the people in town and at the logging camps: avalanche! They had occurred twice since Emma had come to Easthope, but never at one of the camps—they had always happened in unpopulated areas.

Frantic, Emma pushed her mare on. The ground beneath her thrummed and chunks of snow bounded across her path. She kept moving, intent on getting to the cook's cabin up the hill and around the bend—to get to Jason. Where the trail turned sharply upward, a slide of snow hit her and Ruby full force and knocked them down. Ruby landed on Emma and all that saved her from being crushed was the deep snow that she landed in. The horse neighed and rolled off her, but could not regain its footing and slid down the steep slope. Ruby was gone. Emma lay in a depression of snow, unable to move for several moments, her wind gone. Fighting to concentrate, she regained her breath and had to dig her way up out of the hole in the snow. Suddenly, a hand grabbed her by the wrist and yanked her out. It was Kent Barry.

"Mrs. Beck, you all right?"

"Yes," she gasped. "We've got to get to Jason!" The scene swirled around her as she fought for air, panting and rolling on her back.

"Ma'am, you've got to stay away. The snow's still shifting!"

"But it may have hit the camp! I have to see if Jason is all right!"

"I'll go up and see. The cook's cabin is strong; he's probably fine. But stay here and grab onto a tree in case this slide's not over yet. I'll be right back for you."

He looked around and up the snow clogged trail. "Where's your horse?" Emma pointed down the hill. "Oh Christ," he muttered. Kent left his horse and picked and crawled his way up the hill.

Emma waited until he was out of sight, then followed, careful to keep on his trail.

He heard her coming up behind him. "Mrs. Beck, do not follow me! Go back! This snow could cave in!"

"Leave me be," was her terse reply.

Emma had to take Kent's word that they were at Camp Three. All that remained was a field of snow. She staggered, recognizing nothing, even though she had been up there countless times. The little outbuildings, the equipment, and the cook's cabin were gone. Her breath came in painful gasps of terror. "Jason!" she called.

"You've got to be quiet! Noise could bring more snow down on us. It wasn't an avalanche—looks like a pretty heavy snow slide, though. If you're going to follow me, stay in my footprints and step very carefully," Kent whispered.

Kent walked across the sliding snow, looking for signs of the cabin. Jason's horse's legs stuck out of the snow many yards away. He stopped, hearing a muffled sound and stood still, listening. He found the source and picked his way across the snow with care. He lay on his belly and began to dig. The snow shifted and Kent lay still, listened, then dug faster.

Emma tried to keep her voice low. "Oh—no—is he under there?"

"Don't know. I heard a groaning noise," he said. "It's logs popping—rubbing together. Might be the cook's cabin. I can't be sure."

A blast of air hit them and Emma froze. Another slide crashed through the trees less than a hundred yards away. Kent jumped up and grabbed her and they stumbled to a large fir tree.

"Hold on!" he shouted over the ear–splitting roar.

A suffocating cloud of snow passed over them, so thick that she could not see for several moments. Then everything was still. The hole that Kent had dug was gone.

"Jason! Where's Jason?"

"I'll do my best to find him, ma'am. Are you all right?"

"Yes! Let's get to work!"

"No—stay back!" he said as he tried to get his bearings and locate the hole that he had dug moments before.

"I'm going to help you."

From the look of determination in her eyes, Kent knew that arguing with her was useless. "Okay, but you have to do as I say. I've been through a lot of these in Colorado and I know what to do. All right?" Their heads turned downhill. Leo was ringing another avalanche bell. "We'll have help from the workers at the other camps as soon as they can get here."

"We have to find Jason now!" she cried.

They searched, digging near debris and calling out, no longer taking care to keep their voices low. They were not making much progress and were quickly becoming discouraged. Kent had no poles, no shovels, nothing but riding gloves on his hands, but he kept on digging with Emma beside him.

Each breath she drew was stabbing and piercing. "Look for the logs. He has to be near them!" she sobbed as she crawled around the snow. They both continued like this for many minutes. Kent tried to keep her away, but he gave up. "I lost one husband, I'm not losing another. Shea, help me, please. Help me find him."

Kent gave her a sidelong glance. She seemed half mad.

Leading several sled loads of workers, Leo led the rescue parties from the other camps at last. Everyone had long sticks, with which to locate survivors, and shovels. Dogs kept at the camps and trained for rescue were also brought up to aid in the search.

Emma was frantic, her voice breaking as she muttered to herself as she dug. "You're not leaving me, Jason Beck. You're here and I'll find you. Hold on, hold on!" Her efforts were fruitless. She fought a terrible dread that he would never be found. Alarmed at her rising distress, Kent led her away.

"Mrs. Beck, we're all going to keep looking. You're hurt so you rest and let us work. We have search dogs."

"I have to keep trying! He would try to find me!"

He was frank with her. "Mrs. Beck, the dogs will do a better job. Please, please move away and let them work."

A quarter hour went by with no success. Emma stood near the sledges feeling panicked and helpless.

Intruding on the sound of boots crunching on snow and the muffled voices of the men, a hoarse barking was heard from one of the big German Shepherds. The dog began to dig, sniff, dig, bark. The men came running with Emma bringing up the rear. She fell hard on the sliding snow, but scrambled up and kept moving.

"Keep back!" Kent shouted. "The snow's shifting. Someone throw me a pole and a shovel."

Emma pushed her way to the front of the crowd as Kent began to dig. Several times, he lay prone, looking down the hole. He would rise again and dig some more, then when he satisfied himself that the pit was stable, he jumped into the hole and called for more help.

"Two men—no more! I found the logs from the cook's cabin. Dig, men, but dig fast and careful!"

The wait was interminable as Emma watched and waited. No one spoke, waiting for a muffled word from the hole, now almost three feet deep and several feet wide. She fought waves of dizziness and her chest ached as the cold air permeated her lungs. She leaned on the pole in the hands of a man standing next to her. His face was grim.

"Help them, Shea, help them." She repeated the words like a chant. The men exchanged uncomfortable glances among themselves.

Muffled shouts were heard and the message was relayed from the hole. "We need more diggers—now!" Kent shouted.

Emma ran forward, but a logger held her back just out of sight of the hole. "Is he there?"

Kent was crouched nearest the hole. "They're still digging. They've found something—his coat, I think. Please be patient. This takes time. We don't want a cave in."

She stood alone, frightened to the depths of her soul. More men were ordered to dig around the perimeter. "Why don't they tell us anything? Have they found him?" she asked to no one particular. More faint voices rose up from the hole. Kent listened, straightened, and looked askance at Emma. "Tell me!" she cried.

"He's down there, but he's pinned under logs."

"Is he alive?"

"We're working as fast as we can, Mrs. Beck. We think he's breathing," Kent answered.

More men went down into the hole. Three huge logs were pulled up with ropes then chopped into smaller pieces to shore up the walls of the pit. Emma thought that she saw blood on one of them. A slow, creeping dread filled her heart and her hand flew to her mouth. "No," she whispered.

Saws were sent down next, the rasping sounds muted as the men worked. More pieces of the cook's cabin were lifted out. Then a stretcher and a bale of rope were sent down the hole.

"He's coming out! Mind the ropes, men!"

A dozen men pulled hard, slipping on the unstable snow as Jason was brought up, tied to the stretcher. He was quickly covered with blankets. It took six men to lift him into a sledge.

Emma was lifted into the sledge and squeezed in beside him. "Jason! Jason!" His head was bleeding from a deep gash and his hair and face were blackened with blood. She used her skirt to stem the flow. His flesh was cold and hard when she touched his face. "Jason, can you hear me?" She looked up, tears streaming down her face. "Is he alive, Kent?"

"He was breathing when we brought him up." His face was solemn. Kent trotted off to retrieve his horse and rode beside the sledge as it moved downhill.

Ignoring the searing pain from her sore ribs, Emma laid her head on Jason's chest. She listened intently amid the crunching of the snow under the sledge's runners. Then she heard a thump, then another and another. It was a sound that she knew well. She heard his lungs drawing air. "He's still breathing! I can hear his heart! Hurry!"

The trip down the mountain was frustratingly slow. Half way down, Stuart Barlow met them, riding fast in his small sledge. He had heard the bells and had come as fast as he could. The big sledge stopped for him and he climbed in. He quickly looked Jason over. "Anyone else hurt?"

Kent spoke up because Emma did not. "Mrs. Beck's hurt, too. Got knocked off her horse. No one else I know of is hurt. Jason dismissed us all because of the weather. He was the last one at the camp."

"Let's go—hurry!" Stuart said to the driver. "Hey! Somebody bring my sledge down for me." A man jumped off the big sledge and drove Stuart's sled down the mountain. "Somebody ride ahead and alert the hospital." Kent nodded and spurred his horse downhill.

As the big sledge came down Main Street, many people were waiting outdoors, nervous and quiet. They had heard the avalanche bells. Rachel spotted Emma in the sled and ran beside it.

"Jason's hurt! Find Kate for me!" Emma called.

"Okay!" Rachel shouted as the sledge outpaced her.

Jason was carried into a room at the hospital and immediately surrounded by nurses and orderlies. Emma was deposited in the next room while Stuart disappeared with the stretcher bearers into Jason's room. Emma lay back on the bed in great pain, unable to cry, still in shock. Rachel came running in, slipping on the tracked–in snow upon the floor.

"Emma, how's Jason?"

"Don't know yet. Where's Kate?"

"I sent Caleb to get her from school."

Emma took a shuddering, painful breath and told her what had happened at Camp Three. "They had to use the dogs to find him. He was pinned under the logs from the cook's cabin. He's all broken up—his leg looked badly broken. The worst of it is that he's got a huge gash in his head. There was so much blood."

Rachel carefully pulled off Emma's coat. "Where does it hurt?"

"Everywhere—everywhere. Ruby landed on me, then went down the mountain. She's gone, poor thing."

Rachel disappeared for a few moments and returned with cool compresses for Emma's bruises. She had a hospital gown over her arm.

Stuart poked his head into her room. "You okay for a while, Emma?"

"I'll get her in a bed gown, Stuart," Rachel said. "She looks to be pretty bruised up."

"Stuart—tell me!" Emma pleaded.

"I'm trying to save his life," Stuart said as he closed the door.

A moment later, someone knocked at Emma's door. "Come in," she said.

Kent Barry entered, looking very somber. The big lumberjack shifted his weight and fiddled with the brim of his hat. "There are a lot of people outside asking after you both."

"We don't know anything yet about Jason and I'm just bruised up." As he turned to leave, Emma said, "Kent, thank you for all you did today."

He nodded and closed the door behind him.

Rachel helped Emma remove her clothes. She gasped, seeing her torso covered with purple and black bruises. "Oh, Em!" She tugged the gown on her with care. "I'll get someone. You need to get those ribs seen to right away." She disappeared into the room next door.

Emma heard Stuart shout. "Stay out of my way! I'll see her when I'm done. Get out!"

Rachel returned, choking back tears. "Uh, he'll be in soon."

"What's going on in there?"

"There are a half dozen people in there. They were cutting off Jason's clothes and Stuart was cleaning the cut on Jason's head. That's all I saw before he threw me out."

Pounding feet were heard in the hallway and Kate raced into Emma's room and flung herself on her mother. Emma yelped in pain. "Momma! Caleb said there was an avalanche. He said Jason's hurt! Is he all right?" Her eyes brimmed with tears, searching Emma's face for reassurance.

"He's hurt, but we don't know how bad."

"I want to see him."

"You can't right now. Stay here with me."

Kate sat near the bed on a stool, holding her mother's hand. "Your hands are so cold. What happened to you?" As Emma told her, Kate took each of Emma's hands in her own. Emma felt her daughter's warmth revive her frozen hands. "What can I do to help?" Kate asked. Rachel charged her with preparing more compresses for Emma's many bruises.

Emma, Kate, and Rachel strained to listen to the low, subdued voices in the adjoining room, unable to make out anything as Stuart and the nurses worked on Jason.

Emma's dread grew as she waited. Kate sat on Emma's bed and laid her head on her mother's shoulder. Emma stroked her daughter's dark hair. "If they're still in there, it means that Jason's holding on."

"Stop it, mother," she snapped. "I heard the men talking outside. He's hurt real bad. They're saying that he's dying."

Emma ignored Kate's flash of temper. "Shh, don't say that. He's a very strong man."

Kate broke away from Emma and covered her face in her hands. "I couldn't take it if Jason died! I just couldn't!" she squealed, unnerved.

"Neither could I, Kate." Emma took Kate's hand tightly in hers.

At last, Stuart came in to Emma's room. Allison Carruthers followed behind him, forcing a smile. Stuart asked Rachel and Kate to go to the waiting room. He began to examine Emma then wrapped her ribs while Allison held her steady. A million questions knocked at Emma's lips, but she could see that Stuart was very downcast. She clamped her mouth shut, waiting for him to speak.

He then spoke in his crisp, clinical voice. "He's still unconscious, Emma. He's got a very deep gash to his head and he's lost a lot of blood. He's got broken ribs, a broken arm and his leg is broken in three places. There is frostbite on his face and hands." He took a deep breath and looked at her. "His head injury is bad, Emma. I can't be sure, but he might have a fractured skull. I stitched up the cut on his head and wrapped the ribs. I'll set and splint his arm and leg tomorrow when the swelling goes down." She was shocked into silence. "I've sent for a doctor from Spokane—a neurologist who specializes in the head and brain. Maybe he can tell us more." Jason's injuries were severe and he would likely die from them; Stuart wondered how Emma would cope if Jason died. She had not done well when Shea had passed. "We'll take you in to see him for a minute, but then you have to rest and leave him to us," he said when he finished bandaging her ribs.

Her injuries were just beginning to take their toll and she moved stiffly and slowly as Stuart and Allison walked her to the adjoining room.

Jason lay on his back, his head wrapped in heavy bandages. His blood-soaked clothes had been cut off and lay in a heap in the corner. Tears dripped down Emma's cheeks. Stuart and Allison led her back to bed.

"I'm going to give you something for the pain. It's very mild," Stuart added, worrying about her former addiction to laudanum. "Allison or I will be with Jason through the night. We're doing everything we can." He left to get the pain medicine from across the hall. Allison gently laid Emma back down on the bed and covered her.

Stuart returned several minutes later. "Well, there is some good news. Just got word that the neurologist will be here in a couple of days. Now take this," he said giving Emma a spoonful of a nasty–tasting medicine. Whether it was the drug or her own crushing fatigue, she fell asleep in minutes, her pain fading into oblivion.

Stuart came into the waiting room and spoke to Kate who waited with Rachel at her side. "Your mother's sleeping and will be here for a few days due to a few broken ribs and a sore back. Rachel, take her in, will you?"

"How's Jason?" Kate asked. She went pale as Stuart recounted his many injuries.

"We'll know more in the morning. Go with Rachel now. If there's any change, I'll send word."

"Can I see my mother?"

"Sure, but she's sleeping. Don't wake her."

Kate tip–toed into Emma's room and placed a kiss on her bruised cheek. "I love you, Momma."

Emma slept through the night but awoke the next morning with pain radiating from every part of her body. Allison was moving around her room. Emma tried to sit up, but her back was very sore. "Allison? How's Jason?"

"He's still unconscious. But we got lucky. The doctor from Spokane, Dr. Witherspoon, is over in Millersburg on another case. He'll be here soon."

Obeying Stuart's order, Allison gave Emma more of the bitter liquid and she dozed through the morning.

It seemed that hours went by while Dr. Witherspoon examined Jason, then he and Stuart consulted in his office. Later, both men entered Emma's room. She woke up when they entered.

"Mrs. Beck, I'm Doctor Harold Witherspoon." He sat upon the stool at her bedside. "Your husband's head injury is very serious. He hasn't regained consciousness yet. From what I can tell, his skull isn't fractured but the injury to his head caused what is called a brain contusion. That's when the brain is pushed against the skull, bruising it from the inside. Until he regains consciousness, we can't tell what damage he's suffered."

Her eyes widened. "What kind of damage?"

"For openers he could have problems with his memory or speech. He may have difficulty walking, using his arms, standing—things like that."

His brusque manner shook Emma very deeply. She took a deep stabbing breath. "Oh, no!"

"I'm telling you the worst that could happen, Mrs. Beck. We just have to wait and see. He's in good hands with Dr. Barlow."

Emma's face dissolved, but it hurt her ribs to cry. With all her will, she resolved to wait and see, then deal with whatever was to be. But she wondered if she could survive another blow like Shea's death.

Dr. Witherspoon and Stuart talked in hushed voices in the hallway near Emma's open door.

"It's touch and go right now, Stuart. Someone should be with him every minute. I've got to get back to Millersburg right away. I've got a young girl with a head injury from a sledding accident. If you need me, send word to the Millersburg telegraph office. The people there know where to find me."

"Thanks for coming, Harold. I'll keep you informed."

As Stuart reentered Emma's room, she said, "Stuart, I'm scared. How can Witherspoon know if Jason has brain damage if he hasn't woken up yet?"

He sat beside her on the bed. "Witherspoon's giving you the worst that could happen, Emma. His bedside manner isn't as refined as mine," he smiled. "Try to rest."

"Stuart, can I be moved into Jason's room?"

"You can't do him any good, Emma, and it won't do you any good to lie there and worry yourself hour after hour. Your injuries are serious, too."

"I want to be with him. Please. If he goes, I don't want him to be alone."

He considered it while he rewrapped her ribs. "Well, all right, but if you get in the way, you're back in here, understood?"

As she was rolled into Jason's room on her bed, she craned her neck to see him. He was breathing but his face was sunken, just like Shea's was before he died. She suppressed a shudder. His left arm and leg were splinted and his hands and forehead were wrapped in bandages. He was so still.

Allison came into the room. "Try talking to him, Emma. It might help bring him out of it."

She wanted to say something, but no words came. The shock of seeing him so broken up had silenced her. The memory of standing over her parents' grave flashed through her thoughts—no words had come that day, either.

The next day passed without progress. Jason lay unconscious, unmoving. Either Allison or Stuart sat with him for hours on end. Emma slept fitfully, fighting the medicine that Stuart gave her. She fought to stay wake, reassuring herself that Jason lived. This sad routine wore on for a third day.

Each day Rachel, Caleb, and Kate, along with many of the loggers, visited Jason. They came in with hope, but left disheartened.

The afternoon of the fourth day, Emma got out of bed and walked around the hospital. Her back hurt and she moved slowly. Later, as she undressed to take a bath in the washroom, she got a good look at the bruises on her body in the mirror. Her torso was covered in black and red bruises where her ribs were cracked. More bruises were scattered up and down her limbs.

Kate came twice a day and each time left deflated. Emma worried about her and hated not being with her during this difficult time. Emma never told her of Dr. Witherspoon's dire prediction that Jason might be left with brain damage. Better to keep her in the dark until they knew more, she reasoned.

The evening of the fourth day, Emma was sitting up in a chair near Jason's bed, reading aloud while Allison sat near the door. Her eyes were on the book, but from the corner of her eye she saw Allison stiffen. She closed the book and looked to Jason. His good arm flinched and he groaned. Emma leaned over and touched his face. "Jason? Wake up, please wake up. Come on. Open your eyes."

His eyes moved beneath the lids and he opened his mouth, licking his lips. He moaned and coughed, then his eyelids fluttered open for an instant, but quickly closed again.

"I'll get Stuart," Allison said, hurrying out into the hallway.

Emma would not give up. "Jason, it's Emma. Wake up—open your eyes." Stuart came running. "He's trying to wake up."

They watched him in silence while he struggled for consciousness. His mouth worked and he coughed again. Allison took a cup of water and wet his lips. He reflexively swallowed then he was still again.

Stuart put a hand on Emma's shoulder. "He's fighting his way back. It's a good sign. Back to bed with you."

The next day, Saturday, Kate came into the room her parents now shared. She hugged Emma, mindful of her sore body. "How is he?"

"He tried to wake up last night."

Kate looked worried. "I've heard people talking. They all say that he's going to die. It's been too many days. They say that he's in a coma."

"Oh, Kate! That's just talk. They're not here. They don't know how he's doing. Don't listen to the rumors."

"But he won't wake up! They're saying the longer he's unconscious, the worse it is."

"He's had a head injury. It takes time."

"I want to be ready in case, Momma, so tell me the truth. You told me the truth about Dad. I want the truth about Jason—please!"

Emma sat up as best she could. "He did try to wake up last night. He's fighting, I know it—I know him. You know that I wouldn't lie to you, Kate. I've always been honest with you."

Kate sat next to her on the bed. She bit back tears. "I thought that this time you might be afraid to tell me because of what happened to Dad."

Emma thought before she answered. "Did it bother you that I told you the truth about your father's illness?"

"At the time, it did."

"I wanted to do the right thing. You deserved the truth."

"I'm not saying that I don't want you to be honest with me. After Dad died and you went to the hospital, I was afraid that I'd end up an orphan like you."

Emma felt ashamed. "I'm sorry for all of that, I truly am. I work every day to make it up to you, if ever I can." She saw the fear in her daughter's deep blue eyes. "I know all of this scares you. I'm sorry to be away from you right now."

Kate seemed to burst. "It's been hard to live like this! Every time something bad happens, I'm shuffled off to the Barlows' to wait for someone to tell me what's happening. I'm part of this family!"

A jolt hit Emma's heart. She plucked at the covers. "I wish I could fix the past, I do. You've been afraid and uncertain about the stability in your life. You matter more to me than anyone in the world. I'm sorry for hurting you."

There was a very long silence, then Kate spoke. "You want to protect me and I understand. But I've always wondered—you just came home that day from the hospital and we went on as usual. It was like nothing had happened. It was like you were away on a vacation or something."

It was time to tell her the truth. "It was no vacation, Kate. I had a lot of problems to work out. I had a lot of guilt about things that have happened in my life." She continued at length. "I was jealous of your relationship with your father. You were so close to him. I didn't resent you, don't ever think that. But I wanted that closeness with you, too. When your father was dying, I saw you curl up inside yourself. I didn't know how to reach you. I didn't know how to be close to you. I was coping for all of us and took all the responsibility of your father's death on myself." She wiped away tears. "I had convinced myself that I caused his death."

"What?"

"I reasoned that if I hadn't returned to him, he would still be alive today, and I let those terrible thoughts eat away at me. But later on, when I would listen, Stuart asked me if there was a day that I could live without you. It hit me like a hammer. My answer was no—I couldn't imagine a moment without you or with Shea. I would not have you if it had not been for your father. His death couldn't have been prevented, but at the time I thought that it was my fault. I've never spoken of this with you and I should have. You're right— after I got out of the hospital, I went ahead and continued on with our lives. It was my own sick little routine. I was afraid that you wouldn't love me anymore if you knew how messed up I am."

"If you had told me, I could've helped you somehow. I love you, Momma. You're my mother."

"I love you, too, dear. That's why I want to protect you."

Kate was silent as she took it all in. For the first time, her mother was being honest about her own feelings. Emma let few people into her heart and Kate knew that. Then, Emma told Kate the truth of what had happened to her parents that day in Kansas. Kate watched her intently as she spoke then responded, "You were the same age as me, almost. I would've done the same thing." She hugged Emma. "If you would tell me these things, Momma, then you would feel better and I wouldn't feel so alone."

"You're not alone," a deep voice croaked.

"Jason!" Kate was at his side in a flash. "You're awake!"

"Kate? Boy, my head hurts. Where's Emma?"

"I'm right here, Jason." Emma slipped off her bed and knelt beside him, ignoring her pain.

"Emma!" His good arm flopped, searching for her hand. She took his hand still bandaged due to frostbite. "What happened?"

"Shh. Stay still Jason. You're at the hospital. You're pretty banged up. But your green eyes are the most beautiful sight I've ever seen." She kissed his lips. "Kate, would you get Stuart?" Kate was gone in an instant calling for Dr. Barlow through the echoing hallways.

"Everything's blurry," Jason muttered.

"I'm right here, love. I'm right here. Can you feel my hand?"

"No."

"You hand's bandaged from a little frostbite, but I've got you."

Stuart came running in moments later with Kate behind him. "Nice to see you, Beck."

"Stuart? What in hell happened to me? I feel lousy."

Kate came into view above Jason. His eyes squinted. "Shouldn't you be in school?"

Kate spoke without thinking. "It's Saturday."

Stuart put up a hand to silence her. "Take your time and tell me what you remember, Jason."

Emma pulled Kate down next to her on the floor and put an arm around her. "What a relief," she whispered.

Jason took a while to speak and his eyes rolled in their sockets as he fought to stay conscious. Allison came in with water and he was able to drink a little. "Where am I again?"

"You're at the hospital, Jason. Can you tell me what you remember?" Stuart asked.

Jason was fighting against dreams and reality, trying to recall what had happened. His features twisted and for a few moments his memory went blank. "I can't remember." Emma looked worried. "Oh!" he exclaimed. "Emma!"

"I'm right here Jason. I've got your hand."

He gripped her hand tight despite the bandages. "Avalanche. There was an avalanche."

"What else do you remember?" Stuart asked.

His head turned toward her. "Oh, Emma. I lost you. I'm sorry."

"I'm right here."

He shifted as pain stabbed him. "I couldn't hold onto you!"

"Jason, I wasn't with you. I was on my way up to the cooks's cabin when I heard the avalanche. I'm all right."

"Tell me more, Jason," Stuart prodded.

He closed his eyes and relived his terror. Rumbling—the ground shaking beneath him. The walls vibrating and popping as great chunks of snow and ice smashed apart the small cook's cabin. He remembered thinking that he was about to die. He remembered nothing else until the moment he had awaken in the hospital. A tear slid down his cheek. "Emma, I thought you were with me and you had been swept away by the snow. I heard your voice crying out."

Emma had never seen him cry before and kissed his cheek, tasting his tear. "It was just a dream," she soothed.

He was finally able to focus better and his eyes ran over her. "Why are you in a bed gown?"

"I have a few bruises. I'll tell you about it later, love."

"Was anyone else hurt in the avalanche?"

"No. You were the last one on the mountain, remember? You had sent everyone home."

"Yes, yes," he mumbled. "The weather got bad." Pain and fatigue pulled at him and he closed his eyes and slept.

Emma climbed back into her own bed, sagging with relief. "Thank you, Shea," she whispered.

That night Kate stayed at the hospital, keeping vigil with her mother. "Thank you for letting me stay, Momma."

"I never want you to feel left out again, Kate. I'm so glad that you're here."

"You sleep, Momma. I'll watch over him."

For the first time in days, Emma slept. Deeply. Restfully. She was secure in the knowledge that her family was together and safe. Until now, she had never realized how perfectly the pieces fit. Even in the midst of this tragedy, they were united, drawing strength from one another.

Jason's moaning woke Emma the next morning. She looked to Kate who dozed, sitting upright in the chair, her head lolling to one side.

She came to him and kissed his lips. His hand slipped behind her neck, holding her in the kiss for a very long time. Playfully, she touched her nose to his. He pulled her down to him again and kissed her.

"Well, you're certainly feeling better. What do you need?"

"You," he smiled. "But I'm awfully hungry, too."

Allison brought in his breakfast later that morning. Saying that she would rather do it, Emma fed Jason. Relieved of the duty, Allison left to go home. Kate left soon after and promised to return after she had bathed and changed her clothes.

Emma sat on the bed feeding him. "I feel like a baby," he grumbled as she spooned broth for him. "I can do it."

"Your hands are bandaged and you've got a broken arm. Aw, Jason, let me do this. No arguments," she cajoled. "Now eat up."

"How long have I been out?"

"Four days."

Jason's eyes widened in disbelief. "I wondered what Kate was talking about yesterday when she told me that it was Saturday. I thought that it was the next day when I woke up. So it's Sunday now?"

"That's right, but it doesn't matter now. You're going to be up and around in no time, if I know you. Kate's been staying with the Barlows, but she wanted to stay here until she knew that you were on the mend."

"I want to go home as soon as possible."

"I want you to come home too. But you have to do what Stuart says. You're going to be down for a while. Have some patience."

"I'll manage, you'll see."

"Jason Quincy Beck—God help you if I catch you exhausting yourself. I almost lost you, so you're under orders from me to cooperate with me and Stuart. You once told me the same thing when I was released from this place. Now it's your turn to take your own advice."

"Emma, tell me what happened to you. I can see you've got bruises all over your arms and chest."

She kept feeding him as she spoke, trying to minimize the terror of her ordeal, recounting her fall and the loss of Ruby. "When Kent and I got to Camp Three, he heard where you were. He said that he heard logs rubbing together. It was the most incredible sound I ever heard."

"Lumberjack's instinct," Jason said with a proud smile.

"He worked so hard to free you and so did the other men. Kent dug with his hands. All the men worked to get you out."

"How long did it take?"

Emma shifted from her ribs stabbing her. She blinked against the pain, taking a moment before answering. "It took over half an hour. You were about six feet down."

"Six feet under and I didn't die!" he joked, then he became serious. "What else? I can see it in your eyes. Tell me everything, Emma."

She set aside the bowl and dabbed his chin with her sleeve. "Your head was bleeding pretty bad. I'm afraid your clothes are ruined."

"Emma," he pleaded.

She looked at his handsome face and met his soulful green eyes. "Your head injury was so bad that Stuart called in a specialist. This Dr. Witherspoon thought that you might be left with brain damage. He said that your brain was bruised inside the skull. You might have trouble with your memory, or you might not be able to walk normally."

Jason was disturbed by the prediction but managed a smile. "I'm going to prove him wrong."

"I know that you will. Finish your soup."

Later, Emma sat next to Jason on his bed. He managed to put his good arm around her. She flinched. "You're in pain."

"I'm a lot better. Stuart said that I could go home, but I want to be here with you for as long as you're here. It's one of the few arguments that I've ever won with him."

Chapter Twenty-Four

Jason's recuperative powers proved formidable and a week later, Stuart allowed him to go home. He could not use crutches, hindered by the broken arm and ribs. Although the bandages from his hands were removed, the skin was red and crusted and hurt him more than he admitted. He complained all the way home about having to be in a wheelchair. Volunteers from the mill had constructed a zigzag ramp up the front steps of the house. The townsfolk gathered and looked on as he was brought home.

He whined as he was wheeled into the formal parlor. "I am not an invalid. This is embarrassing."

Emma leaned over and kissed him. "They're trying to help, so let them. See?" she pointed. "I had our things moved down here so you don't have to use the steps." Emma had the big keeping room just off the kitchen converted into their bedroom. Their bed, armoires, dressers, and chests had all been brought down. Jason's favorite chair, a leather easy chair built to suit his large frame, had been brought in from the parlor. "Your men did this for you. This is our bedroom until you're well."

"I can get up the stairs with a little practice."

"Jason, remember when I got out of the hospital and you told me to let others help me? This is hard for you, I know, but if I got through it, you certainly can."

"All right, all right. I'll behave." They shared a smile.

Kate hurried home from school that afternoon and hugged Jason the minute she came in. "I'm glad you're home." He accepted her kiss on his cheek. "Hey, can I move into the big bedroom upstairs for a while?"

Despite his initial confidence, Jason's recovery was miserably slow. He put on a brave front, but the myriad of injuries drained him as the weeks passed. Stuart checked on him often, noting that Jason was becoming impatient and irritable. He had always been a strong man and had never had a health complaint other than an occasional cold and the collision with the wayward log long ago. Jason hated the wheelchair and, in the privacy of the makeshift bedroom, tried to walk with crutches. He fell several times, bringing a frantic Emma running to his aid.

"I'm not a cripple! I hate this!" he protested.

Emma understood his frustration all too well and was reminded, more than once, of the hardships that she and Shea had endured after Tyler's attempt to lynch them. Shea's injuries from the hanging had been dreadful and she remembered that time with lingering bitterness. Determined not to go through it again, she remained patient and helped Jason all she could as she herself healed. However, it dawned on her that this time was different. Jason was sensitive to her injuries and employed various men from the mill to help him bathe, dress, and get around town. Allison and Rachel found people to help with housework and cooking until Emma was better. Jason was restless and he despised being perceived as feeble. Being away from his business drove him to distraction.

Weeks later, when she judged that he was stronger, Emma had his office at the mill moved into the large kitchen at the house. The reasons for the move were twofold. One, it gave Jason something to do, and two, she could keep an eye on him. He had dizzy spells and fell from the wheelchair several times, often hurting his already broken bones. Emma was chastised when she suggested tying him in the chair. She backed off and watched as he struggled each day.

In moments alone, Emma wondered if she would suffer another collapse. She was weary with the strain of keeping watch over Jason each day. With his good arm, he managed to wheel himself all over the house and sometimes outside and down the ramp. Many times she found him fighting his way back up the ramp. Whenever Stuart arrived he always took Emma aside and talked with her, not just about her injuries, but also about her emotional state.

"Are you coping with this? I mean, do you feel in control? If there is anything bothering you, we can talk about it, or you can talk to anyone else— Rachel, Allison, Martha Hamlin, maybe?" Stuart said. "Don't bottle this up again. You know you can't do it. I'll get you more help around here. You've got to take it easy too." His concern was genuine for he loved her like a daughter.

"I'm doing all right, but I'll be honest with you, Stuart. Sometimes—sometimes," she emphasized to minimize his worry, "I get worried—like I'm waiting for something to explode. Jason isn't Shea and his temperament is much different, but I can't help the feeling that we're heading for a big fight. Jason doesn't handle being cooped up very well. I'm expecting him to lash out at me." She let out a long breath. "Silly, huh? I don't want to pick a fight with him or do anything to anger him. I'm a little nervous, but I'm doing all right so far."

Stuart understood. "You're right in that Jason isn't Shea. You may have to weather an argument or two, but Jason is not the type to lash out at you. He bottles things up, as I'm sure you already know. My best advice is to keep nearby, but don't baby him."

"True, but when I was sick, he babied me."

"True," Stuart echoed. "That's just the way he is. I'm just saying to resist the urge to hover over him. I think that the two of you will come through just fine."

Weeks later in February, while Emma was clearing away lunch, Jason tried to wheel himself to the sink to wash the dishes, but a dizzy spell hit him and she caught him, or, more precisely, used her body to break his fall. He fell on top of her and she yelped in pain. He was insensible for several moments then came around, panicked.

"Emma, are you all right?" He rolled off her. "I'm sorry."

She rolled on her side then kneeled on the floor. "I'm okay. I'd rather you not hit your head on the floor. Your skull's not that thick." She tried to laugh it off, but Jason gripped her arm. She recoiled, remembering how much it had hurt when Shea had done it to her years ago. He immediately realized that he had gripped her too hard and let go.

"Please Em, don't do that again. Let me fall. I can get back up. See?" Maneuvering himself with his one good arm and one good leg, he managed to hoist himself back into the wheelchair.

"I'll admit that it was a reflexive move on my part."

"Did I hurt your arm?" he asked, seeing her rub it.

"No. I'm okay."

"Let me see," he insisted, taking her arm and rolling up her sleeve. The flesh was unmarked. He breathed a sigh of relief. "I would never hurt you." He watched her face and saw a vulnerable expression in her eyes. "Em, tell me, did Shea hurt you like that? Did he ever hit you?"

She looked away. "Once, he grabbed me by the arm and I had a few bruises. It was after he was hanged. He wasn't himself," she said. "He didn't know what to do with his own anger. He threw things at me and didn't treat me very well back then. But I had to endure it until he was well again."

He put his hand behind her neck and pulled her to his lips. He kissed her tenderly. "I wasn't trying to hurt you. I'm sorry."

"Nothing to be sorry for, my love," she replied as she got up off the floor.

In the evenings after supper, Jason helped Kate with her homework and Emma made sure to leave them alone. This time of bonding and reassurance was what Kate needed. She seemed more content each day.

Unable to walk for weeks, Jason relied on the hated wheelchair as his sole conveyance around town. Emma was dressed down by Stuart on the street one afternoon in March as she wheeled Jason along the walkway in front of the house.

"I told you that you're not to exert yourself. Those ribs are not healed. I'll get one of the men from the mill to come and wheel him around when he wants to go out. Jason, how could you let her do this? Emma, if I see you doing this again, I'll—"

"Sorry, Stuart, but I was feeling good today. And Jason needed some fresh air," Emma appealed to him.

"I don't care!" he snapped as he took over Jason's chair and pushed him back up the ramp to the house.

Jason grabbed Emma's hand and kissed it. "I told you that he'd catch us." They were amused. Stuart was not.

Later that day, Leo Esterling appeared at Beck House on Stuart's order. He wheeled Jason through town as Emma walked beside them. Despite his temporary infirmities, Jason had not lost much weight and poor Leo was winded and sweating despite the cold winter day.

At the mill, ramps had been installed to aid Jason in getting in and out of the buildings. The men gathered around him and it heartened him. Jason's business was still booming, albeit without his constant supervision. He had placed his trust in the men who worked for him, but he was itching to get back to work full–time.

In April when the trails cleared, Jason wanted to go up to Camp Three. He caught Emma's uneasy look when he mentioned it.

"I'll go with someone from the mill. I don't think that you should go. I'm lucky. I have little memory of that day. And I don't want you worrying about me," he said, knowing what she was about to say. "I have to go. It's my business. I have to get Camp Three rebuilt as soon as the snow is gone."

"Why don't you rebuild it somewhere safer?"

"I have to see for myself. Camp Three is my largest operation. If I have to move it elsewhere, I will."

"Please clear it with Stuart before you go up."

Stuart gave grudging approval to Jason's trip, voicing his opinion that it was too soon. "It's too rough a ride. Your bones haven't finished mending. You could make things worse for yourself."

"I have to go, Stuart. I've got lumberjacks who need the work."

Kent Barry volunteered to drive Jason the next afternoon. An early melt made the track slick and muddy, but Kent's wagon and his powerful pull horses made it up the mountain roads. At Camp Three, enough snow had melted to expose the logs of what once had been the cook's cabin. They were scattered like match sticks over a wide area. All equipment, saws, sluices, and tents were obliterated. Jason paled as he took it in.

Kent pulled the wagon to a halt. "That's where we found you, Jason." Kent pointed at a pile of timber. "We had to saw you out from under them."

Jason looked at the stack of heavy logs. He straightened, locking the picture in his memory. It was stupid luck that he had been found at all.

Kent continued. "When I heard the avalanche coming, I was scared out of my head knowing that you were still up there. But your wife wouldn't turn back, hurt as bad as she was. She didn't seem to feel the pain, you know? All she wanted was to find you."

"I want to understand what she went through that day. She won't tell me much."

"You're married to quite a lady," Kent said. "She didn't give up on you for a minute. It was scary how she held on, like her will kept you alive or something." He looked at Jason. "I heard her mumbling something to her first husband, Shea. And I'll tell you alone, it gave me the creeps. I'll tell you plain, we didn't think that we'd find you alive. It had been too long and we were afraid that you had been crushed or smothered. But the logs made an air pocket around you. That's what saved you." He paused a moment. "Maybe it was Shea who did that, like he answered her. Maybe his spirit is in these hills, you think?"

"You may be right, Kent."

That evening after Jason settled into bed, Emma bustled around the room putting clothes away in the dresser. "Come here, Emma." Jason invited her to bed, pulling back the blankets.

She curled next to him, enjoying the warmth he generated. "It's going to be a cold night. I should build up the fire."

"Later." He pulled her close and she snuggled against him. "Kent told me what had happened after the avalanche. I didn't realize how close I came until today, until I saw what had happened at Camp Three."

"But you made it. You're still here with us."

In May, despite Stuart's reluctance, Jason at last managed to get around on crutches once his broken arm had healed. He was reborn. He went to work every day but preferred staying in the office, rarely venturing up the mountain to the camps. He had promoted Kent Barry to manager after the former manager had moved to Seattle. Kent was grateful for the opportunity and he also gave Jason peace of mind. Jason knew the kind of man that Kent was and owed him his life. Kent was put in charge of rebuilding Camp Three.

Life had pretty much returned to normal, except that Emma and Jason's bedroom still occupied the keeping room. Emma could tell when Jason wanted her when he wedged chairs against the doors once they were alone. His broken leg prevented him from doing much to her, but she sure did a lot to him. By June, all was back to normal. Jason had his men move the bedroom furniture back upstairs and the keeping room was put back in order. Despite a limp that lingered for a few months, Jason was himself again.

Kate had one more year of schooling to go and Emma began planning for her college. Kate could pick any college she wanted, but she was reluctant to leave Washington.

That fall, Emma noticed that Kate and Randall Barlow's relationship appeared to become more exclusive. An ominous realization gripped her one afternoon while she baked cookies and apple pie in the kitchen. Now that their children were older, Rachel and Caleb made a habit of taking short trips to Spokane or Tacoma. Although Kate had always spent most of her free time with the Barlow children, Emma now began to worry about Kate's relationship with Randall. She dare not mention her fears to Jason. She lacked the courage to tell him; besides, Jason was so busy these days she did not want to burden him.

During a week that Rachel and Caleb were away, Martin was charged with the task of watching over his brother and sister. He worked at the mill though, so he could not be around every moment. While Emma was in the yard hanging laundry that weekend, she saw Kate and Randall walking together and holding hands. She watched them disappear around the corner, heading for the Barlow house. Her instincts told her to do something, but fear held her back.

Fear became near terror the next day as she washed clothes. She noticed a red watery stain on Kate's underclothes and worked hard to scrub it out. Later on in the week, Emma noticed that Kate's menstrual rags were not in the laundry. Her chest tightened as her worst fear became real. She remembered a similar stain on her underclothes after she and Shea had made love for the first time. She sank into a chair knowing what she had to do.

Jason noticed her distraction that night as they lay in bed. "What's on your mind? You have the strangest look on your face."

"Nothing, nothing."

After the Barlows came home Sunday afternoon, Emma made sure to arrive at Rachel's early the next day. The children were in school, Martin was working at the mill and Caleb was at the bank. Rachel was glad to see her and they visited in the parlor. Rachel served tea using the silver service that Emma and Jason had given to her. Rachel prattled on about her and Caleb's trip to Spokane.

While Rachel poured more tea, Emma took advantage of the lull in the conversation. She came right to the point. "Something happened while you and Caleb were away. Rachel, I think that something's going on between Kate and Randall."

Rachel froze in mid–pour and the cup overflowed. She knew what she meant. "Oh no."

"I think that Randall and Kate were alone in the house and they—" She swallowed hard. "I was doing laundry and I found a stain on Kate's underclothes, but she's not in her monthly time." Rachel's face went slack and she avoided Emma's eyes. "I think that they went to bed together."

The teapot clattered to the tray. "Are you sure?"

"Look, Rachel, I'm not here to blame either of them. We've got to separate them now, before this goes too far." Emma took a deep breath. "I don't need my daughter pregnant with her half–brother's child—and I know he may not be, but I'm taking no chances."

Rachel sat in a big chair near the hearth, shaking and pale. "My God, Emma. I thought they were just friends." Her eyes welled up with tears.

Emma's fears were overwhelming her and she fought for control. "So did I. But we have to keep them apart. Both of them have bright futures ahead of them and I won't risk either of them missing out. Kate's going to college next year and I'll make sure that it's far away. You have to promise me that you'll send Randall to a college on this side of the Mississippi." Rachel's head bobbed in agreement. "We'll work together to see to it, all right?"

"Emma, are you angry about this happening under my roof?"

"No, Rachel. Neither of us saw this coming. Kate will hate me for keeping her away from Randall, but she'll live."

"Emma, I'm sorry. This has been such a mess."

"I agonized about coming here today and I hoped that my fears were unfounded, but this is for the best. Neither of us would survive the scandal if this got out."

"I need to be sure. Emma, do you forgive me?"

She went to her friend and sat on the arm of her chair, slipping her arm around her. "You're like a sister to me and I forgave you long ago." Her brave facade was fast crumbling. She had gathered the strength to say what she had to today; now she wanted to go. "I'd better get home and get dinner ready. We'll make plans later on."

"Emma?" Rachel asked. "Does Jason know?"

"No. And he's not going to. This stays between you and me."

As Jason helped Emma around the kitchen that evening, he knew that something was wrong. He scooped her up in his arms. "You okay?"

"Sure—fine. I'm just tired."

He knew that she was lying and did not press, but he also remembered those same words years ago before she collapsed.

But this one thing would destroy him, Emma knew. Jason loved Kate as his own daughter and knowing that she had lost her virginity to her possible half–brother would be too much of a blow. This was the only thing that she ever kept from him.

The next few days found Emma and Rachel working behind the scenes, scheming to keep Kate and Randall apart, or at least, chaperoned at all times. Helen and Martin were pressed into service without realizing it. There was a harvest dance at the school that Saturday and Kate and Randall were perturbed as Helen and her escort, Warren Brody, the blacksmith's son, dogged them all night.

As the weeks went by, Emma found many excuses for keeping Kate home and encouraged her to see other female friends, sometimes arranging invitations behind her back in order to separate the budding lovers. Rachel did the same, making Randall get a job at Beck Lumber after school and on Saturdays. Unwittingly, Jason assigned him to the logging camps far from town. He was a strong boy and well suited to the heavy work. Randall did not like the separation much either, but unlike Kate's, his ardor began to fade and he began to look around at the other young girls in town.

A couple of weeks later, Emma saw Kate's menstrual rags in the laundry bag. Kate was not pregnant. She then told Rachel who sagged with relief.

More sensitive to the separation, Kate was vexed to no end by the sudden change in her relationship with Randall. She complained that she and Randall were too busy to spend any time together. Emma felt for her. Still, their relationship had gone too far too fast. Because she was fighting for her daughter's future, she never looked back or felt guilty for doing all she did. She attacked the problem with cunning. Kate and Randall still saw each other on occasion, but it was always in public. Their relationship had quickly cooled off.

Emma wrote to Shea's father and with his help, arranged for Kate's acceptance at Bryn Mawr, a girl's college in Pennsylvania.

Emma's relationship with Rachel somehow survived, although it took a long time to bridge the gap that had reopened between them. Many months passed before they drew back together into some semblance of closeness. Jason noticed the distance between them and asked if they had had another fight, but Emma assured him that they had not.

"The bakery's been so busy the past few months, so we haven't seen much of each other."

In June, just before Kate's graduation, Emma announced to Kate that she had been accepted to Bryn Mawr.

Kate gaped at her. "Pennsylvania? That's too far away!"

"I asked your grandfather if you could stay with him while you're in school. He said that he'd love to have you. His house is near the college so you wouldn't have to stay in a dormitory."

"I don't even know him!" she protested.

Jason broke in. "This is an opportunity of a lifetime, Kate. You would meet all sorts of new people and you'd get the best education that we can give you. City life is exciting. You'll love it. We'll miss you, but it's only for four years and we'll be out to see you now that the railroad's finished up here. We can be out to you in a matter of days."

"I know that it's the best college for girls, but I don't want to be so far away from home and living with strangers." Kate brooded over it for weeks and at last consented, mostly persuaded by her girlfriends who expressed particular envy that Kate had been accepted into such a prestigious university.

Emma had not counted on Kate's friends convincing her to go to Bryn Mawr, but she was relieved nonetheless. Her plan had worked. Kate's desire for an education outweighed her infatuation with Randall Barlow. Already, Randall was courting one of Fiona McBride's daughters. Kate's heart was broken, but as Emma predicted, she had lived through it.

One night, Emma and Jason were making plans to take Kate to Pennsylvania. Jason had to broach a difficult subject with her and he worried about Emma's reaction when he told her. "Emma, when you were in the hospital, we asked Donald Sternin to send inquiries to find any of your relatives, in case you were—" He hesitated.

"In case I had been committed," she finished, reliving the spike of fear the thought of losing Kate always generated.

"Well, it was never an issue after you came home, but we managed to locate your father's family in Ohio."

Emma was surprised and a little miffed. "The Jordens? Why didn't you tell me?"

"I was so happy that you were well again, it completely slipped my mind. Then we had all the wedding plans to make. And I also thought it wasn't something that you wanted to deal with."

"Who did you find?"

"Your father's brother, Clay, and his wife, Bridgett. They still live in Point Pleasant, Ohio, the town where your parents came from."

"My father told me that his family objected to his marriage to my mother. It caused a lot of problems between the brothers. My father tried to patch things up. Every time we went to Bockmeier's, he always posted a letter home, but he never got replies."

"Since we're going east with Kate, think about whether you want to meet your aunt and uncle. Point Pleasant is on the way—but it's up to you."

Emma debated Jason's suggestion for weeks, then decided to contact Bridgett and Clay. Writing the telegram was difficult. In it, she had to explain who she was then relate the tragic circumstances surrounding her parents' deaths. She rewrote the message several times because her hands were shaking from nerves. To her surprise, Clay wired back the next day, asking for the date of their arrival.

Shea's father had also been wired and had promptly replied, stating that he was very excited to meet his granddaughter. After all the years of correspondence between them, Emma felt like she could entrust her daughter to the care of the elder Shea. His letters were well–written; she could almost hear his British accent in his phasing.

With fluttering nerves, Emma braced her courage for the trip, the longest of her life, sure that it would be very eventful.

One night, Emma cuddled with Jason after making love.

"When are you going to tell me what's been bothering you all these months?"

She sat up. The sheet fell away from her breasts and he was instantly distracted, fondling and kissing them. "I've never been happier." She cradled his head against her body, relishing every kiss, every caress. Burying her face in his thick, dark hair, she drank in his scent, always so sweet and woody. He kissed her and a while later, slipped into her. She watched him move above her, her mind on him and her own sensations. She lost her worries and he forgot his earlier question.

Kate would be safe soon living far away in Pennsylvania. She would soon forget all about Randall Barlow.

Chapter Twenty–Five

In July, Emma, Jason, and Kate boarded a train at the station in Millersburg for the trip east. To Emma, the journey across the country was astonishingly fast. Jason dozed in a warm streak of sunlight coming in the window of their sleeping car. It was a comfortable trip in the large private coach which had a stateroom, kitchen, and sleeping berths for four people. She and Kate relaxed, watching the scenery change hour by hour.

Emma's stomach flipped, recognizing landmarks that she had seen in her travels from Nebraska to Montana so long ago. The train's route through Nebraska followed nearly the same route that she had taken with Max Cody. She thought of her parents' graves somewhere out on the Kansas prairie. Memories flicked by as quickly as the train moved along the tracks.

The train chugged and jerked to a halt in Point Pleasant, Ohio. Emma did not know what Clay and Bridgett Jorden looked like and scanned the platform for several minutes while Jason had their trunks loaded onto a wagon for the ride to the hotel. Then she noticed an older couple surveying the crowd. As the man turned slightly, she glimpsed a familiar profile, similar to father's.

Emma girded up her courage and, with Kate in hand and Jason at her side, walked toward them. The couple turned at their approach. "Uncle Clay? Aunt Bridgett?"

The couple smiled nervously and Clay greeted her. "Yes. You must be Emma!" he said, bestowing an affectionate hug. He wore an old brown suit that did not fit him well; the buttons on his coat strained against his bulging belly. Emma saw bits and pieces of her father's features in Clay's face. His hair was very dark, almost black like her father's had been, and he had a little gray at the temples. His hazel eyes were kindly.

Bridgett stepped forward with a rather tepid hug for her. She was short and very round with a huge bosom stuffed in a corset. Her hair was dark brown, but patched with white. She stepped back, taking in Emma's fine clothes.

"I—I'm your niece, Emma Beck. It's a pleasure to meet you." Emma blinked away tears. "I'm making a fool of myself. I'm a little overcome." She pulled Kate forward. "This is my daughter, Kate."

"You're just lovely, my dear. What a beauty she is, Clay," Bridgett commented. Clay and Bridgett embraced Kate, but Emma noticed Bridgett's unconcealed scrutiny of Kate's appearance. Kate wore a striped dress in green and gold and her long, thick hair was braided down her back. With her hair off her face, the high cheekbones, inherited from Shea, clearly showed.

Bridgett spoke. "I'm sorry that my daughter Pearl and her husband Marcus couldn't come today. The farm keeps them so busy. It's doing well and it's hard for them to get away. We are planning a barbecue tomorrow afternoon at our home here in town. They promised to come then with their six children."

"I'm looking forward to meeting everyone," Emma said, reaching for Jason's hand. "My husband, Jason."

Jason stepped forward, introducing himself and shaking hands with Clay and Bridgett. "Jason Beck. A pleasure."

Clay led them off the platform. "Uh, well, we live just a few blocks down the road. As soon as you're settled in the hotel, we'll walk to our place and spend the evening there."

The five of them got into the wagon. It took mere minutes to deposit their trunks at the hotel.

During the walk to the Jordens' house, everyone was awkward and quiet except Jason, who was telling Clay about his logging and sawmilling business.

Emma spoke to her aunt. "Bridgett, how long have you lived in town?"

"We've lived here almost twenty years. We couldn't make a go of farming after your father sold us his share, but we'll talk of that later." Bridgett inspected Emma from head to toe. "You have the look of your mother and the tall frame of your father, Emma."

"I hope my coming here doesn't upset you or Clay. Letting you know of my parents' death through a telegram was not the kindest way of introducing myself."

"We have much to talk about, you and I," Bridgett said. Her look penetrated Emma.

Kate strolled next to Clay. "What was Arthur Jorden like?"

Clay answered Kate after somber thought. "He was a good man, strong and handsome, too. I wish that you could've known him, but I can tell you all about him, and your grandmother, Jane."

Emma's father, Arthur, had written to his brother often, she knew, but had never received replies. Emma knew that the brothers had some sort of falling out when her parents married. Her father had not talked about his family often, but had said that they owned a prosperous farm on the outskirts of Point Pleasant.

But Emma found it difficult to keep any kind of conversation going with Clay or Bridgett. Their answers and were short, almost abrupt. Her initial enthusiasm was fading upon meeting Clay and Bridgett. It was obvious that the family quarrel had never been resolved, but she decided to put old recollections aside. She had nothing to do with the brothers' arguments years ago.

Soon, they came to a modest blue house a few blocks away from the center of town. It was a well-kept clapboard structure with a small front yard, and, Emma could see, a large yard around the back. A very tall white picket fence ringed the property, making the house appear smaller than it was. Mature oak and elm trees shaded the front.

Emma, Jason, and Kate were left in the parlor while Bridgett and Clay got refreshments in the kitchen.

"Well, she's got good manners, in spite of everything," Bridgett said to Clay, "and Jason appears to be quite well off."

"He seems like a nice fella. Kate's a lovely girl, too. And Emma's a beauty—very much like her mother."

"Let's hope that she's not too much like her mother. Well, aside from that, the girl made a good match on her second try. She'll want for nothing. Maybe her money will get this family back on its feet."

"You're not going to ask her for money, are you Bridgett?"

"We've been struggling since we lost that lousy farm your brother unloaded on us. She's got the means now to help her own."

"We lost the farmstead because I wasn't good at farming. Emma owes us nothing. Leave this be, Bridgett."

Emma spoke to Kate, who sat stiffly on a sofa near a window overlooking the road. "The split between the brothers happened long before I was born. There may be a little misplaced resentment we have to withstand, but don't take anything they do or say to heart, all right?"

"All right," Kate replied, finding the view out the window particularly fascinating.

"Don't worry, Em," Jason said. "We're making an effort and that's what is important."

Emma spoke low so that Clay and Bridgett would not hear. "They have lived here in Point Pleasant all along. Why did they ignore my father's letters? Even though they moved to town years ago, you would've thought that my father's letters would've been delivered to them. My parents and I didn't disappear off the earth!" She tried to calm herself. "Clay seems nice, and I tried to talk to Bridgett, but she seems to resent me. Maybe it's just that we're strangers. I don't quite know how to take her."

"We're only here for a couple of days," Jason said. "Hold together. Wait and see what happens."

Bridgett and Clay made them welcome but there was tension, particularly between Emma and Bridgett. However, Emma refused to be led by it.

Dinner held polite chatter, but Emma could see a look on Bridgett's plump face—a judgmental, critical look that bothered her to no end.

After dinner everyone moved to the parlor. The ladies sipped wine as Jason and Clay enjoyed beer. Kate sat apart, her gaze directed out the window again. She looked bored.

Emma asked Bridgett, "Aunt, are my mother and father's parents still living?"

Bridgett's voice was grave. "Your father's parents, Ida and Samuel, died two years after Arthur and your mother left. There was a yellow fever epidemic."

"Oh, I'm sorry. We never knew that. Did you ever hear anything of my mother's family?"

Bridgett cut in. "The McLarens—yes. The whole lot moved to Kentucky years ago. They were long gone before your parents met and married."

"What do you mean—my mother's family left her here? She was only sixteen when she met my father. Why did they leave her behind?"

"Jane was sent off to work somewhere in Cincinnati when she was about fifteen. The McLarens were a strange lot. I remember there were seven children. Knowing that Jane had work meant one less mouth to feed, so off they went to Kentucky. When she returned to Point Pleasant a year later, she was shocked to discover that the whole family just up and left without telling her." There was a strained silence until Bridgett spoke again. "Emma,

I've had enough wine to get my courage up. It's time that we talked of other matters." She rose and rummaged in a desk drawer and handed Emma a bundle wrapped in twine. As if she were giving a command, she said, "Open it."

Inside Emma found, yellowed by age, a pack of letters along with Max Cody's articles clipped from the Point Pleasant Gazette. She looked to her aunt, bewildered and hurt. "My father's letters! The Cody articles?" She glanced to Jason. He came to her chair, looking over her shoulder. Kate kept her place. At that second, Emma saw Shea so strongly in her. Kate waited and watched—waiting for Bridgett's game to play out.

Bridgett sat down. "I always picked up the mail you see, because Clay's knees bother him. I was in town more often back then, before we had to sell the farm. That's just the way it all worked out, the way it all began."

Why she retreated into excuses, Emma had no clue.

"When I received the first letter, I couldn't bring myself to open it. I thought that it was your father's demand for us to send the money we owed him for his share of the farm. We fell on hard times after he and your mother left. The bank foreclosed on us and we lost the property—five–hundred acres' worth. We barely had enough left to afford this small house. Clay took a job running the ticket booth at the train station and I did mending and ironing to support us." She became a little haughty for a moment. "Pearl and Marcus were able to buy back the farm years later, so it's in the family once again." She reached for her glass of wine and took a deep drink. "I didn't want Clay burdened with coming up with the rest of the money. I thought that's why your father wrote so often—I was sure that he had fallen on hard times. The return address was in Kansas, not Oregon, as he and your mother had planned. I received other letters over the years and hid them all. Finally, my curiosity got the best of me and I opened them one night. I discovered that Arthur was writing only to tell us of his life—about the loss of the three children before you—and the struggle to survive in such a hostile place. He never once asked for money. I felt very ashamed for hiding the letters. For all Clay knew, his brother was prospering in Oregon and had no desire to contact him ever again."

Emma's mouth opened on a thousand questions.

"Hear me out, dear, please," Bridgett said, curt. "No letters came for a very long time. They stopped coming in '77, I think. Then more than a year later, I read the Cody stories in the paper. Clay read them too, but he never put it together. He didn't know that you existed, you see. He did comment on the Jorden name, though, and thought nothing more of it. As for me, I was shocked when I read of the young girl who had married a renegade half–breed Indian. When I saw the name Emma Jorden Hawkshadow, I knew exactly who you were."

Kate was offended and angered at the 'half-breed renegade' reference to her father. Without protest from Emma or Jason, she rose from her seat and poured herself a glass of wine.

"Your father often spoke of you in his letters. He was very proud of you and how you never complained about the place you lived or the hard work that you had to do. But he did have high hopes for you, that you would marry a soldier and travel around the country." She shifted her bulk in the chair. "Cody wrote of the deaths of your parents, but he never used their names, nor did he say how they had died. I didn't know what to do. The truth would hurt Clay, so I kept silent."

Emma was bewildered. "Didn't you think that he had a right to know?"

"Too much time had passed. I couldn't tell him that his brother and sister–in–law were dead—then tell him that his niece, who he never knew existed, was carried off and married to an Indian and living on a reservation! I love Clay and would not hurt him with such shocking news."

Emma was very annoyed at Bridgett's disapproving manner and how she referred to Shea and his people. Kate came to sit next to her mother on the arm of the chair. "I was not carried off, aunt. Shea saved my life. If he hadn't, your little secret would've been safe because I would have been dead."

"I admit that I did a terrible thing. But it was better having Clay believe that Arthur was alive, not buried on the prairie in an anonymous grave."

"I still don't understand."

Bridgett's eyes glistened with emotions that she tried to keep in check. "I was protecting my husband. You might have done the same. You may think me uncaring about your plight, but that wasn't why."

"Why hide my existence? Because I lived with Indians?" Emma sat erect, her attitude resolute. "I have no regrets about Shea. I loved him. But he was taken from me by cancer eleven years ago. I rebuilt my life. You have no idea how hard it's been. Knowing that I had some family would've been some comfort. At least my father made an effort to stay in touch with you. Why couldn't you do the same?"

Bridgett leaned forward, patting Emma's hand, trying to pacify her. It was all Emma could do to not yank her hand away. "You poor thing. I know the terrible things that you endured living with the savages. My heart went out to you. You might not believe me, but it's true. But then, years later, we received an inquiry from a lawyer in Easthope, Washington state. It was to verify our relationship in case we were chosen to take custody of your daughter." She nodded toward Kate.

Kate took a gulp of the wine and her grip on Emma's shoulder tightened.

Emma's eyes welled with tears. She had expected a few bumps in the road with Bridgett and Clay, but in truth, the visit was not starting out very well. "I was in the hospital for a few months after Shea's death. I won't lie to you. I had a breakdown. If I had been committed, then you and Clay or Shea's father in Philadelphia would've had to raise Kate."

Bridgett was startled by Emma's open confession of her illness. "Of course, if she had come to us, we would've taken good care of her—even though she is part Indian—"

This was the slip that Emma knew was coming. Kate put down her glass of wine and headed for the door. Jason got up and stopped her.

Emma glared at Bridgett. "Kate is not beneath your notice because she's part Cheyenne!"

Clay stood up, went to Kate and took her hand, patting it. "Don't go, Kate. Please hear us out." He led her back to Emma's chair, but not before Kate had grabbed her glass of wine as she returned through the room.

Bridgett flushed and looked to Kate. "I didn't mean it like that. I meant that your life would be difficult when people found out your ancestry, that's all. People are not as tolerant of such things here. Don't take offense, Kate. I had an image of you and your mother as wild things living on the frontier. I wondered if, at my age, I could take on the responsibility of a young child. When Clay asked me who I knew in Easthope, I had to tell him everything."

Jason watched Emma. He could tell that she was ready to explode. Her whole body was trembling with rage.

Clay broke in. "Emma, what your aunt did was not intended to hurt you, but to protect me. After she explained everything, I understood why she did it, but I was very upset when I read Arthur's letters and those articles." Clay looked at her with eyes so much like her father's. "If I had known, I would've done anything to find you. Bridgett and I had some go–rounds about it for a very long time. I wanted to hop on a train to go find you, but she talked me out of it. It wasn't that we didn't care. We were afraid of what we might find. It was fear of the unknown, my dear, not fear or disdain of you. My brother's marriage to your mother caused a lot of problems and Arthur and I had many arguments over it. I'm assuming that you know of your mother's problems before she met Arthur?"

"What problems?"

"When she was arrested?"

Emma was stunned. "Arrested?"

Clay looked uncomfortable and took a deep breath before he continued. "As Bridgett told you earlier, when Jane was fifteen her parents sent her to work as a maid in a hotel in Cincinnati. Months later, she was suspected of robbing a bank. It was said that she took around three thousand dollars. A witness who was at the bank the day of the robbery identified her for the police. She was arrested several days later, but the money was never found."

"My mother was in jail?"

"No. She went crazy when they arrested her. She ended up in an asylum. Since she was branded as insane, no charges were filed."

Emma paled and it took a moment for her to find her voice. "How long was she in there?"

"About a year," Clay answered. "She was released because the doctors said that she was better, but the real reason was that the place was over-crowded. After her release, she made her way back here. When she came home, she discovered that her entire family had moved away. No one knew where they'd gone. She later got work as a waitress at a restaurant here in town."

Feeling drained, Emma fought off old demons. Knowing that she had problems similar to her mother's frightened her. Were her own mental weaknesses inborn? Would she have to battle more collapses the rest of her life? Unable to deal with such fears, she got up and headed for the door. "I need some air, please excuse me."

Jason followed her outside to the porch and hugged her. "Don't take this so hard, Emma. I'm sure that there were a lot of reasons why your mother did what she did."

"I'm more like her than I ever knew."

He held her tight against him and motioned to Kate, who had followed them outside. She came to her mother and put her arm around her shoulders. "Mom, I'm sorry."

Emma smiled weakly. "I'll be all right. It was hot in there. I need to be alone for a while." She left Jason and Kate and walked down the dark street alone. Clay and Bridgett came onto the porch and watched her go.

"I didn't mean to hurt her feelings," Clay said to Jason and Kate.

"It's obvious that she doesn't know everything. There is more to tell her," Bridgett added with a note of foreboding.

"Enough, Bridgett," Clay admonished. "If she wants to hear it, I'll tell her the rest myself, all right?"

"Do as you please," she sniffed.

All of them took up stations on the front porch waiting for Emma to return. Jason stood at the gate, watching for her. A half hour later, she came back.

She had been crying. "I'm so sorry to go off like that," she apologized.

"Not at all, my dear," Clay said. "Please come sit on the porch. It's cooler out here."

Bridgett went into the house to bring the refreshments out to the porch.

"Maybe we should head back to the hotel so you can rest," Jason said to Emma as they ascended the steps.

Emma shook her head and seated herself on the porch. "No. I want to hear it all." There was a flash in her eyes. "Now I know where my mother's money came from. I always wondered why it was all in large denominations—and why the tin had dirt encrusted on it. I think that she robbed the bank, then buried the money until she could get to it when it was safe for her. But I can't understand why she and my father didn't use the money to make their lives better."

Clay continued the story as Bridgett returned to the porch with a tray of drinks. "The Jorden family was invited to a wedding that spring, catered by the restaurant where your mother worked. Jane was there to serve the food. When Arthur saw her, he fell for her in a second. They began seeing each other in secret because he knew that our parents would object. There were stories about her all over town. When their romance was discovered, our family tried to break them up. The arguments continued up until the day of the wedding and didn't stop afterwards. We all drove them away."

Emma braced herself and dared to ask a question that had troubled her since childhood. "Was my mother pregnant when they married?"

Bridgett's hand fluttered to her considerable bosom. After a long silence, she answered. "Yes. She was."

Emma shook her head in wonderment. "So much makes sense now—things she said about Aaron, her firstborn. He lived only a few days."

"What did she say?" Jason asked.

"She said that Aaron was the sacrifice she had to make to turn her life around. I always wondered what she meant. After he died, she got pregnant very soon after and lost Grace, then right after that she lost Elizabeth." She looked at Clay. "Maybe she was afraid that my father would leave her if there were no children to hold him."

"Then you came along, Emma. You made them very happy." Clay said. He rose and went inside the house and brought out the letters. "Take these with you and read them. They will explain a lot."

Emma took the letters out of courtesy, wondering if she would have the courage to read them.

"You'll find, as I did, that your father loved Jane. He would never have left her."

Emma nodded to her uncle.

Jason suggested that he and Clay retreat to the back porch to smoke a cigar. Kate went with them. Jason knew that Emma had much more to say to Bridgett and that they were better off if left alone.

Once they were left to themselves, Bridgett's demeanor changed. Her next question surprised Emma. "You loved this Indian man, didn't you?"

Emma was overcome as memories of her life with Shea flooded back. "I know to many people he was considered a savage, but Shea Hawkshadow was a very tender, loving man. We were happy together. I am a better person because of him, and very lucky to have loved him. He gave me Kate. She has been my strength more times than she knows."

"And Jason?"

She smiled at his mention. "Shea was the husband of my youth. I was naïve, willful, selfish, often foolish, and he tolerated me as I grew up. Jason's the husband of my heart. I love him more each day. And he's become Kate's father without pushing Shea's memory aside. I don't know how he does it." She met Bridgett's eyes. "Sometimes it wasn't easy living with Shea. I have many scars, but no regrets. None. I'd do it all over again."

On the back porch in the warm, quiet night, Clay offered Jason a cigar. "Bridgett hates the smell of them, so I can't smoke in the house. It's all right most of the time, but it's miserable in winter. Can I get anything for you, Kate?" She shook her head.

"We'll be here for quite a while. I think that Emma and her aunt needed some time alone. I hope you don't mind," Jason said.

"Oh, I agree. I need a moment for myself, too. This has been a difficult night for all of us. I regret that we didn't handle the truth about Emma's parents better. We thought she knew." He spoke to Kate. "People shy away from what they don't understand, from what they fear. Bridgett didn't mean to hurt your feelings. It's just the way she talks." He struck a match and lit Jason's cigar then his own.

Kate accepted his apology, but she was still stinging from her first encounter with prejudice. In Easthope, she had been sheltered from it. She was becoming afraid of bigotry that she might encounter at college.

Clay puffed on his cigar. "Emma seems too upset to go into it, so I'd like to ask you, Jason. Do you know how my brother and his wife died?"

He thought before answering, heartened that he could spare Emma the pain of telling Clay of that terrible day in Kansas. "Emma told me that a band of Pawnee attacked the homestead back in '77. Arthur and Jane were killed during the raid. Emma was far from the house when it happened and there was nothing that she could do to save them. She hid near the creek until the Indians had gone, then buried her parents. She had to abandon her home in case the Pawnee came back."

Clay saddened. "What a horrible way to die. So senseless."

"Emma's guilt over it all was very hard for her to overcome and contributed to her breakdown after Shea died. She's survived and endured through very hard times," Jason said.

"Emma did what she had to do, but why stay with savages? Weren't there other settlements nearby that she could have gone to?"

"Please don't call the Indians savages," Kate interjected.

"I'm sorry, Kate," Clay apologized. "I'm afraid the use of that word is commonplace around here. It won't happen again."

Jason continued. "The nearest settlement was more than twenty miles away at a trading post. Emma was going there, but she was on foot because all the horses had been taken by the Pawnee. There was a snowstorm and Emma got lost. Shea found her half-dead out on the prairie and brought her to the Cheyenne reservation."

Clay said, "Don't take this wrong, but after reading all those articles and realizing who Emma was, I found myself disapproving of her. Now that I know everything, I understand, but to go off and do what she did," he caught himself. He looked to Kate who wiped away a tear. "I've offended you again. I'm sorry."

"I loved my father. He was a great man," Kate said.

Jason spoke. "Shea Hawkshadow was the finest friend I ever had, sir. He was brave and he loved Emma and Kate. He was not a savage, but a strong and noble man. He protected his people, his family."

"My Lord, how did Emma manage?" Clay said.

Even though Clay's question was rhetorical, Jason answered. "She managed because she loved Shea. He saved her life and gave her love, which she desperately needed. And if people don't approve, so what? All she wanted to do was live in peace with her husband and child. Events swept her up in the days following her parents' murder. For years, she never had a chance to catch her breath. She witnessed the Cheyenne massacre at Fort Robinson, something I'm sure you read about. She watched dozens of people get maimed and killed. Later in Montana, an old Indian woman she was very close to, Red Leaf Woman, died the day the militia attacked the camp. Then, Shea died not long after they settled in Easthope. It all caught up with her. That's why she was hospitalized—not because she was crazy."

Kate came behind Jason's chair and hugged him.

Clay looked shamefaced. "I didn't mean to insult your friend. What Emma did—all that she went through—must've been hard, but worth it."

"Emma did what she had to do," Jason said.

"I never tried to find out what happened to my brother and his wife. I should have."

When Jason, Kate, and Clay returned to the front porch, Emma and Bridgett had buried some of their initial animosity. It was late and with the letters clutched in her hands, Emma bade her aunt and uncle good–night.

When back at the hotel, Jason said, "Emma, when we left you and Bridgett alone and went to the back porch, Clay asked me about the day your parents died. I told him everything."

Emma sat on the bed. "Thank you for doing that, Jason. I was dreading having to tell him."

After Kate closed the door between their adjoining rooms and Jason fell asleep, Emma read her father's letters. She learned many things she had never known and confronted many truths. Arthur was a very sensitive man and deeply committed to Jane. He understood her grief when Aaron died, patiently waiting a week until she allowed him to bury the child. Her father never regretted his decision to settle in Kansas. His writings showed that he enjoyed the struggles of being self–sufficient. He was also ready to accept the consequences of living in isolation. In the wee hours, Emma finally curled beside Jason and slept.

The next morning, a note was slipped under the hotel room door. It was from Bridgett and Clay, inviting Emma, Jason, and Kate to ride to the Jorden farm to help transport Pearl, Marcus, and their six children to the barbecue. Curious to see the property, Emma hurried Jason and Kate out of bed. They met Clay at his house at nine o'clock in the morning. Bridgett begged off, saying that she had to prepare food for the barbecue, refusing Jason's offer to remain behind to help her.

The Ohio countryside was pretty with rounded hills, thickly wooded, just as Emma's father had so often described. At last, the road dipped into the shallow valley of the Jorden farm. Emma asked Clay stop his buggy for a moment so that she could take a long look at the acreage. Jason and Kate seemed nonplussed. Coming from the lush mountains gave them no appreciation for the lowlands and the fertile ground that needed such careful tending. But the sight of the land moved something in Emma. So often, she had heard stories of this place until it took on almost mythical proportions. As they drew nearer the house, she was crestfallen. The fields were indeed doing well, planted with beans, potatoes, corn, and a kitchen garden near the back of the house. But the farmhouse had not fared as well as the fields. It looked sunken, tired, almost ramshackle. Shutters hung at crazy angles, the entire facade needed paint, and the windows were dirty. Emma's heart was embittered, seeing the state of the place. From her father's description, she had expected more, but had to realize that more than forty years had passed since her father had left his boyhood home.

A woman, Pearl, Emma supposed, raised a hand to them as she hoisted her six children into a buckboard. A tall, slim blonde man who had to be Marcus was stacking boxes between the children's feet at the back of the wagon.

Clay brought his buggy to a halt near the front gate. Jason handed down Emma and Kate while Clay got down with remarkable agility and trotted off to greet his grandchildren.

Marcus grinned and walked over to Jason, Emma, and Kate. "Great to meet you all," he said, shaking hands with them. "Marcus Lange."

Emma introduced herself, Jason, and Kate.

Pearl then came forward, taking in Emma's polished appearance and fine clothes. "Well, hello, Emma." She was only two years older than Emma, but her appearance brought into sharp focus the hardships of farming. Pearl's blue dress was worn and faded. Gray stood out in her light hair, which was pulled into a sloppy bun. She looked far older than thirty-nine.

"Nice to meet you, Pearl, Marcus," Emma said, bewildered at Pearl's churlish tone of voice.

"I'll give you a hand," Jason said to Marcus, excusing himself to help him in loading the rest of the boxes into the buckboard.

Kate noticed that the children who were giggling and playing in the back of the wagon seemed to be about a year apart in age. Their clothes were limp and dirty. And Kate thought that all six children would benefit from a good scrubbing; their faces were gray with dirt and their hair was matted and greasy.

Pearl, Emma, and Kate stood together. "Here you are at last, Emma. You're the last person I'd expect on my doorstep after all I've heard about you." Pearl's disdain for Emma was very evident.

Emma fought to remain polite. "Clay invited us to come. I wanted to see where my father grew up."

"Is it what you expected?"

"It's very pleasant here. Much larger and finer than the homestead where I grew up in Kansas."

"I'm sure it is," she said with a smug glance at the acreage.

"You have five–hundred acres?" Emma asked, remembering that her father had often mentioned the size of the Jorden property.

Pearl seemed exasperated. "There used to be. When Marcus and I bought back the place, two–hundred acres had already been sold off by the previous owners."

"It's still a large property to manage," Emma said, trying to find some common ground with Pearl, but it was proving to be a difficult task. "I always wondered how my parents farmed a hundred and sixty acres. The acreage we had always seemed so huge to me."

"What did they call you—yes, sod busters, right?" Pearl said with a superior laugh. "Or were you squatters?"

Pearl's attempt to humble Emma put her on the defensive. "We were not squatters. My parents owned their homestead in Kansas. And for your information, our fields looked as good as yours." Pearl scoffed and began to make another disparaging comment, but Emma cut her off. "Excuse us," she said briskly, walking away with Kate.

"This is going to be a long afternoon," Kate muttered.

"You said it," Emma whispered back.

Kate went to Jason who had finished loading the wagon. He handed her up into Clay's buggy and turned around, looking for Emma. She had walked off a short distance, ostensibly to survey the fields. She really needed a moment to calm herself after talking with the openly vindictive Pearl. Emma turned to go back to Clay's buggy and saw Jason signal to her that it was time to leave.

Then Jason saw Pearl approaching Emma from behind.

Emma heard Pearl coming as her footsteps crunched on the gravel. "I didn't mean to offend you, Emma. Meeting you—well, you're not what I expected." Pearl's manner had now softened—somewhat.

"What did you expect?" Emma could not bear to look at her and kept her gaze fastened on the fields.

"Well, my mother said that you were married to a lumberjack. I expected a lumberjack's wife."

"I am a lumberjack's wife."

"You're wealthy, that's obvious to anyone," Pearl replied, her arms crossed defensively across her chest.

"Jason owns the lumber business in Easthope and I run my own bakery."

"After all I read about your exploits in Cody's articles, you still landed on your feet, didn't you?"

Emma turned on Pearl. "Why do you resent me for that? Why is it all I've heard from you and your family since we arrived are insults followed by halfhearted apologies? I'll tell you this much, Pearl, I'm sorry that I ever came here."

Pearl's face pinched as she squinted into the morning sun. "Once we discovered that a relative of ours was the subject of those stories in the newspaper, the opinion of the Jorden family fell considerably."

"Well Pearl, you or your parents had to tell people that I was your relative in order for that to have happened," Emma shot back.

Pearl had no defense on that point, but she kept on baiting Emma. "Still, it embarrassed us. You were out on the frontier gallivanting around with Indians, doing God knows what with them."

Emma seethed with rage. "Do not insult the Indians any longer, Pearl.

You know nothing about them—and remember that Kate is the child from my marriage to Shea Hawkshadow. She's one–quarter Cheyenne."

"I know that, but—"

"I don't want to hear any more about it. She's not a little savage, my husband Shea wasn't, and neither am I."

"But your conduct—participating in that illegal outbreak from the Indian reservation—we were so shocked," Pearl scolded.

Emma's voice quavered in anger. "You know nothing about me, except what you read in some newspaper articles written twenty years ago. For years, my father wrote to Clay. He never wrote back because your mother hid the letters from him. Judge that conduct before you judge mine!"

Clay heard the ruckus between Emma and Pearl. He approached them saying, "Let's get moving." His look to Emma was full of apologies. He took Pearl by the arm and led her over to her wagon. "What was that all about?" Pearl only shook her head.

Emma went to Clay's buggy. As Jason helped her up, she declared, "I've had enough of this narrow–minded family."

"So have I," Kate replied. "If my grandfather's family is this rude, I'm coming straight back home with you."

"No argument there," Emma agreed. "Now I understand why my parents ran away from these people!"

"What happened between you and Pearl?" Jason asked.

"I'll have to tell you later," Emma replied as Clay came toward the buggy.

On the ride back to town, Emma fought back tears as she recovered from the spiteful exchange with Pearl.

Clay glanced back at her. "I'm sorry Emma," he said. "Pearl's too much like her mother sometimes. She talks before she thinks things through."

The barbecue at Clay and Bridgett's began at noon. Throughout the day Emma mixed with the guests, comprised of Pearl's children and neighbors of Clay and Bridgett's. She was careful to avoid Pearl at all costs. She glanced around from time to time and saw Jason standing in a circle of people, Kate glued to his side. He was charming and pleasant and the center of attention. She was grateful to him, knowing that he was doing this for her. She had spoken with more than a dozen people who were curious about the newspaper articles about her and Shea. As she recounted the details to an eager audience, memories of Shea became sharper than they had ever been. She was an unwilling celebrity, bemused by the interest in the story of her life.

The day was very hot. Alone, Emma retreated to the shady front porch in the late afternoon.

Later, Marcus came around the house and sat in a chair beside her. "Pearl told me what happened between you two. She feels bad. She didn't mean anything by it."

"Pardon me, Marcus, but yes, she did. I don't hold anything against you, but Pearl made her opinions of me very clear."

"Give her another chance, Emma. She had a picture of you in her head and I guess when she saw you, it threw her off balance. She's not always like what you saw today."

Despite a very strong desire to get on the evening train without a backward glance, she apologized to Marcus for her terse remarks. She felt sorry for him that he was married to such a shrew. But he seemed affable and eager to know her.

"Pearl sees me as the girl from those Max Cody articles. I'm a grown woman."

"And Pearl realizes that, too. Just sometimes her mouth starts running and she can't stop. She feels just awful. When we found out those articles were about a relative, we didn't know what to think. We all thought you'd gone Indian."

Emma laughed out loud. "I did!"

He looked startled, then said, "I'd love to hear all about it."

She opened her mouth to speak, but his hand on her arm stopped her.

Pearl came up the steps. "Emma, I want to apologize. I was rude and didn't mean to say those things. I promise to apologize for my rudeness to Jason and Kate as well."

Marcus smiled at Emma and left them. He headed back to the yard.

"Pearl, we're leaving tomorrow. I don't have the strength to spar any longer. I don't have to explain why I made the choices I did."

"Please, Emma. I don't want bad feelings between us. I was jealous of you. You've led quite an exciting life."

"It wasn't as romantic as you may think, Pearl. I had a lot of losses."

"But look at you now. You're an elegant lady married to a rich handsome man. And your Kate is a beautiful, intelligent girl. I just didn't understand how different things are out west. There is more tolerance for more unconventional ways of living. In spite of everything, you turned out all right." She smiled with a spark of warmth.

"The good things that happened to me fell into my lap. I think that Kate and Jason are my payoffs for just living through it all."

Pearl capitulated. "I don't want you to go back home hating me. I only see the end result before me."

"I knew that I had relatives here. I could've come here any time, but deep down, and don't take this the wrong way, I didn't want this life. I always felt that there was something else for me and I hoped to find it on the frontier. Nothing turned out the way I imagined."

"I understand what you mean, Emma. I'm not thrilled running a farm. I had dreams, too," Pearl confided.

Despite lingering hard feelings, they settled into the twin rockers on the porch and talked. Emma and Pearl eventually reached a truce. Jason saw the two women talking as he came around the front of the house. He smiled and returned to the yard unseen.

Emma was pleased that Pearl, Marcus, and the children, along with Clay and Bridgett, came to see them off on the train to Philadelphia the next morning.

Pearl surprised Emma by hugging her. "I hope you return someday."

As the train chugged out of Point Pleasant, Emma burst out laughing.

Jason turned to her. "What's so funny?" Since the visit with the Jorden family had not gone well, he was puzzled what Emma had found so amusing.

"My mother—a bank robber!" she chuckled. "If you had known her, that would be the last thing you would expect her to do."

Kate grinned. "Why?"

"Because she was a very quiet and reserved person, at least she was when I knew her. I just can't imagine her walking into a bank and saying 'this is a stickup!' She was a tiny woman, barely five–feet tall. I wonder how the bank teller could have seen her on the other side of the high counter! The thought of her doing such a thing is hilarious!"

Jason smiled, not only at Emma's humor, but because even though the visit to Ohio had been rough, she had experienced a breakthrough. In her own way she was making peace with the deaths of her parents. Finding a morbid spark of humor in her mother's act of robbing a bank revived Emma's spirits.

Chapter Twenty-Six

As Emma descended from the train in Philadelphia, her heart thudded in her chest. Not knowing what Shea Russell looked like, she once again had to scan a bustling train platform looking for a stranger. Then Emma stood transfixed. The resemblance was so strong—the eyes and angular features, the same mouth, the tall lean frame. Summoning her courage, she took the hands of Jason and Kate and approached the very well–dressed man. When he saw her determined approach he smiled knowing that she was Emma, from Cody's description of her auburn hair, still worn long and loose to this day.

She extended her hand, battling many conflicting emotions. "I'm Emma." She felt his hand tremble in hers.

"I'm so pleased," he said in a clipped British accent as he removed the bowler hat that matched his dark gray suit.

"This is Katherine, Shea's daughter," Emma said as Kate came forward.

"Pleased to meet you." He shook her small hand, holding it a long moment. Profound emotion welled up in him. "You're beautiful. You look so much like your father."

Kate's eyes welled with tears. "Thank you," she managed.

"And Jason Beck, my husband," Emma said. Jason came forward and they shook hands.

"It is indeed a pleasure to meet all of you," Shea Russell said.

Emma caught herself staring at him. "Forgive me."

"I'm sorry if the resemblance makes you uncomfortable."

"No. It doesn't. It just brings back a lot of memories—good memories."

"I'm glad for that." He spoke to a young, sandy-haired man standing nearby. "See to their luggage, Daniels."

With a warm smile and discreet assessment of Kate, Daniels disappeared into the crowd with Jason to find their trunks. Emma and Kate looked at each other, suppressing a nervous laugh since Daniels was the first butler that they had ever seen.

"How was your visit with your family in Ohio?"

"It didn't go as well as we hoped, Shea—" When Emma said his name, her voice choked off.

"Why don't you call me Russell? Would that do?"

Emma was grateful for his quick notice of her discomfort. "Yes, that would be easier, if you don't mind."

"I want you to feel relaxed and at home while you're here. I have my driver and carriage waiting for us. Daniels will bring your luggage along in another wagon," he said with the ease of wealth. "Shall we find Jason?" He offered his arms to Kate and Emma and they headed across the platform.

"Are your wife and children here?" Emma asked.

"I asked them to stay at home today so that I could enjoy you all without competition. Everyone is waiting for us at the house."

So far, Kate liked him and hoped that her reception in his home would obliterate the ignorance of the Jorden family. After all, she would be spending the next four years living with this man, a grandfather she did not know.

They found Jason and proceeded to Russell's brougham carriage. It was a luxurious black coach, imported from England, Russell told them. Emma ran her hand along the side panels which were decorated with gold scroll work. Four sleek black horses were harnessed and impatient to go. Jason, Emma, and Kate were further impressed with Russell's coachman who was liveried in a black uniform trimmed in gold and a top hat made of silk. He handed them all into the spacious interior that was upholstered in tufted green velvet.

Emma watched the city unfold before her as they rode to Russell's home. Philadelphia was the largest city that she had seen since the honeymoon in San Francisco, but Philadelphia was much more crowded—and much older. The old brick buildings they passed lent a reassuring and conservative atmosphere to the city. As they drove to the outskirts of town, they passed several mansions with manicured lawns. Kate was fascinated. And Emma had never seen such grandeur or wealth. Russell talked about the area and all it had to offer in the way of shops, parks, museums, and theater. He and Jason talked about their respective businesses. Jason was particularly interested in Russell's import/export business which had offices in Seattle, as well as Philadelphia and New Orleans. Emma was amused, knowing that Jason was trying to figure a way to add a new business establishment to Easthope.

Soon, the carriage turned onto a long, curving private road paved with patterned bricks. The grounds were luxuriant with a huge lawn of deepest green ornamented with clumps of trees and carefully trimmed shrubs. Over a hill and within sight of the house, the lawn was embellished with lush beds of orange, red and white flowers. The road ended at the most magnificent house that any of them had ever seen. The handsome two-story facade was red brick done in geometric patterns. Two large one-story wings extended from either end of the main home. The windows spanning the first floor were enormous, probably ten feet tall. Opposite a grand columned porch and across the gravel drive was a marble fountain of carved flowers surrounded by a pond rimmed with stone that was cast in scrolls and bird designs.

As the coach came to a halt, Russell's wife, Margaret, greeted them just inside the door. They stepped into a huge entranceway clothed in gold wallpaper and set with ornate furniture. Margaret was from Boston, Russell had said. She was very beautiful and gracious as she showed them into the parlor. Her hair was still blonde, even though she was more than fifty, and she wore it in a relaxed bun. Her figure was slim and her posture perfect without seeming stiff. Emma admired Margaret's elegant dress of midnight blue satin that rustled with richness as she walked.

As they became acquainted over tea, Margaret did not appear to resent the fact that her husband had led another life before marrying her. She accepted them in her home with ease and grace. Emma liked her. Russell's three daughters, accompanied by their husbands and very well–behaved children, soon appeared from the nether regions of the mansion.

Later, Margaret showed them to their rooms, which were exquisitely furnished. The house was lit with gaslight, a novelty to them all. Emma and Jason were given a huge room decorated in green and beige. Upon seeing the bed, Jason winked at Emma. With the three of them traveling in the same rail car, Emma and Jason had enjoyed little privacy during the trip.

Kate's room was a few doors down the hallway. It was a large and pleasing suite decorated in shades of pink and cream. To the left of the bed was a large dressing room that had walls covered in mirrors. She even had a balcony and bathroom of her own.

As they dressed for dinner, Jason noticed Emma's awe as she talked about all the lavish features of the house and grounds. "We could live like this if you want to," he said.

She laughed as she put his tie around his collar. "We would need a dozen maids to keep a place this big clean and a dozen gardeners to care for the grounds. Thanks, but I'll pass. I love our cozy little home in Easthope."

"I think they do have a dozen maids in this place. They're lurking around every corner ready to wipe up every speck of dust," Jason joked. He pulled her to him. "Do we have time?" he asked, his hands feeling Emma's curves.

"Don't mess up my hair to much," she giggled as he laid her on the bed.

After a sumptuous five-course dinner in the vaulted dining hall with Russell and his family, Emma excused herself from the table and went to her room. She returned with an old cigar box and asked to see Russell alone, before brandy and cigars were produced for the men. With a modest nod from Margaret, Emma and Russell went into an adjoining billiard lounge. She seated herself beside him and placed the box on a small table at his elbow. He saw Kate's name emblazoned on the lid in childish scrawl.

"I'm sorry that Kate's a little bashful around you."

"We are strangers for the moment, but I assure you that she will be well looked after and will always be chaperoned, Emma."

"I can't thank you enough for taking her in," Emma said in deference to him.

"I am grateful to you for bringing her to us," Russell replied with genuine humility.

Emma then handed Russell the cigar box that held the photographs taken of Shea at the cabin years before. "These photographs were taken about a year before Shea died. I wanted to show them to you in private. If you don't want to see them, we can return to the dining room—"

Russell took the pictures from the box and studied the images of his son, abandoned so long ago. Emma saw his face flush with emotion.

"Does this upset you?"

He shook his head. "I'm overwhelmed, my dear. These are magnificent." He looked through them again and again. "Would you mind? I'd like a few moments alone."

"Of course." Emma closed the lounge door behind her and returned to the table with apologies to Margaret and the family. She sat and wondered if she had done the right thing; she could not guess Russell's state of emotion as she left him.

A while later the butler, Daniels, tried to enter the game room but found that the door was locked. He glanced at Mrs. Russell, who indicated with just a tilt of her chin that he was to remain until her husband unlocked the door. Emma, Kate, and Jason exchanged looks of wonder as the young man stood stock-still with his tray of brandy and cigars at the ready.

Soon, Russell emerged, asking everyone to gather in the parlor. Even Daniels followed, at a discreet distance, the half–dozen brandies and cigars perfectly balanced on the silver tray.

Emma stole a glance at Russell as they all went down the hallway; his eyes were bloodshot. She hoped that showing him the pictures had not been a mistake.

Once everyone was settled in the ornate parlor, he passed around the pictures of Shea, speaking of his son with tender pride. "I most admire you, Emma, for ensuring that Shea had love and a family. And for giving him such friends as Jason, of whom you've so often spoken of in your letters and for Katherine, who made his life complete."

Emma was surprised when Kate went to her grandfather and hugged him. "You many keep your favorite photograph, if you wish," Kate offered.

Russell chose one of the close–ups of his son's face.

The next day, Russell had his coachman take himself, Emma, Kate, and Jason on a tour of the rolling Pennsylvania countryside in his elegant carriage. There was no avoiding the subject of Shea, so at length, Russell began to speak.

"I want to explain. I want you to know why I left Shea and his mother."

"There is no reason to reopen old wounds," Emma said in an effort to spare his feelings.

"Maybe the wound will heal at last if I admit my shortcomings to those who were closest to him. Perhaps I can purge some guilt about leaving so long ago."

Emma said, "Shea somehow knew that day that you would never return."

"I meant to return. His mother was a beautiful woman. And I loved her and my son."

"Then why did you leave?" Kate asked.

"That's the hardest part to explain. I could tell you that I met someone else, but that's not how it was. I could not spend the rest of my life on a reservation and I did not have the courage to tell my wife and son. And I could not risk taking them into white society. I started walking that day and just kept going. I ended up in St. Louis and thought that I would return someday. Then one day passed and then another and another until those days became years and it was too late to resurrect that other life." He spoke to Emma. "Your life with Shea was hard. I know what living on a reservation is like. I give you credit for more courage than I possess."

"Thank you, Russell," Emma acknowledged. "But we had good times, especially when we were smart enough to stay in Easthope after Kate was born. The townspeople accepted us and we became part of the community. I can't imagine what our lives would've been like in another town."

"I am glad for that. For years, I worked with Max Cody to find Shea. I was just too late. I got the news of his passing just before Christmas in '87. I hadn't told Margaret about my earlier life until the day I received the message from Max. I was immobilized with grief. It was Margaret who encouraged me to write to you and send the bank draft on Kate's behalf."

"I have always been grateful to you for being so generous to Kate. You didn't even know us, yet you were trying to help," Emma said.

"I knew that my son would choose a woman of extraordinary strength and beauty." He swallowed several times. "He was my only son. My selfishness caused him great suffering." In the photograph of his son that he had kept, the scars of Shea's acquaintance with the noose showed. Russell could not get the image out of his mind.

Jason spoke. "Russell, before Shea died, he talked to me about you. When he and Emma left the Montana reservation, he knew that she and his child had to live among their own people. In leaving the Cheyenne, he understood why you had to go."

"Reservations are sad places," Russell said.

"Shea felt the sacrifice was worth it," Jason returned.

In comparing his behavior with his son's, Russell found that he and his son were not so different after all.

Before Kate was to start college, they decided to tour New York City. After the train ride, a hired carriage took Emma, Jason, and Kate through the bustling city. They were taken to a grand hotel, their stay a gift from Russell, near the Hudson River on the island of Manhattan.

As they checked in, the desk clerk called to a young man standing nearby. He was clad in the hotel uniform of a red jacket trimmed with gold braid and black trousers. The young man was tall and broad shouldered with dark hair and eyes. He flashed a practiced smile at them, but it changed as he took in Kate. His grin deepened.

Instinctively, Jason moved between the two. "Elevators?" he asked.

"This way, sir," he said, tearing his gaze away from Kate.

The young man chattered on about the amenities of the hotel as the elevator clanked to the fourth floor. "Here's your suite," he said, turning the key in the lock. The door swung open on a rather gaudy but well furnished sitting room. Two elegant bedrooms could be seen beyond. "I hope that your stay is pleasant and here's your complimentary newspaper," he said, handing a copy of the New York Times to Jason. He brought in the luggage, his eyes returning to Kate. She knew that he was watching her but she acted oblivious to him. Jason's protective posture negated any attempt on the boy's part to linger and he departed with a few coins in his hand. "Thank you, sir. My name is Robert. Just let me know if you need anything else."

Jason fairly slammed the door in his face. Kate giggled and went off to explore the rooms.

Later, Emma sat at the small dining table at the window and browsed through the paper, snapping the pages in the silence. Her eyes fell upon an advertisement for the Tremont Insurance Company of New York and a name at the bottom of the ad. The copy read: To protect your precious possessions, property or business, pay a visit to our office under the capable direction of Adam Lawrence, 360 Fifth Avenue, New York, New York. She sat back and reread the ad. No, she thought, it couldn't be. It was a common name, she reasoned; it couldn't be her Adam. Her Adam. She remembered the moments that she had shared with him, from their first meeting in the Indian Territory to the day he left her in the stand of white birches. She had never forgotten his devotion and his declarations of love and protection. She jumped a little when Jason entered the room and sat opposite her.

"So, what do you want to see first? A museum—or do you want to visit the shops?"

She looked up and smiled. "Oh, there is so much to see and do here. I hope three days is enough."

"Well, let's all make a list of what we want to do and we'll work it out best we can, okay?"

"Good idea." She paused for a moment, then folded the paper and handed it to him. "I saw this advertisement for this insurance company. Look at the name at the bottom."

Jason's brow wrinkled for a moment. "Lawrence? Isn't that the same name as Shea's friend who was in the army?"

"Yes—Adam Lawrence."

Jason looked surprised. "Do you think it's the same man?"

"I'd like to find out, but I don't want you to be angry with me."

"Why would I be angry? He's an old friend of yours. Shea told me how he saved your lives."

"I'd like to go to the office to see if it's him. But I would like to go alone, just at first."

"Of course, Em."

"I don't want you to be jealous."

"Why would I be jealous? You two haven't seen each other in almost twenty years."

She felt nervous at the possibility that it was indeed Adam. "It's very possible that he doesn't know about Shea. I'd just feel better if I could break everything to him alone."

He leaned across the table and kissed her. "Emma, I understand and I'm not jealous. I want you to go."

"I love you, Jason," she touched his soft hair. "You and Kate should tour the town while I'm gone. Don't wait on me."

His eyes sparked as he took in her beauty. "You know, I hope it's him. I've always thought that the two of you had unfinished business."

"Not unfinished, but just the same, there's a lot of history between us. We had a unique friendship."

"Em, go. If it is Adam, invite him to supper tonight. I'll find a restaurant and reserve a table for seven o'clock. Meet us back here, all right?"

"Thank you, Jason."

Later, Emma spoke with Kate as she donned a lightweight blue cloak that Jason had bought for her simply because it matched her eyes.

"It's best that I see him alone before you meet him," she was saying to Kate.

"But Mom, I want to meet him. He was Dad's friend. I know all that he did for you both."

"We have many years to catch up on and you and Jason would be bored. And if it isn't him, you wouldn't have wasted a trip."

"Oh, all right."

"Maybe it's not him. Maybe I'm being silly."

Kate regarded her for a long moment. "Were you lovers?"

Emma was startled at such an intimate question, but she answered Kate honestly. "Very nearly."

"Did Dad know?"

"Yes, Kate. He did."

That afternoon, armed with the address, Emma took a short carriage ride to a three–story brownstone office building on Fifth Avenue. Inside, she approached a pretty blonde receptionist.

"Pardon me. Does Adam Lawrence work here?"

"Yes, ma'am. Do you have an appointment?" she asked, running a finger down a calendar on her desk.

"No. I'm not sure, but if he's who I think he is, we're old friends."

She looked up. "He's out of the office at a meeting. He's expected back shortly, but he may not have time to see you."

"I realize that, but I'd just need a moment of his time."

"Well, I'll see what I can do. Please have a seat." She pointed out a bank of chairs.

Emma seated herself at the window and waited forty–five minutes. A short, paunchy man entered the office. Emma saw the receptionist speaking with him and pointing to her. She was disheartened as he approached, his hand out, smiling at someone he thought was a potential customer.

"Ma'am?"

Emma rose and took the proffered hand. "I must've made a mistake. I was looking for Adam Lawrence."

"I'm Thaddeus Mahler, Mr. Lawrence's associate. Can I help you, Mrs.?"

"Mrs. Beck. Emma Beck."

The man looked at her, startled. "Forgive me. Emma, you said?" She nodded at his look of confusion. "And you're here to see Adam Lawrence?"

"Do you know when he'll be back?"

"We had a meeting with a client a few blocks away. He'll be along any minute." Mahler excused himself and headed for his office, throwing glances at her over his shoulder. He nearly ran into his office door. She noticed he positioned himself in his windowed office so that he could watch her.

Emma resumed her place and her perusal of the passersby on the sidewalk. Then, a tall man clad in a gray overcoat and felt hat walked past, his back to her. Emma immediately recognized his lanky, purposeful stride. She stood as he entered the lobby and spoke to the receptionist.

"Miss Yaeger, I need the files for Long Island Cartage in my office right away."

The young woman's head turned as Emma approached. Adam seemed annoyed at her inattention and turned as well.

"Hello, Adam."

He came to his full height, astounded at seeing her. "My Lord! Emma!" To her complete surprise, he hugged her, lifting her clear off the ground. His gold–flecked brown eyes shone. "I don't believe it!" He ended the embrace and took both her hands in his. His eyes were as soft and warm as she remembered. Although twenty years had passed, before her was the same handsome man who still carried himself like a soldier. Little had changed, except for some gray in his dark hair.

"Nice to see you, too, Adam."

"What are you doing here?"

"This morning I saw an ad in the paper with your name at the bottom. Thought that I would come by and see if it was really you."

"Do you live in the city?"

"No, we're just visiting for a few days."

"Where's Shea? Why didn't he come with you?"

She at last had confirmation that he had never received her letters. And from his affectionate reception, she knew that he had not been ignoring her. It took her a moment to gather the courage to tell him. "Adam, he passed away eleven years ago. I tried to contact you through Indian Affairs, but I guess you never got my letters."

Adam was visibly shaken. His eyes welled up. "Oh. I didn't know." It took him several moments to regain command of himself. "How?"

She swallowed and tried to hold back her own tears. "It was cancer of the throat. It might've been from the hanging. The doctor was never sure."

Young Miss Yaeger listened with keen interest. Adam cleared his throat several times as the first waves of grief washed over him. He had always considered Shea to be invulnerable. His head snapped up, remembering Shea's own prophecy the night that Emma had danced around the fire in Montana, the prophecy that he would not live long.

"Miss Yaeger, I'm going to be unavailable the rest of the day." His hand closed around Emma's arm and he led her to his glassed–in office. He motioned to a chair near his desk. "Please," he offered. He sat in his large leather chair. "I'm sorry, so sorry." He rubbed his eyes and sniffled. Emma saw that he was crying.

"I'm sorry to just appear like this and tell you bad news."

"I wrote to you at the reservation, but I got no answer."

"Shea and I left the reservation the spring after you went to Washington, D.C."

"Guess we were at cross purposes." His head came up as his memory of those days flooded back. "The child?"

Emma smiled with pride. "A girl. Her name is Katherine Shea Hawkshadow. Shea didn't want our child raised on the reservation. We ended up in Washington state. We lived near a small logging town in the mountains. Easthope."

Adam perked up, smiling his approval of Kate's name.

"Kate's a beauty and the image of Shea. She's here with us. She's starting Bryn Mawr in a few weeks, but we decided to see New York before we head back home."

With her mention of the words 'we' and 'us,' she saw his eyes linger on her wedding ring. "You've remarried?"

"Yes. His name is Jason Beck. He owns the logging and sawmilling company in Easthope."

"I hope that he's good to you. You deserve it."

She caught the look in his eye and knew what he meant. "He's a wonderful man. He and Shea were friends, much as the two of you were." She sat back, relaxing in his presence. "I remember the first day that you and I met back in the Indian Territory. I couldn't stand you at first. I thought you were a know–it–all. But I learned to understand and appreciate you. What I remember most is how you watched over me, especially after Tyler's ambush."

"That was long ago in a different world."

Even after so many years apart, she felt comfortable being honest with him. He had earned her trust by act and deed long ago. "I fell apart after Shea died. But Jason saved me, just like you did that day in Montana. Kate was only seven when Shea died and it was very hard on her. I was a mess and I didn't look after her like I should have." She was not prepared for the flood of memories coursing through her.

"How long will you be in town? Will I have the privilege of meeting Kate and Jason?"

"We're here two more days. Jason wanted me to ask you to dinner tonight at seven, if you can make it. We're at the Chesapeake Hotel."

"Nice hotel. You must be doing well," he smiled. "Yes, I'd like that very much."

It was her turn to glance to his left hand. "And bring your wife and family, too."

"It will just be me, I'm afraid. Udele, my wife, is at our summer house on Long Island with the children."

"A summer house? You're doing well," she echoed his earlier remark. "How many children?"

"Four. Two girls, two boys."

"You didn't waste any time, did you?" They laughed, trying to bridge the gap of years between them.

He still looked at her with that same intensity, penetrating her, mesmerizing her. "Emma, you haven't changed a bit. You look as young as when I left Montana."

She smiled at the compliment, noticing Adam's eyes never left hers. "You've held up pretty well yourself, a little grayer, maybe. But it looks good on you."

"I worked hard for every one of them," he said with an easy smile.

"By the way, whatever happened to your brother Ben? I wrote him at Fort Robinson, but he never replied."

"Oh, he's married with three children and lives in Boston. He's partners in a shipping company. He left the army soon after you left Fort Robinson. He'll be sorry to have missed seeing you. I'm sure he would have come down from Boston, but you'll be gone before he could arrive."

"I wish that I had time too, but we have to get Katherine in school."

"I'll have some coffee brought in. I want to hear everything, Emma."

More than two hours later, Emma finished her story, for once including how she had confronted the truth of her parents' murder.

Adam was not triumphant at her admission. "I remember when I tried to get through to you about your parents. I never understood your reaction. Remember how angry you were? You blocked it out to save yourself. I understand now."

"Not well enough. It sneaked up on me after Shea died. It almost killed me. I ended up in a hospital for three months. There was even talk of having me committed. And I was neglecting Kate while trying to deal with my problems by myself. There were a lot of things I never dealt with. A lot of terrible things were locked away, or so I thought. They got loose on me and I had to face them. But I felt so alone. I thought that there was no one who would understand."

Then she came to the incredible story of how Shea's father had searched for his son. "Cody's stories did some good in the end, even though Russell and Shea would never meet."

"Russell?" Adam raised an eyebrow. He still could read her so well.

"I call him Russell because calling him Shea is too hard for me. Russell's a generous man. And his family is so accepting of Kate, so glad to know her and care for her. She'll live with them while she's in school."

"You're having an easy time for a change. God knows you need it."

"Things are getting better all the time. Except for a visit we made to my father's family in Ohio on the way out here." She told him of the many disasters of their brief visit with the Jordens. "I understand why my parents left. Being around that family is oppressive. They continually pass judgment on you. Needless to say, I gave them a lot of ammunition! They aren't bad people, I'm just not used to how easterners think," she grinned.

The years fell away as they talked. He looked at her with the same eyes, filled with the same longing as before. When she finished her capsulated version of the past years, Emma fell silent. It was clear from the way Adam watched her that some of his feelings for her had never dimmed.

At length, he spoke. "Emma, there hasn't been a day gone by when I haven't thought about you. I sound like a fool, but I'm still in love with you." She opened her mouth to speak, but he continued. "Don't get me wrong. I love Udele, I do, and I love my children. But you've always held a special place in my heart."

"Oh, Adam—don't."

"I shouldn't have said that." He smiled. "I sound like a love–sick boy."

She met his eyes. "You're being honest, like always. Maybe you're still seeing the nineteen year–old girl you knew who was stubborn and unrealistic. I grew up and I've got a grip on things at last. It took a long time for me to realize it, but I know how lucky I am. Other people have been worse off than me."

"You went through things that would've done in most people for good. You're quite a lady, Emma." Their eyes locked. "You are strong, you always were. Maybe that strength was misplaced sometimes, but you always focused on what was important. I always thought that you were refreshing and unconventional."

She laughed out loud. "Unconventional! Maybe I was, but it was because I was making it up as I went along."

"You did right by helping the people you loved. I don't know many people who are that committed. Never lose that, Emma. It is who you are." He paused and poured Emma another cup of coffee. "So, now that you've seen

New York and Philadelphia, is there any chance of moving east someday?"

"Afraid not. We've got roots in Easthope and I like that. I moved around too much in my younger years. Besides, these big cities scare me."

"I know what you mean. It took me a while to get used to Washington, D.C. It was so noisy and crowded."

"I know how you feel," she said. Then she asked, "Adam, why did you leave the Bureau of Indian Affairs?"

He sat back, thoughtful, brooding. "I was naïve, not unlike you back then. I thought that I could make a difference with my wealth of experience with the plains tribes. I thought I would bring a different perspective, but I was mired in politics and corruption. I soon realized that I couldn't do anything. I left the army, moved here, and fell into this, courtesy of my father–in–law," he said, motioning to Thaddeus Mahler's office across the aisle. Mr. Mahler was trying to look busy, but his gaze kept returning to them.

Emma smiled. "I didn't know that he was your father–in–law. No wonder. When I told him my name, he looked as if he'd seen a ghost."

Adam chuckled. "My fault. I told him, Udele, and the children all about you. Thaddeus read those articles by Cody. He was very impressed that I had the inside story on you and Shea. I think it greased the skids when I asked to marry his daughter." He leaned back in his chair and laced his fingers behind his head. "I'm content, but sometimes I crave that old excitement. I miss the adventure of never knowing what's going to happen next out on the frontier. I've got a family to support now and a good life. But I have my memories. Good memories."

"I have never thanked you for being friends with Shea. You meant a lot to him, even if he never said it out loud."

"That's good to know. I often thought of you both living on the reservation. You seemed happy there, although I never understood why. But it was the life you wanted and I had to accept that."

She smiled as her thoughts went back to the day that he had told her he was leaving for Washington D.C. He had kissed her with such passion. She could conjure that moment now, the beautiful birch trees surrounding them, the earthy, sweet smell of him, and her own confused sensations and longings. "I remember how tender you were to me the last day we were together. You have no idea how much I needed that. Shea and I were having such troubles back then."

"I loved you since I first knew you, but I suppose you know that."

"Yes, I guess I did, now that I look back."

Her voice had become hoarse from all the talking, so she sipped her coffee. "Adam, I can tell you this, because I know that you'll understand. Remember when that soldier attacked me at Fort Robinson? Sorry, of course you do. Well, weeks after Kate and I moved to town after Shea passed away, Fulton showed up. Jason had hired him to work at one of the logging camps, not knowing who he was."

Adam went pale. "What?"

"I guess he'd been drifting all those years, but somehow he ended up in Easthope. He'd been around a few weeks when he heard about me. He broke into my house and tried to finish what he began back in '78."

Adam saw how her look became haunted. "What did he do, Emma?"

Her head came up with a morbid look of triumph on her face. "I killed him in cold blood. Somehow the whole thing was hushed up by Jason and that was the end of it. I didn't realize until then how powerful Jason was. I don't know what he said or did, but Fulton's body was taken away and with it, my part in his murder."

Adam was shocked, not at the realization that Emma could kill if she had to, but that Fulton had found her in so isolated a town. "No one will ever know what you just told me."

"I know it bothered you that Fulton was never found. I wanted you to know that he finally paid the price for hurting me." She glanced at the clock on his wall. "I'm sorry for keeping you from your work all afternoon."

A slight shake of his head acknowledged that it was all right.

She stood. "I hope you're hungry. I'm looking forward to you meeting Jason and Kate."

"Well then, we better get going. I didn't realize it's after five–thirty already. Time with you always passes too quickly, Emma."

After Adam introduced Emma to his father–in–law, they went out the back door to a building where Adam's carriage and horses were stabled.

He helped her up into the carriage, then got in next to her. Emma kissed his cheek. His hand touched the faded scar on her cheek, the scar left by his bullet. In silence, they set off for the Chesapeake Hotel.

Anticipating Emma and Adam's arrival, and with a large bribe to the maitre d', Jason reserved a private table at a nearby restaurant for dinner. Adam felt a pang upon entering their suite, seeing Jason's obvious love for

Emma in his tender kiss as he greeted her. As they waited for Emma and Kate to change for dinner, the two men talked. Adam liked Jason and admitted his envy.

Jason returned the compliment. "If it hadn't been for you, she and I would never have met. You saved her life. You will always have my gratitude."

Throughout dinner, Adam could not keep his gaze from returning to Kate. He felt that he was talking to Shea; the resemblance was so striking and she was so much like him, although much more talkative. From Adam, she learned much about her father's life before she was born. To Kate, her father was indeed unique, but until that night she had never realized just how brave he was. Emma and Jason exchanged smiles while Adam and Kate talked almost exclusively to one another for most of the evening. Adam later asked if he could look in on Kate while she was in school. This got an enthusiastic yes from Kate.

But too soon for Emma, it was time to part from Adam. He was heading to Long Island the next day to spend the weekend with his family.

Back at the hotel, Jason and Kate retreated to the large bedroom while Emma and Adam said their good–byes at the door.

"I've always hated saying good–bye to you," Adam said with open and tender affection.

"Same here," Emma said. "You'll never know just how much you did for me. You saved my life and I love you for it."

His soft brown eyes held her transfixed. "Do you think we ever could've had something together? I know you're happy with Jason and he's a good man, but I guess I need to know."

Emma nodded with a sly smile. "Under other circumstances, it might have happened. You have a good heart and you proved your patience with me more than once. I hope that we can stay in touch with each other, now that I've found you again. I hope that your wife won't mind."

"Emma, I told her all about you before we married, even how I loved you. When she hears that she missed meeting you she'll be disappointed."

Emma stepped into his embrace and he kissed her cheek. "I will miss you and I promise to write." He stepped to the door and turned. "What would your life have been like if I had found you on the prairie instead of Shea?"

He had asked her this same question years ago and she could not answer it then, nor could she now. Emma blushed and smiled, feeling his love that she remembered so well.

"On second thought, don't answer that," Adam said with a slight laugh.

They exchanged correspondence with each other until his death twenty–five years later. A telegram from Udele informed her that Adam had died of a heart attack. His loss shook Emma deeply. She went to the funeral alone. Udele delayed the service until Emma arrived in New York.

That night in bed, Emma laid her head on Jason's warm chest after they made love. "You were so quiet during dinner. I know you felt left out."

He kissed her hair. "I didn't feel left out. Adam's from a time in your life before me. I was listening to everything he told Kate about Shea." He nuzzled her and was quiet for a while. "Adam loves you. I could see that plain."

She hugged Jason tight. "What bonded Adam and I together took place a long time ago. I was a different person then."

He ran his hands along her nude body. "I like the person you became." He and Emma began kissing, then she rolled on top of him, the length of her body pressed against his. Jason became aroused and slipped inside of her. She straddled him, taking her time before coming to orgasm. Exhausted and panting, she flopped back onto him and slept. Jason cradled her throughout the night.

Their stay in New York was over and it was time to take Kate back to Philadelphia to begin college.

In the grand entranceway of Russell's home, Jason said farewell to Kate. He tried not to cry, but he did anyway. He stepped away, wiping his eyes.

"I will miss you so," Emma said, tenderly enfolding Kate in her arms. "I love you so much and I am so proud of you. Your grandfather will take good care of you, but if there is anything you need, wire us and you will have it." Her tears fell unchecked. "You will come home during the holidays and the summers, promise?" Kate nodded through her own tears. "You're strong and steady, just like your father. He would be so proud of you."

"If I don't like it here, I can come home, right?" She was afraid of all the new experiences coming her way and needed to know that she had an out.

"Of course you can." Emma and Kate hugged each other for a long time before Emma could at last let go. But she had to. Kate was getting the chance that Emma never had and she would not make her daughter feel guilty for pursuing her dreams.

As Jason handed Emma up into the carriage for the trip to the train station, she turned and took a last look at Kate standing on the steps with Russell. She looked so small, but Emma knew how much strength was packed in
that tiny frame. Emma wept all the way to the station, her head on Jason's
shoulder.

As the westbound train moved through the countryside, Emma proposed
to Jason that they stop in Kansas on the way. "We would have to change
trains in Cincinnati to head south. Then we can rent a wagon once we get to
Dodge City, Kansas." Emma saw the grim look on Jason's face.

"You want to go back to the sod house?" He worried about what the
detour implied. Emma would come face–to–face with powerful, tragic
memories. "Do you think that you can handle being there?"

"I think so."

"I'm worried about your health, Emma. I don't want you ending up back
in the hospital."

"The property reverted to the State of Kansas years ago. There's probably someone living there, cursing Useless Creek, just like my father did.
The soddy and the graves are probably gone, too. But I want to see the place
one last time. I have unfinished business there."

At Dodge City, they disembarked in a noisy, boisterous town. The town's
violent history was a source of pride among the locals. Emma and Jason,
in their fine clothes, attracted much attention as they made their way to a
modest hotel near the railway.

The next day, Emma stepped up into a rented wagon beside Jason. He
snapped the reins. She was going home. Home. It seemed such a strange
concept since she had had so many homes.

Not surprisingly, the countryside had changed much in twenty years. Towns
and farms now lined the roads south to the border of what had been the
Indian Territory, now the territory of Oklahoma. But there were many places
where the swaying prairie grass remained, green–gold and tall, just as she
remembered.

The first night, they stayed at a small inn and set out at first light to try to
find the old homestead. They drove for hours and Emma was worried that
she would never find the property, but then a familiar hill rose to the south.

"Head that way, Jason," she pointed. "I think it's over that rise."

She remembered well. As they crested the hill, Emma was relieved that
the land was unoccupied, but disappointed that she could not see the soddy.

As they drew nearer Emma stood up, keeping a hand on the wagon bench, scanning the property.

The sod house had fallen back into the prairie, reclaimed by the earth and small, burrowing animals. She could see pieces of the crude furniture left behind sticking out of the fallen earth walls. The small barn and outhouse had blown down, the weathered wood lying in the grass. Tufts of wheat crowded together here and there and a few stubborn corn stalks poked up through the swaying cord grass. Other than that, few signs remained that the land had ever been cultivated.

Then her eyes fell upon a row of sticks in the ground. "There," she said in a quiet voice. "There they are. The graves are still here."

Jason pulled up beside the graveyard and handed Emma down. Her memory was still vivid, remembering the freezing night that she had buried her parents.

"It's a miracle that no one disturbed them all these years." Emma went about finding sticks with which to fashion crosses for each of the graves, replacing the ones that had long since fallen apart.

She tripped over something in the grass. She glanced behind her, then bent down to see what it was. She straightened and stood motionless. "Oh!" she sobbed. She held the shaft of a broken arrow in her hand.

Jason quickly came to her side and looked at it. Feathers, faded by sun and rain, were still wrapped along the shaft but the tip of the arrow had been broken off. "Em?"

She could barely speak because her throat had closed tight. "This is one of the arrows that killed my father. I had to break it off so I could bury him." The ground where she was standing had been the spot she had found her father's body. A chill ran through her.

Jason took her hand. "This was a bad idea. Let's get out of here."

"No," she shook her head slowly. "I have to do this. I have to know how I feel here." She pulled away from him and continued to fashion new crosses for the graves, tying the sticks together with strands of long, wild grass.

Jason left her alone to deal with her feelings. He walked around the desolate land, always keeping an eye on Emma. Later, he scrutinized her as she approached him.

"I'm all right, Jason," she said. "This isn't as painful as I thought it would be. The graves don't even look like graves. The prairie is taking them back and that is how it should be. Being here gives me such a strange feeling. I can't describe it. I've changed so much and this land has stayed pretty much the same. It's not what I expected."

They walked to the little creek, almost dry from a hot summer. The bush that she had hidden behind as she watched the Pawnee attack was still there, just larger.

"Around that bend in the river is where I hid that day." She waited for the old guilt over her cowardice to surface but when it did, it did not have the same sting. She walked around, examining the bank, looking for something familiar, but the wind and weather had changed even the course of the creek in twenty years.

"I can guess what a hard life you had here," Jason said as he surveyed the countryside. "So alone. I don't know how you did it."

"I didn't know any better," she answered, her face into the familiar wind. Her hair trailed behind her, bestowing a spark of color against the yellow grass.

Jason spoke with great care, sensing that she needed to do something to alleviate her old guilt. "Emma, what if we had your family's remains moved to Easthope? How would you feel about that?"

"Wouldn't that be desecrating the graves?"

"No. I don't think of it that way," Jason answered.

She walked around a little longer, thinking. "If we did move them, I'd like them to be near Shea up on the mountain. Yes, maybe that's what has been missing in me all this time. There's been a void I can't put into words. I left them behind in many ways and never gave them the credit they deserved for my very life itself. Maybe I do owe them a proper place in those beautiful mountains—near me."

Jason quickly arranged it. He wired Topeka, the territorial capital, for permission to exhume the remains. They learned that the property had never been sold; the dried–up creek had kept prospective buyers away. Although anxious that the remains be handled with care, Emma was thankful that Jason supervised the workers. Though she kept her distance from the work, her mind brimmed with memories of her life in this place. When the bones emerged from the hard prairie, she turned away. Jason oversaw the remains into the five coffins that he had purchased for transport and reburial.

The work went on for hours, so Emma went to the creek one last time. She sat in the sun, absently pulling at the long, tough prairie grass and began weaving circular shapes, almost without thought. Then she stopped.

She had been doing exactly the same thing when she had heard the rumble of the Pawnee horses the day her parents had been killed. She was going to drop the little circle she had woven, but decided against it and kept weaving. She passed the afternoon as she had when she was younger. The rhythm of the work calmed her. So far back in memory had she gone that she half expected her mother to call her home to supper.

Before leaving Dodge City, Jason wired his mill, arranging for his buggy, a freight wagon, a team of horses, and drivers to meet them at the Millersburg train station on the day of their return.

At the Millersburg depot three days later, many heads turned as the coffins were loaded into the wagon, along with Emma and Jason's trunks. In their buggy, Jason and Emma led the way back to Easthope.

Rachel was just leaving Carruthers' store when she saw Emma and Jason coming down Main Street ahead of the massive wagon with its strange cargo. Seeing the coffins, she came running. Jason pulled up.

"Emma! What happened?"

"Rachel, everything is all right." Emma stepped down off the buggy.

Jason snapped the reins and said, "I'm going to the blacksmith's. Harris Brody will store them in his barn. Meet you at home." Emma waved as he drove away.

Rachel was astonished. "Emma, what in hell is going on?"

"You might think this ghoulish, but those are the remains of my parents and my brother and sisters. We brought them here for a proper burial up on the mountain."

"Oh!" she cried, her hand flying to her chest. "I don't know what to say about that. That's the last thing that I'd expect you to bring back from your trip east!" Very shaken, she found a bench outside Murdock's and sat down.

"Relax, Rachel. I will have my family together now. I know it sounds morbid, but I need this. It feels like the fitting thing to do."

Rachel had serious doubts, afraid that Emma would collapse again. "Are you sure that this is healthy? I mean no disrespect to your family, but this is a peculiar thing to do." Her voice faded away.

"I know that you're worried about me, Rachel. And I'm all right. I'm glad I did it, though at first I thought that Jason was crazy for suggesting it."

"Jason wanted you to do this?"

"He knew I needed this. My family will be together. I don't feel so guilty anymore. This is important to me."

"All right," Rachel said, rising. "If this is what it takes to keep you healthy, then you must know what you're doing. I don't understand digging them up. You're quite a puzzle, sometimes. But I trust you know what you're about?"

"Yes, Rachel, I know what I'm about. Quite a lot happened on our trip. Oh, and I found out that my mother robbed a bank. I'll tell you all about that later." Emma chuckled as she walked away.

"What? You can't say something like that then just walk away!" she called after her.

Days later, Jason and Emma were joined by the Barlows and a few friends as the five coffins were interred a few yards from Shea's grave up on the mountain. Emma remained at the graves after everyone had departed. Jason waited for her near the carriage. She knelt in the grass and carefully arranged bundles of flowers on each grave.

"Welcome to my home, Mother, Father, Aaron, Grace, Elizabeth. This isn't the way I wanted my family together, but it will do." She touched the fresh earth. "Forgive me, Mom and Dad. I'm sorry. There are so many things that I would change, but there are just as many I would do all over again. I regret all that I didn't do on that horrible day so long ago. I know what you'd say: I was seventeen, just a child."

She looked at her parents' names inscribed on the temporary grave markers. "If there was one day in my life that I would change, it would be the day that you were killed. I have missed you both so much all these years. I needed your guidance more times than I can count. But the family goes on, though. I wish that you could've known Kate, but she wouldn't be here if things had turned out differently, would she? There isn't much to say about how things work out."

It struck her that her parents' deaths were, in a perplexing way, a release from the strain of their lives. Emma believed that they had gone to a better life, a better existence. As she thought about it, she could not imagine that her parents' lives would ever have changed. Their toil would have continued until they were too frail or sick to continue farming. Would they ever have left Kansas and spent the money on a better piece of land? Probably not. If Emma had, as her father wished, married a soldier, she might have been taken far away from them; she might not have been there when they needed her as they aged. And no matter who died first, one of her parents would have been alone, left to an uncertain fate.

Her thoughts went to the people who had been so important to her, the many people who had come and gone from her life. Her parents, Red Leaf Woman, Adam, Little Fox, and all the Cheyenne that she had known and loved. She sent thanks for Doctors Malley and Cromwell, Max Cody, Rachel, even General Considine, and most especially Shea, Jason, and Katherine. They had all shaped her in their own unique ways. This day, she at last understood how lucky she was. And finally, she forgave herself. All the guilt that she had been storing evaporated and she felt secure and sensible about all the decisions that she had made in her life.

Emma went to Shea's grave and pulled away long grass that had grown up around his crypt. She then stood there, remembering her years with him and fully comprehending all that he had sacrificed for her and for Kate. Her memories of him would always be a precious treasure to her. She conjured his magnificent face in her memory and at that moment believed that she could hear his voice speaking to her in the winds of this wild meadow.

Jason could not read her face when she joined him beside the carriage. He wondered how she was coping. "You all right, Em?"

"Yes, I am all right," she said with a slow smile.

Jason's tender mouth on hers reminded her of how much she loved life and this man, who loved her so completely.

Emma and Jason got into the carriage and headed down the mountain along Hawkshadow Road.

THE END